THE URBANA FREE LIBRARY

3 1230 00898 8967

W9-AHQ-919

DISCARDED BY THE
URBANA FREE LIBRARY

The Urbana Free Library

To renew: call 217-367-4057
or go to "*urbanafreelibrary.org*"
and select "Renew/Request Items"

HARD
RED
SPRING

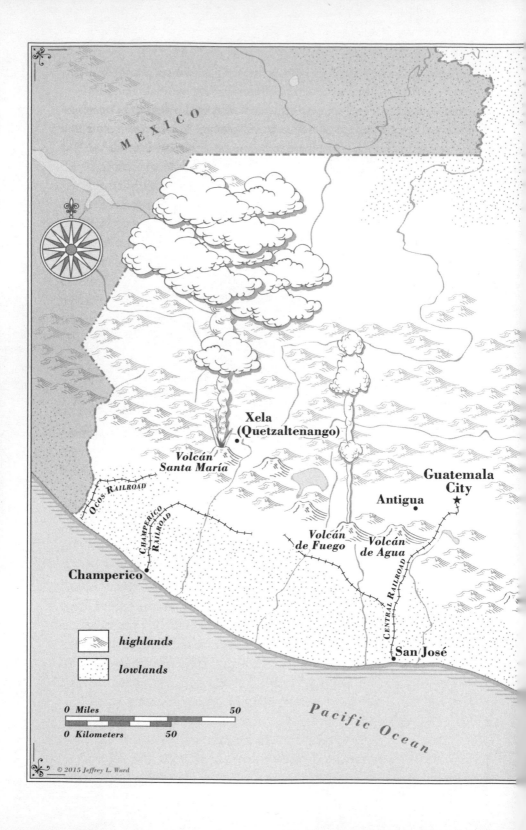

MEXICO

Xela
(Quetzaltenango)

Volcán
Santa María

Ocos Railroad

Champerico
Railroad

Champerico

Volcán
de Fuego

Antigua

Guatemala
City

Volcán
de Agua

Central Railroad

San José

highlands

lowlands

0 Miles   50
0 Kilometers   50

Pacific Ocean

© 2015 Jeffrey L. Ward

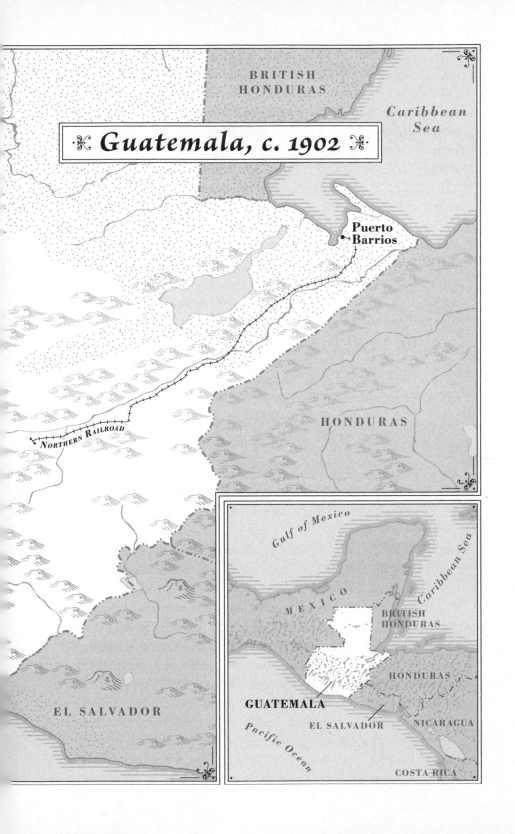

Guatemala, c. 1902

BRITISH HONDURAS

Caribbean Sea

Puerto Barrios

HONDURAS

NORTHERN RAILROAD

EL SALVADOR

Gulf of Mexico

MEXICO

Caribbean Sea

BRITISH HONDURAS

GUATEMALA

HONDURAS

EL SALVADOR

NICARAGUA

Pacific Ocean

COSTA RICA

Kelly Kerney

HARD RED SPRING

VIKING

VIKING
An imprint of Penguin Random House LLC
375 Hudson Street
New York, New York 10014
penguin.com

Copyright © 2016 by Kelly Kerney
Penguin supports copyright. Copyright fuels creativity, encourages diverse voices, pro-
motes free speech, and creates a vibrant culture. Thank you for buying an authorized
edition of this book and for complying with copyright laws by not reproducing, scanning, or distributing any part of it in any form without permission. You are supporting
writers and allowing Penguin to continue to publish books for every reader.

Excerpt from "Guatemala: Memory of Silence" by the Commission for Historical Clarification. © 1999 United Nations. Reprinted with the permission of the United Nations.

"The Jaguar and the Deer" from *Tales and Legends of the Q'anjob'al Maya* by Fer-
nando Penalosa. Yax Te' Books publishes books about Mayan Culture and by Mayan
authors from Guatemala. Used by permission of the publisher.

Excerpt from "I Like Bananas Because They Have No Bones" by Chris Yacich. © 1936
(renewed) Chappell & Co. All rights reserved.

ISBN 978-0-525-42901-2

Printed in the United States of America
1 3 5 7 9 10 8 6 4 2

Set in Bodoni Std Book
Designed by Francesca Belanger
Map by Jeffrey L. Ward

This is a work of fiction. Names, characters, places, and incidents either are the product
of the author's imagination or are used fictitiously, and any resemblance to actual persons, living or dead, businesses, companies, events, or locales is entirely coincidental.

For E

Innocence is like a dumb leper who has lost his bell, wandering the world, meaning no harm.

—Graham Greene, *The Quiet American*

1902

The cave in Father's mountain was just big enough for a little girl to walk inside, though Evie had never done so. She could barely bring herself to look at the cave, let alone breathe its air. Its cold limestone jaws, frozen open, perpetually dripped water. She had never seen anyone in the cave, only the things they left behind, near the entrance: candles, coins, clay trinkets, fragrant half-burned bundles of grass, sometimes still smoking. The Indians came there, trespassing on Father's land, to talk to their dead ancestors. And these sad offerings, cheap even to an eight-year-old's eye, were the presents left for the ghosts.

Once, Evie had been compelled, had been feverish enough with want, to try to take something from the cave: a baby doll set back beyond the fire ring. Dressed like a miniature Indian, the doll was made from an eaten corncob with the husk pulled down into a painted skirt. Its burned silk clung to the top to mimic black Indian hair. Clutching a long stick, trying to snag the doll by the hair, Evie inched close enough to feel the cold cave breath leaking from a small hole, like a throat, in the back. Just big enough for a little girl to be swallowed. Startling herself, she dropped the stick and could not bring herself one inch closer to retrieve it.

She never told anyone about the gifts she saw in the cave. Mother didn't even know the cave existed until Evie informed her. It was too far into the forest, beyond her daily range, which kept her close to the house. Evie had told her long ago, hoping she would order Judas to burn it, which was how she dealt with any trace of Indian activity on their land: corn plantings, altars, huts. Their woods were perpetually on fire. But could you burn a cave away? Could you burn ghosts? Evie suspected not. Now that she had turned eight, she was beginning to understand that some situations were hopeless, beyond even her parents' powers.

Father knew about the cave and generally ignored it, since he had no use for it. Only his fields mattered: wheat and prickly pear, on which he raised cochineal bugs to be killed and dried for dye. Strange Indians using his uncultivated land didn't bother him very much, though these trespasses kept

Evie awake at night, praying to the American God she wasn't sure could hear prayers outside America. Half the time, she feared only the ghosts themselves could hear her pleas for protection. And when she did finally sleep, the ghosts came to her in her dreams.

For all her terror, she felt no surprise when she awoke one morning inside the cave, with her head on a rock. The inevitable, the thing she'd always dreaded, that she knew would happen, had finally come to pass. Had she walked in her sleep, had she been carried? It didn't matter. And there was no use screaming or trying to escape. Feeling a strange calm, she considered the possibility that she had died. That her soul, too far from home, had not known where else to go but where Indian souls went. But once she saw the Indian coming at her with a raised machete, she realized that she was not dead yet, but about to die. His sunken leather chest, his black matted hair and blazing eyes: this was not a ghost, but a man. Filmed with sweat and dirt, he approached, smelling horrifically familiar. At this, she screamed, and that was when her father began to shake her awake. His hands on her were the Indian's, attacking her. Molesting, disgracing. Words she heard almost daily but never understood until that moment. This was what it was to be disgraced by an Indian.

"Start moving, Evie. Get your shoes on! The ash is going to kill the bugs!"

A dream. Only a dream, but she could not place herself. Had she woken again, into another dream? The lumpy handmade walls seemed like another cave. She could not move at first, though she willed it. She began to consider again the possibility that she had died. It could be like this, death, it could certainly be like this in Guatemala.

"Evie!"

"What?" she asked in a strangled whisper. The Indian's hand still on her throat.

She rubbed her eyes, confused. The smell held her back: corn. Warm and slightly sweet, it lingered on her tongue. She blinked again. Her room looked strange to her. Not the things, but the light. The light was strange.

"Evie, Santa María's erupting. We've got to save the cochineal!"

Mother flashed by the door, then Father ran out after her. Things became clearer, but not why she was awake so early in the morning. In her bare feet Evie shuffled to the front door, peered out through the thick brown morning light, and saw what looked like snow. For a moment she thought they were back in New York. It made sense: the slow flakes, the unidentified drifts of darkness all around, the cold bite of highland air. But then Father grabbed her shoulders and shook her again.

"Evie, wake up!" He tried to push her outside. "If we lose this crop, we're finished! The volcano—"

She clung to the doorframe, resisting. "But what about the lava?"

"There's no lava here, just ash. The ash won't hurt you, but it'll kill the cochineal. We've got to protect them."

They all darted through the prickly pear fields, still in their nightclothes, arms full of papers, clothes, blankets, anything they could find, to cover the cacti, where the cochineal bugs lived. Evie folded newspapers over the stiff leaves like a hat. Once harvested, these bugs would make the most vivid red dye, in high demand around the world. Mother, Father, and Ixna rushed around in the dark, with tablecloths and sheets, while Judas—the only field worker who slept at the farm—worked the far side of the field, doing the same with burlap sacks. Evie heard Mother arguing with Ixna, who refused to sacrifice her extra Indian blouse. They were expensive, she protested, a blouse took months to weave and she only had two. Accusations of vanity were exchanged through the flurries and smoke.

"I'll buy you a new blouse! From the Frenchman's shop!"

Ixna balked, offended.

"Oh, you're too good for our clothes, I see. Too good for anything of ours! But I know you stole my last tin of face powder, Ixna! And my mirror!" Mother shrieked. She always pronounced Ixna like a sneeze—*Icksna*—when in reality it was pronounced *Ishna*, like a secret. "I know exactly where I left it, I remember!"

"Mirror?" Ixna repeated the word with difficulty. "What's mirror?"

This ignorance made Mother even angrier. She called Judas over, away from his work, for a translation.

"There is no word for mirror in Quiché," he said.

"How can there not be a word for that?"

Judas shrugged. Father ran to the scene, arms flailing. "What's going on? Judas! Get the southwest corner covered!"

"How do your people know if they look respectable?" Mother pressed, waving away Father's insistence. "If they have food in their teeth?"

Judas glanced at Ixna, who was leaning against the house, hugging her extra Indian blouse, which she had succeeded in wrenching away from Mother.

"I guess we just rely on other people to tell us."

——

With all their blankets, pillows, and sheets draped over the cacti, they could not go back to bed. They had no choice but to stay awake, marveling at their situation and shivering, for they had sacrificed their coats as well. The old church, their home, had been completely emptied of comforts in the effort to shroud the cacti. Evie thought the prickly pear plants—now dressed in linens, pants, and dresses—looked like a crowd of people amassed outside their house, demanding something.

"Doesn't it look like snow, Evie?" Her mother sat beside her in the parlor with a lit lantern, drinking tea. Her coarse black hair hung like curtains parted to show her pale face, reflecting the flame. They sat watching the artificial night through the open front door. "Remember in New York how quiet it would become with the snow? The whole city would just shut down. No noise at all."

Evie nodded. She did not remember much about New York, but snow she did remember, especially the cozy deprivations and disruption it brought to daily life: sleigh rides in the streets, the thrill of not having a stocked pantry when the storm hit. Like refugees, they all three would huddle over a can of peaches for dinner, secretly pleased by the necessity of sharing.

In Guatemala, however, catastrophes were not cozy and did not bring out the best in anyone. In Guatemala, roads were not just impassable in bad weather but could completely slide down a mountainside, burying entire towns alive. No sleigh could glide over the sucking, killing mud of the rainy season. When catastrophes happened here, the Indians believed the earth was angry, and the only way to appease the earth was to feed her more bodies. So in times of distress, like when a bridge in Totonicapán collapsed from the rains, more disturbing developments inevitably followed. Kidnapping, killing. Travelers on the road would go missing and their headless bodies would be found days later. The heads, supposedly, buried at each end of the bridge to "stabilize" it. At least that's the word Judas used to explain the situation.

These, of course, were stories that Evie was not meant to hear, but they always, without fail, came out during Mother's weekly teas with her friend Mrs. Fasbinder, who lived on the other side of the volcano. Since she owned a coffee plantation that employed hundreds of natives, Mrs. Fasbinder knew much more about Indians than they did.

"You know that's how I met your father, don't you? In the snow?"

Evie shook her head and squeezed a point of blood from her finger. The cactus plants were unforgiving.

"He'd arrived from Charleston on the train just before the storm and had never seen snow before. He just wandered the streets, taking in the whiteness and the silence, and then he heard me playing the piano. He followed the sound and that was the first time we saw each other, through a window in my parents' parlor."

"Was he handsome?" Evie asked, knowing the answer. Father was still handsome, with ice-blue eyes, but she liked to hear other people say so.

"Oh yes, but more than that, I loved his accent. I'd never met a boy who wasn't from New York. Who wasn't afraid to go places and talk in his funny way. He was so confident. My mother called him a tramp and chased him away with an umbrella, but she was too late. Ten minutes too late."

"What time is it?" Evie asked, peering out the door into the inscrutable brown night.

"Ten in the morning."

"Where *is* Father?"

"He and Judas went to climb the ridge, to see if we should be worried."

Yes, Father certainly wasn't afraid of going anywhere. At any moment, he could be on top of an erupting volcano, or eating caviar with ladies at a fancy dress ball. His whereabouts often surprised Evie, who had a hard time envisioning a world beyond their lonely mountain.

Ixna appeared, sweeping ash off the porch with hard, sure strokes. A sixteen-year-old house girl, she was beautiful and peculiar, with large liquid eyes and a dimple like a thumbprint pressed into her chin. She'd been cooking her corn tortillas behind the house when the ash began. That's what Evie had smelled in her dream. Why did she eat those flimsy Indian things, when she could have pancakes and pies and bread for breakfast? Father called that the question of the new century. But Ixna was a pagan and did not like questions, though she moved with the calm confidence of someone who knew exactly why the ground rumbled beneath her, why the sun was blocked out, and exactly why a human head needed to be buried underneath a fallen bridge.

Ixna, as far as they were concerned, came with the mountain. When they arrived three years ago she had been waiting at the top, standing there with nothing but her square basket. She was thirteen at the time. At that age, Indian girls in Guatemala got married and had children. But she had other ideas.

Ixna worked without complaint or enthusiasm. Though she had basically forced herself into their home, she seemed to be somewhere else most of the time. Evie could not imagine what Ixna could ever daydream about. She'd never been anywhere, not even to the capital. When Evie asked her about her goals, she didn't seem to understand the concept. She was doing, she said, exactly what she wanted and what she was meant to do.

Ixna did not smile and talk predictably, like Judas, who'd been studying white people for years. She was very definitely Indian and made no effort to act otherwise. She did strange, shameful things that Evie could not even bring herself to mention to her parents. Once, Evie had walked behind the house to see Ixna kneeling and kissing the ground. Kissing the dirt! Not saucily, not like a joke or a greeting, but slowly, with reverence, intimacy. Ixna would not eat their food or even pretend to understand their stories, stories that Mother called universal, like the one about the tortoise and the hare.

"How did a turtle ever win a race?" Ixna had asked in irritation. She then told her own story, about a jaguar and a deer, who had each decided to build a house on the same spot, though they did not meet for a long time. The deer cleared the site with his antlers and left for supplies, then the jaguar arrived, saw the clearing, and built the frame. Then he left and the deer came back and built the roof. They each were so happy to have a helper that when they finally did meet, they decided to live together to make life easier. But one day, the jaguar came back with a large deer he'd killed. *Let's eat*, he said. The deer became very afraid. In the morning, he went and found another jaguar, then found a bull and said to him, *That jaguar over there was bad-mouthing you.* The bull gored the jaguar, and the deer dragged the jaguar corpse home and presented it to his housemate. *Let's eat what I have killed!* The jaguar became very afraid. That night, neither could sleep, thinking of the other in the next room. Deer killing jaguars and jaguars killing deer. The deer had a bad dream and his antlers struck the wall, making a big noise. Both were so frightened by the noise that they ran out of the house and did not stop. And did not return.

"That's all?" Evie had asked.

"What else? That is everything," Ixna told her.

Evie considered Ixna her one and only friend in Guatemala and did not believe she had ever stolen anything from Mother. Though she was poor, Ixna didn't envy any of them or their things. Because of this, she and Ixna could be friends. When Mother first accused Ixna of stealing her last tin of ivory face powder, Ixna had laughed.

Evie had been bold enough to look in Ixna's basket once and had found pine needles and a red Indian blanket inside.

They lived in an old, gutted church on the farm that had been run by a priest years ago. Before this, the mountain had been communal land for the Indians, where anyone could plant or graze or pray. But the government seized it and sold it to the Church. The resident priest then divided the land into small plots that the Indians rented to plant food. But with the regime change twenty years ago, the priest had been thrown out of the country, and the land confiscated by the President, along with all the other "excessive" Catholic landholdings. After that, the government sold the land to a cochineal farmer, who moved in, planted cacti, then failed, or disappeared. Or both. Stories in town conflicted.

The church they lived in was small. Except for the cross on the roof, from the outside no one would even know it was a church. But still, Father had built a porch on the front, where steps used to be, and painted the whitewashed exterior brown, to make it all look less holy. The inside, which had been dark, was then whitewashed for the same effect. It was like the windowless church had been turned inside out.

As the afternoon grew strangely dark, Father was still gone on his ridge climb. As they waited for him, Mother instructed Evie to watch for lava out the one window they had. Father had cut this window to cheer up Mother, but it was almost always used to watch out for disaster: early rains, thieves, wild animals, and now the lava. How would lava come? A sudden lake of fire washing around them, a river cutting through their fields? And more importantly, what would Evie do if she did see lava? Because Judas said once you see it, it's too late to escape.

So many terrible things in the forest: criminals, lava, ghosts, animals.

"What about jaguars? Father left his gun." Evie's fear amplified, seeing her own worried face in the dark glass.

"But he has Judas with him," Mother reminded her.

Judas was Father's number one man because he spoke Spanish, English, and Quiché. And because he would sense a jaguar stalking them. Father said Judas's Indian mother had at first named him in Quiché. He had gone by this name for the first few years of his life. But when his mother became a Catholic, the nuns had encouraged her to rename him from the Bible. And they never could dissuade her from her choice.

When Judas did arrive, around dinnertime, Evie had mistaken him at first for lava. His torch bobbing in the distance was everything she had been dreading. A bright, seething eye seeking them out. Paralyzed with fear, she stood at the window and watched the flame appear intermittently, weaving its way leisurely toward the house.

He walked in the front door a few minutes later, holding a much smaller lantern that brightened the whole room and threw his dignified shadow on the wall. Despite his dark skin and flat Indian nose, Judas always wore European pants, shirts, and shoes. Sometimes Father and Evie went into the men's shop in town and selected pants, a shirt, and shiny lace-up shoes for him. Evie had the idea that Father paid Judas in these elaborate outfits.

Seeing Judas alone and in filthy disarray, Mother clutched herself and cried, "Where's Robert?"

"*Saber.*" *Saber* meaning something like, *Who knows?* in Quiché. Only, Judas never said it like a question.

"What? You've no idea? You lost him?"

Judas was immune to any tone of voice, even that of desperation. He shook the ash from his shoes, tapping the points on the floorboards, as Evie's world crashed all around her. Imagining life without Father, no jokes, no songs, no funny stories about important people drinking too much. Then, just as quickly, everything returned to normal.

"Evie, go get a chicken crate! Hurry!" Father's familiar voice, from the far end of the field, brought everyone to the front door. They could not see him at first. He did not have a lantern and blended into the dressed cactus field like he was on a crowded street.

He mounted the front porch, cleared all three steps in a single leap, with a half-full burlap sack bucking and heaving in his hands. Something huge and powerful, with what appeared to be fists, punched at the fabric. Father held it up triumphantly.

The first thing Evie believed upon seeing this was that Father had found her a sister in the woods. Just last year, her parents had announced to her that she would be getting a new brother or sister. How? She had asked just this. How will my sister arrive? Well, Father explained, she or he will come in a burlap sack. Like the ones we use for shipping? Like the ones for coffee? Yes, he had told her, exactly. But she had waited a long time and the bag never came. When she asked again, they seemed disappointed she had remembered the conversation. "We thought you were getting a sister," Father explained, "but the mail in Guatemala is terrible. You know we're always having problems. They delivered her to someone else, Evie."

Then Mother cried.

"Robert, what is it?" Mother asked now, hugging herself, keeping inside the doorway.

"All I saw was red, blue, and green in my torchlight. Just these fabulous bright colors, down low in a bush."

"But what is it?"

"I thought I was hallucinating. It's the most incredible thing, Mattie. The most beautiful creature. I knew you'd never believe me if I described it to you, so I jumped on it with the bag."

So, not a baby. A creature. With this, a more terrifying possibility occurred to Evie. A ghost. Father had caught one of the ghosts that lived in the cave. In Guatemala, everyone believed in ghosts. Indians—adults and even respected leaders—came from all over to talk to the ghosts on their mountain. Only, they did not call them ghosts, but ancestors.

"You see something beautiful, an animal, you have no idea what it is, and your first instinct is to jump on it and bag it?" Mother asked, amazed.

"It worked on you." Father winked, and Mother blushed with pleasure. That was definitely a part of the story Mother had not shared.

"Evie, hold the bag tight over the crate. Hold it tight and don't let go until I say."

Evie hesitated, then did as her father told her. She imagined a dead Indian ancestor in that bag. A shrunken old mummy man without teeth. It was too late to do anything else. It was in the bag, angry. The only thing to do now was keep this thing prisoner, to make sure it didn't come back for revenge.

Father shook the bag. "Okay, now."

Evie let go, the top of the crate slammed shut, and everyone stepped back. The thing looked at them and they looked at it and saw that it was not a ghost, or an old man, or a baby, but a bird. Just a regular-sized bird, but with two fantastically long tail feathers, nearly a meter long, crammed into a crate. Now out of the bag, it did not buck and punch, but maintained a calm dignity. How had such a small bird made such a scene, how had it filled the bag like it had?

"What is it?" Mother lifted a lantern, putting a hand on Father. Though she scolded his recklessness, she was often half pleased with the fruits of his bravery.

"I have no idea." Father panted with excitement. "I think it's lost. Maybe its home was destroyed by the volcano, maybe he was confused by all the ash."

The bird's spiked green head gave him the air of alertness, his blue neck the posture of calm. His entire breast, a brilliant jeweled red, pounded with breath, like a large, pumping heart exposed to the air.

"It's gorgeous. What are we going to do with it, Robert?"

"Of course, we're going to keep it."

~~~~~

The vigil for lava lasted all day and into the next night. Judas paced the porch with Father's gun, while Mother, Father, Evie, and Ixna sat in the parlor, ready to flee a river of fire at a word. No one could sleep. Ixna probably could have, but since she slept in the parlor on her mat under the piano, she couldn't.

It became Father's purpose to find new ways to distract them from the sound of Judas pacing, the vibrations of the earth under them, which proved to be the most disturbing development all day. More frightening than the ash. The stacked china chattered in the kitchen, the stucco walls let out small explosions of dust. The bird, which Father decided to name Magellan, hunkered down and refused to be interesting. For a while, Mother played the piano, which tempted Father to make up songs to go along.

> *The Indians are drunk*
> *The coffee boat is sunk*
> *Down to Brazil*
> *Where the grounds stay still*

Mother stopped mid-verse, laughing, and pulled the face she reserved only for Father. A face of exasperation and humor, as if she found their troubles both unavoidable and amusing. "If we keep up like this, we won't hear Judas calling."

"Where's Brazil?" Evie asked. "Is it at the bottom of the sea?"

"Now, that's an idea." Mother closed the piano. "You haven't even had your lesson today. Robert, show her where Brazil is. We can't have her learning geography from your silly songs."

Evie fetched her colored pencils and brought them to the table. "This . . ." Father said, making a large shape on a piece of paper, "this is America. And this is Guatemala, and this is South America, and here's Brazil."

"They grow coffee in Brazil? Like they do here?"

"Yes. This is where coffee is being grown." He made a few brown dots over Guatemala, a whole lot of dots over Brazil. "And these are where bananas grow." He painted many little yellow fingers in Honduras, to signify bananas. And a few more on the east coast of Guatemala.

Evie squinted skeptically at the map. "How come if bananas grow in Guatemala, I never see them? I haven't eaten one banana since moving here! You promised—"

"Well, that's a complicated thing, Evie. You see, all the things that make life nice grow under this line." He took a red pencil, made a line below the United States that went all the way across. "Bananas and tea and sugar and chocolate. Now, below this line, all these things grow. But above this line is where all the money is. See?" He switched pencils, adding Europe, Africa, Asia, and Australia. "The people in America and Europe love bananas and coffee, so they have to be shipped there." He made blue lines now. "Americans send money down, and Guatemala sends coffee up."

"Does anything grow in America that doesn't grow down here? Do Guatemalans ever send money up there for things?"

"Not really, Evie. They don't have money to do that."

"But you said America sends money down here all the time!"

"It's not that kind of money, darling. Look." Then he made arrows across all the oceans, showing how all these things move around the world. "The tea is grown in India, and makes it this way by boat to England. And diamonds—" Arrows all over the place, all of them eventually pointing to America and Europe.

"But you grow wheat down here and don't send it up," Evie said. "Right?"

"That's right, Evie. I am a lonely man. Just me against the world."

When Mother bent to see the lesson, she pursed her painted lips and said, "That's not where Germany is."

"Yes, it is."

"Germany does not border Spain," she told Father. "I know that much."

"Have you ever been to Germany?" he asked.

"No."

"Well, I have."

Then he began reminiscing about the time he'd hopped a train, on his way through Germany, to learn how to brew beer. A story Evie had heard before. He'd had dreams once of starting a brewery in New York. That's what brought him to Mother and snow in the first place. In this retelling, he'd timed his train-leap poorly and was holding on for dear life.

These stories always put Evie on edge, as she wasn't sure they would not end terribly. The fact that her father was at that moment sitting before her, relaying the tale, did nothing to reassure her. Her understanding of death and misfortune had been completely altered since they'd moved to Guatemala, a place where Indians constructed portals to talk to dead ancestors, and those dead ancestors roamed their woods, sabotaging their farm. Death had just become a more powerful stage of life, the boundary between the two so fluid that anyone could pass from one to the other. If her family wasn't careful, they could wake up dead one day and not even know the difference.

Mother's patience for Father's European stories wore thin quickly. She had never been to Europe and blamed Father for not taking her.

"Europe's played out, Robert," she reminded him, with the phrase he often used on her. "And Evie, sit like a lady. That's enough geography for today. Maybe we should discuss a plan. How are we going to harvest the cochineal this week?"

"We won't," Father declared, twirling a pencil. "We'll wait until next week."

"What if it's still ashing next week? We're cutting it close as it is with the rains."

The rains, which had come early last year, had drowned half of Father's cochineal crop. Judas later told Evie that an old Indian woman had been in the cave, praying for early rains.

"It won't be ashing next week," he said, with a confidence that put Evie's mind at ease. She did not understand much about her father's cochineal, but she knew that if this year's crop failed, they would be finished. The cochineal was hard work, but it didn't last long. The planting, tending, and harvest only took three months. The rest of the year, Father grew different kinds of wheat. Wheat was what he really cared about, that was his grand experiment, but he had to harvest the cochineal once a year to fund his agricultural endeavors. Once harvested and dried, the bugs were worth more than their weight in coffee.

But so many things could go wrong. For their first crop, Father had not known to keep his workers from the religious festival in town. They all disappeared, tricked into accepting advances from coffee planters while drunk—an obligation they either had to flee or work off on the plantations on the other side of the volcano. Father could not find enough replacements in time, and two-thirds of the bugs were lost.

Evie's father knew how the world worked and, barring two failed cochineal harvests, the world generally worked in his favor. He navigated the compelling dramas, like the mudslides, the beheadings, and even this volcano, with a confidence to rival Ixna's. So instead of worrying, Father announced a game with his magnifying glass. He held the glass up. "I can see everything," he declared, blinking his giant blue eye.

"Can you hold it up and see the volcano with it?"

"No, Evie. It's not for big things you always see, but little things you never see."

They held the magnifying glass up to Magellan, the bird. Father had named him, but Evie would be responsible for taking care of him. This was the first job given to her at the farm, and she took it very seriously. In addition to freeing his crammed tail feathers so they extended out of the crate, she had placed a dish of water near him, along with some dinner scraps.

"Ixna says she's made out of corn," Evie said. "She told me last week that all Indians are made out of corn. Can we see if that's true?"

"Corn!" Father declared. "Ixna, is this true?"

From her cross-legged position on the floor, Ixna nodded, determined to be bored despite the incredible drama of the day. She did not have to sit like a lady. In fact, she refused to sit in chairs at all.

"Well, let's see." Father crossed the room and politely asked for Ixna's hand. She gave it, feigning disinterest, but after a moment she, too, leaned in to see the landscape of her own skin. Her fingerprints, like Father's topographical maps, curved into parallel lines, coming to a point, to a summit, at the tips.

"I sure don't see any corn." He laughed. "Looks like you're made of flesh and blood like the rest of us."

Ixna made a face. For a sixteen-year-old, she had a remarkable knack for delivering severe reprimands with the slightest effort, like an old blue-haired matriarch. She seemed to draw pride from being made of corn.

The pacing stopped and Evie heard Judas cock Father's shotgun. Silent, aiming.

"She thinks it's an insult," Mother said with a laugh, "being made of the same stuff as us."

~~~~~

The next morning it was still ashing, more heavily than the day before. Large, slow flakes taking their time. Father wanted news from town, so he sent Judas down the mountain road with instructions on who to speak to in Xela, and with money for a newspaper. No lava had appeared, at least not yet. Maybe it had slipped down the other side of Santa María, to the plantations on the Piedmont. Maybe there'd be none at all. The situation was completely unpredictable. Volcanoes, Judas told Evie, were like jealous women.

Morning looked no different than night, though Father reassured Evie that the sun was still in the sky. Ash in the atmosphere just blocked its light. The ground groaned like a hungry stomach. Their dishes no longer vibrated but clashed and broke. In the yard, the chickens jumped and ran into each other, but Magellan did not move in his crate. He had not eaten the scraps Evie had left for him, and bit her hand when she added more to the pile.

"I think maybe we should let him go. He's not eating."

"Let him go? But Evie, you've always wanted a pet." This was true. However, things she always wanted always came at the wrong time in Guatemala, in the wrong way, making her realize she did not want them at all.

"Maybe he eats bugs," Father said. "After breakfast, go to the woodpile with a lantern and see what you can find."

When Judas arrived with the newspaper, Father flipped through the entire thing, flipped back, then forward again. "This is incredible," he said, tossing the paper aside.

Mother took up the paper, glanced through it once, then twice. "Oh!" she cried with an indulgent roll of her murky brown eyes. "The Fasbinders' party was a raving success, did you see? The President's wife showed up in a gown cut for the Queen!" She held up the front page, featuring a photograph of the President and his wife.

Xela's newspaper was not written in English, but Mother could usually cobble together the stories by the names, pictures, and few words of Spanish she knew. Indeed, the front page of that day's paper described a gala held at the Fasbinders' coffee plantation a few days before. They knew it had happened a few days before because Father had been obsessed with obtaining an invitation. Mother, however, could not even imagine herself attending. She had nothing to wear. All the dresses she owned, thanks to Ixna's vigorous washing, were shapeless, faded replicas of their former glory.

"Ask her!" Father had commanded on several occasions. "Ask her for an invitation the next time she comes to tea!"

"Why, Robert? What's the point of going?"

Of course, she knew why. Even Evie knew. He harbored hopes of cornering the President and sharing the details of his grand experiment. The economic future of Guatemala, secured. "Once he realizes the possibilities of a year-round wheat harvest, he might come up with some government funds, Mattie."

"Everyone is going to talk to the President," Mother had replied, more than once. "Everyone has a plan for Guatemala. The railroad men, the Boston banana barons, the German bankers. Even Mrs. Fasbinder has a scheme to present to him at the party. What makes you think he cares about feeding Indians?"

"Because starving Indians can't lay train tracks!"

In a high, affected voice, Mother now began reading the Fasbinders' guest list from the paper, names easy to pronounce because they were American. Father held his head in his hands, hopeless, like these influential guests were being introduced and promptly led away from him, one by one.

"Maybe that was what we've been hearing, you think, Robert? We should file a noise complaint. That party has been shaking our whole mountain!"

Father grinned, spreading his fingers to look at Mother.

"And the ash from their cigarettes!" she added with a whoop. "Blowing over here, making a mess!"

It became a happy breakfast, with Mother and Father teasing one another, joking about the newspaper, which failed to make any mention of the volcano.

"Here, Evie, you can color the front page of this one. That's all it's good for."

So there was no news on the lava. In town, there had just been talk of the ash. Judas said so much of it piled on Xela's rooftops that several had cracked under the weight. With that news, Father climbed up onto the church roof to sweep it clear. "I can see the party from here!" Father called down, hanging his arms over the big cross. "I can see the President with his big cigar! They're all eating bananas, over there! Dancing girls, naked dancing girls, eating bananas!"

"Robert!"

There was no more discussion of the delayed harvest, of the ash, which fell more heavily, Evie noticed, by the hour.

The band began playing that afternoon—the drums so loud that they could be heard all the way up at the farm. At first Evie thought that it was the volcano. But this noise felt different. It did not shake the ground. It thumped in Evie's chest like another heart. Mother, standing on the porch, sweeping yet another layer of ash off into the yard, paused, cocked an ear in the direction of the city.

"It's music," she said to no one in particular, although Evie was the only one around. Father had left with Judas, gone to climb the ridge again, hoping for a better view. Ixna worked in the kitchen, whitening their good shoes with the useless newspaper.

Evie held her breath and listened, finding the regularity of the beat.

"It's 'The Battle Hymn of the Republic,'" Mother said, with a peculiar smile on her face. She set the broom against the house and told Evie to run and get her parasol. They were going into town.

They took Ixna with them because they needed a translator. In preparation for the move to Guatemala, Mother had taken six months' instruction in Spanish, only to find that it was useless in most everyday interactions outside the capital. Out here, where the Indians lived, people spoke Ixil, or Quiché, or Mam, or any one of a dozen Indian languages. The only people who spoke Spanish in Xela were the wealthy Guatemalans they did not associate with, the government officials, who preferred to speak English anyway, and other foreigners (mostly German coffee planters), who'd made the same mistake Mother had. Their Spanish, Mother declared, was unintelligible.

Mother held her black mourning parasol like a shield as she walked through the gray flurries of ash. In her other hand, a lantern swayed, revealing frightening glimpses of smoked-out jungle. Today, Evie did not fear the volcano as much as she feared walking to town without Father or Judas. Every foreigner in Guatemala had been warned (by government officials, by the newspaper, by each other) of the dangers awaiting lone white female travelers in the highlands: a familiar refrain from Mother's weekly teas with Mrs. Fasbinder. Men were killed, but the horrors awaiting women were much more unimaginable to Evie, because she had no idea what the words meant. *Taken, molested, disgraced.* All Evie understood was that there were worse things awaiting women on the road than merely being killed.

"They throw girls in the volcano, you know," Mrs. Fasbinder had said not long ago. "They've done it for centuries. *Virgins*, of course. This country is like a bad adventure novel sold to silly women. You'd think the Spanish never arrived."

Why were they walking to town alone? What were virgins? Did they die in the volcano? Terrible thoughts, unmentionable questions that Evie could not even gather the breath to ask. Her mother walked so fast down their mountain that Evie could not keep up. She lagged behind with Ixna, who was barefoot and taking her time.

"Ixna, do you think lava's coming to Father's mountain?"

"His mountain?" She clicked her tongue.

"Yes. His mountain. Where we live. Will lava come?"

"Not his mountain."

"How's that?" Evie asked, kicking the dirt. "My father paid for this land. It belongs to him."

Ixna did not break her calm stride and passed by Evie, leaving her standing in disbelief. "The mountain never belongs to anyone. We all belong to the mountain."

"He paid," Evie insisted, galloping to catch up. How else could someone own something if they didn't pay? "He paid!"

"Who did he pay?"

"The government."

"Ah, but we paid for it, too. Three times. How many times did your father pay?"

Evie didn't know what to say. Conversations with Ixna usually turned on Evie in this way. So she wasn't much surprised, just hopeful that one day she would understand.

"When he pays four times, it can be his." Ixna's tiny, flat-topped teeth came over her lip in an angry imitation of a smile. "Then we eat bread. Then all our problems solved."

There was no view of the city from the mountain, where there should have been a view. Just black clouds, ash falling up, down, sideways, and accumulating on the empty road, and the sound of trumpets and drums in the distance. They walked two miles to Xela. There should have been Indians on the road. Evie imagined them standing, lined up just beyond visibility. They were there, Evie knew they must be there. This road was crowded with shacks so primitive they didn't even have doors and proper walls. These Indians would sneak onto their land to plant food, cut down trees, and worship.

"They have no sense of what ownership means," Mother often said. "Unless they have a claim. Then they start waving titles at you. Illegible titles for communal land, issued over a hundred years ago by the Spanish Crown! But they wanted independence from Spain and they got it!"

The band was still playing by the time they made it to the central park, where half the gas lamps had been blown out and the other half cast a gothic orange light over the busy scene. Visibility had cleared somewhat, because of the protected position of the park plaza. There had been no one on the road, no one to trouble them, and now Evie could see why. Everyone had come here—standing in open doorways or sitting on the wide dingy steps of the Catholic church—to watch the military band. Evie knew they were from the military by the severe, straight lines they stood in, and their uniforms. At least two hundred of them aimed their instruments at the sky, playing so loudly that Evie couldn't hear what her mother said right next to her. A little farther away, near the market, more soldiers marched, yelling into windows and at the people who passed by. The same phrase over and over.

"What are they saying?" Mother asked Ixna.

Ixna shrugged. "They say there's no volcano erupting."

"What?"

Evie watched one of the band members shake the ash from his hat and spit on the ground. He held a trombone at his side, then pointed it at some Indians like a gun.

"In Quiché. They say the President decrees that this is not from the volcano." Evie watched a small flake of ash flutter down and get caught in Ixna's eyelashes. She didn't even blink.

Mother, still holding Evie's hand in her sweaty fist, tightened her grip. "If it's not the volcano, then what the hell is it?"

Rocks fell on the town and littered the street. They burned through the thatched rooftops of Indian shacks and shattered the windows and roof tiles of the government offices and the fancy whitewashed houses. Mother looked around in amazement.

"Europe's all played out, Evie. Aren't you glad we could come to a place with so much promise as this?" She laughed, wiping her eyes clear of something.

A flaming rock the size of a man's fist hit the side of the police station behind them, leaving a hole in the stucco. Ixna turned away. Mother's mood turned sharply at this close call. She reopened her parasol, pulled Evie under its protection, and walked toward the safety of the church.

"Now do you see?" she yelled over a sudden shout of trumpets. "Now do you see our predicament, trying to conduct reasonable and civilized business in a place like this?"

Two young Indian women, Ixna's age, walked past with very large babies, their heads covered in black sacks. Almost all the Indian babies in town had their heads stuffed in black sacks, always, to protect them from evil spirits. A fact that made the image of her own sister arriving in a sack one day very plausible to Evie. Mother eyed these young mothers as if they had walked across on cue to make her point.

The band had come all the way from Guatemala City. They played "The

Battle Hymn of the Republic" over and over, with no flourish or variation. But with all music, there are rests. Not even the Guatemalan Army could deny that. Even as they denied the ash that rained down, clogging their instruments and forcing some to shake their horns clear, even as one of the trumpeters was knocked in the head with a flying rock and fell down and did not move, they could not deny those beats of silence at the end of each verse. And so everyone stood waiting for it. The director tried to hurry through those rests, waving his arms frantically, as if he himself summoned the rumblings in the distance that seemed, along with Mother, to get angrier with each verse.

A crowd had congregated near the church to watch the performance. The huge limestone cathedral sheltered them from the occasional flying, flaming rocks and blocked much of the ash. Mother pulled Evie up the main steps— past the poor Indians sitting at the bottom, then Ladinos, then the rich Spanish-speaking Guatemalans above them. At the top sat the foreigners, like them, the Germans and French, a few Americans. Mother walked past everyone and into the high, hollow church, where the band's song was transformed into ominous echoes.

Evie had never been inside the cathedral and was disturbed by its decadence. Muddy paintings framed in bright gold, the pictures so muddled and dark that it was not until they got close that Evie could see the scenes: men hanging from trees, a man holding his own severed head.

They sat down to wait and rest in safety. Who knew where Ixna had gone? Indians came and went, lighting candles. Up front, Jesus on his cross looked like the saddest man on earth, with his open eyes rolled up to the sky and his ribs showing. Below him, a line of little girls in sack dresses prayed on their knees. At least thirty girls, all dark, black-haired. A nun paced nearby, watching. Evie had never seen so many little girls in Xela, so many so close to her age.

"Mother." She tugged at her sleeve. "Who are they?"

"Orphans."

"What are orphans? Can I play with them?"

"Orphans are children without parents, Evie. You can't play with them."

"How did they lose their parents? Do parents die?"

"Of course not, Evie. Sometimes they just can't afford to keep their children, so they drop them off here."

"What are they doing?" It was shocking to Evie that children could lose their parents at all, although it seemed that orphans could only be little girls.

"It seems they've been instructed to pray the volcano away. Or maybe the army."

~~~~~

The band played for two and a half days without stopping, though the ash had finished by the next day. Father said that they brought in replacements so they could play in shifts. For two days, all through the day and night, Evie could hear those drums all the way up their mountain. She would find herself walking to the beat, chewing, breathing. Even Magellan the bird could not resist the beat. He ignored his food, his water, and any effort on Evie's part to communicate, but he did acknowledge the drums. If Evie sat far enough away and pretended she wasn't watching, he would turn his head almost perpendicular to his body and bob to the rhythm, as if it made perfect sense to him.

She thought often of the orphan girls, too, lined up and praying for two days.

Evie asked Father what all this could be. If it wasn't the volcano, then what was it? He assured her that it was the volcano, that he had climbed the range and seen it himself. It looked like a big mouth smoking a cigar.

"Then why does the paper say it isn't the volcano?" Indeed, the paper had gone from not mentioning the volcano at all to explicitly denying the eruption.

"A hundred years ago, Evie, there weren't newspapers down here. A hundred years ago, no one would deny that volcano erupting. Not even the Spanish. But progress is a funny thing. Newspapers aren't for news, Evie. They never were."

"What are they for, then?"

"For coloring," he said, handing over the latest edition.

And then, just as suddenly as it had begun, "The Battle Hymn of the Republic" stopped. Evie was on the porch helping Ixna, when the beat that had been regulating their lives for the past two and a half days just stopped. Evie looked up at Ixna—who also looked up, cleared a stray hair from her face, and then went back to her sweeping.

~~~~~

Father stood on the porch in a pose of determined, casual calm, a tense smile fixed on his face as he stared down at the newspaper Judas had brought from Xela. The sun was back, high and red. The days now were stuck in perpetual dawn with the ash lingering in the atmosphere.

Mother, standing next to him, did not smile. Not even a little. Not even in her exasperated way. Evie saw a new expression on her face, one of despair. The band had worn her down over the past sixty hours. The assault by music, her beloved medium, had unhinged her. Criminals and thieves she could understand, but absurdity proved to be too much. After a particularly scary story from Ixna, Evie had asked Mother the scariest story she'd ever heard. *Alice's Adventures in Wonderland,* she had replied.

Father, on the other hand, remained calm. To him, Guatemalan politics were akin to natural disasters. No use getting upset, you merely endured and recovered. He'd been executing funny dance steps for two and a half days.

They gave the paper to Evie to color in. She could not read the Spanish, but she knew what it said. They'd been talking about it in escalating whispers all morning, the sound of the drums replaced by their quarrel. On the front page, she began to fill in the picture of the President. She'd give him horns. Every time his picture appeared in the paper, which was quite often, Evie colored him a different way to make Father laugh.

That day's newspaper published two decrees from the President. One: that a volcano had indeed erupted in Mexico five days before. A strong wind had blown the ash into Guatemala and aid was being sent to the affected coffee plantations. This decree, printed in Spanish, English, and German, made everyone laugh—Father heartily, Mother nervously. But the second decree had started the fight. The President had instituted a labor draft to provide this aid. Every male Indian in the highlands would be rounded up tomorrow and taken to the Piedmont to save the coffee. Anyone caught ducking the draft would be whipped and forced to work anyway like the others, but in shackles.

"How can we possibly keep this running now," Mother said, not like a question. Seated at the table, Evie studied her work, trying to come up with something more than horns on the President that would make them both laugh.

"Oh," Father mused, "there are ways."

Turning to the second page, Evie found a picture of the Catholic church, which had collapsed hours after they'd been sitting under its protection. What had happened to the orphan girls? Only the steps remained, perfectly intact, leading up to a pile of grainy black-and-white rubble.

"There is no way to run a farm without workers, Robert."

It had never occurred to Evie that a building could collapse, let alone a church. All this time, she had felt protected somehow, living in their little chapel on the mountain. Now she stared up with fear at the lumpy walls, the pitched ceiling.

"We could sell some things, maybe. It says any Indians indebted to a farmer are exempt. It says here, any Indian five hundred pesos or more in debt. We could loan them money to keep them here."

Evie began to color in the church ruins with a dark blue pencil. She would have used white, but experience had taught her that she needed bold, dark colors when filling in the newspaper. Anything less would just smear the ink and make everything gray.

"What do we have to sell, Robert?" Mother's tone caused Evie to pause, unable to color well and listen at the same time. "Of course, something of mine."

"Well, Mattie," Father joked, feeling her out with his playful blue eyes, "you have such nice things."

"How convenient for you." Mother regained her composure just as quickly as she'd lost it, though her cheeks remained two scorched circles.

"I would if I had anything, if I came from rich folks—"

"I have an idea!" Mother clapped. "How about Evie?"

Evie looked up from not drawing.

"She's half yours. We could hire out Evie! Hey, why not? She'd bring in a good price." Mother's gaze glittered with possibility. "The coffee plantations would take her, for sure. Or one of the new banana farms. You like bananas, Evie."

Father chuckled with horrifying lightness. "Now, that's an idea."

Evie dropped her pencil and choked on the sob in her throat. It had been a long time since she'd wanted to work on a banana plantation, didn't they know that? She had learned what it was actually like from Judas, who had worked on the coast for years. Whippings, rotten beans to eat, yellow fever. And the coffee plantations were no better, according to Ixna. Evie stood up from her chair, shaking, with tears in her eyes.

Mother drew her in, embracing her roughly with a little, harried laugh. "We're just joking, sweetie. We're not going to sell you to anyone. How could you think that? You're old enough to know when your father and I are teasing."

"That's a nice picture, Evie," Father commented, turning the newspaper back to the front page. The President of Guatemala with horns and gold peso eyes. "You understand the situation here more than anyone I know."

They sent Evie to the kitchen, so they could argue in earnest. There, she tried to feed Magellan. He was not doing well. Evie had yet to convince him to eat anything. She had tried worms and flies, berries, beetles, and bread. Everything she pushed into the slats of the chicken crate rotted or crawled away.

How do you force food on someone? He must be starving.

No one cares about bread down here, Mother had begun to mutter to herself a few months ago.

It was true. For two years now, Father tried to sell wheat at market to the Indians, but no one wanted it. He then sent his wheat far away to be ground into flour and then sent back, but still no one was interested. After that, he had Ixna bake breads and cookies, but no one would even try the free samples he offered. They approached his cart, in varying degrees of boldness, to see his blue eyes. Then they walked right on over to the piles of corn on either side. Not one Indian tried the grains, the flour, or the baked goods. Not even the animals would eat bread, Evie realized, watching Magellan defecate on his piece of toast. Not even Ixna, who had once almost starved to death.

From the age of eight until she came to the mountain, Ixna had worked on a coffee plantation, where they paid and fed the workers "per task." By law, a task was supposed to take a day to complete, but tasks had a way of growing and taking three days. So she worked every day but only received food every three days. The coffee trees, however, were shaded with banana trees. Ixna could not help herself. The overseer caught her, whipped her, and she had to work a year to pay for the "damaged" tree.

It took so long to pay off the tree because Ixna was paid with worn-out pretend money to be cashed in every two weeks for real money. With nowhere to safely keep these slips of paper, she had to tie them to her body beneath her blouse while she worked. During the rainy season, as she worked through heavy rains, the strips of paper disintegrated against her skin and she could not get her work credited against her debt.

So when Mother threatened to sell Evie to a plantation, she had cried, thinking of starvation, bananas hanging over her head that she could not eat. Whips and dogs. She pictured Ixna, eight years old, a brown version of herself.

Considering all this, Ixna had no reason to complain about her work on the mountain, but Evie watched her now, plodding around their kitchen like a slave. How many different ways to cook wheat, to mix wheat, to make it look like something else? Breads, cookies, biscuits, cakes, thick floury pies. Something, anything, to convince the Indians.

Ixna did not like cooking with wheat and certainly did not eat it. She handled flour with visible disgust, moaning at the traces it left on her hands, the clouds it formed with a misplaced breath. She squeezed her eyes and mouth shut, averting her face, not wanting to breathe it in. But she made all of the dishes just how Mother told her, baked them for market knowing they would not be sold. Father's favorite wheat, the one he insisted would save the Indians, hard red spring, was reserved for breads. Beaten, risen, baked, and cooled by Ixna's strong hands, the loaves were fluffy on the inside, with a fortress of crust on the outside. By year's end, Father said, he would convert all his fields to hard red spring. The Indians needed to learn a new crop, for the higher, dryer land. The plantations were expanding, the government giving them all the communal corn-growing fields the Indians had used for centuries. They had a choice: adapt or starve. At the moment, they seemed to be choosing the latter.

"Ixna, why don't you eat our food?"

Ixna's forehead rippled in annoyance as she kneaded dough for dumplings. Her fingertips left marks on little balls she twisted away, dented and smiling like little faces. "Our ancestors did not have bread." The water on the fire had begun to boil, the pot rattling like something trapped inside. "So why should we?"

"Because progress is good. My grandparents didn't have telegraphs, but now we do, and we're happy."

"Your family is happy?"

"Goddammit, Mattie!" Father shouted from the porch.

The little faces were lined up, ready for the pot, but Ixna did not put them in right away. She turned to a different batch of rising dough and began punching it down, punching hard, as if defending herself from attack. She asked her question again.

"You think wheat will make Indians happy like your parents are happy?"

Evie ignored the question and pinched a corner of the dough, rolled it into a pill, and squeezed her hand into Magellan's crate to offer it. He swiped down, bit her knuckle with a small, vicious twist.

Hard red spring, at least, had not yet won over Ixna, or Magellan. How could anyone resist it? In addition to being tasty, it was beautiful out in the fields. When the stalks rose, they came up looking like fire.

"Father's very smart," Evie said, sucking the blood from her injured finger.

"Not so smart if he makes the snake angry. It was very ignorant to make him angry." As Ixna spoke, she took the lid off the boiling pot to check the water.

"What snake?" Evie knew she should not ask, but if she did not know she would only imagine the worst. Yet another enemy added to their life on the mountain.

"The big snake in the volcano." Ixna took a heap of dough and rolled it briskly with the flat of her hands, making a long tube, a snake. "He punishes bad people."

Ixna never tried to shield Evie from the horrible truths of the adult world, and because of this she was sometimes her best source of information. As long as she made sense, which she rarely did. "How has Father been bad?"

"Bad is not asking permission of the mountain, not giving thanks. Bad is going against the ancestors. Breaking their traditions." She cut the snake of dough into small pieces and pinched the ends. More dumplings.

"What traditions?"

"Traditions of dressing and praying and eating."

"Like eating bread? Does eating bread make the snake angry?"

"Yes." Ixna took the dumplings and dropped them in the pot one by one. "But what makes him most angry is when someone tries to own this mountain." Ixna dropped the last one in and watched the blanched bodies tumble, fighting for surface space.

Evie watched Ixna watching the dumplings, taming their foam with a spoon. They came out one by one, their little pale faces wrinkly, cooked, hardened into worry.

Evie found Mother in the parlor, alone. In this new red light, she looked beautiful. Until about a year ago, she had been shaped by corsets and padding, her skin dusted porcelain with powder. One by one, these artifices had dropped away. The corset was the first to go, being impractical with the work, the uphill walks, and Father's claim not to notice a difference. She began to wear her hair straight and loose. With the disappearance of her last tin of face powder, she suddenly developed freckles across her nose, which made her look girlish. Only her lipstick remained, and this Mother applied obsessively, *to keep the wolves from the door*, Father had once said. Another terrifying joke Evie did not understand.

Mother was writing a letter.

"Who are you writing to?" Evie asked.

"Just writing a letter home."

Mother composed all their letters to New York. These letters, which Mother read aloud before mailing, usually detailed the most trivial things. Things like: "Evie was chased by a rooster today," "The Indians stare at me when I wear pants." On the day they woke up to ash raining down on their heads, she wrote home: "I ripped my last pair of good stockings today. Will never be able to replace them."

"Is there something you want to say to Grandma?"

Evie did not remember her grandmother, but would never say so. "Are we staying, then?"

"Yes." Mother tried on a smile, fresh and pink. "Your father has a plan."

Evie understood this plan right away. Like every other plan he'd had on the mountain: Mother would write Grandmother for more money. She'd sent more money when they bought the bugs in January, when Father advanced the Indians their pay last year. When the police chief arrested their worker Raffie for startling a white woman and made Father buy him back in time for the second harvest, which ended up drowned in the early rains anyway.

"Is he going to bribe someone?"

Mother paused, her pen point pressed into the paper, and glared at Evie. "Where did you learn that word?"

"From Judas," she lied. Because Judas wouldn't care or blame her if Mother scolded him for it. He understood survival on the mountain more than anyone. Evie certainly could not say that she'd learned it from Mother's teas with Mrs. Fasbinder.

"Well, you surely are getting a Guatemalan education," she observed crisply. "But no, we won't use Grandmother's money for bribes. We pay people to *work*, Evie. Bribes are for cheats and criminals. Your father's not that kind of man." She turned back to the letter, writing in a burst. "I did not marry that kind of man."

"How come the President says the volcano didn't erupt? Did it erupt?"

"Of course it did, Evie. You saw for yourself, didn't you?"

"Yes. But why does he say it didn't?"

"Sometimes, Evie, the truth can be very expensive."

After finishing her letter, Mother began to play the piano. She played "The Battle Hymn of the Republic," which Evie had never heard her play before. She stabbed at the keys with fierce fingers, making many mistakes, trying to reach Father in the fields. Evie knew that by suggesting they sell "some things," he really meant the piano. It was the only thing they owned in Guatemala that was worth anything, outside of the mountain itself. Father didn't have nice things and Mother had left all her jewelry in New York, for fear of tempting thieves.

This piano was like a part of the family. When they left for Guatemala, it accompanied them on every leg of the journey. First shipped by rail across the U.S. to New Orleans. From there, it came on the coffee steamboat with them from New Orleans to the port of Coatzacoalcos in southern Mexico. Then it was loaded onto a car on the Tehuantepec Railroad, hauled across Mexico, to a Pacific port, where men rolled it onto another coffee steamer bound for Champerico, Guatemala. From Champerico, the piano took up a whole compartment in another railroad car to Retalhuleu. Then it was pulled by a team of horses to Xela, where Father unloaded it at the base of the mountain and pushed it onto a wooden cart, to which he attached Tiny, the skeptical mule he'd just bought.

"If you think getting here has been a trial for us," Father had said, sweating and swearing at Tiny, who refused to complete the last mile of their monthlong journey, "just imagine how the coffee planters feel. Whoever solves the shipping problem in Guatemala will be a rich man."

On several occasions, Mrs. Fasbinder had offered increasing sums of money for the piano, but each rising price offended Mother more than the last offer. And though Evie knew she had just been making a point, her mother's suggestion that they sell Evie rather than the piano was not as much of a surprise as one would think. And Father's hint about selling it in the first place made her realize how bad their situation must be.

"Will all our workers be drafted away, even Judas?" Evie asked over "The Battle Hymn of the Republic."

Somewhere else, somewhere civilized, with her eyes closed, Mother tapped a foot to keep time on the old floorboards. "I don't know, Evie. I hope so. No. No, I don't."

"If he goes, will he die?"

"No, Evie. He'll come back, don't worry. This isn't the railroad draft. A lot of Indians get drafted to the coffee plantations and come back."

"But Judas isn't Indian. He's a Ladino, he told me. Maybe they won't take him."

"Ha!" Mother cried over her own song. "Ladino isn't even a real word, Evie. He may spend every peso he makes trying to become white, but according to the government, he'll always be Indian. And for Indians, the government has the last word down here."

~~~~~

Evie watched the labor drafts the next day from an overlook near the road. The sun that day had risen red and progressed to a yellow-orange bright enough for her to see the larger details below, where Xela's central park seethed with thousands of Indians. Bold black lines of policemen then corralled the crowd into smaller groups. The mass halved, then quartered, on and on until they fit into the wagons.

Every male Indian in the area between the ages of twelve and fifty who was not majorly indebted to any farmer was required to go. But since most Indians didn't even know how old they were, the police ignored claims that someone was too young or too old. Indians rarely made it past fifty, anyway, so no one could argue about being too old. If they looked like they could harvest coffee, then off they went. Judas told Evie that his nephew, nine years old, had been taken away and probably wouldn't be back for months.

Father's plan for his Indian workers, however, succeeded. On the faith that Mother's letter home would work, he borrowed from the bank in Xela and registered their debts at the government office to exempt them from the draft. By the time Evie came back from the overlook, they were gathering wood for the cooking shed, repairing the brushes and nets.

~~~~~

Two days after the draft, it was light enough out to venture into the woods again. Judas stood on the front porch that morning, taking instructions from Mother.

"Clear it all out," she told him. "Whatever you find. On our walk to Xela, I saw those shacks right on the property line." She had started using the Indian name for the town (pronounced *SHAY-la*) months ago. The Spanish name, Quetzaltenango, was just too much of a mouthful, too tiring—eventually even for her.

They had not wanted this much land, but the government insisted Father take it all, for a very low price. All or nothing. Then they gave him instructions on how to keep Indians away: hanging a specific dead animal from a tree, sabotaging altars with dreadful omens, shooting trespassers, but Mother preferred fire. It was dramatic yet unconfrontational, and she could see the plumes of smoke, the proof, from the porch.

Judas relaced and retied his shoes before setting off with a lantern in his hand and his machete strapped to his hip. Evie followed with a basket of rolls. Behind them, the piano began, per Father's request. He'd requested a long song, the longest Mother could find, to keep him company while he worked.

"Judas, are you an Indian or a Ladino?" Evie asked, tagging behind.

"I am Ladino," he announced, annoyed. "Do I look lazy and drunk? I work for my food, I buy my clothes."

"But your parents were Indians? And you used to be Indian?"

"Yes, but that's before. Now I speak Spanish, English, some German. Now I am Ladino." He held the lantern out as if lighting their way through the forest, though the sun shone bright enough now that it wasn't needed. In his other hand, he held one of Ixna's rolls, which he ripped with his teeth.

"But you're on the draft list. Have you told the *jefe* that you're Ladino?"

"I am working on that," he assured her, chewing. For a man missing many teeth, the crust was difficult to crack, and his entire face contorted with the effort. But still, Judas ate wheat with pleasure, unlike every Indian in town.

"What about Ixna?" Evie asked. "She works. She can speak Spanish and English. Is she Ladino?"

Judas held a finger up, shook his head. "But her clothes are Indian," he said with his mouth full. "Women cannot change to Ladino. If all men change to Ladino, then Indians have money and dignity. If all women change to Ladino, there are no more Indians. There is nothing left."

Father's forest looked burned. The ash would remain, sticking to everything, until the first rainy season shower. Animal tracks preceded them, and human tracks, too. Evie could tell Judas's tracks from his shoes, pointed at the tips, whereas Father's boots left wide, blunt prints. The largest in the forest. There were so many tracks, tracks of bare feet, Indian feet. Deer, jaguars, and lizards, and the sideways slide of snakes. They could still hear the piano clearly, running through a refrain. Mother's playing not only entertained Father while he worked, Evie drew courage from it when she ventured into the forest.

They ran into Father and Ixna, who was holding her red blanket to her chest. Both coming from another trail, laughing. Father held on to Ixna's tied belt, allowing himself to be towed along the path. They did not see Evie and Judas right away.

"Father!" Evie called. "Are you playing a game?"

They both spun around. "We are!" Father answered, waving. "Blindman's bluff! Though don't tell your mother, you know she doesn't like games so much when we're supposed to be working."

"I know."

The piano suddenly stopped. Birds, insects, unseeable things crawling in the brush. Evie shivered with fright. Father turned Ixna around by the shoulders and pushed her down one of the paths. In a moment, she was gone. In another, Father was gone, too, down a different path.

The music began again. The pause lasted just long enough that Evie knew what had happened. A breeze from the window had blown the sheet music across the room.

"I can never get Ixna to play games with me," Evie told Judas. "Not even I Spy." All Evie's games on the mountain were solitary, dreary endeavors at imitating her parents. Planting pebbles, pecking at the piano. "But it seems she likes blindman's bluff. You think she'd play that with *me*?"

"*Saber.*"

Evie and Judas continued deeper into the forest, where Judas needed his machete. He whacked at branches and vines with big, unpredictable motions, never warning Evie. She appreciated this, his trust that she knew to keep clear.

They soon came upon a small clearing planted with tiny corn seedlings. There had been trees before, but an Indian had cut them down to sun his crop. Evie could see the stumps, sliced up with thin, weathered machete marks, then burned to feed the soil. An Indian could have twenty of these plots hidden all around their land.

Alone, this discovery would terrify Evie, but with Judas, she felt brave. He was just Indian enough in her mind to be able to control the ghosts, and white enough that she didn't fear him. That's what Ladino meant to her. She watched him now attack the earth with his blade, cutting up the corn plants, not six inches high. Evie did her part and stomped on them, too, twisting her heel into the white, surfaced roots. In a minute, they'd destroyed the plot. Evie took three rolls from her basket and left them there, a gift, a hopeful gesture Father insisted on if Mother was going to insist on such destruction. Then they set off to find more.

"Judas, what does Magellan eat? I can't get him to eat anything." This was not the only problem. In addition to not eating, Magellan had begun to peck at himself. A large wound had appeared on his breast, sticky and infected. Evie moved him to a dark corner, hoping no one would notice. Her first job on the farm, and she was failing at it.

Judas made an abrupt right and began to slice what seemed to be a new trail. "Magellan eats fruit and lizards," he told her.

"I tried that!"

"But it's no use. He won't eat. He's killing himself. He's decided not to live."

Evie stopped. "Why's he killing himself? Why would he do that?"

"*Saber.*" He smiled secretly, ducked under a vine, then cut it down so Evie would not have to duck. Yes, he was just Indian enough to be maddening at times, too.

Evie stomped a foot. "When you say *saber*, I know it means you know!"

He shrugged, turning them back onto an old path.

"If you tell me, I'll write you a note for the Frenchman's shop." Amazingly, a note from any white person, even an eight-year-old, even with misspellings, could gain admittance for an Indian to browse. "A note to look at anything you want."

Judas paused to consider, sucking the bread from his teeth and studying his machete for nicks. "Okay. Fine, I will tell you. Magellan is killing himself because he cannot kill you." He seemed very pleased with this statement and swallowed.

"What?" But Judas continued walking. "Why would he want to kill me? My father saved him from the woods!" she yelled at his back, running to keep up. She felt disoriented, had no idea how far they'd gone until she was startled by the appearance of the cave. She had thought they were somewhere else completely, and the shock of seeing the stone jaws, the blackened cavern filmed with smoke, almost made her heart stop. Forgetting herself, she nearly walked into one of Judas's wild machete swings.

"Why would he want to kill me?" she asked again, weakly.

She felt the temperature drop as they neared, and the hair on her arms stood up in fright. She kept close to Judas, holding his belt now, to keep clear of his machete as he cleared the path. Evie hoped that Mother had finally heeded her warnings about the cave and had ordered Judas to burn it. But no, they passed by. And that was when she saw the most startling thing. A gift left for the dead ancestors, nicer than all the others. Among the coins and paper trash, the doll and bottles, she spied a silver glint.

They did not lose speed, coming off a trail and cutting directly through the brush. In front of them, branches shook, a flash of bright colors there and gone. An Indian. The jungle fell away from Judas's sharp blade, finally revealing an altar, a portal to Indian ancestors. The hanging gourds looked like heads knocking together in the wind, the twisted saplings like limbs.

Judas doused the pagan altar with kerosene, then tipped the lantern and lit it all up in a big bright whoosh that sounded like a flock of birds taking off.

Evie took no joy from this fire, which would ordinarily make her believe they could win the battle with the ghosts and Indians. Because now she realized these fires did nothing. They were losing. The piano, its crescendo in the distance, provided no solace. They hadn't even the safe space of their own home. They'd passed so quickly, but she knew exactly what it was: the shape, the size, the glint. What she had seen there in the cave and what she couldn't bring herself to stop and retrieve was her mother's missing mirror.

They burned three altars and dug up four corn plots that day, the communal land reclaimed in the name of civilization. When they returned from the forest, stinking of kerosene, smoke, and black mud, Evie could see her parents from afar, standing on the porch with a newspaper. Evie approached carefully, watching them. They hadn't noticed her skirting the cactus field, still costumed in their clothes and providing camouflage.

Mother closed the paper. "Now we've lost our workers and our money. I told you not to throw money at the problem right away. Now they need all the Indians, no matter if they're in debt. If you'd just waited a few days—"

"Not all of it," Father insisted. "We still have a little money left."

"Yes, what we need to get home. You're not taking our fare money."

Money. Evie walked to the back of the house, uninterested in hearing more. How could they argue about money when much more horrible things were happening all around them? The ghosts didn't want their money, they wanted Mother's mirror for some horrible, unimaginable reason. And, she was sure, they wanted her parents to fight. In the kitchen, she studied the bird and his bloody breast. She couldn't believe Magellan wanted to kill himself. More likely, the ghosts were tormenting him, too. She peered through the slats and met his fierce, black-bead eye.

Evie gathered the heavy crate in her arms. Magellan flapped and hissed in protest as she carried him to the front porch.

"Magellan's sick," Evie said, hugging the crate. But they didn't hear or see.

"They can't take all the Indians away. I'm sure they'll make exceptions."

Agitated with their fight, Magellan hopped from foot to foot and began preening.

"Every bean has to be washed, Robert. Every single coffee bean has to be picked by hand and washed and dried. And they will get every Indian in the country to do it. You got out of the first draft, now you think you can get out of this second draft, but what about the third and the fourth?"

"I just have to talk to the right people. The government—"

"The government *exists* for coffee. Not law and order, not social welfare. Their *only job* is to get the Indians to work. That's all anyone pays them for!"

"But still, they have to see what I'm doing is good for the coffee, too."

"Haven't you figured it out, Robert? Have you yet to realize that feeding the Indians is not in their best interest? Starvation is the only incentive they have!"

In the long, searching silence that followed this proclamation, Mother saw Magellan for the first time. "Oh my God, what is wrong with the bird?" she gasped. "What's he doing?" Sensing her attention, the bird glared up at her with his demented beard of blood and feathers. "Evie, what's the matter with Magellan?"

"He won't eat. I don't know. I tried everything," she cried.

Father took the crate from her. It seemed light in his hands. "Did you try lizards?"

"Yes."

"Berries?"

"Yes!"

"I think we should let him go," Mother said, peering through the rough slats. "He's going to kill himself like this."

Father turned the crate over, observing the situation from various angles. "Ixna knows. I know she knows what kind of bird this is, but she wouldn't tell me."

"Judas says it's not my fault. He said it's in his nature to do this."

Father decided on an angle and held his chin, thinking. "If he can't survive in a crate, with us bringing him food, he certainly can't survive on his own in the woods."

"So we have to watch him waste away in our house?" Mother asked. "While he rips himself to shreds before our eyes? Evie, don't look at him!"

"What is wrong with this country?" Father marveled, sniffing the rotting food. "It's like they all want to starve to make some point, even the god-damned animals."

Done with Magellan, Mother threw her shawl over the crate and turned back to Father. "You care more about these Indians, who don't even want your help, than your own family. Do you think"—she paused, licked the sweat from her upper lip—"this is a nourishing environment for your daughter? Without school or friends or an idea of civilization? Do you know what she's learning down here, following Ixna all day? She doesn't know what a toilet is, Robert, but she knows about bribery! She knows all about a bunch of ghosts that live in a cave and steal our things!"

Evie's face went hot with shame. She should have known her mother wouldn't take her concerns about the cave seriously.

"We're broke. The wheat plan is done," Mother decreed, flourishing her arm. "It was never even feasible. It's not about food, it's about hundreds of years of history. Indians aren't fighting hunger, they're still fighting the Spanish. They're fighting history. They won't win, but they'll starve trying because they have nothing more to lose."

They're fighting history. The phrase struck Evie. How does one fight something that already happened, that cannot be changed?

"I'm hiding our fare money," Mother told Father's back as he walked out the door. "If your plan doesn't require it, fine, but we're not going to be stranded here." Evie followed Father. She had no desire to know where their savings were hidden. She tried to block out the sound of the bureau sliding from the wall. She was afraid one of these days Father would ask her where their money was and she would tell him.

~~~~~

The next morning was a special morning, Mother said, as she tugged and twisted Evie's hair into two tight, wretched braids, then tied them off with blue bows. Evie was going with Father into Xela.

"Is he selling bread? Will we be at the market?" She held her feet up, one by one, for her white leather shoes with the heart-shaped buckles.

"No, Evie. Market is on Sunday. This is special business. Just do what your father says and don't say anything. Act like a lady," she reminded Evie several times, making her increasingly nervous. The worse off they were, she knew, the more ladylike she'd have to be.

"Be careful, Robert," Mother pleaded, burying his gun under some sacks in the back of the cart. "Stay on the main road, and don't give any Indians any rides. They're worked up about the volcano. I want you back here in one piece."

"I'll hope for two," he said, then took Mother's hand and began to sing, "*I lost my head in Totonicapán, over a girl . . .*"

"That's not funny, Robert."

"Two pieces, Mattie. Me and Evie. Don't worry."

The mule cart rocked downhill, shuddering with the excruciating pace of Tiny's stubborn haunches. Magellan, in his crate on Evie's lap, was still despite the rough road.

"What do you think is wrong with Magellan? Is he sick? Did I not take care of him like I was supposed to?"

"It's not your fault, Evie," Father reassured her.

She reconsidered Judas's theory that Magellan wanted to kill her. "He bites me every time I try to feed him. I think he hates me."

"Birds can't hate, Evie. It's scientifically impossible. Their brains are too small. It's not you, it's the bird. I don't know if sick is the word. Maybe he's crazy."

"Are we taking him to a doctor?" She thought they must be going to see someone special, since she was in her best dress and Father had put on his only suit—both rescued from the field and washed just for this trip.

"No, Evie. I don't know what we can do to help him. But maybe he can help us."

Now ten days after the eruption, the view in all directions had cleared. Santa María loomed ahead, looking closer than before. The shacks, too, on the bottom of the mountain seemed nearer their fence, as Mother said. More like skeletons of houses, sticks lashed together and topped with dried leaves. The sticks and leaves, Evie knew, came from their land. She stared down from the cart at shirtless men hauling enormous loads of dried corn on their backs. Bent over double, they wore head straps tied tight to counter the weight.

A little potbellied boy, completely naked, ran alongside the cart, trying to get a look at Father's blue eyes. Sometimes he humored these curious children, smiling savagely so they screamed with terrorized delight and ran away. But today he whipped Tiny into a trot, leaving the little boy behind.

"They're all trying to plant now, before the second draft. With all the men gone, there's going to be a corn shortage, Evie. Dead Indians can't pick coffee. Dead Indians can't build railroads."

But they could do other things. Steal, sabotage her family's crops, haunt their mountain, and possibly much more. "Father, what made the volcano erupt?"

The mountains, to Father, were not holy or evil. They were nothing more than two plates colliding. He demonstrated for Evie how mountains formed over millions of years.

"Our mountain," he said. She did not like that phrase anymore: our mountain, my mountain. Each time he said it, she thought of the snake. Father let go of Tiny's reins, butted his chewed fingertips against one another. But his hands, which always seemed huge and powerful, struck Evie as completely inadequate for what he was trying to demonstrate. "Two opposite forces," he said, "pushing against one another. Now those same forces that made our mountain can release lava and pressure from far below the surface. Pressure you cannot imagine. That's why, too, when the volcano erupted you felt the ground moving. Everything's connected, right below the surface."

Evie didn't find this explanation any more comforting than Ixna's story about the big snake. "And what about the cave? What made the cave?" she asked boldly.

"Caves are just made from water. When lots of water flows for a very long time, it carves out the rock. No ghosts," he reassured her, winking.

Just outside the city's limits, they passed vast, empty fields. No Indian shacks, no crops, no workers. Half the year, the fields grew wheat. The other half, nothing.

"The dirt crop's looking good this year," Father said, making his usual joke.

They'd seen these fields full of wheat on their initial arrival in Guatemala and Evie had cried, thinking someone had beat Father to his idea. But no, this had not been the case. "That wheat isn't grown for Indians," Father had told her. "That's for export, grown in the regular season, and on a much larger scale than what I'm trying."

"Why won't the Indians eat your wheat?" Evie now asked. "I understand they don't like bread, but they won't even try cookies!"

"Indians think that new foods will anger their ancestors. They think they can't be Indians if they change at all. They rely so much on corn that it's their religion, their clock, their food, their everything. Which was fine back then, when people didn't have clocks, but now what's the point?"

"Maybe if we baked them cinnamon cookies. They're the best."

"Now, that's an excellent idea, Evie. I'll try that."

Xela had already moved on from catastrophe. Its white buildings that had not crumbled stood immaculate again in the restored highland sunshine. Trails of whitewash dripped over the road, showing how recent the restoration had all been. The balconies of the rich, columned houses floated above, seeming to inhabit their own separate city fifteen feet above Xela.

They passed the ruins of the collapsed cathedral, looking just as it had in the newspaper. They watched an Indian road crew moving barefoot amid the rubble, perhaps to rebuild, perhaps to clear the way for something else. A white foreman, wearing shoes and carrying a whip, directed them.

"Father, there were little girls in there right before it fell. They were praying, I saw them. Do you think they all died?"

"Probably."

"Can I play with them?"

He gave her a squinty look. "Not if they're dead."

"How could God let that happen? How could He let His own house fall down?"

The road crew coalesced around a task. They pushed and pushed a single stone that would not move. Evie imagined a little girl squashed flat underneath that stone. Father steered around it and the sound of the whip behind them made Tiny bolt. "God has left Xela, for the moment. Of that I'm sure. But someone has already taken His place."

"Who?" she asked with a shiver.

"We're going to see him now."

The government building had walls that went all the way up to the ceiling, doors that properly closed, and even gaslights. A sign in the window read in several languages that the telegraph was broken for an indefinite period of time.

They entered a waiting room full of Germans. Robust men with red, worried faces, each holding a bag on his lap. Upon seeing them, Father groaned and said, "It's going to be a while, Evie. Let's play a game to pass the time."

"What game?" she asked, setting Magellan on the floor.

"A game in which I predict the future. Are you ready?" A secretary called one of the Germans, who stood up and disappeared down a hallway. "I predict that his meeting will be very short. Under two minutes. And I predict that when he comes back out, he won't have his bag."

"How do you know? You don't know what his meeting is about."

"Just count, Evie. And see if I'm right."

He was. The man strolled back through the room and out the front door in eighty-eight seconds, empty-handed. Evie soon learned that every meeting went this way, meaning Father knew something she didn't, which she considered cheating. She showed her displeasure by accepting his predictions coolly, not even giving him the satisfaction of asking what was in the bags.

They sat for hours, watching Germans and some Americans come and go. Evie began to lose patience. "We were here before him," she whispered to Father. "So why is he going in before us? It's not fair."

"I think you're old enough to know, Evie, that life in Guatemala is not fair."

To distract herself, she studied a framed map on the wall: Guatemala. She studied the drawing, seeing railroads all across the country. Railroads she knew didn't exist, because the fact that they didn't exist had ruined their

trip down from New York. The crazy route across Mexico, boarding count-
less boats and trains, had been no fun at all. She shook her head, seeing all
the mistakes, and pointed them out to Father.

"As always, Evie, you understand the situation here more than anyone I
know."

Mr. Ubico, the *jefe político*, saw them last. Evie had lost track of time, had
even fallen asleep in her chair, and woke up to find the waiting room empty.
And then they were all inside an office, sitting on a wooden pew that faced
this man at his desk. Light-skinned, the color of a sugar cookie, he sat on a
sort of red velvet throne and wore a cream-colored suit. He fussed with a
dented gold chalice on his desk, the chalice filled with sharpened pencils,
pointing up. Father took the shrouded crate, placed it on the desk, and un-
covered it.

"A quetzal!" Mr. Ubico beamed. Magellan did not look so bad this morning, as Evie had cleaned out his crate and managed to smooth his feathers
with a damp rag. If he looked sick or crazy, this man did not notice. He
peered into the cage, curling his clean fingers around the slats. Magellan
eyed this intrusion and Evie prayed he would not bite. She drew her eyes
from the bird to Ubico's fingers, then noticed a stack of colorful pesos at the
bottom of the cage, where Evie usually left food. Where had they come from?

"I will name him Estrada Cabrera. After the President!"

Evie crossed her ankles like a lady. An invisible clock ticked audibly
from somewhere. *Tick, tick, tick.* Making her anxious. She wanted to tell
Ubico about all the mistakes in his map, wanted to warn him that Magellan
might bite, and that Estrada Cabrera was a terrible name for a bird, but
knowing she shouldn't say anything, she grabbed one of her braids and
plugged her mouth with it.

Mr. Ubico leaned back in his rigid throne, taking his time. "Do you like
my office?" he asked.

"It's very nice," Father agreed.

"The cathedral!" Mr. Ubico roared unexpectedly, making her heart leap
into her throat. "The cathedral falls and suddenly I have new office furniture!"

"That's very fortunate for you," Father remarked, sounding not at all like
himself.

Mr. Ubico looked content, as if they had just dropped by to give him this
tribute and admire his office. Evie, hoping this was true, began counting in

her head. Under two minutes and they'd be gone. At first, she had thought that Father was joking when he said this man had replaced God. But now the furniture, her father's strange formality, the gift, the chalice, and the fact that her mother had dressed her as if for church made her think that it might not be a joke at all.

"Señor Ubico," Father tried, with a little sitting bow, "I'd like to speak with you about some business concerns I have. I've tried talking with the desk, but they don't understand my special situation."

The ticking clock was maddening, keeping a strict record of Mr. Ubico's silence. Six seconds, before he replied. "Ah, yes. The second draft. It's been all day. Everyone is worried about the new draft. We were hoping the first would be enough, but it wasn't."

Father pitched forward and sat on his hands. "But I have no problem with the draft. I just want to make sure that my men, who are indebted to me, are not taken away."

Father pressed on, for the utter blankness of the man's expression. "I realize the importance of the drafts. With all the Indians wandering around without any desire to work, it's important to utilize them. It is their country, after all, and they need to be responsible for it. But my men are hard workers, I didn't coerce them, they aren't just working because of the vagrancy laws. They've been working for me for years and my crop depends on them."

Evie hit ninety seconds. Just thirty more and this would be over.

"And these men," Mr. Ubico asked finally, "are indebted to you?"

"I have the papers right here." He patted his suit coat, right over his heart. "I advanced money to six of my men. Two years' wages."

"When did you do this?"

"A month ago," Father said.

Evie kicked her legs furiously under her chair for this lie. The heart-shaped buckles clicked against each other as she smashed her ankles together.

Mr. Ubico waved a hand in the air, as if offering absolution or fanning away a bad smell. "No matter, Mr. Crowder. We are sorry it has to be this way, but now we need all the Indians. Have you seen the new decree? The second draft is necessary."

"But you have to make exceptions."

The man made no reaction. Two minutes, gone. Evie tapped her toes on the floor.

"Wheat's a very important crop, not only for export," Father explained.

"If you want to utilize your workforce, it's vital. The Indians can't live on corn like they did hundreds of years ago." And here he launched into a speech Evie knew well. He counted off his points on his fingers. "Corn requires too much land. You can't build a strong economy on a starving population. You can't build a railroad. You can only go so far—"

He stopped suddenly, seeming to forget his own purpose under Ubico's bland stare. Evie wanted to finish for him, to highlight the points he'd missed. Corn exhausts the soil. Wheat can grow at higher altitudes, and requires less water, so it can be irrigated more easily. It can be stored and shipped much more easily. How could he forget all this?

"But if the coffee isn't saved, then everyone suffers. Then . . ." Ubico paused. "Then *there is no one to buy wheat.*" He showed his teeth, pleased at his logic. "We are all working for the same thing down here, Mr. Crowder. We are not enemies."

"No, we're not enemies. So perhaps we could come to a friendly agreement."

"We already have that, yes. Our friendly agreement is that you come to Xela and make your money and I allow you to do so."

"Not if you take my workers! I am an honest man, only asking—"

"As an honest man, it will be better if you see it this way: The Indians belong to the government and we loan them to you ten months of the year. Two months, we ask for them back. We have big projects, roads and trains, and disasters to fix. Projects that benefit you and your business. That is reasonable."

"Not for someone trying to run a cochineal business." Father shook his head. "It's a time-sensitive harvest that requires skilled labor."

Ubico shrugged. "Like coffee. There is nothing I can do. Your workers stay, then everyone will want their workers to stay."

"Just one? Can I keep my overseer? Just one man? Judas Vico."

"Is he literate? Literate is exempt from the draft."

"Yes!" Father shot up to his feet. "He speaks four languages! He writes Quiché!"

Mr. Ubico shook his head. "Quiché is not literate."

Father fell back into his seat. "But my family! What will happen to my family? We won't have food if we can't harvest this year." For the first time since walking into the office, Father acknowledged Evie's presence, pointing at her.

Ubico glanced at Evie, just as she realized she was not sitting like a lady at all. Clearly unimpressed by her slumped, kicking posture, he said, "I understand you are worried about your family, but there are more important things for Guatemala."

Evie gave up counting. They were way past Father's prediction now.

"So I lose my money and my workers."

"Your workers will still owe you money."

Father lost his deferential tone. "But now they'll owe the coffee planters money, too. They'll be indebted to them for years. Do you think they'll come back to repay me?"

"It is not my job"—Ubico stood up, declaring the meeting over—"to think about you and your problems. *My* business is to get these lazy Indians to work." He tapped the slats of Magellan's crate and made his way to the door, walking a little funny due to the gun holstered to his hip. Evie had never seen anything like it before, a gun with a nice suit. She stared at it, unable to match the two things in her mind.

Father remained seated, twisting uneasily in the pew. "You have to make exceptions. I know with all your meetings, all those people in your lobby, all this money moving in and out, you've made exceptions today."

Mr. Ubico held the door open, a different one from the one they had come in through. One that led outside. Father took his time leaving, trying to come up with some way to change the man's mind. He adjusted his suit, dropped his hat, and then fiddled in his pockets for something that wasn't there. His blue eyes were huge and dry, his chin trembling. Evie watched him closely, realizing she'd never seen him speechless before.

She desperately wanted to leave now, but she became very conscious of walking away from the money in Magellan's cage. She knew they had no money and that that was a lot of money. Father left it all behind without a glance. In four steps he passed Ubico and was outside, but then he turned to say something through the open door.

"You know . . ." Father said in a struggling voice. "You know, I have a lot of investor friends in the States. *In Boston.* I know with all the trouble with that eruption, I know that this volcano business would be very interesting. I know . . ." He trailed off, losing courage with Ubico's widening smile.

"Oh, I see, Mr. Crowder." He said their name real slow, and then he repeated it. "Crowder, I see what you are saying."

"Not really," Father stammered. "I didn't mean—"

"Do not worry. Americans are always saying things they don't mean. That's what makes your country so great. Freedom of speech. But I will give you advice," Mr. Ubico mused, lightly touching his gun, just to confirm its presence against his body. "If you are in Guatemala, American laws don't matter. Americans think the laws are here—they think *I am here*—only for the Indians. But I am your *jefe*, too."

Father nodded, and Ubico grabbed his huge, limp hand and shook it many times. At this point, Father noticed that Evie was not outside with him. Their eyes met and he gave her such a peculiar, stunned look that she thought she had done something wrong. She was in trouble, suddenly, she had no idea why, but she tried to move quickly to join him, to fix her mistake. But Mr. Ubico stepped between them and fished into his pocket. "For the little wheat girl," he said, pressing an already-sticky mint into her palm. She had no choice but to accept it, and no choice but to pass under his other arm, which now ceremoniously held the door open for her.

~~~~~

Guatemala was not at all how her parents had told Evie it would be. When they first proposed the idea, they painted pictures in her mind of perpetual spring. Ocean and beaches, year-round mild temperatures, flowers. Father brought home a pamphlet to show them. *Guatemala: The Land of Eternal Spring.* Cheap land, fertile soil, a vast, mobilized, and cheap workforce. A rainy season as predictable as the phases of the moon. The government pamphlet did not show volcanoes or Indians, but white-tiled mansions and flowering vines, pictures that inspired Mother to abandon her campaign for Europe and get behind the plan. In the Land of Eternal Spring, a spring wheat could provide an eternal crop.

In marrying Father, Mother had come down in the world, but she had married for love, she insisted to everyone. And that could not be bought for anything. Love had cost her, however. She had grown up with servants, a summer house in the country, and even a motorcar with a crank. With Father, she had none of these things.

According to Father's initial arguments for the plan, in Guatemala they would be rich, they could own land. In Guatemala, they would have servants. They would be richer than almost anyone but the plantation owners. These were not things they would be able to afford in Europe, he always reminded Mother.

For years, Mother had harbored dreams of moving to Europe. Only distance, she came to believe, would give her marriage dignity in the eyes of her family. In New York, her relatives pursed their lips at Father's accent, his grand plans, which he would outline to anyone, whether or not they asked.

Their humble apartment was a scandal to her mother, who was convinced Father had married Mother only for her inheritance. For all this, Europe seemed to be the answer, the gloss her life needed. But since Europe was played out, according to Father, and since they could afford a nicer life in Guatemala, she finally agreed to the plan.

After arriving, however, it soon became clear that being richer than people who could not even afford shoes was not much of an accomplishment. Nevertheless, Mother kept up appearances. In letters home to her mother, she insisted that she finally had it all: love and money. This proclamation became increasingly harder to make over the years as she periodically had to write a different kind of letter home, asking for money.

The things that had convinced Mother to come were not the same things that had convinced Evie. Evie loved bananas. Once Father informed her that they would be living where bananas grew, she no longer cared about leaving her friends, her school. She'd only had one banana in her life, but the pleasure had been vivid enough to stay with her for years. It was winter in New York and her mother had returned home with two bright yellow bananas. They fit in her hands like two door handles.

"I was walking by the pier and they were being brought off a boat! I paid a dollar each. Can you imagine, a tropical fruit making it to us in the middle of winter?"

The most important thing about bananas was knowing how to eat one properly. On two dessert dishes, Mother laid out the naked fruit and cut them up into small circles. "You must always eat them with a fork," she cautioned. "Like a lady. I didn't know that at first. I made that mistake a few years ago. I bought a banana from the docks and peeled and ate it right there, in front of all the longshoremen! Just ate it with my hands. Can you imagine! I had no idea!"

Evie could imagine it perfectly, but could not imagine what was wrong with eating a banana with your hands.

Sweet, mild, and soft, her first banana felt like ice cream, if ice cream could be warm without melting. She loved the color, the shape. She loved the fact that her mother would pay a whole dollar for just one.

"You can eat all the bananas you want!" Father had promised Evie. "We will even make the journey there on one of the banana boats. What do you think of that?"

This was what she thought: Huge yellow boats shaped like bananas. Curved and fierce as Viking ships. She became nauseous with joy and expectation, barely able to finish out the year at school. She told adults, her teachers, her friends, that she wanted to work on a banana plantation when she grew up. Her favorite color became yellow.

But the incomplete Guatemalan railroad made it entirely impossible to arrive on the Caribbean coast. Father even researched an alternate way of traversing the railroad gap, but the sixty-mile stretch connecting the east coast to the rest of the country was impassable. Swamps, malaria, yellow fever. Evie imagined people turned yellow, turned into bananas.

Instead, they were forced to take the exhausting route they did. On coffee boats.

But more disappointing than all this, Evie soon learned that bananas were even harder to come by in their part of Guatemala than in New York. Again, the incomplete railroad ruined everything. Nothing could make it across from the Caribbean coast, so it all went up to the United States. More and more bananas were making it up. Mother now read letters from New York in which vendors sold cooked bananas in the streets, their discarded peels becoming a public nuisance. Banana editorials and recipes and cartoons in the newspapers Grandmother sent. There were so many bananas in New York now, whole bunches for sale at the grocer's, and they had left just in time to miss out on it.

But even with these disappointments, Father remained committed. On their first night on the mountain, he struck a pose in the open church door and stared up at the wide net of stars cast over their existence.

"This is all ours, Mattie, can you believe?"

"Oh yes," she reassured him. "I believe it."

"We are the richest people on earth."

Mother closed her eyes, took Father's hand.

"Everyone," he continued, "everyone we know back home has plumbing and electricity and couches. But who in New York can say they own a mountain? Who in the world can say they own a mountain?"

~~~~~

Father said nothing on the ride home from Ubico's office—no jokes, no lessons, no songs. When Evie told him that the meeting had lasted for much longer than two minutes, he snorted some phlegm from his throat and spit off the side of the cart. Not knowing what else to do, Evie put Ubico's candy in her mouth. It tasted like it had been in his pocket for years, with old pennies. She turned and spit, too.

At home, after unhitching Tiny, Father stretched and tested his big joints, and smiled tensely at nothing. He went to check on the Indian workers, with the reins still looped around his hand. Evie followed, hoping to glean something, anything, that would explain what had just happened in Xela. Father, she realized, hadn't just been speechless or tongue-tied. By the very end of the meeting, he'd been afraid.

On the ride home she'd come to that conclusion, and then another: It wasn't just seeing her father afraid that frightened her. Despite the smiles, handshakes and apologies, she saw the source. Ubico had said their last name like he was chewing it.

Now she hoped for any word from Father that would convince her otherwise. But he didn't seem to be thinking of Ubico anymore. He remained focused on the harvest. "Why aren't these nets finished already?" he demanded, stepping into the group of Indian workers.

Judas explained that they had finished them; however, the holes in the netting Mani had bought were too large, so that the bugs might fall through. Judas didn't notice at first because he had been stocking the wood.

"Mani, why the hell would you buy this?" Father inspected the old netting, torn in long pieces on the ground. "What the hell is the matter with you?"

Mani's smudged, flat face tilted more intently to his work; he understood his name and Father's tone and nothing else. Everyone just kept working.

"Judas, translate!"

Judas pursed his lips and said nothing.

"Why is it that not one goddamned thing can go right here? Judas, translate!"

Father began to pace the supply shed, kicking at the discarded swaths of net and flailing his arms, Tiny's reins. No one looked up from their work.

"Oh, now I see how dedicated you all are. Translate!"

Judas mumbled something in what Evie guessed was Quiché, which only seemed to infuriate her father more. He kicked the box at Judas's feet. "That's not what I said!" Father yelled, though he understood no Quiché at all. "What did you tell them, Judas?"

"I told them to keep working. What is the point?" Judas asked evenly, using Mother's phrase. "What is the point of wasting time with argument? We have less than three days."

Evie had never seen her father so angry before. A blue vein stood out over his temple like a worm, like his brain was infested with bright blue worms.

She wanted to leave, but became afraid to move and draw his fury. He kicked at the burlap sacks, the dust on the floor.

Father was pacing and kicking and then he kicked Mani, who shot up from the stool, dropping his net to the floor. "Get back to work!" Father cried. He unlooped the reins from his hand with a quick twirl and struck him across the cheek.

The whole mountain became very still.

"The point is that it's always something. Either Mani gets the wrong netting, or Raffie gets arrested, or you all get drunk and take advances from a coffee planter that I have to repay, or your cousin prays for an early rain to drown my crop! I'm helping you! I am helping your pathetic people, can you not understand that?"

They all blinked at him, not understanding a word, except for Judas, who placed a hand in one of the nets, testing its strength with twisting fingers. Mani's dark skin showed no mark from the lashing, but his hands were balled into fists.

"No one's sleeping, no one's eating, no one's taking a goddamned piss until these nets are finished, the wood is stocked, and you are all on your way down *my* mountain and on your way to the Piedmont. I am going to get two years' worth of work out of you in two days. I paid you, and you are going to earn it! And Judas, if you don't translate that, I'm going to break your goddamned back!"

Evie held her breath. She felt it, was sure she felt the snake stirring beneath them, angry. But no, it was Mother, stepping across the rickety floor.

"Robert." She entered, wiping her hands on a towel, putting them all to shame. Everyone looked down, including Father. But her attention shifted to Evie. "Evie, how did you manage to get your nice dress dirty already? Ixna just washed it!"

Evie stared down at herself, unable to come up with an answer.

"How did your meeting with Ubico go?" Mother had put words to Evie's own question. In the beginning, the meeting seemed normal enough, just tense. Like Mother's teas with Mrs. Fasbinder. But then she was sure the end had gone terribly wrong. But now Father seemed to have other worries, like the nets. Maybe she didn't need to fear Ubico, yet another worry added to their life on the mountain. So she awaited the answer with as much hope as her mother.

"He said he'll talk to some people. He really wants to help."

The matter-of-factness, the ease with which her father lied shocked Evie.

She knew Mr. Ubico had never said those words and she now felt more than ever the ground beneath her slipping, as surely as she'd felt the volcano moving beneath them just ten days ago.

"Well, that's good news, I guess. You didn't mention Boston, did you?"

"Of course not, Mattie. I'm not an idiot."

~~~~~

By the time Mrs. Fasbinder arrived for her weekly tea with Mother the next afternoon, Father and the workers were uncovering the prickly pear fields for the harvest. All their clothes and hats and sheets lay in a sooty pile on the porch, a pile that their guest had to step over to get into the house. Usually well dressed for these teas, Evie and Mother wore their everyday clothes. They made up for it, however, by putting on their best white shoes. Evie was always grateful for an opportunity to wear hers.

The wife of a German American coffee planter, Mrs. Fasbinder lived on the other side of the volcano. She was generously proportioned with a pug face, sweaty but sweet-smelling, as if the perpetual gloss on her sallow skin wasn't perspiration at all, but perfume. In Mother's letters home, she always spoke of her dear friend Mrs. Fasbinder, which baffled Evie, since Mother didn't seem to like Mrs. Fasbinder at all. But she was their only visitor. The only reason to use the tea set and to wear nice clothes.

The Fasbinders had no children, but that day Mrs. Fasbinder arrived with a little Indian boy of five, wearing button breeches and a white blouse from one of the nice shops in town. His name was Tomás Raúl Mancha Egardo, Mrs. Fasbinder said, but they were thinking of changing it.

"I doubt that's even his real name. The nuns just make up these ridiculously long names for these orphans, to make them sound convincingly Hispanic. But they're almost all Indian. And this one is definitely, at least, half."

The two women and Evie examined the boy standing in their front room, looking for the Indian in him. His eyes were not Indian, but his nose gave him away.

"They say his parents couldn't afford to keep him, but you know how it goes with Mestizos. More likely, the *father* was Indian. Tomás," Mrs. Fasbinder said, pointing to the floor at her feet. "He doesn't speak English," she explained needlessly.

The boy sat at Mrs. Fasbinder's feet while everyone else remained standing. Mother stepped back, as if from a puddle. "I don't understand. He's yours now?"

"Oh yes, we picked him up last week. He was in the Catholic church when it collapsed. All the other orphans were killed."

"Was he outside?"

"No, he was inside."

"Was he hiding under anything? A statue?"

Evie stared at the boy. An orphan boy, when she had thought orphans could only be girls. She wondered if she would be allowed to play with him, remembering Mother's comment about orphans being unable to play. She had a ball. Maybe she would try that. She so, so wanted someone to play with. Ixna had resisted her attempts at blindman's bluff, though she played it with Father.

"No one knows how he survived. They found him standing. Just standing there, all dusty. Besides"—and here Mrs. Fasbinder shifted easily into territory Mother tried to avoid but that always, inevitably, came up with Mrs. Fasbinder—"no Catholic statue could save anyone. It was a sign, that church crumbling to the ground. The era of repression in the name of God is over in Guatemala."

Evie had been taught that introducing religion or politics to conversation was rude. Though once Mrs. Fasbinder did, Mother couldn't seem to help herself. "And what will take its place?" she asked with determined lightness.

"Freedom and prosperity through the blood of Jesus and through hard work."

"Is that so?"

"Before, the Indians worked while the priests lived off the wealth. But now, with this new economy, everyone works and everyone is paid."

"Everyone certainly works, but I'm not convinced everyone gets paid." Mother pursed her lips and spat out the name like a sneeze. "Ixna worked on the Piedmont and she's told quite a different story. Starvation wages in play money."

"The paper slips are necessary, Mattie. The peso's so depressed we can't get the exact bills to pay them on a daily basis! You've no idea, absolutely none." Still standing, Mrs. Fasbinder worked herself up so that she was almost breathless. "And we pay more than just wages. On every worker we have to pay their tax so the government doesn't draft them away for the road crew or the railroad project. We pay for their food, their children's food, the shelter, we have to pay men wages to round them up all over the highlands to honor their debts, we have to bribe Ubico to favor our debts over the other planters'. Because these Indians take advances from every coffee planter they can! They're just trying to avoid the railroad draft, but not even that works anymore. We advance them six months of wages, then a month later they disappear! We know they go right next door, to the Haussmans'. Their men come in the night to give them new advances, new identity papers, and smuggle them over the fence! So I'd say the majority of them, who are pretty enterprising, get paid very, very well for their work. Then they drink it all away."

"At the plantation cantinas!"

"If we didn't have a cantina, the Indians wouldn't work for us."

"So they drink it all away, and the honest ones are left to starve."

"Exactly!" Mrs. Fasbinder agreed. "That's exactly what I'm saying. It's the lack of morals that's put them in this bind. If we paid more, all of our money would jump the fence and half the population would drink itself to death. Too much drink is worse for them than too little food. And if we left, all the Indians would be dying of yellow fever on that insane railroad project. Right now they are only field workers, but everyone has to start somewhere. With hard work and God-fearing morals," the woman declared, lifting her chin to demonstrate her point, "the Indians will rise."

"That's quite optimistic of you," Mother said, motioning to the piano bench for her guest to sit. "To think that the Indians will eventually be prosperous under a new religion. Not a new government or economic plan."

Mrs. Fasbinder smiled. "We are optimists, but we also have to be realists." She reached across and tested two high keys on the piano, like a chime. "Oh, I miss my piano. However did you get this one all the way here?"

"Is it optimism or realism that makes you think you can eradicate class, eradicate this insane system of advances and bribes, by bringing more money into this country?"

Mrs. Fasbinder touched a middle chord. Mother frowned, averting her gaze, while Mrs. Fasbinder pulled the bench closer to the piano and began to tap out a small tune, a simple one played with only two fingers.

"The truth," Mrs. Fasbinder said as she played, "is that no matter what we want, Guatemala is now a part of our world. And as more money and people and industry come, we can teach the Indians to take advantage and prosper or to resist and be killed in the process. They are very adaptable, these Indians. They've had to adopt many false 'truths' in order to survive the past few centuries. But we're hoping to change that by bringing them the ultimate truth."

"The ultimate truth?"

"I've written my church in Chicago about the collapse of the cathedral, the unique opportunity to break the Catholics' stranglehold on the Indians. They're going to establish a church and a school right away. They're sending missionaries and teachers next month."

They all knew about Mrs. Fasbinder's school. She'd been talking about it vaguely for a year, though there was never any mention of a church. "Missionaries," Mother repeated. "Are you Anglican? Lutheran?"

Mrs. Fasbinder made a face. "Oh no, Mattie, nothing like that. A fairly new church, without all the nasty history and politics. I even spoke with the President about it, at my party. He was very excited about the possibility of reinventing religion down here. We aren't here for empire-building, we're here out of love and compassion and nothing more. It's just what this country needs."

"But," Mother repeated, "what are you?"

"My dear"—Mrs. Fasbinder straightened, offended that it hadn't been obvious all along—"we're American Baptists."

Mother cast a desperate glance around the parlor and into the kitchen, hoping for the tea. "Evie, I don't know where Ixna is. Will you please make the tea?"

"Take Tomás with you, show him how to make the tea," Mrs. Fasbinder called. "He needs to learn these things. Get up, Tomás." She clapped and the boy collected himself from the floor.

"Yes," Mother agreed, "the Indian certainly will rise." She caught Evie's eye, but Evie didn't understand the joke.

"Well, we need a houseboy, and he's much cheaper than hiring a boy out and paying his parents. He was free, in fact. The nuns had nowhere to house him. You know, they had him in a sack dress? They also trained him to cross himself before every meal," she said in a scandalized whisper. "We broke him of that in a day. But at least they taught him straight Catholicism, instead of that pagan-hybrid stuff all the other Indians practice. I can undo what I can understand."

Evie motioned to Tomás, and he followed her into the kitchen, where she added some sticks to the stove. She studied him, trying to recognize him from the line of little orphan girls praying in the cathedral. Maybe they had all been boys, in dresses.

"I'm Evie," she said, patting herself on the chest.

The boy stared at her with shrewd eyes. Not like Indian eyes at all. A Mestizo, Mrs. Fasbinder had said.

"We're getting three hundred new workers from the draft," Mrs. Fasbinder said from the other room. "Almost all our workers took advantage of the confusion and fled. Just disappeared into the smoke. Everything's ruined. The ash was worse than the lava. The cherries have to be harvested quickly and washed. Each one washed."

"Lots of crops will be suffering from the drafts, too. But," Mother chimed happily, "Robert went to speak to Ubico. He says we can get an exception."

"Ubico said that?"

No, Evie thought, ladling water into the pot. She wanted to tell Mother what had really happened, but she had no idea how to explain.

"Yes," Mother answered.

"We paid Ubico five thousand dollars to draft us workers. He better not be handing out exceptions left and right."

"We did not bribe Ubico," Mother announced proudly. "We reasoned with him. He understands workers need to eat. They can't eat coffee, they can't eat money."

Evie listened, realizing that the money on the bottom of Magellan's cage was a bribe. That was the word for it. Of course, now she could not explain to Mother what had happened. She took two big cinnamon cookies from the counter and gave one to Tomás. She nibbled her cookie, thinking of the bribe, waiting for the water to boil.

Tomás didn't say anything and he did not eat the cookie right away. He gripped it with both hands. Then he glanced at the piano room, crossed himself, and shoved the entire thing in his mouth at once. He hunched over, putting his entire body into the endeavor, like a snake swallowing an egg. Evie could not believe her eyes. Triumph! But maybe not, since Tomás was a Mestizo.

He chewed for a long time, staring at Evie's good shoes.

They walked back in once the tea was brewed, balancing the cups with a nervous rattle. Evie had arranged the spoons, the saucers, and the sugar just right on the tray. But Mother did not notice her efforts. Mrs. Fasbinder was telling a story.

"The Indian," she managed, her face red, shucked of composure, "waited on the road . . ." Her eyes cut to Evie and she swallowed the sentence quickly. Evie put the tray down and sat on a chair, crossing her ankles, with her back straight. The tea burned her mouth, but she smiled through it, feigning polite interest in Mrs. Fasbinder's story.

"He *took* her," Mrs. Fasbinder explained.

Mother took her cup up, understanding now. "Oh my! A French girl?"

"He *took* her," she said again. "And now there's a baby."

Mother's eyes widened in horror. Tomás sat down again, just curled up to digest his cookie. "Took her where?" Evie asked, eyeing the sugar.

They turned to Evie with stunned faces, then Mother said, "An Indian tried to take a white girl somewhere. She said no, but he took her anyway."

"Who?"

"I don't know. Just a French girl somewhere."

"Where did he take her?"

"To a restaurant, Evie, of course," Mother snapped with impatience.

How do you force someone to eat dinner? Evie wondered. Would he even allow her to choose from the menu? "I thought Indians weren't allowed in restaurants."

"Stop asking silly questions, Evie. Go play outside, please, with Tomás."

Kicked out, despite her best efforts. She would hear about it later, about proper conversation, about the difference between rude and polite questions. Mother would accuse her of being her father's daughter. Too curious.

Tomás, however, was incapable of playing. He got up again at Mrs. Fasbinder's command, and followed Evie out onto the porch, where he just caught the rubber ball she bounced to him. He would not bounce it back, but kept it in his fist.

"Those CAICO men!" Mrs. Fasbinder exclaimed from the house. "Such charming brutes. Robert would have fit in perfectly at the party! I'm sorry you couldn't make it. It was nice to have some Americans around for once. We're lucky. A few days later, and the whole gala would have been ruined by the ash. But they were all gone by then, thank God, to the Caribbean coast."

"I'm surprised they came all the way here, it's not an easy trip."

"Well, coffee will be their main freight, if they commit to finishing the line. No matter what dreams they have about bananas, coffee is the reality for now. Coffee will pay for the whole rail system in a few years. If they finish it. Personally, I doubt they will. They should pull out now before they lose any more money. They're only a year into their contact. I wonder if they realize the government's been throwing dead Indians at that project for ten years. The terrain's impossible. But one of them told me they've come up with a solution."

"What's that?"

"Jamaicans."

Mrs. Fasbinder asked to play the piano for a while. So she played, and

Mother took the opportunity to go to the henhouse to collect eggs. On the porch floor, Evie laid out a piece of paper and her pencils. She decided to draw a map, to explain to Tomás where she came from.

"This is America," Evie said, making a shape, trying to remember the map Father had drawn for her. "This is New York. This is where I'm from." She thumped her chest and pointed at the map. "This is Guatemala." She drew a small circle right at the bottom of the page.

Across the yard, Mother emerged from the henhouse without her basket, running. Her hand over her mouth. She dashed up the porch steps, her eyes so wide, but she did not see Evie and Tomás there. She tripped over Evie's legs, stumbled right into the doorway, and did not stop. And she did not hear Evie when she asked what was wrong. Or maybe she just couldn't hear over Mrs. Fasbinder's playing.

Tomás stared a moment at the map Evie had just drawn, cocked his head, then took the pencil from her. With it, he redrew Guatemala into a crazy shape. Then he opened his mouth for the second time.

"Guatemala is not a circle," he said very softly in English. Then he dragged his finger over the sea, to North America. "And New York is on the coast."

Mrs. Fasbinder and Tomás left at four o'clock. Mother stood on the porch, rigid as a pole, to watch their cart round the bend. Once it did, the day turned very strange. Mother applied some lipstick expertly, without a mirror, then walked into the kitchen and told Ixna that she was giving her a week-long vacation.

"What is vacation?" Ixna asked, with flour in her eyelashes.

"Vacation means you go and visit your family in Xela. And I'll pay you to do it."

Ixna's vacation started immediately. She was not even allowed to finish cooking dinner. Mother handed her her square basket and pushed her out the front door. Then she tried to cook dinner herself.

Mother had not cooked in a long time. Her feeble attempts at the bread made her cry, as did the soup. She stirred and stirred for over an hour, weeping, while Evie did her best to help. "It's not difficult," she kept reassuring Mother. "Ixna usually doesn't stir it that much. And she punches the bread, but not so much."

"I don't need cooking lessons from some dirty Indian, or from you, Evie. Sit at the table and color the newspaper."

That day's newspaper was all bananas. Big bunches, trainloads, and boatloads of bananas, loaded by smiling Indians. No use coloring them, Evie knew from experience, but she did as Mother said. The yellow didn't work. Too light to show, it just rubbed the ink to make a sickly gray. Like everything covered in ash.

Dinner was impeccably set and awful. The bread burned, the soup boiled into a brown, sour mush. Father, confused, navigated carefully through the meal. As did Evie. Mother's moods sprang from a more mysterious source than Father's. He merely toiled for a harvest, feeling happy when it worked and frustrated when it didn't. Mother's ambitions, however, depended on things like manners, civilization, propriety. Shifting principles, shifting every day, like the plates in the ground Father had told Evie about. So, understanding only this, both Evie and Father ate the miserable meal without hunger, without question, but for the first question:

"Mattie, where's Ixna?"

"Her mother's sick, so she'll be in Xela for the week."

Evie shoved burned bread into her mouth. Two lies now, between them. The difference being when Father lied, he looked right at Mother. But Mother did not see Father once, all evening. Nor had she seen Evie, not even when she picked the floury lumps out of her soup with her fingers. Mother didn't eat any of the dinner she had tried so hard to cook, but stood on the porch, clutching a towel to her stomach like it hurt.

"Evie," Father asked, in a whisper, "did you tell her about our visit to Ubico? What did you say? Did you get confused and say something?"

She had said nothing at all, she insisted, insulted.

"Did Ixna tell you another scary story?"

The cookies, baked by Ixna the day before, were fantastic. Evie snuck them from the kitchen and she and Father ate them secretly, ravenously. They finished a whole dozen, licking the crumbs. Which reminded Evie. She could not believe she'd almost forgotten.

"Father, I got an Indian to eat a cookie today! I was right, cinnamon worked! Though Tomás is a Mestizo. Does he count?"

But he didn't seem to hear, or to understand the importance of this feat. "Did you use that word with Mother today? Mestizo? Is that why she's upset?"

"I think Mother just has a stomachache."

After dinner, Mother put Evie to bed, though it was only seven o'clock. She piled blankets on, not hearing her protests that it was still hot out, it was still light.

"But I have to tell Father that I got Tomás to eat a cookie! I tried to tell him, but he wouldn't listen. Tomás is an Indian, isn't he? Does he count as an Indian?"

"Yes, he certainly does. Don't worry, I'll tell him all about it."

~~~~~

Two things happened while Evie slept. First, Father worked the men until morning and, miraculously, they were ready to harvest the cochineal. But it took at least a week to get a cochineal harvest in, and they had only a day before the men were taken for the draft. But Father seemed to believe in his own pronouncement that Ubico might help him and Evie began to wonder if she had misunderstood the entire conversation between the government man and her father. Maybe the bribe had worked.

The second thing that happened woke Evie up. Ixna had gone to Xela for the night, but now she was back.

"Go back home!" Evie, lying in bed, heard Mother pleading.

Evie shuffled into the piano room to see Ixna on the porch, standing next to the massive pile of ash-blackened clothes still awaiting the wash.

"Go home! We don't need you! I'm giving you the whole week! It's called a vacation, I'm paying you!"

But Ixna merely set down her square basket and began to gather their clothing in her arms, ready to work again.

Whenever Ixna went back to her home in Xela, she'd return with her hair braided in an elaborate crown, with her costume scrubbed and smelling like lemony flowers, earrings glinting on either side of where her smile would be, if she smiled. It seemed all her family and neighbors came together to fix her up and make her beautiful, and this time was no different. Cousins made jewelry, friends braided her hair. Even her father contributed to the effort, weaving her new skirts with thin, multicolored vertical stripes, shot through with strange patterns. She was like a princess the whole community would rally around and love.

"Ixna, is that a new blouse?" Evie asked, helping her carry the laundry out back.

"Yes."

"It looks new. But it looks a lot like the old blouse." She considered the bright, brocaded tunic. "The colors are the same as all the other blouses in Xela. Is that on purpose? Is there only one store for Indian shirts?"

"My mother made it. Every *huipil* from Xela tells the same story in colors."

"And what's the story of Xela?"

"It is very sad," she said in a bored voice, sifting through their ashen clothes.

Evie politely studied the flowers and what looked like eggs and birds clustered thickly around the neck in clashing colors. The bird, she saw, was just like Magellan. A green bird with a red breast and a long, long tail. A quetzal, Ubico called it.

"But not all the blouses in Xela have birds on them, or eggs, or those diamond patterns," Evie said.

"No. Those are my story."

Evie squinted skeptically. How could a bird tell her story? It was hard enough imagining her visiting her family, Ixna doing anything but sweeping, scrubbing, and cooking.

Ixna bent over the cold, weak dry-season stream behind the house, and beat the ash out of their clothes with rocks. She held a dull, round stone in her fist, dunked one of Mother's skirts, and struck it repeatedly, while holding it underwater.

"Mother won't like you being so rough with her clothes," Evie warned her. "You've already ruined all her nice dresses."

"That's okay. You're going back to New York tomorrow. You can all get new clothes there."

"We are? Did Mother say so?"

Ixna nodded. Evie knew this time was different, because Ixna did not lie. She did not lie because she didn't care if her words upset Evie.

~~~~~

Father worked the Indians all day and all night, again. He came into the house a few times for a nap, and while he napped, Judas worked the men.

No one takes a goddamned piss, her father had decreed. *I'm going to get two years' work out of you in two days.*

And he did. When Evie saw an Indian worker in the field, he would look dazed, his hands stained red from the cochineal. The clatter of their brushes and nets, sounding like swords, kept her up all night. She lay awake, thinking of New York, trying to remember anything about it. When she tried to think of the new clothes they would all get, she could only imagine cleaner versions of what they already had.

The draft took all the men at dawn. Even Judas. Transported to the Piedmont in covered wagons, they would not know where they were, so they could not run away, Mrs. Fasbinder had explained. Evie had fallen asleep to the clatter of their tools and had awoken to the sound of her mother packing. Just as Ixna had said.

"We're going home, Evie. What do you think of that?"

She had thought about it all night, and just now, looking around the quiet house, the question came to her. "Is Father coming?"

"I don't know." She vigorously stuffed Ixna's washing into burlap sacks. The clothes still damp and gray from the ash. How gray, they would not be sure until the clothes dried completely. Mother hefted these sacks through the front door and onto the porch, where she meant to pile them with other things she wanted to load onto the cart. But she paused over the trunks and cases, then turned and chucked the sacks over the railing.

With a flushed, smiling face, she strolled back into the house and said, "I don't know why I packed those old things. Of course, once we're back in New York, we'll buy all new clothes! And shoes and ribbons and hats. I'll have my face powder back, and curls and earrings. And you'll need a winter coat. What color do you want?"

Evie didn't know. There were too many colors to choose from, ones that surely didn't exist in Guatemala. So many things existed in New York and not here. There must be colors she did not even know about.

"Well?" Mother's aggressive cheer began to sour with Evie's hesitation.

"Green and orange?"

"A *green and orange* coat." Mother studied her, disappointed. "Those colors don't even match, Evie. You've acquired the fashion sense of an Indian."

Evie sat on the porch and packed the silverware into its velvet-lined box, trying to decide if she was happy to leave. She always thought she missed New York, but she missed things her mother had told her about, not what she actually remembered. And by now she knew her parents' descriptions of a place should not be trusted. Electricity and toilets could turn out to be just as disappointing as being rich in the land of bananas. The best she could do at imagining New York was to picture a bigger version of the Frenchman's shop: a land so full of nice, expensive things that broke too easily to have much fun with them. Of course, that was why manners were so important there.

She had decided upon a cautious joy, convincing herself that of course Father would come along. This was what she was thinking when she saw the lone figure walking up their road. A head rising over the crest, then shoulders, then a body. An odd illusion: someone being born from the road itself.

She watched at first unafraid, because she saw that the figure had shoes on, was nicely dressed. Not a ghost. Then she the remembered Mr. Ubico, how nicely he had been dressed with his pistol and savage smile. And here he was, in the same cream-colored suit. She cried out in fright, remembering how he'd touched that gun and looked at Father. How he'd said he was in charge of everyone, not just Indians.

"Well, isn't that a sight?" Mother frowned, with her hand shading her eyes in the open doorway. "Don't be afraid, Evie. It's just Judas. In a new suit."

Father rolled out of bed to see for himself. He looked as stunned as Evie to find his meeting with Ubico had been a success.

"We're still going, Robert," Mother said, watching Judas part the clinging mountain mists. "You can come if you want."

"No," Father murmured, looking at nothing with his blue eyes, veined with red. "No one's going anywhere, Mattie. There's no money left behind the bureau. I gave it to Ubico."

With a gasp, Mother rushed into the parlor. She struggled with the weight of the bureau, but Father did not help or even turn around. "How did you find it? Evie, did you show him?"

"I didn't!"

"I'm sorry, Mattie." And he did sound sorry. "I don't have the energy anymore to start new somewhere else. I have a plan."

"Do you realize we're trapped here?" She shook her head in amazement, trying to process this terrifying turn, while sinking to the floor. "We have *nothing*. Not a peso."

"That's not true, Mattie. We always have your mother."

"The telegraph's still down, Robert. It'll take weeks for a letter to reach her, weeks for a reply. Your credit's run out at the bank. We have nothing. We couldn't leave if a mob of Indians stormed the house with machetes."

Evie felt her mouth drop open. Machetes? Then she felt a hand on her head.

"Mattie, you're scaring Evie. She doesn't realize you're joking."

"Of course I'm just joking, Evie." Mother stood up, wiped her eyes clear with a trembling hand. Then she steadied herself on the bureau.

Father picked Evie up, smiling. "There are no Indians left, except women. And we processed two bags of cochineal last night. With Judas's help, we'll have more today. We'll have enough to buy tickets in three days if we must." He turned to Mother, but she had already walked out of the room. "You wouldn't have even known it was gone."

Father carried Evie out past the mule shed. "I have a very important task for you, Evie. Can I count on you to get it done?"

"Yes."

"I need you to supervise Judas. There's so much to do, I need you to stay close to him. None of our other workers were exempted, so we have to make sure Judas works extra hard. Can you do that?"

"But I thought we were going home! The Indians are eating cookies, didn't you know? I got Tomás to eat a cookie!"

"Yes, I heard about the cookie, Evie. That's very good, it's amazing you convinced him. But we have a million more to convince, you know."

Evie stared over the henhouse fencing at the hens, which were suspicious at their arrival. Heads cocked midstep, listening. "So, Guatemala's problems aren't solved?"

"Not yet, honey. But thanks to you, we're a little closer. I promise to take some cinnamon cookies to the market. But right now we have to worry about the harvest. It's a big responsibility, I thought you might be too young. If you can't, that's okay—"

"I can! I can watch Judas!"

He let her down at the chopping block, where Judas had begun to stack the firewood the other workers had chopped. "I'm counting on you." Then he strolled back to the house, whistling.

Evie stood a moment, surveying the situation. Judas lifted the logs one by one, to keep his new cream-colored suit clean. "Father's put me in charge," she informed him. "And I say you should pick up more at once. You're wasting time doing it that way."

He ignored her, walking a single piece over and stacking it with the others, then taking the time to dust off his sleeves. Inflamed with her responsibility, with his insolence, she twisted a green branch from a nearby tree and stood a distance away with it. Judas watched her with one eye, like Magellan used to do. From the house, she heard her mother shout.

We will not stay in this situation. You are not going to put your daughter in this situation. You have to fire her.

"Father has put me in charge," she repeated, with sudden tears stinging her eyes. Fire her? When Judas made no reply, she swatted the ground with the whiplike branch.

She could not hear Father's part of the conversation.

I know why you're so desperate to stay! You don't want to leave her!

Stacking, stacking, one by one. Evie took a courageous step toward Judas and snapped the branch again against the ground. "I said—" In one motion, he was at her side, holding her wrist. With her head down, that's all she saw, his big brown hand. He squeezed until her fingers gave up the switch.

I saw you, Robert. I saw! I saw the way you had her bent over the mule trough! Like an animal!

That was enough. Evie twisted free and ran away from Judas, from her parents' terrifying argument. *Stop*, she said to the big-leafed trees clapping all around. *Please stop*, she said, running into the forest, the only place where she could escape. But as she got farther away, Mother's voice worked up to an octave that could sling harsh words to the far edges of the field. Pots slamming.

Evie could not run away fast enough.

Don't blame her. She is a child. A child!

They were talking about Evie. She did play in the mule trough sometimes. She'd float little boats she made from sticks. She played in the trough like an animal. No manners. And now they wanted to fire her. Could you fire a daughter? Was that how orphans were made? She ran out of earshot, too terrified to hear their plan for her. What had she done wrong? Mother believed she'd told Father where to find the money. Money, as always. All she could think of was money. Evie was too expensive to keep. Like the orphan Tomás.

Evie walked the forest aimlessly, trying to get lost. She took all kinds of trails: animal trails, Indian trails, her father's trails. Sometimes there were no tracks and she realized she'd been following the trail of water run dry.

She tried to get lost because she believed that if she did, maybe they would miss her. They would panic, in a desperate search, and Father would return with Evie limp and breathing shallowly in his arms. Her dress shredded from the forest, from the ghosts clawing at her. She savored her fear, imagining these scenes, her parents' realization that they could not live without her, their promises to never fight again. It did not take long for her to come across the cave. She doubled back, trying to get to unfamiliar territory. But several minutes later, she came to it again, then again. All trails seemed to lead to the cave in some way. And when she came upon it the fourth time, she saw people inside.

She immediately recognized Ixna with her basket. An old man stooped inside with her, an old man who must have been a dead ancestor, summoned from the small hole. In tattered pants and no shirt, a chest sunken in where his soul would be, he looked exactly like he had just been resurrected from the grave.

They'd started a fire in the cave and the sweet-smelling smoke drifted over to Evie, burning her nostrils. The old man poured sap in the flames and talked to them, while Ixna handed him a bottle, an egg, and one of Father's golden hens. The man drank the entire bottle in two sucking pulls, then rubbed his old-man ghost hands over Ixna's belly. He cracked the egg open and stared at its mess on a rock. Then he grasped the astonished chicken by the neck and spun it around once, like a noisemaker. He looked at Evie, his dead eyes finding her in her hiding place, as he raised one of their silver knives.

She ran home as fast as her girl's legs could take her. Running so fast that her braid sailed behind, catching on the forest. The branches swiped at her clothes, leaves clung to her hair, but she made it out and within sight of the house in less than three minutes.

"Evie!" Father called from one of the wheat fields. "Where did you go? Judas was supposed to be watching you." But she ran right past him.

"Evie, it's time for lunch," was all Mother said when Evie burst into the house with a strangled sob. "Ixna left your plate in the kitchen."

~~~~~

Over the next two days, workers began to materialize on the farm. Indian men Evie had never seen before. Some solitary figures walking up the road, others arriving out of the trees, holding blankets. Eleven men in all, skinny and universally filthy. They grinned black gums at Evie from a distance. They slept in the woods on their Indian blankets, and Evie could hear them laughing and talking in the night. Sometimes they sang.

No one went into the woods now. Judas carried Father's pistol all day and Father lugged his shotgun between the house and the cooking shed. Evie was not allowed outside, not even on the porch, and had to stay inside with Mother.

"But why?"

"Just because I need you here, to help in the house."

"Where's Ixna?"

"We had to fire her."

"Why?"

"She was too expensive to keep. Plus, she stole."

Evie never believed all her mother's suspicions of Ixna until now. Clearly,

Ixna did go to the cave to command the ghosts, had stolen Mother's face powder and mirror and knife. What could she want from the old-man ghost? At least she was gone now. Too expensive to keep. With that, remembering their fight, Evie became determined to prove her own worth around the house.

Though she insisted she needed Evie's help, Mother never came up with any chores for her to do, so she made them up herself. She dusted the furniture and rinsed pans all morning, while Mother did nothing. She no longer played the piano, hadn't played it since the day of Mrs. Fasbinder's visit. But she had started doing her hair again, and wearing her corsets and lily-of-the-valley perfume. She even changed into her best dress, a silky navy blue dress that Ixna had ruined last year and that Evie hadn't seen since. The hole she'd beaten into the armpit wasn't even on a seam, so could not be easily fixed. But now Mother's solution seemed to be a stiff right arm, pinned perpetually to her side, so that the hole never showed. All day she opened doors, applied lipstick, and even used a fork with her unskilled left hand, while her right arm remained at her side.

Looking so nice with nowhere to go and with nothing to do, every five minutes Mother paced to the window, searching for calamity. She moved carefully yet constantly around the house, like she was trying not to wake some giant beast sleeping beneath them. The snake.

"Why are you afraid of these new workers, Mother?"

"Afraid?" She sat down for the first time that day. "I'm not afraid, Evie. What makes you say that?" She sat straight, her back not touching the chair.

"I don't know."

"Well, I'm certainly not afraid. If anything, I'm just very excited that your father's plan is working. In a week, we'll have enough money to go back to New York and see your grandmother. I guess I'm just excited to go back."

"But where did Father get the money to pay them?"

"That's a good question, Evie. I couldn't put it better myself."

Evie moved to the window and watched as Judas marched the new workers on a tour of the cactus field, their line drooping and wavering like a leisurely snake.

"Mother, what's it like being drunk?"

That was the last Evie saw of them, because Mother shot up from her chair and covered the window with her shawl, with her fumbling left arm. Casting them in near-darkness. "You know, Evie, I just realized we have completely neglected your education this week. What would you like me to teach you today?"

"I want to know what it's like being drunk."

Mother lit two lanterns. "Evie, that's no subject for a lady!"

"But it's in Father's song! And I know a drunk person when I see one. They move like this." Evie swayed and staggered in an imitation of the Indians on the side of the road, in the central park, at the market, just outside their window. "Why?"

"Your Guatemalan education hasn't suffered this week, I see." Mother breathed deeply and searched her mind for a moment. "They move like that because being drunk is like dancing to music only you can hear."

This confused Evie, since it seemed that today everyone on the mountain—the new workers, Father, Judas—was dancing to a tune everyone could hear but her. "But if two people are drunk together, are they hearing the same music?"

"No."

"How do you know? Have you ever been drunk?"

"Of course not! Now, Evie, this conversation is over. We will move on to geography. I saw the map you drew the other day for Tomás. You got it all wrong. Don't you want to see the route we'll be taking home?"

"This . . ." Mother said, making a large shape on a fresh piece of paper, "this is America. And this is where we are, and this is Europe." She'd refused to add to Father's world map, preferring to start a new one herself.

Sitting down, she found she could draw with her right hand, while keeping her elbow at her side. She spent a long time on Europe, telling Evie about France and England and the trip she'd take her on one day. The Mediterranean, the Alps.

"But where's Guatemala?"

"Guatemala is here," she said, making a lonely shape at the bottom of the map, not connected to anything. Not like Tomás's, not like Father's. And this is how we will get home." She made blue arrows to retrace their dismal journey three years ago: up the Pacific coast, across Mexico, then through the Caribbean, then train tracks up to New York. Then more arrows, leading to Europe. "And then we'll go to Italy and see the ancient capital of Rome, and all the art and beautiful things there. Maybe in France we'll find you the green coat you want. Just green, don't you agree?"

"Is France where the Frenchman in Xela comes from?"

"Yes, Evie. That's very smart of you."

"And where do Guatemalans like Mr. Ubico come from?"

"They came from Spain." She pointed to one of the shapes, one that looked like a fist. "A long time ago. Hundreds of years ago." This did not surprise Evie, that Ubico was hundreds of years old. It seemed to explain his power, his ability to replace God, as Father said. So much to learn from this map, though she knew not to ask about Ladinos. Mother would insist it wasn't even a real word, though it seemed Ubico had finally been convinced it was. "And what about the coffee planters? Mrs. Fasbinder and all them?"

"They're German, mostly. Mrs. Fasbinder's parents came from Germany"—she traced the route—"to America. Then Mrs. Fasbinder moved from America to Guatemala."

"And where do Indians come from?"

"Why . . ." Mother seemed surprised at the question. "Indians are from Guatemala, of course. They've never gone anywhere."

"And what about Mestizos, like Tomás? Where do they come from?"

Mother put a hand over her mouth and blushed, averting her eyes. "Oh, Evie . . ."

"Mestizos come from Mestizoland!"

They spun around to see Father standing in the front door. His sleeves were rolled up and his arms were stained red with cochineal up to his elbows.

"Robert!" Mother shrank down in her seat. "Shouldn't you be out there? *Watching* things?"

"I missed my girls. Anyway, Judas has them under control." He walked over to look at the map and studied it over Mother's shoulder. Annoyed, for some reason, for being so startled, she moved away from them both. But her perfume remained.

"Where's Mestizoland?" Evie asked.

"Right here," he declared, pointing smack in the middle of the Pacific Ocean. An island! Tomás was from an island! Evie marked it with a pencil.

"Well," Mother huffed from the other side of the room. "Maybe you should be teaching geography, Robert, since I've been living in ignorance my whole life. Since I've never been to Mestizoland." She crossed her arms. Obviously Mestizoland was another country she wished Father had taken her to, but hadn't.

"Not ignorance, Mattie," he mumbled sadly. His blue eyes glittered in the lantern light like melting ice. "Innocence. Sweet, beautiful, divine innocence. A state we should all live in."

"Where's Innocence? That's a state?"

"Yes, it is. Right here." He pointed to a spot below New York. Evie marked it. "Though I've never been there. They wouldn't let me in, I'm so terrible."

Mother laughed unwillingly, wiping her eyes. "You've been drinking that stuff, too, Robert? It's not even noon."

But time didn't seem to matter anymore in the house. With their one window covered and the lanterns lit in the middle of the day, it was like the ash had come back, stranding them all in a grimy, unchanging light.

"It's made of eggs and spices and, I don't know. It's great stuff. Have a drink with me." Father turned from the map and brought a bottle out from the waistband of his pants. "Let's celebrate."

"Celebrate what?" Mother tightened her grip on herself as he stepped near her.

"Our new workers. Our third harvest!"

"You call a bunch of drunk, wanted Indians workers?"

"What's wanted?" Evie asked.

"Oh yes, she already knows what drunk is, Robert." She explained to Evie, "Wanted means that your Father wanted them very badly. So much so, that he'll probably be wanted himself, which means we'll all be wanting to leave very soon."

Father nodded, allowing this baffling point. "Well, we'll see. But for now, I'll celebrate staying, you can celebrate leaving. In the end, one of us will be happy. That's something to drink to." He uncorked the bottle and held it out for Mother. "Play us a song on the piano, Evie!"

Evie did not move. Despite their smiles, she sensed trouble. They sometimes forgot the old tricks didn't work on her anymore. Evie knew there were different kinds of smiles, and theirs now showed toothy and sad. Father did not notice the lack of music, and began to sing:

> *The Indians are drunk*
> *The coffee boat has sunk*
> *Down to Brazil*
> *Where the grounds stay still*

Mother took the bottle and drank from it with the quick, successive gulps Evie recognized from Indians drinking on the side of the road. Each motion sent her right arm up, showing the white skin through the hole in her dress. Evie watched, unbelieving, as they passed the bottle back and forth. Until today Father did not drink and Mother certainly did not drink. It was a source of pride, which Mother always shared with anyone who would listen. Robert doesn't drink. He may disappear for months, hop trains like a hobo, but at least he doesn't drink. Yet here they were, drinking, not even something respectable like brandy from the Frenchman's shop. No, drinking Indian moonshine straight from the bottle.

> *Now the government's tack*
> *Rides on sixty miles of track*

The song made Mother smile feebly. Father complimented her on her dress, her hair, tracing over her face and leaving a pink smudge. He then slipped his stained fingers down inside Mother's dress and she did not flinch away for propriety but held him there. Evie watched his hand push one of her breasts up, making a mountain that spilled over the neckline. And here were her parents, kissing in the middle of the room. Standing and kissing and making up with violent, desperate movements that sent them stumbling back. Evie, very conscious of her manners, tried to leave, but they blocked the way to the door.

The new workers did not understand the delicacy of the harvest. Judas spent the entire day yelling at them, while Mother spent the afternoon lying down with a wet cloth over her eyes, trying not to hear the yelling. Father promised he'd watch Evie so she could rest.

"Don't you let her out of your sight, Robert," she commanded from beneath the cloth. "Only Judas can bring the baskets, hear? The others aren't allowed to see her."

Father and Evie worked in the cooking shed, keeping two fires. Inside, it was hot and so cramped that two people couldn't fit inside without being all over each other. But Evie enjoyed being so near her father, and found comfort in his complicated, intimate scent: oil, manure, hay, and smoke. She felt a rush of gratitude each time he took a moment to explain something, thinking maybe he had changed his mind about firing her. If she could understand and help with the harvest, she wouldn't be too expensive to keep.

"The pregnant ones are the only ones we harvest. They have the most carminic acid," Father said. "The others aren't worth our time."

Father placed a cochineal bug on the sorting table and held a lantern to it. It didn't look like a bug at all, but like a confectionary from the Frenchman's shop. A small, soft ball, rolled in powdered sugar. Then Father used his thumb to squash it.

"Look," he said, bringing his magnifying glass from the shelf. "Look here." He held the glass over the bug to reveal the suddenly huge smothered body. "That's what we're after," he explained. "See all that?" The bug's demise, amplified a million times, looked like a lake of blood.

Evie stepped back, averting her eyes. "That's terrible, all that blood."

"No, no," Father reassured her. He pushed her to look again. "It's not blood, sweetic. It just looks like blood. That's carminic acid."

Evie reconsidered the crushed body through the eye of the magnifying glass. She looked for any remnants of a face, of limbs, of a mouth. The bugs were pregnant, but there was no sign of a baby, just the red.

"See? It's not so bad. Quite beautiful, really." When he straightened, his huge blue eye filled the glass, finding her. "And it's worth much more than plain old blood."

"But it's still dead."

The bugs went into the stove powdery white and came out gray. Evie helped Father lay them out in the sun, where they dried into pellets. These pellets Father sold to merchants, who powdered and sold them as dye. A deep red, vivid dye.

"Pay attention, Evie. It's important to keep two fires to get an even heat. You make two smaller fires and you keep some hot coals between them, instead of one big fire. That way you can cook more bugs at a time and not burn them."

"You cook them alive? Don't they crawl away?"

"They can't, honey. Once the females get pregnant, their legs fall off."

She held up a cooked specimen. "How horrible. Poor bug."

"Berries," Father corrected. "After they're cooked, we call them berries."

"Berries? Why?"

"Let's put it this way," he said. "If you're a rich lady from Boston, would you rather buy lipstick made from cochineal bugs or cochineal berries?"

"I thought it was used for clothes. Don't they use the dye for clothes?"

"Among other things," Father answered. "Cochineal berries are in everything. In clothes, paint, powder, soap, and lipstick."

"Lipstick? In Mother's lipstick?"

"Oh yes! But don't tell her that. I don't think she knows. Let's not ruin lipstick for her, too." He laughed, and Evie could not tell at whose expense. "That's the beauty of faraway lands, Evie. Something as terrible as a bug's guts gets magically transformed into a berry. All it takes is a short trip across the ocean."

———

"It's going to work," Father said, beaming over dinner with his mouth full. They were able to pick and process five bags of cochineal that day. "If we can do this for a week, everything will be fine. These workers—they're terrible, but I have more of them than I ever did."

"And I helped," Evie reminded her father. "I kept the fires going."

"Yes, you did, Evie."

Pow! A shot rang out from the yard, making Evie and Mother jump.

Mother said nothing, just drank from her glass of the Indian moonshine. The thick yellow liquid reminded Evie of bile, of what she threw up when there was nothing more left.

"What's wrong, Mattie, my love?"

Why did Father keep asking that? He knew, even Evie knew, what was wrong: money, scary Indians. And now this random gunfire, punctuating the evening in unpredictable bursts.

"Don't be scared," Father reminded them for the tenth time. "It's just Judas calling the Indians. It's the fastest way to get them all together."

Mother nodded. Evie studied her lipsticked mouth, the bright bug guts smeared along the rim of her glass and her frown.

"Mattie. I'm sorry. But they're spread out all over the fields, it's the only way—"

"She's still here."

"Who's still here?" Father asked warily.

"Ixna. I saw her in the yard today. I yelled at her, but she won't leave. She's just moved into the forest. She won't leave!"

Pow!

"I didn't see her," Father insisted, unflinching, refilling her glass. "Maybe she forgot something."

"You're going to call the police."

"I can't have the police up here. I'll have Judas find her. In an hour, she'll be gone. I promise." He took her hand. "Will you please cheer up? Things are working out."

"I can't be happy, Robert. Even if Ixna falls off a cliff, even if the harvest succeeds, I cannot relax until I know where the money came from."

"I was advanced money on something that doesn't matter, because I'm going to be able to pay it all back with the money from the harvest. So nothing's lost."

"Something that doesn't matter?" Mother turned the phrase over in her mouth, considering its ingredients. "What is that, Robert?"

"It's more like collateral, really." He glanced at Evie. "Can we discuss this later?"

"Collateral?" A new taste now, this word, one she did not like. "Robert, who did you get this money from? Who do we owe? Who has power over us now, other than a crazy dictator? Other than the coffee planters, foreign investors, bankers, Ubico, and throngs of Indians controlling our mountain?"

"They're friends, Mattie. It's not a bank or some corrupt government official. They're friends and we have a friendly agreement. Let's not bore Evie with the details."

"We don't have friends down here, Robert."

Pow!

Even Father jumped to that one. "Oh, don't say—"

"Who!" Mother slammed her fist down on the table, making a terrific clatter with their dishes. "Who, who, who, who!" Every time she said "who," she banged her fist on the table. Their dinners all shifted to the right and a storm began in their water glasses.

"The Fasbinders."

The answer completely perplexed Mother, who blinked at Father's empty plate. "The Fasbinders? What interest do they have in your experiment? What could we possibly have that they want?"

Evie became very still, thinking this was the moment Father would confess he had sold Evie to Mrs. Fasbinder. She would be a house girl, alongside the Indian boy Tomás. Or she would work in the coffee fields, with all the drafted Indians. Like Ixna, eight years old, whipped for eating a banana.

"Like I said, they aren't getting anything. We can discuss this later, in private."

"In private! Where can we go? I can't step onto my own porch anymore! Shall we go five steps that way and discuss it? Ask Evie to cover her ears?"

"Fine. I'm paying them back in two weeks."

"For what? Their plantation is devastated, Robert. They would not loan a peso to anyone right now unless they're getting something they desperately want. What—" She pounded again. "What do they think they're getting from you!"

"I don't—"

She pounded on the table with both fists now, over and over, almost drowning out Father's eventual reply: "The piano."

Mother's fists froze, midair, and Evie thought she might lunge and strangle him.

"But they're not getting the piano. She wants it for her school. But the school isn't even built yet. The government won't approve it. It was a fight to rein in the damned Catholics. You'll keep your piano and I'll have the money to refund her once the harvest's in. I'll even pay them interest."

Mother's hands lay on the table now, flat. With an eerie formality, she asked, "And if it is built? If, perhaps, the President was at her gala and approved the school?"

"They learned their lesson with the Catholics, Mattie."

"They're after souls, not land and gold, Robert. I think the President is very interested in her *fucking* school. I think he sees a beautiful partnership."

"Even if he is," he sang, twirling his fork, ignoring this astounding language from Mother's mouth, "it won't be built in two weeks." The last time Evie heard Father say that word, Mother made him sleep in the mule shed for two nights.

"Don't play those pretty eyes at me. She's not going to want her money back. She's going to want that piano. She's wanted it for years!" Evie watched her right hand crawl across the table like a spider, hunting the nearest knife.

"I can pay her money back, plus more."

"Because you're sure you'll get this harvest in? You're sure you can control this situation? Indians who skipped the draft, *who are not afraid of Ubico?*"

Pow! Pow!

Mother gazed up at him, her eyes jellied with fear. Her fingers found the knife, gripped it. Father reached for her glass and took it away.

"You're scaring Evie, Mattie. She doesn't realize you're joking,"

"Everything's fine, Evie. I'm just drunk, that's all. People say silly things when they're drunk. They make jokes no one else finds funny."

~~~~~

The next day, Mother played her piano for the first time in days. Possibly Father's promise to stop firing guns cheered her up slightly. She played for hours, not pausing for anything. She suffered no questions, no interruptions, until she pressed the soft pedal with her foot to ask over her own playing, "Where's Ixna? Have you seen her out in the yard today?"

"She's in the cooking shed, helping Father." Evie knew she should have lied about what she saw out the window, but telling would be the only way to ensure Ixna was kicked off the mountain for good. Father would never do it himself; he was too nice.

Mother merely nodded, the music working up her arms, rounding her shoulders, and dipping her chin. She played and played, her eyes set on something not in the room. She swayed on the loose piano bench, her chest out and her dark nipples showing beneath her blouse.

And then the tune was over, or Mother had just stopped, for it didn't seem a proper ending. She stood up. Fixated on the white, closed wooden body where her song expired, she swept her hand over the keys like a magician, knocking the lit lantern over on its side.

The movement of the fire over the piano was so quick that Evie and Mother just watched as the kerosene drew a blue line over the top. By the time the flames rose, Evie yelled, while Mother remained standing, watching the fire with a peculiar half smile on her face. She stepped back, as if for a better view, while Evie ran to the kitchen. All she could find was the cold porridge from breakfast. The heavy, tall pot slopped porridge on Evie's shoes as she ran. With all her might, she hoisted the pot over her head and heaved its contents on the piano. The porridge spread slowly, smothering the fire into smoke.

Mother, still standing behind her bench, had not moved but was no longer smiling. "Well, Evie," she said. "I think we found a new, brilliant use for wheat. Could revolutionize something, I'm sure. And I bet he'll be in here in about one minute, to ask why I've stopped playing for him."

And he was. He walked in a moment later, drawn out of the cooking shed by the piano music's absence.

"I don't know what happened," Mother explained to him. "I was playing I guess a little too hard and tipped over the lantern. Evie saw, didn't you? Was I just playing a bit too hard?" The burned piano still smoked from someplace deep inside, taking up space like a dying dragon. The burned sections revealed strings, pegs, and hammers, looking like lungs, bones, clenched teeth. The porridge coating the parts like an infection.

"Yes," Evie agreed, because she didn't know how to explain what she had seen. Even to think of her mother purposefully setting fire to her most prized possession made her reorder the events in her mind to make it make sense.

Father's eyes darted from Mother to Evie, seeing a similarity, some treachery between them. His anger, rarely stirred, was best diffused by tears, which now appeared like light in Mother's eyes. "Let's just go, Robert. We don't have to repay her. They won't pursue us, it'll cost them more in legal fees. Let's just sell the few bags we have and *go*."

Kneeling for a better look at the piano, Father mumbled, "It looks like it's just exterior damage, maybe I can fix it."

"The exterior's the most important part," she said. "It's what shapes the sound."

"Okay, but still, maybe I can fix it, nail some boards over the top."

She laughed bitterly. "You have no idea what I'm saying, do you?"

"We just have to keep Mrs. Fasbinder away until I have the money to re-pay her. Cancel your tea next week. Send a note. Tell her we're all sick."

"Shall I send Ixna down with the note?"

Father sank back on his heels. "Mattie, I've tried. I swear. She's crazy, she won't go away." Evie saw tears in his eyes now, too, then several traced down his cheek. "She follows me. What can I do? I don't want her here. I've never wanted her here."

That night, Mother baked Evie a dozen cookies. Her version of an apology, for the quiet crying Evie had been trying to control all evening, thinking of the horrors of the cochineal business, her mother's bug-blood mouth, the burned piano, Father's tears. Father had never cried before. Mother was always the one to cry. The piano remained in the middle of the parlor, half burned and horrifying, though Mother pretended it wasn't there. That everything was perfectly fine.

"Don't cry, honey," she said, smearing another layer of lipstick on, like armor. "Eat your cookies. Why would you cry, having your favorite cookies all to yourself?" Mother kissed her, and Evie could feel the dreaded lipstick stamp burning her skin.

Mother wrote a letter to Mrs. Fasbinder, canceling their tea. "What terrible disease would you like to have, Evie? What would keep Mrs. Fasbinder away?"

Mother finished that letter and began another, to her mother. "Guatemala has killed everything," she read aloud, holding up the paper. "My baby, my marriage, my wealth, my beauty. Sometimes I wish those Indians would de-cide to throw me in that volcano. One day, I might just take a walk and never return."

Evie, not wanting to miss a terrifying word, had stopped chewing her cookies. She broke off pieces, put them in her mouth, and merely sucked on them until they dissolved into a paste that made her back teeth ache.

"Raped and headless," Mother wrote and read at the same time. "That's how they find them, Mother. Raped and headless on the side of the road."

What did rape mean? Clearly, it was as bad as, or worse than, being headless.

The letter would not be finished today. Mother exhausted her shallow stores of morbidity and abandoned it, unable to top herself after these opening lines. So she sat with her pen in her hand and asked Evie if there was anyone she wanted to write to. "Do you want to write to any of your friends?"

Evie was surprised to hear that she still had friends in New York. She believed Mother's pronouncement earlier that they had no friends down here. Not that they had no friends in Guatemala, but that moving to Guatemala consigned them to worldwide friendlessness. Her only friend in the world had been Ixna, but not anymore.

Mother pulled a fresh sheet of paper from underneath the letter to her mother. "How about to Sophie?"

"Okay," she agreed, to please her. She remembered Sophie vaguely.

"What would you like to say to her?"

There were so many things that Evie wanted to say, but not to Sophie.

"Dear Sophie," Evie tried. "Life in Guatemala is hard, but rewarding."

It was a phrase Mother often wrote in her letters, but once Evie said it, Mother put her pen tip to the paper, then took it away, leaving a small blue dot.

"Do you really believe that, Evie? That our life here is rewarding?"

Evie nodded. She had believed it until the volcano erupted, anyway.

"I just mean," Mother clarified, "you don't have to write that. You can say what you want to Sophie."

"I know." Evie knew she could say what she wanted, but that did not mean it wouldn't upset Mother. Evie, from now on, would just do her best not to get fired.

Mother hesitated, then wrote down this opening sentence in her tall, leaning script. "What else?"

"I don't know. What do people usually write in letters?"

"Well, that depends. Maybe for Sophie, she'd want to know the best and worst parts about Guatemala."

"The best part about Guatemala is that we have animals."

Mother cocked her head, taken aback by the simplicity of Evie's happiness. Her eyes swimming, trying to understand. "Really, the animals are the best part for you?"

Evie nodded. "And tell her that a volcano exploded near our house and ash rained down on everything like snow." Putting it in a letter like this, the volcano became exciting. She knew anyone in New York would read that and be jealous.

"That's a good simile, Evie. I'll put it down just like that." And she did. "Do you know my favorite part of Guatemala?"

Evie did not want to know.

"My favorite part was having servants," Mother said. "I never thought I'd have them again." Mother used to tell funny stories about growing up with servants, how bad they were, how deceptive. She'd walked in on one of the hired girls trying on her graduation dress. Just spinning in front of the mirror with her hair tied up in a dishrag. "The worst part about Guatemala is having servants, too," Mother concluded cryptically. Ixna's behavior would never be recounted in silly stories like the one about the dress. In Guatemala, you couldn't even fire servants.

"And what's the worst part for you, Evie?"

The worst part, undoubtedly, was their haunted forest, especially Ixna in their haunted forest. But Evie knew enough to use the second-worst thing, so she didn't sound crazy. "Nothing ever changes. There are no seasons like at home, so sometimes you get confused about time. Sometimes it just feels like the same day dragging on forever."

"Yes," Mother agreed. "The Land of Eternal Spring. It sounded nice at first, didn't it?" She put down her pen and Evie felt all the cookies beginning to unsettle her stomach. "I forgot how miserable spring could be."

Evie should not have eaten so many cookies. She went to bed with a tummy ache and woke up later than usual, feeling empty. She lay on her sawdust mattress, listening to the floorboards creak in the other room, someone trying to be quiet. Evie, automatically, matched this caution when she tiptoed into the parlor.

"Evie! Good morning!" Father called from the table in surprise. He was just sitting there, not eating, not reading the paper, not making plans. Just sitting there, staring at his hands, and now at Evie.

"No one woke me up," she said.

Mother spun from the bureau with a peculiar smile. "Well, Sleeping Beauty! Up to join us at last. Sit at the table with your father and I'll bring you breakfast."

Evie took her place at the table across from Father. During a harvest, he usually woke hours before her and did not appear in the house until lunchtime.

From the kitchen, Mother returned with a plate. "Cookies for breakfast! What do you think of that?"

"I don't want any more cookies," Evie whined, pushing them away.

"But you love cookies, Evie. These are your favorite! Cinnamon!" Mother pushed the cookies back, with the same unusual smile, and sat down herself. Something seemed different about her as well.

"Can I just have some bread? I can get it myself." Evie moved toward the kitchen, but Mother blocked her way in an instant. "I'll get it for you! Stay here, sweetie. We need you to keep out of the kitchen today. We're cleaning it."

Mother disappeared again and Evie glanced at her father, who continued to sit there, staring at his hands. She'd never seen him doing nothing before. He did not look up when Mother returned with a thick, buttered slice of bread. Her smile, Evie realized, was someone else's. Pale and open. She breathed through it.

"Can you believe, Robert, Evie has turned down cinnamon cookies?"

Father smiled at his caged hands. "Unbelievable!"

They both watched her struggle to break through the hard crust. Once she'd made it to the soft interior, Mother tapped the table and said, "We have some wonderful news, Evie. Don't we, Robert?"

"Yes, yes." He leaned back and sat on his hands. With this, his leg started jiggling under the table. So hard that Evie had to catch her water glass to swallow down the bread.

"We're going home!" Mother seized Evie's elbow with excitement.

Evie waited for some correction, some protest from Father, but when none came, she asked, "When?"

"Tomorrow!"

"What happened?"

"Nothing *happened*, Evie." Mother's voice turned light and drifting. "It's just, our project is finished. Your father succeeded. So now we can go back to New York."

"The Indians are eating wheat? You convinced them?" She held her water with both hands, as Father's leg continued to shake the table.

"I sure did! It was the cinnamon cookies, Evie. Your idea worked! All the Indians in town are eating them!"

"So Guatemala's problems are solved?"

"They are! Can you believe it, Evie?"

Evie did not believe it. She watched her mother closely as she rose to take her plate away. She seemed to be speaking from someone else's mouth. Unpainted. That was it. She wore no lipstick.

"I'll admit I was skeptical for a while," Mother said. As she leaned in, Evie noticed her housecoat was on inside out. The seams and stitches showing. "We'll be packing today and leaving tomorrow morning. There's so much to do! I was hoping you could help. We have a very important job for you. Can you help, Evie?"

Evie sat very still, trying to think. But her father's leg seemed to be shaking the whole house.

"We need you to go into town with Judas, to mail some letters and get some supplies. Can you go? Judas won't be able to get into the store without you."

"Can I mail my letter to Sophie?"

Once Evie was dressed and ready to go, Father put his hands on her shoulders, and directed her out the front door and around the house to where Judas stood on the mountain road, waiting, with the volcano hulking over his right shoulder, the forest over his left. The three of them walked to the first bend in the road, where Father handed Judas a pistol and told them to take their time in town.

Judas carried the pistol in his waistband and Evie's letter to Sophie in his shirt pocket, along with the letter to Mrs. Fasbinder. If it worked, the Fasbinders would not know they had left until they were already on the boat to Mexico. What terrible disease, Evie wondered, had Mother given all of them in that letter? Malaria, yellow fever?

"Why are we walking to town?" Evie asked. "Why can't we take Tiny?"

Judas shrugged, put his hands in his pockets.

The morning was still, so still that she felt their steps could be heard for miles. So quiet, as if the woods were crowded with people watching them go.

Something was wrong, Evie could tell. Judas with a pistol, in charge of her now. And, except for the fantastic day of the military band's arrival, she'd never been able to walk on this road before. Mother always insisted on the cart. Walking with Father out the door, she'd seen the cart, with Tiny already hitched. In the back was a covered heap.

Something was wrong, more wrong than usual. More than the familiar worries: the money, the harvest. It had all happened the year before with the early rains. Nothing had been much of a surprise in retrospect. Indians acted terribly, her parents fought, money was tight. The one thing that had taken Evie by surprise was discovering Ixna in the cave. What could she be asking for from the old-man ghost? From the snake? And why wouldn't she leave?

"Judas, what do Indians ask for when they go into the cave?"

His shoes stuttered on the gravel, and he turned around to look through his own dust, walking backward. "The cave? Why do you care about the cave?"

"Because I know it's important and that people ask for things there. What is it? Is it bad things?"

"Indians go to the cave for many things. To give thanks, to ask."

"Did someone ask for the volcano to erupt? Did someone talk to the snake and make it happen?"

"The snake!" He laughed. Thick pancake spit, wheat, made long strings between his teeth. "Who told you about the snake?"

"Ixna. I saw her in the cave, Judas. I saw her in there. What did she do last night?"

Judas stopped. "When did you see her in the cave?"

"Four days ago."

"And what was she doing?"

She told him, as calmly as she could, about the old man and the chicken. The broken egg, the ghost rubbing her belly. Judas nodded thoughtfully, actually listening.

"What was she asking for, Judas?" She felt weak from the telling. Her fears and suspicions said aloud took on a physical dimension. Like the dust in her eyes. She rubbed and rubbed, trying to see him clearly. The road was so dusty and dry that every step they took ruined the air. "What has she done?"

He thought for a long time. In the forest around them, birds settled and trilled at one another, something large walked noisily where there was no trail. "She was giving thanks to the mountain," he said finally.

"For what?"

"I don't know. There are so many things to be thankful for."

Unsatisfied with this explanation, Evie decided to ask outright. "What happened last night, Judas? I know something happened."

"*Saber.*" He bent to tie his loose shoelaces.

"If you tell me, I'll show you a better way to tie your shoes. You won't have to stoop and retie them so much. It'll last all day."

He straightened, considering the bargain.

"I promise I won't be scared. I won't tell them I know."

"Okay. Your father murdered one of the workers last night."

"Why?"

Judas shrugged. "He was in the kitchen."

"Murdered. Does that mean he can't work? Are we short one worker now?"

"Yes. Now show me this new way."

While showing Judas how to double-knot, it occurred to Evie that her parents might leave for New York without her. That was why she and Judas couldn't take the cart. They would pack it—clearly they'd already packed something—and flee without her. She began to believe that when she and Judas got back from town, her parents would be gone. Just bits of packing paper, strands of her mother's dark hair left behind where they didn't bother to sweep on their way out. She'd be an orphan, like the Indian boy Tomás. Too expensive to keep. Without her, her parents would finally be able to afford Europe.

The town, empty because of the drafts and still strewn with rubble, seemed abandoned. As Evie expected, no one was eating cookies. Not the Indian women squatting in the park in their bright costumes or the children lurking in the shrinking morning shadows.

When they reached the government building, a sign announced in three languages—English, German, and Spanish—that the telegraph was still broken. Judas told Evie to wait in the arcade while he mailed the letters to Sophie and Mrs. Fasbinder. It took him several minutes to do so and Evie began to lose patience when he finally emerged, empty-handed, the only Indian man in the whole town.

"Judas, you went in the wrong door," Evie said. "That's not the post office. Did you get lost?" She felt almost sure he'd walked into Mr. Ubico's door.

"Ah." He smiled. "I know, I got confused. So many doors! But they all connect inside," he said. "Don't worry."

At the imports store, Judas gained entrance with Evie's verification and bought the supplies on the list. The Frenchman gave Evie change and they walked out into the rising heat of the day. The longer they took, the more she thought, the more her own fears of being left behind became harder to ignore. If her parents left her, she realized, she'd have to live with Judas.

"Judas, I'm sorry I tried to whip you. I didn't mean it. I was just playing."

"I know," he said, buying four bottles of the egg liquor from an Indian woman on the street. She gave him the change, though Evie held her hand out for it.

"Does Father ever whip you?" she asked, shielding her eyes to see him.

"No. I'm a hard worker."

"If you weren't, would he whip you?"

"*Saber.*"

"Does he whip these new workers? He says they're terrible."

Judas laughed a little to himself. "Only machetes. No whips. No one would whip these workers."

"Why not? Would they kill Father? If he whipped them?"

Judas shook his head, blew air out of one of the gaps in his teeth. "Indians don't kill," he said. "People with money kill. Indians just work. They just do jobs."

"Like kill people?"

Judas hefted the bags. "Indians just do jobs," he repeated, though every story Evie had ever heard of killing had involved Indians. "We can't choose the jobs, and we can't say no. It's the law. If we're lucky, though, we get paid."

Mother and Father had not left Evie behind, at least not yet. When Evie returned from Xela with Judas, she nearly wept in relief at the sight of them: Father washing out the cart, Mother hauling bags to the porch. But she remembered her promise to Judas, to show no fear. And so she passed the rest of the day with determined calm, helping Mother pack as best she could. Plates, sheets, candlesticks, picture frames. Their belongings amounted to much more than Evie thought possible.

Evie was put to bed that night with the ceremony of a sick, much younger child. Mother buckled her polished white leather shoes on her before tucking her in.

"Why do I have to wear these to bed?"

"I want to make sure we don't leave them behind. If you wear them, we won't forget them. Now go to sleep. Tomorrow we'll be in Xela. In a month, we'll be home." Her breath was sweet, mystifying, but when she bowed down, her kiss tasted sour. "Your father processed enough cochineal today to buy our tickets."

"Am I going, too? I'll be good. I can get a job!"

"Of course you're coming, Evie." Mother searched her face with concern and cleaned her cheek with her thumb. "What is going on in that crazy little head of yours?"

In a month, they'd be home. Of course her parents would never leave her. She would not be an orphan. Lying in bed, Evie tried to distract herself, thinking of her letter to Sophie. Where was it by now? She imagined Judas in the government building, handing the letter to an Indian on horseback, who immediately galloped to the nearest station. It would travel by road, then train, by boat, by train again, then another boat, and once more by train. Which would make it to New York faster? Her or the letter?

~~~~~

Points of weak red light filtered through the blanket covering her face. She never cried or screamed or said anything, for the gag filling her mouth. She could not kick. She knew she was being carried down the mountain. Rocks scraped under shoes. Desperate for air, she pressed her nose against the fabric and took deep breaths. Body odor, the smell of rank ocean from the red wool, filled her lungs. She convinced herself this was Father, taking her to Xela, for safety. Ghosts didn't wear shoes, and neither did Indians.

Or maybe he had wrapped her up to sell her. Wrapped her up so she couldn't see where she was going, so she couldn't come back. Like the Indians in the covered wagons, drafted away.

Once set down, she tried to move her arms and legs again, but couldn't. She'd been swaddled. Pressing her nose to the light, she took another deep, nauseating breath.

Who knows how long she lay there, unable to move? It seemed to Evie to last forever. But eventually, hands loosened the fabric and rope. Who would it be? Who would she live with now? Then Evie saw Judas.

"Evie, what happened to you?"

She was in the cemetery, laid next to a vault with painted blue and yellow symbols. She sat up and looked around, seeing the broken stones and crosses and desiccated flowers. Seeing these, she began to cry, the wet rag falling out of her mouth so easily. She was in a cemetery, with dead people, ghosts, all of them situated to face the rising sun. Judas wiped her tears with his nice silk handkerchief.

They walked the dirt road to the city, holding hands, past the plantation workers' shacks. No one paid them any mind. At times like this, Evie felt relief not to have her Father's blue eyes. She could not endure the reactions his eyes caused on this road. Unnoticed now, they passed Indian women punching tortilla dough with tender, practiced violence. They walked through their wood smoke like survivors of a great catastrophe.

"Where are my parents, Judas?"

"I don't know," he said. "Soon."

"Did they leave me? Did they go back to New York without me?"

He led her over the seam in the road where the dirt gave way to cobblestone. Judas's hand felt hot and slick. He wore, Evie noticed, a new pair of shoes. Double-knotted.

"I like your shoes," Evie said, because she did not want him to answer that last question. The two of them, in their best shoes, she thought, must look like a courting couple. It would not be so much of a scandal, she thought, if people believed he was Ladino. Indeed, he did look more Ladino every day to Evie.

"Thank you," he said, turning the sides up, one after the other, to admire the embroidery without interrupting their pace.

"Did Father get those for you?"

"No," Judas said. "I got them myself."

"How did they let you in the store? Did you use the note I gave you? I thought I wrote it for socks, though. Did you get the socks, too?"

He jerked her to a stop, right there in the middle of the road. He pulled her in close to confront his angry mouth. His gray, useless teeth like tombstones. "You ask"—Judas shook her—"too many questions. I'm taking you someplace and you won't ask any questions. You won't say anything. If you stay quiet, you can see your parents." She had never been so close to Judas before. He smelled, to her surprise, intensely familiar. An intimate scent she had not smelled in a while and had almost forgotten. Mother, from a long time ago. She could see ivory powder caked on the sides of his nose, dusting his angry eyebrows.

They passed the imports store, where the orphan boy Tomás was tying Mrs. Fasbinder's cart to a post. Tomás looked very different than when she'd seen him last. He wore the same clothes, but those clothes were ripped and filthy and hung on him like rags. Evie watched him hurry to the side of the cart to offer his head as a newel post as Mrs. Fasbinder lowered herself onto the ground.

Evie neared, and they each stared harder, straining, as if they were moving farther and farther apart, instead of closer. Evie held by Judas, and Tomás wrapped in the reins of the cart. By the time they passed within a breath of each other, they could have been miles away, for their mutual helplessness.

At that moment, Mrs. Fasbinder reappeared and swatted his face. "Who do you think you are, gawking at a white girl like that?"

The office was more finished than it had been just one week ago. Everything now had its proper place. Books upright on shelves, knickknacks consigned to their eternal displays, already collecting dust: an Indian warrior lunging, a helmeted conquistador aiming. The Catholic chalice still held its arsenal of sharpened pencils on the desk. The bird, Magellan, with the red breast, presided in a corner. He opened his beak and held it there—a silent scream or laugh, or a yawn—and shifted his weight from foot to foot in a golden cage lined on the bottom with newspaper. He seemed to be doing better. Two tail feathers, one blue, one green, held a long flirtation through the bars, twisting and crossing for a meter before touching the floor. The bird regarded Evie with one hostile eye, possibly remembering her.

"How old are you, Evie?" Mr. Ubico's accent sounded like his mouth was full of food. Was this really the man who had replaced God, as her father had said? The bird, behind him, nodded enthusiastically, then began shredding his newspaper. Evie had never thought God could look so young, or be so short.

She held up nine fingers. There was no good reason to lie, but it was already done. She sat in the same church pew she and Father had sat in before, while Mr. Ubico regarded her sadly from his red velvet throne. She spread her nightgown to show off the lace, secretly pleased to be wearing it in the daytime, in public.

Judas, with a bowed head, stepped outside. Evie listened to his fancy shoes—*squeak, squawk*—make a crazy noise against the arcade tiles. He had told her not to ask any questions, not to say anything, advice that she trusted. Judas had saved her, after all. They had put her in the cemetery like a dead person, and he had saved her.

"Do you know your address in America, Evie? Could you tell the embassy where someone in your family lives?"

She shook her head, ashamed now that she had lied about her age. A nine-year-old would know her address. Probably an eight-year-old should, too.

"Do you know what happened? Do you know why you're here?" Absently, he reached into his pocket and slid four peppermints across his desk in front of her. Behind him, the bird began aggressively grooming himself, feathers drifting to the floor.

"Our parents," Mr. Ubico began, making his first slip in English, "were murdered by their Indian workers. Your father hired criminals and they robbed and murdered your family. Do you understand this?"

Evie nodded, recognizing that word, murdered, from her conversation with Judas. But Ubico had gotten it backward. Father had murdered a worker, not the other way around. At least, the situation had gotten no worse than the day before. Slightly relieved, she ignored the pile of mints, knowing from before that they were old and stale, and tasted like pennies and pocket dust.

"Did you see anything?"

She shook her head. The only thing Evie had seen was the blanket covering her face, the rough weave of wool and light and straw. She had woken up to fabric being stuffed in her mouth, an Indian blanket wrapped around her head. She couldn't scream or talk, but could open her eyes and see that the color of pure dark was not black but red.

"Did you hear anything?"

Just the footsteps that carried her away. The fabric had been scratchy. Nothing her mother would own.

Someone knocked timidly, and Mr. Ubico stood up. He was short, much shorter than Father. Evie watched him walk to his office door, moving easily, without the gun today. Judas. With his head still lowered, Judas mumbled something in Spanish. Evie sat patiently through their hushed conversation. Judas, no doubt, telling him where her parents had gone, how to send her back, returning everything to normal.

On Mr. Ubico's desk sat a mechanical bank that Evie had been resisting for several minutes. Now she pulled it near. On its small stage, a jaguar and a deer stood frozen in the violence of their next transaction: the deer reared up, antlers cocked forward in the direction of the leaping jaguar. Evie found a peso among the clutter of papers, put it in the jaguar's mouth, and pulled the lever. With this, the jaguar shot forward and the coin hit the deer with a fantastic *ping* and ricocheted across the room.

In his corner, the startled bird jumped down to the floor of his cage and began to turn circles, over and over, drawing his tail feathers up from the floor through the bars.

The exchange didn't last long. Evie heard the door close and again the *squeak, squawk* of Judas's exit, leaving her, Magellan, and Mr. Ubico alone. She had to remind herself not to be afraid of Ubico. He had helped her father recently. And he would help her now. If she heeded Judas's advice, he'd take her to her parents.

"You like my bank?" Mr. Ubico asked with unmistakable pride. He fished in his pocket for a coin, and gave it to Evie. "You can't do it with pesos, only pennies. They have different weights."

Evie took the penny and tried again. This time, the jaguar shot forward and deposited the penny into the hole in the deer's chest. *Crack, ping!* The sound, the exactness, the reliability of the action pleased her.

"Do you . . ." Mr. Ubico asked again, sitting down behind his desk, "do you know what happened, Evie?"

Evie picked up the bank and found the hinge in the jaguar's paw, where the coins could be retrieved. She studied it, amazed. It looked like the deer got the money, but somehow it ran right through its body and the jaguar got it back.

"What do you think happened? You must tell me everything you know."

Evie clicked the heels of her white leather shoes together under the pew. She looked down at the heart-shaped buckles, focused, resisting.

"Do you know? I'll need your help if we're going to catch the murderers."

She allowed herself to nod to Mr. Ubico's question. Yes, she knew why she was here, she knew more about it all than her parents had. She set the same coin in the jaguar's mouth and pulled the lever. *Crack, ping!* The bird shrieked in response. Evie had never heard its voice before. It was terrible, like a train braking. Wheels locking, steam rising, people running.

Squeak, squawk, squeak, squawk, squeak, squawk, squeak, squawk. Another knock. Ubico ignored it. "I need your help, Evie. Can you help me?" More knocking, louder this time, more insistent. Clearly annoyed, Ubico glared at the door, but did not rise to answer it. Instead, he shifted his black eyes to Evie, awaiting her answer.

For the first time, she began to doubt Judas's advice.

1954

T wo best friends sat in a rooftop café popular for its view. From here, two volcanoes, Fuego and Agua, dwarfed the crumbling colonial skyline. Antigua, the old capital, lay on the other side of the range. Two hundred years ago, it had been destroyed in one week when a powerful earthquake triggered an eruption from Fuego. Lava poured through the devastated streets and was quickly followed by another earthquake—an aftershock—that cracked open Agua's dormant crater lake, flooding what remained of the town. After that, the government moved the capital here, to Guatemala City, still outrageously, terrifyingly within sight of both volcanoes. Now Fuego smoked perpetually, while Agua loomed in slumber. Dorie hated the view and tried her best to ignore it, though she put up with it since there were so few decent restaurants in the city. Today, however, the volcanoes kept drawing her gaze. She found herself imagining the fiery lava, then the flood washing down in a mockery of relief.

"So, where should we start?" she asked, shifting her attention to her book. "How about with the theme of deception?"

Marcella nodded, her heart-shaped, honey-colored face sinking as Dorie awaited her response.

"But what of the husband? I wasn't sure how I was supposed to feel about him. Do you think his lies were protective or manipulative? I guess they could be both. I shouldn't assume their mutual exclusivity. Right?"

Dorie stared at her friend and the silence grew uncomfortable. Embarrassed, she began to believe what she had long suspected: the book she'd chosen was insultingly terrible. Educated Marcella could not be bothered with its frivolity.

Finally, Marcella shook her head. "I'm sorry, Dorie. I didn't finish the book."

In ten years of these discussions, neither woman had ever come unprepared. Dorie faltered, tried to salvage a bit of dignity. "How far did you get? Maybe we'll just do a scene study? The dinner scene?" Yes, the dinner scene was almost literary. "Did you get that far?"

"I didn't even start it."

Dorie placed the book facedown on the table. "I'm sorry, it really is a silly book," she confessed. "I can't find any good English books down here."

"That's not it." Marcella waved a jeweled hand in reprieve. "This week's been hard. I had to fire my girl."

"What happened? Did she steal something?" Dorie, unable to bear the thought of some barefoot Indian fingering her things, didn't even have a girl.

"I wish she had stolen something," Marcella said. "No, something much worse."

Dorie suppressed a shudder, could not help thinking that the situation involved Tomás. But no, he was too principled for that. But then again, of course, he wasn't.

"I knew we should have gotten a girl with experience. This one, you know, we plucked right out of the mountains. They're cheaper that way, since they don't know about the Maids' Union. But now we've learned our lesson." She paused, collected herself, and said, "She was going to the bathroom in the bushes."

Dorie's eyes widened, shock and relief.

"I don't think she's used a toilet before, she may not even know what it is. She just cleans it. She waits until we leave and goes in the bushes. A few days ago, I went to cut some flowers and I stepped right in shit. Barefoot. And I lost it. I slapped her." Marcella sucked deeply on her cigarette, extending the ashen tip but not tapping it loose. "Actually, I more than slapped her."

Dorie turned from her friend to the view. She registered the odd illusion of Fuego smoldering on the horizon, while she breathed in curls of cigarette smoke. Marcella did a lot of things now that she would never have done a year before. Beat her maid, show up to lunch already slightly drunk, without having cracked the book. She smoked so carelessly that Dorie often found herself following the lengthening ash at the end of Marcella's cigarettes rather than her words.

"So she went back to the mountains?"

"I don't know. I just threw her out the door in a fit. She's never been out of the house, she barely speaks Spanish. She doesn't even speak Quiché, but one of those obscure Indian languages. She certainly doesn't know how to get to the train station." Marcella stared out over the charmingly disheveled city. "And the worst part is, I didn't even feel too bad about her until just now. But telling you and seeing your face. You'd never have done that. You're so *good*—"

"Nonsense." Dorie cut her off. "I'm awful, too," she heard herself say. She struggled a moment, impaled on her own words. She was, after all, faithless. And compounding that, she had been careless. For this, her situation had become so dire that she hadn't the energy or the moral license to scold Marcella for beating her maid. What's more, she could not even muster surprise. She'd become resigned to how things went in Guatemala, simply out of despair.

"Yes. I guess you are awful, Dorie."

In less than a year, Marcella had gone from being the most fun person Dorie knew, to the most trying. Dorie eyed the rainy season clouds in the distance, hoping her new friend would arrive soon. A possible antidote to Marcella's poisonous, cryptic talk. For the first time since arriving in Guatemala, Dorie had sought a new friend. A new perspective, a fresh dynamic, might be all they needed to have fun again. And at that moment, mercifully, she arrived at the café patio. Dorie and Marcella smiled up at the woman in slacks and a straw coolie hat tied with a crude piece of twine under her chin. Despite her peasantlike attire, she radiated the effortless beauty and confidence of a woman cultivated in parlors and music halls.

Naomi the American nun removed the enormous hat from her head. Her shaded beauty, now exposed to the sun, deteriorated with the revelation of tiny pockmarks infesting her cheeks. With her newfound peripheral vision she looked stiffly about and noticed, for the first time, the fourth person in their group: an Indian, seated slightly behind Dorie so as not to be mistaken for a customer. Startled at the oddity, so suddenly at such close proximity, Naomi could not suppress her surprise.

"Jesus Christ." She yanked the twine loose from her throat. "Who's this?"

"This," Dorie lied, "is my maid, Emelda." In fact, Dorie herself had practically forgotten Emelda, who had been seated in this manner by Marcella. Feeling terrible for not having cared before, Dorie moved her own chair and motioned for Emelda to scoot in. The girl hesitated, then obeyed.

Naomi stared at the silent Indian girl, registered her otherworldly blue eyes, the black braided crown of hair, the bottle of wine, the three wineglasses—two half gone, the Indian's full, heavy, and gold. She came to a decision about it all very quickly.

Yes, she offered a new perspective. But possibly one Dorie could not endure.

"Hello, Emelda," Naomi said to the girl, then turned skeptically on her hosts. "You let her wear her Indian costume? You allow her to drink?"

"Oh yes!" Dorie joked, hoping to lighten Naomi's unexpected gravity. "We've been convinced by the Communists. In fact, she doesn't even work. I'm just paying her a wage as reparations for the suffering of her people over the past few centuries."

Marcella bubbled with laughter. Emelda looked more uncomfortable than ever, seated at the table. Her pale eyes seemed worried, reflecting the coming weather. Dorie had to remind herself that every time she tried to change the dynamics in Guatemala, she just made things worse. She had poured the third glass of wine automatically when they arrived, making Marcella laugh then as well. Naomi now frowned.

"It's fine," Dorie told her, "Emelda doesn't speak English. Don't let her eyes fool you, she doesn't even speak Spanish." She watched this statement have no effect and decided to switch to more traditional social tactics. "The rain's coming," she declared. "We'd better order our lunches."

Dorie had met Naomi in the imports store the week before. Usually wary of nuns—both Dorie and Marcella were technically Catholic—Dorie had invited Naomi to lunch, in gratitude for some advice she'd given and in desperate need of a third to make book club enjoyable again. Naomi embodied everything Dorie wanted to be herself; she was strong, independent, opinionated, and managed to be all of these things without a trace of snobbery. Seeing the book in Dorie's bag, she claimed to have read, and liked, *Burning Hearts* years ago.

But that was last week. So much had changed since then. It became tiring for Dorie, pretending she cared about this lunch, about making new friends, about bad books that fed her basest desires. She had cared last week, when friends and books proved her only escape from this filthy capital. At the time, friendship with Naomi seemed like a refreshing possibility. But now, nothing at this lunch mattered. It was something to get through without cracking, without bursting into maniacal laughter or tears.

Marcella, it seemed, had other concerns, too. Possibly she sensed competition and resented the introduction of a third. She had not uttered a word since Naomi had arrived. Sitting in her patented pose of polite skepticism, she watched the glass of untouched ice water sweating profusely in front of her.

"You certainly have your work cut out with all the problems down here." Dorie tried to jump-start the conversation, fanning herself. Everyone could agree on the sad state of Guatemala. Communists, capitalists, pagans, foreigners—no one here was happy.

"Indeed." Naomi pantomimed exhaustion, though she clearly held vast reserves of energy. "Dorie tells me your husband's in United Fruit?"

Marcella barely nodded.

If it all worked out as Dorie hoped, this may be her last lunch with Marcella. It may be the last time she ever saw her best friend.

"So you're both in politics," Naomi concluded with a smile.

"Unfortunately," Marcella said, her first word since Naomi had arrived. "This new government is making everything political."

"They're making everything political, or finally acknowledging the fact that everything always has been political down here?"

Dorie sat back, pretending to listen as she planned her future, away from all this. Away from the Communists, the Indians, the Church, the suits. In Brazil, things were much more civilized. She imagined scrubbed cobblestone streets, white office buildings, bright colonial churches—what she'd imagined Guatemala to be like before she arrived.

"Always?" Marcella asked with faux sincerity. "How long have you been here?" She did not wait for the obvious answer. "My family has been in Guatemala for over a hundred years and I can assure you that before Jacobo Arbenz took office not everything was political. The natural order ruled."

"Natural order?" Naomi took up her menu.

"In nature, there's a food chain. Someone's always on top and someone's always on the bottom. To try to put that under government control is against nature."

"Nature?" Naomi asked, perplexed, turning the word in her mouth like a bite of fruit gone mealy. "Is that how you want to live? In nature there is no such thing as murder or theft, and there certainly is no such thing as property. Nature, my dear"—with this, Marcella straightened—"doesn't suit your argument. Under the rules of nature, I could grab my knife right now, lunge across this table, cut your heart out, and eat it—all to no consequence."

The statement cut through Dorie's reverie and the women floundered a moment in silence. Naomi had professed this scenario with such sincerity that Dorie wondered if she'd missed a joke.

"According to nature," Naomi pressed, "we should not be having this lovely lunch. *Nature* would have your people and ours"—she motioned to Dorie—"separated by an ocean."

Dorie braced herself for Marcella's response.

"Hispanic, *my dear*, is white. Of Spanish descent. Last I checked, Spain was a part of Europe. Dorie and I are as natural together as sisters."

Yes, Dorie realized at the moment. Naomi was strong, independent, opinionated. Just like Marcella. She should have known this would never work.

With that, the waiter arrived to take their orders. Questions about sides and cooking methods brought them all back to civility. Dorie ordered for herself and Emelda, remembering too late her new rule of letting things be. She could not imagine Emelda managing a knife and fork; the girl could barely sit in a chair. Of course, she'd just embarrassed herself and Emelda further. She tried again to change the subject. "Speaking of property," she said, "have you heard about the latest with the Fruit compensation? It's too comical to believe. Marcella, tell us."

Not much of a subject change, but in Guatemala there was only one subject. They all welcomed the suggestion, abandoning the quarrel about race. Marcella seemed satisfied to have the last word, and surely Naomi sensed a sore spot in Marcella she would wisely, compassionately let alone.

"Oh, what now?" Naomi laughed, making up. Everyone in Guatemala, politics aside, could find amusement in the legal battle between a small, self-righteous foreign government and a powerful American business.

"Tomás is up to his neck in this thing right now, with this whole land redistribution. The Communists took a hundred acres of fallow land from Fruit this month, you know, to give to the Indians or whatever. They're supposed to pay Fruit for it, at least, but get this: the government will only pay them as much as they claimed it was worth on their taxes!"

All three of the women laughed at this, genuinely, the Indian girl joining in hopefully with her own silent chuckle. From there, conversation went smoothly enough until three steaks arrived, already cut up. Naomi had ordered a ham sandwich.

"Shall we discuss *Burning Hearts*?" Naomi asked between bites. "I liked the image of fire. How it consumes the lovers, leaving nothing. Not even hope, not even a memory of happiness."

"No hope?" Dorie asked too hastily, her mouth full. "But I thought the fire was supposed to be redemptive. Destructive, yes, but also redemptive."

"Redemptive?" Naomi flipped through Dorie's copy. "I know it's been a while since I read it, but I certainly don't recall anything like that."

"Don't mind Dorie," Marcella said. "I'm sure you're right. I'm sure everyone burned to a hopeless crisp at the end. She's just in love."

Dorie straightened, panic rising in her chest like a caged bird, flapping.

"With an Indian!" Marcella added, flashing her teeth.

Dorie finished her wine. Marcella always said appalling things to entertain herself. At least, in the past, these pronouncements were both shocking and funny. But these days, she mostly laughed alone. Naomi, perplexed, gave up on the book and focused her attention on her sandwich. She frowned, the corners of her mouth stained yellow with mustard, like a child's. The unpleasant sound of chewing overtook the table, making Dorie self-conscious.

"Oh my, I'm so sorry, we haven't even offered you a glass of wine!" Dorie reached for the bottle.

Naomi raised a cool, stiff hand. "No, *thank you.*"

Marcella took hers up and sipped through her grin. At that moment, Dorie realized that Naomi was not a nun, but a Protestant missionary. And she realized that Marcella had known all along.

Emelda ignored her steak, being too preoccupied with the round, crusty roll on her plate. Holding this roll in her hand, she turned it over and over, studying it.

"If someone wants to marry an Indian, that's none of my business," Marcella said. "That's their choice. But what happens after that?" She pointed directly to Emelda now, the girl's pale eyes flashing like a distress beacon. Dorie refilled her glass, steeling herself. "What happens in three generations when a nice white American missionary comes to Guatemala and falls in love with a dashing Hispanic man?"

"Are we done with *Burning Hearts*? Is this another book?" Naomi asked.

"What happens when they have their first baby and it comes out brown? It happened to a Fruit family six years ago. A successful Fruit man. His baby came out so dark, no one could believe it was theirs. So dark that either they both had Indian blood and didn't know, or she was cheating on him with a laborer. In this country, which is more plausible? And now the States are on the same course. With this Brown decision. Brown! Ha! In a century, the whole world will be brown."

The Indian girl took the first bite of her roll. She kept her blue eyes down.

"Marcella, we know." Dorie tried in vain. Since her life-threatening miscarriage, Marcella had begun to say aloud what they all were thinking. Yes, this may be the last time she ever saw her best friend and, horribly, Dorie was happy for it.

"They fired him, of course, for some small thing a tasteful amount of time after. Ruined the family. It wasn't their fault, they had no idea. We're going to suffer the effects of this revolution for a hundred years, I'm telling you now. Don't worry, it won't affect you, of course," she said to Naomi. "As long as you don't fall in love down here."

"I came to work in the government's literacy program," Naomi clarified, offended.

Quickly finishing her sandwich, Naomi left, claiming to be late for "class." Another government idea, where Indian women made traditional crafts to sell to tourists. She thanked Dorie and Marcella for the lovely lunch. "You really should come to Sunday service sometime. It's a shame you don't have a church down here. Are you saved?" Naomi looked at Dorie when she asked this.

"Saved from what?" Marcella asked.

"My church isn't far from the embassy. You really should stop by, just to say hi. And even if you've never considered it before, well"—and here she patted Dorie's hand in a baffling display of sympathy—"we all need a new start at least once in life."

Naomi then pulled her hat back on her head and left, weaving around the empty tables in her pointed coolie hat, to the patio exit and down the street, like a child's top let loose upon the city.

Emelda actually was a maid, though she was not Dorie's maid. The girl had practically been thrust upon Dorie minutes before she left for lunch, by Jim, her husband. How funny, for all his responsibilities in Guatemala, all the important work he did, the American ambassador also happily served as a maid service for United Fruit. It happened often enough, Dorie knew. A Fruit man, out on assignment in the highlands, would come across some young barefoot Indian girl one-third his age and decide to hire her as his "maid" back in the States. Jim, of course, was vital in securing these girls an uncomplicated passage. Before Arbenz, McCarthy, and the Communist takeover of Guatemala, it had been much easier to get papers. Now, Jim said, it was almost impossible. He had never before involved Dorie. It seemed this Emelda would be going to the United States illegally and Jim enlisted Dorie to take her out, buy her clothes, and try to make her look like less of an Indian.

"Definitely play up her eyes, they're her best bet at passing."

"What is this, *Pygmalion?*"

"Please, Dorie. This is important," he had said. "You've no idea how important."

"You're right, I've no idea how important. Why don't you tell me, Jim?"

In response, he had handed her money for shopping.

Dorie agreed because she preferred to agree with him rather than endure his cool and total displeasure. She had two choices in this marriage: to be his cherished child or his enemy. He rarely deemed anything "important" to her, though when he did, she was often surprised by it. Illegal maids, newspaper stories, some minor Honduran official.

"This is just your sort of thing," Jim had said, bafflingly. Dorie hated the city, the whitewashed half-rot, the Indians squatting shamelessly in the streets. She hated the pathetic imitations of American goods in the shops, the crippled beggars and half-dead dogs trailing her with hopeful eyes. Marcella was the shopper, moving about the city, walking around rain-swollen trash, and declaring the children picking through it "adorable."

"I'm not canceling lunch. I'm almost late already, Jim."

"That's fine. Just take her along."

"Can Marcella help?"

"Of course," Jim said, "but I will trust you two to be absolutely discreet."

"Yes, of course, bringing a barefoot Indian girl into the nicest restaurant in the city for a book discussion, I'm sure, will go completely unnoticed."

"Just tell people she's your maid," he said, kissing her lightly on the white line where her golden hair parted down the middle. "It's natural enough."

Dorie now wondered who the lucky Fruit man was. Marcella had a guess—one of the big suits from Boston who'd been sent in to handle the messier land disputes. Tomás had been helping him in the highlands all week.

"Why else would they go to so much trouble? He has to be high up."

They both stared across their uncleared lunches at the girl, who had not touched her wine or her steak. Eating her fourth roll, she pitched forward in the café chair, smiling and chewing and not caring about the mess she made with the crumbs. Sitting exactly how Dorie would be sitting at the moment, if she had the freedom to. No one paid attention to Indians, they had no audience, but the whole world, it seemed, was watching Dorie, and she had to be careful.

The first thing to get, Dorie and Marcella agreed, was shoes. Of course, the shoe store they chose was not one where either of them would shop, but it struck Dorie as completely adequate for a first pair of high heels.

"I'm sorry." A harried Hispanic clerk emerged from a fortress of shoe boxes. "I'm sorry," he said again. He pointed to the standardized sign hanging in all the shops, of a bare foot smote by a red *X*. Since the passing of the discrimination laws, the NO INDIANS signs in all the shops had been replaced by this one, to the same effect. The man continued, in Spanish, to explain, while pointing repeatedly at Emelda's bare feet.

Every time he pointed, the girl's face darkened into an angry bruise. She pressed her stare, like two ice cubes, on the clerk and said, in English, "We understand the sign, señor, but how do you expect someone like me, who has lost her shoes, to be able to replace them if she can't go into a shoe store? You, obviously, have no business sense at all."

No one said anything for a moment—an Indian who speaks English?

"Christ," Marcella whispered to Dorie. "For a maid and a shoe clerk, these two are both quite uppity."

"She speaks English? She understood our lunch conversation?" Dorie blanched, recalling her joke about reparations and Communists. What else had she said? Beyond simple embarrassment, she feared she may have made fun of Jim during lunch. She sometimes did.

"She should be your maid," Marcella said, obviously unconcerned about this revelation. "Can't ever find a girl who speaks English that well."

What, Dorie wondered, would she do if she had a maid? What would she do if no laundry, cooking, or dishes awaited her? She'd just sit around all day waiting for *him* to call. She suspected she'd start drinking as much as Marcella, inventing betrayals, and slapping the girl because there was nothing else to do. Anyway, she could not help but see a maid as a spy, reporting to Jim. Though she knew Jim would never believe an Indian, and surely not over her. She had to stop being so paranoid.

Emelda and the clerk continued to argue, in Spanish now, since the clerk didn't understand English beyond the phrase "I'm sorry." Outside, a few heavy raindrops knocked on the windows.

"Take off your shoes," Marcella told Dorie.

"Why?" Dorie asked, kicking them off.

Marcella interrupted the argument, handing over Dorie's pumps. "Here, Emelda, put these on. Now." She turned to the stunned clerk and delivered the line that could bring any argument to an end. "If you want to send the wife of the American ambassador into the rain for not having shoes, you can do your best."

No response. But when she repeated herself in Spanish, the clerk relented. Emelda took Dorie's shoes, ran her hands over them, then inside the damp, sour interiors, before wedging them on her own feet. After taking two steps, her ankle twisted to the side. She fell down, laughed, and immediately got up again.

"How old do you think she is?" Dorie asked. Emelda, in a new pair of heels that fit her wide feet more properly, walked circles around the store, just barely holding herself together.

Marcella shrugged. "Fifteen? Why don't you ask her?"

But Dorie did not ask because she suspected she might be even younger. This whole venture made her uneasy, Jim asking her to whore up this child for some old banana baron. She imagined two desiccated, liver-spotted hands groping at the girl. It was hard, sometimes, not to see Jim in this way. Dorie had been young, impressed with his wealth and power. He was twenty-three years older than her.

Completing her second circle, Emelda began to admire herself in the tilted three-way mirror. She stepped into its alcove and saw herself projected back and forth between the two sides.

"Where should we go next?" Marcella asked. "What kind of clothes?"

"I guess it depends on where she's going. Emelda," she called. "Do you know where you're going in the U.S.?"

Emelda shook her head fearfully.

"We know," Dorie coached, "that you're going where you're not supposed to. If you don't have the right clothes, you'll stick out."

Panic tugged the girl's face into many expressions at once. What would Jim have said to make her so afraid? Probably that she would go to jail if she told anyone about her new life. Just threaten the girl, Dorie thought, until she does what you want, just rolls onto her back and accepts the elderly American banana baron, telling herself all along how lucky she is.

"You can trust us," Dorie said.

"Miami," Emelda practically shouted, with her eyes squeezed shut. "Please don't tell anyone I told you."

"Okay, well, you could have just said Florida, but fine." She paused. "I guess she'll need some skirts and blouses, some light dresses. Maybe we'll find some good, cheap perfume."

Emelda, less fearful now, turned around and around in front of the mirrors.

"She's just going to be a maid," Marcella said in a low voice. "It's not like she'll be going to clubs and galas. Who knows if she'll ever even leave the man's house?"

As depressing as it was, Dorie agreed. Was this what it was like to have a child? she wondered. A daughter? Dressing a girl as a cheaper version of herself? She instinctively raised her hand to touch her stomach, but caught herself.

"Should we cut her hair?" Marcella asked. "With those eyes and short hair, she'd look Greek, maybe."

They watched Emelda turning, faster and faster, her body amplified in the mirrors that reflected each other infinitely in a long line. Her hair, half up in its black, braided crown and half down, spilled to her waist. It flared as she spun, like a skirt, catching the sallow light of the store beautifully.

"I'm not doing a thing to that hair," Dorie said. "It's gorgeous. The man can't want it gone. I can't imagine him wanting it gone. The eyes are enough. I've never seen an Indian with eyes *that* blue. Have you?" It was a phenomenon rare enough to take her aback when she saw it, though in retrospect she knew she should not be surprised, considering Guatemala's history.

"No. I've seen gray, hazel, dark blue, but nothing like this. I asked her where she got them, and she said from her grandmother. I'm guessing she really got them from a German coffee planter."

Emelda was still spinning, verging on reckless, before she stopped abruptly and regarded hundreds of herself reflected in the two opposing mirrors. She stood straight in her garish Indian costume, like a line of soldiers at attention. And just when Dorie expected the girl to break into giggles and collapse onto the floor, Emelda became very serious. She clicked her heels together and saluted herself.

The Indians were marching through the rain. Drums, shouting, and fireworks. Dorie made it home just in time to see a mass of them clogging the street not far from the embassy. Cars braked and U-turned, rushing away with rain hissing beneath their tires. Dorie hurried inside the gate and Conroy locked it behind her.

The door to the apartment above the embassy was unlocked when Dorie tried her key. A year ago, she would have run downstairs for one of the guards, but now her heart leapt with danger and joy at the discovery.

He was waiting, just standing in the middle of the unswept room, doing nothing but jiggling some change in his pocket. Letting her purse drop near the door, she said the only thing to come to mind. What she had wanted to say all during lunch, what she wanted to say always now.

"Tomás."

But saying this, seeing him again, did not have the same effect as when she said his name to others, when she was anywhere else just wanting to be with him. She felt peeved suddenly at his audacity, but tried to calm herself. If she allowed herself this initial frustration, the whole visit would be spoiled.

"I've got a meeting with Jim in a half hour," Tomás said. "He was able to squeeze me in between Guatemala Radio and some electronics salesman."

"Is he starting his own radio station?" Dorie laughed, trying to banish her mood.

"Freedom of the press," he joked, hooking a finger into her belt. "The Communists want it, they'll get it."

He tried to pull her in, but the belt was slightly elastic. She spun away playfully, thinking she could still escape the quarrel, the revelation—she had yet to decide which it would be. The apartment was an embarrassing mess. She was wet from the rain, spotted, disheveled, and depressed from the business with the Indian girl.

"How was Xela?" She called the town by its Indian name, a sign of intimacy. Jim, all the suits, called it by its Spanish name, Quetzaltenango. But she knew Tomás preferred Xela. Sometimes he slipped in front of colleagues and was embarrassed by it.

He did not answer, but brought a wooden dagger from his inside suit pocket. A crude blade, but with a magnificent handle, decorated with bright blue and green feathers.

"It's for your hair," he said. "But I know you'd never wear it in your hair, so instead it's a bookmark." He pointed to a book on the table, *The Role of the West*. He often brought her English-language books he found, and these comprised her entire, cherished library in Guatemala. He opened it, replaced her bookmark with the feathers, and closed it again.

"It's beautiful," she said, raising a hand to the feathers, but stopping just shy.

"They're quetzal feathers."

"Quetzal, like the money?"

"Yes. Our currency's named after them, as is Quetzaltenango, but before the money and before the Spanish, there was the bird. They're very rare. Do you know why?"

She shook her head.

"Because they're strictly wild. Quetzals can't be held in captivity. If they're put in a cage, they kill themselves. They're the Indian symbol for freedom."

"Well, they're wasted on me, trapped up here in this apartment. Maybe you should give it to Marcella."

"Not a waste, an inspiration," he said, kissing her neck tenderly in forgiveness. "You just need to get out more."

She tried, discreetly, to close the dresser drawers, to clean up before whatever was going to happen, happened. The disarray would wash around them if they quarreled, like wreckage, like an omen.

"I was out today, and it was horrible. Just trash and beggars. They're marching now, did you see? I can't even tell whether they're celebrating or protesting or striking. It's all the same, shouting and explosions. How do they expect to be taken seriously with these bucket drums and fireworks? It's savage, terrifying. What happened to writing opinion pieces in the newspaper?"

"It's a celebration. Fruit lost a big land case today."

"They wanted the Spanish out, and they got it. But then they missed all the money, so they courted American businesses. Now they want to run Fruit out, not realizing they won't have an economy without them. They only appreciate the money after they expel it."

"History repeats itself, but revolutions always think they're different."

"Then they wanted democracy and they got it. Can't blame them for that. But things aren't happening fast enough. They think they can intimidate their representatives with these ridiculous displays. We want this, we want that. Thinking they deserve things we don't even have in the States. Racial discrimination laws, maternity benefits. Who do they think they are? More fires and drums. That's not democracy, it's rule by mob."

"Well, you have a wall here around the embassy. They can't get to you here, at least." He clawed at her, teasing.

"That's my point, Tomás! I feel like Jim's pet. I can't go out, and when I do, I just want to come home. And when I'm home, I just want out. Just like this cat my mother had, always pacing at the door to be let out, then you let her out and she just paced in front of the door wanting to come in. We never had to worry about her because we always knew where she'd be. On one side of the door or the other."

"Come now, Jim hasn't abandoned you. And I certainly have not. You seem to forget that you have friends."

"Don't you feel guilty, Tomás, seeing me right before seeing Jim?" Even as she squandered this visit on politics and remorse—and hated herself for it—she pressed on. "Poor Jim," she said, not quite meaning it.

"Jim will be fine. Trust me."

"So I get to carry all the guilt?" She said this, although she didn't feel guilty. Jim had dragged her to a dirty, impoverished nation and thrown himself so wholly into its demented history that she rarely saw him, though he worked two stories below the apartment. He had chosen a disease-ridden Communist country over her, which was not nearly as insulting as her choosing Tomás over him.

"I don't have the luxury to feel guilt, Dorie. You're everything to me, you're the only future I have." He kneaded her shoulders, pushing her dress straps down. "How do you want to spend these few minutes we have together?"

Tomás Raúl Mancha Egardo differed in every way from the other Hispanic Fruit men. He had come the furthest of anyone, having been raised poor in the highlands. He did not talk about his childhood, beyond the fact that he had worked on a coffee plantation as a young boy and arrived at his current station in life by his own hard work. He was handsome in the usual, exotic Hispanic way, but for his nose—mangled and squashed, broken twice by plantation overseers. Tomás was utterly dignified, above fights, Dorie suspected, even as a young boy. She imagined him taking these beatings standing straight up, with his hands at his sides in small fists.

He undressed her in the same, but reverse way she and Marcella had dressed the Indian girl at the shops. Unzipping the dress, untying her girdle, unclipping her garters, then peeling off her stockings, carefully, like skin.

"Why all this?" Emelda had asked.

"Because men like to delay gratification," Marcella had replied.

For Tomás, however, the act did not seem to rely on any gratification, let alone delayed gratification. Making love to a Guatemalan was not at all how Dorie imagined it would be. She had dreamed of this coupling for years before it actually happened. But during sex, he remained silent and passionless, except for the last moment, when he gave a small cry, betraying his reluctant pleasure. His religion, Dorie knew, was enough to spoil the pleasure for him, but not enough to keep him away. Dorie had been raised Catholic, although if she had to describe herself with a hundred adjectives now, Catholic wouldn't be one of them. With Tomás, it would be first. She had yet to figure out how he justified all this to himself.

After months of his reticence, however, she wanted more. She wanted to turn herself inside out for more. She wanted him to hold her wrists down, to dominate her, but he resisted all her attempts with a pious frown. This frustrated passion, Dorie very well knew, caused her to provoke fights and delight in embarrassingly bad books, like *Burning Hearts*. Books she would have scoffed at normally.

"If Washington replaced Jim tomorrow," she said as they lay naked on the damp bed, after, "if he was called back to the States, would you let me go?"

"I wouldn't prevent you from doing what you want. I wouldn't force anything on you, Dorie." He slipped back into his undershirt and lay back down.

"I mean, if I didn't want to go and Jim made me go, would you let me go?"

"You hate living in Guatemala. All you've ever wanted, from the moment you landed here, was to be back in Boston."

"I would stay here for you," she said, knowing she could never go back to the States now. She didn't have a choice anymore. It would have to be Brazil. "Would you confront Jim if he tried to take me away?"

"I don't understand what you're talking about," he said, with more of an accent than he usually had. "You want to know what I'd do if they fired Jim—which they won't—and if you wanted to stay here, which you'd never want—"

"Forget it." Dorie had to remind herself that she preferred Tomás's seriousness to Jim's lightness. A lightness he only used to deflect real conversation. Outside, more fireworks exploded. A chant rose above the embassy walls.

"I don't like manipulative questions," Tomás said finally, cuddling up. "Why don't you just tell me what you did today, rather than ask all these silly hypotheticals?"

"Fine, then. I had lunch with a Communist."

"Oh," Tomás said, making the slightest effort to sit up.

"Yes, and she threatened to rip Marcella's heart out and eat it right there for lunch. A Protestant missionary."

"Did you tell her it would make a meager meal, that heart of Marcella's?"

They both laughed. It was a triumph, this joke. He was extracting himself from her, finally. Maybe the cruel business with their maid had done it. A young girl, barely a teenager, disappeared into the city without even the language to ask for help.

"Did she let her have it, that missionary?"

"Of course, though there was no joy in it. She used to at least enjoy a good takedown . . ." She trailed off. Tomás had made clear to her, long ago, that Marcella was off-limits. She didn't want to push her luck. Why did she keep bringing her up?

"I'm almost through *The Role of the West*," she told him. "Do you remember the chapter 'Women and New Democracies'? Two hundred pages on the noble cause of freedom, then, out of nowhere, he decides half the world's population doesn't qualify!"

"A pragmatic approach," Tomás added. "For an imperfect world."

"Of course. These impoverished countries should have their religious roots cut, their natural resources, traditional economies, and ancient cities gutted, but to offend their notions of female inferiority is just too much!" She pounded the mattress, and Tomás intercepted her fist, kissed it.

"You sound like a Communist." He laughed.

"The Communists shouldn't have a monopoly on women's suffrage down here. That is a failing of the right, if someone like me sounds like a Communist."

The march had moved on down the street. Tomás glanced at his watch, sat up.

"What are you meeting with Jim about? You know I can't ask him. Are you still trying to get more money for that expropriated land?"

"The taxes are done. Land in dispute is where we have the most pull," he said as he went reaching for his pants. "The courts can be convinced fallow land is vital to the banana business. If a blight hits, all our plantations could be destroyed in two weeks. The whole economy destroyed in two weeks. Fallow land's the only insurance Guatemala has."

"Is there much fallow Fruit land in the highlands? It's too cold up there for bananas, isn't it?"

"The point is law and order. Ownership is the basis for laws."

"It is?"

"You should finish the book. Don't hold that silly chapter against it. Without ownership, there's no responsibility, without responsibility, there's chaos and bloodshed. There's a piece of Fruit land under dispute now that has a history going back to the Spanish. Take a look at the titles and whenever it changed hands, people were killed. Conquest, slavery, outright murder."

"Murder?" She placed a finger on a small wet spot she'd just noticed on the sheets. She'd have to wash them now. No, she wouldn't.

"In 1902, an entire family was murdered there. They owned the land, worked it. Then one morning, they disappeared. Two parents and a little girl, just gone." He pulled on his socks, one by one.

"That's horrible." Dorie felt herself being pulled somewhere she didn't want to go, off track, forgetting what was important for this meeting.

"Yes, and I knew them. At least, the little girl I knew."

"Really?"

"I barely remember her, but I clearly remember the aftermath. Confusion, fear."

"I can imagine."

"And her shoes. What I remember most about her was this pair of white shoes she wore, with heart-shaped buckles. I'd never seen anything like them before. When I heard she'd been killed, I wondered what happened to those shoes, because I wanted them for myself."

"Children are so funny. All that horror, and you only wanted a pair of girls' shoes. Who killed them?"

"Well, the government's trying to find that out, since it would affect the status of the Indians' brief title to the land afterward. Never mind the case was resolved right away. A bunch of the family's Indian workers confessed and were executed. Twelve men in all, including the overseer. But, of course, now the Communists say any verdict back then was racist. That maybe the confessed killers weren't given a fair trial. And if that wasn't enough, some-one just came forward this week claiming to be an heir to that land."

"Who?"

Tomás moved in, clearing hair from her face with a careful, masterly hand. "That's not a very pleasant story for such a beautiful young lady," he said in an excellent imitation of Jim. "Do you really want to hear it?"

What, Dorie wondered, could possibly be more unpleasant than an entire family murdered? But she didn't want to know. She had to stay on course. If she didn't tell him now, she might have to wait days for another opportunity.

"Corporate ownership can't stop the land grab," he continued, "but a bunch of Indians and their petty disputes over a few acres and a chicken brings it all screeching to a halt. The government wants it all to be very fair, you see. Like they're governing a kindergarten class." He smiled, showing small, crooked teeth. Almost translucent, without enamel, the only obvious clue to his past.

"Do you ever carry a gun?" she asked, when she really wanted to ask if he feared Jim. She suspected he didn't.

"You don't need a gun to rule a kindergarten class," he said, pulling up his pants.

She was losing him. His shadow touched the door and she did not know when she'd have him here like this again.

"I'm pregnant," she said as he slid into his black coat.

Tomás met Dorie's tearful, wobbly face with the ecstatic composure of a businessman who'd just pulled off a merger. Amazingly, nothing threatened his peace of mind. Not even Marcella's miscarriage nearly two years before. He existed in a world of ambition and success absolutely no one could touch. He knew, without even having to ask, that the child was his.

~~~~~

Dorie had met Marcella a decade ago at a World Affairs lecture at Ford's Theatre in Boston. Marcella had been there for a class requirement, while

Dorie went for the course of self-education she'd laid out for herself. Her father had refused to pay for her college, thinking it a waste of money to educate a beautiful girl, beautiful enough to snag a rich man. When Dorie complained that she wanted to make her own money, he enrolled her in a typing class, which she loathed. According to him, boys went to college and girls took typing classes, if they were so inclined for a career. Maybe, he hoped aloud to her, she would meet this rich man while typing for him.

So, to defy him, to try to educate herself, she attended the free World Affairs lectures. She hated to admit, but it bothered her that the war in Europe dominated every lecture of the series. Not confident enough to be critical, however, and fearful that this was exactly what a woman would be expected to conclude, she feigned interest and took notes at every one. During a Q&A following the last, especially depressing lecture ("Is Peace Possible?"), Dorie was floored when a bold, dark, and beautiful girl of her own age raised her hand and commented to the aged, supposedly brilliant professor onstage, "After ten weeks of these World Affairs talks, you'd think the entire Southern Hemisphere didn't even exist."

Radicals usually frightened Dorie, although Marcella's proper looks, her calm composure, made her almost approachable. Almost, for it was Marcella who sought her out in the lobby afterward.

"You're not in my class," she observed with a squint. "Who are you?"

Dorie introduced herself, shrinking a little with this scrutiny.

"Are you with another class?" Marcella asked, looking around.

"No."

"Just you?" Marcella seemed surprised. "Well, that's refreshing. I never see any girls at these things, at least not any who come willingly." She paused. "Though these talks are all distraction. There was a revolution in Guatemala a few weeks ago, did you even know?"

"No," Dorie admitted, embarrassed. Her political knowledge extended no further than what she'd learned from the World Affairs lectures, which were now over. In that moment, she envisioned spending the rest of her afternoon in her typing class. If she did not leave now, she would be late. "No, I had no idea Guatemala just had a revolution. Tell me about it."

They went for coffee. After one cup, Dorie had concluded Marcella was not a radical, just devoted to her home country, and was frustrated that its problems were being ignored for Hitler.

"But the thing is, Hitler's so clearly evil. We should defeat him, yes, but there are much subtler things going on in Guatemala. For that, it will go unchecked. And *that* will be the big threat a decade from now. Bigger than Hitler, because it's so much harder to see the evil in it. They're calling it a democracy, they're making speeches all about rights and equality, but really they're Communists who want us all equally poor and miserable. They're already talking about land redistribution. By the time the U.S. realizes the Guatemalan revolution is a problem, it'll be too late."

Marcella was exactly the type of girl Dorie wanted to be. Educated, effortlessly beautiful, and fierce, with a man who appreciated her for all these things. Her new husband, Tomás, paid for her classes at Radcliffe.

A few weeks into the friendship, Dorie began to borrow Marcella's textbooks. She'd asked Marcella for her final paper on English Romanticism and had put her typing skills to good use, transcribing it exactly, hoping to internalize its lessons through the process. The more Marcella shared, the more Dorie learned, the more grateful and enamored she became. Dorie's typing pool friends—suddenly dull in comparison to Marcella—fell away. They did not discuss revolutions, but hairstyles and keystroke efficiency. She stopped showing up for classes.

By the holidays, they were best friends. Marcella invited Dorie to the United Fruit Christmas party, for a double date. Fruit had rented the Majestic Theatre for a tropical-themed celebration during a blizzard that dropped a foot of snow on the city. On the taxi ride to the theater, Marcella gave her the brief history of Tomás and Jim, supposedly the most handsome man at Fruit.

"If he's so handsome and wonderful, why is he single?" Dorie asked.

"He's always been too busy for dates. But his mother's begun to hound him about having children. Now I have to find dates for him! He needs someone who'd fit in as a fourth. Tomás and Jim are terribly close. And Jim's been lonely since Tomás and I got married. He's never needed a girl until now! But you're perfect. You're as beautiful as I am." She squeezed Dorie's arm. "If you were less, it just wouldn't work."

Dorie found this pronouncement strange, as the two looked nothing alike. Hispanic, unmistakable Marcella, with her bottomless black gaze, made a stark contrast to Dorie's ethereal features. With golden hair and green eyes, she often felt transparent next to her new friend. It was a refreshing reversal, anyway, of the jealous dynamic with Dorie's previous, homelier girlfriends. She always felt uncomfortable with her good looks. Not only did she have to endure unwanted attention, but she had also come to resent it for her father's refusal to send a pretty girl to school. Marcella, however, enjoyed admiration, especially Dorie's. And she could make beauty work for them both, procuring sold-out tickets, hailing taxis in record time, even in a snowstorm.

The men were, Marcella admitted, an odd pairing for best friends. Jim had grown up wealthy in Boston—his father worked for Fruit—and as soon as he earned his degree, he secured a job there, too. Tomás, on the other hand, had been a migrant worker in a rural Guatemalan province. A Jesuit priest had taken an interest in his education, taught him English, Latin, and other subjects. Eventually, the priest secured his acceptance to Weston.

"So Tomás is a priest? You're married to a Jesuit priest?"

"No, well, technically, he could have been one, but he never was. They could only afford to pay for a year at Weston, but they put their faith in God."

"Indeed."

"After Tomás's first year, he applied for a job with Fruit as a translator. He hoped to work a year, then have enough money for his second year at Weston. Of course, Fruit only hoped for someone who spoke Spanish, so the fact that he also spoke Quiché and such good English made him a shoo-in. They appointed him to assist Jim's father, who spent months at a time in Guatemala, on labor issues. This was in the thirties, when President Ubico decreed all Indians had to work the plantations a hundred and fifty days a year to pay their taxes. So, suddenly Fruit has more workers than ever, but no way to control them. They were always escaping. You wouldn't believe how much Fruit spent on fencing and police bribes and guards. So he's pulling his hair out over these expenses, and Tomás finally speaks up. He'd been afraid to for months, but he tells Jim's father that he doesn't need fences. All he had to do is hang dead animals in the trees all around the boundary, and make certain shapes with rocks, and the Indians would be too scared to cross."

"Did it work?"

"Of course it worked! In a day, their biggest problem was no longer a problem. And the solution cost no money at all. Jim's father was so pleased that he tried to hire Tomás right away, but Tomás wanted to finish school. So Jim's father offered to pay for the rest of Weston, as long as he came back to Fruit within ten years."

"How long did it take for him to go back?"

"He started as soon as he graduated. By then he'd spent a few summers as Jim's translator. When Fruit sent him to Guatemala for the first time, his father trusted only Tomás to take care of him. Since then, they've been in-separable. Tomás helped Jim in Guatemala and Jim helped Tomás navigate

Boston. They have all these stories of saving each other from malaria and runaway streetcars. I believe about half of them."

"Whose half?"

"That's wicked," Marcella said with a laugh, eyes flashing. "Beauty, brains, and brass. I do like you, Dorie. I'll admit, I'm afraid if Jim chose a girl for himself, I'd die of boredom."

Magnificent and crumbling, the Majestic opened into a mirrored lobby and a corroded marble staircase that led up to murals of heaven and sky. Inside, the heat was up to a steamy eighty-five degrees. A Negro woman dressed in some bright, bizarre outfit (an Indian costume, Dorie later learned) took their coats. Marcella, in a pink satin sheath, laughed when she saw that Dorie had worn a gray wool dress.

"Oh, I forgot to warn you this is the tropics, Dorie!"

Inside the theater itself, Fruit had forested the floor with stunted banana trees in huge glazed pots. They followed a winding path, toward the sound of fast-paced music and the colorful glow of theater lighting that showed between the leaves overhead.

"Did I tell you not to make any jokes? And don't take the Lord's name in vain. Jim doesn't care, but Tomás is very sensitive to that."

The path spilled them out into the party space. Hundreds of summery gowns and white linen suits sipped drinks and began to test the borders of the gleaming dance floor, so polished it looked wet. A giant papier-mâché volcano steamed onstage, amplifying the humidity. The scene was absolutely bizarre, and Dorie remembered thinking that these United Fruit people were savages, with their sweat, their impossibly bright drinks, and oyster forks. How did she end up here, a merchant's daughter enrolled in typing classes? Already she felt uncomfortable, feeling herself perspiring through the lining of her dress, to the wool. The theater held more men than she'd seen in the city in years. Somehow she had stepped into a world where there wasn't a war going on.

Marcella led her to a table where Tomás and Jim sat talking, Jim looking twenty years older than she had expected. Middle-aged! No wonder his mother worried about having grandchildren. At least, Dorie consoled herself, they were good-looking. Jim especially.

Then she noticed the performance onstage, in front of the volcano. A line of near-naked women danced with huge prop bananas. They scissored and turned in perfect unison, hoisting the bananas above their heads, then passing them through their legs.

Both men stood as the women approached, but Dorie found herself blushing for the act onstage. Tomás, short enough to catch her lowered eyes, seized them with his own and brought her gaze up. Age had softened his eyes into an expression of weary compassion. Like a priest. Dorie saw gold flecks sinking, settled at the bottom of his drink.

"This is Dolores."

Dorie felt disheveled from the hot walk through the banana forest. "Hello," she managed, though Dolores was not her real name. It was Pandora. Despite her family's respectable position now, the name broadcast their humble origins like a beacon. What halfway-educated woman would name a girl such a thing? Her mother had no idea about mythology. She had seen the name on a box of tobacco while pregnant. Of course, Dorie had never corrected Marcella's assumption that her name was Dolores.

"She's a friend of mine from Radcliffe," Marcella added, to Dorie's alarm. Another lie, this one purposeful. Now she'd have to be careful to uphold them both without embarrassing herself.

Like some kind of comedy troupe, the men offered her a coordinated greeting—Jim the elaborate one, Tomás the straight man. The type of friends, she realized, who are constantly in on some joke together, feeling no need to inform anyone else of the particulars.

She felt better after standing in the snowy back exit for a moment and having a shot at the bar, then another. She had asked for the drink with gold flakes, not knowing its name. Her mouth burned, then turned sweet with what the barman offered her. When she returned to the table, the party had progressed during her absence, with couples now dancing. Dorie followed Jim, who stepped onto the gleaming wood and held a hand out to assist her, as if she ran the hazard of getting wet.

> *Standing by the fruit stall on the corner*
> *Once I heard a customer complain*
> *You never seem to show the fruit we all love so*
> *That's why business hasn't been the same*
>
> *I don't like your peaches*
> *They are full of stones*
> *But I like bananas*
> *Because they have no bones*

Jim danced marvelously, passionately. Their success required no effort on her part. He let her body fly, but could bring her back in with the slightest movement of his wrist. She'd never danced like this before, had never felt a man sweating so closely, or moving so confidently, powerfully. All the dancing she'd ever done had been wary and stilted, with boys.

> *No matter where I go*
> *With Susie, May or Anna*
> *I want the world to know*
> *I must have my banana*

Rather than spinning through the party, it seemed that the party was spinning around her. She was drunk for the first time in her life, and as the song built more and more harmonies around them, Jim and Tomás flung Marcella and Dorie back and forth between them with ease. The women, drunker than them, passed each other in bright, laughing blurs, sometimes touching hands.

> *I can't bear tax collectors*
> *Especially one who phones*
> *Ah but I like bananas*
> *Because they have no bones*

When the band stopped on an unexpected beat, Dorie found herself paired with Tomás. She stood staring at his breathing chest, while the crowd clapped for the invisible band. Sweat traced down the middle of her back. She felt embarrassed at Tomás's hands still on her waist. She felt embarrassed to find a priest so sexy, sexier than her initial impression. But when she looked up to catch his eye, his meaning, he was staring over her shoulder, at the paper volcano. He had forgotten her completely, even as she panted in his arms.

"This," he said to himself, "is not good. It's never good when a volcano stops smoking." He looked down at her, but without a glint of interest or flirtation. "So, we've finally found a girl just as beautiful as Marcella." He lifted her chin with his finger. "Wait. No, I can't believe it. This—" And she felt his finger touch the mole on her chin, below the corner of her uneasy smile. "Don't tell Marcella, but this"—he tapped again—"sets you a millimeter ahead of her." He glanced again at the breathless volcano. "I give this double date an hour until it blows sky-high."

———

They talked, danced, and drank for the rest of the night, in alternating, cozy pairs. Dorie met a number of Marcella's girlfriends, all Americans. Surprisingly, Marcella did not interact with any of the Hispanic women at the party. All these girlfriends claimed either Fruit or Radcliffe connections, or both. Many seemingly smart, single, and beautiful enough to have made a fourth for Jim. Why had Marcella chosen her?

Well into the night, Dorie found herself sitting in a corner with Tomás, while Jim and Marcella enjoyed some unheard conversation—probably about her—at a nearby table. Still reeling from drink, Dorie tried to recall the maneuvers that led to their pairing.

"What are you studying at Radcliffe, Dolores?"

Panic must have seized her face, not only for the terrible urge to lie, but also for the prospect of lying to a priest.

Seeing her distress, seeing everything in that moment, Tomás revised his question. "What would you *like* to study at Radcliffe?"

She smiled in relief. "I'm not sure. I don't even know all the subjects there are to study," she admitted with drunk gratitude. She wanted to explain the frustrating sense of a world of happiness all around that she could not even daydream about, let alone name. Just a week ago, she had picked up in casual conversation with Marcella that people could study parties like this. Sociology, it was called.

"Knowing that you don't know is the first step to wisdom," he said with a nod.

"What was your favorite subject in school?" She wondered if this was a dumb question. Did they study more than one subject at Weston? Or, more likely, he believed God to encompass all subjects. She prepared herself for some strange Jesuit answer.

"Hope," he answered simply, with a dazzling, very unpriestly smile that sent his nose at a funny angle.

"C'mon, Dorie. Let's go to the ladies'." Marcella pulled her out of her chair.

In the restroom mirror, Marcella retraced her mouth with a pencil, while Dorie watched. When their eyes met in the glass, Marcella spun away, reaching for her zipper.

"Hey, I have an idea! Let's switch dresses!"

"What?"

"You wear this." Marcella had already wiggled out of one shoulder strap of her dress. "And I'll wear yours."

"Why?"

"Tomás has been giving me grief all night, saying I didn't warn you about the temperature on purpose."

"But I'm taller than you. I don't think we wear the same size."

"You're a bit taller, but I'm a bit bustier. I bet you. I bet that I'm just the same amount rounder as you are taller." By now she'd peeled her pink satin dress down to her waist like a skinned animal. "Jim likes you," she teased. "He called you refreshing!"

Marcella was right. Their small differences in frame canceled each other out. Giddily, they returned to the table to the men's applause. With this new perspective, Dorie saw how terribly she must have stood out, to provoke Tomás's pity. Looking just like a typist, Marcella took the seat next to Tomás with a poise that suggested she'd be taking his dictation. Dorie, feeling looser and freer, floated back to her date. Her retrospective embarrassment proved fleeting, as she felt herself drawing the gaze of the entire party with her reentry.

The rest of the night fell into the more familiar dynamics of a double date. Jim spoke to Dorie almost exclusively of his job with the Education Department of Fruit. He talked about creating banana meatloaf recipes for home-ec classes—recipes she had to memorize in school!—and said funny things like, "The trouble with bananas is that everyone loves them, but no one takes them seriously." Later in the night, he escorted her home in a dark cab and whispered theories on the Garden of Eden. How scholars were beginning to believe that Eve did not tempt Adam with an apple, but with a banana.

"I hope you get your gray dress back," Jim told her, as a goodbye.

"You don't like this one?" She patted the silken fabric beneath her coat.

"I like you. I like that you don't act or dress like a girl as beautiful as you are. I told Marcella that, and immediately she switched dresses."

Dorie had no idea what to say to this.

"She can't help it," Jim said. "She always has to complicate things, to entertain herself. To rile me. Don't take it personally. She adores you. We all do."

Jim did not seem prohibitively old to Dorie, merely for the fact that she did not know many young men in those days. The ones she did know, who weren't fighting, struck her as weak or broken in some way. And the ones who came home for leave seemed marked for death. Jim gave the impression of being too important to be wasted in battle. And with him, she felt for the first time above it all, too. For the first time since her childhood, several hours passed without a single mention of the war.

~~~~~

"I'm pregnant, Tomás." She'd been saying it over and over to herself for a week, and to say it aloud seemed, finally, to make it real.

"But this is wonderful, Dorie," he had said, standing in the doorway, already late for his meeting with Jim.

"It is?" she cried, confusing both of them.

"Yes." He tried to hide injury by maintaining his smile. "I think it was inevitable with us, don't you?"

She had never been pregnant before, though she had stopped taking precautions in her marriage long ago. She and Jim had tried to conceive for a few years, but had given up even talking about it. When Dorie suggested a doctor, Jim decreed that they should wait, anyway, because Guatemala was no place to raise a child. This became the explanation he offered readily to their families, friends, and colleagues. Without any medical consultation, Dorie wasn't sure if the problem lay with her or Jim. Now she knew. And, in retrospect, she suspected Jim knew all along.

"I do," she said. She smiled, a watery, wavering smile, to reassure Tomás.

"Good, then we're on the same page. Let's meet up tomorrow, out in the city for lunch. We'll talk more then, we'll make a plan. But now I have to go." He opened the door. "Jim knows I'm in the building, so I can't be late."

"Will we talk more about Brazil?" she asked, her heart beating in her throat.

"That's what you want?"

"It is, Tomás. It's all I've wanted for the past year. Will you find me a book about Brazil?"

They could just disappear in the night. In Brazil, Tomás could still work for Fruit. Going home to the States was too scandalous to consider. No matter what Marcella insisted, Americans, even the U.S. Census Bureau, considered Hispanics a different race.

"Of course, Dorie."

And just like that, Dorie was transformed. Everything around her—the apartment, the wasted city below, the savage, guilt-ridden lunches with Marcella, the Communists—now took on a conspiratorial shine. Suddenly she had everything, and her old life, though she was forced to inhabit it for a little while longer, no longer mattered.

———

Naomi had set up Dorie with a doctor. A white doctor with no connections to the embassy or Fruit families—a French gynecologist who'd come to Guatemala to make it easier for the lowest classes to breed safely. Another Communist program: breeding more Communists. But Dorie had been desperate, had asked Naomi in the imports store for help, assuring her new friend that she merely did not want to worry her important husband unnecessarily with some small problem. But desperation turned to humiliation, as Dorie sat in the damp waiting room with the obscenely pregnant, barefoot, and distressed Indian women all staring at her in amazement. At least she didn't have to pay for the doctor. Jim would not have parted with such a sum without questions.

She emerged an hour later with the confirmation she had been hoping for and dreading. She'd never particularly wanted children. At least, with her unhappy marriage, Dorie maintained a kind of freedom. Too busy to smother or control her, Jim allowed her to do what she pleased with her time. A baby would have ruined that, would have provoked his oppressive concern. But now this baby could secure more important freedoms than reading and shopping.

Naomi never followed up. At first Dorie believed her lie convincing, but after that strange "new start" comment at lunch, she guessed Naomi had seen this all before. Surely Dorie wasn't the first wealthy woman to come to her for help. She felt grateful now that lunch hadn't worked out. What would be the point of a new friend, anyway, now that she was leaving?

As Dorie dressed for the second time that day, she wondered how getting pregnant could be so easy for some and so difficult for others. Almost two years ago, Marcella had lost a baby she had desperately wanted, lost it the night Arbenz signed the land expropriation law. She had been four months along. The doctor asked her all about the previous few days: if she drank any lukewarm coffee at a restaurant, if she had eaten any fresh fruit. She had answered yes to both of those questions.

Since then, Marcella had slowly unraveled with drink. Any recognizable thread that Dorie tried to grasp and nurture came free in her hands. And though Tomás never said so himself, Dorie knew he felt Marcella slipping irrevocably away as well.

In the weeks after the United Fruit Christmas party, Marcella and Tomás wove an enchanting web around Dorie. Dorie had been impressed by Jim, but she'd really fallen in love with Tomás and Marcella that night. Their marriage seemed to be everything Dorie wanted. She had mistaken their dynamic for hers and Jim's—an understandable mistake when nearly their entire courtship took place across some table from them. Powerful, playful, kind, stern, principled, and easygoing, Jim was everything and nothing all at once. Dorie saw what she needed in him, assuming that Jim, like Tomás, wanted an educated wife. They were so close, how could they not agree? Only a week after Dorie and Jim married did she learn he held strong beliefs on the subject.

"Why do you want to take classes, Dorie? Why do you think I'd pay for those?"

"Marcella takes classes."

"And Marcella is the unhappiest girl I know. She's getting all this education and can't do anything with it but lose arguments with Tomás. What kind of job can she get? Only a typing pool would ever take her. Or a school. Can you imagine yourself or Marcella with a classroom of eight-year-olds? There's no point other than frustration."

Dorie never considered Marcella's unhappiness back then, but she surely understood now what Jim meant. All her thwarted hopes had been diverted into the imagined, unrestricted life of a male child. But complications from the miscarriage had left her sterile, and since then, she'd grown indifferent to everything and everyone around her.

"Now, if the world was a different place, I'd be behind you all the way, Dorie. I'd be the first one to sign you up for classes. Believe me."

In the end, despite her best efforts, her father's prediction came true: Dorie did not need an education to escape mediocrity, for she'd captured a bigger fish than he could ever hope for, with her angelic good looks.

A pounding on the apartment door startled Dorie out of this memory. She opened it, hoping irrationally for Tomás, but was surprised by a young Hispanic soldier. Gilberto, recently hired by Jim. The grave teenager gripped his holstered gun in one hand and a woman in the other. It took Dorie a moment to recognize Emelda.

"What have you done to her?" Dorie gasped, grabbing the girl and pulling her into the apartment.

Gilberto replied by thrusting a note into her hand. A note from Jim downstairs:

The clothes weren't enough. Gilberto said he'd cut hair in the
military, but I should have known what would happen. Can you
fix it?

Emelda, still bursting with excitement, obviously had yet to look into a mirror. She smiled and smiled beneath the ragged fringe of what was left of her beautiful black hair. A soldier's cut.

When Jim came home, earlier than Dorie expected, he did not linger with a hello, but walked immediately to the telephone. His legs so skinny it looked as if his suit were walking itself. Jim walked across the apartment, flipped the phone over, and began tearing at it with his hands.

"Jim, what are you doing?"

He fumbled the phone. "I need a screwdriver," he said, a cigarette wagging between his lips. "Bring me a screwdriver, Dorie."

She brought him one from under the kitchen sink and he began unscrewing the phone, taking the bottom plate out to reveal its complicated machinery.

"You're going to electrocute yourself." Dorie did not rush to unplug the phone from the wall. "What's going on? You're going to break our phone."

"We found a bug in my office," he said, without looking up. Ash fell from his words, into the plastic shell. "In my phone," he clarified. "They found a fucking tap on my phone!" He began pulling at the wires more forcefully and something came loose.

"That should do it," Dorie announced. "No one should be able to listen in now." She tried to remain calm, though she ran through her own phone calls in her head. The brief ones to Tomás, her rash, ridiculous proclamations of love.

Jim gave up on the phone, sat on the couch, and Dorie poured him a whiskey. "So you found a bug," she said. "No doubt you have them bugged."

Jim glared, ignoring this attempt at a question. The paranoia on both sides was astounding to Dorie. The Communists paranoid that Jim was masterminding some kind of plan to overthrow them, and Jim paranoid that they were listening in and realizing that he was not.

"Who have you talked to on the phone in the past month?" he asked. He emptied his whiskey glass, drinking back the ice melt.

"I don't know, Marcella, my mother, Tomás." This was how she lied now, by telling the truth as closely as possible.

Would the Communists now know about her and Tomás? Were they all standing around, chuckling at their pathetic dramas?

"I'm going to fire all Guatemalan staff." He tried for another sip, but he hadn't given the ice long enough to melt. It slid in a single, frozen mass, and clinked against his teeth. "Even though it's probably someone closer."

Dorie crossed the room to refill his glass. He watched her closely as her hand betrayed an unsteady pour. She was sweating, elated, pregnant, in love, and terrified. Whenever Tomás left her, she felt like she had a low-grade fever for the rest of the day.

Jim studied her, then let his gaze drift, settling on the table, on *The Role of the West*, with its feather bookmark. For a moment, he focused all his frustration there.

"This is ridiculous, Jim. Are you going to start spying on me now?" She cleared the table in a wifely way, swaying innocently about the room, though fear began to catch up with her.

If anything, Arbenz's reasonableness disturbed Dorie the most. A conservative revolutionary. The top of a reasonable, slippery slope into Marxist hell. That would be the downfall of Guatemala, the world, at a much later date. She could hardly admit it to herself, but even his land reform seemed quite modest to her. With 85 percent of Fruit land lying fallow, with half the population starving, she couldn't blame him for addressing the problem. And Fruit should pay taxes like everyone else. But, as Jim explained to her, it would all be very reasonable, until it wasn't. Until they were all standing in line for moldy bread. Guatemala was no different from Russia, which was no different from China. She'd seen the pictures in *Time*.

Jim, however, believed the disaster would come much sooner than later. He'd become so obsessed with Communists that he did not see the real enemy, in real time, that threatened his way of life.

She continued to tidy up, sweeping away Jim's ashes with her hand. When she looked up, she saw he held a small black handgun.

"Jim!" She dropped the ashtray, instinctively raising her hands. "You're not going to start carrying a gun!"

"I am, and I don't want you leaving the embassy without Gilberto."

"Gilberto! But he's a child! An illiterate child!"

"He's a trained soldier, Dorie." As he spoke, he held the gun out, aiming at the glassed-in bookshelf across the room.

"Yes, you trusted Emelda with him, too, and her hair was absolutely butchered! How could you do that to her? Any woman would kill for that hair." It was too far gone for her to fix, so she'd made a salon appointment for later that week. The loss of Emelda's hair, for some reason, made her almost cry for something she had lost herself.

"It was too Indian. I wouldn't be able to get her through the airport with the papers we have for her." He aimed recklessly now, tracking their belongings.

Dorie kept her eye on the wavering barrel, wondering if it was loaded. "This is ridiculous. Marcella's never had a bodyguard thrust upon her."

"Marcella knows the city, Marcella's aware. She grew up here, nothing gets past her. You've been here for years and you don't even speak Spanish. You stick out."

"I'll stick out even more with a car and an armed soldier following me around everywhere." She realized then what this arrangement would mean. "I can't even go out for lunch tomorrow? I have a lunch date."

"You can go with Gilberto."

She crossed her arms.

"Dorie, do you know, with all this populist fervor, what can happen to a white woman walking alone in the city? These Indian men think they're entitled to everything, and it's not going to stop at land and health care. They will take what they please!"

Dorie felt her resolve slip, the beginning of the slippery slope. She imagined the Indian man without a hand coming at her in the street, the one who always came at her, thrusting his stub in her face, threatening her for change. She imagined him venturing beyond his usual block, imagined him coming at her and not stopping at all.

"I made all my calls about Emelda on that phone."

"I'm sure the Communists have bigger concerns than an illegal maid, Jim."

He glanced up at her darkly. "All the Guatemalan staff must go. But Emelda won't be leaving for a while. I'll send her up every morning. It'll be good training for her. And you should get used to having a maid, anyway."

"I don't need a maid, Jim. I don't need a bodyguard. Is Gilberto even old enough? Is Emelda? The labor department's cracking down. That's probably who bugged your phone. A child labor sting."

He stood up, declaring the argument done. "You aren't allowed out of the embassy without Gilberto, Dorie. Do you want to find out if I'm kidding?"

"Fine," she said. "But don't ask me to get involved in any of your sex trafficking ventures again. It's too depressing, that girl has too many hopes."

Tottering in the street in her new heels, Emelda had proclaimed, "Now I am no longer an Indian." It was the saddest moment of the entire afternoon— sadder even than her butchered hair—this girl believing that a simple pair of shoes changed her place in the world.

"There's nothing wrong with hope," he said, smiling, mending their quarrel while checking the full chamber of his gun. "Things may turn out for her, you never know."

~~~~~

When they arrived at the Gringo for dinner two days later, their friend Christopher Cortez was already there. "Jim, Dorie." He grimaced, looking crushed by everything around him. "Coffee?" He gestured to the untouched cup on the table. His own blend.

"No, no," Jim said. "Scotch for us." He motioned to Eduardo, the owner.

Cortez tried not to frown. A failed coffee planter, his family's vast plantation in the highlands grew much more than he could sell. Hemorrhaging money and unable to beat Brazilian prices, he had resigned himself to a small grove of trees, while the rest lay fallow. Six months ago, the group had rallied in drunken sympathy for Cortez's plight and demanded Eduardo carry Cortez's coffee. And so now Cortez sat staring distastefully down into a cup of his own coffee, which no one ever ordered but him.

"How are things, Cortez?" Jim asked, watching the door.

"Not good, Jim. Not good. I think you may be interested to hear what I've been dealing with in the highlands, with these Communists."

Eduardo arrived at the table, set down two straight scotches with a flourish. Jim shifted his attention back to the door, leaving Cortez adrift.

"Cortez . . ." Dorie tried, taking pity on him. A good friend of the previous ambassador, Cortez was more of an inheritance than a close friend. Jim kept him in the circle, however, for strategic reasons he would never share. "We missed you last week."

Cortez sighed, considered speaking.

"Gilberto!" Jim cried, and thrust an arm in the air. The teenage soldier practically marched into the Gringo, wearing his army uniform. "Cortez, this is my new secretary!"

Of course, Gilberto was not a secretary, but Jim enjoyed using that term to tease both Tomás—who had hired a real male secretary—and Gilberto, who was merely a tough.

Gilberto took a lone seat, near no one, and set his eyes placidly on the wall. Jim raised one finger in the air. "He's an observant fellow. A good secretary! Tell us, what would make a man like Cortez give up all he knows?"

After regarding Cortez a moment, Gilberto said with distaste, "One round of water cure and he'd betray us all."

Jim giggled mercilessly, while Cortez managed a paper-thin smile. Dorie did not laugh, but studied the smooth side of Gilberto's face, appalled. She imagined poor Emelda holding still while this boy wielded scissors around her head.

How could she make her final escape with him following her around? She imagined lowering herself from the apartment window by a tied sheet.

"A good secretary," Jim repeated, to no one. "I'm going to send him to college. What college do you want to go to?"

"Harvard!" Gilberto nearly shouted, like a command.

"Ah, an intellectual. No West Point?" Jim teased.

"Harvard!"

The hiring of Gilberto baffled the entire embassy, but Dorie understood the choice right away. In an office where everyone tried to prove himself, impress someone, and make a career, Gilberto merely obeyed. And he was only interested in obeying Jim. He treated Jim's word as scripture. After hearing him refer to Harvard as the best college in the world a few weeks ago, Gilberto had become set on attending. For his loyalty to Jim, he thought he'd gain admission, despite the fact that he was illiterate.

"My God!" came a voice from the door. "It's a zoo out there!"

"A tequila," Jim ordered, as their friend Marco Jenks strode onto the scene, his face pink, exploded from the broken red veins of his nose.

"A damned circus!" Jenks cried. "I almost killed someone on the way here!"

"Glad you could make it, nevertheless," Jim told him.

Jenks collapsed in the chair on the other side of Dorie, already a good number of drinks into the day. Dorie began plotting some other way to come in contact with Tomás. Maybe a playful nudge of her foot under the table. She had tried it a few weeks ago and had made Cortez choke on his drink.

"What happened?"

"Today's the day of the traffic shift," Jenks explained. "There are signs everywhere." Indeed, signs all over the city announced that in order to make the government center more accessible, the one-way streets had to be reversed. According to the Communists, previous dictators had put traffic patterns in place that purposefully disenfranchised the people.

"If the streets were meant to keep Indians out before, reversing everything will just make it impossible to leave," Jim joked, but Jenks was on a roll.

"But Indians don't have cars! Indians can't read! So I'm driving near Plaza Mayor, and this old woman just goes strolling out in front of me, her head turned the other way! I had to swerve into a cart and donkey to avoid hitting her!"

Eduardo arrived with the tequila bottle and a shot glass. Jenks immediately downed one shot and motioned for another. "Who's this?" he asked, swallowing, leaning forward to look Gilberto right in the face.

"This is Gilberto, my new secretary! He was booted from the army for being a soldier. They're all aid workers now. They tried to make him confiscate land and pass out food! They took away his gun!"

Jenks accepted this explanation with a nod. "I see," he said, shifting his eyes to search for the next topic of conversation. Gilberto made no reaction to the attention so violently thrust upon and wrenched away from him in a matter of seconds.

"Dorie," Jenks resumed. "You're looking well this week."

"I am?"

"You're glowing!"

She tried not to show her distress. She turned to the door, where Tomás and Marcella should be making their entrance. He would be devastated, but he wouldn't show it. She had skipped their lunch date, since Gilberto was at her side the moment she stepped out of the embassy. When Tomás called to ask why she hadn't shown up, she could hear him through the broken phone, like a voice calling up from a well. But he could not hear her. Then she had hung up, for fear of the Communists listening.

"If you ask me," Cortez said, "that traffic shift is an excellent idea. Gets rid of everyone who can't read. The most effective literacy program yet!"

Jenks smiled at this, his body convulsed in one big chuckle. Jim cleared his throat. He'd told Dorie last week that Gilberto couldn't read, but Gilberto made no reaction to this insult.

"We all have to do our part and breed these commies out," Jenks added. "Now that illiterates can vote, traffic accidents aren't enough. I have seven children! But you Americans wait forever to have kids. By the time you start a family, Jim, you won't have the energy for more than one. And by the time he's old enough to vote, you'll be dead! Your vote merely replaced, rather than multiplied. That's no way to build up a decent democracy."

Dorie watched Jim very closely. "But the commies are building up, too," he said, with a ready smile. "You can't compete with the Chinese on that front. We need builders *and* demolition men."

Thankfully, Jenks agreed, ending that conversation. Another tequila arrived, which he, now mannerly, allowed to be set down. "Thanks, Eduardo."

"A pleasure, Consul."

Dorie counted five seconds until Cortez turned to Jim. "You know, it's lovely up in the highlands now. You and Dorie really should take advantage and stay at my villa in Quetzaltenango. It's all yours whenever you want it! Just say the date!"

"Thanks, Christopher, we'll keep that in mind."

"It's just lovely up there," he said to Dorie.

"Sounds lovely," she remarked, wondering how Cortez would ever think they'd go to a dirty Indian town for vacation. But this, she knew, was all he had to offer.

Hospitality did not prompt Cortez to open his villa to them, but rather his desire for an official title. Jim had named Jenks an honorary consul a few months ago for nothing more than the privilege of driving his car. The 1954 Nash Ambassador, with air-conditioning, was much more comfortable than the embassy's 1952 model. The diplomatic plates Jim gave Jenks made drives an easy pleasure, without interference from police checkpoints. Though Jenks did not really need the plates for influence. His family owned Guatemala Radio.

Ever since Jenks became an honorary consul, Cortez came to believe that he, too, could acquire such a title by lending his luxuries to the ambassador. Diplomatic plates might help him with his troubles in the highlands with the Communists.

"Hello!" Marcella and Tomás materialized at the table. Tomás maintained a tight hold of Marcella's waist, possibly to hurt Dorie. His eyes flashed happily everywhere but in her direction as Jim pumped his hand in welcome.

They took seats on the other side of Jenks. Tomás's secretary, whom Dorie had never heard speak (though he could read and write), pulled up a chair behind Tomás. His name was José Efraín Ríos Montt, a graduate of the Latin American Training Center. Baby-faced, he had a crew cut and large ears that betrayed him by turning red with any emotion that overtook him.

"Tomás," Jim said, ready for the fun to begin. "I brought my secretary to meet your secretary. José, this is Gilberto."

"You've a secretary now! Splendid!"

Gilberto and José regarded each other warily. Though they each had the same military haircut, much more than the table separated them.

"Let the king order first," Jenks insisted, as Eduardo bent to take Dorie's order. "Kings first, then ladies."

Everyone laughed as Eduardo straightened, wondering if he meant Tomás or Jim. Obviously, Tomás wouldn't be in his current position in Fruit without the early influence of Jim's family. Everyone knew this. And everyone knew that Jim held the distinction of representing the most powerful nation in the world. But, more and more, and certainly recently, Jim appeared to be taking his directives not from Washington, but from Fruit. More specifically, from Tomás. While Tomás was away in Xela, Dorie had overheard Jim put off a few calls with Washington, saying he was awaiting instructions from Tomás. Their weekly status meetings, Jim had told her, could not be interrupted for anything. Who held more power now? She thought of Jim, aiming his gun. She remembered Tomás pulling on his pants the other afternoon, talking about kindergartners.

Eduardo took Jim's order first.

"Tomás, I was just telling Jim about my villa," Cortez said halfheartedly from his corner. "You and Marcella are also invited to stay anytime."

"Is that so? I may take you up on that," Tomás said.

Cortez perked up, as if he'd been watered. "Splendid!"

"I just found out I'll be traveling there again in a few days, actually. The great land grab continues."

"Fuckers." Jenks played with his silverware. The secretaries eyed each other while the other wasn't looking.

"It's a mess, these land disputes. We've had this piece near Quetzaltenango for over twenty years, and it's involved us in some drama that goes back to the Spanish. If you look at the title, it's like a grocery list, I'm not kidding!"

Marcella, bored with politics, sighed loudly and turned to Jenks. "Has it even occurred to you to offer me your seat so Dorie and I can chat about girl things?"

Jenks grunted and stood to switch seats.

"Coffee?" Cortez asked.

"Yes, coffee at some point," Jim answered for Tomás. "But that's just the tip of the iceberg. Get this: The local Indians have a title issued in 17-something by the Spanish Crown, saying it's communal land. But then I guess they changed their minds, and there's another title that gave it to the Church a century later." He paused, sipped his drink.

Tomás picked up the thread, no doubt summarizing their meeting from the other day. "So for a long time, priests farmed it with Indian labor, but after some reforms they rented plots of land out to the Indians so they could grow food. But then that system eventually became so exploitative that the Indians grew the food and were still somehow starving. So in 1860, a few decades after independence, the priest was expelled by the President and the land was given back to the Indians by the conservative regime."

"A few years pass," Jim added, "and suddenly we're in the coffee boom, and the liberal government deems all titles from the Spanish Crown void. So they take the land from the Indians again and sell it for commercial planting, to some coffee farmer, who doesn't even get his trees going before the coffee bust."

"God, this is boring," Marcella declared, settling in close to Dorie. She placed a cigarette between her dry purple lips, then glanced up to see both Tomás and Jim holding out tiny flames for her. She looked from one lighter to the other, sighed, and tossed the cigarette back into her purse.

"Communal land?" Dorie asked Tomás, playing dumb, hoping for eye contact. "What's communal land?"

"Property that can be used by everyone," Tomás said, glancing at her briefly. "So anyone can plant or graze or sleep there. So this coffee farmer tries growing cochineal instead, but the Indians are hostile. He abandons the property, so then the Indians apply for another title, pay for it again. But the government in power denies them on some technicality and sells it to some wheat farmer from New York. Now, this is where it gets interesting."

Marcella cupped Dorie's elbow to get her attention. "What do you think that little Indian girl is doing right now?"

Dorie imagined the lost maid with a black eye, hiding in a dark alley.

"I bet she's thrown those new shoes in the ditch. They were so pathetically cheap, they must be painful. She'd be better off without shoes. And without English. You know, she told me her grandmother worked for an American. That's how she learned."

"Oh, you mean Emelda?" She listened to Marcella, though she tried to listen to Tomás, too.

"This wheat farmer and his family are there a few years, then one morning they're all hacked to pieces. Even a little girl."

The men looked down in collective shock and shame. Cortez's excitement at having a houseguest had vanished.

"A missing little girl," Marcella confided to Dorie. "There's nothing more horrific than that. A girl went missing near here just last week. Fifteen years old . . ." She kept on, and Dorie nodded, trying to hear the rest of the story.

"Was it the Indians?" Cortez croaked in horror.

"Yes, graphic stuff, according to the confessions. Parents gutted, the little girl raped—"

"Now, now, Tomás," Jim interrupted. "There are ladies present."

Marcella rolled her eyes.

"Well, anyway, no one was surprised by any of it. Their own workers killed them, to finally be able to get the title for their people, which they did. After the murders, no one wanted the land. Investors were pulling out anyway for Brazil." Tomás's eyes grazed Dorie's as he said this.

Cortez raised his hand for a real drink. "Anything," he told Eduardo.

"So the Indians paid for it and got it," Jim said.

"So much trouble a girl can get into, roaming the streets alone." Marcella sipped her golden drink, took a single, purified ice cube in her mouth, and sucked on it.

"So enter Fruit in the thirties," Tomás continued. "Under President Ubico, a judge rules that the Indians had acquired the title through devious means. The Indians argued there was no proof the executed criminals were working for anyone, but the title was revoked anyway, and we got the land along with a good number of acres surrounding it."

"The good old days," Marcella sang around the ice cube in her mouth. "Tomás misses Ubico, don't you? Your job was much easier then. Everything, walking down the street, was easier then, because you carried a whip. Didn't you, honey?"

"What does Fruit want with the highlands anyway?" Dorie cut in. "It's too cold up there for bananas." There, pretend we haven't had this conversation before, tell it all to me again. But he didn't bite. He frowned at them both, troublemakers.

"The point is, with this land reform, that stretch is fallow. The Indians have applied again to the government. But *more* interestingly," he said, cutting his eyes dramatically to Jenks, "there's another player now. Someone who claims to be an heir to that land, which trumps everything. An Indian."

"How the hell does an Indian inherit that land?" Cortez pounded the table.

"Under this government, an Indian could inherit Fruit." Tomás took his second sip of scotch.

"So what are you going to do?" Cortez asked. "Are you going to appeal if they decide for this Indian?"

"We'll strangle that puppy when we get to it," Tomás said. A phrase he and Jim often used, which Dorie didn't like. She had no idea where it came from, but it pleased them to be able to use it. Another one of their private jokes. No, Dorie thought, watching them together, telling this story, Jim would never shoot Tomás. He'd be more likely to shoot her. Dorie excused herself and went to the restroom, where she vomited quietly into the corroded sink.

Dorie lingered in the bathroom longer than she needed. She had had two drinks by now, meaning that the entire bar, the entire world, revolved around Tomás. When he leaned over and spoke to Marcella in Spanish, it was like a knife turning in her belly.

They nearly collided in the small, dark hall.

"Dorie."

"I want to learn Spanish," she said, inexplicably. "Marcella's always refused to teach me, and I know why!" Not, *I'm sorry* or *I was prevented from our meeting.* She intended to say that right away, but his moist eyes, his uncharacteristic wilted expression of hurt uplifted her. He loved her, she was sure of it now.

"Dorie. What?"

"I mean, we need to talk."

"I know," Tomás mumbled. "We were supposed to talk yesterday, over lunch." They stood closely. "Then I called, but you hung up on me."

"I'm sorry, Tomás. I couldn't come. Jim insists that Gilberto follow me everywhere now. He's paranoid I'll be kidnapped by Communists, or raped by Indians in the street. And the embassy's bugged, I couldn't take your call. Jim broke the phone. It rings and rings. If I pick it up, I can hear you but you can't hear me."

"I thought you had changed your mind," he said, his voice trembling. "I thought you decided you wanted to get rid of it."

"God, Tomás!" she gasped. "Never, I would never! How could you think—"

"You were acting so peculiar at the apartment. You kept talking about Jim, and how guilty you feel, and hinting that Jim might take you back to the States. You were picking a fight. Then when I called later you hung up on me."

"I was just scared." They had been gone too long now. But maybe everyone was too drunk to notice. "We have to talk about what we're going to do. Jim's going to find out soon."

"That's why I needed to talk to you. I just found out, Dorie. I'm going to be working this land dispute." He took her hand. If someone came down the hall, nothing could make this meeting seem innocent.

"The one with the murdered family?"

"Yes, Fruit has decided to pursue it. That's why I have to go back to Xela again. And again, and again. They've set a court date six months from now."

"Six months! Tomás! We don't have six months!"

"I know, I know, Dorie. But we're going to have to make it work."

"Why, Tomás? Why do we have to make it work? I don't understand."

"Fruit needs me here now. This is a crisis, and if I left, they wouldn't just give me a cushy job in Brazil. If I left now, I would be fired for abandoning them."

"Six months is impossible. Is there any way to move the court date up?"

"We already moved it up from a year. The system's absolutely clogged with disputes. There are Indians in the highlands taking land by force."

"So what are we going to do?"

"For now . . ." he tried, then started over. "For now, you'll have to tell him."

"Tell him I'm having your baby?" She shook loose of him, appalled.

"No, just tell him you're pregnant."

"I can't do that to Jim. I can't lie like that!"

"You don't have to lie, Dorie. Just tell him you're pregnant, you don't have to say whose child it is. And we both know he's not going to ask. We have nine months, don't we? Jacobo Arbenz is stepping on a lot of toes, he might not even last that long."

"Seven months. And the people love Arbenz, he's not going anywhere. I can't lie, Tomás. It's cruel to Jim. I don't like him very much, but I do love him still, in a way. He's been good to me, he doesn't deserve this."

"You don't have to lie. Just choose your words. We weren't born into all this like Jim and Marcella were. We've made our own way." His hand found her waist.

"Tomás—"

"Everything I've gotten in life, Dorie, everything, I got by deception." He pulled her close. "And biding my time."

"That's not true, Tomás." Dorie did not like where this was going. She felt the scene around her darkening, felt her life re-entwined with the people she thought she was leaving behind. "Everything you got by deception?" she asked.

"Yes," he said without hesitation.

"Even me?"

A high rubber squeal from the street trumped this small dig. Followed by a hard crack. Tomás pushed past Dorie and jogged down the hall. He was the type of person to run toward the unknown instinctively, sure of his usefulness.

There, in the street, lay an Indian man, facedown. At first Dorie thought he may just be knocked out by the black sedan idling a few feet behind. Then she saw the blood blooming on the pavement. Everyone stepped back from it. What had Tomás done in those few seconds before she arrived? Had he tried to revive the man? Had he merely turned the body over to spare them all his smashed face?

Behind the cracked windshield of the sedan, a dapper young Hispanic man sat at the wheel, stunned. Everyone knew what had happened. No explanations necessary. It was bound to happen, with the reversing of the road.

"That could have been me!" Jenks gasped, pointing to the man behind the wheel.

An hour later, they stepped out of the Gringo as the Nash Ambassador glided to the entrance, right through the blood, to pick them up. Conroy opened the door for Jim and Dorie to get inside. When he pulled back into the street, Jim became livid.

"No, no, Conroy, don't go this way. Go the other way." Defiant with drink, he lurched halfway over the barrier, instructing him.

"But the road's been reversed," Conroy said. "It goes this way now."

"Communists drive the new way!" Jim threatened, with a good humor that only entertained him. "We drive the old way. You aren't a Communist, are you, Conroy?"

"No, sir."

Conroy eased the car into an alley, backed up, and began again, driving south carefully, against the red warning signs.

"That's better." Jim sat back, took Dorie's hand. How could she even begin this deception? It bothered her that it fell on her. But then again, Tomás saw Jim more than she did. They were closer. He'd probably have to come up with his own string of lies over the next six months. She was willing to go with Tomás's plan; what other choice did she have? Jim had never been confirmed sterile, so that left her some room to maneuver. A miracle baby, after ten years.

"Conroy, why are you going so slow?"

"Because of all the accidents," he said. "The roads have everyone confused."

"That's absurd. Drive faster. We've an equal chance of hitting someone in either direction now. Half the people will be looking the new way when they cross, half the old way." Ash fell from his cigarette with these proclamations, right onto Dorie's lap. She brushed them away. "We must do our part for the new literacy program!"

The car, obediently, sped through the narrow street. Dorie nervously watched through the windshield, trying to anticipate an accident. If Jim now believed himself potent after all these years, she'd be raising him up to a great height before dropping him. Was she capable of such cruelty?

"Did you have too much to drink?" Jim asked. "Are you feeling okay, Dorie?"

"Yes."

"I'm sorry about Emelda's hair. I'm sorry about that whole day." He apologized, but did not retract his decree that Gilberto shadow her. He did not give up his gun, which she could see underneath his suit coat.

How funny, how sad, she realized: she had thought that by joining Jim's world, she would be leaving the infinite war behind. But just two months after the wedding, peace came and she found her husband enlisted in a truly endless, nebulous war.

The car suddenly went dark. The sun dropped behind the mountains. Night came in Guatemala like the flipping of a great switch. The darkness made it seem like they were going faster, too fast for the confines of the narrow street. Everything in front of them illuminated with cold white headlights.

~~~~~

Marcella and Dorie now shared Emelda the maid, at least until Marcella could find a replacement for her lost employee and Emelda left for Miami. Five days after the Gringo dinner, Marcella called Dorie to insist on a visit. When Dorie arrived at her house, Emelda was buzzing around barefoot in a maid's uniform, with her hair fixed into the shortest bob imaginable. Boyish and clumsy, she brought the coffee out on the balcony, then the whiskey.

"It's going to be impossible," Marcella lamented to her friend. "I interviewed a girl today. Well, I shouldn't say girl. Can't hire girls anymore. This one had already, obviously, had fifty kids. So, not a girl. And do you know what she had the gall to ask for?" She added a glug of whiskey to her mug. "Maternity benefits! Can you imagine, paying an Indian maid every time she gets knocked up?"

"We don't even have that in America. Why does she think she deserves it? What did you say?"

"I told her she wasn't Tomás's type." Her eyes glittered in self-satisfaction. "You know that's how they used to do it. Maids would seduce the husband, get pregnant, then blackmail them for money or land. But now, of course, it's all legal. It's in their union contracts. Now they get knocked up and you *have* to pay. No, I told her she was too fat for Tomás. And just as I tell her this, Tomás walks in. You should have seen the look on her face."

Dorie straightened in her chair, stung. "Tomás is back from Xela? How long has he been back?" She hadn't meant to use the Indian term.

"Two days." Marcella smiled, spooning sugar into her cup. "He's even been to the embassy. You haven't seen him?"

Dorie took the whiskey and splashed some in her coffee. "Was he meeting with Jim? What about?" Tomás had been to the embassy, but had not come to see her.

"Cortez. Turns out he's in big trouble in *Xela*. When Tomás stayed at his villa, the government was in the process of taking *all* of his land away."

"I thought they were just taking the fallow acres."

"They were. But then he tried to fool them. He plowed the unused acres, trying to make it look like he had planted something there. Of course, they knew. It was stupid of him, but he did it anyway. If they catch you trying to fool them, they take it all. It's the law now."

"Poor Cortez," Dorie said, feeling sorry for herself. Not even a phone call or a note.

"They're letting him keep his villa, although it'll be in the middle of fields that don't belong to him. He'll have to look out his window every day at Indians working and doing as they please with his land! And reaping all the profits! He'll go mad!"

"I bet they'll cut down the coffee trees and convert it all to corn."

"Tomás said Cortez paraded him around like a tiger on a leash, introducing him to every official as his houseguest. I have no idea what he thinks Tomás will do for him. Fruit has enough of its own problems. If some drunk Indian worker falls over his own bottle and twists his ankle, they have to pay him injury compensation. It's never-ending. Tomás sleeps four hours a night."

"I've barely seen Jim. Everyone's going crazy. Us versus them."

"Not us versus them. It's more like musical chairs now, Dorie. Someone's started the music. Everyone's got to secure their place. Tomás is so exhausted he can't even—"

Marcella stopped short, rolled her eyes toward the edge of the balcony toward Gilberto: Soldier? Secretary? Bodyguard? Spy? He stood guard closely, as if protecting one woman from the other.

Just as Dorie had suspected, Gilberto was a significant drag on her social life. He just sat there, suspicious of absolutely everything, making her paranoid. But still, he listened, which peeved her the most. They were being ignored and eavesdropped upon at the same time.

Though Marcella could not finish her sentence, Dorie understood the good news. Tomás now claimed to be too exhausted to make love to Marcella.

"Musical chairs," Marcella said to herself. Her foot tapping on the floor. "There are no teams, Dorie. Every woman for herself."

Dorie was forced to imagine this game, since Emelda at that moment turned on her shortwave radio. Marimba music. Marcella sighed. "I swear, it's impossible to find an Indian that isn't attached to one of those cheap little radios. They don't have shoes, but they'll spend all their money on batteries." She nodded in the direction of the kitchen. "But at least it's music. I know someone whose maid listens to replays of Jacobo Arbenz speeches all day. She can't say anything about it, of course. The Maids' Union, freedom of expression. But what about the right to peace and quiet? All night those damned radios are going. Our wall doesn't keep them out. So Tomás can't sleep, even when he does manage to get away from the office."

"Sounds like Tomás's court case isn't going too well. An Indian is inheriting the land, didn't he say? How?"

Marcella blossomed in her chair. "Turns out," she said, "that wheat farmer may not have been very faithful to his wife. Turns out, he may have been messing around with their Indian maid."

"Oh God." Voices—serious, singing, screaming—spun from the radio dial.

"Turn that off!" Marcella cried. The music stopped. "She claimed shortly after the murders to be carrying the farmer's child, but the baby came out looking Indian enough, and no one took her seriously. But now there's a grandchild in that family, born with blue eyes. They've been parading it around for years, like there's an official stamp on his forehead, but there were so many Germans in the highlands for so long. It really proves nothing. At least, not with previous governments."

So this was the dispute. Fruit versus some bastard Indian. "Do you think he has a chance of winning, this Indian?"

Emelda arrived on the balcony with round, terrified eyes. She clutched a broken wineglass in one hand and a sudsy toilet brush in the other. "I'm sorry. The soap is very slippery. I will buy you a new glass."

Both women stared, not at the hand with the broken glass stem. Emelda followed their eyes to regard the toilet brush. Marcella leapt from her chair and slapped her.

"You've been washing our dishes with that?"

Dorie felt ill. She pushed her coffee cup away, but Marcella was not done. With her hand still raised, she bore down on Emelda, who shrank back in confused terror.

"You think you're getting paid this week? You still owe me for your uniform, now the glass, and now for *emotional distress.*"

"I'm sorry, sorry," Emelda stammered, not knowing for what she apologized.

In one motion, Dorie stood to block Marcella's next slap. She caught her arm, bone striking bone. The impact had a strange effect on Dorie, something like a release. "If you hit her again, Marcella, I'll report you to the labor board." She hadn't meant to say the labor board. But who else could hold Marcella accountable? She prepared herself for ridicule.

"The labor board!" Marcella snorted with laughter.

Dorie's grip softened and Marcella took immediate advantage, rotating her hand to now grasp Dorie's wrist. She tried to wrench herself free, but Marcella's fingernails dug into her skin. Surprised by the pain, the twisting force, Dorie watched her other hand come up and strike at Marcella's smiling face. But Marcella ducked, releasing her, leaving her unbalanced and swiping foolishly at the air.

Shocked by her reaction and embarrassed at Marcella's now-hysterical laughter, Dorie turned to leave. "Okay, Emelda. It's time to go back to the embassy."

Emelda did not move. Dorie had to push her toward the door. "We'll go together and gather the laundry. Have you learned dirty laundry yet?"

~~~~~

After a week of waiting, Dorie became convinced that Tomás was avoiding her. His job always kept him busy, but this land dispute also seemed a convenient way to forget her and their mutual problem. Mutual, at first. But day by day, as she paced the apartment, unwilling to leave for the inevitable presence of Gilberto, the burden's weight seemed to shift slowly, exclusively onto her.

Not wanting to invite Marcella over, Dorie found herself thinking of Naomi. But to pursue that friendship would be impossible under the present circumstances, since Naomi had set her up with the free clinic. If Naomi didn't suspect already, she could too easily figure out Dorie's secret. So Dorie's only company, her only link to the outside world, became Emelda. She arrived every other day, carrying her shortwave radio and wearing one of the dresses Dorie had bought for her. Unlike Marcella, she did not make the girl wear a maid's uniform.

"Emelda, are you all right? You look upset."

The girl nodded, brought her hand up to trace her fixed bob. She stood, wavering very slightly, in her heels. Dorie pulled a kitchen chair out for her to sit.

"Is everything ruined? Will he not take me now?" Emelda had become uglier with the bob, but also quite talkative since Dorie had rescued her from Marcella's wrath.

"Short hair is very stylish," Dorie lied. What else could she do but change the subject to something constructive? "Are you meeting a lot of people at the embassy? You've met Tomás, of course. What do you think of him? Have you seen him lately?"

"He's very nice." She nodded. "He gave me a quetzal feather for my hair. I can't wear it out because it's too Indian, but I can wear it when I'm by myself. Once my hair is back." She patted the chopped sides, unsure they would come back.

Dorie tried to smile. Had he bought a whole box of those to pass out to girls? She stood up to pour the coffee, thinking too late that it was Emelda's job. "And what do you think of Jim?"

"He's nice."

"But not *very* nice?" Dorie teased.

Emelda panicked, a seed of fear showing. "No, he's very, very nice, too."

"It's okay," Dorie reassured her with a light touch on the shoulder. She often forgot that she shouldn't joke with Emelda. When she had explained the problem with the toilet brush, she tried to laugh it off, but Emelda did not find the incident in the least bit funny. Mortified and convinced her career as a maid was over, she cried for almost an hour. Then she became distressed that she'd inconvenienced Dorie, and further doomed herself with her tears. The only thing that made her feel better was an armload of dirty sheets.

"Are you nervous about your trip?" Dorie asked.

"No. I feel *good*," Emelda said, confirming this new emotion by straightening her posture. Chairs had been difficult for her at first, but she seemed almost comfortable in this one today.

"Are you happy to be going to Miami? It won't be easy, any of it." What was she going to do, try to talk her out of it? Jim would kill her. "When I was your age, I made decisions that I regretted later. Decisions that I thought would make my life easy, but everything turned out harder. I hope you've thought this through."

"I think it will be easy. Much easier than working on a banana plantation."

"You've worked on a banana plantation?"

"When I was a little girl, all Indians had to work on plantations to pay taxes."

"Was it very hard work? Did they use whips?" She suspected Tomás had whip scars. One of the reasons he moved so carefully over her. Hiding his back, which felt ridged under her fingers. He never lingered naked. His shirt always the last to come off, the first to put on.

"Yes, they whipped my grandmother for being slow. She was old. Then one day they called us out of the fields, but she did not come because of her bad hearing. My mother yelled for her. *Ixna! Ixna!* She was still working and the airplane came and dropped chemicals on her. It was terrible how she died. It took days. Her insides turned to liquid."

"I'm sorry, Emelda," she managed. The coffee's bitterness took hold of her throat.

"It's okay, but now you see going to Miami isn't so bad. I think it will be fun!"

"Yes, I suppose so." Dorie felt a little better now about the situation, but that story skewed her sense of injustice. She thought again of Tomás, his first job with Fruit, under Ubico's term. His insights given to Jim's father had probably trapped Emelda and her grandmother into that fate. Too ignorant, too afraid to walk past some constructed omen, to freedom.

Dorie finished her coffee, the sweet sludge on the bottom cold on her tongue. She hoped, more than anything, that this old banana baron was kind.

On Emelda's way out the door, Dorie gave her one of her more stylish hats to cover her hair and a note to deliver to Tomás at his office. The hat framed the girl's face perfectly, with small, fake berries suspended on short wires, quivering as she teetered to the door in her heels.

———

That afternoon, Tomás arrived like someone with legitimate business at hand, breezing in while straightening, not loosening, his tie. "How's *The Role of the West* coming?" he asked as a greeting.

"You've been back for days." She crossed her arms. "You've been here and you haven't come up to see me."

"I haven't had the time, Dorie, it's been crazy here." He reached out, but before he touched her she collapsed on the sofa. "All these new suits walking around, these eternal dinners and luncheons and briefings. And Gilberto." He sighed.

"I know! Gilberto is a problem. More of a problem that anything else. Do you feel like he's watching you, too?"

"I'm not sure, I don't think so. But either way, we can't go on like this. I'll deal with him, I'll figure something out."

"You could send him to Harvard," she joked miserably. "He'd go."

"Yes, that's a cruel joke, isn't it?" he observed. "He thinks college is like the army. He thinks he can just move up through dedication and obedience. He made it to corporal at one point, it seems. And Jim . . ." he paused, remembering more important things. "You haven't told him."

"No, I haven't. I've barely seen Jim, for all these meetings. How was your trip to Xela?" She reached up for his tie and began to loosen the silk knot between her fingers

"I brought you a present."

Dorie, imagining another quetzal feather, squared her eyes at him. "What?"

"It's not a thing," Tomás teased. "It's a bit of hope."

"Hope?" She laughed, feeling fondness between them returning.

"About that land in Xela. My investigation is turning up some interesting facts."

She pulled his tie free.

"It turns out the little girl may not have died. She may have survived the murders."

Outside, a cloud slipped from the sun, brightening the room.

"How do you know? Did you find her?"

"No, but I thought I remembered seeing her in town once, after the murders, but I was so young. I thought it must be a mistake. But when I was in Xela this time, I found witnesses still alive. Witnesses saying they saw the little girl in town right after the murders, too. That she didn't disappear until later. And there's an older white lady living in Totonicapán. No one knows how she got there. She's a bit nuts, she thinks she's an Indian. Wears Indian clothes and speaks Quiché."

"I heard the Indian heir claims to be related to the wheat farmer," Dorie said, searching Tomás's face for a reaction. "Does he have a good case?"

Tomás frowned. "Who told you?"

"Marcella."

"She shouldn't have." His hands curled in his empty pockets. "She should not have. It's hard enough keeping her quiet when she snoops around my desk, now I have to worry about who you tell."

"Who would I tell? I don't care about the Indian. I care about us. What does it mean that people saw the little girl after? Does it help your case or hurt it?"

"Well, it would hurt Fruit's case, definitely. But it would hurt the Communists' case, too. As a legitimate child, the white daughter's claim would trump everyone's and the judge would throw the whole dispute out."

"And we could leave."

"Ideally. But these Communists need proof for everything. Technically, no one can *prove* there were murders in the first place. That the family didn't just abandon the property, to flee creditors. They were plenty in debt. That would revoke the daughter's claim. The court might demand someone drag the parents' corpses into court as evidence."

"Is that a possibility? That they were never murdered?" She was trapped in the apartment, getting fatter, more obvious by the day, while he ran around in the highlands playing the detective hero.

"This time, instead of claiming the murderers weren't working for the community, like they claimed in the thirties case, the Indians are claiming we can't prove murders even occurred without bodies. Which is true, but from the confessions it sounds like there wouldn't be much left to recover."

"So they got confessions, but no bodies?"

"Dorie, do you even understand what I'm telling you? I'm saying I'm trying to find this little girl. If Fruit knew what I was doing, I'd be fired for sabotaging their claim. I'm sorry I've been out of touch, but I don't even have time to change clothes anymore. If I can find the daughter and convince her to claim the land, we can be free in a week. But I have to be careful, Dorie. No one can know. I've kept that much from Marcella, at least."

"But where does that leave me? Should I tell Jim I'm pregnant or not?"

"Tell Jim, it'll buy us time. The longer you wait, the more suspicious it'll be. Trust me. You have to trust me. You've nearly ruined us already, drunkenly accosting me in hallways, sending letters through Emelda. You have to stop sending letters, Dorie."

"Why? Are you afraid of Jim?"

"Don't talk nonsense." He sat heavily next to her on the couch.

"Have you found my book on Brazil?" she asked.

"Not yet, Dorie. You know English books are impossible down here." When she'd wanted to learn about Guatemala ten years ago, Tomás could only find one book in English, *Popol Vuh*, the native creation myth. A myth! Now, of course, Americans wrote books about Guatemala all the time, books like *The Role of the West*. Her understanding of Guatemala remained stranded between myth and conjecture. Brazil, however, would be different.

"Are there universities in Brazil? Do they take women, like they do here?"

"There hasn't been a revolution in Brazil. To take classes there, you may have to join a nunnery."

Dorie stood up. "Don't make fun of me. I'm serious."

"I'm sorry. I'll look into it." He took her hand and made a knot with his own. "What would you like to study?" If he remembered this was the first conversation they ever had, he did not show it. "Last week you told me Spanish."

"I could," she considered. "I tried so hard to learn at first, but it's no use if no one will practice with you . . ." She stopped herself, avoiding the topic of Marcella. Things were going so well. "Tell me about Brazil. I know nothing. Is it on the coast?"

"It is, but we probably won't be." He pulled her back down, rocked her, kissed her hair, and all her frustration dissipated. "We'll be in the hot, buggy interior," he said.

"Is Brazil where they have that big ancient city up in the clouds?"

"That's Peru."

"Oh." She tried to recall other pictures she had seen that might be Brazil. "What about that giant waterfall?"

"Argentina." Tomás smiled down at her.

"Will our baby speak Spanish?" Dorie asked.

"Oh yes, he'll speak Spanish. And Portuguese and English."

"Portuguese? What's Portuguese?"

"That's the language of Brazil."

"It is? I didn't even know Portuguese was a language." Yet another language added to her life, which she would not understand.

"And there are several Indian languages. Many more than there are here." As he went on and on, Brazil began to sound just like Guatemala. A bigger, scarier Guatemala, with cannibals instead of Communists.

"What about our baby?" she asked, to change the subject back.

"He'll be beautiful, brilliant!" He outlined his plans for the baby, the Catholic education, the son following his father to the Fruit offices—for it never occurred to him this baby may be a girl.

"He'll have your eyes," he said, laying a hand on her waist. His touch electric. The slightest brush against him at a party still jolted her.

"And your hair." Dorie smiled. She could play this game, coloring in the outlines of this anonymous baby. "And let's hope he has my nose." She turned to him, reaching up and tracing down the seam of broken bone, like one would follow a road on a map.

~~~~~

Three days later, Dorie went to Marcella's without Gilberto, practicing for maneuvers to come. She and Tomás had not set a date for their next meeting, but it would have to be after he came back from an investigation of the crazy white woman in Totonicapán. Having no idea what she was capable of until she tested Gilberto, she remembered Tomás's advice: deceive and wait for your moment.

Dorie slipped out the embassy gates—waving to Conroy as she did—went in one direction, rounded a corner, then reversed. She walked the entire way to Marcella's, walked an hour. She arrived to find Marcella reading human-interest stories in *Prensa La Verdad*. She translated aloud an interview with an Indian girl whose father had received land from the Communists. Before, he earned a steady wage with United Fruit. Good year or bad year, he could always rely on making the same wage. With their new land, he quit this job to plow and plant his own fields, but no rain came. They had borrowed money for farming equipment, now they had nothing to repay the loans. Her parents, in despair, started to drink away what little money they had. They couldn't sell the land, because everyone else knew they'd get land for free if they waited long enough. Drunk and desperate, her mother got onto the complicated plow, didn't know how to stop it, and accidentally ran over her father. Just plowed his body into the field. Then she killed herself.

"*Our land,*" she read, "*is only good for one thing, and that's burying my family.*" Marcella performed this translation with a hand on her breast. The fine line between sympathy and mockery perfectly toed.

The story chilled Dorie so that she turned to her coffee for warmth. "How could highlanders work for Fruit? It's too cold up there for bananas."

"Highlanders migrate to the coasts to work," Marcella replied, tossing the paper aside. "Tomás says about half their workers come from there. But still, that story's bullshit. There's nothing worth reading anymore, now that the censors are gone. It's all drivel. Anyone can write any nonsense they want. At least the censors were educated, they had a sense of story, of *structure*. Tomás—"

"Is he in the highlands again?" Dorie hadn't meant to bite the hook so abruptly.

"Of course." Marcella sighed. "There's nothing our men won't do for a missing little girl. A little girl fifty years ago! If they do find her, they'll be disappointed she's an old lady." Marcella wavered in her chair, drunk from spiked coffee. "It's too late for us, Dorie. We're too old for anyone to care if we went missing. Dorie Honeycutt. Such a nice young lady gone missing from Boston, never to be seen in civilization again."

Dorie did her best to sort through this calmly in her chair. Marcella knew about Tomás's investigation. Maybe he'd slipped in conversation or she discovered a document. Small lies and half-truths, she remembered him saying, to cover their tracks.

When she tried to make love to him during his last visit, she only succeeded in taking off his shirt. Usually the last to come off, she went for it right away. But he said he was too scared of harming the baby. Then he scolded her for not telling him before the last time they'd made love. They would take no risks, he made clear. Then he made her promise to boil all her water twice.

"It's important you know," Marcella told her, "that investigation means nothing. It's a decoy."

"A decoy," Dorie repeated, as if she understood. His rejection, no matter how thoughtful, had caused her to resort to desperate maneuvers, which he evaded, claiming a meeting with Jim. "Jesus Christ!" she had cried. An unforgivable offense. He fled, turning his naked back on her for the first time. Showing the whip marks she had only before felt. Long pink ridges, bubbled with old scar tissue.

"I just keep going back to that afternoon in my mind," Marcella said into her mug. "Just two minutes could have made the difference. None of this . . ." She leveled Dorie with a look. "None of this would be happening."

"None of what, Marcella?" But it came out too high and false, as she fought tears, remembering those scars.

"I never told anyone, not even the doctor or Tomás, but I know what caused my miscarriage. If I had been delayed a minute, it could have all been avoided, none of this would be happening."

Dorie did not ask again what she meant by "none of this." Her sadness, her transformation over the past year?

"I'm glad you could give Gilberto the slip. I've never told anyone this. I was walking home by way of the Presidential Palace. You remember the day Jacobo Arbenz signed the land expropriation law. But I didn't know this—I'd been out all day. Suddenly a mob of Indians rushed the palace and I got caught up."

"Did you fall? Did they trample you?" Dorie felt, much like the story, herself being pushed where she did not want to go.

"Nothing like that. The Indians were singing and chanting and pushing forward. The smell was terrible. The next thing I knew, this old Indian man pressed right up against me. He brought his filthy hands up and just started caressing my face. I was so shocked, I couldn't even scream. And then he slipped his fingers into my mouth. It was awful. I tasted them; they tasted like metal. I finally came to my senses and screamed. I ducked and found an opening in the crowd and escaped. That night, I lost the baby."

"So it was all the pushing, you think?"

"No, no, the pushing wasn't so bad. I've had worse at Fruit parties around an open bar. It was that Indian. He did something to me."

"You mean, like a curse, or like a disease?"

"I don't know!" She stifled a sob into her palm. "All I know is that an old Indian man would never think of laying a hand on me a day before. But Jacobo Arbenz did it. Signing that law, making them think they deserved everything. Making that filthy old Indian think he could put his half-dead fingers in a white woman's mouth."

The miscarriage happened while she was home alone. She said she felt it coming, and fled to the bathroom, where she would not ruin anything.

"I know he did something to me. Women have miscarriages all the time, but he did something to make it impossible for me to ever have children again."

"Marcella—"

"But now," Marcella sniffed, "I'm thinking maybe it's all for the best."

Dorie tried to muster pity for Marcella. How did she become the type of woman to steal anyone's husband, let alone her troubled best friend's? But Dorie did not have the luxury to give up an ounce of the meager happiness she could hold on to in her life. And she suspected Marcella would do just the same to her.

"There's something else," Marcella said, more composed. "Something Tomás told me. Something he's never told anyone. Not even Jim knows, I'm not kidding. When I was three months along, he confessed something to me. He said because he didn't want me to be surprised when the baby came."

A knock rattled the front door, but neither of the women paid any attention. They both knew who it was.

"What did he tell you, Marcella?" Dorie leaned forward, her hair dipped into her coffee. She did not care now how suspicious her interest, her dread, looked. The knocks on the door grew louder, trying to save her. She sat there, frozen between two enemies, unable to gauge her chances with either.

"He's an Indian, Dorie. Half Indian, at least. He was an orphan adopted by wealthy coffee planters named Fasbinder. He wasn't a migrant worker. He was a slave."

Horror wrung Dorie's heart, squeezing any hope, any idea of happiness from her. She felt it all leaving her with the force and efficiency of two hands twisting.

"An Indian?" The word she said a hundred times a day struggled now up her throat like bile. "But he doesn't look Indian."

The door jumped from its frame as Gilberto threw himself against it, trying to break in. "Mrs. Ambassador, I hear you! Are you safe?"

"It's his nose," Marcella said, waiting a moment for Dorie to understand. "It wasn't broken in fights. He broke it himself, three times. Reset it three times, then ran away from the plantation when he was thirteen."

Dorie ran the bath as hot as she could, poured a tumbler of whiskey, and made herself, despite the pain, crouch so the water touched her backside. Bracing herself with a swig, she sat down completely, feeling the burn in her throat and on her skin.

She sat in the tub until it cooled and she needed the whiskey to stay warm. Then she drained the water, walked naked around the apartment, until the water heater recharged for another round. She would not let herself cry. To cry, to wallow in self-pity, would only waste valuable time.

If she could not rid herself of it in two weeks, she would have to tell Jim. Telling Jim would not mean she'd have to give up the baths. It just meant that when it finally worked, she would have to endure the pity of everyone she knew. And there was only one thing she could think of that would be more humiliating than being pitied.

The unbearable visit with Marcella did not end right away. Gilberto stalked the house with his gun drawn, while Marcella kept insisting, "If it had come out dark, I don't know what I would have done," over and over, more sure each time, as if she knew exactly what she'd have done but couldn't bring herself to say it. Dorie imagined Marcella climbing Volcán de Fuego, tossing her dark baby into the smoking crater.

Of course, everything about Marcella's behavior over the past year now made sense. Her slow slide into mad drunkenness, her rants about race.

The phone rang. Dorie ignored it, suspecting Tomás.

She had been prepared to run away with a Hispanic man, Hispanics and whites married often enough in Latin America, especially in Fruit circles. Though unacceptable at home, at least they would have the Southern Hemisphere to find peace in. But this relationship would be considered an abomination even in Guatemala. And surely in Brazil. Dorie didn't know any women who'd say hello to an Indian man, let alone have an affair and become pregnant with an Indian baby. There was no one to turn to for help.

She considered Emelda's blue eyes, and the faceless Indian in Xela, claiming land after two generations. She'd seen a handful of gray-eyed Indians just in her limited wanderings around the capital. Then, of course, there was the dark baby born to a respectable Fruit family. Even an act of impropriety committed a hundred years before could, without warning, come back to stamp itself on the face of any child.

He arrived like a specter during her third bath, his black suit moving through the steam-filled apartment.

"It's like a jungle in here, Dorie." Jim swam with his arms, through the bedroom to reach her. His glasses steamed, rendered his face blank and eyeless.

"I'm just taking a bath." She slipped down further into the water to hide her body.

He knelt down, dipped a finger in. "It's so hot! Why do you have it so hot, Dorie? You're going to burn yourself!"

Before she could answer, he opened the cold tap, which spewed instant relief. She waited for him to realize, to think for one moment about his own question. Whiskey and a burning hot bath. So obvious to any woman. She stared down at her body, slightly distorted with the baby and the magnification of the water.

"It relaxes me," she said, sinking down so the water lapped just beneath her chin. "The heat relaxes me." Her breasts, she was sure, had grown a half cup-size bigger.

Thankfully, he took off his glasses before he could notice. "Why do you need to relax? I'm the one that had the scare today. What were you thinking, sneaking out of the embassy without Gilberto? We thought you'd been kidnapped!" His eyes were wet with steam and emotion. He rubbed them, then squinted to find her through the peachy blur of his farsightedness. "Gilberto is here for your protection, Dorie. Do you know what could have happened—"

"I can't have him following me everywhere, Jim. He's awful. He stresses me out. He perches like a vulture, like he wants someone to try to murder me so he can prove himself. He's an idiot, a savage! He broke down Marcella's front door!"

He rolled up his sleeves. "Here, let me wash your hair."

Dorie did not want her hair washed. She lowered her head into the water to escape him, her knees going up. Underwater she discovered surprising sounds—metal banging, voices traveling up the pipes from the lower floors. She heard a voice distinctly say, *"In times of crisis, it's important that the news stays consistent,"* just before she ran out of breath.

"It's been forever since I washed your hair." He worked the shampoo in tenderly with his fingers. "Do you think I'm enjoying this, Dorie? Do you really think I enjoy having you followed?" It occurred to Dorie then that Jim knew everything, had ordered Gilberto to follow her solely because he suspected her affair. But did he know it was Tomás?

"Jim," she said. "This is my life. How can I conduct it in the shadow of that horrible boy? I dread even meeting him in the hallway."

"I know," Jim reassured her, kneading her neck, his fingers curling completely around her throat, massaging. "Everyone does. That's why I hired him."

Jenks, unexpectedly, was her salvation. He burst through their apartment door, Jim's receptionist trailing behind with an apology. Jim left her to attend to him, closing the door, though she could hear every word in their small apartment.

"The newspaper yesterday reported twelve dead from traffic accidents from the road reversals thus far," Jenks panted in the other room. "Have you heard?"

"No."

"There will be more, of course. In response, Jacobo Arbenz released a radio announcement about the changed traffic patterns, in Quiché, Ixil, Kaqchikel, Achí, Q'eqchi', and Mam, and decreed that all stations must play it every hour for the next week."

"So . . ." Jim ventured.

"All our broadcasts are in Spanish!" Jenks cried. "No Indians listen to Guatemala Radio. There's no point! Except, of course, the control. Fucking commie control! It takes fifteen minutes to run it in all those languages! Fifteen minutes, every hour. You wanted me to tell you when they start to interfere with the media."

"What happens if you don't play it?"

"A fine. Another fine! They're sinking us with these fines, which is the whole idea. Tomás says they fined Fruit for a press release stating Arbenz's grandfather owned slaves. Libel. But Tomás says they had an eyewitness source. Freedom of the press, it seems, only applies to the left!"

Dorie, dried and hidden in a robe, recalled her last conversation with Tomás. Before she'd spoiled the visit, she had teased him about his reluctance to make love, called him a prude, believing she could still change his mind. She asked him why he didn't become a priest.

"Development will bring the Indians to Christ," he'd said. "Will eradicate poverty more quickly than preaching at them will. More quickly than voting reforms and child labor laws. Forcing these things is counterproductive. And so I answered my calling in an unconventional way. I'm still converting souls, Dorie."

"You say now that money is the answer, but you worked as a child. I know it was awful. I know they whipped you."

"Yes. But without plantation experience, Fruit would never have hired me. If the government then had been like the one today, if they plucked me from my job and placed me in one of their free schools, where would I be right now? On a plantation."

Jim finally succeeded in pushing Jenks out of the apartment.

"Dorie, I'm sorry. I came up here to talk to you. And now I've called downstairs to make sure there are no more interruptions."

She clutched the robe at her neck.

"Dorie, is there anything you want to tell me? You seem . . ." He paused, searching for the precise word. "Distracted."

"No." She knew her face betrayed her. She turned to the bedroom window.

"You know you can tell me anything, Dorie. Anything at all." Which was true. Jim had the ability to neutralize seemingly impossible problems. When she finally confessed to him that her real name was Pandora—knowing he'd see the name typed out on their marriage license—he merely chuckled and brought her paperwork the next day to have her name legally changed to Dolores. An option she did not know existed.

I'm pregnant with your best friend's Indian baby, she thought to herself. There'd be no way to neutralize that. The problem stretched beyond even Jim's powers.

"Okay, you don't have to tell me, Dorie. But I'm going to give you advice, anyway. Universal advice." He sat on the bed and patted a place for her to join him. "When I was running the Education Department of Fruit, we had a big problem with bruised and overripe bananas."

Dorie stifled a simultaneous sob and laugh with her fist.

"Bananas ripen fast and they bruise easily, when you have to ship your cargo by train, then boat, then train again halfway across the world. Brown bananas were our biggest problem at the time, but I solved it. Do you know how?"

He bent down and found her eyes.

"I don't know, Jim."

"I rebranded them. Brown spots aren't bad, they're good! I renamed them sugar spots. Where the sweetness is. I wrote a whole ad campaign and people began buying brown bananas over the yellow ones! *Creative thinking* was all it took."

Dorie herself still bought brown bananas because of that commercial, with no idea of Jim's connection to it. She smiled despite herself, wiped her eyes clear. "You wrote that commercial? I remember watching it as a girl. The dancing, spotted banana—"

"You see!" He encouraged her, bouncing the bed. "You feel better already!"

"But what about Communists? Land reform? Can they be done away with creative thinking, Jim?"

"Of course!" he said, kissing her forehead. "That's why Washington hired me."

Tomás,

    I'm writing you because I know that if I try to do this in person, I will fail. I would be cruel and would only be able to halfway succeed, prolonging both our despair. So I am writing now and I hope you forgive me for it.

    I cannot be with you anymore, Tomás. I cannot make a life with someone who has made a life of deceit. I have lived this way for a year now and know that I do not have the strength or the cunning for it. I recall you telling me at the Gringo that everything you have gotten in life was by deception. I thought you were exaggerating, but only now do I understand the truth of it. In short, I know about your heritage. It doesn't matter how I know, but I do and you cannot deny that this must change everything for me. You know as well as I do that there is not a single country in this world where we could comfortably make a home. If there wasn't a child, maybe it would work, but how can we be together, Tomás, and be fruitless? Your religion prohibits both birth control and divorce and I have no desire to force you to compromise your most fundamental beliefs.

And what of this baby? Beyond my own fears of exile, you must know that a simple gamble of heredity could ruin you, too. All you have worked for in your life, wagered with frightening odds. I know your success is too important to you to risk. So what was your plan? Did you plan on breaking the baby's nose repeatedly, too? Of continuing this charade for generations until your bloodline is washed clean? For even if our baby came out looking normal enough, what, then, of his children?

There are just too many unknowns here, too much pain to pass on to the generations. So I am stopping this before it can go any further. I am not going to Brazil with you. I am not having your baby. I'll take care of the arrangements myself, and you need not know any more details. It will not be your sin, it will be mine. A sin, as was my own deception in this entire affair: I was only using you to get out of Guatemala. I do not love you, Tomás. If it was possible to undo our entire history, to start again as friends, I would, but I do not think either of us would learn from these mistakes if we treated them as simple folly. A child's game to be restarted when we do not like the results. But maybe you can. If so, I envy you and give this advice: Go back to Marcella. She loves you, in her way, and you've the luck there of a fruitless marriage. It seems the path of least resistance for you and I do not know why you strayed from it in the first place.

She awoke that night with a raging headache from her day of whiskey baths. A dream had startled her awake, a horrible dream she could not shake. In it, she'd been plowing a field and did not realize she'd run over Jim until she felt his bones crunching in the blades. She jumped off and found nothing left of him but a bloody black suit.

She blinked at the walls, trying to calm herself, to get back to sleep. Then she turned and found Jim lying next to her, awake also, still wearing his suit. Rumpled, but clean. She could smell the smoke, the coffee of some recent meeting on him. The bedside clock placed him there at an impossible hour, before midnight.

"I've been thinking, Dorie. Jenks is right. There's always going to be a reason not to, there's always going to be work and travel. I think we should go for it and try again for a baby. What do you think? It will be our patriotic duty."

What did Dorie think, lying in bed, hearing this from Jim? She thought very carefully about her words. And about the brutal irony of Tomás's plan falling into her lap the moment she abandoned it. Of Jim's astounding self-deception. Was he capable of even considering the possibility that he was sterile?

"I don't know, Jim," she managed. "I still don't think Guatemala is any place to raise a child."

"Oh." He waved a hand. "There are worse places."

"Are there? I don't even know the situation down here. I don't even know what you do all day, so I can only imagine the worst. Especially with the fragments I do get." A viable argument that could sustain her for a while, if needed. "Tell me what's going on downstairs, Jim. You never tell me anything. You keep apologizing for the craziness, but I've no idea what it is. Maybe if I knew the situation better—"

"It's only fair," he agreed for the first time in a decade. All these concessions, all this tenderness, suddenly, as if he knew Dorie had planned to leave him. "Confidentially, my most important project went haywire, which is why I've been so stressed this week. We screwed up one of our newspaper stories. This one's about a girl in the highlands. Her father got free land and began farming it. But he can't run the equipment, it's too big, and he's just an Indian. He's used to mules. So he's on this motorized plow and the mother is on there with him, but her Indian skirt gets caught. And he can't turn off the plow. He ends up dragging her along, her body torn up and plowed into his field."

"Jesus Christ, Jim." Dorie sat up. The light from the guard station outlined the dark room in a simple sketch. "What are you talking about? You made that up?"

"Freedom of the press, Dorie. The Communists asked for it."

The phone rang and Jim walked into the next room to answer.

"Tomás!" he called into the receiver, now fixed. Dorie scooped up the sheets to cover herself at the sound of his name. "Yes, tell me all about your trip. What time tomorrow works for you? I've got some things awaiting your approval."

He hung up. "Where was I?"

"The man plowing over the woman." The version from the newspaper, she remembered, being the other way around. Jim abandoned her, spent all his days making up newspaper stories?

"Yes." He returned to bed. "I'm talking about how this is a very powerful story. It needs to be covered by the press. Hernando understands this, he runs it in *Prensa La Verdad*. But then one of the editors changes it so the woman runs over the man, which is absurd. He argues that it will have more resonance with Indians if the woman runs over the man. So now we have two different versions running in the papers. And Arbenz is using it to prove opposition papers aren't reporting real stories, but repeating what they hear from us. And Washington knows, and we all look bad. Papers we rely on look bad and we're set back months in our work."

Dorie lay on top of the blankets for hours, shivering, unwilling to crawl under to join Jim in his warm, dreamless sleep. Jim slept easily, but claimed not to dream. So sure of himself at the end of each day, not a scrap of doubt remained to trouble his rest.

"We can do this, Dorie," he'd said, before falling asleep. "You can even get another maid to help with the baby. A Hispanic, or maybe even a girl from the States. Will you promise to just think about it?"

"I'll think about it."

She watched him sleep, thinking instead of the letter she wrote to Tomás between baths, already sent. She gave it to Emelda that evening to deliver to his house, since new security measures at Fruit wouldn't allow an Indian maid near his office. Had he read it already? She felt the heavy machinery of her plan beginning to grind. If she changed her mind now, she'd be crushed.

~~~~~

She awoke in the early morning to a cool light splintered by the partially open blinds. Next to her, she saw his naked back and felt so grateful that she cried out to touch Tomás. But the skin was smooth beneath her hand. She'd woken him up and Jim turned over to kiss her, thinking she had made up her mind to try again for a baby.

As he made love to her, Dorie stopped worrying that he would even notice her changed body. She found him unbearable, clumsy. She missed Tomás, his almost weightless presence above her. Jim moved too eagerly, twisting the sheets into a rope around her waist. His face too close to hers, breathing too much of her air. She missed wanting more. By the time Jim finished, she had wanted less. About ten minutes less of him than she had to endure.

Jim was pathetic, she realized, an actor sent by Washington to create an illusion of power in a situation they had no control over. An adman, a story-teller. She saw him clearly, in the brightening dark, for this first time.

By midmorning, she sat alone in the apartment, both longing for and fearing the moment she would see Tomás again. Soon he'd make his way up the third-floor stairs, after his meeting with Jim. At any moment, he'd knock on her door and she would have no choice but to open it. Because he had a key.

What part of him would she see? She knew the moment he appeared, her heart would choose a side. Only, she could not predict which. Could she find happiness in exile? In abandoning the respectable position she'd wanted her whole life?

And if this baby was born, a likelihood that grew stronger each day that she failed to get rid of it—as it grew teeth and fingers that clung to her—she would need Tomás. Having an Indian baby with someone she loved would be preferable to having one with Jim. She considered again Tomás's rule: to lie and bide your time. And thought how cruel, to use his own advice against him.

Dorie needed to get the letter back right away. She could not close her options off so finally. Running out the embassy door, she waved to the guards and cleared the gate at a trot, while they looked on helplessly. "I'm going to the salon. I couldn't find Gilberto and I'm late for my appointment already!" They knew they could not stop her, and Jim would never order anyone to physically subdue her. They'd send Gilberto to the salon first, giving her a bit of time. She set off in that direction, but changed course once out of sight. She felt the rain beginning before she'd traveled a block.

When Dorie arrived, soaked and shivering, Marcella announced, while turning off Guatemala Radio, "Thousands of people are protesting across the city—Indians and peasants, demanding that Jacobo Arbenz resign."

"That's funny," Dorie replied, feeling this greeting even funnier, "I just walked across the city and didn't see anything."

"Gilberto's already been here, looking for you. To what do I owe this surprise visit? You never just stop by anymore."

Dorie glanced casually around the room, looking for the letter. She saw Emelda's fruit hat on a peg, heard her working in the bathroom.

"Fearless Dorie," Marcella cackled, "you're going to get in trouble one of these times. But you'll keep having your fun until it happens. And I'll keep losing front doors."

The new front door, paid for by the embassy, looked just like the old one.

"You're soaked. Do you want something dry to wear?"

Dorie shook her head, seeing the letter on the foyer table. Unopened.

"The natives are restless," Marcella said. "It seems they don't like to be saved. How much time do you think you have?"

"Time?" Dorie asked.

"Until Gilberto comes back. You must at least have enough time to change."

When Dorie emerged from the bedroom, wearing a dress of Marcella's that she once coveted, the letter was still on the table. *Tomás*, it read, in her disguised hand that looked like that of a criminal.

"You know, he searched the house for you." Marcella pointed to the white couch, pulled from the wall. "Yet another little girl who doesn't want to be saved." She extracted herself from her chair, made her way across the room to a round gilt mirror, and brought out a tube of lipstick.

"What about that case in the highlands?" Dorie asked. "Did they ever find that little girl?" She hated that little girl now, wanted her to stay dead. That distant court date could buy her time to figure out what she wanted.

Marcella traced a lopsided heart over the pale flesh of her mouth. The clattering down the hall continued. "A fucking hair clog," Marcella said. "How hard can it be?"

"Is Tomás still working on that case?"

"No," she said, finding Dorie's eyes in the mirror. "There's no case anymore. Fruit dropped it."

"Why?"

She shrugged, began powdering her neck. "Because it was too much trouble," she said, patting. "Because they discovered something they didn't like. Because the land is cursed by Indians. Because none of this is going to matter in a month, anyway. Who the hell knows why, Dorie? Fruit is not an open book."

"But Tomás must know."

"Must know what?"

"What happened with the land, if the little girl came back to claim it."

"Oh yes, the girl's getting the land."

Yes, he had done it himself. He had found the little girl and convinced her to claim the land to expedite the Brazil plan. Dorie felt dizzy. "So she wasn't murdered?"

Marcella blinked at herself in the mirror and brought out her eyeliner. "Oh, *that* little girl? A respectable woman like yourself shouldn't be concerned with such ugly stories, Dorie," she said with mocking distaste, sharpening the tip with two efficient twists. "I can tell you what happened to her. She was gang-raped by Indians and killed, didn't you hear? It's what everyone wants to believe anyway."

"What do you mean? You said—"

"You're worse than the men, with your titillated concern."

"I'm not titillated. I am concerned."

"Lost little girls are never found, Dorie," she proclaimed, pulling her lower eyelid down. "They are always raped and they are never found."

In the bathroom, more clanging metal.

"You take all the effort to sneak out of the embassy and you come here?" Marcella spun around with a magnificent, painted expression. "Aren't there more important things you should be doing? Emelda!" Marcella screamed down the hall, and the clattering stopped. "That fucking clumsy girl. It's so simple, just straighten a coat hanger and snake it in. That's all. But I have to fucking do everything myself. You can't trust anyone in Guatemala. If you want it done, do it yourself." She breezed out for a brief moment. By the time she returned, the letter was in Dorie's bag.

"Are you still here?" Marcella turned back to the mirror as she fixed a feather in her hair. A quetzal feather, a hair pick exactly like Dorie's. "You better leave before your brown prince arrives."

Dorie wandered the rainy streets like a refugee in Marcella's blue dress. Though she stuck out, she felt the streets gave her perspective. The beggars and vendors who rushed her did so halfheartedly, their eyes somewhere else. Her misery, out here, did not seem so bad. Everyone shared the eaves to keep dry, making room for her.

Every other person held a battery-operated shortwave radio, which played marimba music, sermons, revolutionary news, or replays of Arbenz's speeches. No matter where she walked, she could not escape the clamor.

Filthy children tagged along, touching Dorie, watching her with pleading, crusty eyes. Not allowed to work in factories or plantations anymore, they prowled the streets, picking pockets or selling the things they picked from pockets. Of course, they did not go to the new schools. They had to eat, after all.

Dorie could not muster the anger to shoo these miserable souls away. So they just grew in number. She walked, the head of a miserable parade, wanting someone else to take control, wanting a car to fly around a corner, screech to a stop, and unload well-dressed Communists in her path. They'd put a hood over her head, and shuffle her in.

She headed in the direction of the embassy, because those were the only streets she knew. But she did not go home. Circling the borders of familiar territory, she kept walking. At one point, just a few blocks from the embassy, she noticed a little storefront church. Inside, safe from the rain, she saw Naomi teaching a literacy class. Thirty Indians, reciting the alphabet. Dorie hesitated, then kept on. Things were too far gone to explain, to ask for help or comfort.

An hour into her walk, she noticed the Nash Ambassador gliding behind at a distance, and once she saw it, she knew that she had been hearing it for a while. She picked up speed, considering the one option she had left. She would run, the car would pursue her, and she would throw herself under it. They were, after all, going the wrong way on the street. An accident. Maybe she wouldn't die. Maybe she would lose the baby, keep Tomás, Gilberto would be fired, and everything would work out.

She ran. Without looking back, she broke into a sprint along the side of the uneven road. Vendors parted, dogs scattered, the Indian children screamed and pointed, some raced behind, trying to keep up. She felt the car accelerate behind her now and tried to prepare herself for the sideways dive.

"Dorie! Dorie, hey!" Tomás called from across the street, waving her down.

Dorie ran faster, but she could see he would catch up with her. Not now, she could not face him now. With a defiant stomp, she stopped in her tracks, turned, and stared down the glaring, opaque windshield until the car proceeded to her side at a crawl. The children dispersed like smoke. She managed a smile—she could not make a fuss now—and let herself be picked up.

Dorie found herself sitting in the back between José and Gilberto. Once the door closed, Conroy accelerated, just as Tomás reached the car. His normally placid face pinched in rare annoyance, looking so Indian. How shocking, how hadn't she seen it before? He stared right through the tinted glass, finding her.

Dorie felt disgust at his gaze. His race so obvious now—why had she not known? Because he never gave anyone a hard look. Because of his nose, a decoy she had grown to love. It looked obscene to her now, a mashed idol of deceit and self-hatred, pressed to the glass. And then gone.

"Where are you going, Mrs. Ambassador?" Gilberto asked.

"Home," she said. "Take me home."

"That is a nice dress," Gilberto said. The most extravagant thing she had ever heard him say. José, on her right, grinned at Gilberto in a chummy way, approving of the joke. The illiterate soldier and educated secretary were now, supposedly, friends. A perverse alliance. Another Jim and Tomás. She hated them both.

The journey back to the embassy seemed much more menacing from the car. Political graffiti dominated the view: CERDO COMUNISTA, CERDO CAPITAL-ISTA. Each time they slowed, Indian children came running to look inside. Their dirty hands pressed to the windows. The children only acted so boldly with cars when some revolutionary milestone was afoot: a fiery radio speech or another reform passed by the legislature. Conroy beeped the horn.

"I know," Gilberto said slowly and deliberately, "I know you don't like me. I know you think I am ignorant. I know you think I am a savage, but that's just my job. That's why your husband hired me."

My God, Dorie thought, I've hurt his feelings. Conroy sped up. The hands pressed to the glass fell away, sarcastically waving goodbye.

"I did go to the American Training Center; where do you think I learned English? But I did not finish," Gilberto explained. "When I was there, the commander gave us puppies. We all had our own puppy that we took care of. I named my puppy Alvaro, he was black with white feet and a white belly. We trained our puppies to run with us and fetch supplies. Then, at the end of training, we were ordered to strangle our puppies with our hands."

His eyes, which had been frantic to keep up with the speeding landscape, settled on her. Dorie stared back. José snorted back phlegm and swallowed elaborately.

"I would not kill my puppy. Instead, I strangled the commander."

Dorie looked away. Marcella's wet dress clung to her. She could not stop shivering in the air-conditioning.

"I was not allowed to graduate, but the embassy hired me anyway because . . ." Gilberto strained his neck, pulled her gaze back up to him. "Because the puppy was training to kill men."

They pulled into the embassy lot. Gilberto leaned in to her and she leaned away with the turn, accidentally pressing up to José.

"Your husband, your friends, all strangled innocent puppies," Gilberto said. "They strangle puppies, they say, to practice to strangle men. But they never strangle men. They hire people like me to strangle the men for them. But they go on strangling puppies anyway, and think they are courageous for doing it. And I am the savage."

A moment later, Jim folded her in his arms, standing stiffly while he enveloped her. He cried, smiling at the same time, happy she had been found and brought home.

~~~~~

After Jim stationed Gilberto at the apartment door, Dorie's life became like a chess game in which she was at first slowly, then all of a sudden rapidly, losing her options. Reading anything worthwhile these days frustrated her for her lack of focus—*The Role of the West* stopped making sense long ago—while romances only depressed her. With nothing else to do, she clung to chores to pass the time. The apartment had never been so clean. But she could invite no one to see it, since Gilberto guarded the door. Every time she opened it, there he was, sitting with a composition notebook, practicing his letters. He'd only permit Jim into the apartment, and Emelda, who arrived to find everything already clean. Three days into Dorie's seclusion, however, she came to say goodbye.

"I walked all the way here from Marcella's house!" She limped into the apartment, then proudly showed Dorie the raised welts on her feet. "I did not fall!"

The heels did look painfully cheap, especially now with wear. Even so, Emelda's new life in Miami offered more promise than Dorie currently imagined for herself. But still, Emelda envied her. She could see it in the girl's hungry gaze, perpetually drinking in the apartment, Dorie's things, which she had learned to clean with obsessive care. The fact that someone still envied her lifted her spirits slightly.

There was nothing left for Emelda to clean, so Dorie invited her to sit.

"I wish I was going to Miami," Dorie halfway joked over wine. This time, Emelda drank with poise, without reservation. She sat elegantly in a chair, transformed in a matter of weeks by relentless practice. The fruit on her hat no longer quivered, but swayed with confidence.

"I won't be gone long," Emelda said. "I'll make my money, come back, and buy myself a house with *real* things. I'll have land and I'll build a house with floors and lights and couches. Closets filled with dresses and shoes! Will you come visit me in Xela?"

How much did Emelda think she would make as an illegal maid? She probably thought she'd get a minimum wage in America, since she got one in Guatemala. At least, that's what Dorie paid her. Dorie smiled sadly and said of course she would come visit. They would shop for these things together. She preferred Emelda to Marcella. Sipping wine, but not too much, chatting, laughing, like happier book club times. She was friends with an Indian, Dorie marveled to herself.

"Do you feel ready for your trip, Emelda? You aren't scared at all, are you?"

"Yesterday, I felt too afraid to walk to work. But then I realized it was just my shoes. I was not confident in the shoes. So Tomás told Gilberto to give me a ride. But not today. Today, I am ready!"

"You mean Jim told him. Gilberto works for Jim." Dorie wondered how long she remained unguarded yesterday. Whenever she thought to look, she always saw the shadow of his feet beneath the door.

Emelda tilted her head sharply, reminding her of Marcella. Of course, she had studied Marcella, had studied them both. "No. Gilberto works for Tomás."

"That's impossible, Emelda."

"He pays him, I've seen it. And yesterday, when Gilberto drove me, he stood there." She pointed to the door. "He stood there so Gilberto could leave. He's a very kind employer."

"Tomás? Tomás guarded my door?"

Sensing tension, Emelda evaded the question. Dorie watched her expressions, her gestures, and her talk regress into that of a maid. Simple, servile, confused. A minute later, when Gilberto knocked, letting them know the airport car had arrived, they did not embrace, though Dorie wanted to hug Emelda and tell her to be brave. Strangely, she saw in Emelda the same hesitation and pity, before she said the most unexpected thing.

"I will pray for you in Miami. If you tell me what you want, I'll pray you get it."

Emelda stood in the open door patiently, unwavering, as Dorie considered this strange offer. "Oh my, I've forgotten to pay you for the week!" She turned for her purse.

"No. Give it to *her*. I owe for my uniform, room and food, the glass I broke, taxes, emotional distress—"

Dorie pressed American dollars into her hand. "I'm not paying Marcella for your services, Emelda. You worked hard. You'll need this if you . . ." She didn't know how to finish the sentence under Gilberto's hard stare. She looked down to see his composition notebook on the floor, where he'd been practicing the alphabet. His letters over the past week had improved markedly.

~~~~~

Two days later, an airplane buzzed the city. From the apartment window, Dorie watched it make passes, lower and lower, over the government zone nearby. She did not fear the plane, she feared being a mother, a scandal. She feared Tomás arriving with a bag and two tickets to Brazil. She feared Gilberto stopping him at the door. She feared Tomás never arriving at all. Watching the plane circle, she began to wish it would come nearer. Just bomb the embassy, putting them all out of their misery.

After a few passes, the plane did drop something. Dorie saw very clearly, a bomb that exploded too soon into thousands of pieces. Elegantly swooping and swirling. Paper. Leaflets. One blew over the embassy wall, sailing on a wind over the barbed wire and cut glass. A sign, a message from God. Dorie was desperate enough now to seek signs from God. She phoned the offices below, ordered one of Jim's assistants to retrieve it.

The flyer gave a message in three languages, though none of those languages were hers.

"Dorie!" Jim arrived in the rumpled suit he'd been wearing for days. "I forgot to tell you we're having a party tonight. It's been so busy here, I completely forgot."

"A party? Where?"

"Here. At the apartment. I'm sorry I forgot to tell you, I thought I had."

She felt herself losing control, even of the few rooms she now inhabited. "What kind of party? Who's coming?"

"Oh, just the usual, with some additions," he said. Dorie cast a worried glance over her small, clean prison. "Don't worry, there's nothing to do. You're a pro at these things. The food's been ordered. I just need you to keep it warm when it arrives at five-thirty. I'd planned on a six p.m. start, but we're sort of dealing with a crisis here. I think seven p.m. now."

"Crisis? You mean the airplane?"

"Arbenz co-opted one of our newspaper stories. I have no idea how, but he ran it today in *El Patriota* a day before our story was supposed to run in *Prensa La Verdad*. But he changed it slightly, made it anti-capitalist."

"Instead of anti-Communist?" Dorie wanted to ask how a slight change could swing a story from one ideological extreme to the other, but it seemed unimportant. Everything Jim did seemed unimportant now. "I think you have much more to worry about than these newspaper stories, Jim. Did you see the airplane?"

"What airplane?"

"The one flying over the government zone an hour ago! It dropped these all over the city!" She handed him the flyer. "What does it say?"

He studied the words, holding the paper out at arm's length. "I don't know. Something about God. I'm not so good at reading Spanish."

"Doesn't this seem important? Can't we find out what it says?"

He promised her a translation, pocketing the flyer and fleeing for yet another emergency meeting.

For the past twenty-four hours, the embassy had been roiling over the latest development: something called *The Voice of Liberation*. A couple of young dissenters, on the run in the jungle and lugging their own radio equipment, had materialized out of nowhere. Twice a day, in the afternoon and the evening, they hijacked a radio frequency and took the opportunity to criticize Arbenz. Reporting news they claimed he kept out of the papers. It sounded a little ridiculous, these kids with a microphone. Dorie had tried to listen to the show, but it was all in Spanish and Quiché.

That evening, Dorie lay on the bed, sweaty and defeated by every cocktail dress she owned. When she stepped into them, they stuck at her hips. When she pulled them over her head, they caught at her breasts. Just as the first knock came at the front door, Dorie zipped up the only dress that fit: a white cotton frock, a bit too casual. She studied herself in the mirror, reminding herself of the truth of Jim's statement. This was an easy role to play. To be graceful, stunning, to make his colleagues jealous of him. For years, she drew pride from these performances, but not anymore. She hadn't enjoyed a Fruit party in years. And in this old, shapeless dress, she felt all confidence leaving her.

She must drink enough to be considered a good sport, while not drinking too much and burdening the fun. The margin of error being about one drink for Dorie. She'd made the mistake last year and argued with some Fruit suit who criticized the Communist push to expand voting rights.

"Why does everyone lump women and illiterates together in these arguments?" she'd challenged him. A grave blunder, according to Jim. "Of course, I know what you mean," he'd said. "But these Hispanics don't. Just let it slide."

Thirteen guests arrived over the next hour, half of whom she recognized but could not precisely place. Often, at times like this, Dorie felt her life in Guatemala was like a play with a small cast. The same people reappearing constantly in different roles.

By seven-thirty, Tomás had yet to arrive, but Dorie knew he would come. In dread and anticipation, she drank too much right away. She could not relax, forget him, or even guess how she'd react to his entrance. Emelda, she decided, had been confused about his relationship with Gilberto. More likely, borrowing Gilberto for small jobs was his way of eventually getting him out of the way.

"You're so tense, Dorie," Jim said, massaging her shoulders, leading her to a quiet corner of the kitchen. "What's going on? I thought a party would cheer you up."

"I'm fine, Jim. Really."

"No, you aren't. You're obsessing over scraps of paper that blow in from the street. You talked in your sleep last night, accusing me of riding a plow and strangling puppies. You just refilled my scotch with brandy."

"I just haven't been sleeping well. I'm sorry."

"No. I'm the one who should apologize. You're locked in this madhouse and it's not fair. I know I haven't been the most reasonable person lately, and that's affecting you. You're not yourself. I think you need a vacation."

"A vacation!" Her life of suspicion and phone taps suddenly replaced with parties and vacations? She glanced desperately around the hot, cramped party, wondering if she was going mad. "Where would I go?"

"Don't tell me you hate the idea of a vacation. You need some fun. I've already talked to Cortez and he's agreed to have you at his villa."

"Of course, a vacation would be nice, but the villa? It's surrounded by Communists now. Poor Cortez is in no position to be entertaining guests."

Jim waved a hand. "Cortez will be fine. He can't compete with Brazil, so he may as well let the Indians have a go at it and fail. Let them pay a minimum wage to their workers, let them deal with the union. It'll serve them right, thinking they can just jump into a global market and succeed because Arbenz told them they can."

"Will Gilberto be coming to Xela?" She felt drunk, disoriented, and unable to fight this strange turn of events.

"No, Dorie. I need him here. Cortez will look after you, he knows what to do. And Marcella's going, too. You won't be alone. When did you start calling it Xela?"

By eight-thirty, their priest, Father Guiar, made his entrance, with Hernando from *Prensa La Verdad*. A few Fruit suits arrived, accompanied by Spanish-speaking wives with flimsy bright dresses and shallow faces. Gilberto and José arrived together.

Tomás's appearance took Dorie completely by surprise, though she had been waiting for it for hours. Alone, buttoned up, and with a gentle smile, he stepped in the middle of the room the moment Dorie turned around from chiseling ice. He moved calmly, sure of himself, looking Hispanic. No hint of the thickly laid scars across his back. His nose, a ruin of jammed bone, looked almost charming again. Dorie could imagine him smashing it, then pinching it into its current, tortured shape, trying to attain a bridge.

She fled to the kitchen.

The party eventually settled into factions. The media men spoke seriously among themselves, while the English-speaking suits stood together quietly watching the Fruit men grow drunk. The Fruit women sipped their drinks gracefully, acknowledging Dorie with polite smiles of indifference as she circled to refill their glasses. When she returned to the main room, Dorie saw Tomás again. She moved toward him instinctively, so quickly she bumped into Marcella, tipping her red wine onto the floor.

"Tomás, you haven't been to see me," she scolded, feeling small and unkempt. She hurried to an empty corner of the room, away from Marcella and the Fruit women. He followed her casually, a few steps behind.

"And you ran away from me in the street. I saw you, you saw me. Why the hell would I come see you? Especially with Gilberto outside the door."

The excuses lined up, she had so many. "Gilberto was following me in the car. You had no idea and you may have kissed me or something. I panicked."

"You've never let Gilberto stop you before." He regarded her closely, unconvinced.

"I can't run like I used to, Tomás. I couldn't even get into my favorite dress tonight!"

"I'm sorry," he said.

"I don't care about the fucking dress," she snapped. "I care about you!" She was off-track already. How could he believe her if she spoke as if she hated him?

She touched his wrist. She didn't care if anyone saw, because no one's opinion mattered but hers. The revelation hit her. Jim had been right. Yes, creative thinking solved everything. For she had never considered the possibility that his Indian heritage didn't matter. She loved him. And she hated all these people, anyway. Why should she care that they ostracize her?

He reciprocated dangerously, twining his fingers in hers. "Then why don't you want to have my child, Dorie?" He said this as if he knew exactly why. His black eyes shining with pain. "I know you're having doubts. I can tell by the way you looked at me when I got here, and in the street. You should have seen your face."

"Because you're treating me like some knocked-up maid." She made an attempt to stack some dirty dishes, to dispel any attention they may have attracted. "I've lost confidence. I hate the fact that I have to sit around and wait for you to wrap up things at work. I can't have this baby on my own—"

"I don't believe that, Dorie. I believe even if I jumped on a plane tomorrow and disappeared forever, you'd be fine. You're not some weak woman who needs me to tell you what to do." His passivity, his opinion of her, were robbing her of her anger. She would prefer it if he made a scene, slapped her.

"I am!" she cried, wanting to collapse in a loud display of tears and breaking dishes.

"You're not," Tomás scolded, with a careful glance around the room. "You've held your own against Gilberto. Everyone's afraid of what you'll try to pull next. They have Conroy watching the window, to make sure you don't climb out with a rope."

"I heard your land dispute was dropped."

"No, Dorie, it hasn't been dropped. Where did you get that idea?" He sipped his drink, his eyes darting to Marcella across the room. "But it's getting very interesting, this case," he continued. "I think I found that little girl. In Totonicapán—"

"I don't care about the fucking little girl!" Dorie hissed. "I care about me!"

"You don't mean that, Dorie. What a terrible thing to say!" He regarded her, disappointed in her lack of empathy for a missing little girl.

A scuffle broke out in the middle of the room, where José and Gilberto bore down on one of the media men. Everyone turned, drawn by the swift movement.

"*The man runs over the woman with the plow, you commie prick,*" José said, loud enough for the room to hear. Everything became quiet as Gilberto backed the man up against the buffet, grinning.

"I'm sorry," the man managed, his hand going into the spinach dip.

"Don't be sorry," José continued. "Run a retraction. Sorry is fucking useless."

Dorie turned back to Tomás, expecting him to intervene, but he'd disappeared, replaced by Jim. At the buffet, the dishes clattered as the accosted man stumbled.

"Jim, aren't you going to do something?"

Jim smiled at Dorie, as he had been smiling all night. A big, ruthless, constant grin. "About what?"

"Gilberto and José! Who do they think they are? I don't want them in my house, starting fights! They've ruined the spinach dip."

Jim sipped his drink, enjoying the scene. "I think they have journalistic ambitions. This is freedom of the press at its finest, Dorie. Newspapers are a merciless business. Who am I to interfere?"

By nine, the drunken crush of the apartment allowed her to escape unnoticed for some air. All that remained of the day was a scarlet cut in the clouds, quickly draining behind the mountains. The city had lost its color, lay simplified in cold shades of blue. Vendors gone, shops closed, one maid passed in her ghostly white uniform. Dorie slipped past the guard station as Conroy admitted a late guest.

The side streets were completely dark, the main thoroughfares losing shape quickly. Dorie hurried, trying to find a safe place to compose herself. Her intoxication compelled her a few blocks farther than she should have gone. After a few wrong turns, she found her destination: an open storefront made of corrugated tin. She walked inside, drawn to the light, the music, the large wooden cross nailed to the back wall.

Naomi was inside. Her little church staved off the night with one swinging light and a battery-operated radio. A handful of Indian women and children worked at tables. There, they painted decorative animal masks, while Naomi hung them up to dry on the walls and from the cross.

"Mrs. Ambassador! What a surprise! How are you?" she asked, and Dorie thought she spied an involuntary glance at her stomach.

No one had asked Dorie how she was in quite a while—Jim asked, instead, what was wrong. And Tomás asked no questions at all. So Dorie shocked herself by answering, "Pregnant. Drunk. Exhausted." The release almost brought her to her knees. She began to cry.

Knowing enough not to ask anything more, Naomi helped her to a chair, clearing it for her to sit. Dorie recognized the stacked notebooks there. They had the same color and pattern as the one Gilberto bent over all day, every day now. She opened one, then another and another. Names. People practicing their names a hundred times in childish handwriting. Seeing these names, for some reason, brought more tears to her eyes.

"I just thought I'd finally drop in and see your church." Dorie smiled in an attempt to lighten her mood. A girl with a clubfoot and a vaccination bandage on her arm teetered across the room. She handed Naomi a painted antler, then grabbed another, unpainted one from a box.

"We're pulling an all-nighter," Naomi explained. "I'm being kicked out of the country, I have to leave tomorrow. So they're trying to paint all the blanks. They can sell them without me." Naomi dropped two wet masks on the table in front of her and stared down at them as if she had no idea what they were.

"Why do you have to leave, Naomi?" Though their friendship had barely begun, though no one could help her now, Dorie felt abandoned. Naomi was the only person she knew outside of her vicious little circle. The only person Dorie could imagine accepting her love of an Indian.

"They're kicking all the missionaries out. Haven't you heard?"

"I thought you were helping with their literacy program. Why would the—" She stopped herself from saying Communists. "Why would they kick you out if you were helping?" The Indians rebelling against Arbenz, then Arbenz kicking out his allies. She felt a parallel to her own nonsensical struggle with Tomás. They both wanted the same thing. Why was happiness so hard, then?

"They don't trust religion." Naomi scraped beneath her fingernails, which were stained green. "And I guess I don't blame them. Baptist, Catholic, Hindu—it's all the same to them. It's all smoke and mirrors to justify poverty."

"You feel like you haven't helped people down here?" Dorie asked meaningfully.

Naomi laughed. "No. I realize there's much more to the situation than teaching the poor to read and sell crafts. Paranoia is stronger than progress."

"Paranoia?"

"People get some food, a bit of land, security, and they become absolutely paranoid of the harm it will do them later. They know things will get worse, that Arbenz won't last forever and another Ubico will take over. It's the cycle down here. When another dictator takes over, they'll be implicated by the land they got, by what union they joined. So they begin to distance themselves. One minute they love Arbenz, but the moment the Catholics and the Americans start a buzz, they become terrified and jump ship. It's all self-fulfilling."

"What kind of buzz?" she asked. "What made them afraid?"

"Father Guiar gave a sermon on the evils of knowledge and the next day a hundred people dropped out of the literacy program. You'll notice they never teach the New Testament." Naomi put a few dried masks in the box. "I agree it's best we all go. Maybe, with fewer foreigners meddling, the people will finally relax and welcome their revolution without fear."

"I'm sorry you'll be going," Dorie said, meaning it. She had never met anyone who spoke about Guatemala like this. She'd never met anyone who was willing to change their mind about what they thought this country needed. "Will you be back?"

"Oh, who knows? Maybe," she mused, smiling. "It's the lovely thing about being saved. You make mistakes, but you can always be reborn into something better than before. It's lovely," and this time she said lovely she seemed to mean it more than the last. She lost eye contact with Dorie, turned two masks over in her hands—a jaguar and a deer. "To just start over. Over and over. Until you get it right."

"It really works that way?"

"Oh yes. Just ask your maid."

"Emelda? She's been here?"

"Many times. After our lunch together, she said she liked what I said about having a fresh start. She came here to find me and I taught her how to pray. The girl had no idea that speaking to, asking things of God was even possible."

The radio static jumped in the background, the music cut off by a girl's voice.

"Have you heard *The Voice of Liberation* yet?" Naomi asked with a frown. The weary missionary limped toward the radio to hear more clearly, then translated the Quiché for Dorie: "*It's a new day for Guatemala. The Communists are afraid, Jacobo Arbenz is afraid for you to hear the truth. The Indians have dignity, they are God-fearing, they believe in the respectability of hard work and morals. Thousands are marching all over the country. They are through being babied, being treated like helpless children. We don't want your land, Jacobo Arbenz! Resign or the people will rise up and throw you out!*"

Twenty minutes later, Dorie slipped back into her own party, where no one had noticed her absence.

Driving Tomás and Marcella home late that night, Dorie never thought the air of Guatemala City could be so clean. Jim drove Jenks's car, with the windows down. The men in the front, the women in the back. Marcella reached for Dorie's hand, then her leg.

"Armando, now, that's a strong name!" Jim proclaimed.

"No, no," Tomás said. "Too strong, not subtle enough. Juan is much better."

"What're you talking about?" Dorie demanded to know. She felt so far away from everything in the backseat, even from herself, making her paranoid.

"We're naming the characters in Jim's next newspaper story."

"Are we being followed?" Jim searched the rearview. "That car's been behind us for a while."

"I don't think so," Tomás reassured him.

Marcella's fingers made small raking motions on Dorie's thigh, right under the hem of her dress. Her eyes, hidden by her hat, betrayed nothing. "You look just like a little maid in that dress," she said. "You want to be my maid? I can't find anyone . . . that Emelda girl owes me money." Then she fell asleep.

Dorie did not believe anything Marcella said regarding Tomás. Of course the land dispute hadn't been dropped. Unhinged by grief and liquor, she invented the most bizarre stories to maintain the mysterious, pathetic scraps of her life.

"Dorie, I forgot to tell you, Tomás translated your note from the sky!" Dorie had forgotten about the leaflet from the plane, though she had considered it very important for a few hours. "It says, 'Resistance is futile. Submit to the will of God.'"

"What an odd message."

"It's from the grassroots opposition, calling on Arbenz to resign. And there's a Bible verse. Which is my favorite part. Something from Jeremiah." Jim fished through his inner coat pockets and gave the flyer to Tomás.

"*They misled you and overcame you,*" Tomás read, "*those trusted friends of yours. Your feet are sunk in the mud; your friends have deserted you.*"

"Grassroots?" Dorie asked. "How do a bunch of peasants get aircraft?" Headlights appeared again behind them, close, illuminating the cab. "*The Voice of Liberation* delivered an ultimatum tonight."

"When did you listen to that, Dorie?"

"During the party. Hernando came into the hallway with me, to listen and translate."

They dropped off Tomás and Marcella without incident. Dorie was tired, so tired. As they drove home, she turned to watch her own face in the side mirror, translucent and strange, caught in the headlights of a car behind. But then it turned away.

"Is it *The Voice of Liberation*? Did something on that show scare you, Dorie?"

"Of course, everyone's on edge."

"She's something, isn't she?"

"Who?"

"María, the *Voice of Liberation* girl. The anger in that sweet voice just gets everyone going. Everyone loves her, there's no way to discredit her. Arbenz must be going crazy over it. You can just see her, can't you, when she speaks?"

"Yes, actually, I can."

"What do you think she looks like?"

"I see a girl in man's pants and boots, standing up in the jungle and yelling into a microphone. A square jaw, those big black eyes. A real Indian."

"That's exactly what I see!" Jim laughed, slapping the steering wheel. "A real revolutionary leader! A Joan of Arc! Who needs my newspaper stories when you have her? She's *real*."

As Jim drove back through the commercial zones, Dorie closed her eyes. The night had been so bizarre. She relived it, then began dreaming it. She woke up, on the verge of identifying the source of her troubles, something much bigger than a love affair and a baby. Seeing flashlights and reflective tape, she realized they were at a police checkpoint. Usually the guards waved them through after noting their diplomatic plates. But now Jim had come to a complete stop at a metal bar blocking their way.

"What the fuck?" He leaned out the window to speak to a policeman in a jaunty cap, bent down to look inside. "Can't you see the plates?" Jim said. "I'm the American ambassador."

"Please, no," the policeman commanded. He tapped his flashlight lightly just inside the open window.

"What does he want?" Dorie peered out her window to see at least ten other policemen. Hulking, armed shadows.

"Listen," Jim snapped, his patience already lost with the small intrusion of the flashlight. "I'm the American ambassador. To search this car is to violate U.S. territory."

The policeman opened the driver's-side door with the ceremony of a chauffeur. "Please, wait here." With his flashlight, he illuminated a patch of grass that glistened with broken glass. "One minute, please."

Jim did not move. "I repeat, I am the American ambassador, this car is a territory of the United States."

"Jim, just get out," Dorie said, making out more soldiers and guns behind them. At that moment, the latch on Dorie's door released with a pop that gave her a start, for the only noise she had been expecting was that of a gun. Another shadow beckoned for Dorie to step out of the car and she did so, too stunned to resist.

"That's my wife! She's American property, too. Don't touch her!"

"Shut up, Jim."

Dorie hoped that her evacuation from the car would compel Jim to follow, out of some instinct to protect her. To resist would make things worse, she believed. Jim, used to automatic deference, could not be trusted in this situation.

"Dorie, what are you doing?" Jim shouldered past the officer to confront her in the high beams of the car. In the concentrated spotlight, he looked maniacal, every stray hair illuminated, his skin pale and eyes tightened like a cave creature.

"It's just a checkpoint, Jim. We see people go through these all the time—"

"Not us!" He turned to the two officers. "I'm the American—"

"Yes, American ambassador," one of them cut in. "Please, come here."

Dorie obeyed, and Jim followed helplessly. "Dorie, stop it."

One man stood between them and the car, while four others searched the cab.

"That's American property!" A broken record, Jim remained stuck to the only line he knew. The only line he'd ever needed with anyone until now.

"No," their guard corrected him. "We borrow it. Guatemalan property right now, but we give you this." He circled his flashlight beam around their feet. "This is American property. We don't bother you there." He made a point of stepping away from their circle of grass. "You are safe in America, don't worry. Just don't step out of America!" He laughed, swept his flashlight across the landscape in a way that made nothing clear. Dorie watched one of the men unfold the wadded paper with the Bible verse on it and stare at the letters before folding it into his pocket.

"Okay, now please come into Guatemala."

Neither of them moved. As if they truly inhabited a sphere of international protection there on the side of the road. The officers placed their belongings back into the Nash with disturbing care.

"If you do not come into Guatemala," the man said, no longer joking, "I will be forced to invade your country. Please do not make me break the law."

Dorie stepped toward the car. Jim followed without a word.

"Now, please." He approached Jim with his hands in front of him, then those hands patted Jim's suit coat. He reached tenderly into the coat and pulled out the gun.

"I see you carry your wife's gun for her." He held it up so the other officers could laugh at its size. "That is very manly of you, very nice." He turned to Dorie, his face a mess of smile and shadow. "This is your gun? For your protection?"

Dorie nodded.

"Good. Guatemala can be dangerous for a lady. But still, it is a nice country. I hope you enjoyed your visit." He handed the gun to Dorie, who had no idea how to accept it. She had never held a gun before and was surprised at how light and easy it felt in one hand.

"Yes, thank you for visiting Guatemala." The officer stepped aside to allow them into the car. "I hope being here a few minutes wasn't an inconvenience. You can return to the United States now. A very clean car. Very nice."

The ride home passed in silence, with Jim enraged and Dorie relieved at their luck. Nothing had happened. They had passed through a checkpoint just like anyone else in Guatemala. Like Tomás, Marcella, Emelda, like everyone at their party. Jim made things so much worse insisting that they were special somehow. And she understood, suddenly, that life with Tomás would be so much easier. Nothing to fear at all.

~~~~~

The train to Xela did not have a first-class option. Indians, Mestizos, and Hispanics stood tangled in the aisles. Seated passengers only accounted for a third of the people packed into the car. Dorie and Marcella sat with their luggage stacked around them like a fortress, with Cortez perched behind them.

Despite the nausea, the inconvenience of Cortez, and the smell, Dorie felt elated as their train picked up speed. But she knew it wouldn't last. Over the course of the next five hours, their train would slow and even idle several times to give United Fruit trains the right-of-way. She wanted to go fast, to increase the feeling of freedom overtaking her. For she was happy with her decision to love Tomás. He, more than anyone, must know that a dark child could ruin him. He had much more to lose than Dorie—his job, his connections. But still, he wanted it. Why? Because he loved her. She no longer cared what anyone thought—in Guatemala or Brazil.

Once she got home, she would tell Jim about her pregnancy, and that would buy her some time. Maybe even some time after the birth. He was deluded enough to believe it. She thought of Emelda and felt better. It was always Indians with white traits she saw, hardly ever the other way around.

They could be in Brazil by the end of the month. The peasants would fight for her. Over the past few days, the impossible had turned inevitable. *The Voice of Liberation* reported marches all over the country, demanding that Arbenz resign. In response, Arbenz announced a widespread military sweep through the mountain jungles to bring the rogue broadcasters to justice.

"He calls them foreign agents," Marcella scoffed. "But half their broadcasts are in Quiché! Of course, they can't just admit this is censorship."

Just as Naomi predicted, the Indians were quickly turning against Arbenz. From there, everything began to fall into place for Dorie. Like God waving His hands over the capital, orchestrating events solely for her benefit. If Arbenz resigned, the land reform would be repealed, and Tomás would no longer be needed for the Fruit land disputes. An easy transfer to Brazil. Dorie even convinced herself that Marcella would be thankful for the loss of Tomás. The temporary injury to her pride would be more humane than forcing her to inhabit a marriage she believed unnatural.

The train came to the briefest stop. A minute later, soldiers, about ten soldiers, came through the front door of their compartment, making the car go quiet. Indian women went wide-eyed with panic, their men shrank back from the aisle.

"Jesus," Marcella whispered. "It's the Communist brigade."

The soldiers shouldered through in an orderly manner, then exited through the back. Not looking for people, but for seats. To Marcella and Dorie's disbelief, two stopped in front of their luggage fortress, surveyed it briefly, before squeezing by and sitting directly across. Two Indians, now facing them. They wore the same green uniform that Gilberto had only recently been persuaded to discard. These soldiers were going to the highlands to hunt down *The Voice of Liberation*. Everyone on the train knew it.

Marcella restacked their bags into a higher wall, then reached into one. "Here, Dorie, I brought a book club read for us." She handed over a thick volume with a simple title, *Brazil*, in flaking gold letters.

Accepting it in her hands, Dorie managed a thank-you. Why did every damned thing that happened to her seem so significant all of a sudden? "In English? Where did you find this, Marcella?"

"Oh, we've had it for ages around the house. I picked it up last week and finished it already. I'm sorry to report, it's boring as hell."

The flowering vines of Cortez's villa appeared to be either holding the whole building up, or tearing it down. Tender green fingers clutched the windows, climbed the decayed stucco. More problematic, the thick hardwood vines pried up the shutters, the roof tiles, destroying and fortifying with the inexhaustible vigor known only to nature.

Inside, everything gave the impression of being slightly damp—the wallpaper, the rugs, the curtains. The magnificent carved furniture gleamed with recent oiling, though the upholstery had all faded into the same tired pinkish hue. A painting of some porcelain-skinned ancestor surveyed the fate of his fortunes with resignation.

The *Voice of Liberation* signal was strong, rare for any radio station in the highlands, Cortez said. "They must be really close."

The soldiers had filed off the train, then piled onto idling army trucks at Xela's station. Gone in less than five minutes, into the forests. In their wake, the town shut itself up, shops closed, children scooped from the street, as if there had been an invasion.

Cortez's old woman cook appeared in the room, a character almost not to be believed. She did not wear an Indian costume but fine Western clothes a bit too tight, too young, and too long for her, making Dorie think Cortez had dressed her from apparel left in the house by his fleeing forebears. She sat with the radio an inch from her ear. Cortez did not sit. He walked about, fussing with books that crumbled at his touch and gazing distractedly out the window at his land, which no longer belonged to him.

Since this broadcast was in Quiché, the cook began to translate the show into Spanish, with a high, troubling wail that not even Marcella could understand.

"They just apologized for signing off so abruptly last night," Cortez translated for the women, peering through the vines. "They had been detected and had to flee. But now they're safe and settled somewhere else."

Dorie had been slightly skeptical of these broadcasts at first, but Arbenz's outsized reaction seemed to confirm their veracity. He'd never cracked down on the press before, not after Jim's fictitious newspaper stories or Guatemala Radio's incendiary reporting. Nothing more than a fine. So something big had to be happening throughout the country to cause him to send the military out.

"They're doing the news now, they say the news you won't hear anywhere else, because Arbenz is controlling the media." He paused, listened. "Thousands of Indians marched in the capital demanding Arbenz's resignation."

And there it was. "Today?" asked Dorie. "They did today? And to think we just missed it! Just!" She threw herself back on the sofa, sending up a cloud of dust. Of course, in response to mass protests, Arbenz had declared the military sweep. That seemed proportional, that made sense. Why would he send thousands of troops out after a radio show?

"They're interviewing a cabinet member now, who wishes to remain anonymous." Cortez, flustered at the dynamic change, struggled as this cabinet member spoke in Spanish, followed by the girl María translating for the Indian listeners. The man spoke, Cortez tried to translate, but then María's Quiché muddled him. All made worse by Cortez's cook echoing a few beats behind, translating María's translation back into the original Spanish, but with that wailing accent no one could understand but Cortez.

"He's resigned, along with other cabinet members, with more to resign and abandon the sinking ship of Arbenz's Communist regime. His reason for resigning, he says, is . . ." He paused. The women leaned forward. "Corruption! Arbenz expropriated land from a neighbor to build a swimming pool. It's part of his master plan."

"Master plan?" Marcella asked. "His master plan is to have a swimming pool?"

Cortez waited for the words to filter back to him through the cook. "No, no. That's not his master plan. The swimming pool was corruption. His master plan is Soviet control! He's slowly spreading the military through the countryside. Soon all opposition will be repressed, freedom of the press suspended, martial law declared, and the Russians will be running the country."

Marcella, during the interview, stood up and crossed the room to be closer to the radio. She listened to this cabinet member with a peculiar look on her face, her arms crossed over her chest.

"Do you know him?" Dorie asked. "Do you recognize his voice?"

"Yes," was all she said. She returned to the sofa, smiling, and said nothing more for the rest of the broadcast.

After the show finished, the party settled in the dining room for drinks and a game of gin rummy. Cortez favored the thick, spiced egg liquor that the Indians made and poured sizable portions for everyone. They drank to the courage of María and Manuel, miraculously spared for another day. Cortez dealt the cards with trembling fingers. He generously laid down runs and tricks the women could play off of, while doing his best not to win.

"It's no fun this way, Cortez," Marcella scolded him. "Let's make it interesting with a bet. I want your cook. Is she in the union?"

The egg liquor was strong, even for Marcella. The night progressed cheerily enough, with Cortez wielding one of his ancestor's swords, staging a mock attack on his shadow against the wall. He did his best to control it, but during one of the more dramatic moments, had smashed a wooden tea cart. Soon after, the evening took a turn. He fell to lamenting the old days, when God and property meant something. The women had left him caressing the sword, asleep.

The drink had the opposite effect on Dorie, making her giddy with the possibilities of her new life with Tomás. She even decided on the subject she'd study in Brazil. She'd always fallen back on literature, but falling back would be no way to start anew. No, she would study archaeology. The decision had come to her that night, in bed, while reading the book on Brazil. Whole civilizations, swallowed by the jungle. Societies with temples raised to nothing, completely alien moral codes. Human sacrifice, animal gods. Nothing about her situation seemed scandalous in comparison. All the obstacles she anticipated fell away, became nothing more than constructs of a failing society.

She dreamed that Guatemala City had vanished just as completely as those jungle cities, obliterated by Agua and Fuego. A plague of fire and water, erasing all evidence of her unhappiness.

~~~~~

The sound of grinding gears woke her in the morning. Dorie went to the window. A red truck full of Communists turned in front of the villa and made its way toward the coffee fields.

Cortez drove to Xela late that morning and brought back three newspapers. One copy of *Prensa La Verdad*, one of *El Diario* from two days before, and one copy of the latest *El Patriota*, a notorious echo chamber for Arbenz. *Prensa's* front page featured a grainy picture of peasants somewhere in the south, rallying themselves with guns. *El Diario* showed similar photos of men, quoted as saying things like, "Communist land is temporary land," and "Ownership is the basis for laws."

El Patriota offered a completely different account of the state of the nation. Three presidential decrees dominated the front page. The first being that Arbenz's cabinet was stable and no one had resigned. The military, also, remained sound. No generals had defected. The third decree insisted that there was no unrest in Guatemala, that a few media outlets had been "hijacked" by a "foreign party," and because of this, the state had no choice but to suspend freedom of the press in the interest of national security. Any lingering doubts Dorie had about the uprising dissolved with this decree. Freedom of the press, one of Arbenz's most beloved accomplishments, tossed aside. Cortez read on. *El Patriota*, however, would remain in print, to keep the nation informed. Arbenz hoped to soon reinstate the radio stations and printing presses.

"Oh my God," Cortez cried. "At last it has come to this. We are living under Stalin. No one can deny it now." He walked to his radio, turned the dial through all the frequencies, to find various tones of static and marimba music. Guatemala Radio had been reduced to an especially jovial song, with trumpets and maracas as well.

"Jenks must be in a state," Dorie said. "He's either roaring around the embassy or passed out in the hall. We got out of there just in time."

Flipping through *Prensa La Verdad*, Dorie found an article with an old-fashioned picture of a little white girl. *¡Muerta!* the headline read.

"What's this?"

Cortez read the story with nervous fingers. "Oh, this isn't very pleasant. Not at all." He folded the newspaper and put it behind his back. "Not vacation reading at all."

"Cortez, what does it say?"

"Just another terrible story. About a little girl who was supposed to be murdered around here in 1902. A long time ago, Dorie. Nothing to be afraid of."

"The girl who was murdered with her family?" Dorie lunged and grabbed the paper back. Cortez, unused to women, could not resist.

"Supposed to be, but this says she wasn't. This story says they just found out that she's still alive, that she wasn't killed in 1902."

"Alive!" Dorie knew it. She knew then Tomás had succeeded, though it didn't quite matter anymore. She studied the blurred image. The little girl with the white shoes that Tomás had so coveted. *Evie Crowder*, the caption read.

"Well, she was alive." Cortez sighed, shaking his head.

"What do you mean?"

"Well, she was alive, but they found out she was alive because they've just now found her dead. Communists found her in her home in Totonicapán and murdered her because she was going to claim their communal land." He took the paper back. *"An old lady,"* he read, *"hacked into pieces for inheriting land from her family."*

Dorie took back the paper and studied the story, published in the human-interest section, where Jim usually placed his articles. It sounded like one of his bullshit stories. Especially that last line.

"Cortez, you have family in Brazil, don't you?" she asked over coffee in the sitting room before lunch. Marcella had yet to emerge from her bedroom and, Dorie assumed, her egg liquor hangover.

"Yes, of course. They moved most of the coffee operation there, leaving Guatemala to me."

"So you've been there? Do they have universities?"

"Oh yes."

She raised her coffee cup to her lips, but Cortez moved in and snatched it away.

"Sorry, sorry!" He shot up from his chair. "I just realized I forgot to tell the cook to boil it twice. Jim made me promise to boil everything twice for you." In a moment, he retreated to the kitchen and returned. "It'll be just a moment."

"Jim said that? Why? I've never boiled twice at home."

"Of course, not before. But now that you two are trying for a baby—"

"Jim said that?" She pushed back from the table, chair legs screeching.

Cortez's face melted in horror. "I'm sorry. I'm so sorry. I didn't mean to embarrass you. I thought . . ." But he failed to articulate what he thought.

Dorie breathed deeply, her hands gripping the edge of the table. Cortez, across from her, looked as if he might suffer a heart attack. "No, I'm sorry. It's not your fault what Jim says. It's just that we're not trying for a baby."

"You're not," he echoed, unmoving.

"No. I'm leaving him, Cortez." It felt incredible to say out loud. "I'm leaving Jim and he has no idea." She felt so good, so safe. She knew Cortez would never repeat this to anyone. She could see that he was trying already to forget it for his own sake. He began chugging around the room, vibrating with coffee and fear.

"Why are you so afraid of Jim?" she asked.

"Aren't *you* afraid of him?"

"No. I used to think I was, but then I realized I was just afraid of the unknown. Of starting over without his sphere of influence." She'd never met any woman she admired who moved through the world without this safety net, until she'd met Naomi.

"But the sphere is everything!" Cortez spun around with crazed eyes. "Without the sphere, we're just bugs struggling in the dirt! We're no different from them out there!" He thrust a hand in the direction of the window, the Communists.

This image chilled her, forced her to picture life in the Brazilian jungle, kneeling in the dirt after some failed civilization. Because she'd been cast out from her own. "What do you think Jim will do for you if I go back and say I had a lovely vacation? What do you think he's capable of, Cortez?"

"*Are* you having a lovely vacation?"

"Yes," she reassured him. "And I will make sure Jim knows."

With this, Cortez turned back to the window, she thought to think of an answer to her question. But then his shoulders shook despite his best efforts. He was crying.

"Arbenz has suspended the freedom of the press, so we, The Voice of Liberation, *are the first and only source to now report that civil war has broken out in Guatemala. The rebel Castillo Armas, with an army of thousands, has invaded from Honduras. This morning, in San Pedro, peasants greeted his army with a parade. There, the locals have joined his march for the capital, increasing his numbers. He and his army have demanded that Jacobo Arbenz resign, and if he does not, they will take the capital by force!"*

Cortez clapped, jumped from foot to foot as he translated the Spanish broadcast. *"Pan y patria,"* he chanted with the radio voices. *"Pan y patria."*

"What's *pan y patria*?" Dorie asked.

"It's bread!" Cortez beamed. "Bread and country! The battle cry of the counterrevolution!"

The cook brought back telegrams from town, one for Marcella and two for Dorie. She opened Tomás's first, anxious for a response to the one she'd sent him the moment they arrived in Xela: *Te amo.* And now she opened his reply:

Guatemala will be the new Brazil.

Dorie stared at the words, wondering what they could mean. Next to her, Marcella ripped her telegram in half and threw it into the cold fireplace.

"A love letter. From Tomás." She sighed, placing her fingertips on her throbbing temple. "It's damned ridiculous. I know he's not there, that he's having all his messages forwarded to and answered by Jim. But he thinks I'm an idiot."

Dorie crumpled her message in her trembling fist. "If he's not in the city, where is he?"

"Miami," Marcella said. "I saw his plane ticket."

Cortez nodded. "I dropped him off at the airport before picking up you two."

Why the hell would Tomás be in Miami, with all the developments in Guatemala over the past week? And if he was there, why would he pretend not to be? Jim could not have written that telegram. Of course, Marcella was lying. She often did now, for no apparent reason. But Cortez? Could Dorie not believe anything anyone said anymore?

There was nothing to do, Jim insisted to Dorie via the second telegram, but for the party to relax, to stay in the villa until this all died down. But Dorie found relaxing impossible, with *The Voice of Liberation* playing all day, relaying stories of uprisings throughout the country that Cortez insisted on translating. Over the course of the day, anxiety gnawed away at all her hopes. She began to suspect that even if everything happened in their favor, Tomás would still come up with some excuse for not eloping. He'd lied to his lover, his wife, and his best friend. Considering this, the idea that he'd snuck off to Miami without telling her became quite plausible. In the middle of the night, Dorie slipped downstairs and retrieved Marcella's note from Tomás, or Jim pretending to be Tomás, from the fireplace: *My love, my white bird*, it read, *to lose you would be to lose life itself.*

Something she could not imagine either Jim or Tomás putting to paper.

~~~~~

According to *The Voice of Liberation*, the rebels were a day and a half away from the Presidential Palace. As Marcella and Cortez cheered the news of their army's progress, Dorie sat immobile, thinking how heartless she had been toward Jim. He had been nothing but kind and protective of her, and she had repaid him with deception. He would never deceive her. While Tomás took secret trips, orchestrating fake messages to hide his where-abouts, his lies about his family, his heritage, his work. Everything in this life, he said so himself, attained through deception.

And poor Jim, receiving love letters from her, intended for Tomás. If he hadn't figured it out before, he certainly knew now. She envisioned a mob of armed Indians descending on the embassy. The fact that the United States had been against Arbenz the whole time probably didn't matter much in a scene of mass hysteria. He'd die, thinking she didn't love him. She did. She loved his smile, his blind confidence, his insistence that he could shape history down here.

~~~~~

She awoke on the day the rebels would be arriving in the city and spent a half hour in the bathroom vomiting. When she finished, she discovered Marcella blocking the hallway, waiting for her. The Communists' truck in the fields groaned up a hill. They both listened a moment, watching each other.

"Are you sick?" Marcella finally asked. "I heard you in the bathroom."

Dorie nodded. "I think the egg liquor's gotten to me."

"I've heard you," Marcella said evenly, "every morning since we got here."

No reason to panic, Dorie told herself. People were bound to find out. "I haven't told Jim yet. I haven't told anyone," she managed.

"But you told Tomás."

"Why would I tell Tomás before Jim?" The silence unnerved Dorie and she thought of ways to answer her own question.

"Do you think I'm a fool?" Marcella asked. "Do you think that all this time you had duped me?"

The thick paste of vomit clung to Dorie's tongue. "I don't know what you're talking about," she said unconvincingly.

"All this time," Marcella clarified, "were you worried for my feelings? Did you hope to spare me from whatever humiliation you thought you were bringing on me?"

The line of questioning confused Dorie. "Yes," she stammered, "I never wanted to hurt you. It's just—"

She could not finish the sentence for the slap that Marcella then delivered hard across her face. "I don't care you're fucking my husband," she hissed. "After all, I'm fucking yours. That's"—she slapped her again—"for your goddamned pity, and for thinking I'm dumb enough not to know." Dorie stumbled against the wall. Marcella slapped her again. "And that's for thinking Tomás would ever leave me for you."

"I don't, I don't."

"And don't think Jim doesn't know, either. We all know. Jim and Tomás agreed on it, and I was asked, too. I'm just tired of watching you float around like you're the chosen one. Like you feel so sorry for me."

Dorie had no idea what she was hearing, had no idea how to even begin to understand.

"Do you really think," Marcella asked, stepping closer but not raising a hand, "he loves you? I didn't want any of this to happen, but I knew I could never stop Tomás from having a son. I agreed because I'd rather it was with you than some stranger."

"What do you mean, Jim and Tomás agreed? Agreed to what?"

"Jim will finally prove his manhood to the world! Though, believe me, he has no idea how brown that baby might be. They even have names picked out. They can't decide between Juan and Armando. Though I'm sure whatever it's named, they'll make it seem like your idea."

"This is ridiculous," Dorie said. "You really think I'd name my child with a foreign name?" But that's not what she meant.

"I really thought," Marcella snarled, "you'd have enough sense to get rid of it and spare us both from their monstrous egos. Why do you think I told you about his race? You considered it, of course. But then all you American women are so deluded, so convinced you deserve happiness, that the rules don't apply to you. You had to convince yourself that he loves you."

"I'm not, I'm not deluded."

"He's not going to Brazil with you, have you at least figured that much out? He's so pathetically in love with me that he confesses to me everything, every time."

"If this is what you want to tell yourself, Marcella, to make you feel like you have some control of the situation, fine. But don't expect me to believe this. I do feel sorry for you. You're the deluded one, with these stories you tell yourself. Tomás's faith would never allow him to do something like that."

"It's not adultery if your wife agrees, if there's no lust involved, if the point is to conceive. It's not a sin if you get special permission from the Church."

Dorie saw then Tomás working above her, too seriously, only their loins touching. "But no one asked me!" she cried in confusion. "I didn't agree!"

"I really cannot believe you could be so stupid, for so long. Have you really figured nothing out on your own? Should we ring Tomás and have him explain? You trust him more than me, but I'm afraid he's too busy running around Miami with your little maid girl to deal with us at the moment."

Dorie just stared. "Emelda?"

"The Indian heir wins the game! She gets a better deal than we do out of all this."

Dorie lunged for her room and slammed the door, locked it with a frantic hand. But Marcella did not try to pursue her.

———

Dorie didn't know what to wear to impress a Communist. Would they respect her more if she wore her best or her worst? In the end, she decided on her best. If nothing else, the events in the capital frightened them, and they might want the opportunity to have someone influential indebted to them. So, with her shoes in her hands, she descended the stairs and slipped out the front door. She started down a path deeply rutted with tire tracks. Unable to navigate in her heels, Dorie kept her shoes off and, to her surprise, did not mind the cool mud sucking between her toes.

From a distance, she watched two Communists load heavy bags onto the truck bed. They were in a hurry, and Dorie, afraid she would not have the courage to go deeper in the fields and catch them again, called out.

"I need a ride to the capital!" She approached, holding out all the money she had. "I need a ride to Guate," she clarified, using the slang term. "I'll pay you all I have, five hundred quetzales, I think." She pointed to the truck.

The moment the two men looked down at the money in her fist, she regretted her tactic. Here, in the middle of nowhere, they could just take it from her, kill her, and bury her in the field. She put the money back into her purse, but still they continued to stare at the same place. At her bare feet sinking in the mud.

The older one spat through an enormous gap in his teeth. A Mestizo, browned around the edges like toast. He mumbled something to the younger one, who was friendlier-looking, but darker.

"*¿Guate?*" the sweaty boy asked.

"*Sí*," Dorie nearly cried for desperation. "*Por favor.*"

"*Guate rebelde.*"

"I know, I know. The rebels are supposed to arrive soon, but I must get there first. My husband is there. My *hombre* in Guate."

The boy nodded and conferred with the older man. As they spoke, their eyes kept cutting to the villa. From where Dorie stood, she saw a wing of Cortez's house she'd not seen before, with a balcony and a large radio antenna on the roof.

"Me to Guate." She laid her hand on her own breast, hitting herself harder and harder. The boy nodded nonchalantly and began securing the truck's cargo, while the older man, unmoved, studied her.

Much to Dorie's relief, the older man stayed behind, leaving the younger Indian to drive the load of coffee to the capital by himself, with Dorie as a passenger. The relief, however, did not last long. Once on the mountain roads, Dorie wondered if this boy had ever driven a car at all. With no mirrors at all in the vehicle, he didn't compensate by turning his head to look anywhere. He only stared ahead, and took mountain curves so wide and fast that the presence of any opposing traffic would prove fatal.

Dorie soon realized she was alone in a truck with a Communist, who knew exactly how much money she had, and who could lose everything he owned in a day in another revolution. But, she reassured herself, this boy might well be a part of the enraged peasant masses overthrowing the President. Maybe they weren't hauling coffee at all, but weapons. Why would this boy be risking his life to deliver sacks of coffee in the middle of a civil war? Would he fight for or against Arbenz? She felt utterly foolish and confused, not even knowing who was on what side, when the sides seemed so clear.

With no conversation, or much of a common language, Dorie began to rethink her fight with Marcella. Clearly, jealousy of Dorie's pregnancy had driven her insane. Something about Jim agreeing to let Tomás impregnate her—as if they had discussed her in their long meetings. As if Dorie were a piece of property to be negotiated.

"My name is Dorie," she said to the young driver. "Dorie," she said again.

He gave her a long side glance. "Simón."

"Why are you driving today? Why bring coffee to Guate when there are dangerous rebels?"

Simón sped up for the next curve that descended through the morning mist. He launched into a long explanation, taking his hands off the wheel to illustrate, Dorie believed, that if the government was overthrown, his land title would be revoked and it wouldn't be his coffee anymore. It would be Cortez's again. He had to sell now.

She could, she realized, very well die today. If not by a car accident or rebel fire, then by the hand of this boy who was probably, most definitely, hauling weapons. Why would he risk his life to sell a few bags of coffee when he could be fighting to keep his land?

"My *hombre* is the American ambassador," Dorie blurted. It worked. He set a wild-eyed look on her, ignoring the road for a good five seconds. Then again, this boy may have just realized he had a valuable hostage.

Dorie swallowed the sobs of frustration rising in her throat. She had to shut up now, she wouldn't say anything more. She placed a hand on the door handle, watching the edge of the mountain road. She could not, for the trees, tell how far the drop was.

For the first time since her illness that morning, Dorie thought of the baby. The stubborn baby that clung to her despite all that she tried to shake it loose, and the baby that slipped through Marcella like a sliver of peeled fruit.

Marcella's baby had been Tomás's, everything normal, until he told her about his race. Dorie remembered her saying over and over that she wouldn't know what to do if it turned out brown. She had been found in the bathtub, covered in blood. Not one drop stained the house. She had done it herself. She had invented the story of the land march at the Presidential Palace. Tomás must know she had done it herself. He had told her about his race in maybe the only moment of trust and weakness in his life, and she had been appalled. How did it feel, knowing your wife would do something like that to herself because she was so afraid to mix her blood with yours? Dorie could imagine Marcella doing exactly what she could not bring herself to do: throwing herself down the stairs, punching herself repeatedly in the stomach, even plunging herself with some astonishingly everyday household instrument. It had not been whiskey and baths. It had left her sterile and had almost killed her.

Beyond that, Marcella's story was too much to believe. It disturbed her that she could see Tomás participating in a plot like that, but never Jim. Sweet, teasing Jim.

Out of the highlands, they drove directly into the morning sun. Dorie closed her eyes for relief, but the effort did not produce darkness, only red. Simón must be a revolutionary, she decided. But a revolutionary for Arbenz? Or, she realized, those fighting Arbenz were considered revolutionaries, too. She was in a country where absolutely everyone was a revolutionary.

And what of Emelda? With all this, Dorie had nearly forgotten what Marcella had said about her. Could it be true? She hadn't been whoring her up for an old banana baron, but for Tomás. Tomás found her during his investigation in Xela, and wanted her in his vacation house in Miami. He was the old banana baron. By the age of fifty-seven, Tomás had acquired an Indian bride, a Hispanic bride, and a white bride for himself.

Dorie refused to believe any of it until she saw Jim herself and, looking at him, could imagine him plotting such a thing—just handing her over to be used like that. For what? For pride. To save face the next time Jenks talked about his children. She would look him in the eyes in a few hours and know. She watched the landscape—everything so green, so brilliantly green with the rains. They passed a verdant cliff, with its red clay exposed to the road, ragged and unhealing, as if inflicted by a swift, immense claw.

———

They entered the capital on a small road Dorie did not recognize. Simón stopped the truck, turned it off, to track the sound of an engine drawing near above them. They both looked up and watched a fighter plane pass.

"*Rebelde*," Simón said as machine-gun fire started up in the distance.

"The rebels are here already? How'd they get fighter planes? How"—her voice rising uncontrollably—"did a bunch of peasant rebels get fighter planes!"

But Simón didn't understand or care. Whoever he had come to help fight needed him. "*¿Dónde?*" he asked, starting the engine again. "*¿Dónde?*"

"Where are we? I don't know, Simón. I can't see anything."

He inched the truck out of the side street, onto a larger, empty thoroughfare. At first she didn't recognize anything. As they crossed the main road, however, Dorie glimpsed a familiar building.

"Stop," she said, closing her eyes to compose a map. "Go right here, on this street." She pointed, and Simón obeyed. They sped the wrong way down one of the recently reversed streets. As they accelerated, another plane, or maybe the same one, swept into view. It bore down on them, dipping low and coming head-on. Simón braked hard in the middle of the street and Dorie caught herself on the dashboard before his arm reached over, grabbed her hair, and forced her down onto the floor. Machine-gun fire cracked as the plane passed overhead, shooting for what seemed like an eternity.

After deciding she had not been hit, Dorie remained on the floor, even as she heard Simón pull himself up, apparently unharmed. She had wet herself and she did not want Simón to see. She felt the warmth spreading under her dress during the assault, but now in the aftermath it began to cool, shameful.

"Okay? Okay?" Simón leaned over, putting his hands out for her. "Okay?"

She bunched her skirt behind her and out of sight as she slid back up to her seat.

"Okay."

Dorie surveyed the truck: no broken glass, not a bullet hole in the stucco buildings around them. Had they been shooting at someone else?

Simón wrestled the truck back into gear. "*¿Dónde?*" he asked just like before, refusing to be amazed by their luck. They continued straight. She looked back out the truck window, and saw nothing but coffee, spilled all over the road like shell casings. Dorie began to cry.

They saw no troops, no Indian rebels, nothing on the remaining blocks to the embassy. When Simón pulled up to the guard station, Dorie jumped out, still holding the back of her dress. "Thank you, Simón." She turned to go, but he did not pull away.

"Quetzales!"

"Oh God, yes." She dropped the money onto the passenger seat through the window. The seat smeared with blood. Simón saw this at the same time she did.

"Okay?" he asked.

But Dorie ran toward the embassy, bent and cradling her stomach as if she'd been sliced open and had to hold herself in. She ran past the gate, where José stood, holding a tray of coffee and snacks, trying to enter.

"José Efraín Ríos Montt," he repeated, twice, for the guard, who checked his name on a list.

Dorie's sobbing arrival through the front door caused a number of people to stop, midstep, to stare.

"Where is Jim!" she screamed at these suits. No answer. They stared, as if Dorie were insane, as if there weren't planes bombing the city. She ran past them, to Jim's office, empty, and collided with Gilberto as she turned to run through the main hall.

"You're supposed to be in Quetzaltenango!" he yelled, gripping his notebook.

She grabbed him by his suit. "I almost died getting here!" But these words didn't seem to convey the message. He merely watched as Dorie stood there shaking and sobbing.

"Where is Jim?" she moaned.

Gilberto grabbed her upper arm, pulled her back into the office.

"Where the fuck is he!"

Restraining her with a force that shocked her into silence, he barked, "Where the hell is Cortez?" He pinned her against the plaster wall. Trying to get away, Dorie wiped red handprints down the front of his shirt. His nostrils flared, the smell of blood rising. "Be quiet," he hissed. "Jim's . . ." He hesitated.

"Oh God," she wailed, feeling her body melt, but he held her firmly in place. "Let me go!" Her left hand flailed at her side, found something heavy on Jim's desk. She swung and hit Gilberto across the mouth with it.

The secretary fell to his knees, as did his composition notebook. He touched his split lip gently as it dripped coins of blood on the floor, onto the open pages, where he'd written his name a hundred times. Dorie looked at the telephone still in her hand. The receiver hanging, droning, spinning in circles at her feet.

"Jesus." Gilberto laughed, making no move to get up. "He's not dead. He's on the roof. He's on the goddamned roof."

The roof? She took off down the hall and Gilberto did not chase her. She passed José coming through the door. Suits stepped out of offices to watch as she ran, feeling her own blood slipping down her legs. Ascending the stairs, she ran past the apartment and turned up the third flight. Wires lined the stairs, dozens of them, going all the way up and through the small half-sized door to the roof. She heard gunfire again, closer than before. She stumbled over the wires as she neared the top and fell into the door, which slammed open into blinding brightness.

The first thing Dorie saw was Jim, standing on the roof in full sunlight, waving his arms maniacally at an airplane flying low and headed right for him.

"Jim!" she screamed, but he did not hear over the engine and bullets.

Dorie sank to her knees, knowing this would be her last sight of him, knowing she'd have to watch him take three hundred bullets in the chest and fall down. Her eyes remained wide open, watching in fixed horror as the plane bore down, firing. But there was no smoke, no sparks. Jim waved his arms to the right and the plane then turned that way, turned away. Jim remained standing, his arms now on his hips, as the gunfire started again. And it was then that she noticed the equipment: a large radio antenna and speakers, dozens of speakers cluttering the roof, their wires tangled in a mass. These speakers blared the sound of gunfire.

"Jim!" And this time he heard her. He turned around. He was smiling.

1983

The military plane shuddered through the steamy mountain air with a violence suggesting the hand of God. He had taken a notion to either hold them up or dash them on the bright, jagged mountains below, Lenore thought. But as soon as it had come, the turbulence settled. God again, telling her not to worry.

But it was difficult not to, in this plane, without proper chairs or even the calm faces of other passengers to reassure her. Neither she nor Dan had ever flown before last week, when they boarded their first plane together, from Louisville to Houston. Then from Houston to Guatemala City. The flights had been difficult for Lenore, although at least in a real airplane she could order a Pepsi to comfort herself. Now, in the military plane, with the bolted metal twitching and long rigid benches reinforcing the sides, there were only two places to look. She could either turn completely around to look out the window, or stare straight ahead at the soldiers.

Lenore didn't know if you could call teenagers with guns soldiers, but there they were, lined up on the opposite side, facing her. Down the length of the bench, their faces all set in an expression that Lenore could only call blank.

Despite the cramp in her back, her fear of planes, mountains, war, heights, and plane crashes, she chose to look out the window. The mountains of Guatemala looked like moss-covered rocks from this height. As they neared the base, a pale road snaked along their route, then gave out. Like the end of the world. Then there was no road at all, just green. She squinted down, searching for anything: a finger of smoke, a glint of metal, anything that could be a guerrilla camp. Her breath kept fogging the glass, which she wiped clear with her sleeve. If she saw anything, she would tell the pilot immediately. There was more than one way of doing God's work.

Dan, next to her, preferred to look nowhere. Instead, he pretended to read a conference pamphlet. For the past half hour, he'd been on the same page, titled "The Mayan Heart Is Ripe for Harvest." His leg rested on one of the food aid bags, which had ruptured and spilled yellow dust—cornmeal—

around everyone's feet. Other than the two of them and the soldiers, the belly of the plane had been filled with these bags (IN THE NAME OF THE LORD stenciled on each) and diapers. The same blue-eyed baby repeated on the plastic packaging, confronting Lenore with a strange middle-aged knowingness.

Lenore spied a break in the canopy, a figure running from the plane's shadow. The Indian costume so bright, like a target itself, then gone. Lenore bit her lip, glanced at the boy soldiers, then ahead to the pilot flipping switches behind the fortification of food aid. She should say something. She had no idea if this plane was armed, but she imagined the pilot dipping down at her suggestion, to fire at the canopy. The figure running, then falling facedown before her eyes.

She turned from the window and said nothing, asking God's patience as she adjusted to her sudden role in this war.

General Ahumada Lobos met them on the airstrip after a landing that made Lenore cry. But no one noticed. She had put on her sunglasses. From behind their dark lenses, the General's face looked yellow and puckered, like dried fruit, his eyes two black pits. Unlike the boy soldiers, his uniform was starched, neatly creased, showing no hint of the man inside. The sight of such a formidable figure reassured Lenore. Yes, someone was in charge around here.

Lenore disappointedly fingered her hair. She'd spent a half hour that morning carefully curling the ends under, but it hadn't even taken five minutes for it to reverse itself into an unflattering flip. Dan, she noticed, appeared doughy and shapeless in the unrelenting sunshine. Too pale, too big, too delicate for the tropical climate. Like a grub accidentally turned with the soil, into the light. He smiled down at her.

The General assured them with rough handshakes that he was glad for their help with the Project. He spoke English without much of an accent.

"This airstrip," he said, "is the Project's first success. Indian work crews finished it in a month. And now we can fly in supplies"—he paused, glowing—"and you! We could make another model village. Good work makes more good work possible."

"Praise the Lord!" Dan said.

"Yes," the General agreed, slapping something off the back of his neck. "Praise the Lord."

"When does the amnesty begin?"

"Yesterday. We've already had many, many Indians surrender. Some are already cooperating and telling us where the guerrilla camps are."

"Are they *all* guerrillas?" Lenore asked, gazing past the General to the mountains, which were softened into pleasant pastels with fog and smoke and distance. They were surrounded by the enemy, without even a road connecting them to the world they knew.

"Mostly," the General said. "Why else would they be surrendering?"

"How can you tell the innocent Indians from the guerrillas?" Dan asked.

The General frowned at the question. "We don't call them Indians. We call them Maya now."

Dan nodded. They had a brochure on that. His rimless glasses floated over his face, making him look so serious. On the sides, only two tiny golden claws showed where the lenses attached to the frames.

"We have ways of knowing," the General went on, scratching fiercely now where he had slapped before.

"Are you afraid of guerrillas making it into the village, General?"

"Yes, we are always on the lookout for that. That's why we'll have the Civil Patrol. Every town in Guatemala has a Civil Patrol. Not just model villages."

"And what's the next job?" Dan was eager to get to work. They'd spent months training at their church, and four days shuffling between seminars and collecting brochures at the conference in Guatemala City.

"Roads," said the General, thrusting a firm hand out to the horizon. "We build roads to break up the guerrilla territory."

Lenore watched him through the rosy tint at the bottom of her glasses. He was handsome this way. Handsome and in charge. When he smiled, she noticed a stubborn line where his lower lip had once been split.

"I know roads." Dan's eyes lit up. "I've worked construction my whole life. I quit a job as foreman to come here," he lied, slightly. He'd been demoted, began drinking again out of despair, then was eventually fired for drinking on the job. Yet he clearly did not consider this a lie. "God must have sent me here to help you." He shook his head, amazed. "Every day He reveals a little more of His plan to me."

While Dan and the General talked roads, Lenore glanced down at her feet. On the dusty orange runway, she noticed a small lizard near the General's right foot. This lizard moved in a very peculiar way. Lenore tilted her sunglasses up to see the ground covered with thousands of ants, hauling it in swarming shifts.

"The model villages are very important work," the General continued. "We're introducing Indians to society. If they surrender under the amnesty, we will take them in, teach them the value of democracy and hard work, of citizenship, and they will learn to love Guatemala. But they have to learn a new way of life—no more politics or superstitions. To pave the way for that," he said, thrusting his arm out again at his imaginary roads, "you must change their hearts and spirits."

"Born again," Dan assured him. "To start anew, we must all be born again."

Lenore watched the ants. She lifted one foot, then the other, marching in place and trying to keep them off her.

A military helicopter approached from the west, pulverizing the fog with its propeller. The still morning air became a storm of dust and activity. Soldiers running in every direction.

"This is the larger picture if I ever saw it," Dan said to Lenore, shielding his eyes.

Inside the base, the General led them through scrubbed linoleum halls that gleamed faintly green, reminding Lenore of a school standing empty for summer break. She breathed in the chemical clean, thinking of home. Already she was thinking of home.

"The war," the General explained with his hands locked behind him, walking, "has been too long. Over twenty years, and now no one knows the sides anymore." Room after room stood empty, but he pointed to each, giving the tour. "The Communists have stolen military uniforms and killed thousands while wearing them. So even the innocent hate us, which means they don't stay innocent for long. They take up the fight with the Communists out of revenge. That's how the guerrillas recruit, they kill Indians, wearing our uniforms, then convince the survivors to join them for revenge. They don't even know who's killing them anymore." He sighed, weary with the explanation he no doubt gave every day to soldiers, missionaries, journalists.

"General—"

"Please." When the General smiled, his lips went white and bloodless on either side of his purple scar. "Call me Gilberto."

"Gilberto." Dan nodded.

"How was the conference?" he asked. "I was supposed to teach there, but I could not leave. Too much going on."

"Very informative," Dan said. "We learned so much. Really gave us an idea of the larger picture." Lenore crossed her arms, annoyed that Dan kept using that term, the larger picture. Pastor May's phrase, a phrase that peeved her. And she had not enjoyed the Open Arms conference. It had been too much—too much information to keep focused on the mission. Politics and horrific pictures she had to close her eyes to.

"And the fun? Did you have fun, too?" The General spoke of fun like it was a foreign country he'd never visit. "Did you do the shark diving?"

"Oh no! That's a bit too adventurous for us. We just stayed at the hotel."

"It was my idea, the shark diving. I see them when I fly over the water!" He laughed. "For you sharks are too adventurous, but you come to guerrilla country to live?"

Lenore found she did better if danger wasn't mentioned at all. She could go where God needed her, where there were people she could help, and that's how she saw it. Saving souls was the same, in Kentucky or in the middle of a guerrilla war.

"You speak English very well, General," she said.

"I went to Harvard!" He beamed with his split smile. "I studied political science."

"Oh my," Lenore gasped, but then said nothing else, hoping she hadn't offended him by being surprised. Neither she nor Dan had been to college, and now the man she believed made perfect sense to her a minute before became utterly incomprehensible. She had no idea what political science even was.

At the end of the long hall, a figure appeared—an animal, running. Lenore could hear the padding of its paws on the linoleum. She froze, fearful. The fluorescent light burned sickly yellow, defying any attempt to understand. The thing seemed to be running faster, seeing them: a puppy, Lenore realized. A black-and-tan puppy loping up the empty hall at an angle, right up to them. Jumping up, it stretched just to Lenore's knee, licking desperately, whining and nuzzling her hands.

"Who are you?" she asked. Its ears, loose and long, felt like crushed velvet in her hands. She squeezed and pulled.

"Hue-la!"

Another figure, a man, came running from the same direction. A soldier, making a stark shape against the sanitary glow of the hallway.

"Huela!"

The puppy ignored him and the soldier stopped, openmouthed, seeing the General too late. It took him a moment to remember to salute.

The General sighed. "This is Mincho, your interpreter. And this is Mr. and Mrs. Beasley."

The young soldier smiled, his boyish face breaking with old man teeth. "Hello, Beasties." He turned to salute them, too.

"Beasleys," Dan corrected him.

"Mincho is a new soldier, but he speaks Spanish, English, and Quiché. He'll be working directly with you in the model village, interpreting your sermons."

"Fantastic!"

"*¡Abajo, Huela, siéntate!*" But the puppy continued to ignore him. Flushing, Mincho scooped it up so it could whine and squirm in his arms. "She's very young," he explained to Lenore.

"Mincho, get ready. You'll be giving them a tour of the village soon."

The boy soldier ran back from where he'd come.

"Are the soldiers here allowed to have pets?" Lenore asked.

"Yes, the puppies are very important. Every new soldier gets a puppy. They train their puppy to help in the mountains. Making a good puppy is as hard as making a good soldier." He nodded down the hall and Lenore saw the puppy padding away, Mincho following with his arms flailing. "And the boys," the General conceded with a shrug, "get lonely. For many of them, this is the first time they leave their homes. So the puppies help with that, too."

"That's very nice," Lenore said. She liked this man: firmly in charge, yet compassionate. Just what Guatemala needed, just what she needed to get comfortable in this peculiar new world. "Teaching both love and discipline, they seem to balance each other out."

The General's joyless laugh echoed down the hall. "Yes, usually, but not with Mincho. His puppy is terrible because he loves it too much."

~~~~~

When Dan spoke of the larger picture, Lenore knew he was referring to problems they'd been having. More specifically, problems she'd been having. Just over a year ago, at the town's annual blackberry festival, she had, as Pastor May later told her, hit rock bottom.

As the main festival sponsor, the church enlisted the Ladies of Vision for the setup. They handled everything from food and pony rides to religious literature distribution to covering the greased pole with Crisco for the kids to climb. And Lenore, as the president of the Ladies of Vision church group, became responsible for those responsible.

The day had been hot, with the heat reflecting off the blacktop and making things at any distance go wavy. Wherever she meant to walk next, no matter where, her destination looked distorted and strange, as if blocked by a wall of invisible flames. Lenore, red-eyed and weary, found herself trekking across impossible distances to yell at the tent salesman, the BBQ pit master, the blackberry juice man, the teenage volunteers, even Pastor May's wife for buying fifteen hundred plain paper plates, instead of the ones with compartments to keep your food from all running together. A headache bloomed behind her right eye. How could anyone forget ice on a day like this? Each dumb face she confronted was like a divine test of her faith.

By the time the festival began, Lenore couldn't even bring herself to attend, but lay in the church nursery with a wet cloth over her eyes.

Near the end of the day, however, a sudden, intense desire overcame her. She walked straight from the church, across the scorched blacktop, past the stage where Miss Teen Blackberry waved and waved, past the pie table, the exhausted pony, and the greased pole. She walked to the prayer circle, where Dan stood with a slice of blackberry pie in his right hand, while holding someone's hand in his left. They prayed against the rain clouds, amassed on the horizon, threatening the festival. Lenore grabbed his wallet from his back pocket and made for the dunk tank, where Pastor May had good-humoredly offered up his dignity to raise money for the church food bank.

He was smiling above his full gut, eating pie, with his bare feet suspended over a placid skin of water, calling for quarters.

"Who wants to give me a second baptism?"

Lenore handed Bobbie Groenig everything in Dan's wallet—thirty-five dollars—and started throwing.

"Is that all the power you got?" Pastor May laughed, spooning his pie. "Keep trying, old lady! Maybe the Spirit will enter that arm and give you a decent fastball!" But after about fifteen tries, the taunting stopped. He just watched her, a worried look on his face, as she heaved balls pathetically at the target. Some missing wildly and actually hitting the grate that protected his head. A silent crowd formed, watching. Then Dan appeared.

"What," he hissed in her ear, pulling her away, "has gotten into you?"

"You know," she said, "as much as I do how absurd all this is. You cannot—" She stopped and twisted under his grip to face him. She raised her voice, hoping others would hear. "You cannot tell me that you feel at all like a man. Sitting there, getting fat on pie and praying for it not to rain on your fun, while there is so much suffering in the world. You even broke the prayer circle! You broke the circle because you could not fathom letting go of your pie."

They both looked down at the blackberry pie in his left hand, while he held her arm with his right. Lenore knew she was being unfair. If she hadn't been in this mood, she'd have been in the same prayer circle, eating pie, too.

He listened to her with the blatant show of patience that infuriated her. He said things like, *I think you're tired. I hear you, Lenore. I hear you.* After fifteen years of marriage, she knew he tended to repeat himself when he lied.

He walked her back the same way she had come. Past the smoldering BBQ pit and the colorful wreckage of the pie-eating contest. He walked her through the sly looks of everyone. Even Miss Teen Blackberry could not maintain her general benevolence as they passed. His grip on her upper arm became gentle as they entered the nursery, where he re-wet her cloth and tucked her into a child's cot. He spoke to her in the empty church quietly, as if there were sleeping babies all around them.

That, it seems, marked the beginning of her troubles. After that, Lenore resigned as the president of the Ladies of Vision, and stopped going to evening church services. At first she told Dan that she had too much to catch up on around the house.

Dan, concerned at her inactivity, started signing Lenore up for clubs at the church. At first he thought exercise would help, so he enrolled her in the married women's volleyball team. But Lenore couldn't muster any enthusiasm for sports and when they lost a scrimmage match to Sacred Heart, her frustration overwhelmed her.

"How could God let idolaters triumph over us?" she'd asked Dan. "If He'd levitated me for one spike, the entire county would be on its knees, praising God."

Dan began chewing his lip, showing real worry for the first time. "I think," he finally said, "your problem might be a bit more fundamental than exercise. I'll sign you up for a Bible study class, Lenore. What do you think of that?"

"But I already know the Bible," she snapped. "I know it backwards and forwards. I've known it much longer than you have!"

Dan did not like to be reminded of this, of the fact that she had been born-again her entire life, whereas he'd only been so for about ten years. "Well, obviously you've forgotten the temptations of Christ in the desert. If you remembered, you'd know not to ask such a silly thing as why God doesn't lift you up for a point in volleyball."

"Just because the Bible mentions it, doesn't mean I'm satisfied with the explanation!"

This shocked them both and Dan left the room. She cried for a good hour, then drove herself to the evening service to repent. She sat in the full parking lot, in the car, but no matter how terrible she felt, she could not convince herself to go inside. The heaviness, the emptiness—was it possible to feel both at the same time?—only got worse when she was at the church. How could this be, if she still believed in its overall message? Faith had carried her before through moments of uncertainty, but now relying on blind faith seemed lazy. Faith seemed a way of avoiding honesty with herself about her part in God's plan. Was she really just meant to bake, scoop ice cream, and rent dunk tanks for God? She sensed a larger purpose for herself, though she hadn't any clue what it might be, since the world she inhabited suddenly felt so small to her.

"What do you want, Lenore? What would make you happy?" Dan kept asking. For weeks, she had no answer for him. Then one day she told him that having a maid would make her happy.

"For what!" he had yelled. "What do you need a maid for?"

"I'm exhausted, Dan. I just can't keep up with the canning and everything."

"But you haven't been doing anything else. You don't work, you don't do anything with the church anymore, you walk through the mall and come home to watch television. How could you be exhausted?"

"I don't know. I just am. I think the maid would be a great relief. I think if it works, I may look for a job."

"A job? Do you think I don't provide enough for you, Lenore?" With this, his pleading had gone from measured and rational to panicked. "Is this about my demotion? Is that it? Are you worried about money? I've applied to other jobs, but no one even wants to interview someone with an arrest record. I'm trying—"

"Of course not," Lenore reassured him. She hadn't meant to poke that sore spot, but he held it in front of him, always, so everything hit it. "I'd just like to have a job. I think I need to be out in the world."

"Where? What would you do?"

"Maybe I could go back to Friendly's. I worked there before we got married."

"I know you did. And I also know you hated it. Why would you want to work a job you hate when you don't have to?" Dan was so perplexed and desperate, his eyes swimming. Ten years ago, in this situation, he would have punched the wall behind her head and shaken her. Now he questioned his own manhood.

"I don't know," was all she could say.

That evening, Dan phoned Pastor May. The three of them met that night, and for two weeks after that, for emergency counseling.

~~~~~

The road from the base to the model village was so new that the survey stakes from its construction still marked its edges. From the hilltop, as they descended into the valley, Lenore studied the village: a grid of sheds spaced exactly, inhabiting only a small area in the center of the valley. Surrounding the fence, and stretching to the jungle in all directions, the earth had been turned in preparation for planting.

Getting closer, Lenore could see tiny solitary forms, wandering slowly and without purpose. Indians. No, Maya.

Huela led the way, running ahead with her too-long tail sailing behind.

"Huela! *Aquí*," Mincho yelled. "*¡Aquí!*"

Several guards stood at the gate, older soldiers without puppies, with dirt on their uniforms. They laughed, ceremoniously holding the gate open for Huela.

"Why so many guards?" Lenore asked Mincho.

"We are in guerrilla country. The Indians in here are under amnesty now, they give up and tell us where the guerrillas are hiding. We must protect them, or the guerrillas would kill them all for being traitors."

"Have you gotten a lot of good information already?"

"Oh yes. I think everyone is ready for the war to be over."

Dan breathed in and out several times, refreshed, as if their downhill walk had brought them to a mountain summit. She waited for him to say something about the larger picture again, but thankfully, he did not. Lenore felt that the world, which was supposed to be expanding for her, had only closed in. She breathed in and out, too, trying to capture Dan's confidence.

Tiny sheds stood like double-wide port-a-potties along the gridded paths. Donated by Operation Open Arms, they looked modern, though without the dignity of doors, and were new and sturdy and big enough for two people to sit comfortably in. For three people to lie down side by side. But Lenore didn't see any people. The figures she had seen from above, crawling the village grid, were gone.

"Where is everyone?" she asked.

Mincho brought them to the water pump—an efficient-looking contraption that moaned and shuddered when Lenore worked the lever, hinting at a vast underground network.

"The secret to the water pump," Mincho said, "is that you have to put in just a little first, to get a lot back." He retrieved a small can of water on the ground, poured it into the curved, humanoid mouth, then worked the lever. Water gushed out, puddling between them. "But," Mincho warned, with a seriousness that must have been imparted to him, "you must remember to refill the can every time, Beasties." He placed the can under the stream and set it back on the ground.

"Beasleys," Lenore corrected him.

They left the pump and followed Mincho into one of the unoccupied sheds. It was dark and smelled like a Tupperware container. Lenore pressed her hand to one of the walls: cool like metal, but when she tapped a nail, she heard the dull thud of plastic.

They stood inside the cramped, dark shed for a moment, with Huela whining outside, distrusting the space. Then suddenly a light revealed Dan's surprised face.

"And there's electricity!" Mincho shouted, pleased at his timing.

Dan put a hand out, palm up in the light, as if feeling rain.

"Every shed has electric light and a hot plate!" Mincho said. "The Indians no longer have to cook over fire. No need for firewood."

"I bet they've never had electricity," Dan said. "I bet this is a treat for them."

"Yes," Mincho said, his hand still on the switch. "They all lived in darkness, all the time before."

Huela sensed the Indians that Lenore could not see. She barked and barked, betraying their whereabouts everywhere. What would they look like, these refugees? In the pictures at the conference, their skin had been dark, with dirt and race mingling deceptively.

"Are you happy to be translating our sermons?" Dan asked. "Is that something you asked to do?"

"I am." Mincho lowered his head in humility, then proceeded to admire his boots. "I asked, but I also knew they would ask me. I am the only one here who speaks Quiché."

"No one else can speak to the Indians?" Lenore was astonished. "I thought Indians . . . Mayans," she corrected herself, "made up over half the country's population."

"He speaks Quiché," Mincho said, motioning to one of the armed guards slouched at the gate. They had made a complete circle. "But he doesn't speak English."

Lenore eyed the razor wire, so new that it glinted cheaply all around the camp like a toy crown. Above, a large bird circled and called. The guards were all turned in, watching the village and not the mountains.

"We're glad to have you helping us," Dan reassured Mincho. "I think you'll have fun, and maybe learn something, too."

"Fun, yes. But not as fun as shooting Communists. Ha ha."

This, they would soon learn, was how Mincho laughed. Saying it, rather than actually laughing. He'd draw his lips back, revealing a mouth full of horrible jagged teeth, and lunge forward. *Ha ha.* Like a terrifying fish taking the bait of a joke.

The education building marked the exact center of the model village and was, by far, the nicest and sturdiest of all the structures, though Dan squinted skeptically at the foundation. They toured inside and were surprised to find carpeting, a television.

"For educational videos," Mincho explained, running his hands over the dead screen in wonder. "All Spanish lessons, sermons, and Lessons in Democracy."

"Sermons? I thought we were going to have a church."

"Oh, not your sermons. The President's sermons. He gives a sermon to the nation every week over the television. I translate for the Indians. I translate the President!"

They moved on to the last stop on the tour, the church. Constructed entirely of corrugated metal, it bordered a small public square that faced the entrance and guards. In front, a flagpole displayed the Guatemalan flag throwing a fit in the wind. At its base, three struggling shrubs provided the village's only greenery.

"Those plants are nice," Lenore ventured. The sight of the television had renewed her, made her think they weren't as cut off as she had believed. "Maybe we should do some more planting around the village to cheer it up?"

"The plants," Mincho said, "are nice because they are in front of the guards. There can be no more, because they will burn the sticks and leaves for their gods."

"Oh my. Okay."

Inside the church, wooden benches faced a stage with a microphone. Mincho hopped up and yelled into the microphone, "The church has electricity, too!" But his enthusiasm died a prompt death. The mic wasn't plugged in.

Though small and spare, their first church, with its bolts and seams showing, made Dan and Lenore hold hands and smile.

"Your first sermon is tomorrow at eight o'clock. I'll be here to translate. It will be good practice. I never told you," he confided as if he had known them for years, "that I would like to be a preacher when the war is over."

"That's wonderful, Mincho."

"But I am worried about education. Do I need to go to school to be a preacher? I'm not good at school."

"No, no." Dan waved his arms in small, strict lines like a referee. "Christianity isn't an exclusive club. Not like the Catholics. If you have the Call in your heart, the only book you need is the Bible. No college needed, no degrees, no fancy connections."

"And no Latin?"

"Nope. No Latin or expensive clothes, no wine or gold jewelry."

"No wine?" Mincho, for the first time, looked worried.

"No wine," Dan repeated, very seriously. "Alcohol clouds your thinking. How can you help others who are confused if your head isn't clear?"

Mincho considered this. As he walked the stage, his boots squeaked, sounding tight and uncomfortable. Finally, he stopped, "But I can have women, right?"

"Well," Dan was able to reply, "you can get married, yes. Getting married is not a sin, although—"

"Ah!" Mincho seemed satisfied. "Priests have wine and no women, but preachers have women and no wine. I think the preacher wins. Ha ha."

An ill-fitting door, cut from the metal wall, then bolted back with three tight hinges, separated the church from their apartment. It opened with a shrill scream and they found a single room with a double mattress, a table, two chairs, and a hot plate. A single bare bulb of too-high wattage threatened to explode from the ceiling. Their luggage had already been delivered and filled the room, making it impossible to step inside. Mincho left them there trying to negotiate their entrance.

"Goodbye, Beasties!" He said he would be back, but did not specify when.

"Where are we going to put everything?" Lenore asked Dan. Their bags were all unzipped. She imagined the boy soldiers sniffing her underwear, stretching the waistbands, frowning at their width. "We don't even have drawers to put our clothes in."

"If there's no place to put our stuff, maybe we shouldn't have brought so much. It's materialism that's the great appeal of communism," Dan said. "We should be setting an example, showing them that the spiritual world is what really matters."

Lenore had never heard Dan use the word materialism before, but it had been a main point at the conference. And in order to show that they were here to combat it, they immediately, and with a strange joy, sifted through their luggage, doing away with everything but the essentials. They even tossed the battery-operated hair dryer Lenore had gone all the way to Lexington to buy. Out it went, along with the twenty C batteries brought along to power it.

Though their room was windowless, the thin metal walls picked up every noise of the village, amplified it, like a large ear. A slow shuffle of feet, the gurgle and hack of the water pump. The model village came alive again in their absence. They had yet to see a single refugee, though a hundred already lived in the village. Lenore sat on the bed and listened. She put a hand to the cold wall, wanting to feel the vibrations of them right on the other side. This was the larger picture, she told herself. If she went to look, surely everyone would be gone.

Dan stacked their newly condensed luggage against the walls, two high and all around, like sandbags. "Mincho seems trustworthy," he concluded. Lenore still had her hand on the wall, waiting for something, when she felt the military truck. She felt it a few seconds before Dan heard it.

Outside, as Lenore suspected, everyone disappeared again. The truck idled under the flagpole, with its back end undone to unload its human cargo. Lenore and Dan hung back near the church entrance, watching, holding hands.

Twenty-three Indians reluctantly lowered themselves onto the ground and lined up where the soldiers pointed, too close to the truck. Lenore watched the exhaust gas around them, but no one noticed or cared. She counted sixteen women, five children, and two men. Scarecrows had more substance, more dignity, Lenore thought, than these Indians. No, Maya. They stood, filthy and exhausted, wavering slightly, like dead trees in the wind.

"God," she thought she heard Dan say. She could not remember the last time he'd taken the Lord's name in vain.

Lenore noticed a woman among the group in shredded Mayan clothes, which she must have been wearing in the mountains for years, to whom all five children seemed to belong. They never strayed an inch from her, all holding what was left of her rough skirt. Lenore wondered if those little fists had fired guns, if they had killed people. If she imagined the worst, she would never be caught off guard—advice the General gave them.

A soldier walked the line, holding a combat helmet from which he prompted the Maya to draw numbers.

Not knowing how to insinuate themselves, Dan and Lenore stepped backward, back into the cold cavelike air of the church. One of the new Indians raised her head to register their slow, guilty retreat. An older woman, with a gaze so startling, so pale and empty, that Lenore thought the woman must be blind. But no, after a moment Lenore could see that the woman was not blind. Her eyes were just blue. Bright blue, sky-blue, and seeing everything.

Their room, which had seemed so bleak a few moments ago, became welcoming, if only for the fact that it had a door they could close.

"We'll give them some time to settle," Dan confirmed, as if he'd been asked. "Then tomorrow we'll get to more important things."

Lenore began to search the supply boxes the church had sent ahead of time. "I think I'm going to organize the children tomorrow. They're so"—she tried to find the word—"serious. I mean, do they even know they're children?" She opened another box. "Those kids need crayons. Where are the crayons?"

"It's awfully quiet, for a war going on," Lenore remarked, after she had found her crayons. "For some reason, I thought there'd be a lot of explosions and screaming."

"Guerrilla warfare," Dan said, "isn't like that. It's ninety percent quiet, then before you know it, you're in the middle of a savage, bloody massacre that lasts five minutes. They use fear and paranoia to break down their enemies. Silence is their weapon."

They both listened to the silence all night, like children trying to scare themselves. A village of a hundred Maya, and no sound. Lenore recalled the pictures at the conference, the ones she had not been quick enough to close her eyes to. Bodies dumped in busy park plazas. Their throats cut open, their tongues pulled through to hang like neckties. A fate reserved for capitalists.

~·~·~·~·~

"You've been active in Church activities since you were a little girl, Lenore. Am I right?" Pastor May had asked in the emergency counseling session, the first time she had seen him since the dunk tank. The king of the festival, sitting on his throne while young girls brought him pie and iced tea. Lenore had wanted nothing more than to drown him that day, to see if he could drown.

For the first few minutes, Dan held Lenore's hand. But by the time the questioning began, he let go to fold and refold a healthy-marriage checklist he'd picked up at the foyer information table.

"Yes," she said. "I was saved when I was eight. Since then, I've been in so many Christian clubs and organizations, I can't count."

"Have you ever had a crisis of faith? Other than now?"

"No," she said. "Never." She looked over at Dan, as he folded with purpose, trying to make something.

"Lenore," Pastor May said, leaning back with the simplicity of what he had to say. Incredible, she thought to herself. Months of chaos and tears, and already Pastor May had figured it out. She immediately wished Dan had brought her sooner. "Your situation, actually, is very common," he continued. "Many people, many women, come to me with these same feelings. And do you know what I tell them?" He did not wait for her to say no. "I tell them that their faith is still stuck in childhood. That their faith must grow to fit their adulthood. Do you know what I mean?" This time, he allowed her to answer.

"No."

"You've been a good Christian since you were eight. It's a great thing, Lenore, but your roots are misplaced." He paused in a gesture of frankness. "When children take on their parents' faith, they do it for childish reasons. To please, to obey, for approval and praise. Being so young, you could not fully understand the choice you made. And you've never questioned it. Your faith has existed, thus far, in the small picture."

Lenore nodded, though she did not like where this was going. She needed a larger perspective, sure, but to call her childish was too much.

"But now your experiences have caught up with you. These old roots aren't strong enough to anchor your faith as an adult. Before, you served your church for selfish reasons. For recognition and reward, like"—he lowered his voice discreetly—"at the blackberry festival."

Lenore felt her face turn hot at the thought of it, pitching baseballs at Pastor May's head. Dan's hand reached across their chairs and found hers, squeezed.

"And when you didn't get recognition for your hard work, you felt as if your faith had no reward. You began to question why you were doing it in the first place. You were working very hard physically, Lenore, but your faith was lazy. You were not glorifying God, you were glorifying yourself. This is acceptable for children, but not for an adult. And now, in order to realign your faith, you must see the larger picture and how you fit into God's plan. Do you understand?"

She said yes, although she wasn't sure. Nothing she did seemed to be for herself. In the Ladies of Vision, she'd cooked for homeless people, visited shut-ins, handed out Christmas toys, and churned blackberry ice cream until her arms went numb.

For two weeks and five more meetings, Lenore pondered this explanation, but Pastor May's insistence that all adults have to go through some sort of crisis, to hit rock bottom, for them to be able to grow in their faith seemed too bleak to her. Why couldn't someone love God purely, instead of needing Him to pull themselves out of despair? Wasn't that a selfish reason in itself? She was too sensible a person to hit rock bottom, to let things get that out of control. But she did not dare say this to either of them, knowing their own personal histories.

Dan had always been bothered by the fact that he was a relatively new Christian, whereas she had known the way her whole life. She had not drank and fought and stolen the first twenty years of her life, like Dan had. She had never been to jail for assault, then for assaulting an arresting officer, for shoplifting and destruction of private property. That had to count for something. Three times, he'd been in jail. The last time, she had bailed him out only after he promised to start attending church with her. But now he had saved her, instead of the other way around. This was not a dynamic Lenore was willing to accept. Saving Dan had been her life's proudest accomplishment.

This stormed in Lenore's mind for weeks, making her resistant to change, unable to sleep. On one of those wide-awake nights, she flipped on *The 700*

Club, and there on the TV screen appeared the new President of Guatemala, José Efraín Ríos Montt.

~~~~~

A scream rattled their small, tinny room, waking them early the next morning. Lenore pulled the scratchy Indian blanket over her head, the terror of her dreams amplified by such a violent awakening. She tried to hide, but Dan was already up and running. She had no choice but to follow, her pajamas flapping, her eyes struggling to see in the raw, early light. The sun had yet to hit the valley, but the military base glinted above them like another sun.

A crowd of Indians had gathered around one of the living sheds. They stood like zombies—filthy and swaying, many with wounds, though none fatal. Through their loose formation Lenore could see a woman collapsed on the ground, wailing like a siren. No one tried to console her. Lenore found Mincho holding Huela on a rope, while pushing and clapping at the congregated Indians.

"What's going on?" she asked.

"This is not good," he replied. "The General does not like idleness."

"No, I mean with her. The woman crying." Moving for a better view, Lenore found a girl on the ground, too, completely enveloped by the sobbing woman. They held each other in a mess of tears, dust, and long black hair.

"And who is that girl?"

"Oh, that's her granddaughter. They just found each other," Mincho said.

"So then why are they crying?" The woman began clawing at the dirt, while the girl held her waist. Held her to keep her in place.

Mincho pointed to a man standing in the doorway of his shed just next door. "The grandmother picked her house number from the hat, but she says she can't live here next to Leandro." Huela pulled on the leash, gasping for breath. "Sit," he commanded. "I mean, *siéntate*."

"Why?"

"She says he's a Communist and killed her son. The girl says he came into her house dressed like a soldier, chopped up her father with a machete, and stole their land. I think the old lady just found out her son is dead."

Lenore and Dan surveyed the man in question. A small, bony replica of a man, unimpressed by the women's tears. Everyone, in fact, seemed unmoved. The strangeness of the scene paralyzed Lenore, and she found herself watching, standing just like the others. The old woman moaned and hit herself, her face, her chest. Through this shocking performance, Lenore spied a flash of her blue eyes.

Forgiveness and national healing aside, Lenore and Dan figured it wouldn't hurt to give this woman some peace and move her to another shed, maybe with her granddaughter. But Mincho shook his head, claiming no exceptions to the rules.

"If one person gets to choose their shed, then everyone will want to choose."

Walking back to the church in his robe, Dan said, "A blessing in disguise. It's terrible, but he's right. Everyone here has lost someone, everyone has someone to blame. It's the cycle of revenge that we're here to stop. This is an exercise in forgiveness. I'll rewrite tonight's sermon to address it."

A half hour later, the Indians gathered under the flagpole, doing their best to sing. Mincho's voice carried above them all, enunciating the words for their benefit. He stood, their choirmaster, directing with both arms. The Indians followed with distressed faces, as if the Spanish syllables hurt their mouths.

Standing, shivering in the church doorway, Lenore searched the crowd for the Indian woman with the blue eyes but did not see her. The singing of the Guatemalan national anthem every morning was a mandatory exercise. The woman had to be there. Lenore hated to think it, but all these Indians looked the same. Except this one had blue eyes. All the Maya, however, kept their heads down. She might never be able to pick her out again.

Back in the apartment, Lenore stood over the hot plate, waiting for water to boil to make instant coffee. Outside, the refugee men split up for their duties. The road crew marched to the forest and the Civil Patrol learned how to raise and lower the Guatemalan flag. It went running up with a clean, fast zip, then immediately back down. Up again, then down, like several days passing in a matter of minutes.

She looked down into the water. Fine bubbles had formed on the bottom of the pot. She stared at them expectantly.

"A watched pot never boils," Dan said, shrugging on his flannel jacket.

While the road crew cut trees all day, the Civil Patrol would keep order in the village. Dan would work with the Civil Patrol, though only ten hours a day, instead of sleeping in shifts like the Mayan men. If anything happened, the village was small enough that she could scream and Dan would hear her. Lenore tried to steel herself against panic as she remembered her dream.

Her first night as a missionary and she dreamt that the ragged, docile female Indians were conspiring to burn her alive in her own church.

"The gang's going," Dan said. "I got to go."

Lenore checked the pot. "It's still not boiling, Dan."

"That's okay. I'll just skip coffee today. Tomorrow we'll start it earlier."

Lenore nodded, wondering why everyone else—President Ríos Montt, Pat Robertson, Pastor May—had such wonderful, significant dreams, while hers only magnified her fears. For months before they had even left Kentucky, she dreamt only of Guatemala. Terrifying dreams about jungles, giant insects, spiders, and snakes.

The first task executed by the Civil Patrol was the orderly distribution of food bags. With their wooden machetes—bestowed on the men so seriously that Lenore thought it a joke at first—the Mayan men guarded the military truck from the crowd of their own women. While these women stood in line, Lenore stood in the shelter of the church, eyeing them. These women, with their strange neon costumes and stone faces, frightened Lenore more than the boy soldiers and their guns.

Lenore had heard much about these peculiar costumes at the conference. A perfect example of the Maya's vanity, such impoverished women spending all their time and money weaving these elaborate outfits. The blouses varied from town to town. An Indian could tell right away where any woman was from by looking at her blouse. But if they wore regular clothes, the lecturer said, tribal divisions would break down and the Maya would begin to feel like Guatemalans. Convincing them to give up their clothes was one of the goals of the Project.

Lenore could think of nothing to do with herself, since the clothing donations from Operation Open Arms had yet to arrive and she had no interpreter. They had no idea there would just be one, and that he would have other duties. Mincho headed the Civil Patrol. And so without any idea how to approach these refugees without him, she spent the day organizing their luggage. Everything they'd decided to do without the night before remained in a pile. The village contained no trash cans, provided no garbage service. She realized this after going to the pit toilets and having nowhere to put the plastic packaging from her new toothbrush.

That evening, Dan and Lenore sat in the dark of their apartment. The lightbulb was so powerful and the room so small that to use it seemed an invasion of privacy. After a few hours of electric light, they stopped using it altogether, preferring to keep their door cracked open to allow a bit of light in from the adjoining church.

Too tired from the Civil Patrol to write his first sermon on forgiveness, Dan picked the first prewritten sermon from his Open Arms pastor's manual. The blue-eyed Indian, whoever she was, would have to wait to learn the significance of her suffering. Dan tried to nap on the bed while Lenore did her best with their first dinner. She stood over the hot plate, staring down at the pot of water, willing it to boil.

"A watched pot never boils," Dan said with a yawn from the pillow.

"It's the same pot, Dan."

"What?" He sat up.

"That's right. The same pot as this morning. I don't know what to do." The water maintained its fizzy promise, but the small bubbles had been there all day. She put a finger in, felt the temperature of a bath. "I can't boil water for drinking like this. I used the iodine today, but it tasted awful, like blood. I had to put coffee in to cover the taste. Barely warm coffee."

"Well, at least we have the iodine. I guess we'll have to use it from now on."

"But what about the Maya? We don't have enough for them, and they probably can't boil the water, either. How are they supposed to drink?"

"They're used to it. They're from here. They'll be fine with the pump water."

Giving up, Lenore mixed warm iodine water with the Open Arms corn mix. Then she poured the gravelly batter onto a warmed pan and hoped for a tortilla. After half an hour, it still would not firm up, leaving them with a gritty soup that tasted like mold.

"Fritos and Swiss Cake Rolls for dinner," Lenore announced. She sliced open their box of emergency junk food supplies, though it shamed her to be doing so. What kind of model village would it be if she did this every day? The whole silent village, she was sure, could hear the plastic packaging crinkle in her hands.

The sermon began at eight o'clock that evening. The Maya filed into the church, orderly and silent, requiring minimal direction from the guards. Herded from activity to activity all day, they'd been kept busy to give them a sense of normalcy, but Lenore had no idea what was normal for Indians. The men didn't normally have jobs, the women did not normally have water pumps and hot plates. Certainly no one had had television. But here they were now, shuffling in from their daily Lesson in Democracy.

Lenore sat on the stage behind Dan, facing their congregation. She watched the Indians, feeling a rush of tenderness and hope for these way-ward souls.

Dan held a hand up for quiet, an unnecessary gesture, then signaled to Mincho. In his uniform, Mincho swung his AK-47 behind his hip to allow him to speak closely into the microphone. In the system they'd worked out an hour before, Dan would speak a sentence and then pause for Mincho to translate into Quiché. To make this work, he had to keep to single sentences that were very concise.

"Welcome, my brothers and sisters in Christ," Dan said. A third, unex-pected voice followed. An echo off the mountains from the speakers. Huela, tied up outside, whimpered at the sound of Mincho's voice.

Lenore scanned the congregation, over the weary faces, watching for a flicker of understanding.

"God has brought you all to this village for a healing.

"You do not need to run from the guerrillas anymore.

"You do not need to run from your sins.

"Here, the military has been called upon by God to protect you.

"They have chosen to forgive you for your subversive acts.

"And now you need to forgive those that have hurt you.

"The military has brought you here to be healed.

"Only when there is forgiveness can Guatemala experience peace.

"And true forgiveness only comes through the Lord Jesus Christ."

Dan tried to slow down, to allow the echo to die off before his next line, but he struggled to tame his momentum. Lenore imagined his words reach-ing the guerrillas camped in the forest.

"In heaven, there is no poverty, there is no lack of food.

"There is land for everyone. But to get there, to get to heaven, you must give up your gods and accept the one true God.

"In the end, God will punish those who deserve to be punished.

"And you will live rich in heaven.

"Do not dwell on what has happened to you here.

"There is no changing the past."

Unable to wait for his small church echo, Mincho, and then the larger Spanish echo from the mountains, Dan kept on. Sentences overlapped so that Dan seemed to be interpreting Mincho. The Maya didn't care. They sat, slumped, as if their bodies and spirits were as threadbare as their clothing. The filth had to have a psychological effect. Nothing to do about it until the clothing donations arrived.

Outside, Huela began to howl and howl in her abandonment, a fifth voice contributing to the confusion.

"In the Bible, there is the story of an evil place. It became so corrupt that God decided it had to be destroyed. A man named Lot was spared, God told him to take his family and flee the city, but to not look back under any circumstance. This is what has happened to you. The mountains have become so corrupt that they are being destroyed. Communism, murder, paganism— all sprung from your corrupt lifestyle. Many have not made it out, but a few have. You. God has chosen you. He wants to give you a chance at a new life. But in order to do that, you must not look back."

At that moment, Lenore sensed someone's stare, which she sought out. From the audience, the woman with the blue eyes watched her. Lenore, startled, turned away.

"God is sparing you, but He's telling you not to look back. To give up the old life, the old ways, and to start new. Some of you, I know, are not willing to give all that up right away. You think that you can maybe do it slowly, one thing at a time, but I am telling you that's not possible. You are being given one chance, just like Lot and his family. It's hard, I know it's hard. It was hard on Lot, especially his wife, who could not obey. She looked back, my brothers and sisters. Lot's family was fleeing the city and his wife could not let go right away. She looked back at the destruction. She did not run back, she only glanced, and do you know what happened?"

A useless question flung up against such a crowd. No one moved.

"She was turned to salt."

Mincho translated with wide eyes, evidently hearing this story for the first time himself. He turned to Dan, shocked.

"Really?" he asked. "Like salt I put on food?"

Dan nodded emphatically. "Yes, she turned into a pile of salt and then the wind blew her away." This last part surprised Lenore. Was that really how Dan interpreted a pillar of salt? A formless pile of grains that blew away, leaving nothing? Lenore always imagined a solid salt rock, like a carved statue of the wife. A beautiful translucent statue people came from miles to admire and fear.

A few of the Indians eyed each other, panicked. Amid the distress and indifference of the others, Lenore found the woman again. With her head tipped down, only her mouth remained visible. Lenore saw that she was laughing. Some joke cracked her lips in amusement and she laughed, silently, through bared teeth.

They celebrated their first sermon by opening two cans of warm Pepsi.

"What did you think?" The empty church reflected off Dan's glasses. Bars of light lay across where his eyes should be.

"I think it was wonderful, Dan, I think it'll only get better. I mean, they've probably never been in a church and heard anyone say anything meaningful before, that applies to their real lives. They're used to burning sacrifices in the woods and caves to ancient animal gods. Who can relate to animals?"

Their church, which had been hot all day, now felt cold. The metal walls seemed to take the mild weather outside and amplify it to the two extremes.

They both sipped, trying to make the Pepsis last. They'd only had room for a twenty-four-pack and knew they'd regret this early indulgence later.

"Do you think," she asked after a minute, "they really think they'll turn to salt if they look at the mountains? They're everywhere, it's hard not to look at them."

"You know that's not what I meant, Lenore. It was a lesson." He blinked, sipped. "I mean, the story is true, but how it applies to them isn't so literal."

"I know it was, I know that. But do you think they do?" She sucked at the brown soda crescent trapped on the top of the can, flicking her eyes up for a brief, serious look. She had been annoyed Dan didn't run the sermon by her first.

"I don't know." His mouth made a nervous downward slide. "Do you think they think that? I just meant they can't go back to fighting and worshipping their old gods. Do they understand figures of speech? It was a sermon from the booklet, you'd think they'd know how these Indians think."

"Maya, Dan."

"Yes, sorry."

Lenore remembered the woman. It had to be the same woman from that morning, crying and now laughing. How many blue-eyed Indians could there be? How could anyone laugh at that story? Possibly the woman didn't understand it. About half the congregation seemed not to understand, but they certainly didn't laugh.

"Well, maybe just keep that in mind for when you write your sermons. Just maybe clarify what you mean. I can help, if you read me drafts."

"You're right," Dan agreed. "I'm sorry, I forgot to run it by you. I'm for-getting our roles already." He drained his Pepsi. "All this Old Testament stuff might be too much for them, anyway. They've seen enough destruction down here. I'm going to write all my sermons from the New Testament from now on. What do you think?"

"I was hoping you'd say that." Lenore beamed. She trusted him, she did. He knew what she'd advise without her even saying it.

And with that, a hearty boom thumped them each on the chest. An ex-plosion, followed by spats of gunfire in the distance. A battle, their first. A spotlight swept periodically through the village, showing the gaps in their church. Dan and Lenore huddled on their small bed and held each other, though the fighting was too far away to threaten the village.

~~~~~

Lenore didn't even know where Guatemala was until the graphic came on the television screen. So close to the United States. She had thought it farther, but on the television map, Guatemala and the United States were only an inch distant. President José Efraín Ríos Montt had taken power in Guate-mala just weeks before, and this would be his first television interview. On *The 700 Club*, of all shows! After listening for a minute about the situation down there, Lenore woke Dan and pulled him into the living room to watch.

"The Lord," Pat Robertson said, "has a plan for Guatemala. This plan was put in motion in 1954, with the ousting of the Communist leader, Jacobo Arbenz. The Guatemalan people, inspired by Christian principles, rose up in civil war themselves and defeated him. But the Communists who brought him to power have not yet been defeated. They moved to the mountains to fight, and have been fighting for the past twenty-five years, to bring commu-nism back to Guatemala. Tens of thousands have been killed by these guer-rillas, even more are being brainwashed to believe that the government is doing the killing. Mostly uneducated, impoverished, pagan natives, who have joined the fight out of ignorance, for revenge, or Communist promises of free land. But now Guatemala has a new leader, who will put an end to the civil war that has been raging for decades. President Ríos Montt is aware of God's plan. He is a born-again Christian."

Ríos Montt's black, oiled hair could not quite hide his large ears, which burned red with divine purpose. His thick mustache shaped his entire mouth into a frown. Lenore studied the man, amazed to see a born-again president at all, let alone one in a third world country. "The Lord," he said with impressive gravity, "showed me in a dream what I could accomplish in my country."

Pat Robertson sipped his coffee. "Some people might be skeptical that you assumed power through a coup, but you have the backing of Reagan. In a country filled with pagans and Communist guerrillas, electing a righteous leader democratically is impossible." Which made sense, Lenore decided. "Sometimes democracy will not work. The Lord knows when to use force, and He is not afraid to wield His power through military means." He paused a moment, in reverence of this power, and then asked, "What did God show you in your dream?"

The new President of Guatemala took his time. He closed his eyes, his lids trembling, the dream coming all over again. "In my dream, there was a war waged on a large map that I held in my hands." He raised two fists to hold up this invisible map. Lenore strained forward, not wanting to miss a word. "The government was fighting the Communist guerrillas, the Communist guerrillas were killing the Mayan peasants, and the peasants were fighting the government. There was blood and killing everywhere." Then the camera zoomed in so slowly that his face grew bigger with the revelation. "And then, one by one, the warriors laid down their weapons and raised their hands to heaven, with fighting still going on all around them. One by one, they began to recognize God." Tears welled in Lenore's eyes. She dabbed at them with her sleeve, realizing how small her problems really were. At least she did not live in a war-torn nation. "These people laid down their weapons and became oblivious to everything else. This continued, until exactly half of the people were praising God. When that one person who made it half laid down his weapon and lifted his hands to heaven, all the fighting stopped."

Right there on the show, Pat Robertson began fund-raising to help Ríos Montt repair his nation. He called for donations to a charity called Operation Open Arms, which would send food, along with housing and medical supplies, to Guatemalans. A number flashed on the screen. Lenore wrote it down and Dan rubbed his eyes, while Pat Robertson said, "More than anything, to help fulfill God's plan for Guatemala, we need every one of you to write your congressman, demanding that the Guatemalan military sanctions be lifted. No supplies can make it down there unless we convince our lawmakers that President Ríos Montt is a righteous man who can save his country. First we need the law, then we need the money and supplies, but most importantly, if our efforts succeed, we need missionaries to help spread the word of God in this suffering nation. The Lord is calling on all of you to help in any way possible. If you can only send a few dollars, that's fine. If you can send more, send more. But if you want to dedicate yourself to this cause, please talk to your local pastor. We are going to lobby our lawmakers and coordinate with churches all over the country, sending our own warriors down there to help fulfill God's plan for Guatemala. Only when half the population has been born again will the nightmare stop. You could be the person who reaches the one who makes it all stop. The Lord is putting out a call, and we need to assemble our army of love."

Lenore stared at the screen, feeling very peculiar.

"I know there are some of you out there who've been seeking a larger role in God's plan." Pat Robertson placed a finger on his temple. "God's telling me *right now* that there is someone out there, someone who has been struggling with despair. Someone in Kentucky." Lenore's mouth fell open. "Who wants to do more, but has not been able to find a purpose." He pointed right through the screen, at her. "God wants me to tell *you* that this is *your* opportunity to do God's work. Do you feel Him moving through you right now? Do you feel Him putting the Call in your heart?"

She did, she felt it, like adrenaline. It began in her heart, which quickly pumped it through her body, out to her limbs. She stood up, with her hands in the air. Dan had fallen asleep again, but the movement woke him, and he blinked at her.

That night, the larger picture became clear to Lenore. She pictured it just as Ríos Montt had said, a large map in her hands. She and Dan had never discussed joining a foreign mission before, as they'd been trying for years to have children. But for some reason, God had withheld that blessing from them. As had the state adoption agency, after seeing Dan's record. And now Lenore finally understood why God had kept them childless. She had been waiting for some more subtle signs about her purpose, but this one was all color and lights, playing on the television and spoken in clear English. Guatemala was the reason; Guatemala was the larger picture Pastor May had been speaking of.

~~~~~

They had to use their iodine in everything, to soak beans, to brush their teeth. It tinted their fingers reddish orange. The drops spread through water like red smoke. It tasted too awful by itself, so they added the Folgers instant powder to everything they drank and Lenore kept a constant supply of warm, weak coffee on the hot plate.

After the pledge and song the next morning, after the road crew marched off into the forest, the Civil Patrol gathered the women for their first day of work in the surrounding fields. The only difficulty in coordinating the women was the children, many clinging to their mothers' skirts and refusing to let go. The children had to be extracted at the gate and Lenore watched the unfortunate effect of the wooden machetes, which the children feared even when lowered.

In the distance, columns of smoke rose from the mountains, from where helicopters had flown thirty minutes before. One, two, three columns of smoke, perfectly spaced and orchestrated.

The women knelt in the dirt, just outside the fence, digging with plastic spades. Their children lingered at the fence with their fingers curled in the links, watching. Lenore eyed these kids, knowing what she had to do. She didn't have an interpreter, but she did have the pamphlet on ministering to children and her phrase book. The day before, Dan had come home exhausted from working the Civil Patrol; the road crew had cut fifty yards of road, and Lenore hadn't even changed out of her pajamas.

The children that Lenore could lure away from the fence were coaxed with offerings of saltwater taffy, held out at arm's length. Some took the candy and remained, while others followed her distantly for more.

Once in the carpeted clean cool of the education building, Lenore felt a bit of freedom from everyone's expectations. She was usually so good with children, though these kids seemed nothing like her nieces and nephews. She remembered Pastor May's proclamation that as a missionary she could be mother to a hundred children, instead of just a few of her own. It had inspired her then, but did nothing for her now.

She and the children eyed each other. She counted forty-three, with no pushing or chatter, not a sound, except for the same openmouthed cough that circulated through the group. Mostly emaciated, they struggled with the taffy. They chewed and chewed with pained expressions, pink foam pushing out of their mouths.

Lenore closed the pamphlet. Waving puppets at these children suddenly struck her as demented. She had two, both with cut felt smiles, one with green hair and earrings to illustrate that you could still be cool and love the Lord. They stared up at her from the bottom of the supply box, smiling and dead.

Lenore could have wept for relief at the sight of the television in the corner. With nothing else to do, she found the power switch and coasted the channels until she found a Spanish-language cartoon. She turned the volume up to drown out the battle sounds in the distance and the shoveling nearby. The children sat on the floor and remained, transfixed in various poses of wonder, for four hours.

The battle went on into the night, closer than the night before. Lenore and Dan, exhausted but jittery from too much Folgers powder, could not sleep. They ate their gritty soup of corn mix and beans and lay in bed, talking.

"How was your time with the children?"

Lenore had prepared herself for this question. The television, she knew, was only meant for the formal lessons. The cartoons appeared moral enough, but then they had ended, and for an hour they had watched something called a telenovela, which seemed to Lenore to be a soap opera. The children accepted it, openmouthed, just the same as they had the cartoons.

"Good," she said. "They're so good. They don't really act like children."

"What did you end up doing? The puppets?"

"No, we worked on our Spanish." It was not a lie.

"But you don't speak Spanish, Lenore."

"I know. We're all learning together."

At some point, Dan fell asleep. Lenore listened to his strangled, weak snore. How could anyone sleep through this? Smelling smoke, feeling an intense heat, she sat up. But no, it was Dan, burning up. She put a hand on his arm, feeling his sunburn, like a dry fever.

~~~~~

The clothing donations from Open Arms arrived at the end of the week. About half of the clothes proved useless, missing zippers or ripped. Other clothing Lenore deemed impractical, like the electric-pink prom dress with a vomit stain down the front. By the light of the open church door she sorted through them all, while the Civil Patrol marched by every fifteen minutes, doing their rounds. Lenore heard Dan counting their steps aloud by fives as they circled the church, then cut through the square to circle the education building, where the women and children were having a Spanish lesson.

How many hours of TV had the kids watched this week? At least thirty, Lenore knew, feeling terrible. The Spanish lessons, democracy lessons, the sermons from Ríos Montt, and then their time with her. They emerged each day from a supposed Bible lesson with their faces sticky with taffy, their eyes glazed with too much sugar and television. She'd run out of candy already and had to write the church for more.

Lenore paused to watch the patrol disassemble, attempting something. Two Indian men crouched below a window with their wooden machetes, and two others stationed themselves at the door. Mincho waved a signal. Dan then repeated Mincho's signal to the others. The two men under the window leapt up and yelled, "Ha!" just as the two at the front door ran away. Dan shook his head, with his machete still raised for something.

By late morning, Lenore succeeded in sorting the donation clothing. One by one, the women approached the altar and Lenore would eye them and any children clinging to them. She'd select a size, and hold an outfit up against their ravaged frames. Sometimes, wanting to be generous, she'd go through a few outfits to find one that was flattering.

They were passive, accepting, not hostile at all, not even the ones at the end of the line who received tie-dye and muumuus. And when she finished, Lenore felt she deserved a small rest, some leisure, and the end of her project just so happened to coincide with the beginning of the soap opera. It really was silly, but also just the thing to reward herself for her success. The conference teachers had warned them that the women would be difficult about the clothes, so she had not expected it to be so easy.

But an hour later, when Lenore emerged from the education building, she saw the women shuffling about in their old clothes. The day that had been so promising now was wasted. Lenore had three hours until Dan came home and asked her what she'd done with her day.

She would go door-to-door with the phrase book, Lenore decided, to try to recruit baptisms. And in doing that, she would also investigate what had happened to the clothes.

She sounded out the Quiché translation for, *Hello. I'm here to tell you that Jesus loves you and that He wants you to accept Him as your savior. Would you like to be baptized and born again as a Christian?* She repeated this over and over, trying to memorize it.

A girl was loitering in the square when Lenore stepped out of the church. Lenore recognized her from the clothing distribution. No more than fifteen, she had surprised Lenore with her dark beauty. It took this second encounter to place her as the girl from that horrible scene earlier in the week, holding her grandmother on the ground. Lenore knew right away what dress to give her. An elegant white linen dress that she had deemed impractical until that moment. When she held it up, the girl had smiled.

"¿*Sí?*" Lenore had asked.

"*Bueno,*" the girl said in Spanish. "*Gracias.*" She patted the fabric.

And just like that, Lenore had spoken to her first Mayan refugee.

But now the girl still wore her tattered costume, the white dress she had admired forgotten. Lenore approached and promptly offered salvation to the girl.

"*Sí,*" she replied to this offer. "*Gracias.*" She smiled the same smile as before.

"¿*Cómo say llama?*" Lenore tried, with her rudimentary, conference Spanish.

"Cruzita Sola Durante," the girl replied, raking a line in the dirt between them with her naked toe.

"Cru-zita," Lenore repeated, writing in her notebook. She couldn't believe how easy this was, saving an Indian. Mayan.

"Your dress," Lenore tried. "Where is the dress I gave you?" She ran her hands down her own body, then put her hands up, asking where.

The girl just smiled and smiled, staring down at her doodling foot.

No one rejected her offer of salvation. All the women gave their names, then the names of their children for baptism, then became afraid when Lenore wrote them down. The calls to the sheds all began to run together in her head. She nearly finished one group when she realized she'd gotten them hours earlier. But they'd answered the question, given her their names, panicked at her pen, again.

Some of the clothing appeared on the shed floors as bedding, others hung as privacy screens or were ripped into cloth for washing at the pump. Near the end of the afternoon, Lenore entered a shed with a belted red dress hung in the doorway, filtering the sunlight. A voice greeted her.

"Hello."

A woman's voice. Lenore drew the dress aside to allow more light. A woman sitting in the dark.

Well, Lenore said to herself. That's a step. No one had tried English with her. But the woman did not move from her place on the floor.

"You know there's electricity here," Lenore said.

She moved her hand toward the switch, but the woman said, "I like it dark."

Lenore's vision adjusted, allowing her to see the blue-eyed woman from that first day, sobbing on the ground, then laughing at the fate of Lot's wife.

Surveying the shed, Lenore spied a small tower of stones and a bundle of pine needles on the hot plate. In a corner, ants swarmed a ruptured corn mix bag. Lenore traced their route back to the door. But this woman was neater than the rest. She hoarded the newspapers the soldiers delivered every day, but did not use them for bedding. Instead, she stacked them neatly. And on the wall, she'd pasted carefully torn-out out articles with spit. Right at her elbow, Lenore read a headline: "*La resurrección de Evie Crowder.*" A story accompanied by a blurred photo of a little girl. So blurred that her nose and mouth were pixelated and lost.

"Everyone in the village is now signed up for baptism," Lenore announced the moment Dan returned, dusted gray from a day of marching. Her success had cheered her completely from her guilt about the TV. To repent for the telanovela, she had also moved the junk food box below several others to make it inaccessible.

"Really? Is that why you were running around all day? You got everyone?"

It was basically true, except for the woman who spoke English. Lenore didn't even ask her. She had been so shocked that she had just left without taking her name. Now she wished she had, because after an afternoon of contemplation, she decided that this woman had violated camp rules.

"Dan," she tried, "I saw in one of the sheds today, someone had what looked like a stone altar, and some pine needles burning."

"Who? Which shed?"

She proceeded with caution. "I can't remember, there was no one inside, but there aren't pine trees here. There aren't stones."

"The road crew. The road crew must be bringing it in."

"Should we confiscate it?" Lenore asked. "Aren't we supposed to?" It seemed so pathetic, so petty. Desperate people smuggling stones and leaves into the barren village. Like people who just missed the forest.

"I can't imagine taking anything from these people," Dan admitted, wiping his hand on his pants. "Can you?"

"I guess it'll mean more if he decides to get rid of it himself." Using the masculine pronoun had been automatic. Why was she hiding this woman from Dan?

"Well, one step forward, two steps back," Dan said cheerfully.

"Two?"

"The clothes. I thought the clothes would be the easiest part. Who would want to wear those filthy rags?"

"I know, Dan. I know."

"At least the men are wearing them," he offered lamely. Of course, he knew that the point of the clothing had been the women. It was almost entirely a village of women and children. And the men mostly wore regular clothes already. "Maybe now that you've got everyone signed up for baptism, you can spend your time convincing the women about the clothes."

Lenore nodded. How could she convince women this traumatized of anything? What could she do, strip them down and force them into the clothes? And Dan had his own problems. "I found out today that a lot of the Indians don't speak Quiché." He sighed, massaging his eyes.

"What do you mean? That's the Indian language, isn't it?"

"Turns out there are several Indian languages. Quiché's only one."

Lenore's pride leaked from her, silently. Never had she saved so many souls, but possibly half didn't understand her. She searched for the phrase book, which was lost already in their cluttered room.

"Mincho was trying to teach the men how to secure a building. But some of the guys had no idea what he was instructing." Dan shook his head, lost himself. "And then the guys who did understand became confused when they saw the others. So half of them fled their positions, and the other half just stood there."

"What's the use of that?" It had been convincing when she saw the setup. She remembered panic flooding her chest for just a moment, seeing the patrol surround the education building full of women and children.

"It's training, that's all. But how can we train a police force when we don't even speak their language?"

"How did you not know before? It must have been obvious the past few days that they didn't speak Quiché."

"I have no idea what Mincho says to them. I think he knew, but he thought he was still getting through to them. But, obviously, only enough to march in time and fold a flag. Anything more complicated is impossible."

"Do you think the General knows?"

"I have no idea. They never mentioned at the conference any language but Quiché. Maybe he doesn't know."

Dan began rewriting that night's sermon, making it relevant to the problem with the patrol. He read aloud, remembering their agreement: "*There is a story in the Bible about a place like here. In this place the people wanted to build a tower to reach God. But God punished them. The tower crumpled and everyone was cursed to speak different languages. Hundreds of languages, and no one could understand his neighbor. This is what has happened here. By fighting your government, by trying to impose an unnatural system on your country, you have tried to play God. And you have been punished. You have been brought here, in a confusion of languages, to repent and be reborn.*"

"That's good." Lenore nodded. "There's a Bible story for everything, isn't there?"

"*God punishes, but He also forgives. He is merciful. He's given you a common language to learn. You can rebuild your nation and finally become Guatemalans under the one true God, one language and one blessed government. All you need is an open heart and patience.*" Lenore smiled, feeling uplifted. The day did not seem like such a failure anymore. Yes, God was merciful, patient. And she needed patience, too. Dan went on, "*The government is providing you with Spanish instruction for free. We are offering you God, for free. All you have to do is accept and be made clean.*" He paused, unsure. "What do you think? I know only half will even understand, but it's better than nothing."

"It's good, it's good," Lenore repeated, stirring their dinner on the hot plate. Then she remembered.

"What?" Dan asked, seeing her hesitation. "What's wrong with it?"

"I think it's good, really I do. It's just, I just remembered. The Tower of Babel. That's the Old Testament, too. I thought we weren't going to do the Old Testament anymore."

Dan tossed his pen aside. "Well, we can't completely ignore the Old Testament. It has valuable lessons, too."

~~~~~

Whenever a truck arrived at camp to deliver airlifted supplies, no one knew what it carried until soldiers unloaded it. Sometimes supplies for the education building, sometimes newspapers from the capital, or more of the corn mix bags. Everyone gathered to watch. With the first food bag that appeared, the women swarmed the truck. If the door opened to reveal more surrendered Maya, the others would walk away or linger, trying to see a relative.

When new Indians arrived, Lenore signed them up for baptism right away. Once they disappeared into the crowd, she knew she wouldn't be able to identify them again. She found it difficult, approaching them in this degraded state, asking, before offering even food or water, if they'd like salvation. And who knew what language they understood? But they always said yes, giving their names up so easily that Lenore wondered if they were afraid to refuse. She banished the doubt quickly, however. The Devil, she reminded herself, is an agent of doubt. And only the Devil could twist the idea of salvation in her mind to make it suspect.

Despite her falling into a routine, too much coffee powder put Lenore on edge. The constant explosions in the distance made her jump, the soldiers marching made her clench her teeth. It had been nearly three weeks since she'd signed everyone up for baptism and she'd still had no success with the children or the clothes. More refugees arrived in trucks now, along with some baked rolls—a recent addition to their diet, one per refugee per day. Lenore took the new arrivals' names with shaky handwriting. When she finished, she turned and almost plowed into someone standing directly behind her.

The Indian stood so close that Lenore detected several smells coming off her body—sweat, excrement, smoke, and mud. She'd never been so close to an Indian. The woman kept her head down, extracted a flaking, raw finger from her right fist, and pointed at the list in Lenore's hand. "Emelda Tuq."

"You'd like to sign up for a baptism?" Lenore studied her, but her head remained lowered. She was sure she had signed everyone up already.

The woman nodded, averting her face. And that was when Lenore knew. Something compelled her, made her unafraid. She touched the woman's chin, directing her face up. A face rugged as bark, with two bright eyes set deep like jewels.

"*You* want to be baptized?"

She pretended not to understand the question.

No one's willingness to have their name on the baptism list surprised Lenore but this woman's. Emelda. She pretended she didn't speak English now. Lenore wondered if she should inform the General of her presence. He said they should report anyone who stood out. This woman certainly did. She'd found something to laugh at in each of Dan's sermons. That disturbed Lenore, more than her bizarre looks, more than her English skills. What did this woman find so funny about all this?

Was Lenore in a position to reject someone's salvation? Yes, probably. Especially if that person had built a pagan altar in her shed. But if she refused her baptism, the General would be informed. Lenore didn't have the courage to make such a major decision yet. The woman, seeing her name recorded, smiled grimly, showing a mouth full of teeth that looked burned.

"Dan, I think I've come up with a good way to minister to the women here."

Dan did not react right away, but merely nodded at the watery corn mix Lenore presented to him, as if nothing were wrong.

"It's just that I've been working so much with the children." The past three weeks had been terrible, nothing but a catalogue of failures. She feared that her creeping despair had weakened her mind, allowing the Devil to plant that first seed of doubt. She needed to start fresh, she needed to get away from those dead-eyed children, she needed to get away from the TV. "And you've been working with the men. I feel like we're neglecting the women. And if convincing them to change their clothes is a big part of the Project, well, then I think I may have figured out a way."

"How's that?"

"I think I'd like to teach the women to sew their own clothes. Their own regular clothes. I think that if they knew how cheap and simple our kind of clothes can be to make, how much more comfortable, then they may be more willing to wear them."

He spooned the corn mix, letting it drop back into the bowl. "But they already have the donation clothes. Aren't there plenty of donation clothes? Shouldn't we just convince them to wear those?"

"You have to admit, Dan, no one would be excited to wear those donation clothes. They're someone else's cast-offs. If we're going to convince them to change their traditions, we need to at least present them with clothes that fit them properly, that were made for them."

He squinted at the thought, as if it were either very bright or very dim.

"If they make their own regular clothes, it won't feel like they're being forced to wear someone else's things. They can be proud." The buzz from the coffee powder had turned from anxious to focused. She practically vibrated with purpose and excitement.

"So," Dan said, nodding, "it'll give them new skills, break down their old ways, and teach them to take responsibility for their own needs. This," he said, "sounds perfect. When can they do all that, though? Their schedule's full."

"I was thinking the ones who want could take a few hours from the fields."

"But there's still work to do out there. The weeding and irrigating. The crops are needed, Lenore."

"Clothes are, too. They made such a big deal out of them at the conference."

Dan nodded, cramming his dinner into his mouth ravenously, without tasting it. He looked thinner than just a week before, dirtier, almost sexy. "You know you're going to have to ask the General. Something like this must be approved."

~~~~~

Their decision to go to Guatemala seemed to solve so many of their problems, so suddenly. At first Lenore only felt her own purpose taking shape, but soon Dan began to claim signs from God pointing him to Guatemala as well. Most significantly, he could now, with divine approval, justify his firing from his construction job. The never-ending shame of his demotion, and his inability to get a better job anywhere else because of his arrest record, had trapped him in a demoralizing situation. He'd been a foreman for eleven years before a buyout had transferred the construction company to a new, much larger owner. This owner and his HR department did not want a foreman without a college education. No matter Dan's experience, no matter that the new, young foreman, though he'd studied engineering, had no idea how to pour asphalt, had never seen a Ditch Witch, and feared the jackhammer. Dan was demoted, his pay cut to a sum meant to make him quit. But instead, he spent his workdays teaching the new foreman and instructing the workers anyway, so they could finish the job on time without a lawsuit. If he didn't do this, the new company might deem his crew (full of friends and a nephew) incompetent and lay them all off, as they'd done with half the employees of the old company. This had been going on for two years before they finally fired him for drinking on the job. During the last six months, Lenore had detected alcohol on Dan's breath as he slept. This, when he'd given up drinking a decade before.

Beyond Dan and Lenore, the lives of the entire church congregation became entwined with the Guatemala mission. Their unlucky congressman received hundreds of calls and letters daily. Pat Robertson met with Reagan himself on a few occasions to discuss the problem of the military sanctions. Then in December, Reagan visited Ríos Montt in Guatemala. By January, Congress approved some military funding, Open Arms had raised a million dollars to help build model villages, and the way was paved for Lenore and Dan.

Their church had always supported missionaries, but these missionaries were people they had never met, photos on the "World Harvest" map displayed in the lobby. But then Lenore and Dan's photo went up on the wall with an arrow connecting them to Guatemala. Lenore studied this photo for a long time, during their farewell party. Their picture differed from the others. They had decided not to smile, because there was nothing to smile about when you thought of Guatemala's problems. But then she realized that everyone else on the wall was smiling—even the African missionaries—which did not make Lenore and Dan look any more serious, just miserable.

"You see," Pastor May said, coming up behind her, "God had a plan for you all along. Women are meant to be mothers, but there's more than one way. Instead of having your own, you can now be mother to a hundred children."

She turned, held her iced tea in front of her, and smiled. The plastic cup cracked as she squeezed. Had Dan really talked to Pastor May about their efforts to have a child?

"You're spilling," Pastor May announced, handing Lenore a napkin. "Are you having doubts?"

She smiled then, with the same look of confidence the other missionaries had. She was peeved at Pastor May for his deciding vote on the dynamic of the mission. The entire thing had been her idea. She knew the Bible better, she had known it longer. But Pastor May and Dan had agreed that Dan should be the one to do the preaching. These native cultures are sexist, Pastor May had said, and they wouldn't listen to a woman preacher.

"No, no doubts." She could not tell what she felt, other than the ice melting in her cup, freezing her fingers.

"Can you believe the fight in Congress over funding Montt?" Someone behind them blew through his lips in disbelief. "Of course because Montt's a Christian."

Thankfully, Pastor May shifted away from Lenore, just a tilt of the hips, but it was enough to allow her to breathe. "They're so obsessed with the supposed separation of church and state," he said to a gathered group, "they'd rather have people killing each other than worshipping God."

"It takes money to win a war. How can Montt save Guatemala if there's no cash? How will he get the money?"

"The Ladies of Vision will miss you," someone said to Lenore's back. Lenore, grateful, turned. "You know," Dorothy Smalls confided, "Pat Robertson put out a call for adoptions. There are so many orphaned babies down there. Brian and I were looking into it for you, but the fee's too expensive.

You wouldn't believe! So I thought the entire church could chip in. Maybe you could pick one out when you go down there."

Lenore blushed, but managed to smile through her embarrassment. Did everyone know that they couldn't get pregnant? Had Dan called the Prayer Chain hotline at some point, to get everyone praying for them to conceive?

The church rec room became crowded with people and their suggestions for Guatemala. In the corner, Pastor May's wife distributed the farewell cake, decorated to look like a Guatemalan flag, limp and overburdened with icing that stained everyone's lips a deathly blue.

Pastor May approached again, accompanied by Dan, who was on his second piece of cake. "I've been waiting to catch you two together," he said. "I just wanted to give some last-minute advice. I know you've gotten a lot, but I've worked with so many missionaries and I know the strain this can put on a marriage."

Dan took Lenore's hand and squeezed it dramatically, as if they were about to jump off a bridge together.

"A mission takes up all your time," Pastor May told them. "You'll often be doing separate projects. Stress and lack of supplies will cause you to blame each other for shortcomings. I know you don't see it now, but it can quickly get out of control. I've talked to several missionaries and I've given this advice. They've come back later to tell me how well it worked, so this is a proven help."

"What?" Dan asked. "Remembering our roles?"

"Oh yes, that, but there's something much simpler. A small exercise that will make all the difference. Whenever one of you is upset with the other, whenever doubts creep in about the mission or each other, just write down whatever is bothering you and mail it home, to Kentucky. Don't fight, don't let doubts take over in such a volatile environment. Once the mission is over, once you have seen the larger picture and are back here, you can go through your mail and read about all your doubts and frustrations. They will seem so little, like nothing, in comparison to what you accomplished."

"That's great advice," Lenore admitted.

"And when you are happy with one another, many times you'll be apart or too tired to share it. In those times, when you are proud of each other, write a small note and leave it on the bed. When the other finds it, it will be a great source of encouragement."

"That seems simple," Dan said, though Lenore knew he was a terrible letter-writer. Her notes, she knew right away, would be more and better than his.

"Yes," Pastor May agreed, "it's simple, but the hardest part will be maintaining a balanced marriage. Don't forget your roles." It would be the hardest part, they both knew. "Your roles as husband and wife balance each other out. If you forget them, everything will go wrong."

He did not have to remind them of their roles—the backbone of all their marriage counseling with him. Dan, as the husband, was in charge. He made decisions, but remained obligated to Lenore as his advisor. Wives were advisors, very important advisors. If a husband recognized that, if he listened to his wife, he would make good decisions. If he ignored her, things would quickly sour. Likewise, it was Lenore's responsibility to advise, but also to defer to Dan's decisions. If she forgot her role, if she tried to be the decision maker, they would be thrown into discord. In a marriage, to avoid strife, there always must be one person in charge. Countries, classrooms, any kind of productive entity follows this model, Pastor May said. God put the man in charge. He had to choose one, and He just chose. It's not because the man is better than the woman, the choice had to be made and He did it.

"What," Lenore had asked, "if a husband and wife agreed to switch roles? They would still balance out, wouldn't they?" She had asked this during their discussion weeks ago on who would preach. It had been her calling, after all, not Dan's.

"God could have just as easily chosen the woman as the decision maker," Pastor May repeated, nodding. "You're right."

"Right," Lenore said.

"But He didn't."

~~~~~

After three weeks, the uphill road to the military base no longer looked new, but as if it had always been there. Lenore and Dan walked, escorted by one of the boy soldiers, for their first status meeting with the General. In the fields on either side of this road, bright green sprouts pulled free of the earth. Lenore had never asked what the women were planting this whole time and she could not tell now. She had the idea it would be several different things, to help round out the Mayan diet.

So many things to talk about with the General, and Lenore tried to calm herself as they navigated the halls of the base. Somewhere nearby a baby screamed, making her tense. She had not heard back from the General about her sewing class idea, and was preparing herself to confront him about it. Not confront, actually. She would simply let him know that communication was important if the model village was to be a success. But once they entered his office, fragrant with cooking smells, the energy for arguments left her.

"You are in time for dinner!" the General said as a greeting. "I thought you two soldiers would like something other than corn mix and dried beans. I'm sorry it has to be that way, but if we fed you steak every day, it wouldn't seem very fair. Not a model village at all!"

They both sat and stared down at steaks, accompanied by sides of creamed potatoes and cooked, buttered corn shaved from the cob. Next to the full plates, silverware reflected the room back up at Lenore in bright, distorted shapes. She didn't think she had ever experienced real hunger until this moment. Three weeks of the same dish: cornmeal and beans. Lenore had yet to figure out how to cook it properly, but she found out that all the women had a hard time getting it to firm up on the hot plate.

"Please," the General said, "eat!"

Dan did not eat. Lenore sipped her water, clean and cold and free of iodine. She drank, noting the matted and framed diploma behind his desk: Harvard, class of 1969.

The General did not touch his food, either, but allowed his face to collapse under the weight of the serious issues before them. He began by updating them on the national crisis: more Maya were flooding from the mountains, fleeing the guerrillas for amnesty. In retaliation, the guerrillas had started massacring innocent villagers, for fear that they would go to the military and betray their whereabouts. He went on, but Lenore could no longer resist. She began to eat. Dan followed a few seconds later. The steak was cooked rare, the potatoes exquisite—creamed to a fine fluff and crusted with salt. The corn tasted like home. Fresh and simple, giving slight resistance before popping with a burst of butter between her teeth.

"With the guerrillas, it is a very sticky situation," he continued. "It is very hard sometimes to tell innocent Indians from the guerrillas, so we must use all our resources to watch for guerrilla infiltration of the village."

"Guerrilla infiltration?" Dan asked. "What would guerrillas do if they got here?"

"They may kill surrendered Indians, or they may try to organize a revolt from the inside. What's important is you two are there all the time, you can be my eyes. If anyone stands out, if anyone seems suspicious, you must tell me. And do not think it will only be men. Most spies in Guatemala end up being women and children."

"What's suspicious?" Lenore asked with her mouth full.

"Anyone who is trying to talk to the Indians, anyone who stands out or tries to ruin the programs we have."

"Like the sermons?" Lenore asked. "If they disrespect the sermons?"

"Yes, exactly! Has anyone been disrupting the sermons?" the General asked with intense interest, his eyebrows crammed down.

"Oh no!" Lenore regretted this tactic. She wanted to be honest with the General, but in that moment she realized that reporting small instances like this made them sound bigger, more significant than they actually were. Since she had yet to even see the General enter the camp, he had no context. Just be quiet and listen, she told herself. Don't cause trouble where there is none.

"These programs," he continued, "are our best weapons against Communist lies. Because guerrillas love ignorance. They take advantage of the Indians' ignorance to convince them of things that are not true. They can easily start a revolt in the camp with their lies." He waved his napkin to dispel Lenore's visible alarm. A revolt from the inside? Orchestrated by women and children? "Education is good," the General continued. "It makes people see things in better ways. When I was at Harvard, I read *Pride and Prejudice*!"

Dan and Lenore nodded, chewing.

"And when I read it, I saw Guatemala! Like the sisters. Guatemala is like a sister in an unfortunate position who has to make a good match, right? A good match to be successful. We have a choice to make a good match, like with Mr. Darcy. Or a bad match, like with Wickham! He's very sexy, Mr. Wickham. He makes promises. Like the Soviets! Promises that sound nice, but cannot be. We must know better. We must wait for our Mr. Darcy!" He heaved forward with this proclamation. "Right?"

"Mr. Darcy," Lenore repeated. She had no idea what he was talking about.

"The United States! Rich and moral and stable. It was the most important book of my education." He turned to Dan. "Do you have the baptism list for me?"

Dan put down his knife to pass over pieces of ripped-out paper from the baptism log. There were just fifty on the list, stamped with Dan's translucent, buttery thumbprint.

"This is all? There are over three hundred Indians in the village now." He frowned deeply. Everything he said with either a smile or a frown, like a man who'd spent his life communicating with people who didn't speak his language.

"There's a long waiting list," Dan said. "Lenore has everyone signed up.

We've just been so busy that we've only had one ceremony, for the sick villagers. It takes a while, because everyone has to have their baptism interview beforehand."

"They can have their interview after," the General declared. "You must start baptizing tomorrow. The President is concerned about delays."

Dan hesitated, then nodded. "Okay, that's fine. Hopefully, soon we'll catch up and be able to do it in the right order."

This pleased the General. "And I understand you have some requests?"

"Yes," Dan said, licking his lips. He swallowed quickly and abandoned his next bite. "First, we're concerned with housing. It seems we'll run out of sheds soon. The pit toilets, too, won't be enough. And I noticed that some of the women aren't getting enough food. I know the men and women are supposed to work for their families' rations, but what about the older widows? It seems they're getting by mostly on the charity of their neighbors, who can't spare much."

The General nodded. "Charity is a Christian virtue, yes?" He stared at Dan.

"Well," Dan said, looking at his plate. "Yes."

"Good." The General clapped twice. "You see, they're learning. This is good."

Lenore opened her mouth, but abruptly closed it.

"Anything else?" the General asked.

"We're curious about plantings. Will the villagers get vegetables?" she asked.

"The Indians are planting wheat."

"Only wheat? That's a lot of wheat for one village."

"The wheat is part of the Project. Every model village plants wheat, then it is all put together with the corn mix and to make the rolls."

"But it's just so much wheat. Maybe you could reserve a small section of the field for vegetables. The corn mix can't be very nutritious—"

"The Indians eat corn," the General proclaimed with a raised fist. "We give them corn mix. They are corn people. They believe they're made out of corn. Just ask them."

"Okay."

"What about interpreters, General?" Dan asked. "We still only have one interpreter. We have at least four Mayan languages in the village and we can only interpret Quiché. When will we get interpreters?" The tone of his voice, to Lenore's surprise, verged on confrontation.

"We are working on that," the General said, now smiling and frowning at the same time, a look of sympathetic pain at their troubles. "There are many model villages and not many people who speak English and Indian. Not everyone here," he added, straightening, "went to Harvard."

"Are there female interpreters? Can I request a woman, please?" Lenore asked.

"Why?"

"I think the women are afraid of Mincho." Dan kicked her discreetly, but she kept on. "At the conference they said that a lot of the guerrillas dressed as soldiers and raped them. They're terrified of Mincho because he wears a uniform. I think if I had a female interpreter they'd be more open to the program. Can I request one, please?"

"Sure," he said, his eyes glinting in polite refusal. "Anything else?"

Dan turned his list over in his hand, skimming down and deeming vitamins, milk, better hot plates, bandages, soap, antiseptic, and antibiotics unworthy of mentioning. He also failed to mention that they suspected that the well was what was giving everyone diarrhea and filling the pit toilets too quickly. Dan refolded the list and said, "I was hoping to talk to you about your road project. I'm a foreman, you know. I've paved highways on government contracts. I've cut fire roads for the Forest Service. I can help you map the best way to cut up this jungle."

They talked about roads for quite some time: grades, soil, gravel, defoliants. The General brought out a topographical map of the area.

"Excuse me, General," Lenore interrupted. "Excuse me. I wonder if you got my note about the sewing class. I have no idea if these notes make it to you. We give them to the soldiers and they just disappear. We never hear—" She checked herself. "I just think it could be a very important part of the program, too. Did you get my note?"

"Oh yes, I'm sorry. I get so many notes." The General leaned back to stare at the ceiling, to page through these notes mentally. "A sewing class to make their own clothes? But they have the donation clothes."

"Yes, but those clothes aren't very nice, General."

"Please, call me Gilberto."

"Gilberto. I think that taking pride in their work and learning a new skill will give them more incentive to give up their costumes. Which is a goal of the Project." She found herself repeating exactly what she'd written in the note. "And I know another goal of the Project is to convince them to participate in the economy. Sewing is a valuable skill, I think something they can work at later once the war is over."

He nodded, fingering the edge of his cherry-stained desk, thinking. He turned a hard profile, like a face stamped on a coin.

"And I fear the women are idle," she said before she could stop herself. This was not something she'd mentioned in the note. "They don't have enough to do." What was she saying? Even Dan turned, shocked. *What?* he mouthed to her.

The General's eyes squared, at something he suspected all along. "Okay, this sewing class seems like a good idea, but it is not a recommended activity on the list. If you can prove its worth, maybe I will put it on the list."

"Thank you, Gilberto."

"If you can get the women to wear these clothes, I will have all the model villages doing the same. It has been a problem," he said. "None of the women in any of the villages are wearing the donation clothes. If this works, it would be a great contribution to the Project."

They sat in their room after, feeling ill from all the food. Lenore regretted the meal, knowing that it had stretched her stomach to an unreasonable size. The next few days, she'd be hungrier than ever.

"I don't think I'm going to get a female interpreter," she said, noticing a line of ants swarming a drop of corn mix on the floor. Ants everywhere. She knew she'd never get rid of them. She also knew Dan didn't think having a female interpreter was necessary.

"Next time," he said, "we should prioritize better. I think maybe we complained too much. We didn't mention one positive thing."

"We didn't mention any of the problems, Dan. Not medicine or water treatment. We talked about roads."

"Lenore, I could see how upset you were, but I just saw that list of problems and it occurred to me that we don't have those things because we don't have roads yet. Everything was airlifted here, even the trucks at the base." Dan gave up on his sermon and moved to the bed, curling up in defeat. "I'm sorry, I meant to mention those things, but I just became so focused on the solution that I never mentioned the problems."

Lenore, surprised by this turn, began to comfort him. "I'm sure he's already aware of all the problems, Dan. I'm sure he's working as hard as he can on them." She paused. Outside, they heard shoveling. They'd come back from the meeting to find soldiers digging more toilets. "I got the sewing class. And he wants us to hold a baptism tomorrow. That's something, he is aware of priorities."

The girl Cruzita would be in the first group, which pleased Lenore. But then she remembered Emelda, further down on the list. The woman did not seem convinced by anything Dan preached. Why would she volunteer to be baptized? And how could these two possibly be related? A sweet, dark-eyed angel and a bright-eyed, cackling heathen.

"I don't know how I feel about baptizing them before their interviews," Dan said. "They need to understand the significance of the ceremony."

"Do you think . . ." she tried, "do you think some of these Indians could be using baptism for something bad?"

"What do you mean? How could baptism ever be bad?" He sat up on the bed, showing that he had been crying.

"I mean, do you think some of them don't believe? They're just going through the motions for some deceptive purpose?"

"It's possible," Dan said with a nod, "that some guerrillas have infiltrated the village, like the General said, that they're going through with it to blend in and fool us. Do you have someone in mind? Have you noticed anyone suspicious? The General wants us to report anyone who's suspicious."

"No." She was not willing to turn anyone in yet. "Everything's just been so easy. I never expected it to be this easy, saving all these people."

Dan quickly fell asleep from all the food. Lenore watched him, fighting the desire to crawl into bed herself. But she needed to write the church for sewing supplies. If she missed one thing, she'd have to wait, probably weeks, for another shipment. So she sat at the table and began to make her list. Scissors, needles, strong thread. The supplies began to sound like weapons, and Lenore wondered if this was a good idea, after all.

When she finished the note, she stood in the doorway of the church, watching the soldiers work. She counted the holes. Five new pit toilets, but they couldn't extend the sanitation building much more, as the only direction they could dig brought it closer to the water pump.

~~~~~

The next evening, Lenore strolled the paths, thinking. Some women nodded hello when she passed, while children trailed wordlessly behind, hoping for some church candy.

"I don't have any candy," she told them in English. "You have to come to church to get candy." Lenore showed her empty hands, but they kept following, the boys in clothes she recognized from the donation pile. They were healthier, no doubt, than when they had arrived. Somehow, the corn mix was more and better than what they had been surviving on in the mountains.

Making a turn, she discovered the Civil Patrol blocking her way. She'd walked in on one of their exercises: practicing a roadblock. From a small distance, Lenore could see Dan wielding his wooden machete, hacking the air at a soldier's command.

She'd never tell Dan, but these drills often looked absurd to her. Like a bunch of boys playing war. Lenore understood the need for a police force to maintain order, but she believed that brandishing those swords gave the wrong idea. Instead of making the villagers feel secure, she noticed that the exercises frightened anyone passing by. Now the patrol fell awkwardly into different formations, like a junior high marching band. Their fake weapons raised, lowered, slicing and stabbing, they marched in place. Lenore chose the long way, to avoid them altogether.

She found Emelda in her shed, alone, holding her daily roll of bread. Just standing and staring, as if it reminded her of something. When Lenore stepped in, she assessed the situation quickly. Still the stacked newspapers, and the clippings pasted to the wall. Her hot plate turned on, a red eye seething in the dark. A hardened ball of sap smoldered on the silver surface, slowly expiring in a thin trickle of upward smoke, making the air medicinal.

"I want to talk about getting you a job in the village," Lenore said.

Emelda did not respond. She considered her roll, scratched at it with a fingernail.

"I know that as a widow you don't have anyone to help earn your rations for you. And with new people coming in, it will just get harder to get food. They haven't been delivering more." Nothing, no reply, not even a glance. "And I need you, I need an interpreter. I can't do my job the way things are now."

The woman tossed the roll up and caught it, replied in an Indian language.

"I know you speak English!" Lenore snapped, then composed herself. "You spoke English to me before."

"I did?"

"Yes."

"I was not well that day." Emelda shook her head and squatted low on her heels. "I have many problems, but I'm not a widow. I don't have a husband. Never did."

"Why do you want to be baptized?" Lenore asked.

"I don't want to be baptized. I need to be baptized."

"Why do you *need* to be baptized?"

"You," she said, laughing miserably through her charred teeth, "are not a good missionary."

"I've seen you during the sermons. You shouldn't mock the Lord. I'm sure you have a boatload of sins on your record, but that is the worst of them."

"I do have sins." Emelda bounced the roll in her hand as if it had significant weight. She bounced it, then cocked her arm back and threw it out the door.

There were two things going on now, but Lenore needed to remain focused. She would scold her later for wasting food. "Well, that's the first step to earning a baptism. What are they?"

"I traded the blood of my people for land and money."

"A lot of people committed those sins. The Communists convinced them to do bad things to get land. They killed your son—"

Emelda gave her a peculiar look. "Communists didn't kill my son."

"But that's what Mincho said, that he was killed—"

Amused, her wrinkled face looked like a map. Thousands of lines, radiating in all directions from her smile. "Of course."

"Where did you learn English?" Lenore asked.

"From my grandmother. She worked for an American family."

"Okay, if you work as a translator for me, I will get you more rations." This had been the deal she'd worked out, before watching the woman throw food into the path.

"No." Her cragged face cemented in refusal. How old was she? She looked old, but all the Indians looked either like children or old. And this woman looked like she'd been left out in the weather for a century.

"Why not? I know you can't have enough food, Emelda."

"Because, no."

How could she refuse? Lenore had not even thought it possible. "The village needs you, Emelda. Everyone needs you—"

"No, no, no!" Her sudden rage stirred the air in the room. Lenore felt it, watched one of the pasted newspaper clippings flutter and break free from the wall. Lenore squinted to see the same headline as before, at her feet. "*La resurrección de Evie Crowder.*" Same headline, same picture, different article. Part Two had been pasted near Part One.

"I mean no. I mean I have worked for Americans before, it never goes well."

Lenore's only hope, worked up for days, vanished in seconds. But she could not give up so easily. Flustered and confused, desperate, she heard herself say, "If you don't work for me, I'll turn you in to the General."

The Indian's eyes drained into flat, icy disks. "Why?"

"Because he told us to tell him about anyone who stands out." She regretted this tactic immediately, even as she saw she would get what she needed out of it.

"You cannot do that! You cannot!" Emelda shot up, terrified, her hands in her black hair, pulling loose her long braid.

"Why not? If you're innocent, then you shouldn't be afraid of the General. Unless you have something to hide. Unless you're a guerrilla."

"I was not a guerrilla!" Emelda stamped her foot and raised a finger in Lenore's face. "I was not a Communist! I worked for *The Voice of Liberation*!"

"What does that mean? Does that mean you'll work for me?"

Emelda spun away, squatted back down on her heels.

"I'll pay you with food."

"I don't want food," she said, shaking her head. "I want pen and paper."

"How could you not want more food? I know you don't have enough."

"Pen and paper."

"Okay," Lenore agreed, dumbfounded.

Emelda, with this victory, set her expression like someone setting a course.

"I have a letter to write and you must mail it for me."

"Emelda, that's against the rules." She was so close to getting what she needed, and she knew she could not turn this woman in to the General now. They both knew.

"Pen and paper," she repeated. "I will translate for you if you get me pen and paper and mail my letter for me."

The light, when Lenore left Emelda's shed, was low. Objects lingered on the verge of shadow. And because of this, distracted by her unresolved standoff with this woman that she both needed and feared, Lenore came upon the Civil Patrol again, after it was too late to turn around. Lenore saw them, though they did not see her. They had stopped an old Indian woman carrying a bucket of water on her head.

Mincho shouted and the men all raised their wooden machetes. Another soldier walked to the first Indian man in line and ordered him to do something. The man did not move. The soldier repeated his command, and after a moment in which no one moved, he took his AK-47 and smashed it against the man's head. The sound was terrible. Lenore opened her mouth to scream, but nothing came out.

The soldier went to the next Indian in line and barked the same order, which Mincho translated, to no effect. Everyone, again, stood still.

That noise again, the next man's head smashed with the gun. He went down into the dirt and now two lay there silent on the ground.

The soldier moved to the next Civil Patrolman in line, Dan. Lenore curled her toes in her shoes, considered running to him and breaking up the entire scene. What could that boy soldier do to us? He would never hit Dan, she reassured herself. He marched with the Civil Patrol symbolically, that was all.

Yet Mincho barked the same order, in the same tone, at Dan. Without hesitation, Dan stepped up to the old woman, knelt down, and ran his hands up her skirt.

The soldier yelled, Mincho translated, "Higher!"

Dan's arms disappeared in the fabric up to his shoulders, his hands moving over her backside, his head against her lap. The old woman, battling the curve of her spine, kept her head high.

Dan extracted himself and stood up. "No weapons," he said, keeping his arms raised slightly in front of him, as if they were wet or dirty.

When Dan came home that evening, he sat at the table and rested his head in his hands. A spot of blood showed on his sleeve.

"You've got to preach in an hour," Lenore reminded him. "Aren't you going to practice? Your notes are right here."

"I'm not going to do that sermon today, I decided. I'll do another."

"Why? What was it supposed to be about?" She rearranged their belongings roughly, for no reason, kicking a box and clattering silverware.

"Obedience."

"And what's it going to be about now?" *Crack, thud!*

"I don't know. I'll do one of the prewritten ones in the booklet, I guess. Tell me about your day," he said as he chewed his daily roll. He slouched in his chair, his head low and to the side, like an old helium balloon.

"Very productive," she reported with a savage grin. "The children are learning to count to ten. Mincho came in to translate for a while. The fact that it was all done at gunpoint seems to make them learn faster."

Dan nodded, swallowing. The trigger in his throat moving.

She slammed a pot. "I can't work with him, Dan. I'd rather work in silence."

"He's all we have, Lenore. I know the gun isn't ideal, but the military acts in forceful ways, we act in patience and love. We're all trying for the same thing here."

"So you're not going to say anything? He scares me."

"I will try. I will," he said carefully, measuring the words for minimal impact.

Lenore shook her head, unbelieving. She pondered the dignity of the men who would rather take an AK-47 in the face than do that to an old woman, and how Dan did it without hesitation. But Lenore said none of this. She also would not tell him about the time she'd spent with the woman Emelda. She'd have to tell him eventually, but just not now. She still had not decided what to make of her. Maybe Emelda could be a great help, or maybe she was a guerrilla. She had promised her pen and paper, a simple enough request that struck Lenore only in retrospect. Maybe she wanted to communicate with the guerrillas on the outside. But no, maybe she just wanted to write to her family. All Lenore knew at the moment was that she did not want the Civil Patrol deciding.

After dinner, Dan chose that night's sermon from his booklet.

"More fire and damnation?" Lenore asked as she washed their dishes in a bucket. She used a drop of shampoo in the water and bent over, scrubbing with violence.

"What's that supposed to mean?" Dan stopped writing to study her. "This is the Good News. We're here to share the Good News with these people, so that's what I'm going to preach."

"From the Old Testament again?"

"What's that supposed to mean?"

"I just don't think everything you preach is such good news to them," Lenore said to the bucket, where the water sloshed and sudsed in her hands.

Dan got up. He walked across the room and she stood to meet him. Her hands, out of the water, went cold. Heavy suds slipped down, dropping off her fingers onto the floor. He searched her face, appalled. "Lenore? What are you saying, Lenore? You know more than I do. You know. If you believe, you have a responsibility to share. The truth . . ." he tried, shaking his head, then began again. "The truth is always good news."

~~~~~

Over the next month, improvements began to show in the camp. The wheat grew into a bright green, hopeful stubble all around, lifting everyone's mood. The national anthem woke Lenore every morning with the promise of an actual melody. The children had gained weight, making Lenore think that maybe the corn mix was sufficient for the villagers. And as the children gained weight, Lenore found herself losing weight. Her pants from home fell loose, her bras sagged. She skipped a period, but thought nothing of it. Going through the donation pile, she picked out new clothes for herself. Jeans. They looked great on her. Dan had lost weight, too, but refused the donation pile, opting instead to stab new holes into his belt.

The children, during their lessons, had begun to use Spanish phrases with one another, shyly. They could count to twenty with Lenore and seemed to be forgetting their fear, which only really returned when a helicopter ripped over the village, on its way to battle. They played with Huela and practiced Spanish commands with her. The puppy, too, improved with the village. Calmer, more attuned to her surroundings, she was becoming loyal to both Mincho and Lenore.

More precise in their movements, yet still unclear in purpose, the Civil Patrol began to take over jobs performed before by soldiers, who now mostly smoked at the gate and smiled, happy the village was running itself. Even the problem of Emelda receded, as Lenore decided to ignore her for a time. No pen and paper, no promises. The longer she put off these decisions, the more perspective she gained. As the village fell into routine, she considered that maybe she did not need the woman after all.

A month of baptisms and reassurance. The children played on the paths now, the women spent less time in their sheds and more time outside. Lenore's sewing supplies arrived. Everything seemed to be working out and Pastor May's statement that problems always seemed smaller in retrospect proved correct. After several weeks, Lenore finally decided not to write a letter home to Dan about the Civil Patrol incident.

~~~~~

The sewing class was not mandatory, Mincho explained that first morning around the flagpole, but the women could take a two-hour break from the fields if they wanted. The Civil Patrol hauled tables from the education building. Lenore really expected no one to show up. But at one o'clock, seventeen women stood outside the church, waiting, looking reluctant, though Lenore knew they had chosen to come. Possibly the first choice they'd made since surrendering.

Emelda was not among them, but her granddaughter, Cruzita, had volunteered, along with the woman who'd arrived with five children clinging to her skirt. Ama.

"Now, I know many of you are skilled at sewing your traditional clothes," Lenore said to her students, facing her with their communal, miserable expression. "But I'm here to show you that you can make much more sensible, comfortable clothes, with a lot less work and money. I've decided to start with skirts, since it looks like most of your skirts are about ready to split up the back."

Mincho barked a remarkably short translation from his position in the doorway. He had brought his gun, which he cradled in his crossed arms, while Huela nosed around the church. Abandoning his regular duties with the Civil Patrol displeased him.

Together, following Lenore's example, the women measured themselves and cut their cloth accordingly. Once the long-bladed scissors came out, Mincho flipped off his safety and circled the class. When he kicked an empty chair out of his way, half the women dropped to the ground. *Ha ha*, he chuckled.

Despite his tendency for self-entertainment, Mincho refused to translate any of Lenore's jokes. Her encouragement turned to threats in his mouth, so after a while she stopped talking altogether.

"Why?" he whined frantically in Lenore's ear, near the end of the class. "Beastie, why did you tell the General I wasn't doing my job? Why did you say the women are afraid of me? I thought we were friends."

"We are friends," she agreed hesitantly. "I didn't say you weren't doing your job. I merely said the women are afraid of the soldiers because of their own experiences. I never said it was your fault. I'm sorry if I got you in trouble."

"The women are not afraid of me," he hissed, spit flying. "They pretend to be afraid, to get me in trouble. Don't let them trick you. They're guerrillas, they trick people."

Lenore studied the women, cutting and stitching so peacefully. The girl Cruzita helped one of her neighbors thread a needle.

"Do you really think that, Mincho? Do you think everyone here was a guerrilla?" She walked away, done with the conversation.

"They trick you," he insisted at her back. "If they trick you and turn you against me, they are guerrillas. It's what guerrillas do."

It only took that first day for Lenore to realize that this sewing class, which could help the women greatly, now brought her back to her original problem. She could not rely on Mincho and she could not rely on the silent routine of the village to make her project a success. She needed a translator, and the blue-eyed Indian she had tried her best to forget began again to occupy her thoughts.

~~~~~

Lenore asked Dan if she could conduct Cruzita's baptism interview. Over five hundred Maya lived in the village now and they were behind on the General's order to have everyone baptized by the end of the month. Dan agreed because he trusted Lenore to do a good job, and because he couldn't do it all by himself.

Instead of using Mincho, Lenore asked Emelda to translate, in the privacy of her shed. Though Cruzita's first language was Quiché, she also understood Ixil. Emelda spoke Quiché and Achí. So between them, if all went well, Lenore might be able to communicate with her women in three languages. Emelda had agreed to a trial run with her granddaughter. No promises yet, no pen and paper. It would be a test for all of them, and Lenore was so nervous that she ate a whole bag of Fritos beforehand.

Outside, the Civil Patrol marched up and down the main path. Emelda still refused to use her light, but the sun was high enough to brighten the ventilation shaft in the ceiling.

Any personal attention in the camp made the Indians nervous and Cruzita mercilessly chewed her fingernails, black and broken from the fields, while Emelda perused a copy of the newspapers that had arrived that morning on one of the trucks. She scanned, looking for something specific. Evidently, she understood Spanish as well.

"Cruzita, I called you in here because you were baptized." Lenore nodded to Emelda, who translated. A rosy alarm spread across the girl's face. Emelda lowered the newspaper.

"Cruzita is afraid she's in trouble. Did she do something wrong?"

"No, no! This is part of the program. Everyone who gets baptized must have a personal interview. This is very good. Please tell her that."

As Emelda translated, Cruzita relaxed slightly. So many people in the camp had already been interviewed, Lenore thought, and, amazingly, word of the interview process hadn't got around. These people were terrified not only of the military but of each other. In her corner, Emelda found something. "I cannot believe this!" she cried. She folded a page of the newspaper into a neat square and began tearing.

"I just have a few points to make about what the baptism means, that's all. The first one being that since she was baptized, she needs to recognize that she's a sinner."

Emelda held up a hand, inked black like a paw. "If I tell her that, she will think she did something wrong. Can't you see how frightened she is?"

"There's nothing to fear. We're all sinners, Emelda. Me, you, and Cruzita."

Whatever she was ripping came free in her hands and she held it up. "Then Cruzita needs to know what sins are in your religion, so she knows what is considered wrong. She needs examples to understand. What are sins in your religion?"

Lenore felt, even as she answered this logical question, the conversation turning in Emelda's favor. "Lying, murder, greed, vanity, envy—"

Emelda laughed, waving her clipping.

"What do you find so funny about Christianity, Emelda? You're always laughing at Dan's sermons. I've been dying to know what you find so funny about all of this."

"It's just, you think you're the first with these ideas. All those are sins for us already, but you think you invented morals. What is a sin that we don't have already?"

How had Dan done this interview with so many people, so quickly? She suspected Mincho, armed, did not entertain questions as he translated.

"Okay. It is a sin to be angry and revengeful. In order to be saved, she must give up her anger and never fight. Terrible things have happened to everyone down here, but she must take the high ground and break the cycle of violence."

Emelda huffed, tossing her newspaper away. "No. I won't tell her that."

"Why not?"

"Why do we have to give up our anger? We have a right to be angry." She walked to the door, spit on her finger, and pasted her new clipping next to the others. "*La resurrección de Evie Crowder.*" Parts One and Two, and now a Part Three. All with the same picture of the little girl with pixelated eyes.

"You do not," Lenore said. "You brought all this violence upon your-selves. Everyone's guilty. Communism is a collective decision, a collective sin."

This, Lenore could see, thawed Emelda's ironic composure. "Cruzita never was guilty of anything. No one here's guilty of this war but me!"

Lenore, astonished, looked to Cruzita to confirm what she'd just heard, but the girl's blank face showed no recognition of the English words.

"Emelda, you're being unfair to yourself. How could you be guilty and everyone else innocent? You alone did not start this war."

"You've no idea what I've done. My voice was so powerful, the whole country listened to me."

"I find that hard to believe. If you had so much power over everyone, why don't you use it now? Why don't you tell them to trample the fence and free themselves?"

Lenore caught herself too late. Why did she use that word, free?

"No one here knows who I am. Not even my own granddaughter. Everyone used to listen to me, but that was a long time ago. Now, if they knew who I was, they would kill me. I want them to. I don't deserve to live, I want them to kill me, but not yet. I have something to do first." She pointed to her pasted clippings. A guerrilla. Lenore was sure of it now, but a woman? Of course, the General had warned them of this.

"As long as you admit your guilt and give up your anger, Emelda, you can be forgiven. The Communists promised everyone land if they did terrible things. Your sins aren't different from anyone else's here."

"Oh yes, I got land." Emelda chuckled. "But not from the Communists." Her eyes seemed to reflect whatever Lenore suspected at any particular moment. Guerrilla, innocent. "I got a whole mountain in Xela!"

Communist. That word caused Cruzita to panic. She patted her grandmother's arm, asking her to translate, afraid they were still talking about her. It was Lenore's turn to speak. She decided to avoid the whole business for the moment. The problem of Emelda was getting no easier.

"Emelda, we're talking about Cruzita. This is her interview. Your interview will come. If you still want to be baptized."

"Yes," she replied. "I do."

"Then your interview will come." Even as she said it, she wondered if they would get that far.

"Yes," Emelda declared, "it will."

Mincho's presence in her and Dan's room did not surprise Lenore when she came back from the sanitation building that night. Dominating the streets and now her sewing class, he had the idea that he was in charge of the village, maybe even in charge of her. She glanced around, knowing she had nothing to hide from Mincho. Huela, however, patrolled the room, sniffing around her feet.

"Hello," Lenore managed in a natural voice.

Was he trying to intimidate her? Reporting him to the General, she knew, would only make it worse. And when she complained to Dan a few hours ago about the women sewing under gunpoint, he'd said, "I guess he's used to working the Civil Patrol. We can't expect him to just snap out of that mind-set. He's very effective, the men need him."

Then they fought. Then they negotiated a fragile peace.

"Do you need something, Mincho?" Lenore asked now. Would he demand something of her in her own room? His uniform no longer looked new. Missing buttons, frayed cuffs, he looked like any other soldier now.

Mincho pursed his lips. The clutter of the apartment was unsatisfactory to him. Without trash service, they'd accumulated piles of empty pop cans, twisted toothpaste tubes, shampoo bottles, soiled face wipes, and plastic food wrappers. Huela circled one of these piles.

"The women finished their skirts today, but they are not wearing them," he said.

"I know, Mincho." Yes, she knew very well. It had not been a good day. "But those skirts were just practice. We're moving on to men's clothes now." She cringed inwardly, but she had decided on this excuse to buy herself more time. "The men are more important. The road crew needs new pants already, they're working so hard they've ripped right through the donation pants. The class will be serving the village, which is much more important than serving themselves." She could convince the women to wear their skirts, surely, with anyone but Mincho as translator.

"Humph." They both watched Huela claw at a box pushed halfway under the bed. Their box of snack food, Lenore realized.

Dan entered then, practically marching, out of breath. Looking unsurprised to see a soldier in their room, Dan handed Mincho the baptism list. "Mincho just came to me with some disturbing news," he informed Lenore.

"Oh?"

"One of the women has been selling herself for food."

"Oh." She tried her best to feign shock. The villagers, who'd arrived in the camp emaciated, were losing the weight they had gained in the beginning. Food shipments had increased, though not in pace with the rising population of the village. The road project was behind due to some strategic guerrilla gains in the jungle and it was nearly impossible to airlift the amount of food and supplies that the village now needed. In addition, the work-for-rations system did not favor widows with children. "Who?"

"Ama."

Lenore imagined the small, serious woman shooing her five children away from the sewing class. The children staring at her through Mincho's legs, making faces, and making her almost smile. Lenore had admired this woman from afar, seeing how dedicated she was to her family. She washed them every day at the pump and had even made a comb from a broken fork to fix their hair. In her mind, Lenore saw Ama as a mother more than anything else. More than an Indian, a refugee, a lost soul.

"She's up for baptism this week and there's no way I can let this happen," Dan said. "I have to write up a report now—"

"A report?"

"Yes, a report. For the General. I have a form to report any infraction." His ears blazed at the tips, as if frostbit.

Lenore said nothing at first, but let the air of out of her nostrils with an impatient puff. And that was enough. Dan wheeled around to look at her, their fight from before stoked so easily. "What?"

"I don't think that's necessary, to get the General involved." Her feelings on this subject surprised her as much as him.

"Are you kidding, Lenore? Not only do we need to tell the General, but the woman needs to be punished. If others see that this is an acceptable way to get food, we're going to be living in a brothel in a week!"

"Ama has five children and no husband to earn rations."

"Ama is a prostitute. Prostitution is a crime."

That word hit her like a splash of water, twice. Somehow, giving it that name made it more difficult to defend. She flushed with shame, but continued despite herself.

"I don't think so, Dan, I don't think so at all." Shame gave way to anger as she yelled, "I think the crime here is not enough food!"

Dan stared at her. "You're telling me you think prostitution is acceptable?"

"I'm saying that some sins trump others and the fact that we're not providing enough food for these people is tempting them unfairly to sin." Indeed, she attributed her own recent sins to hunger. The TV, her meetings with Emelda. Maybe this, too, was a lapse in judgment, but she could not stand down. The jeans from the donation pile no longer fit. They sagged in the seat, in the knees, not making her feel thin, but small and weak. She would begin sewing her own clothes along with the women.

At first Lenore felt pleased at the way village life had carved out a new body for her, but she was becoming increasingly alarmed at the fact that her period was now six weeks late. She often felt the buildup of blood raging, angering her easily, like right now, screaming at her husband, defending a woman she hardly knew.

"The food situation here is meant to promote spiritual cleansing," Dan informed her. "You know just as much as I do the spiritual benefits of fasting."

"Don't give me that, Dan. Don't tell me you really believe that down here." She laughed out loud, suddenly, uncontrollably, like a crazy woman.

Mincho spun to attention. "Beasties, I did not come here to talk about this with a woman," he said. "She is not in charge."

Before Lenore could set him straight, Dan said, "Right."

She stared at her husband.

"There's no question she'll be reported and punished," Dan said. "I have made that decision and Mincho agrees. What we need to decide now is how to prevent this from happening again."

Lenore stood in the center of the room, forcing the men to talk around her. All her delays with Emelda, and now Ama would pay the price. If she'd had the option of talking to Lenore, Lenore could have talked to the General, to get her more rations. She could have prevented all of this.

"The others must see she is punished," Mincho said. "That will help."

"The villagers could be involved in the punishment," Dan said, nodding.

"You can have them all stone her," Lenore offered. "Right there under the flagpole. And they can sing the national anthem after."

They ignored her, like an unruly child. "The General will think this is from idleness," Mincho said. "Idleness is not good. He'll be happy if we have a plan."

"Clearly, this is something the Civil Patrol should enforce. This is exactly the sort of situation we're supposed to prevent."

Lenore stepped from the center of the room. "You better start keeping an eye on me," she snapped in retreat. "I'm getting hungry, too. My Swiss Cake Rolls are almost gone. I just might up and sleep with someone for food!"

She fled through the church, grabbed one of Dan's blank sermon note-books, and ran out into the village. She had wanted to embarrass him in front of Mincho and she surely had succeeded. She walked now, briskly, taking the route she often traced in her mind. She stepped into the shed without knocking, without hesitation.

"Emelda," she said to the sleeping figure on the floor, "I need you to work for me." She threw down Dan's notebook, with a pen tucked into the spiral spine.

"I've worked for Americans before," Emelda replied. "Everyone in my family has. It never ends good."

"I'll mail your letter if you translate for me." If Dan could deny someone baptism for the wrong reasons, Lenore could bend camp rules for the greater good. She was not going to lose another woman, she decided. Not one more.

With the Indian's fearful nod, all of Lenore's confidence left her.

~~~~~

When Lenore returned to the apartment an hour later, Dan was gone. Up to the base with Mincho, she suspected, to report Ama to the General. When she awoke in the morning to the national anthem, he was still gone, but a bunch of crushed, waterless white flowers had appeared on the table. Searching outside, she could find neither Mincho nor Dan. The Indian men of the Civil Patrol oversaw the singing and pledge themselves, herding their own through the Spanish verses.

By the time the sewing class began that afternoon, Dan still had not returned from the base, though Mincho appeared to translate. He refused to answer Lenore's questions about Dan's whereabouts. Blocking the door, he merely stood, staring daggers at Ama, who had no idea why she'd been singled out. Her eyes, in distress, tried to meet Lenore's. Wanting protection, but Lenore had no idea what she could do.

Emelda, who had shown up for her first class, cast her bright eyes from Ama to Mincho to Lenore constantly, sensing something. Lenore knew she could not translate in Mincho's presence. Pressing on, she told the class that they'd move on to men's clothes.

Mincho seethed in the corner, silent, deeming a translation unnecessary.

On top of everything else, Ama and Emelda and her fight with Dan, Lenore did her best to ignore the problem of her two skipped periods. She would not even allow herself to think about it for two more weeks, she decided. False hope and heartbreak had undone her before. She was hungry, voraciously hungry, could think of nothing but food. After Dan disappeared, she ate six Swiss Cake Rolls. The last of them. Then she'd woken up to ants on her face, biting her, carrying away the unwiped crumbs from her mouth.

Each woman cut a pair of practice pants. Mincho watched Ama fiercely, while she hunched over her fabric and did not look up for two hours. She stitched and stitched a single long pant leg from all her material, afraid to look up and learn the next step.

"That's very good, Cruzita," Lenore whispered over the girl's shoulder, watching her small brown hands stitch a crotch. No, Lenore could not lose another woman to the base. She wanted so badly to talk to this girl, to ask her what she needed. But all Lenore could do was run her hands over the stitching and say, "*Bueno*," because she didn't want Mincho to translate.

After class finished, Emelda lingered, the last to leave. Quickly, so not to arouse suspicion, she handed Lenore a folded piece of paper and said, "He doesn't translate what you say. He translates what your husband says, but not you."

"What does he say?"

"When you say something nice or ask us how we do things, he'll say something else. Like, saying the General is watching them with binoculars from the base. That he can see through walls, can see everything we do."

"He said that?"

Dan, when he did return that evening, was filthy. The marks of someone's fingers made a three-pronged slash across his cheek. He limped in, threw his wooden machete down.

"Where have you been!" Lenore shouted at him. "You've been gone almost twenty-four hours!"

"I came back for a few hours last night. You were asleep. You fell asleep hugging your cakes." Had he seen the ants swarming her? She raised a hand to her mouth, feeling the red bumps there. "I didn't want to wake you."

"That's very sensitive of you." The white star-shaped flowers, now in a Folgers can of water, had started to drop their petals onto the table. She swept them away with her hand. Lenore felt appalled with herself. Why had she said that? Threatening to sleep with someone else for food? But she would not be the first to apologize. She knew she should be, but her pride would not allow it.

Dan, however, was not too proud. He touched her with a gentle hand. "I'm sorry, Lenore. I didn't mean to belittle you last night. I value your opinion. I do value your opinion, I hope you know that. I was just so angry, I felt I had failed."

Lenore, melting so easily with his admission, with the assurance that he wasn't dead or on a plane back to Kentucky, reassured him that he hadn't failed. She had failed and she had taken it all too personally, and of course she wasn't defending prostitution, she just thought there were factors to be considered. She had, as Pastor May would point out, forgotten her role as advisor.

No, he was sorry. He hadn't planned on including her in the decision about Ama in the first place, which was unfair. He'd sprung the information on her, forcing her to react suddenly. He promised to consult her from now on before making a major decision like that. He had forgotten his role, and that had made her forget her role.

And in this way, both slinking back to their spheres of responsibility, the thing between them was resolved. They had forgotten how their roles were supposed to balance and complement one another. Almost all of their fights started in this way, and they were both surprised not to have recognized it sooner.

"I like my flowers," Lenore told him later, in bed. "Where did you get them?"

"In the woods."

Lenore sat up. "Out there? How did you get out there?"

"I walked."

"What? Why? Where did you go?"

"I'm sorry, if I knew I was going to be gone so long, I would have told you. I just went up for a meeting, but then I had to see the road sites to give my opinion, so we went out and there's stuff going on you wouldn't believe, Lenore."

"There are guerrillas in those woods, Dan! You could have been shot!"

"That's the point, Lenore. They're everywhere. I saw one of their abandoned camps nearby. The General thinks they have agents here, to communicate with them."

"Communicate how?" Lenore looked at the table, at the letter Emelda had given her to mail.

"I picked them and had to stuff them in my pants so no one saw. I had them in my pants all night. I'm sorry they're sort of ruined."

"They're beautiful," Lenore said, staring at the letter, folded three times. She had opened it earlier, prepared for the worst. Maps, battle plans. But she found only words. Indeed, a letter, all in Spanish. Lenore could not understand a word of it.

"I don't want you to think that I'm not willing to bend the rules here when I think it's necessary. I don't want to be just another soldier, you know."

"I know."

"We're going to have to step up security. This place is constantly on the verge of attack, Lenore. We have to look out for agents, anyone suspicious in the village."

"How do you define suspicious?"

"Anyone who sticks out, anyone who is trying to gather the Indians and talk to them. Anyone trying to communicate with the outside. They're speeding up training, too. A lot of the soldiers are leaving tomorrow for terrain training. Mincho will be gone. So I'm taking over the Civil Patrol for a week. Have you noticed anyone who's suspicious?"

"No."

"You wouldn't believe what's going on out there," Dan said, his eyes awash in fear and nearsightedness without his glasses. "I saw bodies. Burned bodies. They looked like they were made out of paper."

In the dark, Lenore worked her fingers into his knotted shoulders, but he could not relax. The sooner she told him about Emelda the better, the less like a deception it would seem. But what would she say? That in anger she'd bartered with a blasphemous woman, a possible guerrilla, in return for services he didn't think necessary? And she knew he'd turn her in as a guerrilla. The muscles in his back felt thin and tense, like ropes strained by a great force—a sail alighted, unstoppable, on some wind.

"I named the village today," he told her. "The General actually took my suggestion: New Life Village. We're going to get a sign made. But it'll be in Spanish. I don't know how it'll sound in Spanish."

"Did you talk to the General about Ama, too?"

"Yes."

And that was all Lenore could bring herself to ask. Outside, the wheat was just tall enough, knee-high, to make soothing noises in the wind. A whispering that now washed out distant battle sounds, making the nights more peaceful.

Once Dan fell asleep, Lenore returned to Emelda's letter. By the light of the church, she read names, places, and dates that did not need translation: *Evie Crowder, 1902, Ixna, 1954, Guatemala City, Miami.* Lenore looked up repeated words in her pocket dictionary. *Land* and *grandfather* came up often. But the more she understood, the more afraid she felt. The words became political and without context, they took on a sinister shine: *Americans, The Voice of Liberation, American ambassador, United Fruit.* And finally, the last word, a word that appeared several times: *murder.*

~~~~~

Lenore awoke in mute horror, shot up from bed with the rip of helicopters overhead. Taking the soldiers, taking Mincho, away. She heard them and immediately believed Dan was up there, too. She began punching at the blankets, looking for him. He was gone, a soldier now. She envisioned him in the green, buttoned-up uniform with an AK-47. The logic seemed an extension of whatever dream she had awoken from.

Then she saw his shadow. Up before the helicopters, Dan moved in the lighted church, practicing for his first day commanding the Civil Patrol. She watched him as he drilled himself with the wooden machete. He sliced the air into an X, then across the top, decapitating some invisible enemy.

Not long after he left, Lenore found a note from him, placed near the hot plate. *I am proud of you for your work with the women here. The sewing class is such a good idea that I've gone around the General, written Operation Open Arms, to suggest they ask all the missionaries to try it.*

Her first note. She'd nearly forgotten Pastor May's instructions to use notes to encourage each other as well. Holding this compliment in her hands, Lenore wondered if Dan had written home about her yet. Any complaints for them to read once the mission was over. Maybe he knew that she mostly just watched television with the children. Maybe he already knew she secretly recruited a female interpreter. When they returned home it would all be clear, and all this—Ama, Mincho, the helicopters, the smoke, the situation with the well, Emelda—all of it would really seem like nothing.

As she'd hoped, the sewing class relaxed a bit with a female translator. They did not speak, only listened, but with an attentiveness that surpassed anything Lenore had yet to witness in the camp. She explained, through Emelda, that the Civil Patrol would be coming in to be measured for pants. She explained a lot of things that she thought had been explained before, but evidently had not been.

Lenore had no idea how she'd tell Mincho he'd been replaced. The soldiers would be gone for at least a week. What would he say, hearing about an Indian who spoke English? And Quiché and Achí and Spanish? The General, of course, would be suspicious. And Mincho would accuse Emelda of turning Lenore against him, though she did not need to be convinced that he was bad for the women.

"Did you mail my letter, Lenore? To the address I put on the top?"

"Yes," Lenore lied. A necessary lie, as she'd made two mutually exclusive promises, to Emelda and the General. And once she crossed the General, there would be no going back. She must be careful. She had agonized over the address all morning. An address in Quetzaltenango, to someone or something called *Prensa La Verdad*.

"Did you put your own name for the return like I asked? For a reply?"

Lenore nodded. That had not been a part of the original deal, getting a reply. Emelda was pushing it, and she knew. "What's in the letter?" Lenore asked casually.

"It's a letter for my grandmother."

And then everyone dropped to the ground, as someone battered the metal door for entry. Dan, with the Civil Patrol following. "Hup, hup!" he cried. "*¡Uno, dos, tres! ¡Uno, dos, tres!*" They marched into the class, counting their steps.

"Dan!" Lenore rushed to stop him, rushed and found herself shielding Cruzita. The girl lay under her table, on her belly. "What do you think you're doing?"

He looked around him, while his men looked to him. "What?"

"What makes you think you can march into my class and terrify my women?" She used that term, my women, and it pleased her.

"We didn't mean to terrify anyone," he mumbled, noticing only now the women hiding under their tables. "We're the Civil Patrol. We're here to protect them."

"Well, you scared the crap out of me! And I'm married to you!"

"I'm sorry," he said, as Lenore began to help the women up. Cruzita remained under her table, extracting a needle that was sunk deeply in her palm.

"This is my class," she said, "and you have to go by my rules. First, you march your men back out there and leave those silly machetes on the ground. And you walk back in, like decent men. Just walk, I don't even want to hear you counting your steps!"

"I'm sorry," he said, already in retreat. "Okay."

While they measured the men for pants, no one spoke, not even Emelda, because Lenore had no choice but to ask her to remain silent around Dan. Her interpreter asked no questions, did not seem surprised at the request. They sewed pants for two days, with Emelda tactfully lowering her voice every time the Civil Patrol marched around the church. And still, Emelda and Lenore were the only ones to speak. Lenore tried to get the women to speak, she asked them questions, which they would only answer with dull Spanish phrases. *Sí, gracias.* But Emelda finally brought it up.

"They want to know if they're allowed to talk," she said. "They're confused about the rules."

"The rules?"

"Our languages are not allowed. We're only allowed to speak Spanish to each other in the camp."

"But none of you know Spanish. You've only been taking lessons . . ." At that moment, the silence of the entire camp, not only her class, suddenly made sense to Lenore. "Whose rule is that?"

"The General's rule, the soldiers' rule. They told us when we arrived that if we speak our languages to each other, we no longer have amnesty."

"And what happens then?"

"We're punished for being guerrillas."

Lenore eyed the emptied classroom, with its discarded scissors, the half-finished clothing. This was how she saw her church now, as a classroom. When the Civil Patrol folded up the tables every day for the evening sermon, she felt a great disruption. Church time borrowed from her sewing class, instead of the other way around.

She tried to evaluate the wisdom of defying the General, but she was not the decision maker, she reminded herself. Lenore stepped out of the church, into the square, where Dan led the Civil Patrol in an exercise that mirrored his own morning drill. Slicing an X in the air, then slicing off the top.

"*¡Uno, dos, tres!*" he yelled, keeping time. "*¡Uno, dos, tres!*"

Lenore returned to the church.

"Do the women want to speak? They don't seem like they want to anyway."

"Some do." Emelda shrugged. "But they're afraid. And they're confused about me. They think maybe now the rule has changed. They asked me to ask you."

"Well, my sewing class has no rules like that, Emelda." Lenore's anger had warmed her now, making her indifferent to any threat from the General or the soldiers, to Dan slicing and stabbing at the air. "They're free to say whatever they want in my class. We're not running a concentration camp here."

That evening, almost three months into the mission, Lenore wrote her first letter home to Kentucky. Only one sentence: *Dan, do you know about the ban on Indians speaking their own languages?*

~~~~~

Once the women understood that they could speak in Lenore's presence, the sewing class changed. After three days, all the men had new pants, so the students began sewing clothes for the children. Progress was faster and more volunteers opted out of working the wheat fields to contribute. They seemed to be enjoying themselves, despite what Emelda translated to Lenore.

"Carlotta doesn't like the fabric. She says it's too weak and thin," she'd say. Or, "Delmi doesn't want to make any more children's clothes. They killed all six of her children, you know?" Emelda liked to translate their complaints, but Lenore focused on smaller things. Every smile Emelda allowed herself was a victory—every compliment she translated, too: "Cruzita wants to make you a blouse. What is your favorite color?"

Communication improved, though Lenore wondered if she had compromised the mission for this victory. All the women seemed to understand that they could not speak around the soldiers, or the Civil Patrol. Or Dan. What had Emelda told them? The class, despite its success, was becoming a conspiracy of women, Lenore included.

Emelda remained the main translator in Quiché and Achí, while Cruzita communicated through her for the women who spoke Ixil. From there, other women who understood other languages spidered off into their own translation networks. With this arrangement, Emelda and Cruzita grew visibly closer. At first they did not seem to know each other well, having lived in distant villages. But Lenore noticed that they now unofficially shared a shed. They sat for hours in the dark there, talking, braiding each other's hair. This union disturbed Lenore. Her most obedient convert and her most difficult. She watched their interactions closely, suspecting that Emelda would try to corrupt her granddaughter, but there was no way to know because, though all the women talked more now, less and less made it to Lenore through translation.

Emelda and Cruzita plunged so deep in conversation sometimes that they forgot to sew or even pretend to sew. One day, as they whispered with their heads touching, Lenore demanded to know what it was all about.

"I'm telling her how my grandmother died," Emelda said, absently taking up her stitching again. Cruzita did the same. "What she told me right before she died."

"The grandmother that taught you English?"

"Yes." Stitch, stitch.

"The one you wrote your letter to?"

"Yes. Ixna." Stitch, stitch, knot.

"How do you write a letter to a dead person, Emelda? Were you lying to me about your letter?"

The Civil Patrol circled the church in such perfect unison, sounding like one heavy body marching. "*¡Uno, dos, tres!*" Dan spurred them on. "Praise the Lord!"

Emelda made a face, breaking the thread with her teeth. "I did not lie. It was a letter for my grandmother. For? No, about her. Not to her. You are too hard on me with these English words, it's hard to get them right, going back and forth all the time."

Lenore sat on the other side of Cruzita, who was now sewing diligently. She imagined a tug-of-war over the girl. Emelda pulling one arm, and her the other. She didn't know if she believed this latest explanation of Emelda's letter, but it didn't matter, because Lenore still had the letter, had it in her pocket at that moment. She'd decided to mail it the night before, but now, maybe not.

"How did she die, Emelda?"

"It was terrible. So terrible that sometimes I think it was punishment, for what people said she did." Stitch, stitch. The thread was too dark for the material, Lenore noticed, making the seam ugly and obvious.

"What did they say she did?"

"They said she was a murderer."

Morbid stories, possibly made-up stories, circulated through her class. Lenore felt herself losing control of the situation. "Was she?"

"I don't think so, but I stopped the trial. Thirty years ago, there was a trial about my land and United Fruit argued that I did not deserve my land because Grandmother killed for it."

"So they tried to put her in jail?"

"No, this is after she died. But then because I dropped my claim, everyone thought she was guilty and I didn't want it proven. But that wasn't why!"

"Emelda, why are you so upset about this now?" She put a hand out to still the shaking needle.

"I should have rejected their offer, fought their lies in court. But I didn't and that made the ancestors angry. I ignored the one thing my grandmother told me before she died. And because of the one mistake, I had to do many things after that, which made the ancestors angry, too. So many things, just to save myself."

"What did your grandmother tell you?"

"To never want anything a foreigner has. To never take anything they give. Once I do, it will be the last choice I make."

"But you took my pen and paper, didn't you?"

"I had no choice. The lesson's not for me now. I took their money. That was the last choice I made, a long time ago. All I can do is hope Cruzita will not do the same."

Neither of them looked at Cruzita, but at the jumper in her busy hands. The seams were coming together smoothly. The pieces matched, making the shape of a child.

~~~~~

For that week, Lenore took the padlock from their apartment and secured it on the church door, closing it for the first time. Their light suffered, but in this way they could not be surprised by Dan and his Civil Patrol, who busied themselves by searching sheds and investigating the situation of the smuggled stones. Lenore had mentioned this in a roundabout way to Emelda, the night before the first search.

Nothing yet had come of Ama's transgressions. Dan and the Civil Patrol seemed to be awaiting the General's return from terrain training to carry out her punishment, whatever it would be. Another thing that Lenore did her best not to think about. To warn her seemed itself a kind of punishment. All she could do was prevent the situation from happening again. The idea of these Indians having sex was nearly unimaginable to Lenore. But of course, they did. Whatever went on in those sheds at night began to haunt her, and she especially began to worry for Cruzita. The girl was fifteen, old enough for dates. And Lenore had seen too many beautiful girls ruined by the reluctance of adults to address the issue. Emelda herself admitted to being an unwed mother. Unfortunately, there was no way to have this talk without Emelda's help.

"Sex . . ." Lenore began, then immediately stopped for the look on Emelda's face. All around them, the women repaired pants that had come back ripped from the road crew.

"This is what you want to talk to her about?"

"Yes. Just translate, Emelda. Tell her that a man's body and a woman's body were made to fit together. But not to fit with just anyone. She must save herself for her husband. If she doesn't, she'll regret it forever."

Emelda mumbled a translation. A seemingly correct translation, for Cruzita blushed deeply. Emelda held a hand up. "I think this is a lot for Cruzita."

"But does she understand?"

"Oh yes, she understands very well. She thanks you for letting her know."

"Ask her if she understands. You didn't ask her!"

Emelda and Cruzita conversed for a moment, then Cruzita smiled sweetly and nodded at Lenore. With this, Lenore began contemplating her own questions, the ones she did her best to ignore all week. She had no books, no one to talk to, no way to understand how she felt.

"Emelda, what's it like, being pregnant? Did you know right away?"

"Oh no!" She laughed. "I had no idea. Because he told me it couldn't happen between a Hispanic and an Indian. I believed everything Tomás said. I didn't know until I came home and my mother slapped me."

"Were you very hungry all the time?"

"Yes. That's how she knew. I ate too much food and left none for her."

"Were you tired? Did you feel like you were sleepwalking all the time?"

Instead of answering, Emelda put down her sewing and regarded Lenore closely. In the back of the room, a group of women tried to stifle their laughter.

"Sometimes," Lenore said, changing the subject, "I feel like you aren't telling me everything the women are saying."

"I'm telling you everything," Emelda insisted. "You just don't hear it."

"Okay, then maybe you aren't telling them everything I'm saying. Something's missing. The main part of your job is to make them understand me."

"You think that's the problem with the village? That *they* don't understand *you?*"

"Yes, Emelda. I think they would be more open to the program if they understood where I'm coming from. If you—"

Her translator cut her off. "We all know where you came from, Lenore. You came from the sky, from the planes and helicopters. Just like the soldiers, like the General."

"I did not come here as a soldier, I didn't come here because I was paid to or because I was ordered to. I came here out of love. I want to share God's love."

Emelda snorted.

"The hate in your heart has made you very bitter. You can't even accept love. You need to let go of this hate. It will do nothing for you, Emelda."

She had anticipated this. "And what will Jesus do for me?"

"He can wash away your hatred and fill you with love. He died for you, Emelda. He died for me and for you. He died so we can have a new start!"

"He died for you," Emelda repeated, her face, the map of wrinkles, darkening with blood. "And that makes you happy? You don't know what you're saying."

"But I do!" she insisted, gesturing desperately with her arms. How to make her understand? To make her feel that love, to be full of His love, was all Emelda needed.

"No, you do not," Emelda persisted, her face thrust forward. Not much made Emelda angry, except talk about guilt and death. But everything seemed to loop around to those topics eventually. "You've never had anyone die for you; if you did, you'd know it is not a happy thing. I've had too many people die for me already. I don't want another."

Lenore had to be very careful. She did not want a confession right now, she did not want to have to deal with any more information, anything that would compromise the progress she was making with the class.

"Emelda, I'm not going to be able to baptize you if you keep on like this."

"Yes, you will. If you want to keep your interpreter."

"No, I won't." A helicopter ripped overhead. Then another and another, making Lenore shout to be heard. "You say I don't understand, but you don't understand what you're asking of me! It's blasphemous. It's a grave sin. Please—"

Emelda laid a hand on her arm. "Don't be upset. There's no reason, you see, because I was already saved a long time ago. And baptized. So this will mean nothing."

"What? When? Who baptized you?"

"A nice missionary, like you, when I was fourteen. Her name was Naomi. She taught me how to pray."

"But you didn't like it? Did you not get what you prayed for, is that it?"

"Oh no. I got everything I prayed for. Every horrible thing."

~~~~~

Dan ignored his dinner to write a note with fierce concentration, either to the General, to the church, or possibly to her. His forehead creased in bewilderment and Lenore knew that note was going to Kentucky—one of his doubts about her mailed back home for them to read and laugh over later.

He had been meeting with the General on a daily basis since the soldiers had returned, but had not invited her along. She didn't complain at first because she cherished her time with the women, despite Mincho's return.

While Dan and the General discussed roads for hours, however, the village suffered. Nothing on their list improved—water treatment, medicine, food—though Dan seemed renewed by the progress of the road project. Topographical maps added a new element to the clutter of their room. They were huge maps, scrawled with calculations, and impossible to refold.

"Did you meet with the General today?" It was hard for her to act as an advisor when she had no idea what he did with his time. But still, she tried.

He made an affirmative noise and did not look up, transferring his attention instead from his letter to one of the maps.

"Have you mentioned the children are getting thinner?"

"I'll mention it next time, I will. I'll mention it. But it can't be so bad if they're throwing their rolls over the fence. To feed the guerrillas."

Lenore crossed her arms over her chest. "Dan, the birds eat the rolls. What guerrilla in his right mind would walk five hundred yards into a fortified field for a roll?"

"Then tell me why they're doing it, Lenore. No other explanation makes sense."

"I don't know why they're doing it. But just because we don't understand why doesn't mean we should automatically assume it's for evil purposes. Maybe some of them just don't like the rolls."

"Humph." He slashed with his pen through a solid block of green on the map.

"I think there are more important things to worry about. There are some things I think we should mention to him."

"Whatever you want to mention, just write it down." He made tiny, tiny notes next to his slashes.

"I'm tired of writing notes, Dan. They do nothing. Does he even get them?"

"I'll read them to him. Just give the notes to me. I'll be sure he hears them."

"Will he hear them as my silly ideas, or will you stand behind them?"

He shifted back to his notebook, writing. "They will be both of our ideas. You and I are a team, Lenore. We are a team. I don't know why you act like we aren't."

"Well, then, do you think sometimes I can go up and talk to the General, while you stay and watch the village?"

"Do you really mean that?" He finally set down his pen to look up at her. "Do you really want to ride in one of the trucks, up to the base, and meet with him alone?"

"No."

"Which is why I do it." He returned to his notes.

"What do you talk about, Dan, with the General? Other than roads?"

"You don't think the roads are important? If you think we need more supplies, that's the way to get them here. The roads are everything."

"I didn't say roads weren't important. I just thought they were someone else's job. You came down here as a missionary."

"You think I'm not qualified?" He pressed his pen point too hard, making a hole in the map. "You think someone with an engineering degree should be doing it?"

She did not dare tread further. "That's not what I mean at all, Dan. I'm glad you can help with the roads. I'm sure you're doing a fantastic job. I just think the village needs some attention, too. Maybe you can talk to the General about it."

"The General has a lot more on his mind than getting more interpreters. There are guerrillas out there, watching us, waiting to massacre these Indians. He's responsible for everyone's safety." He flipped the map. "What do you have to say, Lenore? Just tell me."

"My period is ten weeks late."

"Oh." He blinked repeatedly at the measured mountains before him. Another problem, another impossible route.

"Ten weeks."

"I'm sure it's just stress. You've been doing too much." He switched to a pencil, testing, tracing something new. "You look great." His eyes flicked up. "Those jeans look great on you."

"Dan, I've been stressed before, and it's never been like this. I don't feel like myself." She began to cry and smile at the same time. "I think I may be pregnant."

He dropped his pencil and looked, really looked, at her. "Are you sure?"

"Pretty sure. I feel it. I just know."

His gaze drifted down. "But how could it be? God's made it clear He needs us down here."

Her thoughts followed his. She stared at the floor, where ants hauled away half a Frito she must have dropped on the floor weeks ago. She bent down and took it from them. Just picked it up, blew on it, and ate it, knowing it was everything to them and nothing to her.

"We'll ask the General for a travel pass," Dan concluded, twirling the pencil around his thumb. "So you can see a doctor. We've just finished a road that connects the way to Quetzaltenango." He showed her on the map. "We can get a bus there. But until we get confirmation, we shouldn't allow ourselves to be distracted from the mission. Or get our hopes up again. I really don't think it makes sense for God . . ." He trailed off.

"I agree, Dan," and she did, although his caution hurt her, made her feel like an obstacle to his new purpose. "I'm going to wait a week, just one more week. There's just too much going on to leave the village now. Because . . ." She watched Dan's eyes drift back to his map. "Because I had an idea today." She sat across from him, demanding his attention. "And if it works, when I'm gone I can get some supplies for it."

"For what? What's your idea?"

"I was measuring the women, and Cruzita, I'm not kidding, that girl has the figure of a fashion model." Dan raised his eyebrows. "And then it came to me . . ." She paused, doubting herself already. "We should have a village beauty pageant."

She had his full attention now.

"It would be fun and it would take everyone's mind off, well . . ." She waved a hand in the air. That was the part that made her doubt the idea. Food was low, the children sick, people were being slaughtered by Communists in the mountains, and Lenore had thought of a beauty pageant. But maybe they'd been so overwhelmed by the larger problems that they'd neglected small joys. To be beautiful and onstage with everyone admiring them. This was the way to win their hearts, to get the women to wear new clothes. Not with threats, but merely by showing them how beautiful they could be.

"It's just that we're supposed to be making a community here, but we've had no real community events. The women could make their own dresses for the competition."

Lenore stopped, for fear of the look on Dan's face. Stunned, no doubt, at this idea. His eyes alight with images: lace and hair spray, satin and music. "Wow," he said. "That's the Holy Spirit talking if I ever heard it. I haven't seen you so excited since before the blackberry festival. I think the General might actually like this one, Lenore."

Her note asking for a travel pass had to be worded carefully, to convey the urgency of her request, without mentioning specifically what her problem was. She could not imagine mentioning her period, or even the word gynecologist, to the General. She hoped that mentioning the pageant in the same note would distract his concern.

The sermon on the other side of the door ran late as she drafted her note. She had feigned illness, claimed her trouble, when it came time for Dan to preach. It gave her a free pass now, this new life growing inside her.

She could not bring herself to attend, because Dan had crafted this sermon to denounce prostitution. More specifically, Ama. Her punishment finally decided. No one knew what was coming and Lenore had no desire to witness the revelation, to watch the panic roll over the frightened Maya in their little church. Merely speaking to an Indian publicly on the paths made them melt, and Lenore could not see anyone surviving this denunciation Dan had prepared, without consulting her.

"Wish me luck!" he'd said before leaving, as if he might possibly fail at humiliating Ama.

Yes, she had failed Ama, but she had convinced Dan, at least, of her pageant idea. And more importantly, she'd convinced him that with new security concerns, Mincho should be with the Civil Patrol all day. She did not need him in the sewing class. Sewing was taught by example, not with talking, she had said. She could manage on her own.

Yes, Dan had said. I'm sure the General will agree. I'll talk to him about it.

And she was pregnant. After twelve years of trying, God had finally answered her prayers. That afternoon, when she prayed for more Swiss Cake Rolls to appear, Emelda arrived with a collection of wheat rolls, which the Indians usually threw over the fence. Just handed them to Lenore without a word. She ate one now, feeling pregnant, feeling nausea, or maybe it was the sermon upsetting her stomach.

"The Lord cherishes the sanctity of marriage, the intimate bond between man and wife," she heard Dan through the wall. Every sermon now would be distrusted, everyone tense, waiting for it to turn on them. According to Dan, this was a good thing, would encourage people to police themselves.

Lenore put all of her energy into blocking out the sermon. But the message traveled too well through the metal walls. She folded a pillow over her ears, thinking of the women in her class, how this would affect them. Did her pregnancy mean their mission was complete, or that they'd failed?

"We all make mistakes," she heard Dan say, "and all of you have indeed made many." But what? Lenore thought. But you're not allowed to make any more? You used up your quota? If that was possible, Dan had certainly used up his in his young days. She'd forgiven him over and over—drunk driving, assault, driving without a license, drunk in public, assaulting a police officer—forgiven him each time, as had God. That grace finally touched and changed him. Yes, everyone makes mistakes, but Dan got perpetual forgiveness, while these Indians got perpetual punishment. He was making a mistake now, he'd feel terrible for it later, but he'd be forgiven.

With the horrible sermon finished, the rest transpired quite silently. She did not hear the soldiers take Ama away, did not hear her screaming. Was Ama afraid even to cry out in her own language, another offense to be used against her?

~~~~~

Both Ama and Emelda were scheduled for baptism, though the next morning only Emelda appeared, ready for her conversion. She stood confidently, while the others scanned the valley uneasily. The mountains had been burning all night.

The situation had grown beyond Lenore's control. What other choices did she have, in retrospect? The sewing class felt like her only success and she wasn't sure if, given the chance, she would do anything differently. For this blasphemous baptism, Emelda would continue to translate, and Lenore took another note from her to mail. The letter seemed to be about the same thing, to the same address. Emelda had become impatient for a reply.

Mincho stalked back and forth in front of the line of converts, translating Dan's ceremony. He had come back from terrain training without Huela. Only once had Lenore asked about the puppy, but he had cut her off, with a demented look in his eye. And now he paced back and forth, reciting Bible verses, scratching his black buzzed hair like a mold had overtaken his skull.

After the scripture reading, Dan turned to the pump. "Someone forgot to refill the can," he said. He set his Bible down and began pumping with two hands. Lenore sighed in relief. "Does anyone have any water to spare?" Mincho translated. Nothing but blank stares, lowered heads.

"Shit, fuck!" Dan punched the air. He stalked into the church as Mincho automatically translated for the astonished Indians.

He emerged seconds later holding a can of Pepsi. One of the last of the twenty-four-pack. The Indians all stared as he cracked the can open with surprising force, as if he had to kill it before consuming it. He considered out loud pouring the can into the pump, but feared what the corn syrup might do to the parts inside. To Lenore's horror, he motioned for Emelda to step forward.

"You have chosen to walk in the path of Christ, shedding your worldly concerns for the Kingdom of Heaven. I baptize you in the name of the Father, the Son, and the Holy Spirit." He dipped his finger into the open can, smeared it into a cross on her forehead, and said, "God now lives in your heart and will protect you as a true Guatemalan."

~~~~~

Dan, convinced now that Lenore couldn't possibly be pregnant, also became convinced that the Civil Patrol could not function without him for two days. So Lenore asked Emelda if she would accompany her to her doctor's appointment, acting as a guide. She did not call Emelda a "translator" in the request, but merely a guide. Quetzaltenango was the closest city with an American doctor, and Emelda came from there. Lenore wrote this to the General, saying that Emelda had proved herself a trustworthy, baptized Christian, and that she would keep a close eye on her. These were not necessarily lies. She did not trust Emelda enough to mail her letters right away; that was why they had received no reply from the first letter. But Lenore had not yet destroyed them. She did trust Emelda, sometimes, in ways she trusted no one else in the camp.

Without asking any questions, the General signed passes for both of them for two days. When Emelda saw the paper with her name on it, a single tear dropped onto her rough cheek, as miraculous to Lenore as if it had been squeezed from rock.

Miserable-looking Maya crammed the bus to Quetzaltenango. Their costumes—cleaner, more complete than in the village—revealed bright, skillful patterns that impressed Lenore. Emelda pushed her way through the clashing neon crowd and cleared a space for herself and Lenore to stand in the aisle. Then the bus lurched forward, leaving the military truck behind. Lenore waved, but the soldiers did not wave back. The bus seemed too silent for the number of people, for the tumult of limbs grasping and adjusting to the whims of the driver. No one voiced any objection to his carelessness. They passed other vehicles racing around mountain curves, and the brakes didn't work well on the descents.

"Emelda, I think you know already, but I'm pregnant. I'm going to a doctor. How are you? Do you need to see a doctor, too? I'll pay, if there's anything—"

"No, a doctor cannot help me. But you? Are you sure?"

"Pretty sure." Lenore smiled. "And I'm so happy. So happy. I've been praying for this for twelve years."

"You're happy? You don't look happy, Lenore."

"I am!" she insisted, wiping her tears and losing her balance at a turn. "Really, I am. It's just difficult for me to understand. It makes me think maybe I'm failing at the village. God told me to come here, so why would He give me a baby so I have to leave?'"

"Why do you have to leave? Why can't you do both?"

"I can't have a baby here!" Lenore laughed, realizing too late that plenty of women had babies down here, including Emelda. Why did she think she was so special?

"I can help you. All the women in the village can help. We all know how to have babies. This is not a problem. Your God isn't trying to confuse you."

"Thank you, Emelda."

Of course, Dan would not allow that, and neither could Lenore. Dan didn't even want a baby now to interfere with their mission. And if he was right and she wasn't pregnant, the possibilities turned frightening: grave illness, early menopause. Dan, with his insistence, didn't seem to understand what he hoped for. *It's just stress. Maybe this is a way God's helping us, too. Your period just slows you down.* The way he presented everything as a blessing in disguise had really started to bug her.

"Get your papers," Emelda breathed hotly in her ear, bringing her back. "What?"

"Your pass, your identity papers." The bus slowed and Lenore could feel the crush of those behind her, straining forward. "This is a military checkpoint."

Everyone on the bus rifled through their pockets and bags. Lenore reached into her purse just as boy soldiers stepped into the aisle from both ends. They shoved through the crowd, demanding papers. One glanced darkly at Lenore before holding out a bandaged hand. Soiled, unraveling bandages with visible leakage.

"*Misionero,*" he read, nodding. He took Emelda's papers, scanned them, and moved on.

Next to them, a man with his child pleaded with a soldier. "*Soy ser evangélico,*" he kept insisting. The soldier jostled him to the front of the bus, the small child, wide-eyed and silent, in tow. Emelda pushed Lenore into their empty seat, then slid in herself. Lenore studied her own identity card. After her name, she noticed the line: *Religión: Evangélico.*

Emelda shoved her papers back into her dress without comment. Lenore felt the warmth of the seat's previous occupants cooling and becoming her own. The bus was moving again in ten minutes. The open windows cleared the air. The jungle's close green walls dropped away abruptly, showing wide valley views. Lenore struggled to get her bearings and to ignore the feeling that they were driving in the direction of the guerrillas. In the direction all the helicopters disappeared. But the General would never send her into guerrilla territory. They were driving toward a city, where people lived. Not where the forests burned through the night. They were moving away from the war, they had to be.

"How long do you think it will be, Emelda? How many hours?"

She shrugged. "It can be three hours to Xela, it can be eight hours to Xela."

"Xela?" Lenore stood up. "What's Xela? We're supposed to be going to Quetzaltenango!" In her panic, she tried to shove her way into the aisle.

"It's the same." Emelda pulled her back down. "Xela is the Indian name for Quetzaltenango. It's the same thing. One is Indian, one is Spanish."

Her terror at being lost in the jungle did not subside easily. To calm herself, she reminded herself of the good news: the General had agreed that Mincho should not waste his time with the sewing class. And he had approved the beauty pageant. She would buy supplies in Quetzaltenango—no, Xela, it was easier to say—for the girls' dresses. A very appropriate community event, he had called it. So much to do, to plan: the dresses, the show, the prize. Maybe she could arrange a talent portion, or a question-and-answer competition. But a talent contest between those girls, she realized, would be dismal. And she could not imagine them answering any question put to them in front of a crowd, not even their own names.

"Mrs. Beasley," the doctor said, and at first she didn't recognize her own name pronounced correctly. In walked the first white person she'd seen in three months, other than Dan. Seeing him, seeing his California good looks, she crossed her legs in her paper gown. For the first time in her life, she was practically naked before a man who wasn't her husband. Too ashamed to visit a doctor, she'd never sought professional help to get pregnant.

"It's a pleasure to see an adult, for once," he said, moving in to shake her hand, businesslike. "It seems all I do is care for babies now."

Dr. Loving sat on a short stool. "Right away, I want to let you know that you are not pregnant. The urine test was negative. Now . . ." his gaze wandered to her knees, as Lenore felt the room collapsing around her. She was not pregnant; she was dying. "Now I think I should do an exam, although I have to tell you that, by training, I am not technically a gynecologist. I'm a plastic surgeon."

With this, Lenore would have stood up and walked out, but her grayed dress hung on the door hook a mile away.

"But I have general medical training, including ob/gyn work. I even delivered my own three kids."

"Why are you in Guatemala, then?" Lenore asked in an appalled whisper. "What could a plastic surgeon be doing here? I asked for an American doctor, I never assumed you weren't a proper doctor."

Dr. Loving laughed at this good-humoredly. "Please, Mrs. Beasley, I am a proper doctor. Not all plastic surgeons do face-lifts and implants. I'm a reconstructive plastic surgeon. Burns, cleft palates, that sort of thing."

"Oh."

"And I do things here in Xela for lack of general practitioners. I've done plenty of pelvic exams and have been able to identify common problems, although if it's not so obvious, I will refer you to a specialist in the capital."

"There are no specialists in Xela? None at all?"

"There is one, but he's Guatemalan. You requested an American doctor. If you'd rather, it wouldn't hurt my feelings if you decided to see him."

When she imagined this Guatemalan doctor, she could only see the General. His pleased face, peering between her legs, talking about Communists and his Harvard degree.

Dr. Loving asked her to scoot to the edge of the table and place her feet on two *X*'s marked in the corners. "But you have to keep your knees open," he said, gently pulling apart the tent she'd made with her legs. If someone had asked her the day before what she would have done in this situation, she would have said pray. But she didn't. Lenore stared up at the ceiling and went through every curse word she could think of.

"Now you're going to feel my finger, and some pressure on your abdomen as I locate your ovaries." She felt more than one finger slide inside her, and the other crawl over her belly, kneading. The fingers met, on either side of her skin, lost each other, then met up again. "How long have you been in Guatemala?"

"Three months," she said, because she hated to be rude. Was she expected to endure all of this and carry on a conversation? His casualness was utterly baffling as he fingered her, searching for some lump that would be her death.

"I've been here for six," he said. "But now I think I'm leaving."

"Why?" Lenore glanced at him.

His fingers stopped their slow crawl. "It's the babies," he said. "I came here to help the babies, but now I don't think I'm helping."

"How could you not be helping? You're a doctor. There must be so much work, with the war."

He nodded, his palm flat and tender on her belly. "The government hired me to work on the babies, to fix up the injured ones for adoption. I've restored tiny ears and noses, erased burns—"

"That's not helping?" Lenore struggled to sit up. "Those babies can have new lives because of you." She wondered if this meeting had been divinely orchestrated. Maybe all her trouble had just been God's way of getting her here, in touch with someone who could help her adopt. Yes, she told herself, watching this man working between her legs as if delivering her a child.

"You'd think . . ." he said, then stopped. "You'd think it was that simple. I certainly did. But now I'm not so sure. Sometimes . . ." His expert tone shifted, so that he sounded like an ordinary man. "Sometimes it seems if I weren't here, they wouldn't be, either."

Lenore had no idea what he meant by this, though it affected her profoundly. She realized they'd been talking like that with his finger inside her the whole time. His frown seemed like another message entirely, one stronger than any God may be giving her. Lenore shivered, thinking of the dead-eyed children of the camp. She imagined having one of her own, following her around for the rest of her life, like a ghost.

"There's nothing definite I can feel or see," Dr. Loving reported after the exam, after he had allowed Lenore to dress in private. The dress she had made for herself in the sewing class felt little different from the paper gown. "I was having a hard time feeling your right ovary, but that may be nothing. Now, you thought you might be pregnant. You've never had children; have you been trying to become pregnant?"

"No," she lied. She did not want Dr. Loving to assume that she was broken in some way. Trying for twelve years would sound that way. Anyway, they had stopped trying last year, so it wasn't a lie.

"It may just be the stress down here. You're a missionary?"

"No," she heard herself say. Why?

Dr. Loving looked confused. "Oh, I'm sorry. I thought you were. Wonder where I got that idea." He searched his clipboard, trying to recollect. "Well, that's a relief, anyway." He laughed.

"A relief?"

"Yeah, that you're not all caught up in that. It's a worse gig than this. At least I feel sometimes like I might be helping."

When Lenore told Emelda she wasn't pregnant, Emelda asked, "Is that good?"

"No," she cried. "It's terrible. They're doing a blood test now. They'll tell me in a few hours if they find anything."

They stepped out of the waiting room into the dingy white streets of Xela. Lenore noticed the fear burning within her, felt it rising. It wasn't the blood test, the possibility of illness, that really scared her. She would know soon enough the results of the blood test, but would she ever know why she had denied being a missionary?

Moments before her denial, she had been in the clinic restroom and had looked in a proper mirror for the first time in three months. She didn't recognize herself. The clothes, her hair, grown out and turned dark, the color of spoiled honey. Her skin dried and darkened as well. She felt like someone else, and when the doctor asked if she was a missionary, she had answered for someone else.

They ate lunch in a dark restaurant that didn't offer menus. Crosses and Bible verses hung in the cemented squares where the windows had been. More beans. And Lenore recognized the taste of the military corn mix, cooked properly so that it rose like cornbread. She'd been looking forward to this meal for days. Now she couldn't gather enough thankfulness to pray over it.

"I'm never going to have children, Emelda," she said over the food. "I think I've just realized for the first time. I mean, before, I knew it wouldn't be easy and I sort of stopped trying, but I always had hope. But now there's none. I can't think of anything worse. I don't even know any women who don't have children. What am I supposed to do with myself? What's my purpose? To stay in Guatemala forever?"

"Don't talk this way, Lenore. There are much worse things. I had a son that I had to give up. I never knew him. And now he's dead and I'm alive and I can't even imagine what he looks like. It is sad to not have children, but it's worse to lose a child. Every dead man I saw in the mountains, I thought was him."

"But you have a grandchild, Cruzita. Does she not make you happy?"

"Cruzita makes me very sad. Every day, all I can think of is the day she finds out who I am. On that day, I will lose her, too. She will hate me and I'll have nothing again. You have your husband, don't forget. He loves you."

"I know you hate Dan." Lenore heard herself almost laugh. "You don't fool me."

"But he does love you. In his man way. He's not different from most men." They both began to eat. Emelda forked her cornbread, inspecting it. "What's this?"

"It's the corn mix. Just cooked differently."

"It rises? Corn doesn't rise."

"They put wheat in it, and some other things. The General told me. All the wheat in the fields goes into the mix. I guess that's why they call it a mix."

"I see." She proceeded to eat the beans but not the cornbread, while she read the newspaper tablecloth. The unwashed, sticky blot on her forehead from her baptism had picked up dirt, dust, and bus exhaust. Lenore studied the dark spot, chewing, hearing the familiar sound of a military truck's arrival.

Emelda isolated a page, turning it toward Lenore. "This is crazy!" She coughed through a mouthful of food. "Why don't they write us back?" She pointed: "The Resurrection of Evie Crowder." Part Four. Lenore had looked up the translation in her pocket dictionary, after seeing the pasted clippings in Emelda's shed. But the translation made nothing clearer. Just another mystery, added to all the others. Who was Evie Crowder?

"Lenore," Emelda said, after clearing her plate of everything but the cornbread, "there's something I need to do in Xela. Something I need you to help me with."

"Of course, Emelda. You helped me, and I'll help you." Lenore welcomed any distraction, anything to get her through the next twenty-four hours. In a week, where would she be? In the capital, in Kentucky, in a hospital? Dead? Or back in the model village, just as before?

"You trust me?"

Lenore had no good answer for this, other than that she considered Emelda her friend, for no good reason. Her need for a friend at the moment trumped her fear and uncertainty. Emelda was the only woman she had spoken to in three months. "I trust you more than a guerrilla I don't know, I suppose," she answered.

Emelda did not correct her. "Nothing bad. I just need you to come on a walk."

"A walk to where?"

"Just here in town."

"Why do you need me?"

"Because my pass says I'm a guide. I can't be a guide by myself."

Emerging from the restaurant, Emelda clutched the newspaper in an angry wad. Lenore looked both ways down the long, baked street and could see a group of men a distance away. She could tell right away from the shapes they cut against a whitewashed building that they were men. Xela's Civil Patrol.

Emelda turned in the opposite direction and Lenore followed her back to the central plaza, where another full bus unloaded passengers. A brief crowd, then, in a matter of moments, everyone was gone. Where did they go? Where were she and Emelda going? Lenore began to distrust her friend when they turned into a decayed alley. Somewhere, a radio voice wheezed through static. Then the sound of tinkling metal, laughing, a story above. A guerrilla network, strung right behind the city's façade.

"You stay out here, do not let them inside see you," Emelda said before entering a smooth building, the color of vanilla peeled away in places to reveal an earthy clay.

What transpired next seemed to Lenore to take hours, though it must have been less than five minutes. From just outside the door, she heard it all, while she frantically checked all routes of escape. Emelda speaking, another voice evading, Emelda slamming the wadded paper down, demanding, *"¡Su dirección! ¡Tiene que darme su dirección!"*

Lenore smelled, sensed, people all around, but could see no one. A door opened and closed. Peeking around the corner, she saw a figure slip out a side exit. The figure running for help. Inside, the man's voice remained calm in response to Emelda's ranting, so calm that Lenore realized he may just be buying time. Emelda fired questions that echoed in the empty alley, which the man answered with no. *No, no, no.*

A few blocks down, Lenore spied the tiny flailing figure, running, leading the Civil Patrol. Their collective afternoon shadow crept dramatically, like a storm cloud overtaking the city.

"Emelda." Lenore found her voice, though she did not recognize the fear in it. "Emelda!" she yelled, and her friend appeared in the doorway. "The Civil Patrol." And that was enough. Emelda grabbed her and they ran together, away.

"What the hell was that about!" Lenore cried, panting. After a few turns, they arrived in the central plaza. Emelda took Lenore by the shoulders.

"Did they see you? Did anyone see you?"

"No, I don't think so. Someone ran out, but they never turned back. I don't think. What was that about, Emelda?"

Her guide pulled her into the open space of the plaza. She held Lenore's hand tightly, forcing a casual pace. "It's about these stories they print. The newspaper office keeps printing this story. It's everything I need to prove my grandmother isn't a murderer."

"Evie Crowder? Is that your grandmother?"

"No, no! I told you my grandmother's name was Ixna."

At the other end of the plaza, the Civil Patrol appeared. Lenore counted them, but they kept pouring in and she lost track.

"Now we find out if anyone really did see you," Emelda breathed, and let go of her hand. Lenore sought it out again, but Emelda swatted her away. "Keep walking just like this. Like this. Breathe slow, like you haven't been running."

This Civil Patrol carried real machetes. And now they marched toward them, preceded by their shadows. The commander, in front, regarded them intently on approach. He held a small pistol low as he walked. Emelda kept her head down. Lenore felt her face flush as she resisted panting from their sprint. She must look guilty, she couldn't help it. Her doubts, her deceptions, her denial of being a missionary. She felt them like weapons concealed awkwardly beneath her clothes. The commander squinted, then he veered slightly away and the men passed more distantly.

Lenore sobbed on their way back to the hotel. "Why, Emelda? Why is your grandmother worth all this? She's already dead! And we could have been killed!"

"Not you." Emelda rubbed her back. "They would not kill you. I would not endanger you, only myself. This newspaper story—"

"It's about your grandmother?"

"No, it's about Evie Crowder. She's alive! She's written to the newspaper, telling them that she is alive and was never murdered!" She held up the shred of newspaper left from the confrontation.

"Wait, I don't—"

"So she is alive and can clear my grandmother's name! But they won't give me her address. They know it, they know where she is, but they won't say."

"So your grandmother was accused?"

"Not until 1954! Not until we tried to claim our land back! Not until after she was already dead! Not until they tricked me!"

"What land?"

"My land. It was fallow, so my mother made a claim for me under the new law. The Fruit company said they'd fight us in court, they said they could prove my grandmother was involved in the murders. We were afraid of the trial and what they would invent about her. They were very powerful, they could prove anything. But then the Fruit man came and said we could have the whole mountain if we just dropped our claim. No trial, no evidence. They would just give it to us. I liked that he spoke Quiché and English, like me. He said we could have our land without a fight. I didn't believe him at first, I remembered what my grandmother always said. I wouldn't take anything from him, at first. But then he gave me money, too. Lots of money."

"So you took the land?"

"Yes, but I should not have. It was very bad for Guatemala. And when people heard we dropped our claim, they thought it was because my grandmother was guilty, that we did not want her exposed in court. But that wasn't why! And I had no idea what it would all lead to!"

Outside, the unmistakable sound of a helicopter neared. They both moved for cover instinctively, and they stared up into the small square of sky above the hotel courtyard, waiting for it.

"I must get Evie's address," Emelda panted. "They have to tell me where she is."

~~~~~

Lenore did not go to the doctor's again. To her relief, by the time they finished shopping for the pageant, it was too late to go back for the test results. But when they left the hotel early the next morning, a note from the doctor awaited her at the front desk. She accepted the envelope in her hands, but did not open it.

Waiting through the various checkpoints, staring out her bus window, Lenore noticed something she had not seen on the way to Xela: villages. So many villages visible in the distance. Small settlements checkered the mountains she thought inhabited only by terrifying animals and guerrillas.

She saw planted fields and paths, houses made of stones, sticks, and leaves, blended into the jungle.

"I don't think I'm going to be in the model village long," Emelda told her after almost an hour of silence. "I think something very bad is going to happen to me."

"But that's the point of the village, we're here to protect you."

The speed of the bus whipped Emelda's long black hair across her face. She gathered the strands and began braiding them together over her shoulder. "They said they did not get my letter."

"Who?"

"The man at the newspaper said he never got my letters you mailed. Which means the General has them. He knows I am in the camp." She finished her braid, which began to unravel the moment she let go.

"No, Emelda. I never mailed the letters. The General doesn't have them." She took her hand to reassure her. "You're safe! I have them still!"

"You didn't mail them?" She wrenched her hand loose. "Why not? We had a deal. I translated for you! I never would have done it—"

"Because I was scared, I didn't know what they were. I didn't know they were about your grandmother, about fixing her reputation."

"You did not mail them! Not even the other one?"

"I was going to. I just needed to work up to it, I guess. Aren't you happy the General doesn't know? But why would he care about your grandmother?"

"Because I know things no one is supposed to know. He doesn't realize I'm in the camp yet. He doesn't remember my name, but he knows my story. Once he finds out, I'm done. But I guess it doesn't matter. We must mail them, anyway."

"I don't get it. You want me to mail them when we get back? Even if it means the General might get them?"

"Please. It's all I can do. I have to find out where she is. Maybe someone there will write back."

Their return trip took much longer than their departure—ten hours to reach the intersection where a military truck awaited them. The ride back on the new road that Dan had mapped and the Indians had cut seemed a little smoother than the day before. Unable to talk to Emelda in the soldiers' presence, Lenore became bored and anxious enough to read the doctor's note. She unfolded the paper and stared at the words. The blood test had come back. She was malnourished. He suggested eating beef and vegetables three times a day and snacking between meals.

They carried plastic shopping bags full of packaged food and supplies for the pageant. No fresh vegetables could be found in Xela. Walking unattended down from the base, they could see the workings of the model village—the Civil Patrol circling the heart in some repetitive exercise, the women in line at the water pump, the children milling purposelessly at the fence. In the nearby jungle, the smoke of the road crew uncurled into the sky. Then, farther out, more smoke spread over the range, a thin gauze over the inflamed evening sun.

"Will you go home soon, Lenore?"

She fell in step with her friend. "Sometimes I want to. I wish I could take you with me. But since I can't, I guess I'll stay. I can't imagine leaving you or Cruzita here by yourselves."

"Don't worry about us. We wouldn't go to the United States, anyway. I've already been there long enough to know it's not for us."

Lenore stopped in the path. "You've been to America?"

Emelda kept walking, passing a stunned Lenore to take the lead as they descended farther into the valley. "You're surprised?" she said over her shoulder. "An *indio* like me?"

"Yes. When did you go? How did you get there?"

"I went to fight the Communists. It was part of the deal."

"Where did you go? When?"

"In 1954, I went to Guatemala City and was interviewed." She seemed amazed, still, at her own history. "He told me another revolution was coming. That I would be punished as a Communist because I got land. I tried to tell him that Fruit gave us the land, we dropped the case, that it was an inheritance, not Communist, but it didn't matter. Things were going to change and I would look bad."

"Who said this?"

"The American ambassador. He said things would go badly for Indians who got land, but that the new government would protect me if I helped them. That I could keep the land when everyone else would lose theirs."

"Where did you go in America?"

"I went to Guatemala City and he told me he needed me to fight the Communists. I'm just a little girl from Xela, remember. I told him I don't know how to fight. But he said he needed my voice."

"The American ambassador," Lenore said.

"Yes. He said he needed an Indian who loved her country to help convince other Indians that communism was evil. I was educated, he said, but

my people were not. He had a plan to free the country and he needed me."
She cocked her head, still amazed at this fact. "He needed someone who
could speak Spanish and Quiché with a convincing accent for a radio program. They called it *The Voice of Liberation*. We told people we were broadcasting from a hiding place in Guatemala, but we were really in Miami."

"You've been to Florida?"

"I thought Miami would be fun, that I could see how great Guatemala
could be. But I was too afraid to leave the hotel. We weren't there legally. If
we got caught, they said they wouldn't come get us. We would go to jail and
no one would believe our story."

"How long were you there?"

"Weeks. I had a radio and a television in my room. I watched so many
shows, *Truth or Consequences*, *Lassie*. I thought America was so nice, even
the dogs were nice. I listened to a radio show where women told how miserable their lives were, then the audience would clap for who had the saddest
story. For the woman with the loudest clapping, they would put a crown on
her and give her a refrigerator."

"What was your job? I don't understand."

"We were supposed to convince the entire world, even Guatemalans, that
Guatemala was having a civil war."

"But there was a war, wasn't there? It's still going on."

"No, not then. Everyone loved Jacobo Arbenz. The war didn't start until
they got rid of him, until Castillo Armas came along."

"I don't understand. How did you convince the world there's a war going
on when there wasn't?" They watched the Civil Patrol's exercise from above.
The men marched in a perfect circle.

"Radio. We reported things to make people afraid to leave their homes,
then told them what was going on, which made them not want to leave their
homes even more. I watched so much television in Miami. All the American
news shows reported a civil war in Guatemala. They even talked about me on
the news. My name was María for the show. I was so proud I jumped on the
bed."

"So it wasn't a war then. But it's a war now, right?"

Lenore remembered watching *The 700 Club*, the graphic on the screen
announcing the civil war. President Ríos Montt's grave report. But all the
evidence she needed surrounded her in the camp. Hundreds of Indians
flooding from the mountains. If it wasn't war, what were they surrendering
from?

"After I came back to Guatemala, the real war began and I knew I'd started it all. I had my land, but I was afraid to leave it, afraid to spend my money to buy the things I'd wanted so badly. People thought I'd gone away to be a maid and came back because I got pregnant by the man. But I was still afraid for a very long time, convinced people would recognize my voice. I never married. The money I hid in my floor dissolved in a bad rainy season. I sent my son away to another village, afraid he would figure out what I had done. Then the war kept getting bigger and bigger and it took my mother and my brother and my sister. I had no one left. I just had my land. Then the Civil Patrol came to Xela last year, they burned my land. I was growing corn, they said to feed guerrillas. Leandro, who lives in the shed next to me, was there, in the Civil Patrol. They held a gun to his head and he raped me. They tried to make him kill me, but he was slow, I think on purpose, and I ran into the mountains."

Lenore pictured Leandro, posed in his doorway, mutely watching Emelda sob that first morning in the model village. Mincho had translated a different story, of Leandro killing her son while disguised as a soldier.

"A lot of guerrillas dress in military uniforms and do those things," Lenore said.

"They chased me with helicopters," Emelda said. "Guerrillas don't have helicopters. They don't even have food."

"But why would the government try to kill you and then invite you back, feed you, and give you a new home? It doesn't make sense, Emelda."

The evening sun found its angle between the mountains. A low knife of light piercing their eyes. In unison, they both raised a hand, a bag, for relief.

"After I realized what I had done," Emelda continued, "I would think of that radio show for ladies, wonder if I could go on there and tell my sad story and win prizes. But maybe . . ." She laughed miserably. "Maybe that radio show was fake, too, just like mine."

In the valley, the wheat had matured and opened into full color. A glowing red amplified by the low sun. The fields rippled and whooshed like fire, completely surrounding the village.

Emelda said she stayed in the mountain jungles for almost a year, running with guerrillas who had found her. From then on, she stopped speaking Quiché, afraid they would recognize her voice from the radio program almost thirty years before. Instead she learned Rabinal Achí, a related dialect, to communicate with them.

"The helicopters burned any crops they found and we had to suck roots during the dry season to stay alive. Some Indians joined the guerrillas to fight, but a lot just followed for food and protection."

"What about you?" Lenore asked. "Did you just follow them?"

"I fought."

"Why are you telling me all this? If you're so afraid of people finding out?"

"Because who can you tell? The only people you can talk to are your husband, Mincho, and the General, and I know you don't want to talk to them. I've been so lonely for thirty years, lonely even when I braid Cruzita's hair. I had to tell someone. Now you're the only person who's ever known me."

At that moment, the stench of the village hit Lenore. The air went dead with excrement and sweat. She raised her sleeve to her nose and mouth. "My God," she said, "was it like this before?" Emelda shrugged. Had the people on the bus, the doctor, had they smelled this on her? A helicopter, she could hear, lifted off from the base and approached from behind. It flew so low that Lenore did not have to raise her eyes to watch it rip over the village. The line at the water pump dispersed, women grabbed their children, the Civil Patrol broke from formation, the whole crowd coming to a sudden boil.

"You're back!" Dan stood in the doorway. She had not understood the words at first, though they had woken her. "What did the doctor say?"

"Nothing to worry about," she said. "I'm not pregnant, I'm not sick. Just stress."

"You see? I told you it was all a part of His plan." Proof of his divine theory pleased him, which was all Lenore wanted at the moment. She didn't want to tell him that she was weak, that despite his energy and health, her body had failed under exactly the same conditions. Her eyes adjusted, then settled on his right hand.

"The soldiers gave me a real machete yesterday," Dan said, noticing her stare. "Which is good, I guess. They had more problems with the road crew bringing back stones and leaves. They've been putting them in their pockets, Lenore. The General has asked that the women stop sewing pockets on their pants."

Lenore didn't reply to this. She did not want to hear about the camp. If she thought about it, she would just wonder where Ama was, or the man and boy taken from the bus. Why no more food or medicine had been delivered to the village, though the new road made it possible now.

She watched her husband.

Dan's body had changed shape a few times over the past three months. From pudgy to lean and boyish. But now the leanness had strength. Made it seem as if Lenore were watching a strange man undress in her presence. From the bed, she reached out and touched his side, damp and gritty. She imagined her fingers leaving a mark. She imagined his Adam's apple, like a trigger in his throat as he spoke.

Lenore reached into his pants, feeling his heart beating furiously in her hand. She wanted to keep the haze of her dream intact, to incorporate Dan into it. She knew that once she was fully awake, things would not be the same.

"Don't cry, Lenore." He slipped into bed beside her, taking her up in his arms. "Are you sad about the doctor?" She nodded, sobbing into his chest. "Don't be. We can adopt. The church has already taken up a collection to pay for it. It was going to be a surprise." He patted her hair back from her wet face, trying to clear a path. "There are so many orphan babies here. There's ten at the base right now, I saw them. They'd be so lucky to have you as a mother. And it's simple here, so much simpler to do. No background checks."

She accepted comfort from him, allowing him to believe that she cried for a baby. But that wasn't it. Not at all. Babies were the furthest thing from her mind. She cried because she realized she didn't smell the stench of the village anymore. It had nearly sickened her upon her return, but now, after she'd fallen asleep and woken up, it was gone.

After they made love, Dan fell asleep beside her. In the dark, Lenore was sure she could feel ants on her. She'd come back from Xela to find them everywhere, swarming the corn mix Dan had absently trailed all over their room. She listened to the wheat, thinking about helicopters, Ama, the little girl back from the dead, her trip on the bus. She wondered if Dan had felt the difference inside her, the lump. This being how she imagined her denial now, her denial about being a missionary, all these doubts. A lump, a death, growing inside her.

Dan stirred. "You didn't say anything about my road, Lenore. Didn't you like it?" She told him she did. "And please don't forget about the pockets." He yawned. "The Civil Patrol already had to rip the pockets out of everyone's pants. We didn't do such a good job. They'll probably need new pants."

Then he fell asleep again. Lenore pictured the Civil Patrol lining up all the men to slice away their pockets. She had the notion now that something terrible had been set in motion and she had no idea how to find out what it was. Before, she had been sleepless for the fear of guerrillas and snakes, but now what frightened her were deeper unknowns. Of being friends with a guerrilla, of trusting her. Of being watched by the General. Of being with someone for fifteen years, sleeping next to him, sharing a life and a bed, thinking that you know him, but suddenly having no idea what he was going to do next.

~~~~~

The next few days seemed the longest Lenore had ever endured at the village. She took Emelda's two letters and hid them under the mattress. When the next truck arrived, she would mail them both, keeping her promise.

The one thing Lenore still believed in, that she should throw her efforts into wholly, was the pageant. Because, if nothing else, it gave them all something to do instead of work the fields, listen to Dan preach, and stand in line for food.

The women worked diligently at their dresses, both excited and nervous to showcase them to the entire village. After much convincing, even Emelda agreed to make a dress for the pageant. "So you will stop bothering me," she had said to Lenore. Too old to compete, she could still wear something nice to the event.

"It's not something I'm giving to you, but that you can make yourself. So your ancestors won't be mad, right?"

"I don't think they can be any madder." She sighed. "After my second baptism."

"I know why you wanted to be baptized," Lenore heard herself say. She didn't think herself capable of bringing up the scene on the bus. "It's hard to see, but the military is trying to help. All they know is force. They want you on the right path, but they have no patience. By enforcing it, they think the rest will follow. It may not be the best way, but it's all for the same end." The more she'd repeated this to herself, the more she believed it.

"I suppose," Emelda replied, "that the fastest way would be to baptize us and then kill us right after. That way, they know we make it to heaven."

Cruzita, sitting on Lenore's other side, played with a gossamer underskirt salvaged from the prom dress in the donation pile. She placed a layer over her face and then cleared it away, like cobwebs, like a lifted veil, smiling.

"Since when is the goal the most important thing?" Emelda asked. "I thought Jesus refused to judge anyone. Mary Magdalene."

"Yes, I suppose that's true," Lenore admitted. "But God is concerned with ends. That's what the Old Testament is about."

"Oh yes, I see. God and Jesus are two different people."

"They balance each other out."

"Like you and the military." Emelda smiled. "Like the ambassador and the Fruit man. I know this story. The nice Fruit man comes along and gives me land, then his friend comes in and threatens me for having it. Gets me to do all sorts of terrible things. I saw the Fruit man again. He came to Miami and pretended to be someone important for the radio show. I think a cabinet member for Jacobo Arbenz. During the coup, he came back to my hotel room, told me a baby can't happen between an Indian and a Hispanic. Jesus and God," she mused. "But you forget that in His end, Jesus broke with God. On the cross, He saw that their ways were too different."

"I don't forget that. You seem to forget the real end. He came back and ascended into heaven. That bit on the cross was only a moment of doubt, Emelda. How could you forget the Resurrection?"

"No, you forget. I know the Bible and I know when Jesus turned human, when He had to experience it, He realized God's way is cruel. When He came back, He wasn't human anymore. He's God again. Jesus only suffered a day. But just that one day made Him declare that God is terrible."

"So you acknowledge the Christian God? You believe He exists? You said before He gave you everything you asked for."

"Of course He exists! He just hates Indians. The foreigners' God loves foreigners and the Indians' gods love Indians. I'm sure your God is not cruel to you. Right?"

Lenore considered this. "Just look at Cruzita. She's happy; she's found new life in Christ. When she arrived she was terrified, but now I never see her without a smile. She seems to get a lot out of the sermons. Do you think God hates her?"

"Cruzita," Emelda scoffed, "is not happy. She acts happy because she thinks they are watching, that if they see her cooperating, they will give her baby back."

"Her baby? Cruzita has a baby?" Hearing her name, Cruzita turned and offered Lenore a bigger version of her perpetual smile, nodding.

"Yes. My son's village was killed and they took her baby."

Lenore's whole body flared with anger. "Emelda, I'm not going to listen to your lies! How could you make up such a horrible story about such an innocent young girl? About your own granddaughter?"

"What do you mean by innocent?"

"She's barely old enough for dates! Now, I'm tired of your stories, period. You're just trying to confuse me. You have to stain everything with horribleness!" Where had the anger come from? Why were Lenore's hands shaking? She felt another seed of doubt planted in her. It had to be the Devil again. Who else could invent such horror, seemingly tailored just to upset her? Spoiled innocence, stolen babies. Despite this awareness, however, she felt the seed sprouting. Every time she saw Cruzita, she would think of this awful story. She would never be able to forget it. She tried to, she took Emelda's dress and tried to correct one of her mistakes. But her hands shook so badly that she ruined the neckline. She slammed her scissors down and held her head in her hands. But she could not calm herself down. In one motion, she overturned the table. The work of five women crashed onto the floor. The whole class jolted at the noise, then stared at her fearfully. They watched her with panicked expressions they had not given her in a long time. Expressions now usually reserved for Dan, Mincho, and the Civil Patrol.

"Don't get so mad about all this, Lenore," Emelda said, stooping to retrieve her dress. No one else moved, though they seemed slightly reassured by Emelda's light tone. "Just remember, you can leave whenever you want." She flicked her hand with the simplicity of it all. "You can just get into one of those military planes and fly away, ascend up into heaven."

Lenore had to remind herself of this daily since they'd returned from Xela. Because she'd begun to suspect that she could not leave the moment she wanted. The past three nights, she woke with an intense desire to just get out of bed, walk through the church, out onto the path, and past the armed guard at the front gate. To just walk past him without a word or a look, to just take a walk up the road. Would he let her pass, or would he gun her down in the middle of the road, in her nightdress?

Even if she could walk away, she would never be able to leave behind the story she'd just heard. But she let Emelda have her point. The fact that someone there thought she could leave was, for the moment, an immense relief.

~~~~~

The children were getting thinner. Watching them run in the streets in their new jumpers, Lenore noticed how the fabric hung loosely on their shoulders, how it tightened around their swollen bellies. She had written to their church asking for anti-diarrhea medicine and iodine tablets and received a day's supply for the entire village. Dan and Lenore discussed giving every child one dose or picking a few to treat thoroughly. But they couldn't bring them-selves to choose among the children. They'd written again to the church to send more iodine tablets.

Dan crumpled a letter and let it drop to the floor of their room.

"What is it?"

"Pastor May. We're supposed to write to Operation Open Arms for sup-plies from now on. The church has given over ten thousand dollars for sup-plies to Open Arms and we have to go through them." He sighed, massaging his face with his fingers.

"Ten thousand?" She couldn't believe the mobilization, the sacrifices her neighbors must have made to raise this sum. "Does that money all come to us?"

Dan shrugged.

"Well, how do we contact Open Arms to get it?"

"Through the General."

He slumped down on the box of anti-diarrhea medicine. Outside, Lenore could hear the soldiers constructing the stage for the beauty pageant. Dan rubbed his temples, rubbed at the drills and hammers in his head. "The Lord certainly does test us," he said.

"So does the Devil."

"What does that mean?"

"I don't know. It just means what it means, I guess."

"As long as we're saving souls, we know who we work for." Dan's bright eyes flashed darkly at her. "The Devil is an agent of doubt."

"I don't agree with that, Dan. I don't agree one bit. Sometimes when facts come up, it's healthy to reevaluate."

"What facts have come up, Lenore? What could possibly change the sit-uation down here to make you second-guess what we're doing?"

"I'm not second-guessing, I just think small adjustments could be made. I don't think it's all or nothing."

"Facts, Lenore, what facts? What do you want to adjust?"

"Well, I think that the Indians should be able to speak their own lan-guages. That has nothing to do with their salvation. God speaks all lan-guages and there's no need to put that added stress on these refugees of having to learn an entirely new language."

"Have you forgotten everything we've learned at the conference? How will they feel loyalty and citizenship if they can't understand what their President, what the newspapers, say? The language is a huge part of the Project."

"I don't think it should be, is all. I think we should concentrate on the religion. That's our specialty and I'm not going to pretend to know anything about politics or foreign cultures. And you shouldn't, either."

Dan's mouth hung open in amazement. "Everything's connected, Lenore. What's happened to make you doubt our mission?"

But it wasn't just one thing, it was several. Not even particularly Emelda's stories, but how Lenore spied echoes of them in everything she had seen on her trip to Xela. The soldiers squeezing their way through the bus, all those villages in the mountains, the direction the bus drove them in. The Civil Patrol. And the village itself. She could not forget walking with Emelda, a new perspective from high up, and watching the line at the water pump disperse as if under attack.

"I was talking with one of the women the other day and she said that military helicopters came to destroy her village. Guerrillas don't have helicopters, Dan."

"You were speaking to one of the Indians? How? Through Mincho?"

Dan's suspicion had been provoked and she knew she could not fool him. She decided on nonchalance. "One of the women speaks a little English and I've learned a little Spanish. She was able to tell me."

"You've learned Spanish." He cocked his head. "Tell me one thing in Spanish."

"Jesús te amo."

This, for some reason, enraged Dan. "Don't play games with me, Lenore! You've begun speaking with a guerrilla and believing her lies and are ready to accuse me and the entire military of killing people before considering that she's brainwashing you. An Indian would have no practical reason to know English unless she was an agent put here to try to confuse you!"

"It's not just her. I've seen it myself. I've seen how they run from the helicopters. I've seen the smoke in the mountains, coming from where those helicopters go!"

"They're burning out the guerrillas! How else are they to do it?" He turned away from her, disgusted, the tiny golden claws of his rimless glasses glinting.

"People live in those mountains! All these people lived in the mountains! There are villages everywhere. I saw them on my trip!"

"They live in the mountains because they're guerrillas. Who is this woman? What's her name?"

"I can't believe you believe that. These people have lived in the mountains for hundreds of years."

"Why would the military destroy their villages, then build them a new one? Who is this woman, Lenore? You have to tell me."

"I do not. It doesn't matter."

Dan's rage crowded their tiny room as he punched his palm, fist in hand, over and over. He had to get away, she knew. He had to defuse the violence in him with a long walk, which was easy in Kentucky, but not here.

"This place smells like shit!" Lenore yelled after him, but he did not turn around.

~~~~~

Two days later, Lenore held an extra sewing class to finish the dresses for the next day's pageant. As soon as they stitched on the last beads and catches, the girls slipped behind the curtain to change. The victory was that simple. They modeled their dresses one after the other, giggling. She wanted to call Dan in to show what a little love and patience could accomplish, but they had barely spoken since their fight. They worked opposite schedules now. Dan, to avoid her, took the Civil Patrol night shift and slept in the education building in the afternoons.

Whenever Lenore returned to their room, however, she saw evidence of Dan's presence: an open Bible, corn mix spilled on the floor, marked-up maps, new roads. All ordinary enough, until lunch an hour ago, when she went back and discovered all their boxes emptied onto the floor, their bed pulled from the wall. A search. Dan, possibly with the Civil Patrol, had searched their own room. They hadn't even bothered to clean up. The place looked pillaged. When Lenore felt under the mattress for Emelda's letters to the newspaper office, they were gone.

She ate in stunned silence, in the ruins of her privacy, before going to the last sewing class before the pageant. The letters, would Dan give them to the General? Or would he confront her himself? She'd been waiting for the next mail truck, which she now heard arriving too late. All around her, girls in dresses spun and laughed. Lenore did her best to smile along.

Emelda and a few of the older women emerged from behind the curtain, holding their dresses. "They don't fit," Emelda said, handing them to her.

Lenore held the dresses up for inspection. The seams seemed fine and sturdy, the proportions looked correct. But she noticed that Emelda's dress was too tall for her frame. And the other dresses were the same size as that one.

"What happened?" she asked. "Did you make the wrong measurements?"

"No," Emelda told her, "the measurements are correct. They just aren't ours. They're yours." She walked over to Lenore, held one of the dresses up to her. "You see? We did a good job. Go try them on."

Lenore's confusion survived a moment after the thin blade of Emelda's smile sliced through her. "These are supposed to be yours, for the pageant," she said. And then it hit her. "Why did you do this?"

"These are your kind of dresses. They look nice on you, but they're not for us." Emelda spoke a few words in Quiché or Achí to the younger girls, all standing around in their dresses, now looking at the floor. One woman disappeared behind the curtain to take hers off.

"Emelda, what are you doing to me!" Lenore's voice cracked in desperation. "I won't have you ruining this. All this." She swept her hand over the class. "This is what this whole project is about. Do you want to ruin these girls' chances of being Guatemalans, to have a regular life?"

"I know you think this is right," Emelda said. "I'm not angry at you for it, I used to think your way myself. But this . . ." She slapped both hands on her chest, then her thighs, indicating her ragged Indian costume. "This is sacred. You can destroy our gods, our land, our families, our ability to feed ourselves, but this is different. You are fighting us down to the last thread of clothing. Why do you want us defeated so completely?"

Lenore wanted nothing more than a mirror right then, a full-length mirror to show Emelda what she was so intent on protecting. The shapeless, rotting rags that made her look like a crazy woman.

Lenore lowered her voice to calm the others, who'd grown fearful at the argument. "Emelda, please tell these girls they have a choice. They can go with you or stay with me. I'm not going to fight with you. It's not God's way. You are free to make a choice. You have always had a choice. You chose to do your work for the government, you chose to take the land they gave you, you chose to go to the mountains and fight that same government who had kept their promise to you, you chose to come back and put yourself under the government's mercy, you chose to eat their food and live under their roof, you chose to be baptized." Lenore's voice had taken on the restrained power of a preacher's. The girls were no longer just frightened, but terrified. Lenore smiled reassuringly at them. "So you can choose not to participate in the pageant. That is what a democracy is about. Any girl is free to choose." She folded her arms, finished, but then realized she was standing in front of the padlocked door. She unlocked it and stepped aside.

Emelda said a few words to the women and then turned to leave, with a handful of the class following.

"What did you say to them, Emelda?"

"The one thing I know. Once they put on those clothes, it'll be the last choice they can ever make."

She walked out. Lenore stood silently, counting the faithful who had stayed behind with her. More than half the girls shifted in their new dresses, eyeing each other. All young, under twenty, the older ones having left with Emelda. Cruzita remained. Lenore watched her take a step in the direction of the door, but only one step. She looked to her grandmother and back, twice, before deciding to stay with Lenore.

That evening, Lenore helped the remaining girls get ready in the church, using her dwindling supply of hair spray to mold their hair into fashionable styles. Lenore didn't like to play favorites, but she saved her curler set for Cruzita. She pulled the curlers from their pile of materialist things that they never could throw away, along with the hair dryer and Dan's hair gel, the useless things now proving their worth to the village. Cruzita sat completely still as Lenore worked on her.

"You're so lucky to be young at a time like this, Cruzita. You really do have a chance to start over." She twisted a thick strand of the girl's hair around her finger like rope.

Cruzita's eyes followed her lips, uncomprehending.

"It's okay." Lenore laid a hand on Cruzita's forehead to smooth her worry away. "I think you know this all already."

Cruzita smiled.

"I don't believe for one moment that you have a baby. You're barely old enough for dates. Why would she make up something so horrible like that?"

She knew not to use Emelda's name. Hearing it, the girl would skew her beautiful face in panic and crack the makeup there.

"She was probably just trying to explain away your happiness. She can't understand how you could be so different, being of the same blood, I guess. You know, she told me yesterday that she got pregnant by that United Fruit man she's always talking about? And she kept your father a secret from him. Your grandfather was a big, successful businessman. Of course, you don't know that. I wish I could tell you. But what good would it do now, anyway? Just make you angry about the proper upbringing she denied you. I think she's threatened by the progress you're making despite all that." She stooped to look at her directly. "You are happy, aren't you? I can tell. *¿Sí?*"

Cruzita shifted her eyes around without moving her head. "*Sí*," she agreed tentatively. Lenore pinned a pink foam curler to her scalp.

"I have to be honest with you, though, Cruzita. I think I owe you that much, after putting you through that crazy facts-of-life talk. And I don't want you to think I'm judging your grandmother for her past." She paused, extracted another long rope of hair, running her finger down the length and finding no resistance. "I didn't wait until I was married to sleep with Dan. It's not that I was lying to you before. Just sometimes, the way things turned out, I really do forget. He is the only man I've been with. And, it's funny. I actually have a fake memory of our honeymoon night, where it's the first time. Anyway, the point is, I do know the kind of temptation that's out there and I know what you're up against. I remember being young, going out on dates, kissing for the first time. All that's just starting for you, and it's so exciting, but it can also get out of control very quickly. How do you say it? *¿Rápido?*"

"*Rápido*," Cruzita repeated, launching one hand off the other, nodding.

"I was lucky, though. I ended up with Dan. I know I'm supposed to regret the fact that I didn't wait, but it was the most romantic night of my life." She snapped another pink roller shut with satisfaction. "On my seventeenth birthday, Dan picks me up from school and takes me out to this lake. He's got a picnic packed and I'm starving. We're sitting in the car, overlooking the water, and I open up my sandwich and I see it's not a sandwich at all, but a silk scarf I had wanted from Sears. And then all the other things in the basket end up being presents, too. He must have spent fifty dollars on me. He'd never even spent that much on himself. Now, it's funny, because for a while I'm kind of disappointed, since I'm still hungry and I thought there'd be all this food. He didn't think to bring actual dinner. But then the sunset kicks in, and the colors just start melting on the water like an ice cube. Dan tells me that he loves me, that we're meant to be together. We start kissing and he starts touching me, like, and, well, I had no idea what to do. But Dan knew what to do. He just kept on going, you know, not letting me be embarrassed or anything. He would just do things like it was perfectly natural. He knew we'd end up together. He knew it was meant to be." Lenore made the conscious effort to still her fingers, which had been twisting Cruzita's hair into knots. "He knew we'd end up together and he just kept saying that, and before I knew it my skirt was up and I was holding my knees together like a vise. He told me that he'd spent a whole week's paycheck on me and that he was in love with me. And he was, I knew he was. And he was so heavy and I just remember how heavy he was and how I couldn't move—and, well, he was right. We ended up together."

She had run out of curlers and, inexplicably, began looking around the church, as if more would appear. All around, young girls twirled and patted their hair. "Well, I guess the lesson there is that mistakes can turn out for the best. But I was very lucky. It could have turned out badly in so many ways." Lenore began fanning Cruzita's damp hair with a piece of paper. "So with how it all turned out, I don't regret it. Dan does, though. He told me much later, after he was saved, that he wished I had resisted him. I was a Christian at the time, he wasn't."

Mincho arrived in the church with a bouquet of lilies and a message that the General had decided on another prize for the winner—a week's travel pass to leave the village. Behind him, soldiers unloaded a piano from a military truck. Another gift from the General, for the pageant. Shipped all the way from Xela.

These gifts, not even asked for or expected, made Lenore feel horrible. She had accused the General of mass murder. She'd believed Emelda when, clearly, Emelda had been planning to thwart her all along. After the pageant, she decided, she would apologize and tell Dan everything.

The women huddled around the flowers. Lenore tested a few keys on the piano and considered the travel pass for the winner. She imagined Cruzita going back to her village, the tearful reunions as she planned for a new life. Feeling renewed, she pulled the girl back into her seat to finish her hair. Lenore used the hair dryer and it screamed hot air all around Cruzita's head. When she found a curler gone loose, she pulled it tight. Cruzita whimpered as Lenore twisted and pinned it back to her scalp.

The ceremony fell together that evening, with the road crew and the Civil Patrol returned from their duties, and the women in from harvesting the wheat. Everyone pledged to the Guatemalan flag. Immediately following, Lenore began the first verse of "On Bended Knee." The piano was out of tune from its long journey over rough jungle roads. She played, trying to find Emelda and the other defectors in the crowd, but they apparently, boldly, had chosen to skip this mandatory event.

Everyone stretched on tiptoe to see the girls file onto the simple stage constructed in front of the church. About thirty soldiers from the base had shown up, too. She had never seen them so animated. The boy soldiers brought to life. They joked, blowing elaborate smoke shapes into the air. Snakes and O's, and a series of puffs like a train.

There wasn't much to the program. With no real charms to display, the girls paraded in groups and individually, in a way that seemed vaguely military. They formed a line, from which each girl walked diagonally by herself. In this way, the group slowly transferred its shy huddle from different corners of the stage. All barefoot, of course.

Running through the three songs she knew, Lenore began again with "On Bended Knee," watching the audience for their reactions to the ceremony. Some swayed, others jumped to see the stage. They're into it, Lenore told herself, they really are. Even Dan looked happy, clapping a rhythm, rushing Lenore's song.

Since the Maya were illiterate, Lenore had decided that the crowd should vote by applause. So Mincho called each girl's name, the girl stepped forward, and the crowd applauded to the appropriate level. When Cruzita's turn came, the crowd absolutely erupted. Even Dan yelled and clanged his machete on the fence, while encouraging the Civil Patrol to do the same. They cheered so loudly that Lenore turned to see if the soldiers would try to impose order, but they'd started clanging, too.

And so, in the village's first democratic decision, Cruzita was crowned the queen. Lenore grabbed the lilies and rushed onstage. Cruzita met Lenore with wide, astonished eyes, her mouth open in a small *o* of disbelief. And instead of taking the flowers, Cruzita hugged her.

That small moment was enough. Yes, just as Pastor May had said, all her troubles seemed so small in retrospect, with her goal accomplished. With the joy evident on Cruzita's face, the smiling deference of the other women onstage, her uncertainty vanished. The crowd, Lenore realized, appeared to be clapping for her. The village suddenly seemed to appreciate all her hard work, to see the point of what she had done. Turning to face them, her doubts faded. She turned and it felt like turning a corner.

Lenore lingered with Cruzita onstage, wanting to make the moment last as long as possible. She felt her happiness leak away just slightly as Mincho mounted the stage to explain that Cruzita would have to go to the base to apply for her travel pass. She seemed reluctant, shy to have all this attention on her, but Lenore encouraged her to go. "It won't take long," Lenore reassured her, through Mincho. "It only took me fifteen minutes to apply for mine. You'll be back before church is over."

Mincho escorted Cruzita to the gate, where one of the armed guards took over and offered a gentlemanly arm. Lenore watched them make their way up the road, like a courting couple. She basked in the image, of a girl being cherished by a young man. As they ascended the hill, up toward the base, Lenore could hear Dan welcoming the Indians to the church service. "Good evening, my brothers and sisters in Christ. And to those who have not yet come to see the glory of Christ."

The night turned windy and in their room, Lenore and Dan could hear the constructed stage shifting and groaning where its nailed joints rubbed. Over the course of several hours, Lenore's happiness had soured with their continuing fight. In a day, her whole situation had been reversed, with the village a success and her marriage in ruins.

"The pageant was nice," Dan offered from the table. He was talking to her again, though he'd not yet brought up the hidden letters.

"I think so." The words trickled out to alleviate the temptation to confess, but they only made the desire worse. Her joints ached, her skin burned. She was so tired, yet she could not nap, for all the Folgers powder she'd consumed. She wiped a line of ants off the wall. "It was very nice of the General to send us the piano and the lilies," she said. She turned to look at the bottom of her paper towel, covered in dying, flailing ants. But there were always more.

"He's very thoughtful when he's not killing people left and right."

"All right, Dan. You know that's not what I meant."

"What, then, did you mean?" He laid his pencil down with a patient click. His handwriting, she noticed, had grown bigger to accommodate the dull lead point. And his sermons shorter, for he measured them by the page.

"I don't know what I meant. I'm not well." She could no longer hold back the revelation, the excuse for everything. "I need better food. I'm malnourished, Dan. It's made me weak and has affected my judgment."

"Malnourished? How do you know?"

"I found out in Quetzaltenango. The doctor did tests."

It was as simple as that to win her husband back and to cast off the guilt of her deceptions and doubts. Suddenly Dan was touching her, brushing her hair back. And with his affections returned, a solvent to all her stubbornness, she became unglued. She cried and admitted that she hadn't wanted him to worry about her, that she thought she could work through the fatigue.

"We can fix this," Dan reassured her. "All I have to do is write the General and I can get you some food within the hour. I've been eating up there a few times a week."

"You have? When?"

"Well, it's not just meals. We're conducting meetings, and there just so happens to be food."

"What have you been meeting about? More roads?"

"And other things. Guerrilla intelligence he's intercepted. I didn't want to worry you, but there are agents here, we've confirmed, planning an attack from the inside."

"Who?"

"We're just beginning to figure that out. A few of the Indians are on a hunger strike. They're even refusing the corn mix now, because it has wheat in it, or something crazy. They're organizing, definitely. But right now"—he picked up his pencil—"I'm going to write about getting you dinner."

She fell asleep, and an hour later Dan woke her, with a plate of fried fish, bread, and green beans. Real bread, not made from the corn mix. She sat up and stared at the plate on her lap, knowing she should desire it, but she only felt nauseous from the fragrant steam.

"Here." Dan placed a cloth napkin over her chest and put the fork in her hand. "Eat as much as you can. Start with the fish."

She forced herself to eat half the fish, while Dan watched. "How does that feel?"

"I don't know." She could not tell sick from well anymore. "If I eat too much, it'll just stretch my stomach and I'll be even hungrier tomorrow."

"That you don't have to worry about. I went up to talk to the General myself, and you'll have all your meals delivered from the base from now on. No more corn mix for you. It was a bad rule. The Indians are used to eating just corn, but we're not. The General apologizes."

She ate the second half of the fish and felt hunger returning. Then she began tearing at the bread with her teeth.

"The General's also interested in your experiences with that woman, the one who you said speaks English and told you those stories about the military. He suspected the agent was a woman for quite a while, but he wasn't sure."

"You mean Emelda?" The name fell out of her mouth with a few crumbs of bread. They landed on the napkin Dan had placed below her chin. She hadn't meant to, but it was done.

~~~~~

The next morning, Lenore remained in bed late, drifting in and out of a shallow, dreamless sleep. Returning from the Civil Patrol, Dan woke her at one point to say—though she wondered in retrospect if this had been a dream, if she had dreamed after all—that he'd be coordinating a counterinsurgency program within the village.

"What does that mean?" she had asked. No answer. He left the apartment bare-chested, with his shirt tucked into the back of his pants like a tail.

He had prepared coffee, but he'd left the Folgers jar open and the ants now carried away the freeze-dried crystals that looked very much like ants, too. There was nothing to do now but to let them take it all away. She sat in bed, watching their line waver over the floor like a crack developing in the foundation.

What else was there for her to do? She had played by the Project's rules and had been rewarded with success, and when she had tried to strike out on her own, had tried to deceive Dan and the General, she had failed. Now that she knew Emelda's intentions, she wondered what the woman had been translating all along. Lenore had given her the power to essentially run her class, and possibly Emelda had used her position to spread lies, to try to organize the women in a revolt. And Lenore had gone along with it, locking the door and allowing them to meet secretly to plot, while pretending to sew their dresses. But not all of them had been pretending. Cruzita and the pageant girls had clearly not accepted Emelda's rebellion.

To go out in the village now, Lenore would have to ally herself with someone. The choice between manipulative guerrilla women and the Civil Patrol did not inspire her either way. She was sick, she should be sleeping. Dan would bring her breakfast soon. Meals, now, were the only thing of certainty.

She slept some more, then woke at the sound of someone in the building. Lenore expected Dan with her breakfast, but Dan didn't come. Instead, she heard a commotion in the church. Pulling the blanket up, she listened to several women arguing, throwing things. The women's revolt. Something struck the door, leaving a dent. Lenore ran to the door, naked but for her robe and sandals, and pulled the latch.

The sanctuary was completely overturned, with the wooden pews thrown over each other in a pile. Emelda kicked and dragged the long, heavy benches, wailing in a variety of languages that echoed against the metal walls, creating the effect of a mob. But it was only Emelda.

"What are you doing?" Lenore ran to her. "Stop it! Emelda!'

"She's gone!" Emelda cried with her black, furious mouth. "She's been gone all night and still she's not here!"

"Who?"

"Cruzita! Why didn't you tell me about this new prize? They took her to the base and she hasn't been back!"

Lenore felt her heart drop three inches into her empty, stretched stomach. "Are you sure?"

"She hasn't been back to the shed!" She kicked the pews, her foot bleeding. "I should have told her more. If she knew about me, she would not have done your pageant. Selfish! Selfish!"

"Maybe she took her travel pass and left already for her village. Maybe she went to see her family."

"They were all dead in the massacre! Her village no longer exists! Our family no longer exists! She has nowhere to go. She's afraid to go to the bathroom at night." Emelda spoke frantically, trying to sort the languages in her head. "I should have told her more. She'd hate me, but she'd be here still. You have to go now," she cried, jerking Lenore's arm. "You have to go save her!"

Overwhelmed, Lenore let herself be pulled out of the church. "Save her from what?"

"What do you think they did with her all night?"

Outside, the low sun blinded her. Lenore resisted for a moment, unable to see her next step. She shielded her eyes, seeing everything backlit: the stark shapes of soldiers and their guns; what remained of the pageant stage, dismantled with the help of ropes, looked like a gallows. "Oh God." Lenore breathed hard, but could not catch her breath. Emelda dragged her to the village entrance, where Mincho stood, regarding the Civil Patrol's formation. The Indian men with their wooden machetes and Dan, too, with a real machete in hand. Still shirtless, gleaming with sweat. His skin was the color of baked clay. Of bricks.

"What's going on?" Dan asked Lenore, frowning at her arrival in the middle of their exercise.

Emelda remained silent, not knowing Dan knew about her English. Lenore, forced to say it herself, crossed her arms over herself for modesty. "Cruzita hasn't been back from the base yet." She gulped in shallow breaths, but they went down like water, only making speech harder. "She's been there all night."

"Oh." He lowered his head, thinking. "Did she get her travel pass and leave?"

Lenore suddenly realized how stupid that sounded, how stupid she must have sounded to Emelda a minute before. Cruzita could not have gone anywhere last night because of the nationwide curfew. She tightened her hold on herself and managed to say, "No, Dan. We have to do something."

He nodded, looked over at the other men, their dissolving formation. Mincho anchored the center, his hands balled in fists, furious at the intrusion.

"Where's Cruzita?" Lenore asked him.

His face maintained composure, though his knuckles went white with tension. "She went back home with her pass, to San Marcos. She'll be back in a week."

Behind Lenore, Emelda yelled in English, "She's not from San Marcos, she's from Valle Lejos! Where is she?"

"Okay." Mincho shrugged, with his preacher's smile. "She went back to Valle Lejos. She'll be back in a week."

At this, Emelda lunged and the men of the Civil Patrol fell on her, bringing her to the ground. Lenore noticed Dan switch his grip on his machete, readying himself for something. For killing her? Mincho remained where he stood, watching the struggle, pleased.

"What's her name?" he asked Dan.

Before Lenore could stop him, he said, "Emelda. She's the one I told you about. I think she's the one who wrote those letters."

At that moment, Lenore broke down, thinking of all she had told him the night before. Emelda, too, wailed, with her fingertips clawing at the dirt. Just as she had done her first morning in the village.

"Dan," Lenore sobbed, "this isn't right. I'm going up there."

"Just calm down, Lenore. You know you can't just go walking up there. We'll write a note and make an appointment."

An enormous pressure rose up from her gut. "Fuck the notes!" she cried.

Again, Lenore saw him switch his grip on his machete. "Watch your language, Lenore."

"What is wrong with you? They're holding her captive in there and you
want to make an appointment?" He stared at her blankly, like a soldier.
"Fuck you," she said. "I'm going myself."

Lenore pushed past him and the Civil Patrol men. They all looked at
Mincho for instructions, but he just watched with an amused smile on his
face. Dan grabbed her arm, with his machete slightly raised in his other
hand.

"What are you going to do, slice me up? With your new toy?" She laughed
at the absurd way he had always held that machete. Fidgety and unsure of
the proper grip. "Go ahead," she said, and shook free of him. "Prove you're
a man."

Lenore cleared the gate, started up the dirt road, and got about thirty
paces before Dan rushed up behind her, grabbed her by her hair, and
dragged her back toward the borders of the village. "Don't you defy me in
front of these men. What kind of example are you?"

Lenore heard the men laughing. Her robe was flung open, revealing her
nakedness underneath, but she couldn't bring her hands down to close it.
They were in her hair, trying to ease the pull on the back of her scalp. With
her head forced down, she watched her own pale body struggling gracelessly,
retracing her footprints back, back into the village. She then saw Emelda's
bare feet floating an inch off the ground, back toward the education building,
escorted by boots.

"You think you're special, that the rules here don't apply to you? This is
a war! You're lucky I was here. Any one of the soldiers could have gunned
you down." Back inside the fence, Dan released her with a violence that sent
her stumbling to the ground. Her hands, unable to decide whether to break
her fall or clasp her robe shut, froze, doing neither, and she fell into the dust
on her back, her legs spread, her robe almost completely off now, the back
sliding down to her elbows. Dan sighed and looked down at her as if she had
hurt him immensely.

"Go back to the church," he said.

It took all of Lenore's energy to gather herself up from the ground without
screaming. She could hear Dan talking to Mincho as she tried to walk away
with dignity, but her knees were shaking and useless. "The Lord says that a
woman's duty is to obey her husband, while the husband's duty is to protect
his wife. There's a lesson in this," he said somberly. He paused, allowed

Mincho to translate to the others. "Even if the woman fails in her duty, even if she insults and mocks you, you still have to fulfill yours. No matter what, you have a duty to protect her. That's love."

Lenore noticed she was barefoot. At some point during the struggle, she had lost her sandals. But she didn't turn around for them.

Lenore spent all day in bed. No one brought her breakfast or lunch. Now she regretted the meal the day before. She regretted so many things. Epiphanies washed over her, one after the other, as she waited for his inevitable arrival.

He came home almost sheepishly, without a word. Instead, he searched his Bible, as if for what he wanted to say to her. But she didn't want to hear it. She knew the Bible better than him. Suddenly she saw everything more clearly than him.

"Do you realize, Dan, that we've set up nothing but a huge Communist experiment? No food, bad water, cramped shacks. Everything is supposed to be for the good of the village, but the men work constantly to build military roads. The women harvest wheat that's driven away in a truck. It's worse than communism, if you ask me. It's a labor camp."

The open Bible hung heavy and limp in his hand as he stood up. "What's wrong with you, Lenore? This isn't what you thought last night. It's what you thought the day before. You're erratic, you change your mind every day. You used to think the women were idle. You used to think that working for the good of the village was the best thing!"

Yes, she knew she had reached the point that whatever she said would be used against her. Her own words bent into loops and snares to trap her. And his words were like heavy stones, stacked between them. Impassable.

"A woman tells you a story, a girl disappears, and you forget absolutely everything we've seen and learned down here. This is Guatemala. Hundreds of people disappear every day. We can't forget our purpose and get caught up in every small injustice. We have a higher calling. Nothing would get done here if we stopped for every crime."

"Dan, I spent hours yesterday dressing Cruzita, curling her hair, giving her lipstick. And I just handed her to those soldiers to take away—"

"I think you're imagining the worst scenario, and we don't have any facts. She could have just gone home."

"Don't give me that! You know exactly what happened to her and you don't care. You care more about your roads than about an innocent girl being passed around—"

He kicked the chair, which clattered on the floor. She flinched.

"You think I'm going to hit you? You think I'm an abusive husband because I had to hurt you to save your life? Should I have let them shoot you?" Blood rushed to his face and he could barely spit his words out for the anger collected there. "I warned you and you brought it on yourself. Don't blame me for your failure. You failed in your duty, but I held up my end."

"I don't care about us," Lenore said, pulling the blanket over herself. "I'm talking about Cruzita and Emelda. Where's Emelda? Did they take her away?"

"The General wanted to see her."

"For what? She didn't do anything, she was just worried about Cruzita."

"She obviously will never trust the military. Those letters she wrote are full of the most typical Communist lies. Blaming America for the war! And she's trying to convince others. She even had you believing her. I had to tell the General everything you told me. She'd compromise the whole program. Guatemala is too unstable—"

"Now, wait, I never said anything like that. If this is about you and me, if this is about our problems, let's not drag an entire country into it."

"Yes, Lenore, let's not drag an entire country into it. You don't trust me, you don't think my roads are important. You hear fantastic stories about helicopters and military massacres and American corruption from a stranger and you believe them because you don't trust me. She speaks English! She's a Communist agent put here to sabotage us."

"My distrust of the program here has nothing to do with you, it has to do with what I see here every day. Where is Emelda?"

"The General and I decided that taking her out of the village was best."

"Emelda is a good woman. She was just hiding in the mountains, she was defending herself! This isn't right, Dan. Don't let the General decide!"

"You're not qualified to make that decision. They know her, where she's been, and who she knows. So they decide. You," he said, "just taught her sewing."

"She was my friend! I know her! I'm the only one who knows her!"

"Guerrillas don't have friends. They're killers."

"Emelda's never killed anyone! This is all my fault! Take me up there, take me instead of her. I can explain!"

"I've spoken with the General, I've seen the evidence. You're willing to believe a strange Indian woman over me, your husband, who loves you. You,

Lenore, are the one dragging an entire country down with our personal problems. You're the one who can't see the larger picture."

Dan went back to the Civil Patrol. Lenore watched them conduct some exercises in the square, switching their machetes from the relaxed to ready position. They held a meeting there, then resumed their drills. Lenore sat on her new piano bench in the darkened doorway of the church and watched them for a long time. It wasn't until hours later, after Dan and the patrol had marched out of sight, that she came out of the church. Stepping onto the path, feeling the gravel, she remembered that her feet were bare. At the gate, a soldier stood guard. Lenore walked to the fence, hooked her fingers in the links, and looked out onto the road that rose to the military base, opaque and terrifying in the distance. She could see her sandals in the middle of the road, several yards away. One in front of the other, frozen in step. She glanced at the guard and knew he would not let her retrieve them.

1999

Two aging soldiers, used to more exciting things, guarded the gate. One leaned inside the frame of the metal detector, which clearly didn't work. It was nothing more than a freestanding doorway for its tacit acceptance of the AK-47, hand grenades, pistol, ammunition, and bowie knife strapped to his uniform. The first soldier stood in the hall, funneling the wary, weary passengers in the direction of the second.

It was either the most dangerous or the most secure border crossing Jean Roseneath had ever experienced. She was accustomed to the small, tyrannical absurdities of third world countries from her less conventional travels abroad. Maya, however, was not. Jean could feel her sidling close, could feel the musky heat coming off her, like that of a baby stirring after a long sleep.

"It's okay," she told her daughter. "Just do what I do."

The two feet of cautious distance that had separated them for the past several months was suddenly, so easily gone. Fifteen-year-old Maya took her mother's hand and made her bare shoulders very small. Jean could not remember the last time Maya had held her hand. She preferred men with guns to her daughter's moods and hoped all of Guatemala was like this. Maybe, under the threat of violence for the next three weeks, their relationship would become more civil.

Jean glanced down on the top of her daughter's hair—angry, matted from failed midflight naps. Her altered part revealed a faint pink scar that disappeared the moment Jean bent to confirm its presence. It was unfair, she knew, to wish this fear upon her daughter. She was fifteen. She was beautiful and furious and popular and, Jean suspected, brighter than she let on.

The first soldier's face twitched from its trance to look from daughter to mother, then back again. He took his time to point them in the direction of the other soldier, who squinted at them as if from a much greater distance. At once these two men became very alive and alert, as if all their training had been in preparation for this moment—a white American woman entering their country with her child. Maya squeezed her mother's hand hard before she was forced to let go. They were directed to walk separately through the plastic metal detector gate that didn't work. They both went through, then Maya was asked to step back and walk through again.

No alarm sounded, no lights, of course. The soldiers looked satisfied that they had accomplished their goal with these two tourists, which seemed nothing more than to slow them down and force them to walk with reverence into the single and only baggage claim in all of Guatemala.

The passengers gathered around the raised mouth of the baggage machine and waited for their possessions.

Jean studied her flight companions, trying to find Telema. She had not noticed the pile of black, knotted hair, the elegant hands coming up to tighten the nest mercilessly, until it was too late to do anything about it. They had already been seated in the plane in Los Angeles and Telema had arrived late, like an omen. The sight of her after four months had felt like an ambush. In order to calm herself, she'd had several Bloody Marys on the flight. From more than ten rows back, after three drinks, Telema could have been anyone.

But she was not anyone. She had followed Jean like a shadow cast by the abstractions that plagued her: love, history, guilt. Jean constantly scanned the baggage area to try to catch her, determined not to be taken by surprise again.

And then they began to arrive. One by one, bags heaved up the throat, clattering down to the circular conveyor belt, where they were either claimed or doomed to make circles for hours with other unclaimed baggage. Jean's and Maya's suitcases appeared. Jean hoisted them both and turned, and that was when she encountered Telema standing directly behind her, her teeth biting her lower lip in an angry smile. She wore combat boots underneath her long black skirt, wore them seriously, tightly laced, not loose and clomping with irony.

"That's a lot of baggage, Jean," she said, looking not at her, but at Maya, who stared back at this beautiful tan-skinned woman with unmistakable sexual awe. Automatically, Jean stepped between them. Telema, of course, did not have baggage. And she stood proudly with her black purse as if not having a suitcase were a moral decision. What could she fit in that big purse of hers? Several notebooks, one change of clothes—no underwear—a few books, a gun.

"Telema. How are you?" Jean tried her best at sincerity, for her own sake.

To show displeasure, to show anything, would just provoke Maya's interest, her cruelty. She asked how Telema was, but nothing would have pleased Jean more than a thick, phlegmy hack in reply, the news that she was ill, dying.

"I'm fantastic," Telema proclaimed as she tightened her black hair scarf with a vicious twist of her small hands. "Clean nose, clean conscience. Can't ask for more, but maybe"—she turned to scan the crowd—"to lose the goon who's following me."

Jean followed Telema's gaze to the exit, where a white man in a dark suit waited. He did not eye the circulating baggage and ignored the taxi drivers swarming around him.

"Tag." Telema tapped Jean's shoulder. "You're it!"

Indeed, Jean took that as her cue. No more questions. If she left now, the encounter would appear brief, casual. She nudged through the crowd with her luggage, Maya following behind with a skip. They were almost clear, almost free of the drama, free of any association, when a Latina woman grabbed Jean's arm and began speaking in Spanish. She then put her other hand on Jean's suitcase and began pulling. Jean could feel Telema watching the scene, amused. Possibly she had planned it. A diversion. Jean imagined her coming through the commotion, taking Maya's hand, and walking away with her. An abduction. But that was absurd. Telema hated children, a hatred that would trump any idea of revenge.

The woman kept pulling, motioning for Jean to check her baggage claim ticket. Jean had read in her guidebook about local thieves using diversions like this. Read this, look at that—then she'd turn back to find everything she owned gone.

She glanced around for security and saw none. The woman kept pulling and Jean noted her cheap attire, her shoes made of black rubber. Not wealthy enough to fly in a plane, she was sure.

"This isn't your bag!" Jean took her other hand off Maya's suitcase (never let go of your bags, the guidebook said) and yanked back with both hands. The woman fell over like a toddler, in a surprised heap on her backside. Jean collected their luggage and her daughter and ran to customs.

Neither of them mentioned the woman, and by the time they made it outside, they had forgotten her: Jean by the force of will, Maya because further embarrassment had awaited her in customs, where more soldiers with guns had opened her suitcase and seen her underwear. They did not search Jean's suitcase, only her carry-ons.

They walked in the direction of a taxi, away from Telema, away from any involvement or accusations, away from the beggars stationed at the exit. Their square, mismatched luggage dragged behind them in the gravel, the wheels jammed, leaving four neat trenches where they dug in.

Guatemala City was a city of constant motion. Not progress or renewal, merely motion. Trash and plastic shifted and resettled constantly with the weather. The recent hard rain had turned everything to mud. Mud the color of baby shit, Jean thought. Pale, thin, and stinking. And it covered everything. It was the rainy season and it would get no better. The rain here did not wash, but only made more mud. Their taxi rushed through, splashing vendors and pedestrians.

Alone, Jean would be walking this street, taking beautiful pictures of the misery and mud. But Maya was unaccustomed to poverty, and this trip was for her.

Next to her, in the seat-beltless taxi, Maya sucked on a swatch of her black hair, a disgusting habit that accompanied deep thought. Maya stared through the smeared taxi glass, seeing people who looked just like her, in various poses of degradation—some naked, some dressed in too many clothes, like the beggars in Los Angeles. Many went barefoot, many more wore black sandals made from recycled tires. Very few looked like the Maya in California, buttoned up in the maid, nanny, and restaurant outfits that did not belong to them.

Jean watched several weeks of exhausting work—arguments, promises, stories meant to stoke Maya's enthusiasm for this trip—turn meaningless in two minutes.

"It will be better in the highlands," she said. "These people are displaced."

Maya removed her hair from her mouth. "Why did they do that with my bra?" she asked. "They were just trying to humiliate me. There was no reason."

Jean often forgot the minor, daily humiliations of adolescence, especially with Maya. It was easy sometimes to forget her age, as she tried her best to appear much older.

"They didn't do it to humiliate you, Maya. They were looking for drugs."

"In my bra padding?"

"Yes."

Maya, unconsoled, said nothing.

"It's a tasteful amount of padding," Jean lied. "It's nothing to be embarrassed about. All bras have it now."

"Then why were you laughing?"

"I was laughing?"

"Yes, you were laughing as the soldiers went through my bag. You looked crazy."

"I was not." But had she? She had thought nothing funny about customs. She had been standing there, paranoid she may have overlooked something, the way they were going through their bags. Shaking her purse upside down, fingering the lining. She had stood there reminding herself she had nothing to hide.

Commotions seemed to be staged in the street with the purpose of slowing the taxi every few blocks. When this happened, the driver leaned on his horn and vendors approached, said to the closed windows, "Chiclets, Chiclets," "Twinkie," or "Coca-Cola."

The inside of the cab began to sour with heat and body odor, so Maya lowered the window to allow a cautious, experimental crack. "I wonder where Brett is right now." She sighed in despair. "Probably at football practice."

Yes, Jean thought, probably. Whenever Maya mentioned that boy, all she could see was a strutting heap of football padding. Maya had first pointed him out to Jean on the field, after flag line practice. An older boy. A sophomore.

On every block, evangelical churches had taken up storefronts, looking identical, with their recycled names. Victory in Christ, Christ the Redeemer, Victory Redemption Center. Each competing for the most hopeful combination from a very small vocabulary. The Victory Redemption Center was guarded by a man with an AK-47.

Yes, Jean preferred an armed military presence and the glue-sniffing child zombies—swaying now in the streets, as the taxi avoided them like potholes—to watching her daughter tanning at the beach with her alarmingly boy-crazy friends. It was not a proper Roots Tour, with a professional guide and tickets and people expecting you, ready and with information on hand. But it was something.

The taxi stopped again and a girl, no older than Maya, stood close to the car, holding a bundle to her chest. Maya watched the baby nurse beneath the flowered native tunic, while her own mouth worked again at her hair.

"There's no education for young girls down here," Jean explained. "Girls marry and become mothers at your age."

Maya watched the girl through the pane of taxi glass. The baby's head lolled back so its face became visible. It fixed its eyes on Maya, calmly revealing a section of pink-gummed skull. Its lip drawn up in a heart-shaped snarl.

Maya made a startled noise in her throat.

"A cleft palate," Jean managed. "It's just a cleft palate."

The girl stared back at Maya, her tunic still raised, her brown nipple slicked with saliva, obscene.

Maya rolled up the window. "What a horrible, beautiful culture."

Yes, Jean told herself, even this was a vacation from Los Angeles, where her daughter preferred insipid flag drills to reading, where summer break turned her slice of tactful, private beach into a meat market of savage nymphets. Los Angeles, where she thought she had left the unresolved problem of Telema behind. But, it seemed, Telema would not be left behind. She'd follow you across the world in order to make a point.

Political signs for the upcoming presidential election—the first since the signing of the Peace Accords—threw large, cool shadows in which people congregated. Other political endorsements were less formal, graffiti scrawled on buildings or over traffic signs: orange triangles, an ear of corn, initials, the most abundant of these being the stencil of a raised blue hand painted on rocks and trees, at times showing up on a proper billboard. The blue hand made a peculiar signal, with three fingers raised, the pinkie and ring fingers curled down. A greeting, a warning, almost always on a white background. Jean, however, could identify no one who seemed to have the energy or passion for politics. People stood dazed in the sun and wind and trash, as if they had no idea how they'd gotten to the city.

They had to get out of the capital, Jean decided, as soon as possible. Already her itinerary was useless. What was Telema doing? She had to have known she had boarded the same flight as Jean. She had to have done it on purpose, but what was the purpose? If they left the city now, they wouldn't have to see her again.

"Not the hotel," she said to the driver. "The bus station. Are there any buses to Xela? *¿El ómnibus a Xela?*"

The driver nodded, and turned a sudden corner. Maya raised a hand to brace herself and Jean noticed a diamond-looking ring on her left ring finger. Groaning inwardly, Jean considered two possibilities; neither pleased her. Turning away, she looked through the windshield. Ahead, a child no more than six and disfigured by mud, sexless, crouched in their path. A lighter in hand, it waited, then struggled to light a firework stuck upright in the middle of the road. Then it was gone, scrambling barefoot out of their way, just in time. The driver did not brake for the child or for the fuse that they cleared a few seconds before it exploded. *Crackcrackcrackcrack!* Children rushed the street, waving their stick arms and laughing. "*¡Es golpe!*" they cried. "*¡Golpe de Estado!*"

The taxi swerved around the impromptu celebration. Pushed against her daughter in the backseat, Jean felt the rush, the fear. It was not the degradation, the desperation, and the casual violence playing outside that seemed so foreign to Jean. It was the touch of her daughter that thrilled and terrified her. Maya held her mother's arm as the taxi driver plowed through one stop sign, then another. Each with the blue hand painted over the face, making its bizarre yet intimate signal to Jean, like a greeting between members of a secret society.

This was Guatemala, the horrific country from which Maya had arrived, fourteen years before, in the Los Angeles Airport, with a sickly wail, a long scar across the top of her skull, and a diaper that had not been changed in a day.

~~~~~

The past several months with Maya had been a nightmare. Jean hated to use such a dramatic word, but it was always the word that came to mind, before she corrected herself: challenge, struggle, even the more biblical trial. When she did hint at problems to other parents, they nodded knowingly. Hormones, independence. But no, this was nothing like that. Maya's anger was needy and, it seemed, plotted for the greatest effect.

Jean remembered something her mother had said on their last visit to Iowa, about how children are always convinced of the atrocities of their parents. It was a fact of parenting. But, of course, she had not put it as eloquently as that. "You and me," she had said to Jean cheerfully, while stuffing clothes into the washing machine, "will always be monsters." And not even by becoming parents themselves, and being accused, did children ever change their minds, her mother said, giving her a meaningful look.

But Jean was innocent, of this she remained sure. At that time, she could not imagine what Maya could ever accuse her of.

One day this past winter, Jean was making breakfast before taking Maya to school. For some reason that morning, Maya crowded Jean in the kitchen, staying close like a toddler. Jean sliced banana into her own cereal, making lunches and coffee all at once. She stepped to the left, toward the refrigerator, and accidentally bumped into Maya, eating her own cereal right behind her. It was not a hard collision, but enough of one to set Maya back one step, and to send a large splash of soy milk over the lip of her cereal bowl.

Maya screamed and then fell over, sending her cereal in the air and her bowl smashing on the ceramic tiles.

"Don't push me!" she had cried from the floor, her palms pressed in the milk, in the porcelain shards. "You're hurting me!"

Jean had been so shocked that she rushed over to help her up, but that sent Maya nearer the edge of hysteria. She scuttled across the tiles like a crab. "Get away from me! You big dyke, get away!"

The scene that ensued was so baffling and violent, of a girl beating herself on her chest and accusing her mother of the worst abuse, that Jean felt under attack. *You big dyke.* She had backed up against the fridge and watched as Maya's beautiful face darkened into startling shades. She writhed on the kitchen floor like a toddler, anger with eddies of insecurity and neediness showing at the margins. She swore like an adult, kicked like a child. Then, before Jean had soaked up the cold mess with paper towels, Maya stood up and got ready for school.

They rode in the car together thirty minutes later in absolute silence. Jean focused her eyes on the road unraveling unpredictably before them, the road she drove every day. She braked and realized she had no idea of the speed limits of her own neighborhood. When the cop pulled her over less than a block from the school, Jean and Maya waited in silence. Cars passed, familiar faces giving Jean expressions of disbelief as if at their suddenly divergent, tragic lives. Maya slid down into her seat.

"I'm sorry," Jean told the cop through her open window. "Was I speeding?" Her heart pounded like she had been speeding.

The cop's sunglasses were huge and unnecessary.

"I guess I just wasn't paying enough attention. I'm just so used to these roads—"

"Is that your daughter, ma'am?" he asked, cutting her off.

"Yes."

He watched them, registered Maya wilted in her seat. Jean could see Maya's reflection in his glasses, could see what he saw. "Miss . . ." he said more gently, "miss, is this your mother?"

Jean turned to look at her daughter and watched her hesitate, considering something, before finally saying, "Yes."

"I'm sorry, I don't understand why you've pulled me over." Jean's voice cracked. Don't cry. "Was I speeding?" She must speed through this area on a daily basis, always five minutes late dropping Maya off. Jean felt herself losing control for no good reason. Was she speeding? Was she crying?

"No," the cop relented. He placed his hands on his hips and gazed out over the schoolyard. "You were going too slow. Going too slow in a school zone is suspicious."

"Suspicious?"

"Yes, it's worse than going too fast nowadays. I have to pull over anyone going too slow."

Fucking cops, Jean thought, so unimaginative, always pulling over the wrong people. She hated him for adding to her distress that morning. Moments before, she had imagined her own arrest. Reckless endangerment of a minor, drunk driving. Was she still drunk? She had opened and finished an entire bottle of wine by herself last night, because she did not have anyone to share the bottle with. Maybe that was why the morning had been so surreal. She was still drunk. And she could not decide which was worse, drunk-driving her daughter to school or that scene in the kitchen.

Jean passed the rest of the day in stunned silence in her office, wondering what could have happened. She replayed the scene obsessively in her head, wanting to find real fault in herself. Possibly she had bumped Maya too hard. But she could not forget the long pause, the single splash of milk, the settling of the bowl's contents, which she had clearly seen (more than she'd seen Maya), before the whole thing went flying into the air.

And her hesitation with the cop. What had Maya been thinking, right before admitting the identity of her mother? Had she been considering denial? Of repeating her kitchen performance and watching the cop drag her mother away? The look that flickered on her daughter's face was one she had never seen on Maya before, though she recognized it for what it was. Temptation.

By the end of the day, Jean deemed the whole scene a hormone-induced fluke. Maya was pubescent, Jean was menopausal. And indeed, when Maya returned from school the equilibrium seemed to have righted itself. Jean even apologized and Maya accepted. Maybe they had both momentarily lost their reason. But then it happened again a few days later. Jean had reached out to gently guide Maya through a crowd in the mall, and she had screamed and fallen. The shoppers parted, a sea of accusation.

It went on and on, to the point that Jean feared what her neighbors would think. She expected the police to come to the house; she dreamed repeatedly of being interviewed by child services.

"I'm a liberal," she'd insist. "I've never even spanked her." The policeman interrogating her never believed her, always had sunglasses on. He confronted her with pictures of Maya's naked body: bruises and cuts and indecent poses on Polaroids.

"She did all that to herself," she'd say. But it didn't even seem believable to her.

"Who took these pictures?" she'd demand. "Who's taking pictures like this of my daughter?'"

"You took the pictures," the policeman would tell her. "We found them in your house, in frames."

Sometimes, in the dream, she'd confess.

During Maya's first therapy session, Jean sat in the waiting room for an hour before her daughter came out and said the therapist wanted to speak to her. The therapist—a young, sincere woman—had come highly recommended by a coworker. But Jean noticed right away that she was not nearly old enough to have a teenager. She looked and dressed closer to Maya's age than Jean's.

"I know you're eager to get to the heart of the matter, and so we'll just start with that," the therapist said as Jean settled in, feeling Maya's warmth in the upholstery. "Your daughter seems to think you're racist."

"Excuse me?" She thought she had said "racist."

"She believes that you saddle her with different expectations because of her race."

Jean felt the whole room tipping beneath her. "Where the hell is she getting that? How can she call me a racist? I give to the NAACP! Where the *fuck* are *you*—"

"Please. Ms. Roseneath. I didn't call you that. I don't think you're racist and I told her so. A very confused little girl with a very unique background thinks this, and it's my job to facilitate communication between you. Now." She consulted her notes. Pages and pages of notes, all Jean's failures, right there in writing. "She mentioned an incident a few months ago and I think it serves as a good example of what makes her believe this. She told me that when she did something wrong, you told her that"—she skimmed down, locating and then quoting—"Latin American immigrants have it hard enough and that she shouldn't give them a bad name with her bad behavior."

"She was shoplifting!"

"Yes. You mentioned that before."

"Well, did she mention she had stolen shoes when I said that? A pair of two-hundred-dollar high heels!"

"Yes. And when you refused to buy her the shoes weeks before and she said she'd 'die' if she didn't get them, you scolded her for her language and reminded her of Guatemala's civil war. Of all the innocent people who died every day, who didn't even have shoes."

Jean had known the session would turn out like this. Maya, with her long-lipped, oppressed expression, her large, liquid black eyes, could wring any-one's heart dry. She knew, the moment she submitted her daughter to therapy, the blame would shift onto her. But still, she took her, because the woman made Maya feel better, and really, that was the point. To settle her tantrums and give her an outlet, even if that outlet turned out to be blaming her mother for everything. Yes, the therapist concluded, the problem *was* her. Not Ma-ya's vapid friends or the degraded moral framework of a life spent at the mall, those were not causing her daughter to lash out, frustrated and unful-filled in life. Because this was what Jean believed. No. The problem was eight million unlucky, faceless Guatemalans, thousands of miles away, cramping her style. Jean should not mention them anymore.

"But that's her heritage. You're telling me we need to completely forget where she came from?"

"I'm saying she needs to understand her past in a different way. She doesn't understand Guatemala beyond the struggling population here in Los Angeles and what you've told her about the war. It's not a source of pride for her, it's punishment."

"You think she needs to see Guatemala? Do you think she's old enough?"

"She's definitely old enough for a Roots Tour. I know many children her age benefit from them, although I don't think Guatemala's the best place to travel at the moment. For children from more dangerous places, I usually suggest that the parents take a class, to learn more and share more positive information about the culture with their children, in informal ways. Kids usually see a class as punishment, but many parents enjoy the challenge. If they have the money and time. I know you're a single mother."

"I love taking classes." Jean straightened. "I have two graduate degrees."

Jean negotiated a fragile peace with Maya. She did not touch her, did not criticize her for her dull friends or her grades, she did not mention Guatema-lans in general, and she found a Twentieth Century Guatemalan History class at a nearby university. She even paid for cable. When she cooked in the kitchen, she allowed Maya to watch terrible things: sexist music videos, sit-coms that reinforced gender roles. There had been only one incident over the summer. It had been the worst, but it had also been the last. Jean believed this to be progress. She even became convinced that she was not to blame for whatever psychological trauma caused these tantrums. For after two months of peace, they had started up again soon after a visit to Jean's parents' house in Iowa. Right after Maya's first visit to a church.

~~~~~

On the four-hour trip in the garishly painted, corroded school bus to Xela, marimba music blared, getting louder as civilization drained away. Airplanes replaced with cars, replaced with carts, then donkeys, replaced by the hunched figures of humans hauling their belongings on their own backs.

The bus driver looked about as old as Maya. He'd covered the windshield with so many Catholic stickers and sexy magazine pictures that he often had to put his head out the window to see something clearly. His business partner, an even younger itchy boy with a light crust about his eyes, squeezed through the crowd, collecting the fares and selling Chiclets.

A storm, which they never saw, had preceded them on the dirt road. The bus tires stamped the smooth, new mud with long, wavering scars. Maya hunkered down with one of her fashion magazines, while Jean stayed vigilant with her sunglasses up and her back straight despite the busted seat springs. Below, over the ambiguous, slick edge of the road, a river ran orange and thick with clay.

"Boy, I'm ready for the hotel pool, Maya. How about you?" The promise of a pool, a shopping district, and frozen fruit drinks had inspired some excitement from Maya in the past few weeks. Anything that made Guatemala sound like California.

"Does it have a diving board?" she asked skeptically.

"I'm sure it does."

Maya flipped pages, her ring flashing. "Mom, that was your friend Telema, wasn't it, at the airport?"

Jean grabbed the seat in front of them, feeling the tires slip. "Yes." Maya and Telema had never met, though they knew about each other. Jean had purposefully kept them apart. The fact that Maya had used the term friend suggested she knew more than Jean wanted her to know. She didn't call Jean's real friends friends at all, she just used their names. "How did you know it was her?"

"You called her Telema. She was on the same flight as us?"

"It seems so, Maya." Jean studied the roadside, amazed that the painted political logos had made it this far. The rocks and trees now had party affiliations.

"Did you know she was coming to Guatemala, too? What's she doing here?"

Jean could not decide on an answer. Telema often claimed her travels were tied to her research. But it was entirely possible she was following Jean. Or she came here for some other reason that had nothing to do with Jean, something charitable, something illegal. Bank accounts, drugs, aid, fighting her Great White Beast. She claimed she was being followed, but knowing Telema, it could have just been a young admirer she had acquired on the plane.

"Baby, why don't you look out the window? It's lovely countryside."

Maya glanced up and, on cue, their window framed a starved cow, grazing in a pile of wet, swollen roadside garbage.

"Lovely," she declared.

"Well," Jean tried, "at least it's free-range."

"Trash-fed."

They both smiled, taken aback at the intersection of their jokes. Maya allowed a few moments before lowering her head again to her magazine. Jean glanced over her shoulder: "How to Talk to a Man."

Being interested in his interests will automatically make you interesting, Jean read from a bolded section in the middle. *For starters, ask what he does for a living. Even if you know nothing about his line of work, you can find common ground with it. For example, if he's in advertising, talk about your favorite commercials.*

"You won't have anything to read on the plane ride back," Jean tried. "How about we read some of the Mayan folktales instead?"

"You brought those?"

Maya had not heard these folktales for a long time. She had claimed, when she first heard them, that they were boring. "Nothing happens," she had complained at the age of six. But now Jean would try again. She and her daughter slid down into their seat like school friends and Jean read the tale of the Jaguar and the Deer:

A deer went to look for a place to build himself a house. There was also a jaguar who was out looking for a place to set up a house. He came to the same place the deer had chosen, and thought he would build there also.

The next day the deer came and thoroughly cleared the ground with his antlers. The jaguar came later and said: "It seems somebody is helping me." Then he stuck some big poles in the ground and set up the framework.

The next day the deer came back and when he saw this, he said: "It seems somebody is helping me." Then he covered the house with branches and made two rooms, one for him and the other for whomever was helping him.

The next day the jaguar saw that the house was finished. He went in one room and fell asleep. The deer came later and went to sleep in the other room.

One day the two came at the same time. When they saw each other, the jaguar asked the deer: "Was it you who was helping me?"

The deer answered: "Yes, it was me."

Then the jaguar said: "Let's live together."

"Yes, let's live together in the same house," said the deer. They went to sleep and the following morning the jaguar said: "I'm going hunting, so sweep the floor, prepare wood and water, because I'll be hungry when I come back."

The jaguar went to the woods to hunt and got a very large deer. He brought it home and said to his companion: "Let's eat what I have caught."

But the deer didn't want to eat; he was very much afraid. He couldn't sleep all night long on account of fear. Early the next morning he went to the woods and met a very large jaguar. Later, he met a large bull and said to him:

"I met a jaguar who was bad-mouthing you."

The bull went looking for the jaguar and found him resting. The bull came up to him slowly, leapt on top of him and gored him. Then the deer went off dragging the dead jaguar. When he got home, he said to his companion:

"Let's eat what I have caught."

The jaguar approached him, but he didn't want to eat; he was very frightened. That night he couldn't sleep thinking about the deer killing jaguars; and the deer couldn't sleep thinking about the jaguar killing deer. Both were very frightened.

At midnight, the deer moved his head, his antlers struck the wooden walls of the house. The jaguar and the deer were frightened by the noise, and both of them ran out of the house without stopping. And so the deer and the jaguar each went his separate way.

"What do you think?" Jean asked Maya, who was sucking on her thick ponytail in concentration, watching out the window. "Do you still think nothing happens?"

"No, I think it's interesting," she said, reopening her magazine. But her eyes skimmed above it, studying the seat in front of them.

Triumph! But Jean knew not to push it. Maya would have to ask for more herself. She closed the book and returned it to her bag.

As they made their way through the highlands, more people squeezed into the bus to stand in the aisles. A generously proportioned woman in Mayan costume took the liberty of nudging Jean and taking over the outer corner of their seat with one formidable buttock. Not feeling she had the right to protest, Jean moved in closer to Maya. At every curve, their arms and thighs touched, and Jean no longer worried about the driver's recklessness. She stopped imagining identical buses barreling the other way around those curves. Outside, along the edge of the road, a large stone sculpture of a Mayan warrior faced the direction from which they had come. Jean took a chance, put an arm around her daughter. She did not resist. For the first time since seeing Telema on the plane, Jean felt the possibilities of this trip returning.

~~~~~

She was elegant and terrifying, half Nicaraguan, an invasive species who used her body when she spoke, wrapped it around her students' "American notions," and patiently squeezed. Mostly, it took only minutes, but she could also take an entire semester, enjoying the last dying kicks as much as the student inevitably did. With her dark hair piled on top of her head (she couldn't be bothered to style, comb, or cut it), she moved carefully, deliberately, as if to maintain its precarious balance. The black scarf always tied tight around like a tourniquet. Students constantly milled in the hall outside her office. The professor put out no chairs for them, so they stood, shifting from foot to foot in a loose line, like cattle bringing themselves to slaughter.

Jean had waited with these young hopefuls two hours for her first meeting with Professor Telema Espejo de la Hoz. With nervous dread, she studied flyers taped all over the hall, advertising alternative lives she could have chosen for herself decades ago. *Join the Aikido Club! Teach English in Egypt!* Things unthinkable then: *The Gay/Straight Alliance* and, more cryptically: *Government Secrets: We worry so you don't have to. Join us for a panel discussion on the American Social Conscience in Daggett Lounge.*

When she finally made it into the cool disarray of the office, it occurred to Jean she had no idea why she was there.

"You're a bit older than the rest of them," the professor said, pointing at the closed door that separated them from the undergraduates. She said older like a compliment, and Jean took it as one. She was forty-nine. She was older than the professor.

"I'm not a full-time student," she managed, her mind reeling. "I already have my bachelor's. And two master's degrees."

"What did you study?" Telema asked, sucking on a piece of hard candy.

"English undergraduate, then two MFAs."

"Two MFAs." The professor rarely smiled, but now she did. "Painting and photography? Theater and music?"

"No, fiction and fiction."

Telema laughed out loud. It gave Jean great pleasure to think of the bewildered undergraduates hearing this outside the door.

"I love made-up things," she declared. "So what does a professional liar find interesting about Guatemalan history?" she asked. "What will your paper topic be?"

And there it was, her purpose. But she paused, reconsidering her plan to tell the professor all about Maya, about the therapist's advice to take this class. In three seconds, she abandoned it. She became convinced then that a child would be a turn-off for this successful woman, presiding from her academically shabby office chair, who owned herself completely. Jean had lost women before, mentioning Maya too soon.

Jean felt the hand on her knee, landed there for a brief moment, like a butterfly, like a blessing. "If you're interested in fiction, Guatemala is the perfect subject."

"Yes, but you didn't like my paper topic. You gave me a C on my proposal. I've never had a paper proposal graded before," she retorted, able to recollect her frustration. The C had disturbed Jean. There was no reason to care, really. She was taking this class for personal enlightenment, for Maya, and she had tried to convince herself for a week that she didn't care about the grade. She had a degree, a 4.0 grade-point average, from a much better school, had two master's degrees from much better schools. She wanted to write a paper on what interested her. But more and more, she began to feel differently, like she was getting a C in parenthood. And that was why she was here, why she stood in line for two hours instead of going to work.

"What's your paper topic?"

"I called it 'Hot Blood, Cold War: The CIA-Orchestrated Coup in Guatemala.' It's about—"

"I know what it's about." The professor sighed in practiced weariness with depressing histories, politics, or maybe just Jean already. "But it's completely boring. I have to read this, you know."

"You're grading based on entertainment value?"

"No, I'm grading based on what I believe the grade will do for you."

"And what will a C do for me?"

"It won't ruin your life or cause trouble for me—in this complex discipline, I can always prove someone deserves a C—but it will completely discourage you from thinking you know history. And it will discourage anyone from hiring you for anything that will allow you to shape history any more than the average consumer. Whatever you write about I'll give you a C, your paper topic doesn't matter. But don't tell them that out there," she said, flicking her eyes to the door. "They're all getting C's, too."

"I don't understand," Jean said, wanting desperately to understand. She liked this woman. The C no longer bothered her. What bothered her was being lumped in with the undergrads in the hall.

"Your paper topic is a complete delusion, all paper topics are. The Cold Warriors did not have hot blood, Ms. Roseneath. The CIA was and still is stacked with literate gerbils stuck in the résumé wheel, toppling governments for the 'experience.' Buffoons who got A's in history and thought it meant something. I refuse to give the CIA any more recruits. I've always given everyone C's."

"I'm forty-nine years old, I'm a successful editor. I'm not going to join the CIA."

"Everyone is more involved than they think, and life is unpredictable."

"Not mine. I'm too old. My life is practically over already," she joked. "The CIA wouldn't even take me. Legally, I can't testify in court, for the drugs I did in college."

"So what are you saying?" The professor cracked down on her candy. "You want to get an A?"

"I'd like to earn an A. I have a personal stake in this class."

"A personal stake," she repeated wistfully. "A personal stake for a fiction writer. What else would you like to write about?"

"Could I research the height of the civil war? The eighties?"

"No, you may not. That's not history."

"It's not?"

"No. The university has defined history as anything that happened twenty or more years ago."

"When did they do that?"

"Last year, when I told a theater full of students that Pat Robertson helped murder over ten thousand Guatemalans through his little funding scheme called Operation Open Arms. The students complained that I was being political, so now the official policy is twenty years or more."

"But the class is called *Twentieth* Century Guatemalan History—"

"Oh, don't worry. It's too bad for you, of course. Right now the history's stuck on Carter. He's lovely, the only real deviation in a century. In two years, I'll have more fun." She stared at Jean, deciding something. "Okay, your new paper topic is 'Cold Blood, Cold War: The CIA-Orchestrated Coup in Guatemala.'" The professor was done, shuffling papers, tapping them square as if closing the file on Jean. But Jean did not want to leave.

"Can I ask you a question about your grading policy?"

"Sure." She opened a metal drawer, dropped the papers inside, and slammed it shut with a dramatic, morgue-like finality.

"Doesn't it get you in trouble? Do students complain?"

"Hardly anyone notices my grading policy because everyone knows to take my class pass/fail."

"Pass/fail? That's an option?"

"Oh yes, these days it is. Kids just take it pass/fail and they never know what their real grade was anyway. They pass, simply that. How narrowly, they have no idea. So they're happy and I'm happy and uncompromised in my stance."

"But you told me. Aren't you afraid I'll complain?"

"You're too old, and probably have too much to do to file a lawsuit. And your parents aren't going to call the dean demanding an explanation, are they?" The professor grinned and tilted back in her chair. "Plus, I'm a visiting professor. Distinguished visiting professor of the humanities. What can they do to me?"

"You're visiting? From where?"

"Austin."

There it was, a handle, a beginning. "Austin. What a great place to be from—"

"No, no." The professor dispelled the fledgling conversation with a hurried wave. "I'm not from Austin. I was a distinguished visiting professor there before I came here."

~~~~~

They came off the bus dried out and dazed, under a healing Xela sky. No one lunged, offering to help with their bags, offering a taxi ride or a box of

Chiclets. The first native faces they saw shared a common pride that refused to be moved at the arrival of two tourists with wheeled luggage. It was clear now that if they needed something, they would have to ask.

Jean had been right to suspect that the Maya in the highlands were more dignified than those in the capital. Many still wore the traditional clothes, though with sandals made from recycled tires. This dignity, however, allowed them to stare boldly at a white woman with her clearly Mayan child.

In her jean shorts, black tube top, and glitter sandals, Maya made a peculiar spectacle. A line of old women squatted on the perimeter of the market and studied them. Jean smiled vaguely in their direction, but did not make eye contact. Maya moved uneasily, snapping the gum in her mouth, as they walked through the busy, landscaped central square. The Maya stared hard at them and only Maya stared back. When people did approach, it was unclear who was selling tourist services and who was begging.

"Quetzals, quetzales?" asked a desiccated, leathery man, holding out the stub where his elbow should have been.

Aged buildings stood reinforced with whitewash. Many of the houses were graffitied with the same political logos they'd seen earlier, which no one bothered to wash away or paint over. They found their hotel, El Gringa Perdida, only a block from the central park. The building, newly whitewashed too thin, showed its cool, dark substance in brushstroke streaks. A regal, crumbling home in a line of equally charming and crumbling two-story colonial homes. Near the entrance, on the house, someone had graffitied the blue hand, like a formal greeting.

They could not check in until after dinner. They had arrived two days early and the Latina proprietor said she needed time.

"Oh, are you full?" Jean asked. "Can you not take us?"

"No, not full." She studied the guest book, weighing her next comment. "We are empty. But we need to clean your room."

It seemed rooms weren't cleaned once a guest left, but before the next one arrived. "Could we just sit inside, then, and wait for our room? We're very tired."

"We are not ready for you, not ready at all," the woman declared with a shaky, upheld left fist. "But there's a restaurant for tourists near the central park. If you'd like, you can leave your baggage with me."

Jean and Maya looked at one another.

The proprietor handed Jean an envelope. "If you are going into town," she said, as if this were only a possibility, as if they might just stand there for the next three hours, pining at the gates, "take this, please, to the mail, to the government building." She pointed to a roof in the direction from which they had already come.

They walked the city with difficulty with their luggage, awaiting the preparation of their hotel room. Jean literally dragged both suitcases behind her. They found the government building easily. The letter the woman gave them fit perfectly into the little slotted mouth in the wall.

The restaurant had no name, only a picture of a hamburger with *Vegetarian* written beneath. It lay a safe distance from the park, but still close enough that they could watch and become accustomed to the new city. Jean knew not to force this. Anything with Maya these days had to be slow and careful. She had a few vacation-like activities planned before they went to the orphanage to see the records.

A party of young white men and women in polo shirts of varying colors filled the far half of the small restaurant. NGO workers. The eyes and ears of the famous Historical Clarification Commission.

"So what do you think?" Jean asked Maya, turning her suitcase upside down to register the damage done to the wheels by the cobblestones.

Maya peered at the English menu. "I think I want the California sprout sandwich on whole-wheat bread."

Jean frowned. "That doesn't sound very Guatemalan."

"Guatemalans eat puppies, Mom. I'm not going to eat puppies."

"They do not, Maya. They don't eat puppies. They eat tortillas and fish and rice and beans." She paused, considering the joke, but it came too late. "They also eat trash-fed free-range beef."

Maya rolled her eyes, a dark flash of moody weather. "Fish and puppies are the same to me. They're both pets."

They were both vegetarians, but for different reasons. Jean could not bring herself to support the toxic and cruel meat industry, while Maya dwelled on the cuteness and innocence of animals. If Jean did not live in Los Angeles, if she owned a gun and had the time and a truck, she would hunt one deer every year and make the meat last. A lifestyle she could see herself getting around to once Maya started college. Telema would've fit perfectly into this plan. Jean would shoot the deer, and Telema would gut it.

The open-air dining room turned pleasant with fry oil and the familiar buzz of the English language. Nearby, the patrons in matching polo shirts gesticulated over nachos. They were weary, but reviving themselves with beer. Americans.

"How many?" one asked another.

"Three."

"Well, I just finished six."

Competitive drinking? Jean made the effort to block them out. Twenty years ago, she would not have been eating at a restaurant like this, comforted by the presence of Americans. She'd spied a shack nearby, which served the local population. Jean set herself the goal of convincing Maya to eat there by the end of the week.

"So what do you think of Xela, Maya?"

Maya squinted out the glassless window, as if it were smudged. "Am I supposed to think something?"

"This is your homeland. During colonial times and during the civil war, it was a city of resistance. This is the home of Mayan warriors and guerrillas."

"I thought you disapproved of violence, Mom."

"I disapprove of violence, but not of self-defense. And don't think all the struggle was violent. It was much more sophisticated. Repression became so ingrained that, after a while, their enemies didn't need violence to control them."

"What did they do? Brainwash them?"

"Sometimes just theater was enough. The Santa María volcano is a good example. In 1902 it blew up, but the government denied it. They sent a band here to play over the noise. The sky turned black and it was raining ash, but the government insisted to the townspeople it wasn't happening."

Maya's face pitched from dejection to delight. "There's a volcano here?"

"Yes, Maya, but you're missing the point. The band was a threat. The band was an implication of violence. Big metal instruments, pointed to the sky—"

"Is it an active volcano?"

"I think so. But don't you want to know why the band threatened the town?"

"Not really," she said, twirling something invisible through her fingers with a determined incuriosity meant to test Jean. Until a couple of years ago, Maya asked the why of things all the time. Jean never tired of providing the answers. These days, Jean had to supply both questions and answers. A lonely enterprise, talking to herself all day. Since Maya had hit puberty, Jean had felt the emptiness of her thirties returning. She felt the need to drink, the need for a romantic relationship, more keenly than ever. She'd been driven into Telema's eager, octopus arms. Yes.

"So what do you think of Xela?" Jean tried again, nudging Maya playfully.

Maya concentrated on the park, a deep furrow showing between her eyes. "I think the women are fat and ugly," she said finally. "Does that mean I'm going to turn out fat and ugly?" Her hair in her mouth again, her hand clutching the sill as if they were in a car going too fast.

Anger was not a feeling Jean felt she was entitled to, but the accumulation of disappointments, she suspected, might be worse for both of them. She wanted a beer more than anything, but this vacation was for Maya. Jean had promised herself that she wouldn't drink on this trip before five o'clock. It was four-fifteen.

She turned to where Maya had been staring, at the line of women squatting on their heels, passing secrets. At that moment, the waitress appeared with a beer Jean hadn't even ordered. The bottle's mouth smoked from recent opening. Jean accepted the bottle, not wanting to complain. She took her watch off and laid it on the glass. Four-sixteen.

"They aren't fat, Maya. They're stout. They have a different body type. These are strong women who haul and plant and walk all day."

"Am I going to be stout, then?" Maya looked genuinely worried. Jean's daughter, who marched in glittering tights, hoisting a jaguar flag for crowds of football fans, worried about her figure. Flag line had become her most serious endeavor.

"These women are not obese, they are not lazy. They eat fresh food from markets and work all day. They are not fat like people who sit and watch television all day. Their body types are of strong, capable women. Don't you want to be strong?"

"They do everything right, and they're still fat." Maya sighed.

Jean knew she would never succeed in making this point. Maya lagged behind her friends developmentally, so she still had her svelte girl's frame, bolstered by her padded bra. With her creamy coffee skin and large black eyes and narrow hips, Maya was the exotic beauty, the ringleader of her pack. Now she felt her empire slipping.

"You are going to be whatever you make of yourself," Jean replied automatically. She realized too late it was something her mother always said, one of her very few reasonable mantras. Her mother said lots of things. On their last visit to Iowa, she had begged Jean to cancel this trip. *God gave me a sign,* she had claimed, *told me you shouldn't go!* Jean watched more of the painted buses disgorge passengers onto the square: several locals, a few NGOs, a white man in a suit. Jean watched closely with a feeling of dread she couldn't shake.

Maya did not eat her California sprout sandwich when it arrived, staked on two tall toothpicks. Instead, she chugged down her virgin colada. Jean ate her avocado melt despite the fact that she no longer felt hungry. The dirt from the journey had filled her hair, her clothes, and her lungs. Every few breaths, she coughed, feeling a rattle. She sipped her Guatemalan beer when it turned 5:01. But she found no relief in the local beer. It had turned warm, rank, and completely undrinkable. She ordered her own piña colada instead, which was weak and tooth-piercingly sweet. When she blew her nose on her napkin, it came away black.

She decided, after three drinks, it would be good for Maya to lose her looks a little bit. Maybe if she did grow stout, she'd make more meaningful friends and focus on her schoolwork. She was proudly, defiantly a C student at an alternative private school where everyone else did well. (There were no grades at the school, but Jean knew what a 3 meant.) And the worst of it was that her teachers loved her for it, thinking this defiance something nobler than laziness. The art teacher reported recently that Maya had a great interest in abstract expressionism—an unconvincing explanation for the random splashes displayed with the still lifes, landscapes, and portraits of her classmates. The therapist, too, wrote off Maya's shoplifting as a mere symptom of Jean's shortcomings. Jean was beginning to suspect her daughter was a shape-shifter, a pleaser. Except, of course, with her.

"Are we going to see Telema here? Is she meeting us in Xela?" Maya asked, testing new waters. She drew out one of the tall toothpicks, which came out clean. "She has a good body and she's Mayan, isn't she?" She propped it between her thumb and forefinger, pressed the sharp point into her fingertip and held it there.

Jean coughed, sucked at her drink. Another bus unloaded and Jean studied every passenger.

"No."

Maya sighed, pressing the toothpick even harder, smiling at the possibility of blood and waiting for Jean to intervene.

———

"Hello, hello, Americans! We are ready for your authentic Guatemalan experience! Welcome to the Land of Eternal Spring!"

The Latina proprietor greeted them as if she had not met them a few hours before, and also as if she had not moved in those few hours. She did not look twice at the mismatched mother and daughter. She took up her pencil dramatically to make some mark in the book to signify their arrival.

After stuffing their hands with various tourist pamphlets—*Guatemala: The Land of Eternal Spring*; *Tikal: Stories of the Past, Predictions of the Future*; and *Rainforest Secrets of the Maya*—the proprietor opened the gate. The newly arrived indigenous staff—three women in Mayan dress—stood barefoot on the black-and-white tiles, paralyzed by the sight of Maya. Jean and Maya carried their own suitcases past them. The woman led the way down the hall, past a beautifully planted courtyard with a hammock. Jean noticed the shabbiness of her dress, which looked more like a nightgown. The fabric pilled, yellow under the arms and dingy at the wrists with smudged lead.

There was no sign of any other guests.

"This," the proprietor said, opening a door, "is the meditation garden."

Behind the house, beige pebbles encircled the painted shore of a blue, kidney-shaped pool. This whole patio was protected by a high concrete wall topped with barbed wire.

"A pool!" Maya clapped, then strained forward. "But there's no diving board."

"You speak English very well," Jean remarked to the woman.

"It's the universal language," she declared, as if Jean might disagree. "Anyone who goes into tourism must learn English. If they want to succeed."

Upstairs in their room, nothing seemed as if it had been touched in a year. Dust saturated the Mayan blankets on the two twin-sized beds. On the long wall, small squares of Mayan fabric hung, heavily matted and framed in a series of three.

"That woman is creepy. She kept smiling at me like she knows me," Maya declared, and said nothing else on the matter.

"Do you want to shower?" Jean opened her suitcase for some fresh clothes. "What the hell?" She shoved the contents aside, digging deeper. "This isn't my suitcase!"

"Whoops!" Maya leaned over to look. "I guess that lady was right."

"Jesus Christ." She held up a man's suit, a silk nightie. Fucking Telema. Fucking racist guidebook, making her paranoid and now ashamed, for having heeded its warnings. She glanced at her daughter, who was mercifully oblivious to the implications of the whole situation.

"That's nice," Maya said, touching the lingerie. "Maybe it'll fit." She threw herself back on her mattress. "I wonder what Brett's doing right now. He's probably at the beach with everyone. With Maureen." Her eyes narrowed in suspicion. "Is there a beach here? It would be nice to swim in the same ocean as him."

"No, Maya. There's no beach. And we lost one of our guidebooks, the one with the best descriptions of Xela." At least they still had the smaller, racist one in her purse.

Jean called the airline to report the suitcase and found out that the other woman had already reported hers stolen. By Jean. She'd have to return to the capital to get hers back. A seasoned traveler from a previous era of her life, Jean had wisely packed the bare necessities and one clean change of clothes in her carry-on.

"He's been flirting with Maureen for weeks." Still in bed, Maya twisted the ring on her finger, confirming Jean's worst suspicion. She'd rather Maya had stolen it. Brett. He treated Jean with ironic respect, smiling too big, calling her *Mrs.* Roseneath. A typical fucking football prick. So good-looking, she couldn't even describe him beyond that.

"If you're worried he'll cheat on you with Maureen, then it sounds like he's not worth worrying over, Maya."

"But it would be my fault. Because I *abandoned* him."

"Three weeks is not abandonment. If he can't control himself for that long—"

"I'll just *die*," Maya declared. "If we're gone one day longer. One hour longer than that."

Jean said nothing. Before the therapist, she would have corrected her language, reminded Maya of real death, of war, whole villages wiped out with armed helicopters. Instead, she counted to ten now, and during those ten seconds, she kept herself busy. The first few times she'd tried this, she just stood doing nothing but counting, and Maya had shrunk back, frightened.

"You look like you're having a stroke!" she'd cried.

They retraced their tour. In the courtyard, the three Mayan women stood against the wall, perfectly spaced and doing nothing. Possibly, Jean thought, they were placed in series of three all over the hotel. Near the entrance, Jean noticed a guest book. There, previous guests had filled in their names, the date, from where they had traveled. On the far right of the page Jean read, *What does Guatemala mean to me?* typed as a heading in several languages. Not many guests had visited—the past three years fit on the first page. Jean picked up the pen and wrote her name, the date, Los Angeles, then paused over the last question. *What does Guatemala mean to me?* She scanned down the answers of the other guests, reading the ones in English:

> *Is there a single decent beer in this country?*
> *So sad to kill each other, why not rock paper scissors instead of war?*
> *Your country has the most beautiful children in the world!*
> *Nothing.*
> *Cold War cemetery*
> *An affordable, fascinating paradise! Why hadn't we come sooner?*
> *Jesus Loves You*
> *Colonialism, Imperialism, NAFTA*
> *Good luck with your first-ever democratic election!*

One comment had been crossed out violently in pencil, Jean supposed by the proprietor. Jean could make out: *I excavated 37 bodies today.* In the middle of the page, someone named Will, from Buffalo, had drawn a picture as his comment. A cave? An old man's face? Jean had to stare at it for quite a long time to see a crude drawing of a vagina, which the proprietor had not understood enough to cross out.

"I want to get a better look at the pool," Maya announced. "For a night swim!"

Jean left her comment blank and sorted through the pamphlets the proprietor had given them. Among these brochures, Jean found what she was looking for—climbing tours of the Santa María volcano:

> *Eco-Tours of Volcán Santa María! Take in the breathing beauty of an ancient volcano, sample the Mayan culture, and give back to Guatemala. Most tours molest the landscape, but Eco-Tours improves the land. Join us Tuesday mornings for a trash-collection sunrise hike up the most sexy summit in Guatemala. All tours led by traditional Mayan guides.*

"It's only four feet deep, Mom! It's a kids' pool."

Maya, sullen, walked back into the courtyard from the pool patio and threw herself into the hammock. Jean noticed someone's shadow lingering around a corner, listening. With this, Jean turned on the television to give them some privacy. After a deodorant and a shaving cream ad, a political one came on. A candidate meeting with Mayan leaders, touring the market. The female voice-over sounded compassionate, convincing. An aging Latino man of slightly deflated rotundity met a Mayan man on a grassy plain. They shook hands as the sun rose up from red in the background. "Gilberto Ahumada Lobos," said the voice, accompanied by the logo of the blue hand.

"Does the fable book have the quetzal story in it?" Maya asked, rocking herself.

"Which story? There were a bunch with quetzals in them."

"The scary one. There was a scary story. I hated it, remember?"

Jean had forgotten about this one, had forgotten her daughter had ever been afraid of anything, other than getting fat. She nodded. "The one that explains how the bird got its red breast. You had nightmares about it." After these nightmares, Maya had insisted on sleeping with Jean every night. They continued to sleep that way for years, until Maya ended the practice at the age of eleven, claiming, suddenly, that Jean snored.

"Really? What's the story? I don't remember."

The book was in their room, thankfully packed in Jean's carry-on. Jean knew this curiosity was fragile enough that going to get it would ruin the moment. She closed her eyes, thinking. "It's a story about a famous Mayan warrior. I can't remember his name. The day he fought the conquistador Alvarado, a quetzal flew overhead. When the conquistador killed the warrior, the quetzal flew down and dipped his chest in his blood, which is why the bird has a red breast."

Maya made a face. "That's not scary. It's just gross. Will we see quetzals here?"

"There used to be a lot of them. The Spanish name for Xela is Quetzaltenango, the place of the quetzals. But the guidebook says now they're mostly gone. Much of their habitat has been cleared by plantations, or burned in the 1980s scorched-earth operations. And they can't be bred in captivity."

"Why can't they be bred in captivity?"

"They kill themselves when they're captured and confined. That's why they're a symbol of freedom."

"That's crazy, Mom."

"It is. It's crazy, but it's also kind of beautiful."

Where, Jean wondered, was Telema at that moment? She could be any-where: meeting with the President, distributing clean water in a slum, cross-ing the border into Mexico with cocaine hidden in her hair, or sitting at a long table in a library, poring over hundred-year-old books.

"What do you want to do tomorrow, Maya? Do you want to see the guide-book?"

"Shopping!"

"C'mon."

Maya shrugged. "Why do you ask me what I want to do, if you don't care?"

"We're here to learn, Maya. We can shop, but we can't *only* shop. Is there anything in particular you want to find out? Anything you've always wanted to know?"

"Not really."

"I find that hard to believe. We come all the way here and there's not one thing you want to learn about your heritage? About the food or religion or the forest? Or the clothes? The Mayan fashions are certainly interesting, aren't they? *Cosmo* could do a whole issue on this place." It sounded lame, even to her.

"This is a vacation. You're not supposed to learn on vacations, you're supposed to relax and have a good time."

"Then I'll need to make sure there isn't any learning on this volcano hike. If there is, we can't go."

"Volcano hike?" It was as easy as that, reeling her daughter in. She was not a difficult girl to please. Walking the mall, lying at the beach, watching TV were the easiest things in the world. But Jean refused to give herself, and especially her daughter, such easy delights.

"Will we see lava? Will it explode when we're at the top?"

"It's possible, Maya. It's an active volcano. There's a disclaimer, saying a tourist was hit in the face with flying lava at the crater a year ago. We must go at our own risk."

"Yes! Oh my god!" Her skinny silhouette swung wildly in the hammock.

Jean hoped the expectation of such a spectacular end (the teenage death wish: Was Maya hoping for Jean's death or her own at the mouth of the cra-ter?) would be enough to appease her daughter for the next few days, through the more serious business, the revelations, awaiting them.

~~~~~

"So, Guatemala," Telema said, peering through the clear curve of her tipped bourbon glass. "What is your personal stake in Guatemala?"

They were at a bar of Telema's choosing that catered to graduate students and serious undergraduates. Foreign, expensive beer consumed in dark, roomy booths, although Telema did not drink beer. On a wall over her shoulder, Jean saw again the campus flyer, slightly different from the one outside Telema's office.

> *Is Our Social Conscience Destroying Our Happiness?*
> *Join us for a panel discussion in Daggett Lounge.*

Instead of answering Telema's question, Jean talked about her paper. The subject of Maya was too raw tonight, after another fight. Maya's words, just hours before, had been sharp, well aimed. More than anything right now, Jean needed escape. The professor, dressed darkly, became elusive in the dim bar light. This was their third student-teacher conference. The class had moved on from proposals to first drafts.

"Like I said, I'm interested in aspects of American intervention. The CIA-orchestrated coup in 1954. That was their first successful covert operation, wasn't it?"

Telema nodded, sensing evasion. "Their first to go more according to plan rather than less." She swirled her drink. "But I'm not talking about your paper. I mean, why, personally, are you interested in Guatemala?"

Jean panicked, wondering if to tell her about Maya would mean she'd been lying before. She felt this going somewhere, and could not sustain the fiction of childlessness for long. But in her last lecture, Telema had touched upon international adoptions. *Assimilation*, she'd decreed, *is violent. A violence upon the psyche.*

Plus, if she talked about Maya now, after several drinks, she feared she'd cry.

"A writer with two graduate degrees doesn't pay to take an undergraduate class. You're educated. You know how to learn. Why didn't you just use your library card?"

"I'm not that self-motivated," Jean said, feeling unmoored. They both had drunk way too much for a simple student-teacher conference. And Telema kept insisting she didn't care about Jean's paper. Jean felt, more and more, that this was a date. The idea thrilled her. She'd only been on a handful of dates in fifteen years, since Maya.

"For a fiction-teller, you aren't a very good liar." Yes, flirtation.

"I'm not sure what you mean."

"You're writing a book." It was clear that the idea of it thrilled Telema. "You're writing a fiction book about Guatemala."

"Yes," Jean lied, wanting to please her, not wanting to ruin her chances by introducing a sullen teenager to their date. Jean did have two MFAs in fiction, although she was no longer a writer. She was an editor. With no desire to write a book, she knew she'd never write one about anything, let alone Guatemala.

"I've always thought that fiction was the best way to approach Guatemala. You see, there are more lies than truth in the history of that little country." Telema held up two fingers spaced slightly, to demonstrate how small the country was. Then she brought them to her teeth to work on a hangnail she'd been mercilessly pursuing all evening. "Are you writing about Guatemalan women?" Back in teacher mode now, Telema wrote something in her notebook.

"In a way. Maids and nannies." Jean had no idea what she was saying, but those were the only Mayan women she'd ever seen in Los Angeles.

"Little bombs," Telema proclaimed.

"Excuse me?"

"Little bombs," she enunciated, as if Jean just hadn't understood the words. "A long time ago, the profession was a tool of strategic warfare. The Maya were so desperate for land that sometimes they'd send their teenage daughters to white and Hispanic landowners as maids. Their job, of course, was not to clean and cook. It was to seduce the patriarch, to get pregnant."

"Seriously? How do you know?"

"It was my doctoral thesis. A little girl of fourteen, dressed up and educated in the ways of seduction," Telema mused, jostling the melting ice cubes in her glass. "The hope, of course, was to blackmail the man into giving her a bit of land, to just go away and keep quiet. And if that didn't work, when the man died and his family went back to Europe or the States, he might leave some of his Guatemalan land to his half-Indian children."

"That's incredible. Did it work?"

"Desperate measures. A lot has to go according to plan over a very long period for it all to come about, but I'm sure some were successful."

"You actually found evidence of this?"

"Circumstantial evidence. Records from that era are hard to come by, plus I couldn't get down to Guatemala to research because of the war. The deeds I could get copied and mailed were so poorly preserved they were nearly illegible. But yes, overwhelming circumstantial evidence."

"Little bombs," Jean repeated, thinking of Maya standing in their terracotta kitchen with a lit fuse at her feet.

"I just love bars and restaurants like this. Every war this past century, I bet you, was orchestrated from bars and restaurants. Fat cats stuffing themselves with booze, steak, and power. That is your history lesson for today, Ms. Roseneath. Every world event begins in a restaurant."

The scene before them, Jean thought, did not look so ambitious.

"Who do you think is plotting a war here right now?"

Telema swirled the last sip in her glass. "I am."

Jean laughed. "And who is the enemy?"

The professor's black eyes glittered with sincerity and mischief. "You are." Finishing her drink, she crushed the last bits of ice between her teeth. Her hand went up to signal the waitress.

"Please," she told the disheveled girl when she arrived, "another for me. And bring my friend over there a drink, a martini, on me." She pointed to a young man sitting alone at the bar, self-consciously filling a suit. "A gin martini," Telema clarified. "If he's going to dress the part, he's got to play it. You tell him that."

"Who's that?" Jean asked. "You know him?"

"He's my best student."

"Which class of yours is he in?"

"All of them. But he won't come to office hours. I'm dying to see what his paper will be about."

"Your best student." Jean studied the young man, not recognizing him from class. But all guys in suits looked the same to her. He appeared overserious, but in the wrong way. An obedient student, not a curious one. When he received his gigantic, potent martini, the waitress explained, pointing at Telema, but he refused to look at her.

"Is he going to get a C, too?"

"Oh yes. Definitely a C."

Feeling a pang of jealousy, Jean kept an eye on the boy, long after Telema forgot about him. Jean watched him test the murky liquid placed before him. He brought his head down to it, sipped from the side, and winced.

———

And then, miraculously, they were at her place. Telema probably shouldn't have driven and Jean probably shouldn't have, either. When they pulled up in front of a disappointingly ordinary one-story ranch house, Jean looked across the street, then down. Mailboxes, carports, sprinklers hissing in the dark. They had arrived, and Jean would have been less surprised if Telema had brought her home to a dark cave half submerged in ocean.

Everything the woman wore was a wrap—her shirt, her skirt. Jean found an end and pulled and everything fell away at once. Underneath, another layer presented itself: blacks, greens, blues, and purples. Smoke and flames, birds, trains, trees, and mountains, strange pictorial writing. The professor did not wear underwear, but she was covered in tattoos. Jean ran a hand up her sternum, on the hard bone where antlers curved out over her high-set breasts, just big enough to hold.

She watched Jean's hand trace over her. The professor's skin felt damp and smelled faintly musty, as if she'd been left out in the rain.

To undress Jean proved less dramatic, with buttons and zippers and a stubborn, hooked bra. Telema struggled with it a moment, then gave up, as if the contraption were completely foreign to her. It took too much time, there would be no more play, and so all that came off was her pants. Jean let her knees go loose as they stood, kissing, and Telema breached there with a powerful thigh that bore the image of a train flying off its tracks. She took Jean's weight with her arms and took two stumbling steps to get the wall's support. Jean slid up and down on Telema's thigh, moving over her own trail of moisture, while Telema studied her. The journey along Telema's thigh became easier and easier, until she was gliding to her climax.

They stood that way a moment, Jean limp and pressed to the wall, like an enemy impaled on Telema's knee. From this position, Jean examined the house for the first time. It was as surprisingly ordinary on the inside as on the outside. Beige carpet, eggshell walls, white trim, and a picture window dull and listless in the dark.

"You're right," Jean finally said. "Someone with two graduate degrees doesn't pay to take an undergraduate class." She slipped down the professor's leg, away from the banana trees colored on Telema's flat belly. "Actually," Jean said, "I don't pay. I'm not even enrolled. I just show up. Have you even once looked at your class roster?"

"I know exactly how your book should start," Telema said, her eyes closed, her own personal ecstasy coming on.

———

Jean could not believe that she'd just had sex for the first time in a decade. And it had all been so easy. A date, in a regular bar. No curious or angry glances from anyone. In the eighties, nothing had been this easy. Jean, all her friends, everyone closeted. Except, maybe, the freaks in San Francisco. The men who made the news and made her circle of friends groan. Jean dated casually then, for there was no other way to date. Being seen too much with the same girl would provoke suspicion, and they all had careers to protect. Maybe they were all paranoid, but eventually Jean tired of the game, deciding to make a real family for herself. A family the world would acknowledge and could understand.

The choice to become a single mother shocked and dismayed Jean's family. But Jean only begrudgingly acknowledged them, anyway, for answering her mother's calls every month proved easier than ignoring them and enduring their increased, panicked frequency. Only very recently had Jean changed her number and cut them out completely. Anyway, their disapproval of single motherhood did not affect her, for they'd disapproved of her sexuality, her atheism, her education, her friends, for decades. Her mother, once, had told her that in addition to being a sin, homosexuality would deprive her of the joys of motherhood and family. Unsurprisingly, her parents did not believe that adopting a child would provide this missing aspect, it would merely pervert the institution. She could never get it right.

What truly affected Jean during this time were her friends' reactions, which, amazingly, didn't differ too much from her family's. At least they tried to be understanding, but eventually they dropped away. Working, taking care of Maya, Jean no longer had time for them. And they had little patience for a screaming infant. And so Jean's social and sex lives pretty much stalled, outside of a few dates where she'd mentioned Maya too soon. On the flip side, she'd had just enough dates to feel the need to come out to her daughter. Maya, eleven years old, accepted Jean's awkward talk with equanimity, then began to sleep in her own bed. *Big dyke* didn't make it into her vocabulary for another few years.

So yes, Jean sat in Telema's house now, a novice in this new, exhilarating world of semi-acceptance. She watched Telema, like a vision, still naked but for her head wrap and combat boots, walk unself-consciously to her bare picture window. She paused to study the street, then she proceeded to the kitchen. There was no excess on her buttocks. On her back, a small, colorful bird perched on her left shoulder blade, with a spectacularly long tail that curved all down her back and nestled around her right hip. A quetzal.

"Are you hungry? Do you want anything?"

"Do you have any coffee? I've got to drive home soon."

"No coffee," Telema declared, standing in the angelic light of the open fridge. "Coffee is against my moral code."

"How about tea, then?"

Telema frowned. "Are you kidding?" She turned to the bright innards of the refrigerator and began fussing. "I have water, soy milk, bourbon, and red wine."

From the couch, Jean eyed the house, empty but for the essentials: a couch, a kitchen table with one chair, a rotary telephone on the floor. All the windows bare, like open eyes in the dark. Seeing this, Jean dressed quickly in a corner.

"So you don't drink coffee or tea. You only buy used clothes because of sweatshops. You don't wear underwear because to buy used underwear is gross. You don't buy new furniture because of illegal logging. You don't eat bananas, of course. Or meat, for obvious reasons, or vegetables, because of exploited immigrant labor. What do you survive on, Telema? This is our second dinner together, but I've yet to see you eat."

"People eat too much anyway."

"You have to eat something. You can't survive solely on booze. You have to choose your battles, right? As one of my favorite writers said, *If you don't hunt it down and kill it, it will hunt you down and kill you.*"

"What?"

"Your conscience."

"You see? You are a perfect CIA recruit."

"What does your conscience allow you to eat?"

"I hunt."

"You hunt? When do you hunt?"

"As distinguished visiting professor, I only teach in the spring. During the fall semester, I hunt."

"What were you going to offer me, a deer leg to gnaw on?"

"I have cereal."

Cereal wasn't the most sobering thing to be having. The soy milk and the bourbon mixed in Jean's stomach, making a vile alcoholic soup.

"Imogene Roseneath. Your name is Imogene?" Telema held Jean's wallet, splayed up to the light. "That's wonderful." She flipped through the contents with the nonchalance of a cop.

"Do you usually card your lovers after the fact?"

"Yes. The investigation's the fun part. The sex is just foreplay." Telema returned with a glass of water for Jean. "Water shouldn't be this easy in the desert, but I'll make an exception for you tonight. I'm writing a book, too, you know. It's not as fun as fiction, but it's a book. An alternate history. Maybe you could edit it. What house do you work for?"

"We don't do academic stuff," Jean lied. In fact, Looking Glass Press would publish just about anything, for a large fee. The pricing created the much-desired illusion of prestige for her writers. She made plenty of money publishing self-help books and romance novels by retired moguls and anyone else who could afford to be added to their list. But Jean would never admit to anyone that she worked at a vanity press. And beyond that, Jean sensed that Telema would be a nightmare to work with. "What's your book about?"

"It's about lots of things." Telema tightened her hair scarf with a reflexive yank.

"Name one thing, then."

"Volcán Santa María," Telema said, with an extravagant accent.

"What about this volcano?"

Telema moved a boot between Jean's legs, teasing. "It exploded in 1902, at a very unfortunate time."

"Is it ever a good time for a volcano to erupt?"

"No, but 1902 was a big year for Guatemala. It's the coffee bust. The country was getting a reputation of being unstable—socially and geologically. Investors were pulling out for Brazil, where there were no earthquakes, volcanoes, or Indian unrest." She stretched her leg up and rested it on the back of the sofa, exposing herself completely. By now Jean realized that sex and politics, to Telema, were indistinguishable. She slipped from lover to teacher with eager ease.

"I bet your neighbors wish you'd get curtains," Jean said.

"Why do I need curtains? Everyone else has them, so it doesn't matter."

"What about people in the street?" Jean stared out the picture window to the line of parked cars. Inside one, a dark silhouette sat at the wheel. A neighbor.

"I've forgotten what we were talking about," Telema said.

"The volcano. The coffee bust. The economy running through Guatemala's fingers?"

Telema bounced her knees open and closed, flashing the entire neighborhood. "Yes, yes. So Estrada Cabrera panics, invites all kinds of foreign investors to visit, to show them the promise of Guatemala. The Land of Eternal Spring. There are parties and galas, he decrees new schools to show how civilized the country is. He was especially desperate to convince a railroad company to stick with their contract to complete the line connecting the two coasts. The project wasn't going well, but the whole economy, everything, depended on it. It was all done but a tiny sixty-mile section, dismal with swamp and disease. But that same week the investors arrive, Santa María blows. The highlands are a mess for it. Now the President decrees that all is well in the mountains, Santa María is fine. And if there is any disturbance, it's blowing over from Mexico. The papers all publish it, but that's not enough. The President knows he must convince everyone in Xela to keep their mouths shut while he tours the Americans around the country. So he sends the military band to play over the noise and announce there is no volcano erupting."

"Why didn't he just threaten them? Why the band? He was a dictator, right?"

"The band is more subtle when you have foreign guests. But more importantly, to the Maya, the military band says, 'See how many of us there are? How scary we are with instruments? If we can play over and deny a volcano erupting, do you think anyone will hear your screams?'"

"Did the Maya take the hint?"

"Of course they did."

"Was the railroad ever finished?"

"Oh yes. With a complete clampdown on outgoing mail and telegraphs, news of the volcano never reached the railroad company, which was owned by United Fruit's founder and vice president. Estrada Cabrera completely sold Guatemala to get the track done. The real power of the United Fruit empire didn't come from bananas, but shipping. They just completed the railroad, set the prices, and were given a complete monopoly on shipping. They operated the railroads in Guatemala under the name of CAICO then. They owned the telegraph lines, the only Caribbean port, and the railroad. And their contract guaranteed they didn't have to pay taxes. Estrada Cabrera gave them control of the Caribbean coast, then thirty years later Ubico gave them a similar contract for the Pacific coast. By 1931, they owned virtually everything. Complete control of the infrastructure. Two dictators is all it took."

"Any why do you care? You want to know why I take your class. I want to know why—"

"And one democratically elected president," Telema said, ignoring Jean's question, "with one rewritten constitution, could have brought it all down."

Telema, Jean noticed, ignored personal questions and did not ask many basic ones herself. Jean was beginning to feel like a whetstone, just an inanimate object against which Telema kept herself sharp. She didn't mind so much, she decided. She enjoyed the semblance of conversation, especially now that she couldn't speak to her own daughter for fear of being tattled on to the therapist. Jean missed Maya at that moment, but she could do nothing about it. She missed her daughter perpetually, she missed her while standing in the same room with her.

"Imogene, Imogene," Telema mused in her empty house, like an echo. She brought her hand down to her open crotch and fiddled absently.

"I prefer Jean. Are you close to finished with your book?" Jean could still see the silhouette in the car, a rhythmic elbow. Telema, Jean realized, had been playing to him all along. Had been playing Jean to him, too. The thought of a stranger watching her make love did not horrify Jean, as she expected. How did she feel? Sexy, dangerous, wanted.

"I haven't written any of it yet, but I've been investigating for quite some time. I'm close. I'm going to Boston in a few weeks to track down my subject."

"You've not written any of it? Not even an outline?"

"No. But I have the title."

"What's that?"

"It's called . . ." And here she paused pensively, pornographically. She reclined, considering the value of the information, before finally handing it over with an opening palm. The one that had been in her crotch. "Lost Little Girls: The Myth of the Sexual Savage in U.S. Economic and Foreign Policy."

~~~~~

The next morning, Maya was up and in her bikini in five minutes, ready for her vacation to begin. She strutted, showing off the black bikini with pink piping. It had been a concession in the Guatemala battle, her first bikini.

Sipping her coffee, Jean made her way down to the screen door of the meditation garden. Maya already lay in the morning sun, talking to herself.

"So, what do you do? Oh, that's interesting, *very* interesting. I love clothes!"

It took Jean a moment to notice a man sitting a distance away. A white businessman in a black suit, lounging in the shade, sucking on a banana drink.

Maya flipped onto her belly, flipped out the tag on her suit bottom. "This bikini was made in Guatemala. Isn't that funny? Maybe it was made in your factory!"

The man, in vintage horn-rimmed glasses, listened with disinterested politeness.

"Do you recognize it?" Maya posed, tipping her sunglasses down. "Why don't you put on *your* bathing suit?"

That was enough for Jean. She strolled in at that moment, overdoing the act of just arriving. "Maya!" she called with a jolly wave. Behind her, the screen door slammed like a shot, startling everyone. "Do you want to come to the Catholic church?"

"No," Maya said flatly, turning back to the sun.

The Catholic church had been the site of the orphanage during Maya's time. The orphanage had moved since then, just outside town, taking all its records along.

"Maya, c'mon. Let's go to the cathedral together. It's supposed to be beautiful." She tried the maneuver from the day before, placing her arm around Maya's shoulders, but Maya shrugged her off.

"I don't care how beautiful it is. It's just a trick so people mistake beauty for God."

Jean stared, knowing exactly where this came from. She counted to ten and watched her own warped reflection, pointy head and shovel jaw, in her daughter's plastic gaze. "Wherever did you get that idea?"

Maya propped herself up on a saucy elbow. "Grandma. She says that Catholics worship statues because they don't know the difference between beauty and God. She says Satan is very beautiful, too, and one day I'll meet him and shouldn't be fooled."

Not even in Guatemala could Jean escape it. How long would she have to knock down the ridiculous straw men her mother continually placed in the path of her daily life? So breathtakingly stupid, so easy to defeat, but after decades Jean felt exhausted. Lately, Maya had become an unlikely ambassador of these ideas. She had yet to figure out that she'd never see her grandparents again. That was a conversation Jean would save for after the Roots Tour.

"Grandma doesn't know a thing about Catholics, Maya. I don't think she's ever even been in a Catholic church."

"Neither have I, but I know what they look like. I've seen pictures and TV."

The TV, too, would haunt her forever. She had walked in on Maya not long ago, watching some evangelical preacher. When Maya was younger, science and reason had been enough. Jean had bought her a science kit to make rainbows when she had asked why the sky was blue. But now that she'd grown older, Maya had begun to have a disturbing respect for mystery. She no longer asked the why of anything. That was the one thing Jean feared more than boys. Much to her distress, her daughter had become curious about God.

"Catholics don't worship the statues," Jean told her. "The statues are just symbols. They're art meant to capture the essence of their belief."

"Why are you defending them? You don't believe in God. You think Catholics are just as silly as Grandma does."

"I don't think they're silly. I just don't believe what they believe."

"And neither does Grandma or me. So we don't go to their church. Why do you even go if you don't believe?"

"There are more important things than believing, Maya."

"Like what?"

"Like appreciation. I don't believe what they believe, but I can appreciate their architecture, I can admire their belief."

"You don't admire Grandma's belief."

"I don't have to admire it, I was raised in it. And I know that their belief is the belief that everyone but them is going to hell. There's nothing to admire in that."

"Grandma doesn't believe I'm going to hell. I'm saved. I was saved when I was eight." Yes, her daughter knew just how to provoke her. Angry, no doubt, about the shallow pool, the lack of ocean, the inevitable union of Brett and Maureen, the embarrassment of simply having a mother in front of the sexy businessman.

Jean needed a beer. She considered going to drink with the NGOs, instead of the church. Raising a teenager, she guessed, was about as stressful as documenting atrocities. Glancing up at the man in the suit, she could see he had been listening. Jean changed the subject, slightly. "Grandma shouldn't have said that about you meeting Satan. Does that scare you?"

"It did a long time ago, but not anymore."

How old had she been? Of course Jean's mother would say that, even to a four-year-old Maya. Satan stalking the streets, very beautiful and looking for her.

"Because there's no such thing as Satan. People invented him to explain away the evil in their own hearts."

Maya pondered this and nodded, the whole sky tilting in her lenses. "Yeah, I believe that." Jean's parents had won a battle, but not the war. Maya believed she was saved, but to her it didn't mean much to her everyday life. She was saved, much like other people were insured.

"I totally forgot Grandma telling me that, until I saw your friend Telema," Maya admitted. The situation, though diffused, had moved on to a matter just as painful.

"You never met Telema before the airport, did you?"

"I saw her once, when Brett drove me home. She was pulling out of the driveway in a horrible car. The exhaust made me cough and burned my eyes."

"You thought she was Satan?"

"It was very childish." She spoke of decisions she'd made just months ago in this manner. She was constantly improving herself, she believed, aging years in a single day. "I just remembered what Grandma said, for some reason. Telema is very beautiful. And I started to wonder why you never introduced me to her."

Jean knew churches never changed much, and so, walking inside Xela's cathedral, she imagined these were the same saints, in the same slow shafts of light, that had, in 1983, set their mournful, painted eyes on baby Maya. Perhaps she had been left underneath one of the statues for the nuns to find. Jean summoned the dried-out, emotionless scream the infant Maya had let out at the Los Angeles airport. A scream that did not expect to be appeased. That scream, which endured for much of a year, drove away the last of Jean's old friends.

For almost twelve years, Maya had given Jean everything she needed. Companionship, purpose, love, acknowledgment from the world. Jean did not much miss her friends or her sex life. She'd always loathed her own parents, felt no kinship to them, and now finally she understood what others meant when they spoke of family with devotion. Even the stigma of single motherhood couldn't ruin her newfound contentment. Almost everyone, in the end, respected motherhood. For years, Maya mimicked the way she read, walked, and used her phrases with pride. A whole, happy child grew from the screaming, scarred infant that arrived in her arms. In a few months, a black mat of hair grew in on Maya's head, hiding the scar for good.

In Xela's cathedral, Jean tried to imagine Maya's infant scream changing the expression of the saints presiding above in painted indifference. Was that on purpose, Jean wondered, with Catholics? Were the statues meant to stare you down, make you feel you had committed some great wrong, even if you couldn't remember what it was? Guilt was useful, Jean believed, and too much was better than not enough. She had been raised Pentecostal, where guilt only occurred in retrospect, generations later.

Jean was here, she felt vaguely, to repent for her parents, who were masters in evading their own guilt. They would never know the destruction caused by their beliefs, though indisputable evidence had arrived in their mailbox months before, bound with a binder clip, and highlighted in the relevant sections. Her parents had given money to the thing called Operation Open Arms.

Jean, aware of the civil war in Guatemala, was applying to adopt when her parents called to tell her of their latest charitable cause. They, who forever clipped coupons and could not afford air-conditioning, gave a hundred dollars to Pat Robertson and his friend Ríos Montt. And despite the scholarship coming out now, despite the years of research and investigation by the Historical Clarification workers she'd seen in the vegetarian restaurant, despite the recent UN report cataloguing their findings and the abuses of Ríos Montt's rule, her parents still would never know. Truth, now, was filed away in library catalogues, filed into oblivion. Truth did not make the news.

One hundred dollars. How many rounds of ammunition would that buy? How many yards of road would it build? Jean imagined the receipt her parents received in the mail, after their contribution. One hundred dollars buys you one heathen soul. She imagined them stapling the receipt to their tax return, to get the deduction.

On her last visit, Jean had confronted her mother directly about her contribution to Open Arms, and had been amazed (though she shouldn't have been) to have made no impression at all. The human life span, Jean marveled, was just long enough to avoid the truth with willful, tactical ignorance. Just long enough for evil to thrive.

Thinking of evil, Jean remembered the man in the suit with his banana drink. So out of place in the meditation garden, in Guatemala, and in 1999 in general. Even his haircut seemed from a different era, a very Cold War look. He would have to have his hair cut every week to keep it up. Who did that anymore? Jean distrusted men in suits, and as she pondered the nature of evil, she envisioned men in suits. She replayed Maya flirting with the man, cocking her hip, tipping her glasses, flipping the tag out from her bottom.

The man watching her with his mouth attached to his banana drink. Jean had thought he was politely ignoring Maya, but now she began to think that maybe that wasn't what he had been doing. Was he even a guest? She imagined the two alone in the meditation garden, Maya completely set on impressing this man with her new bikini. The hotel empty but for the proprietor sweeping remote corners, mumbling to herself.

Jean ran out of the church before she could decide if she was being irrational. Pushing off the pews for speed, she ran five blocks, to find the proprietor standing at the front door in the same nightgown dress, scrubbing away at the blue hand graffiti. A man in a green NGO polo shirt argued at her back.

"There's no vacancy," she said repeatedly.

"Can you let me in?" Jean gasped. Both the NGO and the proprietor turned to her, but neither of them moved beyond this.

"I need in, please!" Jean repeated, but it became clear that the more frantic she sounded, the less willing the proprietor would be to help her. "Have you seen my daughter in there? Is she okay?" Jean asked, more calmly.

"Your daughter is at the pool. She's fine," the proprietor replied, turning back to her scrubbing. For a moment, Jean thought she was scrubbing at the blue hand itself, but she could see now that someone had graffitied the graffiti. Red paint spurted from the two fingers so that instead of curled into the palm, they looked as if they had been lopped off and were bleeding. The proprietor, with a brush and soapy water, attacked the red paint.

Jean hooked her fingers into the ironwork gate. "When's the last time you saw her?" She felt calmer now, seeing one of the staff enter the meditation garden.

"She says there's no vacancy. Do you have a room here?" the NGO demanded.

"Yes," Jean said.

"Well, are the rooms full?"

"Listen, I just want to get inside to my daughter. Can you please let me in?"

"Were there other guests here last night?"

Jean shrugged. "I don't know."

"I want a room for the week," he insisted again to the proprietor, whose own knuckles bled from the stucco. "Everyplace else says they're full, too. I'm not fucking leaving." He dropped his bag on the ground and put his hands where his waist should be. He had the body of someone on the verge of going to fat, probably from all the drinking the NGOs did here. Jean had run by the vegetarian restaurant and had seen a few of them starting already. They worked and drank in shifts, these young devotees of truth.

"It's not good for business," the proprietor admitted with a shrug. The paint began to come up. She thrust her hand into the pink water, renewed by her progress. "We have a tourist," she said.

"I don't mind," Jean said, but no one paid attention. "I just need to get inside. Please." She thought from the depths of the hallway she heard Maya laugh. Her desperation began to seem ridiculous, even to herself.

"Fine," the man huffed. "You know there won't be any more tourists, so I'll make you a deal that's good for business, okay? I take a room here and I don't talk to the tourist." He pointed at Jean. "I'm out of here in the mornings and back in the evenings. No one will see me. One week."

He slammed a handful of colorful paper bills down on the sill and the proprietor pursed her lips at them. "My sons won't like this."

"I won't talk to your sons, either. They won't even see me."

"Okay." She thrust her wet hand into her apron for the key. She pointed a wrinkled pink finger at them both. "But no talking."

Jean opened her mouth, but the woman squared her eyes at her.

Maya was in the meditation garden, lying very still in the sun. She had not moved since Jean had left, save for the slow, rotisserie turn to make sure she tanned evenly. She bubbled with sweat, blackened and laid out on her side.

The man in the suit sat at his table, reading the newspaper with another frozen banana drink. Jean did not enter, but stood at the screen door, watching, knowing she couldn't run in and hug Maya. She could not endure her daughter's rejection again, so she just watched, calming herself. After a few minutes, Maya sauntered over to the pool. She sauntered, Jean was sure, for the man's benefit, and he glanced up from his newspaper with practiced aloofness. Maya dipped a toe into the water, but did not get into the pool. She walked the circumference, testing at different locations, swinging her narrow hips.

The man looked down at his newspaper, turned a page, then glanced up again, watching. Maya hesitated and turned to the side, striking a thin profile in Jean's direction. Her bikini was half wedged into her bottom. Jean watched, with horror, as she giggled and pulled it out with a snap.

~~~~~

Jean had not seen Telema for a week, outside of class. They met up on the campus green, to have lunch, but Telema seemed to have forgotten that. She arrived late and began walking in the opposite direction of the graduate student pub.

"How was your trip?" Jean asked, trying to get a better look at Telema's face. A nasty cut marred her cheekbone. Recent, inflamed.

"What?" Telema glanced back, like someone might be following them.

"Your trip to Boston."

Telema was in the throes of her investigations, although for professional and funding purposes she had to call it research. She would spend a week at a time on the East Coast, only coming back to teach her class. There had been a few trips already, and Telema was often cool about the results.

"Very productive." She smiled to herself.

They walked across campus in silence. Where were they going? Telema, lost in her own head, probably didn't know herself. A troubling state, since Jean had set herself a specific goal for this lunch. To tell Telema about Maya's origins. But already they were off to a bad beginning.

"Where are we going?"

"To Daggett Lounge."

"What's there?"

"The panel discussion. Haven't you seen those offensive flyers tacked all around campus? I can't believe no one asked me to be a panelist."

Jean remembered, vaguely. "The ones about American happiness?"

But she'd retreated again, her dark eyes alight like stoked coals. Whatever went on in Telema's head was almost always more interesting than whatever happened around her. Telema knew she had a daughter by now. However, Jean did not mention ethnicity or adoption. Jean's family life didn't interest Telema, so she'd asked no questions about Maya. Children, it seemed, were boring. And after a month spending weekends with Maya at the mall and evenings with Telema in varying degrees of inebriation outdoors, Jean was beginning to agree. At least, after learning Jean had a daughter, Telema still agreed to see her. Another miracle of this new era.

My daughter is a Guatemalan war orphan. She'd been saying this proudly for fourteen years. But she could not see Telema acting overjoyed about it. She'd just assigned an article she'd written herself called "The Economy of Love," in which affluent white parents paid huge amounts of money for nonwhite children to love. Assimilation, conquest by humanitarianism. Jean had thrown the article aside in tears, unable to finish reading it. For weeks Telema had been like an antidote to Maya's rejection. But as the class progressed, Telema and Maya, though they'd never met, seemed to be allied in the goal of making Jean feel guilty.

Would it be better for these children to die of starvation in their home countries, without parents, than to become a part of a white family? Jean wanted to ask. No, Jean wanted to *tell* Telema this. For once, she felt she knew a topic better than Telema. Just look my daughter in the face and tell her she belongs in a cholera-ridden slum. She'd mapped out a whole confrontation, a whole defense, over the course of the week.

In Daggett Lounge, young men in blue uniforms already filled the first row. ROTC. Telema chose their seats in a middle row. Jean found the clock. Five minutes till one.

"Can we talk, Telema?"

"Yes, of course. We've lots to talk about!"

Jean was forced to sit on the same side as Telema's cut. She spied slight swelling around the eye. "We do?" she asked thankfully. Jean dreaded the adoption conversation, even as she knew the longer she put it off, the more difficult it would become.

"Yes! I've fucking found her!" Two ROTC guys turned to register the disturbance. Four minutes until the panel began, and Telema wanted to do all the talking. "I can't believe I finally found her." In her excitement, she picked at her scabby cheek, beaming.

A few more people walked in, taking seats. A photographer with the campus newspaper, and a few students. Up front, the panelist table remained empty, with five chairs and a pitcher of ice water. "In Boston? Who did you find?"

"The old bat who wrote the letter claiming to be a dead girl."

"What dead girl?"

"My subject! Evie Crowder. My lost little girl."

"Who's that?" Already, all hope for this conversation, lost.

"She was supposed to have been murdered in Guatemala in 1902. No one doubted it. But then, out of the blue in 1983, a Guatemalan newspaper called *Prensa La Verdad* got a letter from an old woman claiming to be Evie. The letter was from Boston. Of course, the paper runs with it and rehashes the whole horrible crime, the history, the trials, with these terribly written, sensational installments. But I guess I can't complain too much. It was those articles that led to me to the story of Evie in the first place. I was researching the volcano and came across the archive."

"And so you found Evie Crowder?"

"Nope, I found a woman in a mental institution named Dorie Honeycutt."

It turned one o'clock. The small audience, mostly ROTC, quieted expectantly. Jean shifted to see the door. "Hey, isn't that your best student? Sitting in the back?"

Telema turned. "Of course."

"He looks like a Young Republican."

"How's your paper coming?"

"I haven't gotten far. I've been busy with my book." No, she'd been busy with Telema. Even when the professor was in Boston, Jean was busy with Telema. Upholding small lies, constructing narratives that inevitably produced more lies. Inventing arguments, defenses. The woman inhabited the mind, took it over, like a vine.

"Who said that any book worth writing is like trying to construct scaffolding around a huge beast you don't even know the dimensions of? Who said that?"

"I don't know."

"The danger, of course, is finding yourself trapped inside. Has that happened to you yet?"

"No," Jean answered in confusion. She felt, more than anything, Telema constructing some network around her. Just hammering and screwing away, without looking, without seeing Jean at all. How could she still think Jean was writing a book?

Someone arrived in the room and the whole audience turned. A girl, a student with a ponytail. Everyone looked at her expectantly and she clapped a hand over her mouth and ran out, laughing.

"Your book is no excuse," Telema said. "You're still required to turn in that paper on time. 'Cold Blood, Cold War,' that was it, right?"

"I've done all the research. And have my new thesis." The thesis was the easiest part. Everything they learned in class fed into the thesis.

"And what is that?"

"The lengths our government will go to protect powerful American businesses abroad. All the ties between United Fruit and the major players in the coup. How everyone, the Dulles brothers, the American ambassador, the CIA men, and even Castillo Armas—how everyone who planned the coup had an economic stake in Fruit. Well, everyone but Eisenhower."

"And so you think Guatemala was the victim of one big fraternity prank?"

"Yes, exactly that."

"Unflagging devotion? A homoerotic hazing around a roasting pig sort of thing? Government jacks off business and business jacks off government?" she said too loudly.

The entire ROTC line turned to give Telema a look, and she waved at them.

"Yes, yes," Jean agreed.

Disappointment touched Telema's face. She shook her head at Jean. "But what about the lawsuit? All the things you're saying are true in a way, but you've not gotten to the meat of it."

"What lawsuit?"

"The suit brought against United Fruit five days after Jacobo Arbenz fled the country."

"There was a lawsuit? What was it? Who brought it?"

"Your State Department. Antitrust, my dear."

Ten after one. The photographer left. One of the aspiring soldiers stood up and walked back to the door. They heard him stepping down the hall in his uniform shoes.

"Why would they do that?" Jean asked. "That makes no sense at all."

"Use your fiction skills. Your imagination."

Jean considered a different, more powerful company, a woman getting in the way. "I don't have much of one," she admitted.

The ROTC student walked back into the room, walked right up to Telema in their empty row, and said, "Are you in charge of this clown show?"

"No," Telema replied, straightening. "I thought you were. I thought this was a circle jerk, not a clown show."

The aspiring soldier blushed beneath his buzzed blond hair. "That's funny." He grinned. "We were all so sure you'd be Exhibit A."

"Exhibit A?"

The boy at the moment looked like the happiest boy in the world. All his buddies turned to hear him deliver his line. "Yeah, for the conscience destroying America's happiness. I took your class, Professor. And I think everyone at this university can agree you're the most miserable cunt on campus."

~~~~~

The short drive to the orphanage was mostly uphill, with jungle piling up all around them. The eyes of the Latino driver flicked constantly in the mirror at

Maya, watching her more than the road. His smell crowded the taxi and Maya was not discreet about rolling her window down. Jean watched the trees, hoping for some birds.

"Quetzals?" she asked the driver.

"Three quetzales." He replied, holding up three fingers. "Do you want me to wait at the top? Five quetzales." The driver enjoyed practicing his English.

"No, not money. Birds." She made a bird with her hands and held it up to the rearview. "Quetzals here?" She pointed up to the trees.

He shook his head. "Quetzals at the Biodiversity Park. I take you there, six quetzales."

"What's the Biodiversity Park?"

"It's very nice, a nice building with animals and scientists. The quetzals have two babies there, behind the glass."

"That's not possible," Jean said. "Quetzals can't live in captivity, and they certainly can't breed in captivity."

"I saw them," he said into the mirror, "last week. Two babies."

"But that's the whole point of the bird, isn't it?" Maya asked. "Don't they kill themselves in captivity?"

"Oh yes, before. But now they figured it out. They fixed that problem."

They ascended in a fury of potholes and dust, gaining speed on an uphill road called Calle Emelda Lupe Tuq. Hardly any of the roads outside the town center had signs, but this one was new and deliberate, a stone obelisk. This cut monument had not been spared the political graffiti: a stalk of corn, an orange triangle, green letters, and the blue hand. This one, too, spoiled with red paint, bloodier than the effort on the hotel.

Jean blew her nose, and the tissue came away black.

The top of the small mountain was a surprise. A vast, bright lawn surrounding a stucco and glass building. So much less depressing than Jean had expected. Near the parking lot, a field had just been turned as if for planting. The grass scraped away in a large, perfect rectangle, to reveal black, wet volcanic soil.

Maya found a bench outside the front door and sat down. "I think I'll just wait here with my magazine, Mom. If that's okay."

"Maya." Jean held open the glass door. "Please come in with me."

"I'll be happier out here with my magazine. Seriously. It's the Fall Fashion issue."

"Honey." Jean closed the door. "I know you think that makes you happy, but it doesn't. That's not happiness, it's entertainment. Can we please do this together? I think you'll be happy later that we did."

"I think I'll have a better time out here. What's happiness if it's not having a good time?"

"This is *important*, Maya. If nothing else, do it to make me happy. You're the only person in the world I want to be with for this."

Maya collected herself slowly, resentfully, into a standing position. "Fine. But you should know, Mom, that the things you claim make you happy only piss you off. You should see your face when you're reading your *New Yorker* every week. All those articles about poor people and pollution. It's giving you wrinkles."

Inside the modern lobby, three American couples waited. Too nervous for the scattered magazines, they were engrossed in the television playing high up in the corner. The smiling woman at the counter asked Jean, in English, her purpose. She said it just like that, referring to Jean's purpose.

"I'm here to see my daughter's records," Jean said. She hesitated, then pulled Maya into view with a gentle hand. Maya allowed herself to be pulled, infected by the tense air of the lobby. The woman nodded tightly, as if she had been warned of this situation, but had yet to deal with it. She seemed to take great relief from the protocol of pushing the sign-in paper across the desk.

Everyone, Jean could feel, was staring. So she tried to lighten the mood. "What are you planting out there? Vegetables for the children?"

"Yes." The woman smiled, probably not knowing vegetables. "Children."

"That's a lot of vegetables. That whole field?"

"Not vegetables. A soccer field. For the children. AstroTurf."

Jean pushed her paper back across the desk and the woman studied it.

"What was her name?"

"María Tierra López," Jean said, for the first time in fourteen years.

The woman squinted. "What year?"

They sat down to join the nervous parents-to-be among the stacks and stacks of newspapers, magazines, and books. The mere volume of reading material implied decades of waiting. These couples watched Jean and Maya through blurred eyes, as if they had read every article available to them and still their names had not been called.

"Who's María Tiara López?" Maya asked, sitting in a molded plastic chair.

"That's you. That was your name at the orphanage."

"It was?" Maya said the name a few times, under her breath, deciding on an accent. She pronounced Tierra like tiara. "Did my mom name me that, or did the orphanage?"

"I don't know. Maybe we'll find out." In truth, Jean had no idea what the records would say. They could say everything, or nothing at all. She suspected the latter.

Their attention wandered up to a preacher, speaking in a Mayan language on the high television. Jean followed the English subtitles: "Only Jesus has the power to raise up a nation. Only Jesus has the power to know the truth. And Jesus will punish those who need to be punished. Jesus is the one and only Truth Commission!"

The preacher just missed being handsome, with a bright row of cartoon teeth for a smile. He thanked his sister church, watching from Colorado, and for whom the subtitles had been provided. Then he took prayer requests, while Maya's lips moved, reading. "I lost my whole family," she mouthed along with a Mayan woman on the screen. "But I am thankful for what the Lord has given to me. I do not want revenge, I want to break the cycle of violence. There are people who only care about the past, they are infected with a sickness of the past. Let's pray for them."

The pastor prayed for the sickness of the past, read from the New Testament, something about forgiveness, then sang a solo. The audience clapped, waved their hands, and wept in one cohesive wave of emotion. Then the screen split to reveal the Colorado congregation mirroring their motions of praise.

"*The Healing Hour*, with Pastor Mincho Escalante-Lincé, will be right back."

The preacher was in the process of laying hands on an old blind woman when the receptionist appeared with a slim file and directed Jean and Maya to a room behind the counter. This room had been primed but not painted, giving the walls a bright, uneven veneer. Maya took the only chair. Jean knelt beside her and pried open the gummed seal of the orphanage file. The first thing to fall out was Maya's baby picture, the one Jean had received and had cried over in 1983. She felt those same tears now, returning. A color photo, the kind tinged red, making the tiny, emaciated body look burned with fever. Maya wore nothing but an obscenely large plastic diaper that accentuated her starved body. Thankfully, her skull wound did not show from this angle.

"Oh my God," Maya breathed, leaning in. "What's wrong with me?"

"You weren't that bad, Maya. It's the color, it makes it look worse," Jean lied, taking her hand. "They used old, damaged film. Seriously."

In fact, seeing this picture, Jean felt the room collapsing around her. She knew this picture, knew it so well, so why did she feel like she'd been punched in the stomach? For the first two years, she had carried this photograph in her wallet, to remind herself to be patient with her new daughter. Single motherhood had not been easy. So she looked at this raw, wounded baby during many sleepless nights and screaming fits. But eventually Maya began to sleep peacefully in her crib and new images and memories eased Jean's frustrations: Maya eating spaghetti, Maya playing in ocean waves for the first time. At what point had she stored this photograph away? She had no idea.

With her free hand, she placed the picture facedown on the table and read the two pieces of paper that made up the file. One a medical record. Jean remembered it well: jaundice, malnutrition, dehydration, double ear infection. On her copy at home, there'd been no mention of a knife wound on her head. Through her limited Spanish and the watery gloss of tears, she saw words that referenced it now. Not wanting to upset Maya further, she turned it over and lifted the second paper, which Jean wasn't sure was supposed to be in there. It gave Maya's birth mother's information: fifteen-year-old Cruzita Sola Durante, from Nueva Aldea de la Vida, had given up her baby because of poverty. The girl had been the same age then that Maya was now.

~~~~~

Despite her reputation as a miserable cunt, the professor had many admirers, and Jean was becoming jealous of the young coeds who cluttered the hallway outside her office. With Maya perpetually in the company of Brett, her friends, or at flag line practice, Jean began to have enough free time for jealousy. She had put her ear to Telema's office door one day and had heard a young hopeful trying to explain herself.

"Little bombs," Telema interrupted her dramatically. "A little girl of fourteen, dressed up and educated in the ways of seduction . . ."

Jean did not stay to hear the rest. She was enraged, and had no reason to be. She could not claim Guatemala for herself, especially in a class in which she wasn't even enrolled. The only thing to do, Jean decided, was to claim Telema for herself, to extract some level of commitment from her. This had been the idea when she invited Telema over one evening, just before Spring Break. But everything they'd done over the past few weeks had begun with some hope, soon thwarted. Jean felt as if they were having an affair, with complications, people to take into consideration, though there were none. Why, then, was this so difficult?

Because she needed to tell her about Maya's origins first, to begin with her. *My daughter is a Guatemalan war orphan.* How could Telema have a problem with that? Because she had a problem with everything. She constantly surprised Jean with her pronouncements, decrying what was generally accepted as good—humanitarian aid, breast cancer awareness—while praising things like handguns, cacao farming, and the kidnapping of the aid worker in Colombia. And her article "The Economy of Love" proved that Maya would be a bigger obstacle than Jean had ever imagined. Scandals, stolen babies, baby brokers, a whole vile economy teeming under the surface of American domestic life. In Telema's opinion, no brown baby in the world could be adopted under moral circumstances. After forcing herself to finish the article, Jean became determined to prove her innocence to Telema and herself. Just yesterday, she'd bought the plane tickets to Guatemala. She would track down the records herself.

But this plan lay months away, and nothing would be easy tonight. Telema was in a mood. The dean had launched an investigation into the American happiness ghost panel from the day before. No panelists had ever arrived. Every faculty member denied involvement. A subversive prank, with Telema as the main suspect.

"As if I have the time for shit like that," Telema said, settling into a chair, her black eyes scanning Jean's beach from the deck. Fifty yards away, someone was trespassing. Jean sat across from Telema, sipped her wine, and watched the dark, solitary form take its time, toeing the high-tide line.

"Have you ever done something for love?" Jean asked, testing. "Something other people disapproved of and couldn't understand? Something you wholly believed in, but others considered evil?"

Telema smiled inwardly, her lips stained with red wine. "Oh yes."

"What was it?"

Telema's naked foot found Jean's under the deck table. "The Sandinistas. I was young, still in high school. But I worked evenings at the library and sent everything I made to my brother, who was fighting with them. I think two hundred dollars in all."

"Are you still happy you did?"

"Of course."

"And your brother?"

Telema just shrugged, and Jean saw her opening.

"I thought you opposed anything that funded any cause, just improving the circulation of the Great White Beast. Isn't that what you told me?"

"I meant any cause that's legal. Anything accepted by the corrupt powers is, in itself, corrupt. If you give money to charities deemed acceptable, that means they're part of the machine. It's one great circulatory system. If the charity makes the Beast happy, that means it's not effecting any great change. Like cancer research."

"But the Sandinistas were?"

"The only charity that makes change is the charity that fights the Great Beast. That is the only cause that will truly help people. You give money to cancer research and you get all kinds of stickers and congratulations. You sabotage Dow, which makes the cancer, and you get arrested. The Great White Beast loves research, Jean. We already know what causes cancer, though we pretend not to."

"The Great White Beast sounds very biblical, Professor."

"Christians don't have a monopoly on beast metaphors. They think they invented everything." She sighed, tired of having a retort for everything. "The FBI has a file on me for that two hundred dollars, for the fact that I'm related to my brother, and for my research."

"How do you know?"

"The Great White Beast is clumsy. It's so powerful it never had to learn subtlety or grace." She raised her wineglass. "They probably have a file on you now, too. For seeing me." She grinned. "Actually, I'm sure of it."

Jean pursued the conversation fearfully. "And what about Boston? Did they follow you there?"

"Of course. They are the ones who turned them against me."

"Them?"

"The staff of the mental institution. Well, maybe that's the wrong word. It wasn't a straitjacket sort of place, more like a retreat for exhaustion. I got what I needed from them, though. Most of what I needed."

"About Evie Crowder?"

"No, no. I told you, Dorie Honeycutt. A friend of mine in Guatemala broke into the *Prensa La Verdad* records and got the address of that crazy letter-writer from Boston claiming to be Evie. I traced it all back, then had to do some records magic of my own to find out who lived in that room in 1983. A sixty-year-old woman, definitely not old enough to be Evie. Checked in almost thirty years before by her big-shit husband."

"So did you get to talk to her?"

"No. She's dead. She died shortly after she wrote the letter. Like, a week after she wrote it. And this is what one of the nurses who remembered her told me. She said this Dolores had an elderly, important husband who would come and visit her a few times a year, but she never said a word to him. She seemed almost perfectly normal otherwise. Just quiet and fragile. Insisted on getting dressed every day like she was going somewhere. For almost thirty years, she did this. Never any drama or worry. She seemed content there, and that was what made them believe she belonged there, how content she was. Normally, people stayed there for a few months or a year, but her husband kept paying the bills. Then, not long after she wrote that letter, her husband arrives for his visit. She sits there for a while, listening to him talk, then she just gets up from her chair, runs across the room, and throws herself out the window. Never said anything, never screamed. Breaks through the glass, falls five stories, and dies."

"Jesus!"

"And the best part is, Honeycutt is the last name of the American ambassador in Guatemala during the coup. She was that fucker's wife! That's as far as I got before the goons shut me down. But it doesn't matter. She wasn't Evie, could not be. But she did get me thinking that maybe this Evie was alive. No one ever found her body, or her parents', though there were supposed murder confessions. But the funny thing about the confessions is they were all in Spanish originally. Eleven illiterate Mayan field hands, and one Ladino overseer. He probably spoke Spanish, but the others? No way. Not to the level of detail they supposedly provided."

"Ladino? Is that the same as Latino?"

"No. Ladino's a native or someone with mixed blood who's Westernized. Gets rid of his traditional clothes, acts white. It's only a word in Guatemala. Anyway, how would this Dolores even know about Evie Crowder unless the little girl was still alive in 1954? Maybe even still in Guatemala? She seems to have known a lot of things. My friend copied the letter she sent to the newspaper and there's a lot more than her claiming to be Evie, there's a lot more than what they printed. She wrote about a conspiracy between United Fruit and the U.S. government. Some of it true, some of it believable, some of it completely bonkers. She said she was Evie Crowder and that someone named Tomás—I have no idea who that is—had been looking for her, had finally found her and told her who she was. And that she was moving with him to Brazil."

"How strange," Jean marveled, preferring these stories to the confrontation she had planned. "Will you find out more?"

"Yes, in time. She had to have known something. Lots of digging to do, but I had to come back to teach this fucking class." The sun disappeared below the water and the scene on Jean's deck darkened. "Imogene, Imogene."

"I hate that name," Jean said, loving it on Telema's tongue.

"Of course you do. So why don't you change it? You know, my real name's not Telema Espejo de la Hoz."

"It's not? What is it?"

"Evangeline."

Telema's laugh was a startling animal-like cackle. The cut on her cheek glimmered with a slight infection. They both laughed so hard that their bodies slid down into their chairs, their legs tangling under the table. Imogene and Evangeline.

"I'm going to Guatemala in August," Jean said, feeling so unexpectedly confident. Yes, she could keep Telema. No need for a fight now. When she went on the Roots Tour, she'd track down the adoption records. If she found the facts to exonerate herself preemptively, Telema could hold nothing against her. And Maya would surely benefit, just as the therapist said. Suddenly the solutions to all Jean's problems lay in Guatemala.

"Are you going to research your book?"

"Sort of."

"Guatemala's beautiful," Telema said vaguely. Jean still did not know if she'd ever been there. "But there's always been the war. You're quite brave to be going so soon without an *organization*."

Jean knew it wasn't the best time, but if she waited any longer, Maya would be old enough to resist. And now Jean's own peace of mind depended on it. "The Peace Accords help," she said.

"Yes, I suppose a signed document is the best gauge anyone has. Peace Accords bring peace. A paper peace, paper justice for a war begun on paper." Her eyes narrowed, following something in the dark, something distant. "Listen, maybe this is a good time to go. I have my own investigation to do down there, for my book."

"Really? Will they follow you there, too?"

"If they don't fuck it up, which they often do. But they've covered their asses in the usual cowardly way. I received a letter from a distant relative of Evie's today. Of course, the suits contacted him about my book."

"What does the letter say?"

"Oh, so and so about harassment, libel. If I publish the story of Evie Crowder, I'll have a lawsuit on my hands."

"But why would the FBI care about your book?"

"They don't, really. The CIA does."

"Your book about Guatemala? Or about Evie?"

"One book about everything, which just so happens to feature Guatemala."

"A book about everything, with a lawsuit already pending. How do you begin to write that? You're still going to do it?"

"Sure."

"What about the lawsuit?"

"To sue me, they have to find me a few more times. And they have to get the right name on the paperwork. They certainly didn't have it this time around."

"But they can find you, can't they? I mean, they know where you are now."

"They know where I am now because I've allowed them to find me. Sometimes it's easier to have them along for a while. They're stunningly incompetent, you know, especially when they have stiffies."

"Aren't you afraid they'll arrest you?"

"Oh no, they want me to lead them somewhere."

"Where?"

"Someplace I will never lead them, but they don't know that." She said this exactly in the way she had referred to her own students, weeks before, oblivious to the fact that they would all be getting C's.

"Would you let them follow you to Guatemala?"

"Maybe, I'm not sure. Actually, I think this summer might be the perfect time for me to go. The best time to get information, records. The world's eyes are on Guatemala, so they've got to play nice, right? Truth and reconciliation. In a year, once the world's forgotten, it'll be much harder. Also, you'd be a good decoy. If we're both down there, they won't know who to follow. When do you leave?"

Jean told her, flushed with excitement at this development. A vacation together, a relationship milestone. Then, remembering Maya too late, she backtracked. "Listen, Telema. I'd love for you to come, but I'm taking my daughter. I can't involve her in—"

Telema held up a hand. "That's fine, Jean. I completely understand. Don't think a second more about it." She refilled her wine. "How's your paper coming?"

"I don't know." The paper was going nowhere and she knew Telema would hold it against their relationship. "I'm having a hard time understanding the point."

"Your thesis, you mean?"

"No, the point of the coup."

"But that is your thesis, right?"

Jean acknowledged this. "I read about the antitrust suit. It just makes no sense at all. Everything, absolutely everything points to the fact that they did it to save Fruit, so why would they dismantle them right after? They got the dictators they wanted lined up, ready to give the company everything they wanted."

"Is that person trespassing?" Telema interrupted, staring wistfully out at the darkening curve of beach.

"I suppose so."

"Do you have a gun?"

"I do not."

"That's too bad. Not one court in this country would convict you if you shot him."

"Listen, Telema. I love you," Jean blurted, warmed with wine. The wine was warming her, but cooling Telema, which Jean could very well see. She hadn't meant to say that, but it seemed the closest approximation to her feelings without using more pathetic, accurate word "need." It was better, anyway, than I'm not writing a book. I give money to breast cancer research. I have an assimilated, adopted daughter, who is currently on a date with a football player.

Telema withdrew her foot from their game beneath the table.

"It would never work," Telema said after taking a long drink, finishing her wine.

"Us? Why not?"

"Because emotions are always exploited, they become distraction."

"Distraction from what?"

"From what matters, Jean. Those articles from 1983 I stumbled upon, detailing the little girl's murder, the ghastly details of her rape, the confessions, everything. Conspiracy theories, alternate endings. Now, why, after all those years, would someone dredge up that stuff?"

"Because they want justice? Because they received that letter?"

"Distraction! The newspaper published that shit during the bloodiest months of the civil war! And this was the news the people got. The smallest bit of investigation would have proved that this Dolores was not Evie. But they didn't even bother to find out. They just ran with the story. Of course, the people ate it up. They loved it because it provoked their most private fears and desires. Emotions are our own enemies, Jean. They distract us from real problems. Especially love. Especially horror."

"I wouldn't distract you. I could help you with your research."

"Still, it would never work."

"Why not?"

"Because you would never give up your private beach."

"I'd give up my beach, sure. It doesn't mean a thing to me."

"Sell it to me, then. Sell it to me right now for a dollar forty-eight an acre."

"A dollar forty-eight?"

Telema was drunk, but this new game pleased her, and Jean felt it leading somewhere other than a joke. Possibly reciprocation.

"That's fine."

Telema reached a hand down to her purse. "How much land do you have?"

"Less than an acre."

Telema laid a dollar on the table and Jean took it too quickly, before she realized she shouldn't have. She was drunker than Telema and she had the vague feeling it had all been planned. That Telema had the deed in her purse and would force Jean to sign it after a few more drinks.

"Now," Telema said, sitting back, "you are my guest. You cannot move from your chair or look at the ocean. You are only allowed to be in that chair and you can only look at me. If you move, I will shoot you for trespassing."

Jean laughed. "But we're together now?"

"Yes. And you cannot leave. You're mine."

Jean knew she should be happy. It was all she had wanted, this simple declaration. She had no idea what she would have done if Telema had rejected her, but now that it was accomplished, she had even less of an idea of her future. What does one do with Telema? The moment she had her, Jean began to suspect it would be painful, but easier, to live without her.

"Our fates are now intertwined, Jean. When you are on my land, you must obey my rules. I paid, so I get whatever I think I'm entitled to. Refill my drink." Here, Telema brought a small, black .22 out of her purse. Jean, astonished, laughed.

"You carry a gun?"

Telema cocked it and Jean could see the weight of it on her palm, loaded. "Refill, Jean."

"Um, okay," Jean said, trying to get into the game but unable to.

"And where's Maya, Jean?"

"Maya? What do you want with her?"

"She's mine, too, now. I paid. She lives here, doesn't she? Or is she just a myth? I've never even seen her. Why are you hiding her from me?"

"You paid for the land, not us."

"But you live here. And you will continue to live here. My land, my rules. Where else would you go? You have a dollar. Where else can you go?"

~~~~~

The Santa María ecotour convened at the base of the volcano the next morning, in darkness that soaked everything brown. It was four in the morning, too early even for perverts. They had made a clean break from the hotel, no one following. Jean had no idea where the paranoia had come from, other than Maya's own ridiculous behavior, but she made a concerted effort now to avoid the man in the suit.

At the volcano's base, Jean shivered in her hiking shorts. She had forgotten how cold spring could be. Eternal Spring felt more like late winter during the nights, and a wet, dank fall during daytime hours. Jean would be cold and underdressed for at least another hour—her coat packed in her lost luggage. When she moved close to Maya for warmth, her daughter moved away, shivering, too. For the past twenty-four hours, she'd turned more sullen than usual, not even perking up for shopping. In desperation, Jean had bought her everything she pointed to. Piles and piles of factory-made shit from the Latino shops that Maya demanded but took no joy in, as she normally would. Three purses, silk scarves, beaded jewelry, and an expensive silver jaguar (her school mascot) that Jean knew wasn't made of silver. A present for Brett. Jean bought all these things, then she had to buy bags to carry it all home. This strategy only made their small room more crowded and Maya's discontent harder to avoid.

What had been in the orphanage file, to affect her like this? To make her so needy, yet remote? The medical notes, the mother's name, the picture. Baby Maya, a red-tinted bundle of pain.

Maya, in moving away from Jean, neared the others.

"What's your name?" a kindly woman in a polo shirt asked, speaking as if to a much younger child. As if to a lost child. For her refusal to stand near anyone, everyone was having a hard time placing Maya. They tried their best not to stare.

"María," Maya replied. "María Tiara López."

"Are you with the Truth Commission?" a member of the tour group asked Jean.

"No," Jean said, pointing to Maya. "We're on a Roots Tour."

"Roots Tour," the woman repeated, possibly trying to decipher the acronym for Roots. Jean did not clarify, pleased to be mistaken for an aid worker. Revenger of Oppressed Tribes, Jean thought. But the joke came too late. The woman turned away, spoke with a man in a different polo shirt.

Their guide did not look like a traditional Mayan guide, but more like a Latino youth with a woven Mayan belt holding up his pants. Disappointed, Jean could not imagine challenging him. Whatever his ancestry, he knew English well. "I'm a tourism major," he said as an introduction. "The climb will be about two hours, and along the way there will be plenty of trash to pick up. I come every week and always there is new trash. The townspeople desecrate their own volcano," the guide reported gravely.

The group, except for Maya, lowered their heads in collective neutrality, torn between their love of the environment and of an ancient culture.

Everyone received a black trash bag and leather gloves, stained brown and stiff, as if by aged blood. They all put them on, opened and closed their hands to achieve some kind of harmony with the fabric, then began up the path. The two Truth Commission workers headed the parade, followed by the man in the white polo shirt, the woman whose organization was unclear though its symbol marked her shirt, and one man directly associated with the United Nations.

It wasn't just Maya's photo that had unsettled Jean. She also could not forget the mother's information. Not information, really, just a name. Cruzita Sola Durante. In 1983, she had been alive, but was she still?

Within an hour, the bags up front filled up and trash filtered down to their position in the line. Maya leapt on the silver shimmer of a food wrapper, then a Coke can. Her enthusiasm dwindled quickly and Jean made up for it with her own efforts. She collected what she could, wondering if a name was enough information to find someone in Guatemala. Had Cruzita really given up Maya because of poverty? Possibly Jean could find her and simply ask.

The rocks underfoot crunched smaller and smaller, into cinders. It became difficult to walk, like hiking uphill on sand. The woman just ahead fell back, out of breath, and began talking to Jean. "He"—she pointed to the man in the white polo shirt—"is with the Truth Commission."

"Is that the same as the Historical Clarification Commission?"

"No. They're different."

"How so?"

The woman shrugged, gave the short answer because of her lack of breath. "Historical Clarification published their findings already, the Truth Commission hasn't."

"And what are they finding? Anything new?"

"Nothing new. Just counting the dead."

"A shoe!" Maya held up a tire sandal triumphantly. "This is the sixth shoe I've found. How are these people making it up the volcano without shoes?"

The woman and Jean looked at each other.

"I don't know, sweetie. Why don't you leave the shoes? People," she managed to say, "might come back for them."

What were the chances this Cruzita was still alive? The bloodiest year of the civil war was 1983. Mostly likely she was dead. Most likely Maya was a true orphan, no matter what Telema's irate article implied.

"I think," the woman ventured, "the Truth Commission is more personal, helps people find loved ones. They'll be here forever. The Historical Clarification Commission worked on the bigger picture, identifying perpetrators, influence, and money flow. They published their report in February."

"And who are you with?"

She pointed to her shirt. "I'm with the Accuracy League. I interview survivors."

"And what do they tell you in these interviews?"

"My interviews are more about the dead. Past injuries they had, dental details, what they were last seen wearing. Stuff like that, helping people find loved ones in the mass graves. Sometimes we identify and return remains to families."

Jean shuddered. "Is that important to the Maya, new burials?" A dumb question.

"Oh yes. Honoring ancestors is always their main concern, even above their own safety. Improper burial is excruciating psychic anguish for them. As is any implication that a dead relative ever did anything wrong. It's hard to get accurate information a lot of the time, because they won't allow themselves to say anything bad of the dead. So, say a father was forced into the army. They won't say so. They'll just report him missing, but if they told us he was in the army, we'd have a much better idea of where to search."

"So how do all these organizations fit together? I mean, the Truth Commission finds the bodies, then you help identify them?"

The woman made a face. "The Truth Commission's full of pompous assholes. Fortunately, we have our own forensic anthropologists."

The bags, heavy and full, could not be carried to the top. Everyone left them on the trail, to pick up on the way down. As they approached the summit, the trail abandoned its switchback pattern and led them on a direct assault of the crater. The sun threatened to break over the ridge without them, but the more they hurried, the longer it took. One step forward could cause Jean to slide three steps back. Maya doubled over, employing her hands to work with her legs. Everyone sweated, so that the fine dust settled on their skin and turned to a thin black mud. The litter near the top was the worst on the trail. Now it seemed they should have hiked up, then collected trash on the way down.

Jean's body locked into a rhythm as she considered the mystery before her. Cruzita. But really, what could she find out? Jean knew the story already. A poor Mayan woman, surrounded by death, unable to preserve her own life, let alone one of a child. To find out more was to open herself only to bad news. Because there could be nothing but bad news for a Mayan woman in the mountains in 1983.

Maya reached the rim of the crater half a minute before the rest of them. She paused, not moving, her arms slightly raised at her sides. The spectacle of her wonder compelled the others to hurry, and when they reached the end of the path, none of them could believe what they saw.

There, above the sunken, smoking crater, a young blond woman presided in a gold bikini, leggy and gigantic. Below her, in the distance, Xela lay in a misty stupor. The hikers had no time to navigate an alternate route, but stood amazed at this goddess blocking their path, ignoring them. And then a miracle happened. The sun mounted the horizon and appeared between her legs—a reverse birth—and began a slow crawl up her thighs.

"Lift your chin," a voice called, to their left. "Open your legs a little more."

The girl obeyed, which caused a flurry of activity off to the side, where a camera crew adjusted to the new angle.

The girl, with light spreading up her body, turned to the camera and held her mouth out, as if for a kiss. "Gilberto Ahumada Lobos," she purred.

"It's a political ad," the UN worker said. "They're filming a presidential ad."

"No, no," the director yelled. "Roll your *r*. Like this. Gilberrrrto."

The girl tested the word on her tongue.

"We've got two minutes to get this right, or we're back up here tomorrow night."

The girl no longer looked immortal, but panicked and cold in her bikini as the sunlight moved up her legs, not warming her.

"Gilberrrrto," she said, over and over.

"It doesn't matter. We're doing a native voice-over for that."

"But it must look real," the director yelled. "Her mouth must look like it's saying that word. No Spanish speaker will believe her lips are saying those words! Baby," he pleaded, "move your mouth like you're making love."

She pouted, crossed her arms over her chest. "Why am I in fucking Guatemala pretending to be able to speak Spanish? We could have shot this back in California. It's a fucking mountain. We have mountains in California! We have the sun! We have people who speak Spanish!"

They eventually made their way around the crew, to a ledge where soldiers with AK-47s sat guarding the view. Behind them, the blue hand gave a ten-foot-tall salute.

"Ahumada Lobos is FRG," one of the Truth Commission people said, staring at the hand. The woman from the Accuracy League disappeared off the trail for a moment and returned with her polo shirt turned inside out.

It was unclear whether the shoot had been a success. The girl, wearing a coat now, huddled on a rock and smoked a cigarette. Maya approached, asking her something Jean could not hear.

"No, I'm not running for President," she replied, crushing her cigarette onto the rock. "But I bet I'd be better at it than anyone running the show now. I can't even get a decent cigarette in this country." She moved her tongue around inside her mouth elaborately. "Tastes like ashes. Like it's already been smoked and resold."

Jean turned her attention to the view, which was clearing and intricate. Daylight seeped into the valley, the sun a bright yellow yolk broken over everything. The mists, dissipating, clung in small depressions scattered through the valley. The woman with the inside-out shirt pointed at them, taking notes. In the outskirts, wheat fields flamed red in the angled sun. No one spoke. From this high, Jean thought, it could be any era they were looking out on. It could be 1902 just as well as 1999.

"This is the most beautiful place I've ever been," Maya panted, with her hands on her hips. "I could just *die*, I could just *die* right here!" She approached the large blue hand and pressed her own hand to the image, like a greeting. "It's wet," she said, surprised at her blue palm. She stamped a naked part of the rock with her own imitation, a miniature close-fingered salute, then wiped her hand down the side to get rid of the paint.

~~~~~

"It's a big day for Guatemala," Telema announced the morning after their date, from her classroom podium. Jean could barely remain in her chair for her excitement, her happiness. She had woken up that morning on her deck, with Telema already gone. And an hour later, here she was, probably sharing the same hangover. Jean stared up at the stage and told herself, This brilliant beautiful woman is my girlfriend. Telema Espejo de la Hoz, she decided, was the most passionate, interesting person she'd ever met. She'd held that gun as if she'd taken hostages before.

All around, undergraduates slumped in their theater chairs, some with their eyes closed.

Telema hoisted a stack of papers and passed them off for distribution. Jean saw the black purse tossed carelessly on the lectern, wondered if the gun was still inside. The first secret between them, the gun in a crowded theater. Jean took two copies and passed the stack across three chairs, to Telema's best student, who was wearing a paisley tie. Jean had never noticed him in this class until now. He took his copy and removed his horn-rimmed glasses to look it over seriously as Telema began her lecture.

"I know we haven't yet studied the years after the CIA coup in Guatemala, but this was just released yesterday." She held up the paper, which went limp in her hands. "The Commission for Historical Clarification has published their report on the thirty-six-year civil war that followed the coup."

Jean felt her heart constrict. This had been released yesterday and Telema hadn't mentioned it to her? She was forced to hear it, like the others, as a lecture.

Telema held the unwieldy report with two hands. She read from the middle:

"During the armed confrontation, the State's idea of the 'internal enemy,'

intrinsic to the National Security Doctrine, became increasingly inclusive. At the same time, this doctrine became the raison d'être of Army and State policies for several decades. Through its investigation, the CEH discovered one of the most devastating effects of this policy: state forces and related paramilitary groups were responsible for ninety-three percent of the violations documented by the CEH, including ninety-two percent of the arbitrary executions and ninety-one percent of forced disappearances."

The students were writing on their tablets—91 percent, 92 percent, 93 percent—afraid the numbers might show up on a test. Jean knew it had been the majority, but such a vast majority surprised her. It may, also, have taken Telema aback. It would have explained her mood the night before, waving a gun around and ordering Jean not to look anywhere but at her.

"Three percent of the human rights violations were attributed to the guerrillas fighting the government. Four percent remains undetermined." No one bothered to write these figures; they knew Telema enough to know the first ones were the ones that mattered.

"Victims included men, women and children of all social strata: workers, professionals, church members, politicians, peasants, students and academics; in ethnic terms, the vast majority were Mayans."

A door slammed open in the back, changing the light, as a handful of students walked in, late.

"Through its investigation, the CEH also concludes the undeniable existence of racism expressed repeatedly by the State as a doctrine of superiority, as a basic explanatory factor for the indiscriminate nature and particular brutality with which military operations were carried out against hundreds of Mayan communities in the west and northwest of the country, especially between 1981 and 1983 when more than half the six hundred twenty-six massacres and scorched earth operations occurred.

"Acts such as the killing of defenceless children, often by beating them against walls or throwing them alive into pits where the corpses of adults were later thrown; the amputation of limbs; the impaling of victims; the killing of persons by covering them in petrol and burning them alive; the extraction, in the presence of others, of the viscera of victims who were still alive; the confinement of people who had been mortally tortured, in agony for days; the opening of the wombs of pregnant women, and other similarly atrocious acts."

She was reading and flipping so quickly. The students, not able to keep up with their note-taking, looked around, bewildered and unsure of what they were hearing. The door opened again, with a burst of sunlight, as more students wandered in late, adding to the confusion.

"The CEH accounts among the most damaging effects of the confrontation those that resulted from forcing large sectors of the population to be accomplices in the violence, especially through their participation in the Civil Patrols, the paramilitary structures created by the Army in 1981 in most of the Republic. The CEH is aware of hundreds of cases in which civilians were forced by the Army, at gunpoint, to rape women, torture, mutilate corpses and kill. This extreme cruelty was used by the State to cause social disintegration. A large proportion of the male population over the age of fifteen, especially in the Mayan communities, was forced to participate in the Civil Patrols . . . The coexistence of victims and perpetrators in the same villages reproduces the climate of fear and silence."

The theater seats moaned as new arrivals sat down.

"Estimates of the number of displaced persons vary from five hundred thousand to a million and a half people in the most intense period from 1981 to 1983 . . . Through its investigation, the CEH has confirmed that those who fled were forced to move constantly, mainly to evade military operations directed against them despite their being defenceless, and partly to search for food, water and shelter . . . From 1983 onwards, Army strategy toward the displaced populations was designed to bring it under military control: amnesties were offered and those who accepted were resettled in highly militarized communities, marked by activities that included psychological operations to re-educate the people and the construction of model villages in the most conflictive regions."

She flipped further.

"Article II of this instrument defines the crime of genocide and its requirements in the following terms: Genocide means any of the following acts committed with intent to destroy, in whole or in part, a national, ethnical, racial or religious group, such as: Killing members of the group; causing serious bodily harm or mental harm to members of the group; deliberately inflicting on the group conditions of life calculated to bring about its physical destruction in whole or in part; imposing measures intended to prevent births within the group; forcibly transferring children of the group to another group."

Jean closed her copy.

"In consequence, the CEH concludes that agents of the state of Guatemala, within the framework of counterinsurgency operations carried out between 1981 and 1983, committed acts of genocide against groups of Mayan

people which lived in the four regions analyzed." Back to the beginning now, no one tried to find the page as she read.

"The CEH recognizes that the movement of Guatemala towards polarization, militarization and civil war was not just the result of national history. The cold war also played an important role. Whilst anti-communism, promoted by the United States within the framework of its foreign policy, received firm support from right-wing political parties and from various other powerful actors in Guatemala, the United States demonstrated that it was willing to provide support for strong military regimes in its strategic backyard. In the case of Guatemala, military assistance was directed towards reinforcing the national intelligence apparatus and for training the officer corps in counterinsurgency techniques, key factors which had significant bearing on human rights violations during the armed confrontation."

She dismissed the stupefied class, to "take full advantage of the day." She added, quite emotionally, uncharacteristically, at their backs, "And one last thing."

Jean, still seated, looked at Telema's purse on the lectern. This is it, she thought. She's going to shoot someone to make her point. She knew exactly who it would be, too. It was a completely ridiculous but plausible thought. Jean found the unfortunate freshman, the willowy boy who insisted on using abstract terms, like freedom, when arguing with Telema. Who insisted that sweatshops gave jobs to previously jobless people. Whose sole criteria for a country's health was its GDP. They had nicknamed him the Quiet American. Jean watched him walk between the chairs, alone, a perfect target.

But she did not go for her purse. Instead, Telema put her head on the lectern and cried.

After class let out two hours and twenty minutes early, Jean had nowhere to go. She had hoped to catch Telema in the empty auditorium, as she stuffed her papers back into her black purse, literally stuffing the report in handfuls. She threw Jean a look of absolute contempt, as if Jean herself had orchestrated those Guatemalan deaths from her private beach. Jean sat, her sole audience, as Telema made a dramatic exit.

She went, then, to the bar Telema had introduced her to, hoping to run into her.

Jean ordered an Irish coffee, to maintain the semblance of normalcy and to push her hangover back a few more hours. There was no reason, she told herself, for Telema to be angry with her. It was the first day of the relationship, the first hours, really, and Jean hadn't even had time yet to screw it up. Nothing had changed since the night before, nothing but Jean's understanding of it. She flipped through her copy of the report, which she set on the bar in front of her, finding again the definitions of genocide.

Forcibly transferring children of the group to another group.

"She acts like our country's some great evil, stomping around destroying everything, but she still lives and works here," one of the boys at the bar said. "She seems to be quite comfortable with the privilege of being here."

No one in the group was familiar to Jean, but that didn't mean anything.

"If she has a problem with how we do things, she should leave."

It sounded, for a moment, like a rally, people working themselves up with beer and indignation, to run someone out of town. But these kids didn't have it in them. The comment was met with embarrassed silence. The girl who'd just spoken stared into her beer.

"Did you see her crying? She would've been the perfect subject for the panel discussion."

"That was the best! How long did she sit there waiting for it to start?"

"Twenty-five minutes!"

They all laughed and finished their beers, ordered more.

"Is self-hatred the only way we can be saved?" another boy asked seriously. "Because that's all I've learned in that class. Self-hatred. If I wrote my final paper on everything I hated about myself, I'd get an A."

"'Lost Little Girls.'" One of the boys giggled. "'The Myth of White Innocence in Everything Bad That Has Ever Happened to Everybody.'"

"No, no," a girl corrected him, "'Lost Little Girls: America's White College Coeds and My Goal to Seduce All of Them.'"

The students laughed, their eyes popping out at one another. Jean, in her head, argued with Telema, with the United Nations. Define forcible. War, she supposed, qualified as forcible, but so did poverty. So did death and illness. All these horrible things, forced on baby Maya, and Jean was wrong to help? Doing nothing, it seemed, was the new humanitarianism. In another twenty years, it'd flip again, and the people who did nothing would be implicated. The perfect business model for these peddlers of guilt.

Jean took two copies of the Historical Clarification report home. That evening, she overnighted her extra copy to her parents without a note, just highlights on the rule of Ríos Montt. She wanted them to see what their hundred-dollar donation had bought. The package would arrive two days before she did, for their Spring Break visit.

~~~~~

By late morning the volcano hike was over and Maya offered no protest when Jean suggested they try the shack for lunch. They showered first at the hotel in the tiny, flaking bathroom without hot water. Jean watched the water run black, then gray, then clear, off her body. In thirty seconds, she was clean. Then Maya took her turn.

The proprietor was fussing in their room when Jean returned. More red paint had appeared on the outside wall sometime during the night and Jean suspected she did not yet know. With zest, she ripped the sheets off the bed for washing, while Jean clutched her towel, making a puddle on the floor. Maya's sheets and the mattress beneath showed a large urine stain.

"I'm sorry," Jean managed. Bed-wetting, at fifteen? A small, creeping devastation took root in her mind. She knew it would only grow over the course of the day, the week. "She's had so many of those banana drinks. I guess too many, too late in the day."

"It's okay. I know children. I have two," she reported, bunching the sheets. "Two boys her age."

"Oh?" Jean knew she sounded surprised, relieved. Whatever her failures as a mother, Jean knew they probably paled in comparison to this strange woman's. How big was this hotel, that she'd missed two teenage boys? Possibly the proprietor kept them locked in a room. Jean felt slightly better, feeling sorry for those two kids. "Are they around? I think Maya would enjoy some other kids to keep her company."

"Wonderful!" The proprietor's creased face lit up like an old paper lantern. "They're good boys. They would love to meet your daughter. They get lonely in the hotel."

Then the proprietor handed Jean another letter to mail.

Jean politely put the envelope in her bag without looking at it. If these boys were handsome, Jean thought, maybe Maya would forget about Brett for a while. And the man in the suit.

At the end of the hall, the shower stopped. Jean leaned through the doorway to see this man waiting outside the bathroom.

"I see there's another guest in the hotel," she tried. "The man in the suit. Do you know him?" Jean kept one eye on the hall, ready to confront him if he touched Maya.

"He is an important guest. You must not disturb him."

"Are we disturbing him?"

"Your daughter. She follows him, upstairs, downstairs." She frowned at Jean. "She makes him uncomfortable."

"How is he important?"

"You see his suit? He is an American here on business."

"Business in Xela?"

"Of course." She sighed, hugging the dirty sheets. "There is too much business here now with the Americans. This business of truth."

The bathroom door opened. Jean watched the suit slide in and push Maya out. "Over an hour, it's been!" The dead bolt slammed and Maya stood at the door, listening, making a face. Jean checked her watch, knowing he was right. She and Maya had been monopolizing the bathroom for some time.

"Poor guy," Maya said, dripping a trail back to Jean. "I told him not to have so many of those banana drinks. He drank, like, five yesterday."

The restaurant was made completely of corrugated tin sheets, apparently balanced like a house of cards. No floor, no windows, no menus, no waitresses. Maya collapsed into a flimsy plastic chair with an air of determined remoteness, wanting nothing to do with this class of people. She opened the Spanish translation book and briefly focused her attention there. Jean cast a long look around, wondering if to wet the bed at the age of fifteen was less fucked up than openly stalking a grown man around an empty hotel.

"Why does that lady keep giving you letters?" Maya asked, pointing to the envelope in Jean's purse.

"I don't know. Maybe she's too busy to mail them herself."

"She's not busy. She was sitting in the courtyard at four in the morning. Sitting there like a dead person. We passed her when we left for the hike and you didn't even see. I almost screamed. Who's she writing letters to?"

Jean took the envelope out of her bag. "This one's to Kofi Annan."

Maya laughed at the name. "Who's that?"

"*Yanqui,*" someone hissed from across the room. "Hey, *¡yanqui!*"

Women without men and men without women filled the restaurant quickly. The women silently distributed plates with one eye, it seemed, on Jean and Maya. All customers would eat what was given, and Jean felt the success of the volcano summit draining away a bit more.

"*¡Yanqui!*"

Jean opened the guidebook and turned deliberately from her purse: *The natives are generally polite. Any rudeness toward Americans usually comes from a basic jealousy of their bigger, wealthier northern neighbor. Be polite,*

never lose your temper, and if all else fails, smile and merely pretend you do
not understand.

Jealousy! Of course, the lost guidebook was much better, written later. Nevertheless, Jean sat back, practicing a smile of good-natured confusion. She aimed it at the women, hoping for some sympathy.

"Mom, I just remembered we forgot our bags."

"What?"

"The trash bags. We all slid down the volcano so fast, we forgot to pick up the trash bags."

"Oh my. I guess we did." She began fanning at her face, spreading herself out in her chair. The cold morning turning rapidly hot. A hot flash?

"Pssst. *¡Yanqui!*"

Jean smiled and smiled. A Mayan woman appeared with two full paper plates.

"*Hola.*" Jean smiled at the woman. "*¿Tienen comida vegetariana?*"

The woman set the plates down and left, walking stiffly away in her patterned skirt.

"Should we go back, Mom? Do you think the guide would take us to get them?"

"We'd have to wait until the next tour next week, and we'll be gone by then, to the ruins at Tikal."

"Can you call the guide and tell him, at least? Maybe he can go get them."

"I'll do that, yes." But there was no number. There had been no reservations, no contact information on the flyer. They had just shown up at the designated crossroads and paid one hundred quetzales each. Nothing to do about it now. Possibly the next group would collect the bags on their way down. She had more important things to worry about. Jean took a map from her purse and opened it. Nueva Aldea de la Vida lay less than a hundred miles outside the city. She looked up the English translation, New Life Village.

"Mom, what's jaundice?"

"It means your skin's turned yellow because of unfiltered bile in your blood."

Jean sat, calculating the hours and mileage. Two hours by bus. But what would she do once she got there? Even if this Cruzita had survived the war, she most certainly wouldn't be able to converse—Jean doubted she knew English, or even Spanish.

"*¡Yanqui, yanqui!*"

"What's that guy's problem?" Maya lifted her face above the Spanish translation dictionary to give the man a withering, adolescent look of contempt.

"Just ignore him, Maya." Jean paged through the guidebook: *Outside of major towns, armed robbery of tourists is not uncommon. If anyone approaches you with a weapon, give whatever they ask for without hesitation. They will shoot. Avoid empty roads and towns without tourist services, but also be alert on well-worn routes. Packed tourist buses are also targets for recently disbanded guerrilla groups. Armed guerrillas have stopped buses to Tikal, checked passports, robbed only the Americans, then lectured the traumatized tourists on imperialism.*

"What's a cranial laceration?"

Jean looked up. "Maya, what are you reading?" She reached across the table. The medical records from the orphanage. "You stole this?"

"They're *my* records. *They've* been stolen from *me*."

Jean studied the paper, saw where Maya had made careful notes with the help of the dictionary. "Maya."

"What? Isn't this why we came here in the first place? To see these dumb papers? You didn't even read this one! So I ask you again, what is a cranial laceration?"

She'd find out anyway, once she had an English dictionary. At least this way Jean could maintain some control of the information. "A laceration is a deep cut. A cranial laceration is a cut on your cranium. Your skull."

"How did I get a cut on my skull?"

"I don't know."

"Did I need stitches?"

"Yes."

"Where? Where was the cut? Did you see it?"

"On the top of your head." Jean pointed to her own scalp, making a line near the back. "Here. It's not even visible now, Maya. Your hair covers it. You didn't even know it was there." Which was true. The scar was so faint, so hidden by Maya's thick hair, that Jean suspected her imagination in the moments when she thought she could detect it.

"Was it bad?"

Jean decided on half-truth. "It was mostly healed when I got you. I only saw the scar. Just a little scar, Maya. I knew a girl in graduate school who had a baby and he had a cut, too, on his head. From a cesarean section. That means he had to be cut out of his mother's belly. It's very common. The doctor just slipped a little bit. It wasn't a big deal. Just a little cut that healed and his hair grew in and no one ever saw it."

"So you think I was born that way? Cesarean?"

"Probably," Jean lied. God, she hadn't meant to.

Maya accepted this explanation with a nod, closed the translation book, and poked at her plate with her plastic fork. "Is this vegetarian?"

Jean inspected their lunches, tortillas and beans with ambiguous green flecks that could never be accused of being meat. "It's okay. These people can't afford meat."

Maya ate a few bites, chewing, thinking. She touched the top of her head tenderly. People were staring at Maya and Jean with side glances while they ate. Jean became so self-conscious that she did not notice the NGO from the hotel until one of the women handed him a plate.

"Hello," Jean said when he walked by with his lunch.

He squinted at her. Rays of mock disapproval appeared around his mouth.

"Hello, tourist," he said.

"Join us?" Jean asked, hoping for a happier conversation. Maya always perked up with a male audience.

But he only laughed. "Oh no. It's not good for business, talking to you." He stood, chewing his meal rapidly like a rabbit. His eyes focused off to the sides, at their audience. Attentive, ready to bolt. Forking, chewing, swallowing all at once.

"We don't have to talk," she said, too flirtatiously. She merely wanted to know who he was and why the proprietor did not want him in her hotel. A slight movement caught his eye and he noticed, for the first time, Maya. He looked from daughter to mother, twice.

"I don't like to linger," he said. "Anyway, a tourist doesn't want to be seen with me. The wildlife will run away from you. Your film will come back all blurs."

Jean stared at him, trying to get his meaning.

"Mom."

She turned to her daughter, paused mid-chew, her mouth open and her tongue pushing chewed food out onto the table. Her hands up and waving frantically around her face.

"What's the matter with you? Stop it! Maya!"

Maya cried and pointed down at her plate, to the beans cleared away to reveal a pig's tail. Curled, pink, and fetal. Maya wailed, spitting and making a scene. The NGO slipped away and the entire restaurant stopped.

"Murderers! They're all murderers!" Maya cried, lurching forward like she might vomit. "Baby pigs, mama pigs, whole pig families! Murdered!"

"Maya, calm down," Jean hissed, trying not to add to the hysteria. "Use your napkin. Just spit it out in your napkin. Don't offend these people. Don't." Before she knew what she was doing, she grabbed Maya's wrist, hard, to still her. "Don't make a spectacle of yourself. We must be careful," she pleaded, but her daughter wailed, spit, and sucked helplessly at the air with the fury of an infant. "People stare at us constantly, Maya. Please don't make a scene, please don't give them any more reason to stare."

It was not a proper market day, but many vendors still sold on the streets. Fruit and masks, packaged bread and masks, fabric and masks, Fritos and masks. Jean did not recall seeing the painted masks at the market before, but now they hung everywhere, and Jean had the odd feeling they'd been put out for their benefit alone.

"Do you want a mask?" Jean asked Maya, who wandered among the stands and fingered some, noncommittally. All colorful animal faces, clashing in the rising wind of an approaching rainy season storm. Jean watched her daughter closely, afraid she might try to steal from these impoverished people. Afraid of so many things, suddenly.

"I'll buy you anything you want," she said, each time Maya paused.

Although the scene in the restaurant had been horrible and embarrassing, Jean felt more disturbed by her own reaction to it. During Maya's tantrum, she had seen the screaming, scarred infant in the orphanage photo. She had seen pain and helplessness, but still she had handled Maya roughly. Just reached out, grabbed her, shook her. Why? For once, she had not been afraid of Maya, but of all the Mayan people around them. Jean could not even guess what she thought they would do.

But still, Jean glimpsed progress in the scene. No fits, no accusations—at least none directed at her. She was thankful to be somewhat spared today. The tantrums were becoming rarer, but not easier. In fact, they made up for their infrequency with their severity. The last tantrum, the only one that summer, had been the most terrifying. It had taken place at home, the day Jean announced the trip to Guatemala. She presented the tickets, a surprise, not realizing Maya would miss the last two weeks of summer flag line training.

Maya brooded the rest of the day, bemoaning the unlearned drills, the lost time with her friends and Brett. Grilling portobello mushroom burgers on the deck, Jean went inside for a butter knife for the mustard. On her way out, Maya had rushed past her, on her way in, and bumped against her. Jean had stiffened, knife in hand, expecting the fall and the scream, but nothing happened. Maya disappeared inside. But then she came back out again, slowly, holding her arms crossed in front of her. She walked up to Jean and uncrossed her arms. There, on the tender undersides of her forearms, she had squeezed ketchup. A bright red line of gore that ended in a splatter where the bottle had given out.

Maya did not scream or throw herself to the ground. It was not an actual fit, more like a fit of the mind. She held her arms out for Jean to see and said in her martyred voice, "You cut me."

They left the market by a narrow side street confined by high, dilapidated walls. The vagrants they passed maintained a silent dignity. Women, in their flowered costumes, crossed their path purposefully, like swooping birds. Maya lingered behind, bumping into walls, shuffling her feet in protest of this tour.

Jean powered on, thinking if she lost Maya in these back streets, maybe the girl would finally understand. She would panic and sob and realize where she would be without her mother. She'd be grateful, for once. It was a cruel idea, pounding in Jean's chest, compelling her to break into a run. She searched out dark alleys and sharp turns she could just disappear into. She imagined herself running and Maya not able to keep up in her flip-flops.

Less than a block away, Jean spied a dark figure crossing ahead of them. There and gone in five steps across the alley. Like Jean's own shadow preceding her. It had not been brightly colored, like the Mayan women. It had been tiny and dark, like a dancer cutting across a stage. Out one door and into another. The piled black hair, the long scarf trailing behind like a tail. Telema.

Jean froze. "Did you see that, Maya?"

"See what?"

"Did you see someone cross just now, in front of us?"

"I didn't see anyone," she said, touching her scalp through her hair. The gesture had become obsessive by now, unconscious. "Can we go back to the hotel? It's going to rain."

"Sure, Maya. Did I mention there are teenagers at the hotel? Maybe we can go back and meet them. Two boys your age."

She perked up, lifting her face into a gust of wind. "Are they cute?"

~~~~~

Their flight to Jean's parents' house in Iowa left two days after Telema's ten-minute-long class. Jean had not been able to say goodbye, had not been able to find her anywhere. She had no idea where they now stood. They had been a couple for less than twelve hours and already Jean had managed to do something unforgivable. Had she said something insensitive while drunk? Jean could see that. Telema waving a loaded gun around, then becoming upset at Jean for a poorly chosen word.

Jean's mother, her face gleaming with age-defying lotion, greeted them when they pulled up in the rental car.

"Oh, Maya!" She bent to hug her granddaughter. "Dinner's ready, and I made it without meat. Just for you!"

Inside, it smelled like every meal her mother had ever cooked, very much like meat. Jean's father presided in the living room in his overstuffed recliner. "How are you, Dad?"

"Starving!" he gasped dryly, maybe the first word he had uttered in days. "And I'm not going to graze in the backyard like a rabbit."

The drama stemmed from Maya, who found it upsetting if people ate meat in her presence. Or even if she saw leftover meat in the fridge. Jean told her mother repeatedly over the phone to just ignore the fuss, to eat whatever they wanted. But this was her offering to her granddaughter now. Everyone would sit around the same table and eat a vegetarian meal. But Jean knew right away that her father would only move from his recliner for what he believed to be a proper meal.

Once the three women sat down to dinner, the smell of the house finally made sense to Jean. Her mother had made a pot roast, minus the meat. Not minus, exactly. As the vegetables and mashed potatoes and gravy made their way around the table, it became clear to Jean that her mother had literally cooked everything with the roast, had even made a gravy from the drippings, and had merely hid the meat away at the last minute. It was also clear that she had no inkling this wasn't a vegetarian meal.

Maya, of course, had no idea. She ate the fat-glazed carrots and the smooth gravy happily, seeing no objectionable chunks. "This is fantastic!"

"Sweetheart"—Jean's mother beamed across the table—"how's school? Do you have a boyfriend?" She perpetually feared that, raised by Jean, her granddaughter would grow up to be "warped" like her mother. For this, she bizarrely, relentlessly encouraged Maya's involvement with boys. Clearly, to be knocked up at the age of fifteen was preferable to being a successful, educated lesbian.

"Yes! His name is Brett."

"And what does Brett do?"

"He plays football and basketball."

"Oh!" Jean's mother clapped. Her heart-shaped, lopsided face looked like a Valentine made by a child. "He sounds wonderful! Good for you!" She smiled and smiled, beaming with the certainty that her granddaughter's boyfriend was popular and handsome.

After the fake vegetarian dinner, they all watched television together. In front of the screen, Jean, for the first time, forgot Telema. It was nice, for once, not to think at all. *Jeopardy!* turned out to be the only show the adults could all agree upon.

Jean's mother braided Maya's hair during the show. With surprising deftness in her elderly fingers, she wove circles around Maya's head. "You're going to look like an Indian princess, Maya. Just like that Disney movie."

Jean closed her eyes and counted to ten, remembering the therapist's recent advice. Of course, Maya would never accuse her grandmother of being a racist, though she had disapproved of Jean adopting Maya in the first place. Interracial adoption was unnatural, she argued. *Those children need to be raised by their own.* Funny. Jean never imagined Telema and her mother could ever be in agreement on anything.

"A princess with lipstick?" Maya asked.

"Oh, I think I can spare some lipstick."

"I wasn't allowed to wear lipstick until I was seventeen," Jean observed calmly. She had only reached the number five in counting.

Maya crushed her palms into her mouth and laughed hysterically through her nose. "Mom says lipstick is meant to make your face look like your private parts!"

Everyone turned to stare at Jean. Her mother, mid-twist, her father mid-rock in his recliner. Eyes wide with scandalized amazement. Who was this daughter of theirs?

Maya patted the sculpted black crown of her hair cautiously, trying to discern its dimensions. "How does it look?"

"It's beautiful, Maya," Jean said, just as her mother appeared with a can of Aqua Net and unloaded it with a toxic hiss from a safe distance.

"If you like it, I can do it just like this when you go to prom in a few years."

"You'd come all the way to California to do my hair for prom?"

"Of course, Maya. Prom's the best night of a girl's life. I wouldn't miss it for the world. Now sleep carefully tonight and it will be just as beautiful in the morning!"

After Maya went to bed, Jean slipped into the basement to drink from a fifth of whiskey she'd hidden among old Christmas decorations. She knew she'd need it at some point. Her father, coming down to the basement refrigerator to gnaw on the hidden pot roast, caught her.

"Be easy on your mother," he told her, chewing on a hunk he'd ripped away with his hands. "She has a weak heart, you know."

"I know, Dad."

"Her pacemaker's going to need a new battery after you leave. It always does."

"What the hell does that mean? That's not how pacemakers work."

"*I* know how your mother's heart works, Jean. And I know it's weak from loving you so much, despite everything. You have no idea. She tries and tries. She'd rather starve me than give you an ounce of trouble."

They stared at each other in the dark, by the light of the open fridge. Jean sipped from the bottle and he chewed his meat, neither caring what the other thought.

~~~~~

When Jean asked Maya what she wanted to do for the rest of the day, she said she'd like to read her magazine at the hotel and meet the proprietor's sons. Jean allowed it, no longer fearing the man in the suit. It must be difficult, Jean realized, to be a man alone. Everyone skeptical of your intentions with the children. Why was it that everyone, even Jean, always thought the worst? Anyway, there were other things to worry about now. The suit faded into irrelevance. Telema had landed in Xela, and Jean had to keep her away from Maya. The hotel now became the best place for her daughter.

Jean took the opportunity to tour Xela alone, without the pauses, the stares that she received when walking with Maya, which made her feel as if she had committed some great wrong. Alone, in her khaki shorts and YWCA T-shirt—the outfit she'd packed in her carry-on—she could be one of the NGO workers. She walked among the Maya in sacrificial deference, her head low and her eyes averted in guilt. Almost wanting someone to steal her purse, she held it loose and low—reparation no one would take.

During their various shopping sprees, none of the Mayan crafts had appealed to Maya, and for that Jean was thankful, for she didn't have the heart to bargain with these women wearing shoes made out of tires. The guidebook said to offer half of what they asked, but Jean could not deny these people their price. She watched the man in the suit, just yards away, bargaining hard for a cornhusk doll dressed in tiny Mayan clothes. For a daughter? A wife? He looked lonely to Jean now, instead of depraved. He looked familiar.

The woman held out ten fingers, but he held out five. She shook her head and held up seven fingers, he answered with three.

The proprietor had confirmed his business with the Truth Commission: A lawyer? A desk NGO? He was able to get his doll for one quetzal.

Jean hadn't the heart for bargaining, but it didn't matter. She toured the market and the women shouted numbers at her anyway. When Jean shook her head, they began the bargaining themselves, yelling ever-decreasing prices at her back. A few of the women became angry, their prices increasing as Jean walked away.

Navigating through the first raindrops of the afternoon storm, Jean felt herself drawn to the knives—small, fixed blades with orange-stained leather hilts in the shapes of animals. She picked up one that was cut into a bird, with a green stone glued on for an eye and a long, curved tail signified by the blade. A quetzal. It did not have a red breast. Instead, a groove ran from the tip of the blade to the hilt, where the breast connected with the blade.

"How much?" she asked the woman, who was packing up to flee the rain.

"Seventy quetzales."

"Okay."

"No. Two hundred quetzales."

Jean smiled, as if she didn't understand. "Okay."

The suit had moved on and Jean caught him a small distance away, snapping a photo in her direction. He snapped a few photos, taking his time, like a tourist. She spun around, befuddled. No, she told herself, he was taking a picture of the beautiful church behind her.

Jean found the alley where she thought she'd seen the professor. If Telema was here, it had to be for her volcano research. Or the sexual savage. Were they separate books? Either way, she could think of no reason Telema would be following her. No reason at all.

Telema had come out of the government offices, a back exit. Jean entered the same door to escape the rain and eventually found herself in the front lobby. Remembering the letter to Kofi Annan in her purse, she pushed it in the slotted mouth, then considered the scene around her. The front desk, manned by an NGO, serviced a long line of NGOs and Guatemalans. Jean joined the line and waited, listening to the storm batter the roof.

"Records request?" the polo shirt asked her when her turn came.

"Uh," Jean stammered, "not exactly."

"This is the records request line," he informed her impatiently.

"Well, I'm looking for someone."

"The missing persons line is over there," he said, pointing.

"No, no. I mean, someone who was just here this afternoon. I was wondering if you saw her. A woman in black, with her hair up in a scarf?"

The NGO straightened. "You know her?" He called over to the woman manning the missing persons line. "She says she knows that woman with the black scarf."

"I don't know her, really," Jean lied. She sensed Telema tugging at her again, after all these months, involving her in something. "I just saw her running out of here an hour or so ago. I thought I recognized her from somewhere, but I don't think so."

"Where was she running? Did you see where she went?" The woman stopped her line and stepped out from behind her counter.

"Out the back, in the alley. She ran out the alley door."

"We really have to start making sure that door is locked." The records request man sighed. "This is the third theft this week."

"Theft? She stole something?"

"And we should start locking the reading room. Just lock them in there with their records requests."

"Yeah," the missing persons woman agreed as her line twitched and fidgeted. "How's there to be truth and reconciliation if people keep stealing the records? I'm sure they have fine motives, but a single record can be tied to thousands of cases! And now, gone. One case solved, three thousand tied up forever."

"Listen, if you run into this woman, you tell her that. You tell her she's obstructing justice, which is a crime," the records request man expounded from behind his counter. "You tell her to bring that folder back! She has to sit in the room and read it like everyone else. Who does she think she is?"

"I don't know," Jean said. "What did she steal?"

"You know, you're the third person today to come asking that."

"I guess it's not that important," the missing persons woman said, stepping back to her line. "It was records from before the war. Way before the war. No one asks for that far back. I think the folder was still sealed. No one had looked at it ever before."

"But still," the man argued, "it's the principle! You never know how things are connected, you just never know! That file could have been everything!"

The woman beckoned her missing persons line into motion again. An old Mayan woman stepped up, holding a photo, ripped in half. "It could have also been nothing, though." She turned, startled at the picture being pushed into her face. Two halves coming together. "Now, who do we have here?"

"So she came in to read some records and she ran out with them?" Jean asked. "What records?"

"Oh, I have no idea," the man said. "Like we said, they were still sealed. It was from 1902. Police records." Jean exhaled in relief. Telema was here, doing her own research. About 1902, the volcano, Evie Crowder. She had really expected the man to say she'd stolen records from 1983.

"Do you have records on people?" Jean asked the man, realizing what line she was in. She eyed the impatient people behind her, but didn't care.

"Yeah. Police records, military, government, tax, and criminal records. Death records, missing persons reports. Who are you looking for?"

"A woman named Cruzita Sola Durante."

The man typed the name into his computer. It was incredible, these NGOs. The chaos, the displacement of millions of people over forty years, and now an indigenous woman could be found by typing her name into a computer. *Here's her address*, the man would say. Or, *She was exhumed from this mass grave three years ago.*

"I'm sorry," he said. "I'm not getting anything."

"Is that good or bad?"

"Well, I'd say it's hopeful. She hasn't been reported missing, or identified in any of the graves yet."

Jean showed the man the door Telema had escaped from, wondering if she should have given him Maya's name to search instead of Cruzita's. María Tierra López. She stepped through the threshold and turned to ask, but he'd already closed the door, leaving her in the bruised, post-storm air, in the alley from which she had come. She heard the sound of the key turning on the other side.

~~~~~

After Jean's father finally went to bed, Jean and her mother sat alone. This was how it always went on these visits. This was when her mother kneaded the loose skin beneath her eyes and talked about what was bothering her. Usually something she'd heard from a preacher about how the Antichrist would be a half-human, half-dolphin hybrid made by "scientists," or how a fallen building from a California earthquake looked just like a fetus in an aerial photo. She inhabited a world of paranoid nonsense, instilled by the blue flicker of late-night religious television. The Christian Broadcasting Network saved the hard stuff for these vulnerable hours, sparing insomniacs from the threat of self-reflection.

While flipping channels, her mother finally said, "Jean, I'm worried."

What would it be this time? Surely not any of the real atrocities going on in the world. Kosovo, the Rwandan trials, the lingering devastation of Hurricane Mitch. Maybe the year 2000 worried her. Jean had seen bottled water stockpiled in the basement.

"What is it, Mom?"

"I'm worried about this trip to Guatemala. I don't think you should take Maya."

The simplicity of this worry, its relation to an actual event, struck Jean, even as she disregarded it. She'd made a mistake telling her parents about the trip so soon, before she'd even told Maya. "I know you're worried, Mom. But you were also worried when I went to college, when I went to Mexico, when I went to Africa, even Europe. You were worried when I moved to California, because of sharks in the ocean. You are worried about bears when I go hiking on an island where there are no bears."

"Oh, Jean." Her mother sighed with the tedium of these visits already. Jean knew how she sounded when she came here. Paragraphs rolling off her tongue, increasing in speed and volume. But what they didn't notice were the passes she gave them. Her mother had no idea what she'd held back with the vegetarian dinner, the derogatory "Indian princess" reference, or the ridiculous talk about high school boys with Maya, the prom comment. To her, Jean fought everything, when in fact she fought less than half the time.

"What is it, Mom? What's worrying you about this trip? Other than flying, the fact that it's a foreign country, that the people there are poor and brown?"

"Oh, Jean." Her mother shook her head. "I know it's easy for you, but you have to think of Maya now."

"I am thinking of Maya," Jean insisted. "I'm doing it all for her!" On the television, the late-night rerun of *The 700 Club* began. Music, lasers, pictures of saved brown people abroad, waving. Jean took the remote and muted it. "What it is, Mom? Can you even name what you're worried about?"

"I have a feeling, Jean. I just do. God spoke to me and said you shouldn't go."

"Why not? Did God give a reason?"

"He didn't speak, exactly. He gave me a vision."

"A vision. A vision of what?"

"It doesn't matter, Jean. What matters is the message that you shouldn't go!"

"What are you afraid of, Mother? What did you see? The oceans boiling, the sky rolling up?"

"What I saw wasn't like that, it was just you. But you were different."

"Tell me! Name it! What are you afraid of?"

"The guerrillas!" her mother cried, pounding the couch with a weak fist. "I'm worried about the guerrillas!"

The word, the clarity and brevity, shocked Jean. Her mother cried, and the television light reflected off the tear trails, making it look like the blue lasers were on her face.

"The guerrillas," Jean repeated skeptically.

"Don't act like this isn't a real worry, Jean! A few years ago, they were all over the television. All the news stations covered it."

"Mom, did you even read the report I sent to you a few days ago? The report about Guatemala's war?"

"I looked at it. I don't know. I don't know why you send things you know we can't read."

"I highlighted the section for you. Did you even look? Where is it now?"

Lost, thrown away. Her mother shrugged.

"The report says that the guerrillas were fighting a genocidal government. The guerrillas were right. Reagan was funding and arming genocide."

Jean watched the furious blush of patriotism take hold of her mother. "Reagan was the most honorable man to ever lead this country! He defeated communism!" She placed her hand on her heart. Jean wanted to laugh, but then realized this was not a patriotic gesture.

Jean spoke carefully, in a calm voice. "Mother, Reagan did not defeat communism. Communism defeated itself. Reagan defeated hundreds of thousands of shoeless Central American peasants with helicopters. Armed American helicopters."

"This report. Who wrote it? You, Jean, have the bad habit of believing everything you read."

"And you believe everything you see on television!"

"You're always telling me about people being biased. Pat Robertson is biased, Pastor Wayne is biased, the Bible is biased. But you never seem to consider that the things you read are. Ever since you went to that liberal college—"

"It wasn't a liberal college, Mom. It was liberal arts. That has nothing to do with politics. It means you're supposed to come out well-rounded. Not political."

"But everyone who goes there comes out a liberal. How can you say that's not political?"

They'd had this conversation, too, a few times. The difference between education and indoctrination. Education, reeducation. On the screen, Pat Robertson prayed with raised fists.

"And you're saying the money you gave a Guatemalan dictator wasn't political?"

"I gave money to Operation Open Arms," her mother said, straightening. "A humanitarian organization."

"Operation Open Arms was a major artery of cash flow to that government, Mom!"

"You didn't say who wrote the report, Jean."

"The UN."

"Oh!" Her mother threw her hands up and threw herself back into the couch cushions. "The UN! Well, that explains everything."

"Whatever could you have against the UN, Mom? Do you even know anything about the UN?"

"I know they let China have a say. A veto, even! They let China have a big say in what goes on in the world! You claim to care so much about people, what about China?"

"We aren't talking about China, we're talking about Guatemala. You gave a hundred dollars to a dictator to murder people!"

"I did not! I gave a hundred dollars for food and diapers. Corn mix, actually. Those people really like corn, the pamphlet said. You can't kill people with food and diapers, Jean." Her hand went again to her heart. But Jean would not give her an out so easily. The gesture enraged her. No one else in the world could duck the truth so easily.

"You marked a box on a piece of paper and you really think that's where your money went?"

"God spoke to me when I saw that footage, Jean. I was sitting up late at night. I just saw the footage of those big-eyed children and God spoke to me. God is not wrong."

"God did not speak to you, Mother. That was you. You heard yourself, your conscience, which is not infallible. I heard a voice when I saw those pictures, too. It's me. It's my thoughts. My conscience. Not God."

Her mother became defensive, hugging a pillow to her chest, her face shaking with disapproval. "I believe that. You've shut God out. How could you hear Him? How can you hear Him when you're drinking? When you spend all your time shouting at people?"

Just a few nips of whiskey. Her mother smelled it on her, thought she was drunk.

"Mom, that dictator, those soldiers you funded, massacred entire towns. They've found mass graves filled with women and children. Beaten and tortured. Over four hundred villages destroyed in seventeen months!"

Her mother's face spasmed into horror, real worry, but not at what Jean had hoped. "Why, Imogene?" she gasped. "What is the matter with you? Why are you so obsessed with such horrible things?"

"Because I want them to stop!"

"But you don't even know what happened. You just read that paper—"

"Clinton apologized. Our government has even recognized the report, recognized that our military trained Guatemalan soldiers to kill, to maim, to psychologically terrorize the population. He apologized to Guatemala."

"Oh, so now Clinton is our moral compass?"

That was it. Jean reached over and grabbed the pillow from her mother. They struggled a moment, push and pull, until Jean wrenched it away and threw it across the room. "I don't care if Clinton got a blow job! Are you hearing me!" she screamed.

"Jean!"

"Killing children, Mom. Raping them, gutting them, bashing their heads against trees!" She got the disturbing urge to grab her mother by the hair, to shake her, to throw her on the floor. Instead she grabbed her own hair and pulled it down over her ears. "You paid for that! Torturing families in front of each other, setting people on fire! It could have happened to Maya!"

At the mention of the name, both women turned automatically to the dim hallway, where the leggy shadow of Maya stood. In nothing but a T-shirt and underwear, she was unmistakable, and she had been there for a while.

"Oh, Maya." It was Jean's mother who said this, who went to her without hesitation. The thin shadow retreated back to the bedroom and Jean's mother followed.

Jean sat by herself, her brain pounding like a heart. It was always like this, always the same. She felt empty and defeated. On the television, Pat Robertson's talking head was accompanied by a phone number at the bottom of the screen. Jean grabbed the remote and turned him off.

She walked to her old bedroom and pressed an ear to the closed door.

"She screams at her family because she cares about people, sweetheart. I know it's hard to understand. It took me a long, long time to understand. She cares very deeply about faraway people she doesn't know."

"But what about us? How could she say that to you, Grandma?"

"I don't know, Maya. But I know she loves you very much."

"No, she doesn't," Maya sniveled dramatically. "She hates how I am, she hates my friends. She only cared about me when I was a baby in Guatemala."

"I know for a fact that's not true, Maya. Your mother loves you so much. You know, when she first told me she wanted to adopt a baby from Guatemala, I was against it. I'm ashamed of that, it was a weakness of mine, but now I'm so glad. I am so glad your mother went against my wishes. I didn't love you until I held you for the first time. I guess I'm simpler in that way, but in the end, we both love you just the same."

The next morning, Jean woke up late to find the house empty. Sunday. She knew right away what was going on. She had never allowed Maya to go to her parents' church, but they'd snuck out while Jean slept in.

They came back four hours later. Maya, strangely silent, walked very straight, as if her own body had become alien to her. The braided crown on her head tilted to one side, the shorter hairs around her ears floating loose. Jean knew Maya had agreed to go to church just to enrage her. When she asked, innocently, how it had gone, Maya said, "They brought me up front and Pastor Wayne put his hands around my head and prayed for my people to be delivered."

Jean could see it. She knew how Pastor Wayne prayed for people, wrapping his large hands around their heads and pulling them to his chest, like a basketball he was about to pass.

Within five minutes their bags were packed and Jean's mother and father crowded the front door, her mother begging them not to go, her father with both hands twisting his hearing aids on.

"I hate you," Jean spat, once Maya walked out of earshot.

"No, you don't." Her mother smiled in the open doorway. Her father waved to Maya and had not heard. Maya did not wave back. She merely let herself in the backseat of the rental car and closed the door, done with all of them.

This trip marked another change in Maya. She held herself differently after, as if she existed in a delicate bubble. She walked with caution, held herself straighter, as if she knew she'd been called to God's attention and He was now watching her. As if her actions spoke for her race and, based on what He saw, He would decide whether to deliver her people—eight million strangers in a strange country she had never visited.

Her daughter had had the weight of God thrust upon her. Jean knew exactly how it felt, and pitied her. Three days later, Maya's fits started up again, worse than ever. She threw herself to the ground, screaming the most bizarre accusation: *Dykes go to hell, you know that, Mom? Don't you care? Don't you care that I'll be stuck in heaven without you?*

~~~~~

More paint had appeared on the hotel wall, next to the blue hand. In addition to the red embellishments from the day before, a full red handprint had been stamped to the right of the blue hand, stamped with too much paint, then scraped down. Jean, for the first time, found the graffiti truly disturbing.

Maya was not at the pool. Jean ascended the stairs, but found their room empty. With panic rising in her chest, she jogged the halls, calling her name.

"Mom!" Maya appeared out of one of the empty rooms.

"What are you doing in there?"

"Hiding."

"Great, Maya. Thanks. You almost gave me a heart attack."

Checking both ways in the hall, Maya walked over and pulled Jean to their own room. "Not hiding from *you*. From the proprietor." Maya closed the door.

"Why are you hiding from her?"

"Because she's *fucking nuts*!"

"Language, Maya."

"She's convinced I'm going to marry one of her sons! All I did was ask where they were and she pulled me into her room and tried to get me to put on her old wedding dress!" Her face melted fearfully. "Where were you?"

"Did she hurt you? Are you okay?" She placed a hand on Maya's head, but she ducked under and away, out of reach.

"She didn't hurt me. She's really nice, it's horrible how nice she is. I don't think she's well," she concluded, maturely. "She just makes me feel so guilty, smiling at me, giving me things. *Where were you?*"

"I toured town. You said you didn't want to come. I'm sorry to have been gone so long." Jean sat down on her bed.

"That woman is crazy, but her sons are cute." Maya smiled to herself. "She showed me pictures. They're not here today, but she says I'm just their type."

"*Their* type? You plan on going on a date with both of them?"

"Maybe. Maybe to the vegetarian restaurant. They aren't vegetarians, though, she told me."

"What would Brett say?" Jean asked, too sarcastically.

Ignoring her, Maya strutted back and forth in their tiny room. Her shadow, on the wall, was enormous and pleasing to her. She watched herself, working herself up for something. Angry for Jean's long absence, her Brett blasphemy. She prepared herself, then said over her shoulder, "Your friend Telema came here while you were gone."

"What!" Jean leapt up. She did not catch herself in time. Maya grinned, enjoying her reaction. She'd figured out that much from the airport. "When was she here? Why?"

"She came to the meditation garden. The proprietor showed her in."

"What was she doing here?'

"I don't know. Maybe she was looking for a room. But I don't think she's staying here. She liked the meditation garden, though, she stayed for a while and we talked."

"You talked to her? What did you say? What did she say?" She'd been wrong. Telema had followed them here.

"Geez, Mom. You don't have to flip out. I thought she was your friend."

"She was. Is. She is my friend." Jean tried to calm herself. The worst had happened, but nothing had come of it. Why was Telema even here? Crossing in front of them, Telema had known they were in that alley. It was just how she would follow someone, by lingering in front instead of behind.

"She said she's here to research her book. She's trying to find out about a little girl who disappeared, like, a hundred years ago. An American girl in Xela who was abducted and raped by Indians!"

Jean crossed the small room, crossed back. Telema was stalking her, that was the word. They had to leave as soon as possible. "Maya—"

"It's okay, Mom. I know what rape is. I know all that stuff. They taught us about condoms in school, too. We put them on bananas."

Drink, Jean needed a drink. Alcohol first, then packing.

"But she says the little girl wasn't raped." That word again. "She wasn't raped or even taken by Indians. Her parents abandoned her, just left her and their debts to start a new life. Her dad was so sketchy and had all these money schemes going on and he just had to flee. So the parents abandoned the little girl and the government just sent her back to New York and completely made up her murder. It was a story the white power structure was always telling to keep people afraid of Indian men, to justify enslaving them. She called it a myth. The myth of the sexual savage!"

"So that's what you talked about? The myth of the sexual savage."

"Some. And other parts of her book. She wants to interview me for it."

Jean, very deliberately, said nothing. All of her energy went into her silence, so she didn't realize she'd grabbed Maya's suitcase and begun stuffing clothes inside.

"I told her I'd love to be in her book. She thinks I could have an entire chapter."

"An entire chapter? An entire chapter on what?" Jean tried to laugh it off.

"On me."

"What about you?" Jean spat, anger traveling to the far reaches of her body, making her flutter her fingers. She stuffed everything into one suitcase. She struggled to close the bulging mass, and was able to subdue it with a knee and slam the clasp down. "What would she write about you? About how your favorite place is the mall? How you're too cool to be interesting in any way? About your insipid friends, who'll get knocked up in a year? There's nothing to write about!" It all came out so quickly, so harshly. Jean sensed someone at the door, listening. She took deep breaths and counted, reassured herself. Her daughter was safe. On the bed, Maya cried discreetly into the pages of her magazine.

"You aren't going to be in her book, Maya," Jean said evenly, repentantly. There was no way to take it back, to even apologize for what she'd said, so instead she apologized for something else. "I'm sorry. I'm telling you that right now. You are a minor, I'm your parent. Legally, you need my approval."

"You aren't my real mother." She flipped a page and wiped a tear. "And it's too late anyway. She interviewed me already. She wrote everything down in her notebook."

"She interviewed you. About what? What did she ask you, Maya?"

"All kinds of questions. And she told me quite a few things, too. Like, I wasn't born by cesarean. People down here are too poor for that." Her hand went up to her scalp, tracing through her hair. "She said she could see it. She said it's a big scar!" Maya's face twisted in rage. "And you'd been gone for hours and hours and I just kept thinking of her book, and the little girl left behind by her parents. And I started to think you'd left me, too. Because you hate how I am! You think I'm dumb and you hate Brett. You hate Brett, but he's the only one who loves me! He loves me exactly how I am! And I know you'd rather find yourself another Guatemalan baby down here, to start over! I thought you'd left me with that crazy woman. She kept saying crazy things about me being her daughter, about one of her sons marrying me!"

"Maya." Jean tried to collect her daughter in her arms, but Maya melted through her grasp, collapsing into a heap on the bed. "I don't hate you, Maya. I love you so much. I'd never leave you, you know that. I just get so frustrated, and I say things I don't mean. Just like you say things you don't mean. We used to get along so well. Do you remember?"

She nodded with her face pressed against the mattress.

"And I don't hate Brett. I just think you invest too much in him because he's your first boyfriend. And I wish," she heard herself say, "you were half as excited to spend time with me as you are to spend time with him."

Maya turned her face up so that Jean saw her eyes peering out through her tangled hair. "And I wish you were as excited to be with me as Telema. But you were too embarrassed to even introduce me to her!"

Mother and daughter studied each other, as if from a great distance. Neither moved toward the other, neither moved away.

After careful consideration in the meditation garden, Jean wasn't sure if the best decision was to leave Xela or to stay and ignore Telema altogether. Jean suspected that to run would only provoke her more. It was too late for a bus anywhere safe or useful, so they stayed another night at the hotel. NGOs filled every other hotel in town.

Jean, however, could not sleep. As soon as she lay down, she just began to think. She could not stop the thoughts, ridiculous constructions of the past, the future. Maya and Telema drinking banana drinks at the pool with conspiratorial cackles, Maya as a fifteen-year-old bride, Telema accepting a Pulitzer for her groundbreaking work in Guatemala, for solving a hundred-year-old non-murder. A hundred-year-old Indian man—the sexual savage—released from prison, into the arms of the media, because no one else was left.

Telema's appearance at the hotel, her conversation with Maya about rape, the disturbed proprietor, the possibility of being under CIA surveillance— none of these things much surprised Jean. What she failed to process was Maya's belief that Jean would abandon her in Guatemala. She'd come to be- lieve this after speaking with Telema, of course. Why would Telema inter- view Maya in the first place? A whole chapter? What did Maya have to do with her book? Jean got the feeling her daughter would be made into some horrible anecdote, supporting evidence for some abstract, half-true theory.

Telema had followed them, this much was obvious. Why? She had broken up with Jean. But still, Telema was following her, though she claimed that she herself was being followed. The government goon. The black suit, the glasses at the airport. From that distance, he could have been any guy in a suit. He could have been the man at the hotel.

Jean had a vision—no, vision would be her mother's word—Jean dreamed of a parade trailing her across Guatemala. Jean followed by Maya, followed by Telema, followed by the suit. And Jean, all along, following the trail of Maya's records. The impulse to flee felt so strong, as strong as Jean's curios- ity. To finally be so close to Maya's story, just two hours away by bus, a story she never believed she could know.

Nueva Aldea de la Vida, at least, still existed. She'd seen a bus in the central square painted with the name. So, the town had survived the war. Had Cruzita? If so, the woman could offer a new beginning for Jean and Maya, a new love for them to share, instead of these insane, romantic competitions.

Jean, wearing the nightie from the stranger's suitcase, wrapped herself in a Mayan blanket and made her barefoot way over the chilled hotel tiles, down the steps, into the courtyard. She eased into the waxy hammock, hop- ing Maya would not wake up to find her gone. She needed air desperately.

"You know you'll get in trouble being down here with me." The voice came from a hedge on the courtyard's border. She knew exactly who it was.

"Don't worry, we won't get you in trouble. We're leaving tomorrow."

"It's probably for the best. Xela's not very pleasant at the moment."

"Why? What are you doing here?" she whispered, hearing footsteps somewhere.

"I'm an anthropologist with the Fact Finders."

Jean swung herself in the hammock. She had stopped trying to remem- ber the difference between all the NGOs.

"A forensic anthropologist."

A breeze moved over the courtyard. All around, the tall plants spoke among themselves. The man appeared, walking toward her. He, like her, hugged one of the Mayan blankets around his shoulders.

"It seems anthropologists are bad for business."

"Indeed, we are."

"Isn't it also bad for business to turn away customers?"

"Well, that depends on what kind of business you want." He sat down on one of the planters, bringing the musk of cheap marijuana with him. Was there a single sober American in this country? "If you want a bunch of NGOs reporting how horrible your country is to the world, and who'll be gone in a year—then, yes."

"Is there another option?" she asked.

"The business class prefers to take the long view. They want tourists. They want people to come and have a nice time and to hear nothing about the violence. Then they will go back and tell all their friends how lovely and cheap Guatemala is. Tourists beget more tourists. Anthropologists just beget dead bodies." He handed her the joint, mostly smoked and smoldering close to his fingers.

"But there aren't any tourists."

"There's you. You are the seed."

Jean smoked, blowing hard at the sky. She stared up at the stars for a moment, noticing them for the first time, appreciating them. They made patterns that weren't constellations. "So I'm it? I'm everything they've been waiting for?"

"For some of them, yes. For others, you're quite the opposite."

"And who do you agree with?" She pulled at the joint, then passed it back. When was the last time she'd smoked? Years ago, in one of the MFAs.

"I'm not here to agree with anyone. I'm just recording what I find," he said.

"And what have you found in Xela?"

"Something that is very bad for business. They know by the color of my shirt."

"Poor anthropologist," Jean teased. "No room at any of the inns."

"Exactly."

"So they've found some bodies?"

"Some isn't the term I'd use. Some are found all the time, no problem."

"How many?"

"At least fifty. All decapitated."

Jean breathed her own secondhand smoke sinking around her head. "Fuck."

"Well, I feel worse for the guy who finds all the heads and has to excavate them."

"You mean the heads aren't even there with the bodies?"

Jean already felt higher than she thought she'd be. She felt herself falling through various perspectives. Suddenly realizing she didn't understand anyone's motives.

"And why are you here?" the shirt asked her.

"I'm a tourist, remember?"

He nodded, unconvinced. "She loves tourists."

"*She* is fucking nuts. I don't even like the idea of leaving Maya alone upstairs."

"She's harmless, really. We all know her. She gets like this whenever we find a grave. It's quite horrible, actually. She lost her whole family in the war."

Jean sank deeper into the hammock, embarrassed. "She has two sons still. She's told me about them. They're here somewhere in the hotel."

"No, they aren't. She doesn't have anyone."

"How do you know? Did she testify to the commission?"

"Oh no, she'd have nothing to do with the commission, but the story came out anyway, from others who testified. From what the commission's put together, in 1982, she had two sons and a husband. Her oldest was sixteen. He was playing soccer one day in the central park and the army just came and scooped up all the boys for the military. Just gone. For six months, they heard nothing of him, then one day he showed up here. Filthy, starving. He'd deserted. She hid him in one of the rooms, but soon masked soldiers came looking for him, found him, brought him out in this courtyard, and shot him in the head for desertion. Then they shot her husband for trying to protect him. They left her and her younger son, who was about fourteen, to bury them."

"How awful." Jean took in the dark shapes of the courtyard, looming shadows like men. But the story was not finished.

"Then three days later, a group of guerrillas arrived with handkerchiefs over their faces, demanding that she turn over her older son. She tried to tell them that soldiers already came and killed him, but they didn't believe her. They see her younger son and think that's the older son. They bring him out into this courtyard and tell him that he is guilty of atrocities. That he's guilty of the army massacre at Lorotenango. They read off a formal charge. One hundred and fifty-two people massacred by his platoon. She keeps trying to explain that this is not her older son, but they just kept reading the charges. Read the names of one hundred and fifty-two people aloud. It takes them, like, fifteen minutes to do this. Then they shot him in the heart."

"How awful," Jean repeated. "That poor woman . . ." She trailed off.

"So you can understand she's not really well. But she's harmless. She just locked herself up for the rest of the war with a bunch of English-language tapes, planning for her business when it was all over. She takes tourism very seriously. She's had plenty of guests and she never hurts anyone. She just talks about her sons. And cries."

"She wants to set Maya up with them."

He crushed the joint into the floor tiles. "She tries to set them up with our local volunteers, too. It means she likes her. Don't be too disturbed by it. We're all used to it by now. I hated to be so mean the other day, but I needed the room. I'd walked miles, all over, before I came here. This place is always a last resort. I don't like to upset her."

Around the corner, the iron gate creaked open. They both rose, expecting to flee the proprietor like teenagers, but no one arrived in the courtyard. Together, they made their way down the hall and to the front entrance. Jean, still caped in her Mayan blanket, peered into the street. In the distance, the market loomed pale and empty in the moonlight, the cobblestone expanse looking like the back of a great, sleeping reptilian beast. Shadows collapsed in corners, looked vaguely human, vaguely dead. Jean thought she saw the cobblestones rise and fall, breathing.

No one appeared. Turning around, Jean saw that someone had made more red handprints on the hotel. They were everywhere, scraped down at all levels and angles, like the scene of a massacre.

"Election fun." The NGO sighed.

The hands were all the same size, the work of a single person. Small and delicate in a way that could not be hidden by the gore. A woman's, a child's? Jean put her own hand next to one of the prints. The same size. They were still wet. Stepping away, Jean collided with someone running around the corner. A bag dropped, and Jean felt the hand on her chest before she saw who it belonged to.

"Boo!"

Telema barked right in her face, smiling like a cat. Long shadows made her teeth looked sharpened. Jean felt the contrast of their expressions: horror met with laughter, fear met with bravery. Telema pushed hard off Jean's chest. She retrieved her big black purse from the ground and Jean watched her run awkwardly away with it looped around her shoulder and a half-full bucket sloshing at her knees.

"That's some balls there," the NGO said. "What does she think this is, a democratic election?" Jean didn't know what he meant until he pointed at the silk nightie, stamped with a red handprint.

"No balls," Jean said, covering herself with the blanket again. Her heart raced, as if the paint had made a mortal wound. "I've checked."

A paper had fallen from Telema's bag. Jean picked it up and opened it. Too dark to read. Her companion pointed to a dark figure following Telema's path. A suit creeping along the perimeter of the square, tripping over a shift in the stones. He fell onto a knee, cursed, then limped on his way.

Back in the courtyard, at one of the tables, the NGO produced a twelve-pack of beer. Jean drank, convinced herself there wasn't a single reason Maya would interest the professor. Whatever she had been doing with that bucket of paint seemed to compel her more. Telema stamping her handprints everywhere. A variation of the blue hand.

"What about the blue hand?" Jean asked her companion. "On the white background, the blue hand painted everywhere. What is it?"

"That's FRG. The political party started by Ríos Montt a few years ago."

"He's started his own party? From jail?"

The NGO grinned miserably. "He's not in jail. He's a congressman, the president of the legislature."

Jean took a moment to process this information. Why hadn't she learned this in Telema's class? Of course, because anything that happened in the past twenty years didn't count as history, according to the university. "What about the mass grave you found? You can't tie that to him?"

"Of course, it's definitely military. But hundreds have been tied to his term. There's nothing to do about it. Truth and reconciliation." He peeled the label off his beer bottle. "That was the deal. No subpoenas, no convictions."

"I knew that, but I didn't realize it applied to Ríos Montt. Lowly soldiers, guerrillas, people taking orders, sure. But it goes all the way up?"

"Some human rights organizations are disputing that, saying that Guatemala's signing of the Geneva Conventions trumps the amnesty, but the big players have already covered their tails. According to the new constitution, you can't be charged with a crime while in public office. You have to be suspended first, by the courts, which are appointed by the people in power."

He pushed his bottle around the table, making circles.

Hearing this, Jean finally understood Telema's purpose in Guatemala. She was, if nothing else, a multitasker. In a single day, she'd spend hours in the library researching Evie Crowder, lounge at a pool and amuse herself with the deranged views of a teenager, then risk her life with that bucket of paint. Jean felt the whole courtyard breathe and she let herself, finally, relax. Telema was here for several reasons. Research, justice, and a little amusement on the side by stalking her ex. Stalking, as a goal, would not appeal to Telema, who valued her time too much to give in to romantic obsession.

"And their candidate, Gilberto Ahumada Lobos, will win. There's no doubt." He shook his head. "I have a theory. The other political logos, I swear, they're painted by his party, too, to make people afraid."

"Afraid of what?"

"Afraid to vote. I have friends working the political end, trying to register Mayan voters. They're too terrified, they won't sign up. All the options, or semblance of so many options, scares them. They're scared they won't pick the *right* candidate. The right candidate being whoever wins. All they want to do is vote for who will win, so the winner won't kill them for voting for someone else. They don't believe that their votes could actually *determine* the winner. It's so fucked up."

"Does all this make you angry? Like the work you're doing is for nothing?"

He shrugged. "You better drink faster," he told her. "If it's not ice-cold, it tastes like ass. They've already been out of the fridge for fifteen minutes."

Jean sipped, already tasting the faint notes of ass. To overcome it, they chugged together, Jean drinking half her bottle in one pull.

"That girl with you . . ." her companion began, but faltered. Instead of finishing the sentence, he finished his beer.

Jean took her time to reply, "She's my daughter."

"Oh." He smiled the empty smile of someone changing course. "Your real daughter?"

"Yes, she's my real daughter."

"And where's her father, if I may ask?"

Jean glared at him. "Possibly Nueva Aldea de la Vida."

"Your daughter . . ." he tried again. "Does she usually make scenes like that?"

"Only recently." The scene in the lunch shack had made quite an impression. Telema's phrase "little bombs" came to mind. "But she's getting better."

"She doesn't look like you, not at all." He laughed uneasily. "She looks like her father, I suppose. Her father's Mayan?"

"I'm not sure," Jean snapped. "I was drunk, it was dark. I couldn't see his face." It was incredible, the personal questions that always came up when strangers saw Maya.

The NGO put his hands up like a referee. "Whoa, whoa! Calm down. I don't really care, you know, I didn't mean it like that. I just want to make sure . . . How do I phrase this?" He opened a new beer. "Yes, people are jumpy. Half the population should be in jail and the other half is too terrified to think straight. There are tens of thousands of armed soldiers without an army now, forming their own gangs. I just want to make sure you don't take that little firecracker to the wrong place."

"What's the wrong place?"

"Ten miles or more outside Xela," he said without blinking.

"How about Nueva Aldea de la Vida?"

"Good God, definitely don't go there."

"Why not? What's there?"

"A new garment factory, an old model village, and a lot of terrified, superstitious Maya who endured the brunt of the war. My organization pulled out of there a couple of months ago, after interviewers received death threats." He tapped on the table to command her attention. "Listen, if you're looking for the father, if you have to engage Nueva Aldea de la Vida at all, don't go there. I'll get a contact for you. There's one woman left there, I think. Last I heard, she was still there. I'll get her in touch right away."

Several beers later, Jean slipped back into her room. At the sound of the door, Maya shot up from sleep. "Where did you go?"

"Only to the bathroom, Maya. Do you need to go? I think maybe you should try."

Half asleep, Maya admitted with a whimper, "I'm afraid."

"You're afraid to go to the bathroom at night? Is that the problem? What are you afraid of?"

"Snakes."

"Well, I was just in there and there are no snakes, I promise." Jean walked her down the hall, holding her hand. Maya peed with the door open.

~~~~~

Jean's first task upon arriving home from Iowa was to search for Telema. They had not spoken since their night on the deck, since the UN report had been released. And now, after Jean had had some time to absorb the report, its implication of her, she needed to confess. Things with Telema simply could not progress without a discussion about Maya. After going to Telema's house and her usual bar, Jean finally found her that night in her office.

"How long have you been here? I've been to Iowa and back!" Jean said *Iowa and back* like she meant *hell and back*. "I've called you—"

"Imogene, Imogene. Why do you write books and papers about things you cannot even begin to understand?" Telema said as a greeting.

"I guess . . ." Jean tried, unsure of her footing among the piles of books. Something crunched underfoot, glass. How long would she have to pretend to be writing a book about Guatemala? "I guess I hope that the writing will help me to understand."

"You cannot understand from afar, at your computer, any more than you can understand it up close, Imogene. The perpetrators and the victims don't even understand. They become indistinguishable. That is violence for you. Real violence. Everyone becomes a victim and a perpetrator simultaneously. Do you know why?"

"No."

A streetlamp outside the window illuminated everything just enough that Jean could sense the things all around that she could not see.

"Because the masters of the violence don't have to do a thing. It perpetuates itself. It hits you so hard you become incapable of understanding anything but your own survival. The soldiers become as terrified as their victims. Blunt-force trauma. Would you like a drink?"

Jean recognized the shape of a bourbon bottle on the desk. Telema switched on a weak desk lamp, to search though its green glass glow.

"I broke the other glass," Telema said, "but you can have mine." She pushed a jelly glass over, then looked over the clutter on her desk. Choosing a black plastic pencil cup, she emptied it, blew inside, then filled it with four glugs.

"I got a call from the dean this evening. I've been reprimanded for teaching politics again with the UN report. I crossed the magical twenty-year threshold that separates fact from opinion. And several students have complained that I'm un-American."

"Un-American?"

"What is this, 1954? I'm sure there'll be more complaints after they all come back from their beachy, third world, Spring Break paradises. But fuck them. I have real work to do." She took up a small index card from her desk and waved it at Jean.

"What's that?"

"Evie Crowder's phone number."

Headlights passed outside, turning the shadows upside down and throwing the bookshelves into tumult.

"She's alive?" Jean asked. "She has a phone number?"

"Yes, but she's not very good at the phone. She's over a hundred years old. She can't hear a thing, actually. I tried. But I'm going to see her next week."

"You're the most productive person I've ever known," Jean concluded sadly. Her shame about Maya was temporarily alleviated by this new pang of remorse. In this relationship, Jean knew, it would never end. Her guilt would constantly change shape faster than she could reconcile it.

"How's your work going, Imogene? Have you figured out your thesis yet? Have you figured out the point of it all?"

"I told you the other night I hadn't. If the coup wasn't orchestrated for the money, then what?"

"Something much worse. How about this: There was no point. The theater of the absurd. A performance for performance's sake."

"So not even United Fruit. The coup had nothing to do with Fruit at all?"

"That's not what I said. How about this: No one believed that the Guatemalans had risen up to oust Jacobo Arbenz themselves. The CIA, Eisenhower, and his crew could control a mass delusion in a tiny country of petrified, uneducated people. They could control the American press, but once the story leaks out into the larger world, it is beyond their control. The UN cried foul and so, to thwart suspicions that they overthrew a democratically elected president for the sake of United Fruit, they told the State Department to immediately bring the company down."

"I never thought anything could make money look like a noble cause. They were bad leaders and bad friends?"

"Self-preservation is the strongest instinct. The money was important enough to spark thirty-six years of civil war, to destroy the lives of five million people. It was important enough to kill a few hundred thousand Guatemalans, but it wasn't worth tarnishing ten American reputations, so they abandoned it."

Jean held her bourbon.

"Did you read the Truth report, Imogene?"

"Most of it, yes. On the plane. It's a little dry, though." It was a good sign, she decided, that Telema used her real name, her pet name. She began to practice her defense, counting off all the horrors she'd saved Maya from, though Telema began her own accounting.

"Indeed." Telema held up the report to read by the light of the desk lamp. *"The Foundation's principal objective will be to facilitate the implementation of the recommendation made by the CEH, regarding five principal areas of activity ordered by the mandate: a) Direct implementation of specific recommendations; b) Backing and assistance in the implementation of the recommendations; c) Monitoring the adequate implementation of the recommendations; d) Promotion of and support for historical research; e) Assistance in seeking funds to finance projects for the implementation of the recommendations."* She took a sip. "They are very careful with their prepositions, very precise. Reconciliation by grammar."

"Telema, I don't understand why you're so upset. I mean, I understand, it's horrible, but this isn't anything you didn't expect. What do you want?"

"I want Reagan prosecuted for war crimes. I want Eisenhower and Dulles exposed in the history books. I want the D.C. airports renamed. As of now, we can completely gut a country for nothing and know that in fifty years, some paper like this will come out and outline how to make it all better." She took up the report again.

"Measures to preserve the memory of the victims: a) Designation of a day of commemoration of the victims (National Day of Dignity for the Victims of the Violence). b) The construction of monuments and public parks in memory of the victims at national, regional and municipal levels. c) The assigning of names of victims to educational centers, buildings and public highways."

A car passed, turning the room upside down in shadows.

"There are not enough roads in Guatemala," she concluded, then tipped her pencil cup back to drain it. "I want there to be only one National Day of Dignity for Americans. Right now, every day is a day of dignity here, but I think there should be only one, like everywhere else."

Jean could only agree. Her shame so overwhelmed her in that moment that she wanted nothing less than punishment. To be disgraced and chided by this merciless woman seemed the only answer. She no longer wanted to save the relationship; she merely wanted to save her sanity at this point. Only after Jean was held accountable could she and Maya move on.

"Telema, you know, this report is sort of personal for me, too. My daughter's Guatemalan." Telema watched Jean's mouth as she spoke, as if she were reading subtitles. "Mayan, actually. I knew you'd disapprove of me adopting her. She was a year old. She arrived at LAX malnourished and reeking of shit. A war baby."

"No, no, I think it's swell. Just swell."

Jean stiffened. The professor refilled their drinks. "It's very selfless of you, very humanitarian. Why bring your own child into the world when there are so many who need good homes, right, Imogene?"

Jean nodded tentatively. She felt her name was being used as a weapon now.

"No!" Telema slammed her cup down, spraying bourbon all over the report, all over her arm. Jean felt it splash on her face. "If you fucking want some legacy, if you want to mold some helpless child in your pathetic image, then have your own fucking children! Raise them to be fucking conscientious Americans! Don't steal the children of an endangered minority, then raise them with your bullshit self-righteous version of cultural appreciation!"

Jean felt a tremendous release as her embarrassment dissolved into anger. Telema's tirade sounded as abstract, heartless, and meaningless as the report. Not a single question about her little girl, her baby who'd been attacked with a knife, who still had the scar, who wasn't a human being to this monstrous woman but a *member of an endangered minority.* "This . . ." Jean growled, rising from her seat, "this is bullshit. You're telling me it would be better for Maya to have grown up in an orphanage, without an education, in a war-torn nation, to die from childbirth at the age of fifteen, rather than be here with me."

"Yes."

"Then you're no different than the people who kill for ideals." Jean stepped back, toward the door, through the broken glass. "You're no different than the people you want to see strung up."

"It's just trading one kind of poverty for another, Imogene. What makes you think yours is better?"

"What the hell are you talking about? If you think Guatemala's so great, why are you here?"

"Maybe there's a road somewhere, in Guatemala, named after your daughter. That would make it all right, yes? Just fill the country with memorials, with concrete penises pointing to the sky, so we can all feel better about your selfishness."

"You have no idea where Maya came from. You know less than I do."

Jean could not walk out carefully on the glass without looking unsure of herself. So instead she stomped recklessly, sending shards skittering across the floor. Telema leaned back in her office chair, studying her calmly, but underneath, Jean knew, she was a mural of smoke and teeth and jungle. Antlers cocked and pointed in her direction.

"How much did you pay for her, Imogene? To whom did you write your check?"

"Money has nothing to do with it. I would have given everything I have. I love my daughter."

Telema nodded. "Oh yes, you love. You are full of love, Imogene. But have you finally realized, in scaffolding your Great Beast, that it just keeps getting bigger and bigger? Bigger and bigger, until you realize you're part of it, too? That you are its heart?"

Jean closed the door on this, and found herself alone in the hall. For once, there were no admirers awaiting their turn. Emergency exits burned at both ends. She felt disoriented, could not tell the way out.

~~~~~

Jean had lost track of how many beers she'd had in the courtyard. She slept heavily through the night and into midmorning, when a knock woke her.

"Where's my daughter?" she asked, half asleep, confused at the sight of Maya's empty bed.

"She is at the pool. You have a phone call," the proprietor said, politely refusing to see Jean in her nightie. Or the red handprint stamped there. "Guatemala phone calls are one quetzal per minute. And it's three minutes already."

The phone call was brief, productive, though Jean still felt drunk. The NGO from Nueva Aldea de la Vida had heard through a chain of two others that Jean wanted to speak with her. No matter the drinking, these Truth workers had set up a highly efficient system of communication. She also claimed to know Cruzita. "I was coming to Xela this afternoon, anyway," the woman said. "Let's meet at your hotel."

Jean hung up, reeling from the sudden possibilities of the day, the whole trip. Cruzita was alive. Only one person separated them now, and by the end of the day Jean would know everything. After dressing, she found Maya in the pool and asked, "Honey, what do you want to do this morning?"

"I thought we were leaving. I was getting one last swim in."

"How about we stay one more day? What do you think? Let's do something together. Anything you want. Shopping?"

"Can we go to the coffee plantation?" She smiled, paddling toward Jean.

"I liked the guidebook description. I think we'd both like it. They have a gift shop."

According to the guidebook, the coffee plantation lay twelve miles outside the city. The taxi, like all the other vehicles in Guatemala, seemed only capable of speeding. The driver swerved and skidded as if they were being chased. But Jean kept an eye out, to make sure no one followed them.

Jean's brain threatened to explode right behind her eyes—the thin wedge of a headache driven deeper with each bump in the road. She pressed her palm into her left eye, feeling that made a difference. Of all the days to feel this shitty. But she could not regret the night before, for the anthropologist had kept his promise. He really did not want Jean to go to Nueva Aldea de la Vida. No matter. When the time came, Cruzita could come to Xela. Jean watched out the window, imagining a reunion. The city petered out and the roads had just turned from cobblestone to dirt when they hit something big, something that made the wheels pop. The driver punched at his gearshift.

"What was that?" Maya spun to look through the back window. "Oh, stop! Stop!" she cried out. "Stop the car!"

Jean tried to see what her daughter saw, but her head screamed with the movement. Nausea rising.

"Mom, tell him to stop!"

"*Pare*," Jean commanded. Had they hit someone?

The man braked hard, Jean braced herself, and Maya hopped out and sprinted away. Jean, easing herself out of the cab, could see nothing but the empty road materializing from the dust of their journey.

It was a dog. One of the scavengers that slunk around the city, so emaciated they seemed to run on nothing but fear. The head lay obscured, down in the ditch, the back legs knocked out and twisted around. It was still breathing.

"Mom!" Maya crouched near it. "Mom!" Her shriek found its mark behind Jean's eye and she pressed it harder as she trotted after.

"Don't touch it, Maya. It could have a disease or something."

"So? We got shots, didn't we? For the trip?"

Jean watched her daughter lay her hand on the spasming rib cage.

"Maya!" The name came out like vomit, Jean gagged, and her stomach heaved. "These dogs aren't used to being petted. You're just scaring him more."

This explanation convinced Maya and she withdrew her hand. The hand that had been on the dog now wiped at her eyes.

"It's horrible," she cried. "He didn't even care. He just kept going."

Jean searched her purse for a baby wipe. "Don't touch your face yet. Here." She looked back at the driver, who leaned against the car, smoking, watching them.

"What do we do? We can't just leave him here." They both looked down to see its blond face, undamaged. Just like a dog resting.

"There's no way this dog is going to survive, Maya. Its entire back end has been crushed. They don't have vets in places like this."

"There has to be someplace."

"There isn't. Most people don't even have a doctor."

"What about the television preacher? The one that cured the blind woman?"

Jean decided on a generous reply. "He's hours away, in the capital."

Maya stood up. "Then we have to put it out of its misery."

"Maya, we don't have to do anything. It's terrible, but there's nothing we can do." She thought of the knife in her purse that she had paid too much for in Xela. No matter how humane, she knew she was not capable of stabbing a suffering dog repeatedly with a small, decorative tourist knife.

"Make him," Maya said, pointing to the taxi driver. Before Jean could reply, she ran toward the man with her angry girl's legs. "You did this, you shithead!" she yelled at him, loud enough for her voice to carry up the mountains. Jean tried to pursue her, but the road tipped and thwarted her progress. "You put that dog out of its misery. You think you're so tough, let's see if you're tough enough to finish it, you fucker!"

Her fearlessness and her language were astounding and Jean knew she should stop her, but instead she stood admiring her anger, her bravery, her small-picture call for justice. Maya was, if nothing else right then, her daughter.

The man, whose English was better than he let on, threw away his cigarette and walked past Maya, then Jean. Shit, Jean thought to herself, the knife turning in her head. Shit, shit.

"And he's a litterbug," Maya called to his back. "Can you believe this guy?"

The man continued past them both, right to the ditch, and with his foot lifted the dog's head to get a good look.

"You see?" Maya whimpered. "See what you did?"

The man knelt down, cradled the dog's head, then, with surprising force, snapped it to the side. The noise was horrible, even from afar. Like walnuts cracking.

He walked back, another cigarette in his mouth, and got in the cab, started it.

Jean had to make a choice then, very quickly. She brought both palms to her eyes and pressed hard. They were in the middle of nowhere, somewhere between town and the plantation. They could refuse to get into the cab with this man who could snap their necks, as if he'd been trained to, or they could take their chances on the road. Armed robbers, ten miles outside Xela. Maya, next to her, was crying again.

"He's horrible. I'm not getting in the car with him. Did you see that? He just killed that dog like he enjoyed it."

Jean made the decision, quickly, to get into the cab. Sensing danger, trusting her mother, Maya followed without question. There was just one of him, whereas on the road they could be accosted by a gang of criminals. Jean found her knife in her purse, unsheathed it with her thumb, and held it there as they drove. In her other hand, she held Maya's shoulder, bringing her close. No one said a word. Maya sat straight and stunned, Jean, straight and ready to stab his brown, hot neck if the car wavered.

They arrived in time for a plantation tour, but neither of them felt up for it. Jean and Maya went instead to the adjacent café, where large, woven fans made slow circles overhead and where the windows framed orderly fields of coffee trees. Jean ordered them both coffee.

"It tastes like death," Maya declared. "With pennies mixed in."

She pushed the cup away and stared hard out the window.

Jean studied her daughter fearfully. Maya, however, did not seem to be working herself up for anything. The tour group they should have been a part of appeared in the glass. All khakis and polo shirts. One of them lingered behind, standing in a slight depression, looking down at his feet.

"I want to go home," Maya said. "I don't feel safe here." Confronted with her daughter's frown—licked, worried free of its glitter lip gloss—Jean felt, more than ever, her failure.

"I'm sorry, Maya. Maybe this was a mistake, maybe it's too early to be coming here like this."

"I didn't want to come."

"Yes, well, it's important, you know. This is your homeland."

"This is the most horrible place on earth. I want to go home and go to school."

My God, Jean thought, she's turned the tables on me now. "Then I ruined it for you. I should've waited. It's only going to get better."

"It'll never be as good as California," she said, "so why ever come back?"

"There are some things that are more important than safety."

"Like what?"

"Like family."

Three people now stood in the depression in the ground, bouncing slightly on their knees. A possible grave? Watching them, Jean realized she'd just paraphrased the therapist. After their trip to Iowa, after Maya's fits had started up again, she'd tried to explain how her parents were to blame. "I'm cutting them out, for Maya's sake." But the therapist only stressed the importance of family. No, she argued back, Maya's outburst about dykes and hell proved that Jean's parents were poisoning Maya's mind against her. They meant well, they meant to save everyone around them. But how could she and Maya live like that? In the end, it was Jean's decision, not the therapist's. By April, she'd changed her phone number.

"When she came to the pool, Telema told me that family is something white people don't think they need. They think they can just buy love, like they buy groceries. She said that after white people take the land and all the money from a place, the only thing left to take is their love. They hire maids and nannies from here to love their children and old people. Then they get their children from here, too, because they're too busy for sex and real relationships."

"She said that, Maya?"

"She also said that when white little girls go missing, the whole world stops. Even when it's a lie. But when a brown little girl goes missing, for real, no one cares."

"I suppose that's true."

Maya's black eyes glittered with sadness. "She called me a lost little girl, Mom. I don't think I'm lost, I didn't like her calling me that. I didn't really tell her anything. I don't want to be in her book. I just said that to make you mad."

Jean nodded her thanks to Maya. She took her daughter's cup, added cream and sugar, and pushed it back over. Maya tasted it thoughtfully and accepted it. Outside, the tour group had moved on, out of sight.

"Maya, I have one more thing to do here. Just give me the rest of the day, okay? You can stay at the hotel, read your magazine, swim, drink all the banana drinks you want. I won't ask you to do anything more. We'll skip the ruins and fly straight home."

"I can spend the last week of summer vacation at the beach? With Brett?"

"Yes."

"You promise?"

"I promise. Just give me a day, honey."

"Okay, but I don't want to stay in the hotel with that sad woman. Can I go out with her sons, to the vegetarian restaurant? She said they'd be back today."

Jean ordered more coffee and began to explain about the proprietor, a less detailed, altered version of the story the NGO had told her. She did not mention that the murders took place in the courtyard, sure that Maya would not want to stay there for another day if she knew.

Nodding, intent, Maya listened, while sipping her coffee. Surprisingly, she did not freak out at being set up with dead boys. "How awful," she concluded, just as Jean had. "That poor woman."

"You don't have to see her. You can just stay in the room if you want, or maybe I can tell her you aren't feeling well and you need to rest by yourself at the pool."

She stirred her cup absently. "No, I'll play cards with her. She likes cards. She must be very lonely in such an awful place." She sighed at the blue-black mountains in the distance. "I'm starting to understand why she never goes outside."

Jean hired one of the plantation workers to drive them back to the hotel. Maya insisted on a white driver.

The Roots Tour had not gone as Jean had hoped, but she believed it could still be salvaged. She believed that if she could bring Cruzita to Xela, if she could help the woman in some way, it might turn out better than she had ever expected. Maya had already forgiven her; maybe Telema would, too, once the truth came out.

Maya took a nap after the plantation visit, claiming coffee didn't work on her.

Jean's guest arrived an hour later. Seeing her polo shirt, the proprietor shut the gate and would not let her through until Jean heard the commotion and insisted she be let in for coffee and lunch. "She's just my friend," she promised her. "We're old friends."

In a dated pair of jean shorts and an official polo shirt, sunglasses, and an air of purpose, the NGO surveyed the courtyard. The logo on her shirt stated her business with the Truth Commission.

"Hi, I'm Jean."

The woman raised her sunglasses. She had the sensible expression of all the NGOs, painfully pink despite the smears of sunblock on the edges of her face and neck. She looked Jean's age, mildly unattractive. Not fat, exactly, but not fit, either.

The woman glanced down at the YWCA logo on Jean's shirt and frowned. "Who are you with?" she asked in a sweet Midwestern accent, tainted with a boozy sourness.

"I'm not with anybody," Jean said.

In a place where everyone was interviewing survivors, counting the dead, and writing accounts of it, this seemed to be the right answer.

The woman downed her coffee in several quick gulps and brought a bottle out of her bag. From it, she filled her empty mug with a thick yellow liquid that looked like eggnog. Grateful for the opportunity to stave off her intensifying hangover, Jean dumped her coffee out and accepted a generous pour as well. An unexpected calmness, patience, overcame her as she enjoyed these last moments with her imagination. After this, she'd know the real story. She found comfort in the fact that she couldn't imagine things getting any worse than that cab ride a few hours before.

"Cruzita's never said anything about giving up any children to me," the woman said, opening a battered notebook with a spiral spine. "After you told me on the phone, I went through all my notes, years of them. I can't think—" She stopped herself, shook her head. A gamy scent wafted Jean's way. She sat back, away from it.

Jean pointed to a Polaroid that had slipped onto the table. "What's that?"

The woman held it up. A house. A painted, cheerful two-story house with a balcony. "That's Cruzita's house."

Cruzita not only wasn't dead; in fact, she had emerged from the war a success.

"Does she have a job? How did she get such a nice house?"

"I don't know. There's a factory in town, a sweatshop. Almost everyone works there, making clothes. Some Ladinos have higher positions."

Jean took the photo. Cruzita had pulled herself up by her bootstraps, worked hard in the factory, been promoted. An American Dream girl made in Guatemala. This certainly was not the ending Jean had ever expected.

"But can you tell me? Was Cruzita impoverished during the war? In 1983?"

"Impoverished?"

"Did she have the resources to take care of herself? To feed a family?"

"Hell, no. Everything she had was destroyed." And there it was, reprieve. Jean wanted this woman to write that down, sign and stamp it with a Truth Commission seal. She wanted now to know everything she could about Cruzita. She no longer felt afraid. "What have you talked to Cruzita about?"

"Her family," she replied. "Her old village." Her eyes narrowed. "Her grandmother Emelda Tuq." She set her gaze on her drink, tilted the mug.

"What about her?" Jean felt herself a part of a large, unexpected family. A family she cared deeply about. "Is she still alive?"

The woman threw her egg liquor back with violence, so the thick remainder hit the back of her throat. The action deemed that line of questioning done. She was off, Jean decided. The woman was definitely not all there. And yes, she smelled. Each time Jean leaned in with interest, she had to pull back for air.

"Is Cruzita trying to find her family?"

"No." Despite drinking hard liquor before lunch, this woman clearly took her job with the Truth Commission very seriously. Too seriously to bother with a shower, or to comb her hair.

"Cruzita has no one?" Jean considered the idea of a family in Guatemala. Since Jean had disowned her parents six months ago, she had no one as well. She and Cruzita needed each other. She envisioned Christmases spent in Guatemala, Thanksgivings in California. Cruzita with a passport.

The NGO refilled her cup from the bottle. "She's the only survivor of the Valle Lejos massacre. She lost everyone there. At least that's what she's always told me."

"When was that?"

"In 1982."

Jean raised her cup and took a sip. The taste was heavy, sweet, pleasant. But then she swallowed and it took her by the throat. She coughed, felt the burn descending. "Maya was born in 1983. Has she not even mentioned a baby?"

"The only baby she's ever mentioned is her baby boy. He disappeared

during the massacre. I can't imagine, I don't even know how this could be."
The woman flipped through her notebook, looking for something specific.

"And where did she go after the massacre?"

"Wherever she could go. She ran to the mountains and wandered alone
for months, hiding from the helicopters. She was lost."

"Was the military looking for her? Did they know she was a witness?"

"No. They were just looking for anyone. They wouldn't think anyone had
survived the fire."

"They burned Valle Lejos?"

"They burned the church." She isolated a page in her hands but did not
read from it. "They filed everyone into the church, sprayed the crowd with
bullets, locked the door, and set it on fire." The paper trembled. "Cruzita
played dead, hiding under the pile of bodies: her husband, her parents. She
dipped her skirt in the blood and held it to her mouth to breathe through the
smoke. The church collapsed before she could be incinerated, but she was
afraid to come out. She hid under the bodies of her friends and family for
over a day before she got the courage to come out."

Jean watched the woman turn the page, accidentally ripping it.

"I'm sorry." The woman seemed to gain confidence with her third mug of
liquor, just the weight of it in her hand. "It still gets me, after all these years,
all these interviews."

"Why did they do that? I know about the broader genocide, but why Valle
Lejos specifically?"

"Guerrillas had ambushed the army a few miles away. The soldiers were
convinced the village had to be selling them food. Over a hundred people
burned in the church. No one knew there were any Valle Lejos survivors. I
still don't think anyone knows. She's too afraid for any kind of attention." She
paused, nailing Jean down with a look of suspicion. "So why are you here,
looking for her?"

"Like I said, she's Maya's mother."

"No, she's not. You are."

Jean finished her drink with the same hard motion the woman had.

"So why? Why did you bring your daughter all the way down here to a
dangerous country to meet a stranger that didn't want her in the first place?"

"Now, I don't think that's fair to assume," Jean said. "The records say she
gave her up because of poverty."

"Poverty doesn't exist for these people. It exists for us, to explain things
we can't understand. Why," she repeated, "are you here?"

Jean stared at her empty, yolk-coated cup and understood it would give her no relief. The heavy liquid sloshed behind her eyes, deepening her agony.

"We didn't come to see her mother. I didn't even think she would have survived the war. Finding Cruzita was never my intention, but now my feelings on the whole trip have changed. I think maybe . . . I think I came here for the wrong reasons. I said this was all for Maya, and it started out that way, but then I read about all these horrible adoption stories. The trip became about me, about clearing my conscience. And about making Maya grateful to me after seeing this place."

"And is it clear?" the woman asked with smiling mockery.

"Yes, but it's a moot point now, with all this misery, the mass graves. My daughter never wanted to come here. I've helped no one but myself. But now I want to help Cruzita. You said she has no one? She lives by herself in that nice house?"

"Yes."

"Where does she get her money? Her adoption papers said she gave up Maya because of poverty. You said she had nothing. How has she pulled herself up from that, by herself, an indigenous woman in this country? Does she work at the garment factory?"

"I have no idea where she got, or gets, her money. She doesn't have a job now. There's a gap in her story"—she pointed to her notes—"I can't pin down. She avoids it whenever I ask. I noticed a while ago that the time line was off. But I didn't press it, I didn't want to make her relive the trauma."

"The burning of the church?"

"No, not that." She drilled her palms into her wet eyes as she spoke. "She was gang-raped by soldiers, over the course of several days, when she was fifteen."

It was now clear to Jean why the woman drank, why the NGOs drank mass quantities of vile beer in the vegetarian restaurant. The American Dream Girl story was descending into origins darker than Jean could imagine. She could not have anticipated this nightmarish beginning, any more than she could have guessed Cruzita's prosperous end.

"What year?" she heard herself ask.

Bringing her hands away, she blinked at Jean, trying to regain her sight through her tears. "The magic year: 1983. After she surrendered for amnesty."

Jean accepted the logical conclusion immediately. Maya, a product of such violence. Part soldier, part victim. A little bomb. With this, Jean felt herself descending into deeper unknowns, pondering the stories that eluded her, but to which she remained surely tied. The girl Cruzita, running from helicopters. Gang rape. Giving birth, by herself. Jean wished, for the first time, she knew what birth felt like. This Cruzita gave birth to a soldier's baby, to a hundred soldiers' baby, then slipped down into Xela in the middle of the night, to give baby Maya to the nuns. The woman was right. Poverty was not the word for it. Jean pressed forward, no longer caring about the smell.

"Can you ask her about Maya? When do you meet her next?"

"This afternoon. But my talks don't go like that. I've been here for years, on and off, and some people are just getting the courage to report missing relatives. They might talk at you, but once you ask a question, they freak out. And they freak out if you write anything down. I have to try to remember everything and write it all down afterwards."

"But she trusts you. She's told you this much already."

"She tells me because she has no one else to tell. She tells me because I'm the only one who knew she had anything to say. Believe me, it's against her best judgment."

"Can I go back with you, to Nueva Aldea de la Vida? Just to see it?"

"No. No, no, no." She closed her notebook. "You can't go there. It isn't safe. The Maya are very suspicious of a white woman traveling alone."

"Suspicious? How about you?"

"I live there, it's my home. At least, it's the best home I can come up with. I've been back to the States, I've tried, but I always end up back in Guatemala. It's never easy. I receive threats. A lot of them don't want me there."

"What kind of threats?"

"Painted on my door, people yelling from alleys, sometimes they break into my room and steal my notebooks."

"Of all the things to be suspicious of, after all this war, a white American woman? What do they think we'll do?"

The woman laughed, a thick, egg-coated laugh. "There are lots of scary stories about Americans going around, lesbian witchcraft—"

"What! Lesbians?"

"Kidnapping kids because they can't have their own. Others believe Mayan children are being stolen for their organs. To harvest for surgeries in the United States."

"They'd think I was prowling around their town to do *that*?"

"Who knows what they'd think of you? All I know is that they'll decide on a story very quickly. Maybe good, maybe bad. You shouldn't take the chance, though. It's crazy out there, away from the bigger towns—fear's taken over. Some people, it's all they can feel anymore." As the woman said this, it became clear to Jean that she was speaking for herself as well. Who was this pitiful, drunk woman sitting across from her? Embarrassed, she realized she hadn't even asked.

"What's your name? I'm sorry, I'm so rude and self-absorbed with my own inquiries. I forgot your name from our phone conversation."

She shrugged and gave her name as if it weren't even her own. "Lenore."

"And what are you researching, specifically, in Nueva Aldea de la Vida?"

"Just interviews. Cruzita's my main subject, always has been, but I only recently convinced her to talk to me."

"How did you convince her?"

"She needed help with some paperwork. She was trying to get a road named after her grandmother who was disappeared. The Calle Emelda Lupe Tuq, just outside of town. I helped her with the application to the memorials committee. The stone went up last week. That's why I'm here in Xela, to make sure it did."

"Honoring her ancestor. That's very important to them, I heard."

"I'm only just starting to understand now how important these things are to them. It's incredible. What principles do we have that we'd die for?" Her tremulous gaze wandered over Jean's shoulder. "Nothing. Plenty we'd kill for, but nothing to die for."

"Can I ask you something?"

Lenore barely responded, her head tilting to the side in assent.

"You said Cruzita was gang-raped by soldiers. I just can't get it out of my head, I just can't help but think that Maya was the result."

She held up her notebook, a shield. "There's no way. What they did was way too violent—broken bottles, bayonets . . ." Her fingers grasped an end of the spiral spine and pulled it straight, into a lance. "You wouldn't know it to look at her, but she's completely disfigured from it on the inside. She's sterile."

Jean felt a little better as the horror piled up between them on the table. Thank God, she thought to herself, thank God for that, at least. The proprietor entered the courtyard, set down two bowls, then left. "So do you think Maya was born in the mountains, on the run?"

"It's possible. Maybe Cruzita was pregnant during the massacre, she wasn't pregnant in the camp. She certainly does pick and choose what she tells me."

"So why is the Truth Commission so interested in her? Why is she your subject?"

"Actually," Lenore confessed, "I'm not with the Truth Commission. I'm not with anybody. I got this shirt"—she plucked at the logo over her heart— "from a friend in the Truth Commission. It makes things easier. At least, it used to."

"Oh."

"When you have this shirt on, people are more likely to tell you their stories."

"I suppose so." Jean folded her arms over her chest.

"I guess I'm a freelance truth commissioner."

"For what? For a book?"

Lenore ran her fingers up the straightened spiral obsessively. Polishing, sharpening. "I wish I could write, could do something with all this, but I can't. I'm not educated. I was a missionary once. That's what I'm educated for, if you could call that education. It only made me dumber."

"Then why are you doing it? Why all these interviews?"

With her free hand, Lenore began eating her sliced bananas in milk, eating as if she hadn't eaten in days. "I don't know," she said with her mouth full. "I guess I can't stop. I guess it's the only thing I can think to do with myself. Until they let me know what I can do." She finished her bowl as quickly as it took to explain herself. "Maybe one day they'll tell me what they want."

"What do you mean?"

"I mean I'm not going to try to guess what they want. There's no way I can. So I'll just wait until they tell me." Her words slurred, making no sense. The bottle, Jean saw, emptied.

"Who?"

"The Maya. Maybe they'll kill me, maybe they'll ask me to write a book. But I have to do something. I just can't leave."

"I'm in publishing." Jean offered her own bowl of bananas, which Lenore accepted. "I can write. I may be able to help you with a book."

Lenore just stared at Jean, unable to focus on her.

"I'm serious," Jean reassured her. Maybe this would be her chance to write a book, to have a subject, a purpose. She and Lenore needed each other.

Lenore shook her head, blinked in confusion. "You can't write this book."

"I can't? Why not? I studied writing. I've studied Guatemala."

"Okay, you studied. So tell me, what would be the point of this book, if you wrote my book? What would Cruzita's story be?"

Jean paused a moment, if only to look thoughtful. She knew exactly how to write it, of course. "The horrors of money and power. Of what people will do—"

"People?" Lenore scoffed, bits of banana flying from her mouth. "Does it really surprise you what people are capable of?"

"I guess so. Though it shouldn't. But to stop being surprised is to give in, to accept it as inevitable—"

"I watched my husband drive his knee into an elderly Mayan man's back for what he thought was right." She brought Jean's bowl to her lips and drained the milk. "Fifteen years, we were married. Once I stopped seeing things as right and wrong, once I stopped thinking I understood anything, I began to think clearly."

"Your husband, he's Guatemalan? Was he in the military?"

"My ex-husband is in Kentucky. He's probably lying on a couch right now watching baseball, eating delivery pizza, at peace with the world. He's nothing, he's irrelevant. It took me a long time to realize that. I'm talking about something bigger than right and wrong. I'm talking about God. How can you know? How can you know how to show people they are mistaken about God? The book's impossible. I hope they don't ask me to write it."

"I don't believe in God," Jean insisted in bewilderment. "I'm an atheist."

"That sounds comforting." Lenore sighed, spearing the last slice of banana. She turned it over on her fork, studying it. "But it's not enough. Not even nearly enough."

After Lenore boarded her bus back to Nueva Aldea de la Vida, Jean lingered in the courtyard, contemplating her next move. Lenore needed her, she needed Lenore. Cruzita remained elusive, and she considered her options: to forget all this and leave Xela, or to wait for Lenore's next phone call. The only place she could go herself, to try to find out more, was the orphanage.

Searching for her guidebook, Jean spied something in her purse. The paper Telema had dropped when they collided the night before. She had almost forgotten, for all the beer and pot. Very old, and so fragile that it broke into four neat pieces where she unfolded the paper. Jean arranged these pieces on the table. A letter dated 1902.

Dear Sophie,
    Life in Guatemala is hard, but rewarding.

Before reading on, her eyes were drawn to the middle of the page, to a passage underlined in red pencil. Faded, but undeniable:

    The Santa María volcano erupted near our house and ash rained down on everything like snow.

The suit entered the courtyard, limping. Jean returned the broken letter to her bag. He proved no more detailed upon closer inspection. Still a suit, with generic looks. He had no qualms about approaching her directly now, like a man who knew she could never describe him.

"Ms. Roseneath," he said.

"How do you know my name?"

"It's written in the guest book." He sat down across from her. The skin beneath his eyes was pummeled, puffed blue with insomnia.

Jean would not pretend she didn't know what this guy was. She had a day left in Xela and she refused to get pulled into Telema's drama.

"I thought we could talk. Do you have a minute?" He stretched his injured knee out, tenderly, off to the side.

"Not really. My daughter should be waking up soon."

"Well, this won't take long. I only want to ask you about Evangeline Cazador."

"Who?" Jean remembered a few seconds too late. "Oh."

The suit made a small cage with his hands.

"What do you want to know about her? I haven't really talked to her in months."

"Now, that's not true, Ms. Roseneath." Grinning, he showed clean square teeth and the receded gums of someone who brushed too often and too hard. "I want to know why she's following you."

"It's not like that." She hesitated, knowing fear had blanched her voice. "Listen, I don't care about her, I'm not trying to protect her or anything. I really have no idea what she's up to. She's not following me, not really. I mean, I think she's enjoying running into me in town and giving me a scare, but that's all."

"A scare? Are you scared of her?"

"It's not how you think," she explained, though she had no idea what this suit thought. "It's really very stupid. She's my ex. We planned this trip for fun, to take together. She bought the ticket before we broke up and it wasn't refundable. She's here doing her own thing."

"She bought her ticket a month ago, Ms. Roseneath. You two broke up in March." And then Jean recognized him. Telema's best student.

One of the Mayan maids came to clear the table. She slumped inside the stiff fabric of her costume, wiping up the milk that had dribbled from Lenore's meal. The proprietor, from the doorway, smiled emptily in their direction.

"Are you still leaving tomorrow?" she called to Jean.

"I'm afraid so. I'm sorry to have to cancel." Jean regarded the suit calmly, telling herself that he could do nothing to her. She was not involved.

The girl finished cleaning and shuffled away, leaving a greasy mess behind.

"You're leaving?" he asked. "Your reservation was for a week."

"You don't intimidate me. I know what you are. And I know I have nothing to hide. I told you everything I know about Telema."

"What about her ties to a terrorist organization? Did you maybe leave that out?"

"I have no idea what you're talking about," Jean managed, her feet running in place under the table. "We dated a few months. I barely saw her, she was always away doing research."

"We know about her research." He chuckled humorlessly. "Breaking and entering, records theft. Stalking an elderly woman in New York, telling her she's someone she isn't. The old lady has dementia and your ex barges in and plants all these notions in her head. She's starting to believe she lived in Guatemala as a little girl, that her parents abandoned her there. Her family finally got a restraining order after she head-butted a nephew. Your girlfriend has some strange extracurricular activities. But we're more interested in her funding scheme."

"I have no idea what you're talking about, but I am pretty sure that your definition of a terrorist organization is a bit skewed. I know quite a bit about your line of work and I would argue that you are the terrorist in this country. Not Telema."

With this, his composure cracked. He'd probably never been called a terrorist before, and surely he had never had an assignment as baffling as Telema. Jean imagined him tailing Telema on deer hunts, to the bar, and into the library stacks for seven hours at a time, then sitting in his car, watching her parade naked through her lighted house.

"Is your outfit supposed to be ironic? Are you trying to look like a Dulles brother? Of course, I wouldn't expect you to know the history of your organization down here. You want to talk about funding, what about funneling money and weapons to genocidal dictators to kill a couple hundred thousand people? Providing helicopters and bullets to strafe villages? Training death squads? That is your legacy down here."

"This is a vintage suit," he said, straightening. "I didn't even have to have it altered."

"Yes, that suit was fate. I believe it. Some goon fifty years ago, stumbling around with your exact measurements. Your exact poor taste."

Hurt touched his mouth. He'd been trained for moles, bullets, car chases, and torture, but not a fashion critique.

"I'm sure you're the envy of your colleagues, being assigned to follow a beautiful woman around the globe. Peeping in her windows, jacking off on your notes, sniffing her underwear, though I'm sure you've reported back by now that she doesn't wear underwear."

He wilted in his chair, blushing. How dangerous could Telema be if they sent this sapling after her? But, possibly, there were more. Jean had seen several suits in Xela, but were they all just this guy? With glasses, without. His one effort at disguise.

"I get more enjoyment out of my interviews with your daughter, believe me."

"Don't even mention my daughter, you fascist prick!"

He grasped her weakness, pulled himself up with it. "Don't play mama bear with me. I've spent more time with Maya over the past few months than you have. And I say you got your money's worth of trouble there. Shoplifting, sex in cars—"

Jean lunged for him. "You filthy shit!"

He spun away, out of his chair, laughing, limping slightly. "Don't kill the messenger. Maybe you should talk to Maya. She did it because of you. Right here, poolside, she reassured me how experienced she was. She fucked Brett to prove she wasn't a big dyke, like you." He blinked, remembering. "Yes, that's just the term she used. *Big dyke.* I guess people at school were giving her a hard time about it."

The proprietor shuffled in again. "I can't trust my maids with anything," she declared, running a finger over the smeared glass table. "Don't let them fool you. They act like they're enslaved, but they make three times as much as the other Indians in town." As she wiped, the streaks of grease shifted, but would not disappear.

The suit threw Lenore's white napkin onto the table like a gauntlet. A poor sense of imagery, this boy had. "She passed off a letter to you last night. We know you are involved, Ms. Roseneath, that fact is undisputed. It's only a matter of time until we find out how."

"A letter," the proprietor echoed, reminded of something. She gave up on the table, fished into her apron pocket, and handed Jean another letter to mail.

Jean did not go upstairs to talk to Maya. Whatever awaited her in Guatemala now seemed much less daunting than that encounter. The suit could be making it up, but the only way to know would be to ask her. She'd already given Maya permission to call Brett and tell him they'd be coming back early. Fifteen minutes, she'd told the proprietor, on my credit card. The peace must be maintained until they returned to California.

In the taxi, driving back up to the orphanage that afternoon, Jean tried to block out images of Maya having sex in a car with Brett. Brett on top, of course, smothering little Maya into the sweaty upholstery with his football padding. The suit, certainly, was fucking with her head. He'd probably been trained to exploit mothers. Telema had warned her against love. Our biggest weakness, and therefore our biggest enemy.

In the orphanage yard, the construction of the AstroTurf soccer field had attracted a crowd of polo shirts. One person shoveled cautiously while the others watched.

The girl at the front desk was not the same one from before. Feeling absurd, but desperate, Jean walked briskly through the waiting room up to the desk and demanded of the stunned girl, "Do you speak English?"

"A little."

Jean pointed to her YWCA shirt and said, "I'm from the Fact Finders and I'm here for a records request."

The girl's mouth fell open.

"You have records of the mothers here? The mothers who give up their babies?"

"*Sí.*" She looked around for help, but there was no one. Siesta time. She then strained to see out the glass doors—the polos and khaki shorts all peering over a hole.

"I'm with them," Jean clarified. "I need the records of Cruzita Sola Durante."

"Cruzita Sola Durante," the girl repeated, without moving. "Cruzita is one of the bodies?"

Jean had never been required to think so quickly in her life as she had in Guatemala, in the past few days. But she had three cups of coffee in her by now, shored up by Lenore's liquor. "We're not sure. But I need your file on her. Please."

The girl hesitated and glanced around again for help that would not come. She had to be one of the orphans, Jean realized, never adopted. A shuffled pile of papers, a week's delay, and she could have been Jean's daughter.

Outside, someone lowered himself into the shallow hole, just a few feet deep. The others gathered around the rim expectantly.

The girl reappeared with a folder three inches thick. The size and weight of it had terrified her more, and she handed it over with fear brimming in her eyes. "Please," she said, pointing to the reading room.

The file, dropped on the table with a thud, frightened Jean as well. How could there be so much for such a common story? *Gave up her baby because of poverty. Gang rape, village massacre.* At least, common enough for Guatemala. What else could there be? She pulled out a photograph of a lovely young woman, a Mayan teenager, wincing slightly as if she wasn't sure what the camera pointed at her was. Cruzita Sola Durante.

Though beautiful, she looked nothing like Maya. Everything seemed wrong, down to the chin. Maya must be her father's daughter.

No hometown listed for Cruzita in these records, no address. Under contact information, she read the name General Gilberto Ahumada Lobos. The name was vaguely familiar to Jean, but she did not linger on it. She flipped through the file, which contained nothing but the pictures and records of children. Files combined accidentally, shoved in so the paper-clipped pages became entangled. Just a filing mistake. She paged through the children with urgency and found Maya's picture and file, with Cruzita's name listed at the bottom. But then, looking at the other babies' files, she noticed Cruzita's name on those, too. In a kind of shocked daze, she went through every one, counted them, noted the dates. In the span of a year, Cruzita Sola Durante had given ninety-six children up for adoption.

Jean shoved the glass doors open and tried to breathe, to think. In the soccer field, the crowd hoisted one of the polo shirts out of the hole. Jean felt the ground move beneath her, pulling her in their direction.

"How many?" someone asked.

"I see three," he said. "But it's old. Much older than the war. I could be wrong, but look at their shoes." He held what looked like a small, shriveled foot in his hand. Everyone stared at it. An old-fashioned child's leather shoe—a tiny shoe, caked with black volcanic soil. He turned it in his hands, to point out a corroded, barely visible heart-shaped buckle.

"Well, shit. Where else can we put the goalpost?"

Jean needed to get in touch with Lenore. Six hours until sundown. She returned to the taxi waiting in the parking lot. The man, uninterested in the scene on the field, listened instead to some vile preacher on the radio. *¡Jesús!* Through the static and Mayan language, his tone was clear: fire, damnation, redemption, hope.

"Nueva Aldea de la Vida," she told the driver. "And turn that the fuck off."

For once, she wished a Guatemalan taxi could go faster. She dropped two hundred quetzales on the driver's lap and told him so. As they raced even farther from Xela, the roads deteriorated into rough paths, nearly into jungle. Civilization fell away and Jean felt nothing, not even anxiety. Despite all the information, the numbers and dates, the facts refused to cohere in her mind. Ninety-six children in a year. All she could think of was some kind of computer error. But records of the children had been handwritten.

In ninety minutes, the taxi hit a main road, then passed the sprawling modern clothing factory Lenore had mentioned. Past this, they descended into the valley below, into a shantytown made of sticks, plastic, leaves, and corrugated tin. It looked, from high up, like a garbage dump.

Everywhere in the town, some step of the factory process showed. Mayan men loaded trucks with the assistance of boys; women and girls walked to or away from the factory glinting atop the hill. The taxi dropped Jean at a stand selling clothes too warped for the outlet stores in the States. Grotesquely uneven arms, one-legged pants hung on display. The Mayan woman who sold them did not look Jean in the eye as she chanted, "Polo, Gap, Kathy Ireland. Polo, Gap, Kathy Ireland," like an incantation.

The rest of the small, inadequate market sold packaged food: potato chips, packaged bread, snack cakes, and Coke. An ancient-looking woman engaged in the only traditional activity Jean could see. Stooped in a stall, she dipped strings of wool in buckets of dye. Blue, black, red, purple. She scooped handfuls of cochineal powder, added them to a boiling bucket, and stirred the thickening dye. Her hands, stained red, trembled with purpose. Behind her, a girl wove these dried threads together into the rough, traditional blankets with her backstrap loom.

"*Estoy buscando Lenore,*" Jean told the woman, who dipped a strand of wool and brought it out dripping red, like entrails.

Jean moved on. A man appeared, mercilessly whipping a donkey over the flat road. He stared hard at her with one good eye, the other askew, lifted up to the sky.

"*Estoy buscando Lenore.*"

The man did not stop whipping, but used his free hand to point her in the other direction, from which she had come.

The village center was flat and crowded with fading, cracked plastic shacks erected on a grid. Bulwarks of plastic wrappers, cans, and bottles reinforced the flooded paths between from erosion. A Mayan girl—maybe eight years old—wearing a tiny replica of the traditional costume, finally took mercy on Jean, after much searching and asking that startled the villagers. Children were scooped up from bucket baths, from games. The streets emptied as the girl pulled her along.

"*Ixchel!*" a woman called, from some unseen location.

When the girl pointed to a leaning shack made of an old Coca-Cola sign, Jean shook her head. But she confirmed, pointing and saying, *Yanqui*. Supposedly, Lenore lived in a shack like all the other shacks, but for the painted graffiti, which did not look political. No symbols, just words: *¡Váyase Yanqui! ¡Niño Ladrón!*

No one answered her knock, and the door looked as if it had been kicked in at one point. The hinges screamed with rust.

Lenore wasn't there. By the light of the open door, Jean made out one chair, one table, a sleeping mat on the beaten earth floor, which sloped severely to one corner. Notebooks everywhere. Some stacked, some gutted, some damaged by water, and others preserved in clear plastic bags. Yes, unbelievably, this must be Lenore's home. Jean found a notebook open on the table, the spine folded over to a single page:

> *In their testimony, the soldiers confessed that they dropped Emelda alive in the Pacific with four others. They cut her breasts off, so she'd bleed in the water. Then they hovered in the helicopter*

and watched the sharks rip them all apart. They took bets on who
would be the first and last to be eaten.

As she stepped back, her foot slid over a puddle of vomit. Coffee and
banana from their meeting, and the yellow egg liquor, looking no different
than it had in the bottle.

"*Ixchel!*" a woman called from somewhere. Then a man. "*Ixchel!*"

The town spread out with better and better houses toward the mountains.
Jean found the little girl again, licking a piece of plastic packaging she'd
found. She knew where Cruzita lived as well and she pulled Jean in another
direction.

"*¿Cómo se llama?*" she asked her.

"Ixchel."

The shadows of people shrank before her in the street. Doors closed. The
old woman at the market, who still refused to acknowledge her presence,
continued dipping and hanging, dipping and hanging.

The political graffiti looked the same as Xela's: orange squares, a corn-
stalk. Along walls, on rocks and trees, the blue hand waved its bloody salute.
Telema had been here. The suit said Telema was following her. Jean imagined Telema just a few yards ahead, painting as she went. She turned
abruptly, confronted alleys and shadows, preparing to see her. She checked
her back repeatedly for the Guatemalan parade. Telema, the suit, an armed
robber, angry peasants, and the last to join: ninety-six children trying their
best to keep up. No, ninety-seven.

"*Ixchel!*" But the girl just grinned at Jean and skipped on.

Cruzita's house stood on a street that curved up the surrounding mountain range. Molded of smooth white stucco and huge for the area, it looked
even nicer than in the photo, with a yard and a flower garden. It was nicer
than the hotel in Xela.

She thanked Ixchel, who demanded payment. *Five*, she showed her, with
her tiny, grimy hand. She gave her twenty. The girl scuttled away with the
money, hooting at what she believed to be Jean's mistake, leaving her at the
gate. Lenore must be inside. She would know what the file meant, or at least
she could find out. If only Jean could walk to the front door and knock. If
only she could leave it alone.

Jean found shade a small distance away from Cruzita's gate. A massive
tangled vine heaved itself over the wall and into the street, allowing her to

watch the gate while remaining somewhat hidden. The minuscule flowers weighted the air with an impossibly sweet fragrance.

"Ixchel! Ixchel!" The girl ran down an alley giggling, flouting her summons.

Standing there, waiting for Lenore or Cruzita, for something, Jean remembered the letter Telema had dropped. She reached into her purse, felt the paper, and brought it out. No, it was the proprietor's letter, given to her to mail. Jean, amused to see Bill Clinton as the addressee, opened the envelope, thinking she would readdress it when she returned to Xela.

Dear Mr. President Bill Clinton,

I listened to your apology to Guatemala on the radio and was happy to hear your hopes that our country could be turned into "a marketplace of ideas." Many of us in Guatemala believe this, too, and have tried to overcome our sad history by establishing businesses that will build Guatemala's future. But I am distressed to hear that you support this truth commission that is plowing through our country, digging up bodies and claiming that it is in the interest of truth and its healing powers. The truth is terrible and the truth does nothing to help the widows and orphans. What would help us recover is to be able to run successful businesses. Tourism is Guatemala's great hope, but your truth workers are destroying that hope. They make the world afraid to come here and instead of helping us to heal, they only make more victims.

Last year, eight men were interviewed by this truth commission, five soldiers and three guerrillas, who confessed to murdering my family. I watched my family die, and then these men confess and they are promised they will not be punished because they told the truth. I'm telling the truth and what do I get? Why is it that killers who tell the truth are free, when everyone else is imprisoned by fear? These eight killers live still in my town. They go to market, they go to church, one lives next door to me and there is nothing I can do. I can either live my life and see these men every day, or I can cease to live. I have chosen the second. Many women in the town are in the same position as me. They are afraid to leave their homes, afraid to run into the murderers. This truth commission forces people to hear the truth, but there is no reconciliation. It turns our neighbors into murderers. It makes me afraid to leave my house, afraid to turn off my lights at night because I know who lives next door to me. I know I would be better off if I never knew who killed my family. Peace in Guatemala will not come by degrading the families of victims with such injustice, forcing them to hear confessions then to watch these murderers raise families and run things and be criminals only in more secret ways. I do not want a road named after my sons. I want to be able to live and run my business without being afraid that the next election will set them all killing again.

My older son, forced into the army, deserted and was executed for it. I didn't know why he deserted, he could not speak when he came home to me. But two years ago, I learned why. His friend survived the war and came to see me and to tell me that he helped plan my son's escape. They were in the army together, he said, they fought together. The training had been hard, but he said it was harder if you did not complete it. Because the Americans were there telling them they were being trained for war. So they completed their training and lived through a few battles against the guerrillas. But they did not always fight guerrillas and something happened that made my son decide to fake his own death. This is what happened: One day, my son and the other soldiers were ordered to attack a village called Lorotenango. Half the soldiers set the huts on fire, while the other half gathered the people at the edge of a ditch— mothers, children, old people. My son and his friend did their best to look busy and to hang back, but their commander saw that they were shy and not doing their jobs. The villagers were lined up and shot and put in the hole, while the commander chose a girl from the line and brought her out into the road. The girl was very pregnant and the commander threw her on the ground and called my son and his friend to assist him. They are terrified to disobey this commander, who inflicts on his soldiers whatever they refuse to inflict on their victims. My son had already been burned badly on the bottom of his feet for refusing to burn someone else. So they follow the commander and hold the woman down as they are told, while the commander strips the girl naked, takes his machete, and cuts her belly open all the way across. The girl is still alive and screaming and thrashing, but it is easy to hold her down because she is so small and young.

He said it was like holding down a mouse. They hold her down and the commander brings out the baby. The mother is still alive. She is lying there with her arms out and everyone can see inside her. Blood and muscle and intestines. The soldiers are kicking up dirt that settles inside of her. The commander cuts the cord and cleans the baby's mouth so it can breathe. It looked like a skinned kitten, covered in blood and a few patches of fur, he said. The commander handed the baby, a little girl, to my son. Told him that his job was to take the baby down to the base at Nueva Aldea de la Vida, fifteen miles away. My son carried that baby over the mountains for fifteen miles on burned feet. He bathed her in a stream and wrapped her in his coat while he shivered at night. He dressed a cut on her shoulder, because the commander had not been too careful and cut her, too, with his machete. He carried the baby because he could do nothing else. It was the best thing he could do for her. The baby was given to a woman there, who would take her to the orphanage in Xela as her own. Two weeks later, he faked his own death in battle and walked one hundred miles home to me.

There was more. Two more pages, but skimming down, Jean could see it fell into hysteria. Written in stages, with different pens, during difficult hours. Jean tried to refold the letter, but her hands shook and she could only manage to crumple it and shove it back into her purse.

Jean recalled the photos of all those babies in Cruzita's file. All about the same age as Maya, but some in much worse shape. One baby had been missing an ear, another looked blind in one eye. What had become of them?

"*Ixchel!*" The search for the enterprising, mischievous girl had gained urgency, more voices calling. "*Ixchel!*"

It was five-thirty. What was Maya doing at that moment? She may have convinced the hotel staff to turn the lamps on in the pool so she could swim in the glamorous white light. She might be trapped in the courtyard, listening as the proprietor planned her marriage to one of her sons.

"*Ixchel! Ixchel! Ixchel!*"

Jean did not want to see Lenore. Suddenly Jean was standing in the last place in the world she wanted to be. And at just the moment she decided she did not want to see her, Lenore appeared. She ducked through Cruzita's gate, into the street, putting on her sunglasses. All Jean had to do was step into view and ask. But she did not. Jean shrank back, behind the vine, watching

Lenore through its twisted green, grasping stems. She watched, unmoving, as a crowd of Mayan women swiftly cohered around Lenore. In two seconds, the street went from empty to full. Where Lenore stood, thirty yards away, the women made a clashing wall of neon stripes, embroidered flowers, over which Jean could still see Lenore's head, several inches above the rest.

"*¿Dónde hay Ixchel?*"

Lenore turned a full circle, almost like a dance. Jean, transfixed, watched this odd scene, not understanding it, until all at once the women raised their hands in the air: machetes, clubs, metal pipes. Jean felt as if she'd been hollowed and filled with cement. She could not move, could not cry out, could not even close her eyes. Her eyes remained open, seeing Lenore bow her head before they all fell on her. She did not fight, did not push or try to explain. She lowered her head, making an easy target for the metal pipe that smashed against her ear. The sound. Like a hammer hitting a watermelon, over and over, as the mob closed in on her body, which collapsed from view. Only sound, only that sound. No one screamed, not in fear or rage. Everyone played her part in dedicated silence. Even Jean, as witness. Even the woman who must have been Cruzita, who ran out her gate empty-handed. She clawed at the mob, trying to pull them back. In Mayan dress, she blended into the crowd. She disappeared a moment, until someone pushed her away. She fell hard onto her knees, spun around, seeking help, and spotted Jean.

The horror of eye contact jolted Jean, bringing her back. Cruzita saw her, and in that moment Jean thought she'd point and turn the mob onto her. How long had Jean been standing there? How long could this go on? Forever. Cruzita gathered herself from the ground and ran toward her, and that seemed to take forever, too. Her skirt made her running steps small. Cruzita became no clearer to Jean, even as she grabbed her wrist and pulled her down the street, away.

They ran together. Cruzita did not let go of Jean's wrist and did not look back. She dragged Jean through alleys, over ditches, keeping away from the main road. Her hair, braided down her back, whipped Jean in the face at several turns.

They emerged into the dusty bus lot, where one of the painted buses revved up, ready to leave. Green, with lightning bolts and blaring pop music, it emitted an acrid black cloud. Cruzita yanked Jean toward it, pushed her up the child-size steps, and into the seat behind the driver.

"*¿Dónde?*" For the first time, she saw her clearly. Jean spied the teenager in the file picture, could see the beauty still evident in aged echoes. Fifteen years of sun, wind, and war had almost eroded her away. She tried to find Maya there. She tried to see a monster.

"*¡Dónde!*" Cruzita shook her.

"Xela," she gasped, the situation abruptly plain to her. If Jean had walked those few yards to Cruzita's gate, if she had not sheltered in the vine for shade, she would be dead, too.

Cruzita spoke to the driver with authority, giving instructions. She drew a wad of money out of her blouse and withheld it until he repeated what she'd said. Then she leapt down, out of sight. No goodbye, not even a glance.

The bus headed in a direction Jean could only identify as down. Where would down lead? She could not ask the people packed in around her. Anything, she feared, could provoke them. If she cried, if she showed weakness, they would turn on her. But she needed to cry out, to call the police, to tell others. But out here there were no phones, no mail, no one to tell. The police staffed by exonerated genocidal maniacs. There would never be anyone to tell. Nothing to do. There was nothing she could do. Lenore had realized that, had not even fought for her life. She merely deferred to their decision, which she had claimed to be awaiting. The scene came back to Jean in pieces that she tried to reassemble. In the moments before Cruzita touched her, Jean had been counting the blows. The only witness, she'd fixated on the number, thinking it important. She had counted to thirty-six before Cruzita wrenched her away.

For over an hour, Jean's thoughts skated in obsessive circles: Someone's been murdered, tell someone, there's no one to tell, because everyone's been murdered; my child's been stolen, so my child's been saved, because she's been stolen, so she could be saved; I almost died today, but I did not, but I almost did. She imagined standing in line in the government office to report these crimes, like everyone else: fill out this form, submit a picture, go home. Three more added to the millions already in their computers.

The bus stopped in a tiny mountain town, to the protests of the passengers. The driver motioned for Jean to follow him. She did, helpless, no longer in charge of her own fate. She trusted him more than anyone else, because he'd been paid. Money, she could still understand. Money made more sense than anything.

And then she saw it across the street: *Xela.* A pink bus with bald tires, overloaded with passengers. The man paid her fare and left before she could show she had the money herself. No explanation was offered to the new driver. She became an ordinary passenger again. A tourist with nothing to report.

On the two-hour ride to Xela, Jean's adrenaline ran dry and she began to think more clearly. She was not helpless, she realized, there were plenty of things to do. To find Maya, to pack, to leave, to forget what she could not change. To just save Maya.

Where was Maya at this moment? Jean imagined her again, swimming in the lighted pool with loose limbs. Swimming, not with skill or intent, but simply to admire herself. Nothing to report but adolescent troubles. And if Jean did, even if she did bring Maya to the government office, if they typed her stats into a computer and came up with a list of likely mothers, what would be the point? To return her to Guatemala? Impossible. Truth down here was not followed by justice or reunion or remedy. Reconciliation had been decreed for a reason, for people like Maya, the small number of those who could be saved.

Everything was taking forever. By the time the bus arrived in Xela, the atrocity Jean had witnessed had migrated to a different part of her consciousness. The excruciating process left her exhausted. She felt as if a new groove had been carved into her brain over the past three hours. Slowly, deeply carved as the images moved through tissue, to become memory. A new groove, through which every action, every thought for the rest of her life, would have to travel.

She could barely walk the block to the hotel. To run, to attract attention, proved unthinkable. To collapse into a defenseless heap even more so. So she walked, like a tourist. The moment she entered the hotel, she meant to scream Maya's name, but the immediate presence of the bright, cheerful maids rendered her speechless with terror.

Jean did not find Maya at the pool, or lying out in the courtyard with a banana drink. She found her in their room, huddled in a corner with her head on her knees. The proprietor, sitting on the floor, too, held her, shushing.

"Maya." Jean rushed at her, to pull the demented woman away. "Maya!"

Her daughter glared up with a red, twisted face. Snot and tears and saliva glossing an ugly expression. Mouth open, eyes squeezed against the light. A noise escaped from her, a low primal groan of pain.

"Maya! Are you okay?" On her knees now, Jean handled her daughter. Lifting her limbs, searching her face. Maya gave in, limp and remote. The proprietor allowed this transfer of ownership by standing up. "Maya, I'm here! Did she hurt you? Did she say something to you again?"

"He dumped me!" she cried with her furious mouth. "I called him to say we were coming home early and he dumped me! For Maureen!"

Jean wrapped her arms around Maya without fear of rejection. She brought her close, smelling her coconut suntan oil. "Oh, honey." She found herself crying as hard as Maya. "Oh, honey." Inconsolable.

Still standing over them, the proprietor began a tactful exit. "I'm sorry," she told them both. "They're good boys. I don't know why they would be so cruel. This Maureen sounds no good. They love you, Maya. I know. We all do."

She stepped out on stiff knees, closing the door behind her.

"If we hadn't gone on this stupid trip, it wouldn't have happened! I knew it would, I didn't want to leave them alone! I told you! I told you!"

Jean just rocked Maya and sobbed. And in doing this, miraculously, Maya said exactly what she would have said: "He didn't love me." She went on, hiccupping with agony. "He never said he did . . . but I thought I could convince . . . him. I gave him what he . . . wanted and I told him I loved him . . . and I thought that would be enough . . . to make him love me . . . eventually." Jean rocked and rocked her daughter, who settled into her arms. Finally, talking became easier and the frantic hiccups subsided. Then, another miracle. Maya began to rock Jean, without breaking their rhythm. "It's not your fault, Mom. Don't cry. He's an asshole. You knew he was an asshole. Don't be upset, don't cry." She wiped her eyes clear and straightened, freeing herself. "You know, I'm glad we came on this trip."

"You are?" Jean picked wet black strands of hair from Maya's face. There were so many. She cleared and cleared, like someone finding an overgrown trail.

"Yes, because it's made me realize who loves me and who doesn't."

"And who loves you, Maya?" Jean cleaned Maya's tears, as she herself continued to weep. The same tears, it seemed, transferred by touch.

Maya did not answer right away. Instead she asked, "Can we go home now?"

They packed Maya's suitcase together, handling the glittery bottles, the spandex, and the lace with a great deal of care. Jean became determined not to act like they were fleeing, though she wanted nothing more than to collect Maya in her arms and run for the bus station. Keep calm, for Maya's sake. These are things she should never even suspect. The last bus to the capital would leave in twenty minutes and it took almost that long for Maya to locate her belongings throughout the hotel. Lipstick forgotten on a windowsill, sandals at the pool, a barrette rusting in the bathroom. Each piece she found became a treasure, as if it could not be replaced the moment they got home. As for Jean, she would leave everything here. She would not even pursue her lost suitcase.

After several minutes of fruitless searching, Maya deemed everything found. She closed her suitcase, tested the clasps, and sat down on the bed, just as Jean rose to leave Guatemala behind forever.

"Mom. I feel like I should tell you. Telema was here again looking for you. Looking for a letter she said you stole from her."

"She said I stole from her? Why would I do that?"

"Because you've become a CIA informant. You're helping them sabotage her important book. The sexual savage book. What's a CIA informant?"

"It's something that I'm certainly *not*, Maya."

"Well, she says you are and that you're helping the government hide the truth. She found a letter that explains what happened to that little girl. A very important letter. It's changed the whole course of her book, she says, proving her point more than ever. And you stole it."

"Telema says a lot of things, Maya. Only seventy percent of them are true."

Her daughter agreed, understanding Telema's nature after just two encounters, more quickly than Jean herself had. "She told me you paid the Guatemalan government twelve thousand dollars for me. Is that true?"

"Yes," Jean admitted, feeling a strange relief. Forgive me, she wanted to say. Forgive me, Maya. I have a weak heart. She imagined twelve thousand obstacles, suddenly, between them. Twelve thousand fights. Twelve thousand corpses.

"That's a lot of money," Maya ventured, caught on an uncertainty that thawed into a lopsided smile. "You really love me that much?"

"Yes," Jean answered, for this was the greatest truth she could offer. For the first time in a long time, happiness touched her. An untuned string within her plucked, reverberating. How unexpected, how encompassing, how close to disappointment it felt.

1902

The office was more finished than it had been just one week ago. Everything now had its proper place. Books upright on shelves, knickknacks consigned to their eternal displays, already collecting dust: an Indian warrior lunging, a helmeted conquistador aiming. The Catholic chalice still held its arsenal of sharpened pencils on the desk. The bird, Magellan, with the red breast, presided in a corner. He opened his beak and held it there—a silent scream or laugh, or a yawn—and shifted his weight from foot to foot in a golden cage lined on the bottom with newspaper. He seemed to be doing better. Two tail feathers, one blue, one green, held a long flirtation through the bars, twisting and crossing for a meter before touching the floor. The bird regarded Evie with one hostile eye, possibly remembering her.

"How old are you, Evie?" Mr. Ubico's accent sounded like his mouth was full of food. Was this really the man who had replaced God, as her father had said? The bird, behind him, nodded enthusiastically, then began shredding his newspaper. Evie had never thought God could look so young, or be so short.

She held up nine fingers. There was no good reason to lie, but it was already done. She sat in the same church pew she and Father had sat in before, while Mr. Ubico regarded her sadly from his red velvet throne. She spread her nightgown to show off the lace, secretly pleased to be wearing it in the daytime, in public.

Judas, with a bowed head, stepped outside. Evie listened to his fancy shoes—*squeak, squawk*—make a crazy noise against the arcade tiles. He had told her not to ask any questions, not to say anything, advice that she trusted. Judas had saved her, after all. They had put her in the cemetery like a dead person, and he had saved her.

"Do you know your address in America, Evie? Could you tell the embassy where someone in your family lives?"

She shook her head, ashamed now that she had lied about her age. A nine-year-old would know her address. Probably an eight-year-old should, too.

"Do you know what happened? Do you know why you're here?" Absently, he reached into his pocket and slid four peppermints across his desk in front of her. Behind him, the bird began aggressively grooming himself, feathers drifting to the floor.

"Our parents," Mr. Ubico began, making his first slip in English, "were murdered by their Indian workers. Your father hired criminals and they robbed and murdered your family. Do you understand this?"

Evie nodded, recognizing that word, murdered, from her conversation with Judas. But Ubico had gotten it backward. Father had murdered a worker, not the other way around. At least, the situation had gotten no worse than the day before. Slightly relieved, she ignored the pile of mints, knowing from before that they were old and stale, and tasted like pennies and pocket dust.

"Did you see anything?"

She shook her head. The only thing Evie had seen was the blanket covering her face, the rough weave of wool and light and straw. She had woken up to fabric being stuffed in her mouth, an Indian blanket wrapped around her head. She couldn't scream or talk, but could open her eyes and see that the color of pure dark was not black but red.

"Did you hear anything?"

Just the footsteps that carried her away. The fabric had been scratchy. Nothing her mother would own.

Someone knocked timidly, and Mr. Ubico stood up. He was short, much shorter than Father. Evie watched him walk to his office door, moving easily, without the gun today. Judas. With his head still lowered, Judas mumbled something in Spanish. Evie sat patiently through their hushed conversation. Judas, no doubt, telling him where her parents had gone, how to send her back, returning everything to normal.

On Mr. Ubico's desk sat a mechanical bank that Evie had been resisting for several minutes. Now she pulled it near. On its small stage, a jaguar and a deer stood frozen in the violence of their next transaction: the deer reared up, antlers cocked forward in the direction of the leaping jaguar. Evie found a peso among the clutter of papers, put it in the jaguar's mouth, and pulled the lever. With this, the jaguar shot forward and the coin hit the deer with a fantastic *ping* and ricocheted across the room.

In his corner, the startled bird jumped down to the floor of his cage and began to turn circles, over and over, drawing his tail feathers up from the floor through the bars.

The exchange didn't last long. Evie heard the door close and again the *squeak, squawk* of Judas's exit, leaving her, Magellan, and Mr. Ubico alone.

She had to remind herself not to be afraid of Ubico. He had helped her father recently. And he would help her now. If she heeded Judas's advice, he'd take her to her parents.

"You like my bank?" Mr. Ubico asked with unmistakable pride. He fished in his pocket for a coin, and gave it to Evie. "You can't do it with pesos, only pennies. They have different weights."

Evie took the penny and tried again. This time, the jaguar shot forward and deposited the penny into the hole in the deer's chest. *Crack, ping!* The sound, the exactness, the reliability of the action pleased her.

"Do you . . ." Mr. Ubico asked again, sitting down behind his desk, "do you know what happened, Evie?"

Evie picked up the bank and found the hinge in the jaguar's paw, where the coins could be retrieved. She studied it, amazed. It looked like the deer got the money, but somehow it ran right through its body and the jaguar got it back.

"What do you think happened? You must tell me everything you know."

Evie clicked the heels of her white leather shoes together under the pew. She looked down at the heart-shaped buckles, focused, resisting.

"Do you know? I'll need your help if we're going to catch the murderers."

She allowed herself to nod to Mr. Ubico's question. Yes, she knew why she was here, she knew more about it all than her parents had. She set the same coin in the jaguar's mouth and pulled the lever. *Crack, ping!* The bird shrieked in response. Evie had never heard its voice before. It was terrible, like a train braking. Wheels locking, steam rising, people running.

Squeak, squawk, squeak, squawk, squeak, squawk, squeak, squawk. Another knock. Ubico ignored it. "I need your help, Evie. Can you help me?" More knocking, louder this time, more insistent. Clearly annoyed, Ubico glared at the door, but did not rise to answer it. Instead, he shifted his black eyes to Evie, awaiting her answer.

For the first time, she began to doubt Judas's advice.

"Do you know what happened? Judas says you don't, he says you're only six. But you're a big girl of nine. I think you understand a lot. I think you can help me."

No one had ever asked Evie what she thought was happening, she had always been told. But yes. She knew the point where everything had changed. One thing leading inevitably to another, forces beyond their control driving them hard to failure. Yes, just like a train barreling down long-laid tracks. Tracks that others had ridden before them: the priest, the cochineal farmer.

History, as Mother would say. There had been no avoiding it. Ghosts, the snake, the awakening of the cave. Yes, she knew exactly the moment it all began.

Ubico turned over a piece of paper on his desk. She recognized Mother's stationery right away. My address in America is there, she wanted to say.

"Can you tell me what happened two weeks ago? Do you remember that far back?" He selected a sharpened red pencil from his arsenal and underlined something in the letter.

Judas opened the door. Flustered, Ubico shot up from his chair and yelled in English, "I do not pay you for your opinion!" Then he remembered his Spanish and Judas shrank back and disappeared at the few words Ubico spoke.

"Stupid Indians." He grinned confidentially at Evie. He fumbled at the edge of his desk and Evie heard a bell, trilling somewhere inside the building. "You can't trust them, not even with a simple job. They just make it harder for me. You're big enough and smart enough to understand that. Didn't your parents teach you to never trust Indians?"

Evie nodded, realizing so much at that moment. Clearly, Ubico had the power to help her. He had replaced God, after all. And Judas, like the stupid Indian he was, made him angry. On top of that, he'd told Ubico that *she* was stupid, that she was only six—six!—and could not even remember what had happened two weeks ago. Changing strategies, she did something unthinkable a moment before. She put one of the peppermints in her mouth. She sucked on it, feeling it burn a tender welt in her cheek.

Another government man in a suit sailed in on a smile and a handshake, from a different, interior door. As they spoke in hushed Spanish, Evie walked to Magellan's cage. Up close, she saw that Magellan was not better. He was worse. The golden cage had confused her from afar. The red breast feathers were completely gone, replaced by blood. And Magellan was sitting on his newspaper, the one featuring Mrs. Fasbinder's party, ripping up the picture of the President's face. Bloody feathers and newspaper shreds that had fallen from the cage stuck to her shoes, her good shoes. Ruined.

Poor Magellan, poor me, she thought, holding back tears of horror. She remembered Judas saying, *Magellan is killing himself because he cannot kill you.* That, Father told her, would be scientifically impossible. Of course, Indians were stupid. But not her! Why couldn't she answer Mr. Ubico's questions? She was not crazy or stupid or useless. She wanted them to know this much. Because she now suspected that her parents had fired her for just those reasons. Had left her to start a new life in Europe.

"I remember everything!" Shouting over her fear made her sound sassy, though she hadn't meant to. The men turned in unison. "I know what this is all about. I know everything started with the volcano!"

And it worked. The government men closed their mouths like traps. They regarded her differently now, not like a child at all. Father, wherever he was, would have been proud, would have laughed and taken her back, for the astonishment on both their faces.

With his eyes still on Evie, Ubico found the knob of his office door and pushed it wide open. Judas was gone. In his place, cold light, fresh air, the busy morning noise of Xela rushed in.

"Thank you. We will take you to your parents now," Ubico said, holding out his hand. "They are waiting for you." Evie let out a little smiling sigh of relief and stepped toward him. Everything fixed, so quickly and completely. The blood on her soles made a tacky sound on the tiles and she hesitated, glancing back at Magellan. The bird, hunkered in misery and contempt, was beyond hope. She remembered Father's pronouncement: *If he can't survive in a cage, with us bringing him food, he certainly can't survive on his own in the woods.* But walking all the way back up Father's mountain, escorted by a policeman, she could not forget him. Poor Magellan, who could not live in a cage and who could not be free.

Historical Time Line

August 31, 1900—The Central American Improvement Company (CAICO) signs a contract with the Guatemalan government to complete the Northern Railway. The railway, built by the government with forced labor drafts, is mostly complete, but for a sixty-mile section infested with swamp and disease. The contract stipulates that the section must be finished in thirty-three months. Once completed, it will connect Guatemala's coffee-rich Pacific coast to its Caribbean ports. CAICO, an American company, was formed earlier that same year by the founder and vice president of the Boston-based United Fruit Company. According to the contract, CAICO will retain all profits from the line for ten years, before selling it back to the government.

October 1902—The problematic section of railroad is far from finished, proving much more difficult than predicted. On the west coast, the coffee bust is decimating the entire economy as planters move to Brazil, which offers both stability and easier shipping. On October 24, the Santa María volcano erupts outside Xela, while foreign investors are visiting President Manuel Estrada Cabrera. The town crier reads a proclamation from the President: No volcano is erupting in Guatemala. The military band plays over the noise of the continuing eruption. Within a week, the forced labor drafts are instituted to help the coffee plantations recover.

January 12, 1904—With the economy struggling more than ever, CAICO—soon to be renamed the Guatemalan Railway Company—demands a new contract to complete the Northern Railway. This contract gives CAICO complete control of the line for ninety-nine years, rights to 168,000 acres of prime banana land, and exempts it from local taxes or export duties on bananas for thirty-five years. It also acquires the docks at Puerto Barrios, along with all stations, telegraph lines, and buildings at the main Caribbean port. CAICO gains authorization to build and acquire railroads throughout Guatemala and the government also guarantees CAICO a 5 percent annual profit on its investment for fifteen years. For all this, the government will have no legal right to intervene in CAICO's affairs: no audits, regulations, taxes, or duties. More contracts like this will be signed over the next forty years, allowing the company to consolidate and expand its power over the entire infrastructure, economy, and population of Guatemala. In return for this exploitative contract worth over $58 million, President Estrada Cabrera receives shares of CAICO amounting to $50,000.

September 1904—Of the 168,000 acres given to the Guatemalan Railway Company (GRC) in its second contract, the company gives 50,000 of those acres to United Fruit to make its first banana plantings in Guatemala. It also negotiates preferential terms with the legally "separate" company. The agreement subordinates the railroad to United Fruit, requiring GRC to haul all freight according to the timetables and needs of Fruit. Additionally, all trains carrying United Fruit bananas receive right-of-way over all other rail traffic. They also receive a steep discount on shipping. Other banana companies will have to pay double the rates United Fruit pays. Over the next decade, as granted in its contract, GRC buys up existing railroads and docks throughout the country. By 1912, the company will be called International Railways of Central America (IRCA), and will have a complete monopoly of Guatemalan railroads.

January 19, 1908—President Estrada Cabrera drives the golden spike into the completed Northern Railway. But it is too little, too late for the west coast coffee planters, who do not utilize the Caribbean port as hoped. The government, however, must make up for the shortfall by paying IRCA the 5 percent annual profits guaranteed in its contract for fifteen years. With Guatemala's railroad problem now solved and coffee not cooperating, IRCA's future profits will depend solely on an expanding banana industry, mostly contained on the Caribbean coast.

April 8, 1920—Estrada Cabrera is declared insane by the Guatemalan legislature and relieved of the presidency.

February 14, 1931—A former *jefe politico* in the highlands, Jorge Ubico, is inaugurated as President of Guatemala, having won the election by a vote of 305,841 to 0.

May 1931—Ubico signs a contract with United Fruit to expand business from the exhausted soil of the Caribbean coast to the Pacific coast. Fruit gains a fifty-year monopoly on the Pacific port system, preferential treatment for all Fruit ships at the port, and a one-cent export tax. By this time, the company controls five hundred thousand acres in Guatemala, for which it paid the government less than $1.48 per acre. Maya in the countryside are forced to work on plantations for at least 150 days a year to pay their taxes. By 1936, United Fruit will own controlling stock in IRCA.

June 1944—Using Franklin D. Roosevelt's "Four Freedoms" speech as a rallying cry, Guatemalans, led by teachers, hold mass protests against Ubico's rule. A few days later, amid increasing international pressure, Ubico resigns. At this time, 2 percent of landowners own 72 percent of Guatemala's land and 90 percent of the people own just 15 percent of productive acreage. Ninety-five percent of the Mayan population is illiterate, with a life expectancy of forty years.

December 1945—In Guatemala's first truly democratic election, a former teacher, Dr. Juan José Arévalo, is elected President with 85 percent of the literate male vote. By March, a new constitution guarantees a balance of powers, freedom of speech and press, voting rights for women and illiterates, limited presidential power, the right to organize, the criminalization of racial discrimination, and other reforms. This constitution also bans monopolies and grants the government the authority to expropriate private property under limited circumstances.

October 1946—Guatemala's Congress approves the first social security law. Inspired by the New Deal law, it mandates workplace safety, injury compensation, maternity benefits, basic education, and health care. A year later, it passes a labor code modeled after America's Wagner Act, which guarantees workers the right to organize, bargain collectively, and strike. It also establishes minimum wages and regulates child labor.

December 1949—The Guatemalan Congress passes the Law of Forced Rental. It gives any peasant who owns less than 2.47 acres the right to petition to rent fallow acreage from neighboring plantation owners.

November 13, 1950—Arévalo's defense minister, Jacobo Arbenz Guzmán, is elected President with 65 percent of the vote. At this point, 2.2 percent of landowners still own 70 percent of Guatemala's arable land. Less than 25 percent of these four million acres is cultivated. The vast majority of the economy belongs to American corporations, mostly United Fruit, which owns five hundred fifty thousand acres. Eighty-five percent of these acres lie fallow. Within a year, the World Bank releases a report on the Guatemalan economy, stressing the importance of recent reforms and calling for further reconciliation of income inequality to create a modern capitalist state.

June 27, 1952—Jacobo Arbenz's Agrarian Reform Law is passed. The act authorizes the government to expropriate only uncultivated property from large plantations. The government pays for these confiscated acres with twenty-five-year government bonds with a 3 percent interest rate. The amount of compensation is assessed from the land's declared taxable worth in 1952. Expropriated land is then given to landless peasants in parcels no larger than 42.5 acres. Over eighteen months, the program gives a hundred thousand families 1.5 million acres, for which the government pays $8,345,545 in bonds.

March 1953—In addition to expropriating 1,700 acres of his own land, Jacobo Arbenz and his government expropriate 234,000 acres of uncultivated land from United Fruit. The company is compensated with the amount it had claimed it was worth on its taxes: $2.99 per acre.

February 1954—After more expropriation proceedings, 386,901 acres of United Fruit land are under dispute.

April 20, 1954—The U.S. State Department issues a formal complaint on behalf of United Fruit, demanding $75 per acre for its expropriated land. Guatemala's foreign minister refuses to accept the complaint.

May 1, 1954—*The Voice of Liberation* goes on the air. The announcers accuse Jacobo Arbenz of communism and other atrocities, such as witchcraft and murder. Claiming to be reporting while on the run from Arbenz's military in

Guatemalan jungles, they are actually stationed in Miami and completely co-ordinated and funded by the CIA.

June 18, 1954—The rebel Castillo Armas "invades" Guatemala from Honduras with 170 mercenaries paid by the CIA. Over the next several days, *The Voice of Liberation* reports a much larger army composed of "Guatemalan peasants" and large battles, with heavy casualties for Arbenz's military.

June 25, 1954—American pilots, paid by the CIA, buzz Guatemala City, bombing a few strategic military targets and smoke-bombing other targets. Other planes in the preceding days drop leaflets. On the roof of the American embassy, speakers play a recording of bombing attacks, as *The Voice of Liberation* reports Castillo Armas's march toward the city.

June 27, 1954—Jacobo Arbenz resigns, declaring to demoralized and frightened Guatemalans, "For fifteen days, a cruel war against Guatemala has been under way. The United Fruit Company, in collaboration with the governing circles of the United States, is responsible for what is happening to us . . ."

July 2, 1954—In response to international uproar over involvement in the coup, which the U.S. denies, the U.S. State Department files an antitrust suit against United Fruit.

July 13, 1954—The U.S. government officially recognizes the Castillo Armas government. A few weeks later, United Fruit and Castillo Armas sign a contract, guaranteeing the return of all expropriated land and a new, lower income tax. Castillo Armas also cancels the Agrarian Reform Law and bans illiterates from voting. By mid-August, he outlaws all political parties, peasant organizations, and unions, and restores Ubico's secret police chief. Some forms of union activity become punishable by death.

1958—The antitrust suit is resolved, with United Fruit agreeing to give up some of its commerce and property to businesses in Guatemala.

1961—The first guerrilla band forms to battle the series of U.S.-backed presidents who control Guatemala for the next thirty-six years. By 1966, the country falls into complete civil war. The United States gives more than $20 million between 1966 and 1970 for military and police training and equipment, increasing the Guatemalan national police force to thirty thousand by 1970. State-sponsored right-wing terror squads permeate the country by 1968.

1972—United Fruit sells its Guatemalan land holdings to Del Monte.

April 1977—Since the beginning of the civil war, the U.S. has given the Guatemalan military $33 million in aid. However, prompted by President Carter and alarming reports of human rights abuses, the United States Congress cuts off military funding. But the sanctions do not apply to previously approved military hardware and indirect funding. Between 1978 and 1982, the Guatemalan government will receive $7.9 million from the State Department's Military Assistance Program and the Foreign Military Sales Program.

March 23, 1982—Army general José Efraín Ríos Montt assumes power through a coup. A born-again Christian, Ríos Montt played a small role in the 1954 coup and promises to end Guatemala's civil war by defeating the guerrillas and bringing the country to Christ.

March 28, 1982—Pat Robertson, the host of *The 700 Club*, flies to Guatemala to conduct Ríos Montt's first interview as President.* Robertson begins a lobbying campaign directed at Congress and President Reagan to lift Guatemalan military sanctions in order to defeat the guerrillas. He also partners with the California-based Gospel Outreach to raise money for Ríos Montt's government through International Love Lift, a fund meant to provide food, medical supplies, and missionaries to Guatemalan refugees.

December 4, 1982—President Reagan visits Ríos Montt and—despite rising evidence of massacres in the highlands, reported by both Amnesty International and Americas Watch—declares that Ríos Montt is "getting a bad rap on human rights."

January 7, 1983—The U.S. Congress approves $6 million in "nonlethal" military hardware for Guatemala, including parts for helicopters used in counterinsurgency raids. Through the CIA, Reagan funnels weaponry that Congress will not approve. Over the seventeen months of Ríos Montt's rule, the bloodiest years of the civil war, over 400 Mayan villages are razed, a scorched-earth policy is adopted, and the first model villages are set up to control and reeducate the displaced Mayan population. International Love Lift sends 350 missionaries to Guatemala on the day that the sanctions are lifted. Before Ríos Montt is deposed in another coup, Love Lift will raise approximately $1.5 million for relief and building supplies to resettle the refugees.

March 29, 1994—An American journalist is beaten into a coma by a mob of Maya in San Cristóbal, after a child she'd taken a picture of disappears. The child is later found, unharmed.

December 29, 1996—Government and guerrilla leaders meet in Guatemala City to sign a peace agreement. After thirty-six years, the longest war in Latin American history comes to an end. As part of the agreement, truth and reconciliation will prevail, with no subpoenas and no prosecutions for any of the players.

February 1999—The Historical Clarification Commission, established by the UN under the peace agreement, publishes its report on the war: more than two hundred thousand casualties and forty-five thousand "disappeared," with the state responsible for 92 percent of arbitrary executions and 91 percent of disappearances, and the United States identified as a major contributor to the violence. Over half of the massacres and scorched-earth operations are tied to Ríos Montt's term. Of the forty-five thousand "disappeared," five thousand are children. Later government reports will conclude that the Guatemalan Army

---

*The dialogue in this interview is fictionalized in *Hard Red Spring*, since requests for copies of the interview went unanswered by the Christian Broadcasting Network.

stole Mayan children to sell for adoption in the U.S. and Europe. A few days after the UN report is released, President Clinton arrives in Guatemala to offer a formal apology.

July 1, 2006—The Central American Free Trade Agreement (CAFTA) goes into effect for Guatemala, allowing U.S. businesses to relocate their factories there to take advantage of cheap labor and lack of regulations. At this time, 39 percent of Guatemala's employment is rooted in agriculture, mostly small-scale farms.

2007–2008—The influx of cheap, subsidized U.S. corn into Guatemala forces traditional Mayan farming and food supply into a global market. Many small-scale farmers cannot compete, and sell their land to large monocultural enterprises geared toward exporting bananas, coffee, vegetables, sugar, and palm oil to the U.S. The number of farms in Guatemala falls dramatically as land is reconcentrated into the hands of a few large producers. By 2014, 1.86 percent of farms will own 52 percent of the arable land. Many of the former farmers must find work in the exploding number of U.S.-owned apparel factories.

2008–2009—The global recession hits the Guatemalan manufacturing sector particularly hard. By 2011, the unemployment rate more than doubles from the pre-CAFTA rate. By 2014, apparel exports to the U.S. fall almost 40 percent due to decreased demand. Once self-sufficient in food production, Guatemala is now dependent on imports for half its cereal grains supply. The price of corn spikes 240 percent due to the global food crisis.

January 14, 2012—The proportion of the population that is food-insecure has increased by 80 percent since the 1990s. Amid rising hunger and out-of-control drug violence, retired general Otto Pérez Molina is elected President of Guatemala. The head of Ríos Montt's security apparatus from 1982 to 1983 and a former member of the *kaibiles*, the elite right-wing death squad, he promises to take a "hard line" against the cartels. That year, the UN Office on Drugs and Crime rates Guatemala as having the fifth-highest homicide rate in the world—higher than the war-ravaged Democratic Republic of the Congo. Thirty-four percent of Guatemalans report that someone in their household was the victim of crime in the previous year.

May 10, 2013—After months of testimony that also implicates current President Pérez Molina, former president José Efraín Ríos Montt is found guilty of genocide by a Guatemalan court and sentenced to eighty years in prison. He is eighty-six years old. That year, the price of tortillas in Guatemala doubles due to rising global corn prices and increased American ethanol production.

May 20, 2013—Ríos Montt's genocide conviction is overturned, 3–2, by the Guatemalan Constitutional Court on a procedural technicality.

October 1, 2013–September 30, 2014—Guatemala ranks among the twelve worst countries in the world for income disparity, with the top 10 percent of earners accounting for 47 percent of national income—up five percentage points from the pre-CAFTA era; 54.8 percent of Guatemalans live in poverty, with 29.1 percent living in extreme poverty; 49.8 percent of Guatemalan children are chronically malnourished. During this period, 67,339 unaccompanied minors flood the U.S.–Mexico border in hopes of gaining asylum. Seventy-six percent of the children come from CAFTA countries. The rest are from Mexico. Twenty-five percent of the children—some as young as five—come from Guatemala. According to USAID and the Department of Homeland Security, the children are fleeing violence, forcible recruitment into gangs, and poverty. Nearly half of the children are girls, many of whom are routinely raped during the journey. Nearly 80 percent of these unaccompanied minors travel with smugglers, making them vulnerable to trafficking. Approximately one-third have made the journey in hopes of being reunited with their parents, who work in the United States illegally for lack of jobs in their home countries.

January 5, 2015—The retrial of former president José Efraín Ríos Montt begins. The defense immediately seeks the recusal of one of the judges for bias, based on her graduate thesis on the war. The motion is accepted. With a limited number of judges in the country even qualified to hear complex cases in high-risk court, and with the defense having challenged a number of them already, finding a replacement judge will be difficult. For this, the trial is suspended indefinitely on the same day that it began.

June 10, 2015—Guatemala's Supreme Court rules that President Pérez Molina should be investigated for his involvement in a multimillion-dollar customs fraud ring. On September 1, the Guatemalan Congress strips him of presidential immunity. By September 3, in response to mass protests and increasing evidence that he may have led the vast fraud ring, Pérez Molina resigns the presidency. Within hours of his resignation, he is jailed to await trial.

July 7, 2015—Guatemala's forensic authority determines that due to his dementia, Ríos Montt is mentally unfit to stand trial.

August 25, 2015—The court rules that Ríos Montt will still be retried. The new trial is set for January 11, 2016. However, due to his cognitive deterioration, a special trial will proceed in which all evidence and witnesses will be presented behind closed doors, with a defense representative. Ríos Montt will not be required to attend his genocide trial. Nor will he suffer punishment if found guilty.

Acknowledgments

I must thank my A-Team: Anthony Walton, Alice Tasman, and Anjali Singh. Anthony patiently suffered my first draft and my million frustrations. Alice, my agent, led me and this book through the desert. And Anjali, with fresh eyes and insight, tamed this beast at long last into something reasonable.

Hard Red Spring is built upon many years of research. The following books proved especially vital to my understanding of Guatemala: *Bitter Fruit* by Stephen Schlesinger and Stephen Kinzer; *Doing Business with the Dictators* by Paul J. Dosal; *Secret History* by Nick Cullather; *Unfinished Conquest* by Victor Perera; and *I, Rigoberta Menchú* edited by Elisabeth Burgos-Debray.

Thank you to my editor, Kathryn Court, for your confidence and gentle hand.

Thank you, Sarah Stein, first mate of my Viking crew.

I am indebted to Liz Shesko, my friend and guide to Guatemala. As well as showing me cities and villages, she fearlessly led me through jungles, around army ant nests, up to active volcanic rims, past the gauntlet of machismo, through ruins and the ruination of twenty-five-cent mojito night.

Mitch Fraas, Dave Cole, and Sharon Gonzalez, I am grateful for your expertise.

And lastly, firstly, this book is dedicated to E. For E, for everything, for making me notebooks when I ran out.